THE WORKS OF TOBIAS SMOLLETT

Poems, Plays, and *The Briton*

THE WORKS OF TOBIAS SMOLLETT

Jerry C. Beasley, General Editor
University of Delaware

O M Brack, Jr., Textual Editor
Arizona State University

Jim Springer Borck, Technical Editor
Louisiana State University

This edition includes all of the works by which Tobias Smollett was best known in his own day and by which he most deserves to be remembered. The edition conforms to the highest standards of textual and editorial scholarship. Individual volumes provide carefully prepared texts together with biographical and historical introductions and extensive explanatory notes.

Poems, Plays, and
The Briton

TOBIAS SMOLLETT

Introductions and Notes by
BYRON GASSMAN

The Texts Edited by
O M BRACK, JR.

Assisted by
LESLIE A. CHILTON

The University of Georgia Press
Athens and London

© 1993 by the University of Georgia Press
Athens, Georgia 30602
All rights reserved

Set in Janson
The paper in this book meets the guidelines for permanence
and durability of the Committee on Production Guidelines for
Book Longevity of the Council on Library Resources.

Printed in the United States of America

97 96 95 94 93   5 4 3 2 1

Library of Congress Cataloging in Publication Data

Smollett, Tobias, 1721–1771.
　　Poems, plays, and the Briton / Tobias
Smollett; introductions and notes by
Byron Gassman; the texts edited by
O M Brack, Jr.
　　　　p.　cm.
　　Includes index.
　　ISBN 0-8203-1428-5 (alk. paper)
　　I. Brack, O M.　II. Title.
PR3692.G37　1992
821.6—dc20　　　　　　　　　91-36319
　　　　　　　　　　　　　　　　CIP

British Library Cataloging in Publication Data available

CONTENTS

ILLUSTRATIONS

PREFACE

The works included in this volume represent three of the non-novelistic genres to which Tobias George Smollett applied his literary skills during his busy career: poetry, drama, and political journalism. Most of the works have never been reprinted in the twentieth century, and only a very few have ever been subject to the kind of editorial concern that our age has come to expect in a scholarly edition of literary works from an earlier age. Such circumstances might argue either the need, or the lack of need, for the project of editing and republishing them. One might argue negatively that writings almost forgotten by most readers have thereby demonstrated their general lack of merit or continuing significance. I recognize that most of Smollett's writings herein printed are properly labeled "minor," and I would not want to justify my labors by a foolish fanfare heralding the resurrection of long-forgotten masterpieces.

On the other hand, present scholarly interest in the literary and social currents of eighteenth-century England, and particularly in the role of the prolific Smollett as a conduit of those currents, would seem ample warrant for editing and publishing the texts chosen for this volume in a form that makes them most useful for and accessible to the twentieth-century student and reader. I explore the significance of the individual works for understanding Smollett and his age in the introductions to the separate sections of this volume; here I shall simply remark upon what I hope is quite obvious: Smollett's literary stature will continue to be based on his great novels, but the reintegration of the writings included within this volume into the Smollett canon should add both depth and breadth to the twentieth-century reader's appreciation of Smollett's achievement and its enduring significance in the English literary heritage.

Although there were reprints of some issues of Smollett's political journal, *The Briton*, during the period of its initial run from 1762 to 1763, and although a few excerpts were printed subsequently, the journal as a whole has never been reprinted since its first appearance. Because collections of the original sheets are extremely rare—perhaps heretofore the least available of any publication with which Smollett was connected—the *Briton* is included here so that students of Smollett and eighteenth-century England will no longer have to depend on long-distance travel or microfilm copies to get acquainted with one of Smollett's more significant journalistic enterprises.

Smollett's poems and plays, most of which were published separately throughout his career, were first collected into a single volume by an unknown editor in 1777, six years after Smollett's death. That volume remains the basis for defining the canon of Smollett's poems and plays. Several editors and publishers during the next century issued new editions of the contents of the 1777 volume, usually as part of some collected edition of Smollett's works. The poems were also republished on a number of occasions as part of more comprehensive collections of poetry, such as the well-known Chalmers collection of *The Works of the English Poets* (1810). Thus texts of the poems and even of the plays have not been overly difficult to come by, but the editions containing them make little or no pretense to textual accuracy or scholarly annotation. Since the last decades of the nineteenth century, editors and publishers have by and large ignored the poems and plays until the present volume was projected. Donald M. Korte did reprint the texts of Smollett's two satires, *Advice* and *Reproof*, in the Spring 1967 number of *Thoth*, and, along with the texts, provided fairly full annotation that has been helpful to me in my undertaking. And, of course, modern biographers and critics of Smollett such as Lewis M. Knapp have often had occasion to look at old texts of the works contained in this volume and have provided in their studies significant commentary and information about the subjects and material they found in them. I trust that my introductions and notes will make clear the value of such previous attention to these works.

In the introductions to the three separate sections of this volume, I have been most concerned with identifying the circumstances and occasions that prompted Smollett to undertake the respective writings. I have sought also to trace the history of their publication and to account for their contemporary success or lack of it. Although I have not intended to make extended critical pronouncements on any of the works, I have tried to identify themes and motifs and forms that connect them to significant achievements both of Smollett and of other writers and thinkers of his day. These discussions undoubtedly are slanted toward my own considered opinions about what is significant and valuable in the mind and art of Smollett and his contemporaries. I hope most readers will find them well considered.

Recognizing that an edition of these works is unlikely to be undertaken again in the foreseeable future, I have tried to make the annotation as comprehensive and definitive as possible. With the exception of *The Regicide* and a few of the lyric poems, all of Smollett's writings in this volume are very topical, filled with allusions to persons, events, places, and news of the day. Without turning the notes into a history of the times, I have tried to provide sufficient identification and explanation to help the reader understand clearly what Smollett must have had in mind when he inserted a name or other topical reference into his text.

Like most educated and intelligent persons of his time, Smollett was widely read in the classics as well as in the literature of his own nation and age, and he used the knowledge and material thus gained to embroider his own writings. All recognizable literary allusions and quotations in the texts herein have been noted and identified as precisely as possible. English translations of passages and phrases from Greek and Latin authors, unless otherwise indicated, are from the Loeb Classical Library. Quotations from Shakespeare have been checked against the text and line numbering of *The Riverside Shakespeare*, ed. G. Blakemore Evans and others (Boston: Houghton Mifflin, 1974). Quotations from Pope have been checked against the text and line numbering of *The Poems of Alexander Pope*, Twickenham Edition, 6 vols. (London: Methuen, 1939–61). Substantiating information about passages identified as proverbs has been found in such standard reference works as *The Oxford Dictionary of English Proverbs*, 3d ed. (Oxford: Clarendon Press, 1970). *The Oxford English Dictionary* has been an invaluable resource for finding out about and preparing notes on all the words and usages with which Smollett felt comfortable but which are likely to perplex the twentieth-century reader.

The poems included in the volume represent Smollett's entire achievement as a poet, and they are reprinted basically in the order of their composition or publication, as far as that order can be determined. The lyrics to *Alceste* are printed last because of their problematic status in the Smollett canon and because they existed only in manuscript at Smollett's death and remained largely unpublished until the twentieth century. A small group of five poems, all attributed to Smollett but never certainly proven to be his, is included in an appendix. Line numbers have been added to the texts of all poems by the present editor as a convenience to the reader.

As was fairly common in the printing of eighteenth-century plays that had been produced upon the stage, the first-edition copy-text of *The Reprisal* marks off passages omitted from the acting script, using internal and marginal double quotation marks. These passages have been included in the present edition, but, for the sake of clarity, they are enclosed within bold brackets instead of quotation marks.

A special feature of this volume is a key to the *Briton*, which appears following the notes to the texts. In the *Briton*, Smollett—or perhaps it was his printer—adopted the old practice of omitting letters in certain words and substituting dashes. This practice, called "gutting," was originally used (most often by satirists, including Smollett himself in *Advice* and *Reproof*) with names only, as a way of avoiding charges of libel; Smollett's use of it in the *Briton* extends to titles, place-names, and other nominative words. The key lists all separate instances of this practice, thus providing the reader with a convenient reference that should prevent ambiguity or confusion.

As the author of a multivolume history of England and the compiler and editor of other historical material, Smollett was an expert on historical matters, and his other writings, particularly the *Briton*, are filled with examples and lessons drawn from former and contemporary history. Wherever such material does not sufficiently explain or orient itself by its own context, additional information has been supplied in the notes. With these notes, as with the others, my intent has been to provide the kind of historical information and insight that will enable interested readers everywhere to increase their understanding and appreciation of the wide-ranging career and accomplishments of Tobias George Smollett.

ACKNOWLEDGMENTS

No volume such as this one can be completed without advice, criticism, encouragement — and sometimes appropriate discouragement — from many people. My main obligation is to those who at various times gave suggestions on how I should go about my task and who generously followed up on their suggestions by reading parts or all of both the text and my introductions and notes and providing me with their strictures, further suggestions, and corrections. These include Albrecht B. Strauss, O M Brack, Jr., Robert Adams Day, Donald J. Greene, James G. Basker, Paul-Gabriel Boucé, Jerry Beasley, and Jim Springer Borck. I owe additional thanks to Nicolas Gross, Hugh Amory, James E. May, and Mark Cronin for their last-minute help in tracking down points of information that had previously eluded me in preparation of the notes to the *Briton*.

An expression of my gratitude is due also to Gwin J. Kolb and the late Donald F. Bond, who many years ago guided my initial investigations into Smollett when I first became acquainted with the *Briton*, and to George S. Rousseau and the late Lewis M. Knapp, who helped give impetus to the initial labors on this project. William Kupersmith helped with tracking down a number of the Latin quotations that Smollett was fond of. Thomas Mackay and Gary Lambert, colleagues in the language departments of Brigham Young University, helped me find answers to questions in their areas of expertise. Graduate assistant Laura Wadley did considerable legwork during the early phases of my work, and I have received additional aid from Brigham Young University in the form of travel grants and released time to pursue my research. Several weeks spent searching through materials at the British Library (then still known as the British Museum) while the project was taking form were made possible by a travel grant from the American Philosophical Society. To all those who have in any way been helpful in bringing this work to fruition, I express my deep appreciation.

ABBREVIATIONS

Adventures of an Atom	Tobias Smollett, *The History and Adventures of an Atom*, ed. Robert Adams Day (Athens: University of Georgia Press, 1989).
Buck, *Poet*	Howard S. Buck, *Smollett as Poet* (New Haven: Yale University Press, 1927).
Buck, *Study*	Howard S. Buck, *A Study in Smollett, Chiefly Peregrine Pickle* (New Haven: Yale University Press, 1925).
Carlyle	Alexander Carlyle, *Anecdotes and Characters of the Times*, ed. James Kinsley (London: Oxford University Press, 1973).
Complete History	Tobias Smollett, *A Complete History of England*, 4 vols. (London, 1757–58).
Continuation	Tobias Smollett, *Continuation of the Complete History of England*, 5 vols. (London, 1760–65).
DNB	*Dictionary of National Biography*.
Ferdinand Count Fathom	Tobias Smollett, *The Adventures of Ferdinand Count Fathom*, ed. Jerry C. Beasley (Athens: University of Georgia Press, 1988).
Humphry Clinker	Tobias Smollett, *The Expedition of Humphry Clinker*, ed. Thomas R. Preston (Athens: University of Georgia Press, 1990).
Johnson, *Dictionary*	Samuel Johnson, *A Dictionary of the English Language*, 2 vols. (New York: AMS Press, 1967). Reprint of 1755 edition.
Knapp	Lewis Mansfield Knapp, *Tobias Smollett: Doctor of Men and Manners* (Princeton: Princeton University Press, 1949).
Letters	*The Letters of Tobias Smollett*, ed. Lewis M. Knapp (Oxford: Clarendon Press, 1970).
Moore	John Moore, "The Life of T. Smollett, M.D.," in *The

Works of Tobias Smollett, M.D., 8 vols. (London, 1797), 1:xcvii-cxcvi.

OED   *Oxford English Dictionary.*

Parliamentary   *Cobbett's Parliamentary History of England*, 36 vols. (New
History   York: AMS Press, 1966). Reprint of 1806–20 edition.

Political   *The Political Controversy; or, Weekly Magazine of Ministerial*
Controversy   *and Anti-Ministerial Essays*, 5 vols. (London, 1762–65).

Present State   Tobias Smollett, ed., *The Present State of All Nations*, 8 vols.
                        (London, 1768–69).

Voltaire   *The Works of M. de Voltaire: With Notes, Historical and
                        Critical*, ed. Dr. Smollett et al., 25 vols. (London, 1761–
                        65).

Walpole,   *The Yale Edition of Horace Walpole's Correspondence*, ed.
Correspondence   W. S. Lewis et al., 48 vols. (New Haven: Yale University
                        Press, 1938–83).

Walpole,   Horace Walpole, *Memoirs of the Last Ten Years of the Reign
Memoirs*   *of George the Second*, ed. John Brooke, 3 vols. (New Haven:
                        Yale University Press, 1985).

Poems

INTRODUCTION

Sometime between the early part of 1742 and May of 1744, Tobias Smollett established his residence in London as a surgeon and would-be author. Just behind him were his few years of service as a surgeon's mate in the British navy. His experiences during the ill-fated expedition to Carthagena in 1740–41 had made him, a young man still in his early twenties, a witness to some of the harshest examples of brutality and official stupidity that his age had to offer—examples that a few years later were to be given fictional form in the violence-filled pages of the work that first brought his name to the attention of the English reading public, *The Adventures of Roderick Random* (1748).

Exactly what Smollett's hopes were as he settled down in London we do not know. He must have wanted to pursue the literary ambitions he nurtured when he first arrived in London from Scotland in 1739, carrying the manuscript of his blank verse tragedy, *The Regicide*. He must have looked forward to the cultural stimulation of the nation's capital. And almost certainly he hoped to find the recognition and success that literary talent and merit deserved, a hope carried by many young men drawn from their native cities into the metropolis by the vitality of London life.

Whatever his expectations—and we need not think he was particularly naive about them—he soon found that much of London life was for him merely a more refined version of the callous and self-serving world he had encountered on the expedition to Carthagena, a world in which few men of place and power were concerned with the quality of life, a world where merit most often seemed to be measured in terms of success in bribery, flattery, and cultivating the acquaintance of the great. At least this was a popular contemporary view of London in the early 1740s, and there was little in Smollett's experience during his first few years of struggle there to draw him toward any other conclusion. A half decade of rebuffs, of observations of a brutal, hypocritical society, was to culminate in Smollett's first significant publications at the end of 1746 and the beginning of 1747. These came not in the form of a novel, the genre in which he was to gain lasting fame, but in the form of an emotional ode, *The Tears of Scotland*, and two verse satires, *Advice* and *Reproof*.[1]

Throughout his life Smollett manifested two personal qualities that often seem part of the satirist's makeup. He had a sincere, charitable concern for the well-being of others, particularly those who were in distress. But he was also very quick to take offense and was almost abnormally sensitive to both physical and moral ugliness. In his preface to *Roderick Random*, Smollett struck off a phrase that very aptly sums up these qualities in his character and describes the tone which frequently informs his writing: "that generous indignation, which ought to animate the reader, against the sordid and vicious disposition of the world."

Apparently Smollett's possession of such indignation prompted him at an early age to express himself satirically. According to his friend and early biographer, John Moore, Smollett, while a surgeon's apprentice in Glasgow in his later teens, began writing satire "against such green and scanty shoots of affectation and ridicule as the soil produced," not only the "youthful circles of coquetry and foppery" but also the "more formal and serious assemblies." Moore reports that the chief concerns of the citizens of Glasgow were commerce and religion, wealth and piety, and that those among them whom the young Smollett considered to be hypocrites, satisfied with only the reputation of piety, were exposed to his satire. His youthful squibs, none of which has been preserved, were effective enough and became well enough known, according to Moore, to offend some of the good citizens of Glasgow.[2]

With a native disposition toward satire and with a certain amount of youthful success in discomfiting moral frauds, Smollett was not likely to endure the disappointments of his first years in London without giving vent to his generous indignation through some sort of rhetorical or poetic expression. Undoubtedly a key stimulus for his earliest "professional" poems was the trouble he endured in trying to get *The Regicide* produced on the London stage. The difficulties he experienced with deceptive patrons and playhouse managers for almost a decade after his first arrival in London were so vivid and exasperating to him that he devoted two chapters (62 and 63) of *Roderick Random* to the interpolated story of Melopoyn, the unfortunate dramatist whom Roderick meets in the Marshalsea Prison and whose account of his unfortunate career rehearses many of Smollett's own disappointments and betrayals. In 1749, when Smollett finally published the still unproduced tragedy, he affixed to it a preface in which he gave a new narrative description of the bad faith of such theatrical managers as James Lacy and John Rich as well as certain aristocratic patrons.[3] In both accounts, the poet-playwright's difficulties arise from a world much like that in the two satires Smollett was composing toward the end of this period of frustration, a world in which true merit was the least of considerations in gaining recognition for a person or his work. The history of *The Regicide*, as both fictionally and literally narrated by Smollett and as an impulse to satiric verse, is a history of praise never acted upon, of flattering promises casually broken, of commitments forgotten at the behest of subtle bribery, of self-serving negotiations moved by whim and opportunism, and, ultimately, of brutal disregard for the feelings of anyone not in a position of power. In fact, as suggested above, the polite world of London letters and society depicted in Smollett's narratives of his difficulties with *The Regicide* seems only slightly different from the world of moral callousness and brutal power that Smollett had witnessed in the British navy.[4]

A more public instance of the brutality and prostitution of power that galled Smollett into writing his first published poems was the smashing of the Jacobite rebellion that broke out in the late summer of 1745. The mismanagement and panic that initially marked the English response to the appearance of the Young Pretender, Prince Charles Edward Stuart, on British soil, the turnabout in the Bonnie Prince's fortunes, and his final defeat at Culloden with the bloody aftermath of Cumberland's pacification of the Highlands, were events bound to rouse Smollett's generous indignation. Smollett was certainly no Jacobite, although he had a Scotsman's sentimental view of the numerous misfortunes of the Stuart line. But the conduct of British military and governmental leaders in the whole Jacobite affair was to Smollett further evidence of the corruption and injustice fostered by the Hanoverian rule of the first two Georges. He was provoked not only by the incompetence and apparent cowardice of such military leaders as Sir John Cope, who commanded the government troops defeated by Charles in his victory at Prestonpans at the beginning of the rebellion, but also by the way such incompetence and cowardice were whitewashed when the rebellion was successfully quelled. (About the time that Smollett's first poems were published, a military board of inquiry was in the process of investigating and eventually exonerating Cope's behavior. The exoneration became an important element in *Reproof.*) And, of course, Smollett's basic humanity was appalled by the indiscriminate slaughter committed by Cumberland's troops as they carried out their orders to snuff out the last traces of rebellion in the Scottish Highlands.

Smollett's first response to the news of Culloden was both ironic and indignant. As recorded by his friend Alexander Carlyle in an account of the arrival of the news in London, Smollett exclaimed, "John Bull . . . is as Haughty and Valiant tonight, as a few Months ago he was abject and cowardly, on the Black Wednesday when the Highlanders were at Derby."[5] Written over a decade later, Smollett's angry account of Culloden in his *Complete History* again shows the depth of his indignation. He calls Culloden and its attendant massacre the "triumph of low illiberal minds, uninspired by sentiment, untinctured by humanity." After a description of some of the specific atrocities, he remarks that "the humane reader cannot reflect upon such a scene without grief and horror."[6]

Just such grief and horror are the emotions of *The Tears of Scotland*, written soon after the battle of Culloden and probably about the same time that *Advice* was beginning to take form. The temper of Smollett in mid-1746 is indicated not only in the lines of the poem itself, but also in an anecdote related by John Moore concerning the poem's early history. Moore tells of how the circulation of the poem, with its authorship fully avowed by Smollett, caused Smollett's friends to fear that its outspokenness "might raise him powerful enemies." Moore continues: "Through the whole course of Smollett's life he was little influenced by prudential considerations, and never intimidated from avowing his sentiments by the fear of making powerful enemies. The caution of his advisers, instead of prevailing with him to suppress the verses, or conceal his being the author, made him avow them more openly than ever. He even added an additional stanza [the seventh], in which he braves the malice of those whom he considered as the enemies of his country."[7]

This story was later elaborated by William Richardson, who recorded an anecdote communicated to him by Robert Graham, one of Smollett's trustees. Richardson tells of some gentlemen playing cards in a tavern "while Smollett, not choosing to play sat down to write." One of the company asked Smollett about his writing, whereupon Smollett read the first sketch of *The Tears of Scotland*. When the friends expostulated with Smollett about the potentially offensive expressions of the poem, Smollett "made no reply, but, with an air of great indignation, subjoined the concluding stanza."[8]

This anecdote, although not fully authenticated, is valuable as the only external evidence of the immediate circumstances surrounding the composition of any of Smollett's poetry. Even more valuable is the suggestion that the traditional persona Smollett adopted in *Advice* and *Reproof*, the indignant and incorruptible poet affronted by the corruption about him and refusing to be silenced by the voice of prudence, was a role into which Smollett fell quite naturally. The callous brutality of life in the British navy, the refined brutality of London patrons of the arts, the climactic (for Smollett at least) brutality of the 'Forty-Five and the subsequent exoneration and glorification of its knavish leaders had developed within Smollett an indignation that eventually subsided but never completely cooled during a writing career that lasted for the next quarter of a century and that was appropriately launched in public print with the outbursts of *The Tears of Scotland*, *Advice*, and *Reproof*.

The view of English life that Smollett expressed in his two satires may have had its roots in his own experiences and observations, but it was far from being merely a personal view. Most of the ideas of the poems had long since become traditional in satiric complaints. Indeed, the basic rhetorical conception of the two poems is an echo of material that was thoroughly conventional — one must almost say trite — by the time Smollett first dipped his pen in the acid of Augustan satire. The political and social milieu Smollett treats in his two works had been thoroughly scanned by satirists for some years before Smollett's ventures, and his works are but a couple of minor links near the end of a literary chain that had been strongly and effectively forged in the three decades since Hanoverians had assumed the rule of Britain.

In February 1742, the month when Smollett's ship, the *Chichester*, returned to England and when Smollett may have left naval service, Robert Walpole had finally been forced out of office as prime minister after a tenure of more than two decades. The political opposition to Walpole, a loose coalition of many forces, had been assisted in the years immediately preceding his ouster by an outpouring of satiric and polemic literature decrying the state of public morality and exposing the corruptions allegedly spreading throughout English society. During the 1730s *The Craftsman* and *Common Sense*, to mention but two of the opposition periodicals, carried numerous brilliantly executed attacks by Bolingbroke, Pulteney, Chesterfield, Fielding, and others on Walpole's policies and the English milieu they were creating. The direct polemics of the journalists were turned into more imaginative fare by an army of playwrights, satirists, versifiers, and poets who alternately berated and entertained the public with their fanciful exposés. John Gay, in *The Beggar's Opera* (1728), had identified Walpole and his supporters with a band of tawdry, venal highwaymen. Henry Fielding, among others, picked up where Gay left off in using the theater to make pungent comments on England and its corrupt leaders. His series of dramatic burlesques culminated in *The Historical Register for the Year 1736*. The following speech from the *Historical Register* is representative of much of what was said in the last stages of the fight against Walpole: "Why, sir, it is a discovery lately found out that a man of great parts, learning, and virtue, is fit for no employment whatever. That an estate renders a man unfit to be trusted, that being a blockhead is a qualification for business, that honesty is the only sort of folly for which a man ought to be utterly neglected and condemned" (3.18–23).[9]

More traditional and elegant literary forms were also employed to express the feelings — from discontent to outrage — prompted by the supposed drift of English life away from traditional, formerly stable social institutions and moral norms. Samuel Johnson's poem, *London* (1738), translated Juvenal's satiric ire at the corruptions of imperial Rome into a conventional but nonetheless intense and significant statement of England's social and moral ills.

The fact that Johnson's imitation of Juvenal was perhaps more a literary exercise than a strongly felt personal statement helps to confirm the pervasiveness of the indignation it registers:

> Since Worth, he cries, in these degen'rate Days,
> Wants ev'n the cheap Reward of empty Praise;
> In these curst Walls, devote to Vice and Gain,
> Since unrewarded Science toils in vain;
>
> . . . .
>
> Grant me, kind Heaven, to find some happier Place,
> Where Honesty and Sense are no Disgrace.
>   (lines 35–38, 43–44)[10]

According to James Boswell, the very day in May 1738 when *London* was published was also the day when another typical verse satire of the age, Alexander Pope's *One Thousand Seven Hundred and Thirty Eight*, appeared. The conclusion of Pope's poem, now usually identified as *Epilogue to the Satires: Dialogue I*, gathers up much of the indignation that satirists and polemicists had been expressing in the preceding years and strikes the tone that Smollett was to strive for not quite a decade later:

> The wit of Cheats, the Courage of a Whore,
> Are what ten thousand envy and adore.
> All, all look up, with reverential Awe,
> On Crimes that scape, or triumph o'er the Law:
> While Truth, Worth, Wisdom, daily they decry—
> "Nothing is Sacred now but Villany."
>   Yet may this Verse (if such a Verse remain)
> Show there was one who held it in disdain.
>   (lines 165–72)[11]

Indeed, Pope's piece and its companion epilogue, *Dialogue II*, published a month later, may well be considered the most direct literary progenitors of *Advice* and *Reproof*. Not only do Smollett's two poems share with Pope's many of the conventional features of the formal verse satire,[12] but they also exhibit a Juvenalian directness and elevated moral indignation that strongly relate them to Pope's dialogues in a single literary and moral tradition. Pope's influence and fame can, of course, be taken for granted in the 1740s. The matter and manner of Pope's two 1738 dialogues may seem to be particularly strong influences on *Advice* and *Reproof*, but Pope's entire output of satires during the 1730s—with its multileveled exposures of corruption, perversion, self-indulgence, and bad taste, and with its attempts to inculcate a harmonious, humane ethic—must be seen as a significant part of the literary and moral ambience in which Smollett picked up his pen. Indeed, Smollett's compatibility with the Popean ethos is affirmed numerous times throughout his career by the many quotations from and allusions to Pope in virtually all his novels and by admiring references to him in many of his other writings.

Like Pope in his two dialogues, Smollett forms his satires as dialogues between the poet and a friend. The friend is the voice of popularity and compromise, of tempering one's views to the prevailing moral tone, of getting ahead by writing panegyric rather than satire. His is the ironic voice, so frequent in the eighteenth century, that notices no ambiguity in the word *great*, accepting without question the equation of position and power with goodness or at least unwilling to risk offending the great by calling into question the quality of their greatness. The poet's voice, on the other hand, is that of conscience and integrity. The more Smollett's poet is urged to yield, the more uncompromising he becomes in his determination that there be at least one voice speaking the truth about the corruption in society.

Out of the exchange between the voices comes an exposure of a sycophantic society in which attention to the public weal and the promotion of taste and morals consistently give way to the prostitution of position and power and to half-concealed obscenity. Although Smollett is far from the near sublime of the last book of *The Dunciad* or the exquisite scorn of *An Epistle to Dr. Arbuthnot*, he conveys Pope's sense of a world almost overwhelmed by dullness, a world of "great" men with puny and dirty minds, a world succumbing to the onslaught of artistic fraud and intellectual dishonesty. In the midst of this onslaught stands the poet-satirist, not very hopeful of stemming the tide but nonetheless steadfastly refusing to be silenced or corrupted:

> Th' indignant muse to Virtue's aid shall rise,
> And fix the brand of infamy on vice.
>
> (*Advice*, lines 129–30)

As Pope had done a decade earlier, Smollett takes the position that, since society is hierarchical, nothing is more morally devastating to a nation than an effete, tasteless aristocracy or oligarchy, maintaining itself in political and social power by bribery and patronage of mediocrity. Like the great Augustans, Smollett sees a powerful connection between bad taste, prostituted talent, and the decay of a society's moral values.

To achieve his exposure Smollett uses a number of devices and elements that continually remind the reader of Pope. It is difficult, however, to fix precisely the Popean echoes of the poems, because most of them represent traditional elements of satire or eighteenth-century poetical conventions that find their most masterful use in Pope but that are widespread among many other poets and satirists with whom Smollett would have been familiar. The following couplet, for example, certainly has a Popean cadence to it:

> Too coy to flatter, and too proud to serve,
> Thine be the joyless dignity to starve.
> (*Advice*, lines 235–36)

Conceivably Smollett might have composed such lines in 1746 even if, by some strange circumstance, he had never read Pope. And yet one feels, after encountering many such lines, that Smollett quite certainly had read and re-read Pope and was consciously or unconsciously responding to and imitating the Popean flow of language throughout his two poems. Here is another example of the many that might be quoted to make the same point:

> There shall he shine, with ming'ling honours bright,
> His master's pathic, pimp, and parasite . . . .
> (*Advice*, lines 79–80)

Similarly, Smollett's strewing the poems with proper names—many of them actual names of contemporaries, some given only with an initial letter followed by a dash, some Latin type names—imparts to the poems a Popean flavor. Smollett's occasional use of a proper name for comic or grotesque effect is a particularly striking echo of the Pope of *The Dunciad*. Here are two examples:

> Insatiate *L[a]sc[elle]s*, and the fiend *V[a]n[ec]k*
> Rise on our ruins, and enjoy the wreck . . . .
> (*Reproof*, lines 127–28)

> Condemn'd by *C[lar]k*, *B[an]ks*, *B[arro]wby*, and *C[hit]ty*,
> And all the crop-ear'd critics of the city . . . .
> (*Reproof*, lines 195–96)

Smollett has few of the brilliant exempla that enrich Pope's satires—the numerous "characters" such as Atossa and Atticus, the description of Timon's

"modest merit" must struggle in the novel. And the homosexuality attacked in *Advice*, like Strutwell's in the novel written a year later, is for Smollett a metonymic construct for the whole social ethos the satirist is attacking. To this extent at least, Smollett's venture into the field of formal verse satire did give a daring imaginative twist to one of the commonplace literary forms of the day.

Thus both private and public concerns, both individual indignation and literary tradition, combined to provide the ingredients of Smollett's first significant appearances in print. Unfortunately, although much can be inferred from the works themselves about their genesis, details are scant as to their publication and reception. There is even some uncertainty as to which was printed first: *The Tears of Scotland* or *Advice*. It appears that *Advice* was published in August 1746 – the *London Magazine* for that month includes it in a list of new titles; but whether *The Tears of Scotland* was in print before then we do not know. Apparently the first publication of *The Tears of Scotland* is a rare four-page leaflet presumed to have appeared sometime in the last half of 1746, but possibly later. This may be the publication to which Alexander Carlyle referred in giving the only data related to the appearance of Smollett's poem that has chronological significance: "I saw not Smollett again for some time after [receiving news of the battle of Culloden in April 1746], when he Shew'd Smith and me the Manuscript of his Tears of Scotland, which was published not long after, and had such a Run of Approbation." [13] Carlyle's vague "not long after" may suggest a period anywhere from a few weeks to a year or longer, but at least his remark does indicate that the poem was printed within a comparatively short time after the events it memorializes.

The only word from Smollett about the publication of his first poems is a passage in a letter to Carlyle written probably sometime in 1747: "If I had an Opportunity, I would send you the New Play [new version of *The Regicide?*] and Farce [unknown], Two Satires called Advice and Reproof which made some Noise here, and a Ballad set to Musick under the name of the Tears of Scotland, a Performance very well received at London, as I hope it will be in your Country which gave Rise to it. The Truth is I have a paternal Concern for that and the Satires above mentioned." [14] The musical setting referred to by Smollett is undoubtedly that by James Oswald, which must have been composed almost immediately after the poem's appearance, for by December 1746 the *General Advertiser* announced a musical volume entitled *The Land of Cakes*, which included a musical setting of *The Tears of Scotland*. This may represent the performance to which Smollett alludes and may even be the first authorized publication of the work. At any rate, it is clear that within a year or two after the battle of Culloden, Smollett's verses were fairly well known. They were reprinted several times during the following years and set at least once again to music;[15] and thus there seems little doubt that the "Run of Approbation" of which Carlyle speaks and the good reception of which Smollett writes were phrases justified by the poem's popular acceptance.

Less can be said about the reception given *Advice* and *Reproof*. Had not the poems been published together in a second, revised edition within a year and a half of their first appearance—a venture it is unlikely any bookseller would have underwritten had not the first editions successfully sold out—one might almost suspect that the verses had fallen stillborn from the press.[16] The text of *Reproof*, published in January 1747 (four months after *Advice*), alludes to the attention given the earlier poem. In the dialogue between poet and friend, the friend comments on the poet's earlier satiric remarks:

> Yes, season'd with your own remarks between,
> Inflam'd with so much virulence of spleen,
> That the mild town (to give the dev'l his due)
> Ascrib'd the whole performance to a Jew.
> (lines 23–26)

In the first edition of *Reproof*, a note presumably supplied by Smollett amplifies the thought: "Various have been the conjectures concerning the Author of ADVICE, who has been represented as a *Jew*, a clergyman, a templar, an independent Elector; nay, some have not scrupled to ascribe the whole performance to the spirit of the late counsellor *Morgan*." This note may merely be part of the satiric fiction, but if it has some basis in fact, it must refer mostly to town gossip, since none of these conjectures has shown up in print.

The only report Moore gives concerning the reception of the satires is his observation that *Advice*, "though possessed of considerable poetical merit, was far more calculated to injure him, from the resentment it kindled in the breasts of individuals, than to be useful to him by the display of his talents."[17] But Moore gives no specific reactions. Some of Smollett's accusations may even have been actionable, but apparently those attacked by Smollett did not deem his words worthy of a formal reply, much less any legal action. However, the softening or obscuring of some passages in the second edition may be a response to resentment from certain quarters. Although Smollett may have taken some satisfaction in the reception given his satires, the noise they made must have been very local and temporary. After the second edition of

1748, *Advice* and *Reproof* were apparently not reprinted until 1777, when they appeared in the first collected edition of Smollett's poems.

However minor the success of these early ventures into print, they at least carried Smollett in the direction he desired to go. Smollett had found a tone, an outlook on English society, and a number of themes that were soon to be transposed from poetry into prose fiction. *The Tears of Scotland, Advice,* and *Reproof* helped Smollett to set his feet on promising paths. Soon, with the outpouring of his "generous indignation" in defense of "modest merit" in *The Adventures of Roderick Random*, he found himself on the highroad of success.

The popularity of *Roderick Random*, published in January 1748, swept Smollett into the mainstream of London literary life. For the next two decades his pen was rarely idle as he launched into a strenuous career of novel writing, journalism, and other enterprises of an astonishing variety. There scarcely seemed time for such polished literary ventures as the writing of poetry; in fact, with the exception of *Ode to Independence*, all of Smollett's poetry subsequent to 1747 appears to be fugitive or the by-product of other projects.

Ten of Smollett's poems appear in the texts of his novels—five in *Roderick Random*, four in *Peregrine Pickle*, and one in *Humphry Clinker*.[18] A couple of these seem to have been written specifically to fit the needs of plot or character development: "Thus have I sent the simple king to hell," the parodic rant written by Narcissa's eccentric aunt in *Roderick Random* (chapter 40); the brief travesty of John Dalton's adaptation of Milton's *Comus* in the same novel (chapter 53); and "Come, listen ye students of ev'ry degree," Peregrine's lampoon of his tutor Jumble in *Peregrine Pickle* (chapter 25). The composition of the other poems in the novels may have a similar origin, but these others (five love songs; the parody of George Lyttelton in *Peregrine Pickle*, "Where wast thou, wittol Ward"; and "Ode to Leven-Water," in *Humphry Clinker*) might equally well have been poems written for other occasions that Smollett conveniently found a place for in his prose fiction. With at least one poem such circumstances seem certain: a four-stanza version of the poem entitled "On Celia playing on the harpsichord and singing" in *Roderick Random* (chapter 40) was published with a musical setting in 1745, about three years before the poem appeared in the novel. Thus it would appear that Smollett used the occasion of his novel to give an ephemeral lyric a new life.[19] The lyric "Adieu, ye streams that smoothly flow" from *Peregrine Pickle* (chapter 21) may also have been written sometime before it found its way into that novel: there exist two different musical settings of this lyric which were apparently printed sometime shortly before, during, or shortly after the year 1751, when the novel first came out.[20] But copies of these two songs, like most sheet music of the day, bear no date of publication, and one therefore cannot be sure whether the poem was indeed published as a song before or after its appearance in the novel, or whether it was written for an occasion other than its appearance in *Peregrine Pickle*.

Although there is little or no evidence that any of the other poems in the novels were published elsewhere, it is quite possible that a few were poems Smollett had on hand from some earlier project or merely from a few moments of poetic trifling, work which he then conveniently inserted into the texts of his novels. The context in which "Ode to Leven-Water" appears in *Humphry Clinker*—Matthew Bramble appends it to his letter of August 28 as a composition by Dr. Smollett—makes that possibility especially strong. The inclusion in the novels of a wide variety of poems, from burlesques to odes, may imply that Smollett was strongly committed to a view of himself as a poetic talent who deserved a hearing and who had a poet's genuine concern for developing his skills.

Smollett's assumption of the editorship of the *British Magazine* at the beginning of 1760 afforded him another opportunity for getting his poetry into print. During that year, four poems certainly attributed to Smollett—they were identified as his in the posthumous collection of *Plays and Poems*, 1777—appeared in the magazine as contributions to a small section of "Poetical Essays" included in each monthly issue. Five additional poems, also published in the *British Magazine*, have been assigned to Smollett by modern scholars, though somewhat doubtfully;[21] these are included in an appendix to the present volume. Of the origins of these poems, including the certain attributions, practically nothing is known. They were all published anonymously. It can be reasonably inferred that "Ode to Blue-Ey'd Ann" was written by Smollett in homage to his wife, Ann (or Anne) Lassells. And the subscription to the "Ode to Sleep," "intended as a chorus in a tragedy," has created speculation that the ode might have originally been written for *Alceste*, the never-produced stage piece for which Smollett was commissioned to write the text and George Frederick Handel the music in about 1748. But the lyrics to *Alceste* that have been identified as Smollett's seem not to bear out that speculation.

However fortuitous and self-serving the publication of the poems in the novels and the *British Magazine* may have been, they at least got into print; not so the poetic lines that Smollett wrote for *Alceste*. Although a fair amount is known about Smollett's involvement in John Rich's enterprise to produce a spectacle on the theme of Alceste with music by Handel, very little can be guessed about the actual work. Handel, well known for borrowing from himself and for mixing parts of one work into another, did later use some of the songs completed for *Alceste* in performances of *The Choice of Hercules*, *Hercules*, and *Alexander Balus*, but apparently no one acknowledged Smollett as the author of the lyrics.[22] Had not some of Smollett's lyrics set to music by Handel been preserved in manuscript and eventually published, this part of Smollett's poetic production would have disappeared as completely as has the full text of *Alceste*. Until O. E. Deutsch ferreted out these lyrics in 1948, *Alceste* was known to editors and biographers of Smollett only as a brief episode in the life of their author.[23]

Smollett's only later poetic production that did not appear in conjunction with some other literary enterprise is his posthumously published *Ode to Independence*. William Richardson, who wrote the "Observations" affixed to the first edition of the poem (Glasgow, 1773) and to many of the subsequent printings, provides most of what little information is available about its history: "[Smollett's] *Ode to Independence* was left in his own handwriting, with some other papers, to the late Robert Graham, Esq. of Gartmore, who was one of his trustees, and who gave it to the author of the present publication, under whose inspection the first edition was elegantly printed, by the celebrated Messrs. Foulis, printers to the University of Glasgow."[24]

The composition of the poem quite clearly belongs to the last decade of Smollett's life. As in the earliest poems, strong personal feelings and experiences are at work in the text. Particularly in the period following his dismal experience with the *Briton*, when he had been terribly abused by the opposition writers and then increasingly ignored by his patrons, Smollett must have had occasion to reflect on the virtues of independence. In May 1763, writing to Richard Smith, an American admirer who had inquired about the facts of his career, Smollett expressed just such reflections: "the truth is I have neither Pension nor Place, nor am I of that Disposition which can stoop to Sollicit either. I have always piqued myself upon my Independancy, and I trust in God I shall preserve it to my dying day."[25] Another expression of Smollett's satisfaction in his own independence is found in his self-portrait in *Humphry Clinker*. Jery Melford, in reporting on an afternoon spent with the writer S—, describes their host as "one of those few writers of the age that stand upon their own foundation, without patronage, and above dependence" (Jery Melford to Sir Watkin Phillips, London, June 10, p. 123).

A more specific autobiographical note is sounded in the scorn poured out upon the wealthy "minion" in the last strophe of the ode. Biographers of

Smollett have long identified this as an allusion to the ingratitude and contempt he suffered at the hands of one Alexander Campbell, who had been befriended by Smollett before seeking his fortune in India but who ignored his benefactor upon his return early in 1768.[26] The experience is also said to be the basis for the Paunceford-Serle episode in the Bath section of *Humphry Clinker*.

There are other kinds of evidence in the poem that help to establish the approximate date of its composition. The reference to Pascal Paoli suggests a period around 1766, when James Boswell was trumpeting the cause of the valiant Corsican through England. And Howard S. Buck has identified fairly striking similarities in general conception and imagery between *Ode to Independence* and Thomas Gray's Norse fragments, "The Descent of Odin" and "The Triumphs of Owen," which were published in 1764.[27] On the assumption that such similarities suggest contemporaneity of composition, one can consider the last half of the 1760s as the period when Smollett wrote *Ode to Independence*.

Why Smollett did not publish *Ode to Independence* during his lifetime can only be conjectured. Little in the poem could be considered offensive to readers in general or to any reader in particular, even if such a consideration had ever had any weight with Smollett. His reputation, despite the personal and political difficulties he had suffered, was such that a publisher should not have been hard to find. The poem appears to be finished, but perhaps Smollett still hoped to polish it more. And perhaps, having given form to his thoughts but no longer feeling the intense urge to get his work before the public that had pricked him in his youth, he was indifferent to its publication.

Whatever Smollett's own concerns or judgments, the ode was greatly praised after his death. Richardson's "Observations," printed with the first Glasgow edition, praise highly both the sentiments of the poem and their imaginative expression. Richardson's praise seemed to set the pattern for commentators during the next generation. The advertisement to the first London edition (1774) notes effusively: "It has all the Enthusiasm and poetic Colouring which suit the Ode; and it breathes a Spirit of Liberty that would not have disgraced a Citizen of Sparta, or of Rome." Despite such puffery, the poem upon its initial publication seems to have made no great stir among either the Scottish or the English reading public. It is only the comments of subsequent biographers and critics which suggest that it gradually came to be thought of as the finest of Smollett's poetic endeavors. By 1810, when Alexander Chalmers included Smollett's poems in his comprehensive *Works of the English Poets*, he could write in his introduction: "The Tears of Scotland

and the Ode to Independence, particularly the latter, are equal to the highest efforts in the pathetic and sublime. In the Ode to Independence there is evidently the inspiration of real genius, free from all artificial aid, or meretricious ornament. It may be questioned whether there are many compositions in our language which more forcibly charm by all the enchantments of taste, expression, and sentiment." [28]

Although individual poems and selections of Smollett's poetry continued to be reprinted throughout the nineteenth century, his reputation as a poet, never very high, had peaked before that century was well under way and has generally been in decline ever since. This fact is not particularly surprising. Clearly, Smollett is not a great poet, and individual works might not be included even in anthologies of poetry (as they occasionally are nowadays) were it not for his reputation as a novelist. In diction and versification, the lyrics sound like hundreds of ephemeral verses descended from the Elizabethan and Cavalier tradition of song writing. It is futile to look for immediate models or sources, because they are stylistically so undistinguished.

The more ambitious odes have a more specific pedigree and probably possess greater interest for the student of eighteenth-century poetry, related as they are to the descriptive and allegorical odes that Thomas and Joseph Warton, William Collins, Thomas Gray, and others began writing and popularizing in the 1740s. These odes leaned heavily on personification (inspired in part by Milton's "Il Penseroso" and "L'Allegro"), apostrophes, and a kind of rhapsodic form inherited from Abraham Cowley's experiments a few generations earlier with the Pindaric ode. Such works increasingly appealed to English readers as the picturesque and the sublime became aesthetic qualities that were more sought after in the last decades of the eighteenth century. (Indeed, Richardson's reasons for praising Smollett's *Ode to Independence* so highly in his "Observations" provide an excellent index to standard criteria of poetic taste and judgment in the 1770s.) The satires, as suggested earlier, owe much to Pope and his tradition of verse satire. And the burlesque and parodic poems explain their own origins in the ideas and styles they mock. They are interesting examples of Smollett's talent for burlesque and caricature, a talent much more in evidence in the personal caricatures of the novels and one that Fielding and Gay, among many others, had prepared eighteenth-century readers to appreciate.

Thus, even though Smollett's poetry may not stand up under very close critical scrutiny, it clearly helps to define his world, the actual world in which he was living—its tastes, its concerns, even its pretensions and clichés—and, more importantly, the world as he saw it, often with remarkably clear eyes and penetrating vision, sometimes through eyes conditioned by disappointment and disdain, sometimes through eyes affected by sentiment and generous indignation. Modern readers will find in his poems, at the very least, a vivid record of feeling and thought, a record that helps illuminate the nature of the genius that raised him, on many occasions, to the status of literary master.

Notes

1. Although *The Tears of Scotland* and *Advice* and *Reproof* were Smollett's first significant publications, his earliest printed work was a four-stanza lyric entitled "A New Song," which James Oswald set to music for a song collection of 1745 called *Universal Harmony*. The text of the lyric is included in the present edition. A shortened and revised version of the same poem was inserted into *Roderick Random* (chapter 40) under the title "On Celia playing on the harpsichord and singing." See Otto Erich Deutsch, "Poetry Preserved in Music: Bibliographical Notes on Smollett and Oswald, Handel, and Haydn," *Modern Language Notes* 63 (1948): 74–75. "On Celia" is reprinted in the textual commentary, pp. 553–54.
2. See Moore, cxi–cxii. Moore observes earlier that "the first sprouts of Smollett's poetical genius appeared while he was at the grammar-school of Dumbarton, as I was informed by an old school-fellow of his; they were verses to the memory of Wallace" (p. cviii). Knapp, 15, argues that, with regard to Smollett's memories of his youthful poetic endeavors, a passage in chapter 6 of the first edition of *Roderick Random* should be given a fairly literal autobiographical interpretation: remembering his university days, Roderick records, "I valued myself on my taste in the *Belle Lettre*, and a talent for poetry, which had already produced some morceaus, that brought me a great deal of reputation."
3. See Smollett's preface to *The Regicide*, pp. 89–93, and see the introduction to the plays in this volume, pp. 71–72.
4. The spectacle of virtue and merit neglected by a nearly obscene society continued to gall Smollett. Another example related to the satires is the case of the "melting *Scot*" who appears in line 122 of *Reproof* and who reappears in chapter 106 of *Peregrine Pickle* as M—(MacKercher), the honest lawyer encountered in the Fleet Prison by Peregrine.
5. Carlyle, 98–99.
6. *Complete History*, 4:673–74.
7. Moore, cxvi.
8. William Richardson, *Poems and Plays* (Edinburgh, 1805), 1:125. Robert Anderson, the most indefatigable of early Smollett biographers, implies that Graham may have heard the anecdote from Thomas Bontein, supposedly present when the incident took place and later also one of Smollett's trustees. See Anderson, *The Life of Tobias Smollett, M.D.*, 4th ed. (Edinburgh, 1803), 30.

9. Henry Fielding, *The Historical Register for the Year 1736 and Eurydice Hissed*, ed. William W. Appleton (Lincoln: University of Nebraska Press, 1967), 39.
10. *The Poems of Samuel Johnson*, ed. David Nichol Smith and Edward L. McAdam, 2d ed. (Oxford: Clarendon Press, 1974), 69.
11. Alexander Pope, *Imitations of Horace*, ed. John Butt, 2d ed. (London: Methuen, 1953), 309.
12. The standard discussion of these is found in Mary Claire Randolph, "The Structural Design of the Formal Verse Satire," *Philological Quarterly* 21 (1942): 368–84. Also helpful in analyzing the traditional satiric elements in Smollett is Donald M. Korte, "Smollett's 'Advice' and 'Reproof': Apprenticeship in Satire," *Studies in Scottish Literature* 8 (1971): 239–52.
13. Carlyle, 99.
14. *Letters*, 5–6.
15. For a list of early reprints, see *The New Cambridge Bibliography of English Literature*, ed. George Watson (Cambridge: The University Press, 1971), 2:962. The musical settings are described by Knapp, 60–61.
16. The second edition, combining the two satires into one volume, appeared in March 1748. A suggestion of a favorable response to the two satires from Lord Chesterfield might be inferred from a passage in chapter 102 of *Peregrine Pickle*. See Smollett's preface to *The Regicide*, p. 91, n. 10.
17. Moore, cxviii.
18. In a full consideration of Smollett as poet, one should also note that there are four songs and a conventional prologue and epilogue in the text of *The Reprisal*.
19. See above, n. 1.
20. Lewis M. Knapp, "Smollett's Verses and Their Musical Settings in the Eighteenth Century," *Modern Language Notes* 46 (1931): 231.
21. Buck, *Poet*, 52–68, provides the only sustained discussion of the poetry Smollett published in the *British Magazine* and is the source for four of the doubtful attributions; the source for the fifth doubtful attribution is James G. Basker, *Tobias Smollett: Critic and Journalist* (Newark: University of Delaware Press, 1988), 201.
22. See introduction to the plays, p. 76.
23. See Deutsch, "Poetry Preserved in Music."
24. Richardson, *Poems and Plays*, 1:124. Luella Norwood provides a full account of the acceptance of the ode into the Smollett canon in her study, "The Authenticity of Smollett's *Ode to Independence*," *Review of English Studies* 17 (1941): 55–64.
25. *Letters*, 113.
26. Knapp, 290–92, gives the fullest account of this episode.
27. Buck, *Poet*, 74–75.
28. *The Works of the English Poets* (London, 1810), 15:552–53.

THE
TEARS
OF
SCOTLAND.

MOURN, hapless *Caledonia*, mourn
Thy banished Peace, thy Laurel torn!
Thy Sons, for Valour long renown'd,
Ly slaughter'd on their native Ground!
Thy hospitable Roofs no more
Invite the Stranger to the Door;
In smoky Ruins sunk they ly,
The Monuments of Cruelty!

II. The

The Tears of Scotland, Recto of First Leaf, First Edition, 1746.
(The Bodleian Library, Oxford, Shelfmark Don.e.230.)

A NEW SONG
Set by Mr. Oswald, the Words by Mr. Smollet[1]

1

When Sappho[2] tun'd the raptur'd strain,
The list'ning wretch forgot his pain;
With art divine the lyre she strung,
Like thee she play'd, like thee she sung,
Like thee she play'd, like thee she sung.   5

2

For while she struck the quiv'ring wire,
The eager breast was all on fire;
And when she joyn'd the vocal lay,
The captive soul was charm'd away.
The captive etc.   10

3

But had she added still to these,
Thy softer chaster pow'r to please,
Thy beauteous air of sprightly youth,
Thy native smiles of artless truth.
Thy native etc.   15

4

She ne'er had pin'd beneath disdain,
She ne'er had play'd and sung in vain,
Despair her soul had ne'er possess'd
To dash on rocks the tender breast.[3]
To dash etc.   20

THE TEARS OF SCOTLAND.
WRITTEN IN THE YEAR MDCCXLVI.

I.

Mourn, hapless CALEDONIA, mourn
Thy banish'd peace,[1] thy laurels torn!

Thy sons, for valour long renown'd,
Lie slaughter'd on their native ground;
Thy hospitable roofs,[2] no more,   5
Invite the stranger to the door;
In smoaky ruins sunk they lie,
The monuments of cruelty.

II.

The wretched owner sees afar
His all become the prey of war;   10
Bethinks him of his babes and wife,
Then smites his breast, and curses life.
Thy swains are famish'd on the rocks,
Where once they fed their wanton[3] flocks:
Thy ravish'd virgins shriek in vain;   15
Thy infants perish on the plain.

III.

What boots it then, in every clime,
Thro' the wide-spreading waste of time,
Thy martial glory, crown'd with praise,
Still shone with undiminish'd blaze?   20
Thy tow'ring spirit now is broke,
Thy neck is bended to the yoke.
What foreign arms could never quell,
By civil rage, and rancour fell.

IV.

The rural pipe, and merry lay   25
No more shall chear the happy day:
No social scenes of gay delight
Beguile the dreary winter night:
No strains, but those of sorrow flow,
And nought be heard but sounds of woe;   30
While the pale phantoms of the slain[4]
Glide nightly o'er the silent plain.

V.

Oh baneful cause, oh! fatal morn,
Accurs'd to ages yet unborn!

William Augustus, Duke of Cumberland, commander of British troops
at the battle of Culloden. Studio of Reynolds.
(Courtesy of the National Portrait Gallery, London.)

The sons, against their fathers stood,[5]   35
The parent shed his children's blood.
Yet, when the rage of battle ceas'd,
The victor's soul was not appeas'd;
The naked and forlorn must feel
Devouring flames, and murd'ring steel!   40

VI.

The pious mother doom'd to death,
Forsaken, wanders o'er the heath.
The bleak wind whistles round her head;
Her helpless orphans cry for bread,
Bereft of shelter, food, and friend,   45
She views the shades of night descend,
And stretch'd beneath th' inclement skies,
Weeps o'er her tender babes, and dies.

VII.

Whilst the warm blood bedews my veins,
And unimpair'd remembrance reigns;   50
Resentment of my country's fate,
Within my filial breast shall beat;
And, spite of her insulting foe,
My sympathizing verse shall flow,
"Mourn, hapless Caledonia, mourn   55
Thy banish'd peace, thy laurels torn."

ADVICE:
A
SATIRE.

——*Sed podice levi*
Cæduntur tumidæ medico ridente Mariscæ. ——
O Proceres! censore opus est an haruspice nobis?
                                    JUVENAL.[1]

POET. FRIEND.

P. Enough, enough;[2] all this we knew before:
'Tis infamous, I grant it, to be poor:

A D V I C E:

A

S A T I R E.

Sed podice levi
Ceduntur tumidæ medico ridente Mariscæ.----
O Proceres! cenfore opus eſt an haruſpice nobis?

J U V E N A L.

L O N D O N:

Printed for M. C O O P E R, at the *Globe* in *Pater-nofter-Row.* MDCCXLVI.
[Price One Shilling.]

Title page of *Advice: A Satire*, First Edition, 1746.
(The Pennsylvania State University Libraries.)

And who so much to sense and glory lost,
Will hug the curse that not one joy can boast?
From the pale hag, O! could I once break loose;   5
Divorc'd, all hell shall not re-tie the noose!
Not with more care shall *H*——[3] avoid his wife,
Not *C—pe* fly swifter,[4] lashing for his life;
Than I to leave the meager fiend behind.

    Fr. Exert your Talents; Nature, ever kind,   10
Enough for happiness, bestows on all;
'Tis sloth or pride that finds her gifts too small——
Why sleeps the muse? —— is there no room for praise,
When such bright names in constellation blaze?
When sage *N——c——tle*,[5] abstinently great,   15
Neglects his food to cater for the State;
And *Gr—ft—n*,[6] tow'ring *Atlas* of the throne,
So well rewards a genius like his own:
Gr—nv——le and *B—th*[8] illustrious, need I name
For sober dignity and spotless fame;   20
Or *P——t* th' unshaken *Abdiel* yet unsung:[9]
Thy candour, *Ch——ly!*[10] and thy truth, O *Y——nge!*[11]

    P. Th' advice is good; the question only, whether
These names and virtues ever dwelt together?
But what of that? the more the Bard shall claim,   25
Who can create as well as cherish fame.

    8. *Not* C—pe *fly swifter.*] A General famous for an expeditious retreat, tho' not quite so deliberate as that of the ten thousand *Greeks* from *Persia;* having unfortunately forgot to bring his army along with him.

    15. *When sage* N——c——tle, &c.] Alluding to the philosophical contempt which this great personage manifests for the sensual delights of the stomach.

    17. *And* Gr—ft—n, *tow'ring* Atlas *of the throne*, &c.] This Noble Peer, remarkable for sublimity of parts, by virtue of his office, conferred the laureat on *C—lly C—bb—r*, Esq;[7] a delectable bard, whose character has already employed, together with his own, the greatest pens of the age.

    19. Gr—nv——le *and* B—th, &c.] Two noblemen famous in their day, for nothing more than their fortitude in bearing the scorn and reproach of their country.

    21. *Or* P——t *th'* unshaken Abdiel, &c.] *Abdiel*, according to *Milton*, was the only seraph that preserved his integrity in the midst of corruption——

    Among the innumerable false, unmov'd,
    Unshaken, unseduc'd, unterrify'd——

A Race from Preston Pans to Berwick.

Satiric print representing the alleged cowardice of General Cope at the battle of Prestonpans.

(Courtesy of the British Library.)

But one thing more,——how loud must I repeat,
To rouze th' ingag'd attention of the Great
Amus'd, perhaps, with *C*——'s prolific bum,
Or rapt admidst the transports of a drum;   30
While the grim porter watches ev'ry door,
Stern foe to tradesmen, poets, and the poor.
Th' Hesperian dragon[13] not more fierce and fell;[14]
Nor the gaunt, growling janitor of hell.[15]
Ev'n *Atticus*,[16] (so wills the voice of Fate)   35
Inshrines in clouded Majesty,[17] his state;
Nor to th' adoring croud vouchsafes regard,
Tho' priests adore, and ev'ry priest a bard.
Shall I then follow with the venal tribe,[18]
And on the threshold the base mongrel bribe?   40
Bribe him, to feast my mute-imploring eye,
With some proud Lord, who smiles a gracious lie!
A lie to captivate my heedless youth,
Degrade my talents, and debauch my truth;
While fool'd with hope, revolves my joyless day,   45
And friends, and fame, and fortune fleet away;
'Till scandal, indigence, and scorn, my lot,
The dreary jail entombs me, where I rot!
Is there, ye varnish'd ruffians of the state!
Not one, among the millions whom ye cheat,   50
Who while he totters on the brink of woe,
Dares, ere he fall, attempt th' avenging blow!
A steady blow! his languid soul to feast;
And rid his country of one curse at least!

---

29. *Amus'd, perhaps, with* C——'s *prolific bum.*] This alludes to a phænomenon, not more strange than true. The person here meant,[12] having actually laid upwards of forty eggs, as several physicians and fellows of the R—y—l S—ci—ty can attest; one of whom (we hear) has undertaken the incubation, and will (no doubt) favour the world with an account of his success. Some virtuosi affirm, that such productions must be the effect of a certain intercourse of organs, not fit to be named.

30. *Transports of a drum.*] This is a riotous assembly of fashionable people, of both sexes, at a private house, consisting of some hundreds; not unaptly stiled a drum, from the noise and emptiness of the Entertainment. There are also drum-major, rout, tempest and hurricane, differing only in degrees of multitude and uproar, as the significant name of each declares.

Fr. What! turn assassin?

                    P. Let th' assassin bleed: 55
My fearless verse shall justify the deed.
'Tis he, who lures th' unpractis'd mind astray,
Then leaves the wretch to misery, a prey;
Perverts the race of virtue just begun,
And stabs the public in her ruin'd son.   60

  Fr. Heav'ns how you rail! the man's consum'd by spite!
If *L——km—n*'s fate [19] attends you, when you write;
Let prudence more propitious arts inspire:
The lower still you crawl, you'll climb the higher.[20]
Go then, with ev'ry supple virtue stor'd,   65
And thrive, the favour'd valet of my Lord.
Is that denied? a boon more humble crave;
And minister to him who serves a slave:
Be sure you fasten on promotion's scale;
Ev'n if you seize some footman by the tail: 70
Th' ascent is easy,[21] and the prospect clear,
From the smirch'd scullion to th' embroider'd Peer.
Th' ambitious drudge preferr'd, postilion rides,
Advanc'd again, the chair benighted guides;
Here doom'd, if nature strung his sinewy frame,   75
The slave (perhaps) of some insatiate dame;
But if exempted from th' *Herculean* toil,
A fairer field awaits him, rich with spoil;
There shall he shine, with ming'ling honours bright,
His master's pathic,[22] pimp, and parasite;   80
Then strut a Captain, if his wish be war,
And grasp in hope, a truncheon and a star:[23]
Or if the sweets of peace his soul allure,
Bask at his ease in some warm sinecure;
His fate in consul, clerk, or agent, vary,   85
Or cross the seas, an envoy's secretary:
Compos'd of falshood, ignorance, and pride,

---

62. L——km—n's *fate.*] To be little read, and less approv'd.

A prostrate sycophant shall rise a *L——d:* [24]
And won from kennels [26] to th' impure imbrace,
Accomplish'd *W——n* [27] triumphs o'er disgrace.   90

   P. Eternal infamy his name surround,
Who planted first that vice on *British* ground!
A vice that 'spite of sense and nature reigns,
And poisons genial love, and manhood stains! [28]
Pollio! [29] the pride of science and its shame,   95
The muse weeps o'er thee, while she brands thy name!
Abhorrent views that prostituted groom,
Th' indecent grotto and polluted dome! [30]
There only may the spurious passion glow,
Where not one laurel decks the Caitiff's [31] brow,   100
Obscene with crimes avow'd, of every dye,
Corruption, lust, oppression, perjury:
Let *Ch——n* [32] with a chaplet round his head,
The taste of *Maro* and *Anacreon* [33] plead;
"Sir, *Flaccus* [34] knew to live as well as write,   105
And kept, like me, two boys array'd in white."
Worthy to feel that appetence [35] of fame
Which rivals *Horace* only in his shame!
Let *Isis* [36] wail in murmurs, as she runs,
Her tempting fathers and her yielding sons;   110
While Dullness screens the failings of the church, [38]

88. *A prostrate sycophant shall rise a* L —— d.] This child of dirt, [25] (to use a great author's expression), without any other quality than grovelling adulation, has arrived at the power of insulting his betters every day.

90. *Accomplish'd* W —— n.] Another son of fortune, who owes his present affluence to the most infamous qualifications.

103. *Let* Ch —— n *with a chaplet round his head.*] This genial Knight wore at his own banquet a garland of flowers, in imitation of the ancients; and kept two rosy boys robed in white, for the entertainment of his guests.

109. *Let* Isis *wail in murmurs, as she runs,* &c.] In allusion to the unnatural Orgies said to be solemnized on the banks of this river; particularly at one place, [37] where a much greater sanctity of morals and taste might be expected.

111. *While Dullness screens,* &c.] This is a decent and parental office, in which dullness is employed; namely, to conceal the failings of her children: and exactly conformable to that instance of filial piety, which we meet with in the son of *Noah,* who went backward, to cover the nakedness of his father, when he lay exposed: from the scoffs and insults of a malicious world.

Nor leaves one sliding Rabbi in the lurch:
Far other raptures let the breast contain,
Where heav'n-born taste and emulation reign.

Fr. Shall not a thousand virtues, then, atone   115
In thy strict censure for the breach of one?
If *Bubo*[39] keeps a catamite[40] or whore,
His bounty feeds the beggar at his door:
And tho' no mortal credits *Curio*'s word,[41]
A score of laquies fatten at his board: 120
To Christian meekness sacrifice thy spleen,
And strive thy neighbour's weaknesses to screen.

P. Scorn'd be the bard, and wither'd all his fame,
Who wounds a brother weeping o'er his shame!
But if an impious wretch with frantic pride,   125
Throws honour, truth, and decency aside,
If nor by Reason aw'd, nor check'd by Fears,
He counts his glories from the stains he bears;[42]
Th' indignant muse to Virtue's aid shall rise,
And fix the brand of infamy on vice.   130
What if arous'd at his imperious call,
An hundred footsteps echo thro' his hall;[43]
And on high Columns rear'd, his lofty dome
Proclaims th' united art of *Greece* and *Rome*:
What tho' whole Hecatombs[44] his *Crew* regale,   135
And each *Dependant* slumbers o'er his ale;
While the remains through Mouths unnumber'd past,
Indulge the beggar and the dogs at last:
Say, friend, is it benevolence of soul,
Or pomp'ous vanity, that prompts the whole?   140
These sons of sloth who by profusion thrive,
His pride inveigled from the public hive;
And numbers pine in solitary woe,
Who furnish'd out this phantasie of shew.
When silent misery assail'd his eyes,   145
Did e'er his throbbing bosom sympathize?
Or his extensive charity, pervade
To those who languish in the barren shade,[45]

Where oft by want and modesty suppress'd,
The bootless talent warms the lonely breast?   150
No! petrify'd by dullness and disdain,
Beyond the feeling of another's pain;
The tear of pity ne'er bedew'd his eye,
Nor his lewd bosom felt the social sigh!

   Fr. Alike to thee his virtue or his vice,   155
If his hand lib'ral, owns thy merit's price.

   P. Sooner, in hopeless anguish would I mourn,
Than owe my fortune to the man I scorn! ——
What new Resource?

         Fr. A thousand yet remain,
That bloom with honours, or that teem with gain: 160
These arts, — are they beneath — beyond thy care?
Devote thy studies to th' auspicious Fair:
Of truth divested, let thy tongue supply
The hinted slander, and the whisper'd lie;
All merit mock, all qualities depress,   165
Save those that grace th' excelling patroness;
Trophies to her, on others' follies raise,
And heard with joy, by defamation praise:
To this collect each faculty of face,
And ev'ry feat perform of sly grimace;   170
Let the grave sneer sarcastic speak thee shrewd,
The smutty joke ridiculously lewd;
And the loud laugh thro' all its changes rung,
Applaud th' abortive sallies of her tongue:
Enroll'd a member in the sacred list,   175
Soon shalt thou sharp[46] in company, at whist;
Her midnight rites and revels regulate,
Priest of her love, and dæmon of her hate.

---

177. *Her midnight rites,* &c.] These are mysteries perform'd, like those of the *Dea Bona,*[47] by females only; consequently it cannot be expected, that we should here explain them: We have, notwithstanding, found means to learn some anecdotes concerning them, which we shall reserve for another opportunity.

P. But say, what recompence, for all this waste
Of honour, truth, attention, time, and taste?　　　　　180
To shine confess'd, her Zany and her Tool,
And fall by what I rose, low ridicule?
Again shall *Handel* raise his laurel'd brow,[48]
Again shall harmony with rapture glow!
The spells dissolve, the combination breaks,　　　　　185
And *Punch*, no longer *Frasi's*[49] rival squeaks.
Lo, *R——l* falls a sacrifice to whim,
And starts amaz'd in *Newgate* from his dream:[50]
With trembling hands implores their promis'd aid;
And sees their favour like a vision fade!　　　　　　190
Is this, ye faithless *Syrens!* — this the joy
To which, your smiles th' unwary wretch decoy?
Naked and shackled, on the pavement prone,
His mangled flesh devouring from the bone;
Rage in his heart, distraction in his eye!　　　　　195
Behold, inhuman Hags! your Minion lye!
Behold his gay career to ruin run,
By you seduc'd, abandon'd and undone!
Rather in garret pent, secure from harm,
My muse with murders shall the town alarm;[51]　　　200
Or plunge in politics with patriot zeal,
And snarl like *G——ie*[52] for the public weal;
Than crawl an Insect, in a *Beldame*'s power,
And dread the crush of caprice ev'ry hour!

Fr. 'Tis well; — enjoy that petulance of stile,　　　205

187. *Lo, R——l falls,* &c.] The person here meant, by the qualifications above described, had insinuated himself into the confidence of certain Ladies of Quality, who engaged him to set up a puppet-shew, in opposition to the oratorios of H—d—l, against whom they were unreasonably prejudiced. But the town not seconding the capricious undertaking, they deserted their manager, whom they had promised to support, and let him sink under the expence they had entailed upon him: He was accordingly thrown into prison, where his disappointment got the better of his reason, and he remain'd in all the extasy of despair; till at last, his generous patronesses, after much sollicitation, were prevailed upon, to collect five pounds, on the payment of which, he was admitted into Bedlam, where he continues still happily bereft of his understanding.

199. *Rather in garret,* &c.] These are the dreams and fictions of *Grubstreet*, with which the good people of this metropolis, are daily alarmed and entertained.

And, like the envious adder, lick the file:[53]
What 'tho' success will not attend on all?
Who bravely dares, must sometimes risk a fall.
Behold the bounteous board of fortune spread;
Each weakness, vice and folly yields thee bread;   210
Wouldst thou with prudent condescension strive
On the long settled terms of life to thrive.

    P. What! join the Crew that pilfer one another,
Betray my Friend, and persecute my brother:
Turn usurer, o'er *cent. per cent.*[54] to brood,   215
Or quack,[55] to feed like fleas, on human blood?

    Fr. Or if thy soul can brook the gilded curse,
Some changeling heiress steal——

                P. Why not a purse?
Two things I dread, my conscience and the law.

    Fr. How? dread a mumbling[56] bear without a claw?   220
Nor this, nor that is standard right or wrong,
'Till minted by the mercenary tongue,
And what is conscience, but a fiend of strife,
That chills the joys, and damps the schemes of life?
The wayward child of vanity and fear,   225
The peevish dam of poverty and care;
Unnumber'd woes engender in the breast
That entertains the rude, ungrateful guest!

    P. Hail, sacred pow'r! my glory and my guide!
Fair source of mental peace, what e'er betide;   230
Safe in thy shelter, let disaster roll
Eternal hurricanes around my soul;
My soul serene, admidst the storms shall reign,
And smile to see their fury burst in vain!

206. *And, like the envious adder, lick the file.*] This alludes to the fable of the viper and file, applicable to all the unsuccessful efforts of malice and envy.

Fr. Too coy to flatter, and too proud to serve,   235
Thine be the joyless dignity to starve.

P. No;—thanks to discord, war shall be my friend;
And moral rage, heroic courage lend
To pierce the gleaming squadron of the foe,
And win renown by some distinguish'd blow.   240

Fr. Renown! ay, do—unkennel the whole pack
Of military cowards on thy back.
What difference, say, 'twixt him who bravely stood,
And him who sought the bosom of the wood?
Invenom'd calumny the First shall brand,   245
The Last enjoy a ribbon[58] and command.

P. If such be life, its wretches I deplore,
And long to quit th' unhospitable shore.[59]

REPROOF:
A
SATIRE.

——*nam quis*
Peccandi finem posuit sibi? quando recepit
Ejectum semel attritâ de fronte ruborem?
JUVENAL.[1]

POET. FRIEND.

P. Howe'er I turn, or whereso'er I tread,
This giddy world still rattles round my head!
I pant for silence ev'n in this retreat—
Good heav'n! what Dæmon thunders at the gate?[2]

---

243. *What difference, say, 'twixt him who bravely stood,*

244. *And him who sought the bosom of the wood?*] ——This last line relates to the behaviour of a General on a certain occasion, who discovered an extreme passion for the cool shade during the heat of the day.[57]

R E P R O O F:

S A T I R E.

THE

SEQUEL to *ADVICE*.

————— *nam quis*
Peccandi finem pofuit fibi ? quando recepit
Ejectum femel attritâ de fronte ruborem ?
                                    JUVENAL.

L O N D O N:
Printed for W. OWEN, at Homer's Head, near Temple-Bar, Fleetftreet;
and M. COOPER, at the Globe in Pater-nofter Row. 1747.
[Price One Shilling.]

Title Page of *Reproof: A Satire*, First Edition, 1747.
(The Pennsylvania State University Libraries.)

Fr. In vain you strive, in this sequester'd nook,
To shroud you from an injur'd friend's rebuke.   5

P. An injur'd friend! — who challenges the name?
If you, what title justifies the claim?
Did e'er your heart o'er my affliction grieve,
Your int'rest prop me, or your purse relieve?   10
Or could my wants my soul so far subdue,
That in distress she crawl'd for aid to you?
But let us grant th' indulgence e'er so strong;
Display without reserve th' imagin'd wrong:
Among your kindred have I kindled strife,   15
Deflowr'd your daughter, or debauch'd your wife;
Traduc'd your credit, bubbled³ you at game;
Or soil'd with infamous reproach your name?

Fr. No; but your cynic vanity (you'll own)
Expos'd my private counsel to the town.   20

P. Such fair advice 'twere pity sure to lose;
I grant I printed it for public use.

Fr. Yes, season'd with your own remarks between,
Inflam'd with so much virulence of spleen,
That the mild town (to give the dev'l his due)   25
Ascrib'd the whole performance to a Jew.

P. Jew's, *Turk*'s, or *Pagan*'s, hallowed be the mouth
That teems with moral zeal and dauntless truth!
Prove that my partial strain adopts one lye,
No penitent more mortify'd than I;   30
Not ev'n the wretch in shackles, doom'd to groan
Beneath th' inhuman scoffs of *W——ms—n.*⁴

Fr. Hold — let us see this boasted self-denial —
The vanquish'd knight⁵ has triumph'd in his trial.

P. What then?

Fr. Your own sarcastic verse unsay,   35
That brands him as a trembling runaway.

P. With all my soul!—th' imputed charge rehearse;
I'll own my error and expunge the verse.
Come, come,—howe'er the day was lost or won,
The world allows the race was fairly run.   40
But lest the Truth too naked should appear,
A robe of fable shall the goddess wear:
When sheep were subject to the lion's reign,
Ere man acquir'd dominion o'er the plain;
Voracious wolves fierce rushing from the rocks,   45
Devour'd without controul th' unguarded flocks:
The suff'rers crouding round the royal cave,
Their monarch's pity and protection crave:
Not that they wanted valour, force or arms,
To shield their lambs from danger and alarms;   50
A thousand rams the champions of the fold,
In strength of horn, and patriot virtue bold,
Engag'd in firm association, stood,
Their lives devoted to the public good:
A warlike chieftain was their sole request,   55
To marshal, guide, instruct and rule the rest:
Their pray'r was heard, and by consent of all,
A courtier ape appointed general. ——
He went, he led, arrang'd the battle stood,
The savage foe came pouring like a flood;   60
Then pug[6] aghast, fled swifter than the wind,
Nor deign'd in threescore miles to look behind
While ev'ry band for orders bleat in vain,
And fall in slaughter'd heaps upon the plain:
The scar'd baboon (to cut the matter short)   65
With all his speed could not out-run report;
And to appease the clamours of the nation,
'Twas fit his case should stand examination.
The board was nam'd—each worthy took his place;
All senior members of the horned race.[7] —   70

70. *Horned race*.] It is not to be wonder'd at, that this board consisted of horned cattle only,
since, before the use of arms, every creature was obliged in war to fight with such weapons as

The wether,[8] goat, ram, elk and ox were there,
And a grave, hoary stag[9] possess'd the chair. —
Th' inquiry past, each in his turn began
The culprit's conduct variously to scan.
At length, the sage uprear'd his awful crest,   75
And pausing, thus his fellow chiefs address'd. —
If age, that from this head its honours stole,
Hath not impair'd the functions of my soul,
But sacred wisdom with experience bought,
While this weak frame decays, matures my thought;   80
Th' important issue of this grand debate
May furnish precedent for your own fate;
Should ever fortune call you to repel
The shaggy foe, so desperate and fell. —
'Tis plain (you say) his excellence Sir Ape   85
From the dire field accomplish'd an escape;
Alas! our fellow-subjects ne'er had bled,
If every ram that fell, like him had fled;
Certes,[10] those sheep were rather mad than brave,
Which scorn'd th' example their wise leader gave.   90
Let us, then, ev'ry vulgar hint disdain,
And from our brother's laurel wash the stain. —
Th' admiring court applauds the president,
And pug was clear'd by general consent.

 Fr. There needs no magic to divine your scope,   95
Mark'd as you are a flagrant misanthrope:
Sworn foe to good and bad, to great and small,
Thy rankling pen produces nought but gall:
Let virtue struggle, or let glory shine,
Thy verse affords not one approving line. —   100

 P. Hail sacred themes! the muse's chief delight!

---

nature afforded it, consequently those supplied with horns bid fairest for signalizing themselves in the field, and carrying off the first posts in the army. — But I observe, that among the members of this court, there is no mention made of such of the horned family as were chiefly celebrated for valour; namely, the bull, unicorn, rhinoceros, &c. which gives reason to suspect, that these last were either out of favour with the ministry, laid aside on account of their great age, or that the ape had interest enough at court to exclude them from the number of his judges.

O bring the darling objects to my sight!
My breast with elevated thought shall glow,
My fancy brighten, and my numbers flow!
Th' *Aonian* grove[11] with rapture would I tread,   105
To crop unfading wreaths for WILLIAM's head;[12]
But that my strain, unheard amidst the throng,
Must yield to *L—ck——n*'s ode and *H—b——y*'s song.[13]
Nor would th' enamour'd muse neglect to pay
To *Stanhope*'s worth[14] the tributary lay;   110
The soul unstain'd, the sense sublime to paint,
A people's patron, pride and ornament!
Did not his virtues eterniz'd remain
The boasted theme of *Pope*'s immortal strain.[15]
Not ev'n the pleasing task is left, to raise   115
A grateful monument to *Barnard*'s praise;[16]
Else should the venerable patriot stand
Th' unshaken pillar of a sinking land.[17]
The gladd'ning prospect let me still pursue,
And bring fair virtue's triumphs to the view!   120
Alike to me, by fortune blest or not,
From soaring *Cobham*[18] to the melting *Scot*.[19]
But lo! a swarm of harpies intervene,
To ravage, mangle and pollute the scene!
Gorg'd with our plunder, yet still gaunt for spoil,   125
Rapacious *G—d——n* fastens on our isle,
Insatiate *L—sc——s*, and the fiend *V—n——k*,[21]
Rise on our ruins, and enjoy the wreck;
While griping *J——p—r*[22] glories in his prize,

---

108. *L—ck——n's ode and H—b——y's song.*] Two productions resembling one another very much in that cloying mediocrity, which *Horace* compares to—*Crassum unguentum, et sardo cum melle papaver.*

110. Stanhope's *worth.*] The Earl of *Chesterfield.*

122. *Melting* Scot.] D—l M—k—r, Esq; a man of such primitive simplicity, that he may be said to have exceeded the scripture-injunction,[20] by not only parting with his cloak and coat, but with his shirt also, to relieve a brother in distress.

126. G—d—n, L—sc—s, V—n—k.] A triumvirate of contractors, who scorning the narrow views of private usury, found means to lay a whole state under contribution; and pillage a kingdom of immense sums, under the protection of law.

129. *Griping* J—p—r.] A Christian of bowels, who lends money to his friends in want at the moderate interest of *50 per cent.*

Wrung from the widow's tears and orphan's cries.   130

Fr. Relaps'd again! strange tendency to rail!
I fear'd this meekness would not long prevail.

P. You deem it Rancour then? — Look round and see
What vices flourish still, unprun'd by me:
Corruption roll'd in a triumphant car,   135
Displays his burnish'd front and glitt'ring star;
Nor heeds the public scorn, or transient curse,
Unknown alike to honour and remorse.
Behold the leering belle,[23] caress'd by all,
Adorn each private feast and public ball;   140
Where Peers attentive listen and adore,
And not one matron shuns the titled whore.[24]
At *Peter's* obsequies[25] I sung no dirge;
Nor has my Satire yet supply'd a scourge
For the vile tribes of usurers and bites,[26]   145
Who sneak at *Jonathan's*[27] and swear at *White's*.[28]
Each low pursuit, and slighter folly bred
Within the selfish heart and hollow head,
Thrives uncontroul'd, and blossoms o'er the land,
Nor feels the rigour of my chast'ning hand: 150
While *Codrus*[29] shivers o'er his bags of gold,
By famine wither'd, and benumb'd by cold;
I mark his haggard eyes with frenzy roll,
And feast upon the terrors of his soul;
The wrecks of war, the perils of the deep,   155
That curse with hideous dreams the caitiff's sleep;
Insolvent debtors, thieves and civil strife,
Which daily persecute his wretched life;
With all the horrors of prophetic dread,
That rack his bosom while the mail is read.   160
Safe from the rod, untainted by the school,
A judge by birth, by destiny a fool,

139. *The leering belle*.] A wit of the first water, celebrated for her talent of repartee and double entendre.

143. *Peter's obsequies*.] *Peter W—t—rs*, Esq; whose character is too well known to need description.

While the young Lordling struts in native pride,
His party-coloured tutor[30] by his side,
Pleas'd, let me own the pious mother's care,   165
Who to the brawny sire commits her heir.[31]
Fraught with the spirit of a Gothic monk,
Let *R—ch*,[32] with dulness and devotion drunk,
Enjoy the peal so barbarous and loud,
While his brain spues new monsters to the croud;[33]   170
I see with joy, the vaticide[34] deplore
An hell-denouncing priest and sov'reign whore.[35]
Let ev'ry polish'd dame, and genial lord
Employ the social chair,[36] and venal board;
Debauch'd from sense, let doubtful meanings run,   175
The vague conundrum and the prurient pun;
While the vain fop, with apish grin, regards
The gig'ling minx half choak'd behind her cards:
These and a thousand idle pranks, I deem
The motley spawn of ignorance and whim.   180
Let pride conceive and folly propagate,
The fashion still adopts the spurious brat:

164. *His party-coloured tutor*.] Whether it be for the reason assigned in the subsequent lines, or the frugality of the parents, who are unwilling to throw away money in making their children wiser than themselves, I know not: but certain it is, that many people of fashion commit the education of their heirs to some trusty footman, with a particular command to keep master out of the stable.

170. *Spues new monsters to the croud*.] Monsters of absurdity.

He look'd, and saw a sable sorc'rer rise,
Swift to whose hand a winged volume flies:
All sudden, gorgons hiss, and dragons glare,
And ten-horn'd fiends and giants rush to war.
Hell rises, heaven descends, and dance on earth,
Gods, imps and monsters, music, rage and mirth,
A fire, a jig, a battle and a ball,
'Till one wide conflagration swallows all.
                                        Dunciad.

174. *Employ the social chair*.] This is no other than an empty chair, carried about with great formality, to perform visits, by the help of which a decent correspondence is often maintained among people of fashion, many years together, without one personal interview; to the great honour of hospitality and good neighbourhood.

174. *Venal board*.] Equally applicable to the dining and card table, where every guest must pay an extravagant price for what he has.

Nothing so strange that fashion cannot tame;
By this dishonour ceases to be shame:
This weans from blushes lewd *T——w—y*'s face,[37]   185
Gives *H——ly*[38] praise and *In——d—by*[39] disgrace,
From *Mead*[40] to *Th——p——n*[41] shifts the palm at once,
A medling, prating, blund'ring, busy dunce!
And may (should taste a little more decline)
Transform the nation to an herd of swine.   190

    Fr. The fatal period hastens on apace!
Nor will thy verse th' obscene event disgrace;
Thy flow'rs of poetry, that smell so strong,
The keenest appetites have loath'd the song;
Condemn'd by *C——k, B——ks, B——wby,* and *C——ty,*[42]   195
And all the crop-ear'd critics of the city:
While sagely neutral sits thy silent friend,
Alike averse to censure or commend.[43]

    P. Peace to the gentle soul, that could deny
His invocated[44] voice to fill the cry![45]   200
And let me still the sentiment disdain
Of him, who never speaks but to arraign;
The sneering son of calumny and scorn,
Whom neither arts, nor sense, nor soul adorn:
Or his, who to maintain a critic's rank,   205
Tho' conscious of his own internal blank,
His want of taste unwilling to betray,
'Twixt sense and nonsense hesitates all day;
With brow contracted hears each passage read,
And oftens hums and shakes his empty head;   210
Until some oracle ador'd, pronounce
The passive bard a poet or a dunce;
Then, in loud clamour echoes back the word,

---

186. *H——ly praise.*] A General so renown'd for conduct and discipline, that, during an action in which he had a considerable command, he is said to have been seen rallying three fugitive dragoons, five miles from the field of battle.

195. *C——k, B——ks, B——wby, C——tty.*] A fraternity of wits, whose virtue, modesty, and taste, are much of the same dimension.

'Tis bold! insipid — soaring or absurd.
These, and th' unnumber'd shoals of smaller fry,   215
That nibble round, I pity and defy.

FINIS.

THUS HAVE I SENT
THE SIMPLE KING TO HELL[1]

Thus have I sent the simple king to hell,
Without a coffin, shroud, or passing-bell: —
To me, what are divine and human laws?
I court no sanction but my own applause!
Rapes, robb'ries, treasons yield my soul delight;   5
And human carnage gratifies my sight:
I drag the parent by the hoary hair,   ⎫
And toss the sprawling infant on my spear,   ⎬
While the fond mother's cries regale mine ear. ⎭
I fight, I vanquish, murder friends and foes;   10
Nor dare th' immortal gods my rage oppose.

THY FATAL SHAFTS UNERRING MOVE[1]

I.

Thy fatal shafts unerring move,
I bow before thine altar, love!
I feel thy soft, resistless flame
Glide swift through all my vital frame!

II.

For while I gaze my bosom glows,   5
My blood in tides impetuous flows,
Hope, fear and joy alternate roll,
And floods of transports 'whelm my soul!

III.

My fault'ring tongue attempts in vain
In soothing murmurs to complain,   10
My tongue some secret magick ties,
My murmurs sink in broken sighs!

IV.

Condemn'd to nurse eternal care,
And ever drop the silent tear,
Unheard I mourn, unknown I sigh,   15
Unfriended live, unpitied die!

TRAVESTY[1]

Would you task the moon-ty'd hair,
To yon flagrant beau repair;
Where waving with the poppling vow,
The bantling fine will shelter you, &c.

LOVE ELEGY
In Imitation of Tibullus[1]

I.

Where now are all my flatt'ring dreams of joy?
Monimia,[2] give my soul her wonted rest; —
Since first thy beauty fix'd my roving eye,
Heart-gnawing cares corrode my pensive breast!

II.

Let happy lovers fly where pleasures call,   5
With festive songs beguile the fleeting hour;
Lead beauty thro' the mazes of the ball,
Or press her wanton in love's roseate bow'r.

III.

For me, no more I'll range th' empurpled mead,
Where shepherds pipe, and virgins dance around;   10

Nor wander thro' the woodbine's fragrant shade,
To hear the music of the grove resound.

IV.

I'll seek some lonely church, or dreary hall,
Where fancy paints the glimm'ring taper blue,
Where damps hang mould'ring on the ivy'd wall,   15
And sheeted ghosts drink up the midnight dew:

V.

There leagu'd with hopeless anguish and despair,
A-while in silence o'er my fate repine;
Then, with a long farewel to love and care,
To kindred dust my weary limbs consign.   20

VI.

Wilt thou, Monimia, shed a gracious tear
On the cold grave where all my sorrows rest?
Strow vernal flow'rs, applaud my love sincere,
And bid the turf lie easy on my breast!

ADIEU, YE STREAMS THAT SMOOTHLY FLOW[1]

I.

Adieu, ye streams that smoothly flow,
Ye vernal airs that softly blow,
Ye plains by blooming spring array'd,
Ye birds that warble thro' the shade.

II.

Unhurt from you my soul could fly,   5
Nor drop one tear, nor heave one sigh,
But forc'd from Celia's charms to part,
All joy deserts my drooping heart.

III.

O! fairer than the rosy morn,
When flowers the dewy fields adorn;   10
Unsullied as the genial ray,
That warms the balmy breeze of May.

IV.

Thy charms divinely bright appear,
And add new splendor to the year;
Improve the day with fresh delight,   15
And gild with joy the dreary night!

COME, LISTEN YE STUDENTS
OF EV'RY DEGREE[1]

I.

Come, listen ye students of ev'ry degree,
I sing of a wit and a tutor *perdie*,
A statesman profound, a critick immense,
In short, a meer jumble of learning and sense;
And yet of his talents, tho' laudably vain,   5
His own family arts he could never attain.

II.

His father intending his fortune to build,
In his youth would have taught him the trowel to wield,
But the mortar of discipline never would stick,
For his skull was secur'd by a facing of brick,   10
And with all his endeavours of patience and pain,
The skill of his sire he could never attain.

III.

His mother an housewife neat, artful and wise,
Renown'd for her delicate biscuit and pies,
Soon alter'd his studies, by flatt'ring his taste,   15
From the raising of walls to the rearing of paste;
But all her instructions were fruitless and vain,
The pye-making myst'ry he ne'er could attain.

IV.

Yet true to his race, in his labours was seen
A jumble of both their professions, I ween; 20
For, when his own genius he ventur'd to trust,
His pies seem'd of brick, and his houses of crust.
Then, good Mr. Tutor, pray be not so vain,
Since your family arts you could never attain.

BURLESQUE ODE[1]

Where wast thou, wittol Ward,[2] when hapless fate
From these weak arms mine aged grannam tore:
These pious arms essay'd too late,
To drive the dismal phantom from the door.
Could not thy healing drop, illustrious quack, 5
Could not thy salutary pill prolong her days,
For whom, so oft, to Marybone,[3] alack!
Thy sorrels dragg'd thee thro' the worst of ways?

Oil-dropping Twick'nham[4] did not then detain
Thy steps, tho' tended by the Cambrian[5] maids; 10
Nor the sweet *environs* of Drury-lane;
Nor dusty Pimlico's embow'ring shades;
Nor Whitehall, by the river's bank,
Beset with rowers dank;
Nor where th' Exchange pours forth its tawny sons; 15
Nor where to mix with offal, soil and blood,
Steep Snowhill rolls the sable flood;
Nor where the Mint's contaminated kennel[6] runs:
Ill doth it now beseem,
That thou should'st doze and dream, 20
When death in mortal armour came,
And struck with ruthless dart the gentle dame.
Her lib'ral hand and sympathising breast,
The brute creation kindly bless'd:
Where'er she trod grimalkin purr'd around, 25
The squeaking pigs her bounty own'd;
Nor to the waddling duck or gabbling goose,

Did she glad sustenance refuse;
The strutting cock she daily fed,
And turky with his snout so red;   30
Of chickens careful as the pious hen,
Nor did she overlook the tomtit or the wren;
While redbreast hopp'd before her in the hall,
As if she common mother were of all.[7]

For my distracted mind,   35
What comfort can I find?[8]
O best of grannams![9] thou art dead and gone,
And I am left behind to weep and moan,
To sing thy dirge in sad funereal lay,
Ah! woe is me! alack! and well-a-day!   40

SONG "While with Fond Rapture"[1]

I.

While with fond rapture and amaze,
On thy transcendent charms I gaze,
My cautious soul essays in vain
Her peace and freedom to maintain:
Yet let that blooming form divine,   5
Where grace and harmony combine,
Those eyes, like genial orbs, that move,
Dispensing gladness, joy and love,
In all their pomp assail my view,
Intent my bosom to subdue;   10
My breast, by wary maxims steel'd,
Not all those charms shall force to yield.

II.

But, when invok'd to beauty's aid,
I see th' enlighten'd soul display'd;
That soul so sensibly sedate   15
Amid the storms of froward fate!
Thy genius active, strong and clear,
Thy wit sublime, tho' not severe,

The social ardour void of art,
That glows within thy candid heart;   20
My spirits, sense and strength decay,
My resolution dies away,
And ev'ry faculty opprest,
Almighty love invades my breast!

A DECLARATION IN LOVE.
ODE TO BLUE-EY'D ANN.[1]

I.

When the rough North forgets to howl,
And ocean's billows cease to roll;
When Lybian sands[2] are bound in frost,
And cold to Nova-Zembla's[3] lost;
When heav'nly bodies cease to move,   5
My blue-ey'd Ann I'll cease to love.

II.

  No more shall flowers the meads adorn;
Nor sweetness deck the rosy thorn;
Nor swelling buds proclaim the spring;
Nor parching heats the dog-star[4] bring;   10
Nor laughing lillies paint the grove,
When blue-ey'd Ann I cease to love.

III.

  No more shall joy in hope be found;
Nor pleasures dance their frolick round;
Nor love's light god inhabit earth;   15
Nor beauty give the passion birth;
Nor heat to summer sunshine cleave,
When blue-ey'd Nanny I deceive.

IV.

  When rolling seasons cease to change,
Inconstancy forgets to range;   20
When lavish May no more shall bloom;

Nor gardens yield a rich perfume;
When Nature from her sphere shall start,[5]
I'll tear my Nanny from my heart.

ODE TO SLEEP.
INTENDED AS A CHORUS IN A TRAGEDY.[1]

Soft sleep, profoundly pleasing pow'r,
Sweet patron of the peaceful hour,
O, listen from thy calm abode,
And hither wave thy magic rod:
Extend thy silent, soothing sway,   5
And charm the canker care away.
Whether thou lov'st to glide along,
Attended by an airy throng
Of gentle dreams and smiles of joy,
Such as adorn the wanton boy;   10
Or to the monarch's fancy bring
Delights that better suit a king;
The glitt'ring host, the groaning plain,
The clang of arms, and victor's train.
Or should a milder vision please,   15
Present the happy scenes of peace:
Plump autumn, blushing all around,
Rich industry with toil embrown'd;
Content with brow serenely gay,
And genial art's refulgent ray.   20

AN ODE TO MIRTH.[1]

Parent of joy! heart-easing mirth!
  Whether of Venus or Aurora born:
  Yet goddess sure of heav'nly birth,
Visit benign a son of grief forlorn.
  Thy glittering colours gay,   5
  Around him, mirth, display;
  And o'er his raptur'd sense
  Diffuse thy living influence.

So shall each hill in purer green array'd,
And flower adorn'd in new-born beauty glow: 10
The grove shall smooth the horrors of its shade,
And streams in murmurs shall forget to flow.
Shine, goddess, shine with unremitting ray,
And gild (a second sun) with brighter beam our day.

   Labour with thee forgets his pain,   15
And aged poverty can smile with thee:
   If thou be nigh, grief's hate is vain,
And weak the uplifted arm of tyranny.
     The morning opes on high
     His universal eye;   20
     And on the world doth pour
     His glories in a golden show'r.
Lo! darkness trembling 'fore the hostile ray,
Shrinks to the cavern deep and wood forlorn.
The brood obscene,[2] that own her gloomy sway,   25
Troop in her rear, and fly th' approach of morn.
Pale shiv'ring ghosts, that dread th' all-chearing light,
Quick, as the lightning's flash, glide to sepulchral night.

But whence the glad'ning beam
That pours his purple stream   30
   O'er the long prospect wide?
'Tis mirth. I see her sit
In majesty of light,
   With laughter at her side.
Bright-ey'd fancy hov'ring near,   35
Wide waves her glancing wing in air:
And young wit flings his pointed dart,
That guiltless strikes the willing heart.
Fear not now affliction's power,
Fear not now wild passion's rage,   40
Nor fear ye aught in evil hour,
Save the tardy hand of age.
Now mirth hath heard the suppliant poet's pray'r;
No cloud, that rides the blast, shall vex the troubled air.

A NEW SONG "To Fix Her" [1]

To fix her — 'twere a task as vain
To count the April drops of rain,
To sow in Afric's barren soil,
Or tempests hold within a toil. [2]

2.

I know it, friend, she's light as air,   5
False as the fowler's artful snare;
Inconstant as the passing wind,
As winter's dreary frost unkind.

3.

She's such a miser too in love,
Its joys she'll neither share nor prove;   10
Tho' hundreds of gallants await
From her victorious eyes their fate.

4.

Blushing at such inglorious reign,
I sometimes strive to break her chain;
My reason summon to my aid,   15
Resolv'd no more to be betray'd.

5.

Ah! friend! 'tis but a short-liv'd trance,
Dispell'd by one enchanting glance;
She need but look, and, I confess,
Those looks completely curse or bless.   20

6.

So soft, so elegant, so fair,
Sure something more than human's there;
I must submit, for strife is vain,
'Twas destiny that forg'd the chain.

ODE TO LEVEN-WATER.[1]

On Leven's banks, while free to rove,
And tune the rural pipe to love;
I envied not the happiest swain
That ever trod th' Arcadian plain.

Pure stream! in whose transparent wave   5
My youthful limbs I wont to lave;
No torrents stain thy limpid source;
No rocks impede thy dimpling course,
That sweetly warbles o'er its bed,
With white, round, polish'd pebbles spread;   10
While, lightly pois'd, the scaly brood
In myriads cleave thy crystal flood;
The springing trout in speckled pride;
The salmon, monarch of the tide;
The ruthless pike, intent on war;   15
The silver eel, and motled par.[†2]

Devolving from thy parent lake,
A charming maze thy waters make,
By bow'rs of birch, and groves of pine,
And hedges flow'r'd with eglantine.   20

Still on thy banks so gayly green,
May num'rous herds and flocks be seen,
And lasses chanting o'er the pail,
And shepherds piping in the dale,
And ancient faith that knows no guile,   25
And industry imbrown'd with toil,
And hearts resolv'd, and hands prepar'd,
The blessings they enjoy to guard.

†The par is a small fish, not unlike the smelt, which it rivals in delicacy and flavour.

ODE TO INDEPENDENCE.[1]

STROPHE.

Thy spirit, INDEPENDENCE, let me share!
Lord of the lion-heart and eagle-eye,
Thy steps I follow with my bosom bare,
Nor heed the storm that howls along the sky.
Deep in the frozen regions of the north,   5
A goddess violated brought thee forth,
Immortal Liberty, whose look sublime
Hath bleached the tyrant's cheek in every varying clime.
What time the iron-hearted Gaul
With frantic Superstition for his guide,   10
Armed with the dagger and the pall,
The sons of Woden to the field defy'd:
The ruthless hag, by Weser's flood,
In Heaven's name urg'd the infernal blow;
And red the stream began to flow: 15
The vanquished were baptized with blood![2]

ANTISTROPHE.

The Saxon prince in horror fled
From altars stained with human gore;
And Liberty his routed legions led
In safety to the bleak Norwegian shore.   20
There in a cave asleep she lay,
Lulled by the hoarse-resounding main;
When a bold savage past that way,
Impelled by Destiny, his name Disdain.
Of ample front the portly chief appear'd: 25
The hunted bear supplied a shaggy vest;
The drifted snow hung on his yellow beard;
And his broad shoulders braved the furious blast.
He stopt: he gazed; his bosom glow'd,
And deeply felt the impression of her charms: 30

---

16. *Baptized with blood.*] Charlemagne obliged four thousand Saxon prisoners to embrace the Christian religion, and immediately after they were baptized, ordered their throats to be cut.— Their prince Vitikind fled for shelter to Gotrick king of Denmark.

He seiz'd the advantage Fate allow'd;
And straight compressed her in his vigorous arms.

STROPHE.

The Curlieu[3] screamed; the Tritons[4] blew
Their shells to celebrate the ravished rite;
Old Time exulted as he flew;   35
And Independence saw the light.
The light he saw in Albion's happy plains,
Where under cover of a flowering thorn,
While Philomel[5] renewed her warbled strains,
The auspicious fruit of stoln embrace was born——   40
The mountain Dryads[6] seized with joy,
The smiling infant to their charge consign'd;
The Doric muse[7] caressed the favourite boy;
The hermit Wisdom stored his opening mind.
As rolling years matured his age,   45
He flourished bold and sinewy as his sire;
While the mild passions in his breast assuage
The fiercer flames of his maternal fire.

ANTISTROPHE.

Accomplished thus, he winged his way,
And zealous roved from pole to pole,   50
The rolls of right eternal to display,
And warm with patriot thoughts the aspiring soul.
On desart isles[8] it was he that rais'd
Those spires that gild the Adriatic wave,
Where Tyranny beheld amaz'd   55
Fair Freedom's temple, where he marked her grave.
He steeled the blunt Batavian's[9] arms
To burst the Iberian's double chain;[10]

---

53. *On desart isles*.] Although Venice was built a considerable time before the æra here assigned for the birth of Independence, the republic had not yet attained to any great degree of power and splendour.

58. *To burst the Iberian's double chain*.] The Low Countries were not only oppressed by grievous taxations; but likewise threatened with the establishment of the Inquisition, when the seven provinces revolted, and shook off the yoke of Spain.

And cities reared, and planted farms,
Won from the skirts of Neptune's wide domain.   60
He, with the generous rustics, sate
On Uri's rocks in close divan;[11]
And winged that arrow sure as fate,
Which ascertained the sacred rights of man.

STROPHE.

Arabia's scorching sands he crost,   65
Where blasted Nature pants supine,
Conductor of her tribes adust,[12]
To Freedom's adamantine[13] shrine;
And many a Tartar hord forlorn, aghast,
He snatched from under fell Oppression's wing;   70
And taught amidst the dreary waste
The all-chearing hymns of Liberty to sing.
He Virtue finds, like precious ore,
Diffus'd through every baser mould,
Even now he stands on Calvi's rocky shore,[15]   75
And turns the dross of Corsica[16] to gold.
He, guardian genius, taught my youth
Pomp's tinsel livery to despise:
My lips by him chastised to truth,
Ne'er payed that homage which the heart denies.   80

ANTISTROPHE.

Those sculptured halls my feet shall never tread,
Where varnished Vice and Vanity combin'd,
To dazzle and seduce, their banners spread;

62. *On Uri's rocks.*] Alluding to the known story of William Tell and his associates, the fathers and founders of the confederacy of the Swiss Cantons.

65. *Arabia's scorching sands.*] The Arabs, rather than resign their independency, have often abandoned their habitations, and encountered all the horrors of the desart.

69. *And many a Tartar hord.*] From the tyranny of Jenghis-Khan, Timur-Bec,[14] and other eastern conquerors, whole tribes of Tartars were used to fly into the remoter wastes of Cathay, where no army could follow them.

76. *And turns the dross of Corsica.*] The noble stand made by Paschal Paoli and his associates against the usurpation of the French King, must endear them to all the sons of liberty and independence.

And forge vile shackles for the free-born mind.
Where Insolence his wrinkled snout uprears;   85
And all the flowers of spurious Fancy blow;
And Title his ill-woven chaplet wears,
Full often wreathed around the miscreant's brow:
Where ever-dimpling Falshood pert and vain,
Presents her cup of stale Profession's froth;   90
And pale Disease, with all his bloated train,
Torments the sons of Gluttony and Sloth.

STROPHE.

In Fortune's car behold that minion ride,[17]
With either India's glittering spoils opprest:
So moves the sumpter-mule,[18] in harnessed pride,   95
That bears the treasure which he cannot taste.
For him let venal bards disgrace the bay;
And hireling minstrels wake the tinkling string;
Her sensual snares let faithless Pleasure lay;
And all her gingling bells fantastic Folly ring;   100
Disquiet, Doubt, and Dread shall intervene;
And Nature, still to all her feelings just,
In vengeance hang a damp on every scene,
Shook from the baleful pinions of Disgust.

ANTISTROPHE.

Nature I'll court in her sequestered haunts,   105
By mountain, meadow, streamlet, grove, or cell,
Where the poised lark his evening ditty chaunts,
And Health, and Peace, and Contemplation dwell.
There, Study shall with Solitude recline;
And Friendship pledge me to his fellow-swains;   110
And Toil and Temperance sedately twine
The slender chord that fluttering Life sustains:
And fearless Poverty shall guard the door;
And Taste unspoiled the frugal table spread;
And Industry supply the humble store;   115
And Sleep unbribed his dews refreshing shed:
White-mantled Innocence, etherial spright,
Shall chace far off the goblins of the night;

And Independence o'er the day preside,
Propitious power! my patron and my pride.   120

LYRICS FROM *ALCESTE*[1]

Overture
ACT I

Grand Entrée
Recitativo — Tenor

Ye happy people, with loud accents speak
Your grateful joy in Hymenean verse;[2]
Admetus and Alceste claim the song.

Soli and Chorus

Triumph, Hymen, in the pair;
  Thus united,
  Thus delighted,   5
Brave the one, the other fair.[3]

Solo and Chorus

Still caressing and caress'd,
Ever blessing, ever blest,
  Live the royal happy pair.   10
This is, valour, thy reward,
This, o beauty, the regard,
  Kind Heav'n pays the virtuous fair.

Aria — Tenor

Ye swift minutes as ye fly,
Crown them with harmonious joy!   15
  Let soft quiet, peace and love
  Still each happier hour improve.
  While as day each day succeeds,
  Lovely and heroic deeds

In fair virtue's path alone   20
Add a lustre to the throne.
Ye swift minutes as ye fly,
Crown them with harmonious joy!

Chorus

O bless, ye powers above,
  The bridegroom and the bride,   25
  Whose willing hands
  Hath Hymen ty'd
  In Love's eternal bands.
Ye little gods of love,
  With roses strew the ground,   30
  And all around
  In sportive play
  Proclaim the happy day.

[ACT II or III?]

Calliope's Song[4]
Admetus sleeping.

Aria—Soprano [first version]

Gentle Morpheus, son of night,
Hither speed thy airy flight!   35
And his weary senses steep
In the balmy dew of sleep.
  That, like Phoebus, blithe and gay,
    He may rise
    With surprise,   40
  And retake the cheerful day.
Gentle Morpheus . . . (Da Capo.)

Aria—Soprano [final version]

Gentle Morpheus, son of night,
Hither speed thy airy flight!
And his weary senses steep

In the balmy dew of sleep.   45
  That when bright Aurora's beams
  Glad the world with golden streams,
  He, like Phoebus, blithe and gay,
  May retaste the healthful day.
Gentle Morpheus . . . (Da Capo.)

ACT IV

Scene, The River Styx.
Charon, *Aria — Basso*

Ye fleeting shades,[5] I come   50
To fix your final doom!
Step in both bad and good,
And tilt it o'er the flood;
To Pluto's dreary shore
I'll waft you safely o'er   55
With this my ebon pole
Tho' high the waters roll.
The monarch and the slave
Alike admission have,
Nor can I brook delay;   60
  Haste, haste, ye shades, away!
Ye fleeting shades . . . (Da Capo.)

Chorus in Pluto's Palace

Thrice happy who in life excel,
Hence doom'd in Pluto's courts to dwell,
Where ye immortal mortals reign,
Now free from sorrow, free from pain.   65

To Alceste

Aria — Tenor [Pluto?]

Enjoy the sweet Elysian grove,[6]
Seat of pleasure, seat of love;
Pleasure that can never cloy,

Love the source of endless joy.
  Thus, thou unpolluted shade,   70
  Be thy royal virtues paid.
Enjoy . . . (Da Capo.)

Chorus

Thrice happy . . . (Da Capo.)

[Another Scene]
Calliope sings to Admetus[7]
Aria—Soprano [first version]

Come Fancy, empress of the brain,
And bring the choicest of thy train
To soothe the widow'd monarch's pain!
  Let fair Alceste still display   75
  Her charms, as on the bridal day.
Come Fancy . . . (Da Capo.)

Aria—Soprano [final version]

Come Fancy, empress of the brain,
And bring the choicest of thy train
To soothe the widow'd monarch's pain!
  Close by his side   80
  In mimic pride
  Let fair Alceste still display
  Her charms, as on the bridal day.
Come Fancy . . . (Da Capo.)

[Finale Scene]
Symphony
Before and during the entry of Alcides [Hercules]
Recitativo—Tenor (Attendant)

He comes, he rises from below,[8]
With glorious conquest on his brow.   85

Chorus

All hail, thou mighty son of Jove!
How great thy pow'r! how great thy love!
  Fiends, Furies, Gods, all yield to thee,
  And Death hath set his captive free.
All hail . . . (Da Capo.)

Sinfonia
Recitativo—Tenor (Apollo)

From high Olympus' top, the seat of God,   90
Descend Apollo and his tuneful choir,
With all their sportive train, to celebrate
Thy great and gen'rous triumph, son of Jove,
And hail Admetus with his happy bride.
Sing ye, ye shepherds, sing, and tread the ground   95
In mazy dances, and let shouts of joy
Return in echo from the vaulted sky.

Aria—Tenor [Apollo]

Tune your harps, all ye Nine,
  To the loud-sounding lays,
While the glad nations join   100
  In the great victor's praise!
Sing his praise, sing his pow'r,
That in the joyful hour
  Bless'd our monarch's arms
  With the fair in all her charms.   105

(Segue il Ballo.)
Ballo Primo
L'ultimo Ballo
Chorus

Triumph, thou glorious son of Jove,
Triumph, happy pair, in love!
  Valour's prize, virtue's claim,
  Endless love, eternal fame!

FINIS

[Additional, or rejected, Air:]
Aria [—*Soprano*] (*Syren*)

Thetis bids me hither fly 110
   With this treasure of the main,
Emblem of the circling joy
   That shall crown thy blissful reign.

Plays

INTRODUCTION

To Tobias George Smollett, an ambitious nineteen-year-old entering London fresh from his native Scotland sometime in the summer of 1739, the quickest entry into the world of renown seemed to be the theater. At least so much may be surmised from the fact that he carried with him from Glasgow, in addition to a number of letters of introduction to well-placed fellow Scots, the manuscript of a five-act blank verse tragedy on the subject of the assassination of James I of Scotland in 1437. During much of the next decade—with time out for naval service—he was to devote himself to a futile attempt to get his tragedy, entitled *The Regicide*, before a London audience.

According to John Moore, it was during Smollett's grammar-school days at Dumbarton that the young author had been first impressed with the story of James I's tragic end. Moore writes that at the Dumbarton school Smollett became acquainted with the works of the Scottish humanist George Buchanan, particularly Buchanan's history of Scotland, *Rerum Scoticarum Historia* (1579), which "became an incitement to his studying and a means of his attaining a knowledge of the Latin language." Buchanan's account of the heroic and pathetic circumstances of James I's assassination, reports Moore, "made so deep an impression on Smollett's imagination, that he afterwards founded his tragedy of the Regicide, written at the age of eighteen, on the assassination of this prince."[1]

Since no text of the play has survived except that which Smollett managed to publish in 1749, more than a decade after he set out for London, it is impossible to know just what the original version was like. Smollett's preface to the published text makes it evident that the play was revised numerous times over the years at the suggestion of friends and theatrical acquaintances to make it more suitable for the stage. But on the nature of the revisions Smollett is silent, and there is no evidence on which to speculate about its original form.

That the young playwright was advised to make numerous alterations in his drama during his quest to have it produced is not surprising when one considers, among other limiting factors, his lack of any firsthand experience with the stage. Presbyterian prejudice against the theater was strong in Scotland throughout the eighteenth century, and Smollett as a youth is unlikely to have seen many plays; possibly he saw only an occasional performance in a private house or on a makeshift stage in some public hall. Such limited opportunities could not have left even a promising writer very sophisticated in the techniques of theatrical writing.[2]

Smollett probably got most of his ideas of what a historical tragedy should be from his reading of the classics and favorites of the eighteenth-century English stage. It is clear from the allusions in his later writings that he was extremely well read. Thus we may assume that, as he took up *The Regicide*, he was well acquainted with the works of Shakespeare, whom he often quoted throughout his career, and of other Elizabethans as well as such Restoration and eighteenth-century practitioners of the heroic and pathetic as Dryden, Otway, and Rowe. So he probably possessed considerable knowledge of the drama, in spite of his having had limited opportunity to witness it on the contemporary stage.

For an eighteen-year-old youth from the theatrical hinterland, Smollett must have been surprisingly well aware of what were the dramatic tastes and trends of the times, even though he could not himself quite handle them effectively. At least we can say that *The Regicide* in its final form, presumably still basically the same work as the original, is an excellent example of the typical eighteenth-century subgenre that Allardyce Nicoll has labeled "Augustan tragedy." Augustan tragedy, Nicoll has pointed out, usually demanded a historical theme (such as the episode of Scottish history chosen by Smollett), handled in a form that was "an amalgam of diverse forces—pseudo-classicism influencing it externally, pathos entering in to colour certain scenes and characters, Shakespearean style directing occasionally dialogue and theme, and heroics flickering luridly if spasmodically over the whole production."[3] The reader of *The Regicide* will readily see how neatly Smollett's play exemplifies these qualities. For example, it adheres quite faithfully to the classical unities—Smollett makes a specific point of this in his preface—and to the classical principles of stage decorum. Its concern with the consequences of rebellion against established order connects it thematically with Shakespeare's history plays, and the blank verse is stiltedly Shakespearean. The character Stuart, who claims to be a law unto himself, reflects the ranting figures of Restoration heroic tragedy, and the heroine Eleanora, in the dilemmas she faces and in her pathetic death, belongs to the tradition of earlier she-tragedies. Although theatrical history provides numerous examples of plays from 1700 onward that fit, like *The Regicide*, into Nicoll's category of Augustan tragedy, as a group they never had a great audience appeal. Thus, although the young Smollett would never have been willing to understand the judgment of the playhouse managers, they had practical considerations on their side—even assuming Smollett's play to have been better than it was—in their doubts about the audience appeal of the youthful playwright's tragedy.

Moore's few comments on Smollett's youthful enthusiasm for Buchanan provide the only information extant about the genesis and composition of *The Regicide*. But the history of the play after Smollett first arrived in London was quite fully, if somewhat waspishly, spelled out by the author himself in his preface to the play when, after finally despairing of ever seeing it staged, he submitted the work to the public in printed form in 1749. The 1749 preface was, in fact, the second time Smollett had reviewed in print his woes with *The Regicide*; the first account had been masked in the fictional guise of Melopoyn's tale, chapters 62 and 63 of *Roderick Random*, published a little more than a year before the preface. The tale, recounted to Roderick in the Marshalsea by the unfortunate Melopoyn, presents the efforts of the poet-playwright to get his tragedy staged, only to be met with a series of rebuffs, disappointed hopes, and calculated dishonesty that ends in his imprisonment. Smollett himself did not land in prison while pressing for a production of his play, but in outline at least the tale of Melopoyn is essentially the same story as that told in Smollett's preface. Since this preface, with a small number of annotations, recounts the story in detail, it should suffice here to note just the highlights of Smollett's struggles from 1739 to 1749 to gain an audience for his play.[4]

Upon his arrival in London, Smollett was encouraged by several friends and in particular by one highly placed but unidentified patron to hope for an early production of his play, but he soon perceived the real indifference and neglect of his supposed patron. He then laid aside his project for approximately two years while he served in the British navy. Sometime after he returned to England in 1742, Smollett submitted the play—apparently extensively revised—to Charles Fleetwood, then the patentee of the Drury Lane Theater. Fleetwood kept the play for several months but made no moves toward a decision, so that finally Smollett indignantly recovered the manuscript. It was then (sometime in 1743) placed in the hands of another prospective patron, "a nobleman of great weight," but with results similar to those of his earlier experience with patronage from high places—nothing was done.

After another two years of indifference and neglect, Smollett managed in 1745 to present the play to James Lacy, the new manager of Drury Lane, who promised a production but never made good on his promise. In the spring of 1746, having secured some support from Lord Chesterfield and David Garrick, Smollett turned to John Rich, manager of the "other" London theater, Covent Garden. Rich "bluntly rejected" the work. With the encouragement and support of "a humane Lady of quality," possibly Lady Vane (whose sensational memoirs were to become part of *Peregrine Pickle* a few years later), Smollett again submitted the play to Lacy in the latter part of 1746. Lacy wavered for several months, now showing interest, then again being very neglectful. Finally, after Smollett had received what he thought was a firm commitment to produce the play sometime during the 1747–48 season, Lacy flatly and without explanation renounced any further interest. This last rejection apparently caused Smollett to give up all hope for a production of his tragedy. By this time (probably about the middle of 1747) he would have been well into the writing of *Roderick Random* and undoubtedly faced the fact that his energies could be better spent than in trying to promote a project that now seemed ill-fated almost from the start.

Smollett, however, could not bring himself to abandon altogether the darling of his youth. Following the great popular success of *Roderick Random* in 1748, he decided to justify his confidence in the play and perhaps gain a measure of revenge on the slippery and dishonest playhouse managers by publishing it with a preface exposing the wretched behavior of patrons and producers. In a letter to Alexander Carlyle written 14 February 1749, Smollett revealed his plans: "Meanwhile, despairing of seeing my old Performance represented, I have at last taken the advice of my Friends, and opened a Subscription for publishing it, which in all appearance will answer my warmest Expectations."[5] A notice of the subscription had appeared a few days earlier in the *General Advertiser* for 11 February 1749, where potential subscribers were informed that "the singular way in which this performance has been excluded from both theatres (as will appear in the Preface) obliges the Author to publish it in a way otherwise not agreeable to his inclination."[6] Two thousand proposals were circulated publicizing the terms of the subscription, but how successful the subscription was is unclear since no list of subscribers is known to have survived. Smollett's concluding comment in the published preface about "the uncommon encouragement I have received in the publication of the following Play" would seem to indicate his satisfaction with the results, but might also be interpreted as his putting the best face possible on a not too successful project. At any rate the subscription edition of *The Regicide* appeared early in May 1749 and was followed by a book-trade edition in the following month. The subscription edition on royal paper cost five shillings; the book-trade edition one shilling six pence.

The publication of *The Regicide* was enthusiastically received in at least one quarter. A review by John Cleland in the newly launched *Monthly Review* was effusive: "The diction is every where animated, nervous, and pathetic. The character of the virtuous, brave, and gentle *Dunbar*, is finely contrasted to that of the headstrong, fierce, ambitious *Stuart*. *Eleanora*, esteeming most the first, but loving the latter, and distracted between her passion and her duty, is a character both natural and well touched. We shall say no more here of it, than that we think it no hazarded judgment to pronounce it one of the best theatrical pieces that has appeared these many years." Cleland was equally enthusiastic about the preface, which, he said, "not only abounds in strokes of humour, and portraiture, peculiar to the author of *Roderick Random*, but is justly calculated for a warning to adventurers in writing for the stage."[7] Indeed, the *Monthly Review* reprinted the entire preface.

But Cleland's enthusiasm was not contagious. Little else is heard of *The Regicide* at the time of its publication or in the years to come. One late note was sounded in 1761, when Charles Churchill, attacking Smollett in *The Apology. Addressed to the Critical Reviewers*, made fun of the hapless tragedy:

> Who ever read the REGICIDE but swore
> The author wrote as man ne'er wrote before?
> Others for plots and under-plots may call,
> Here's the right method—have no plot at all.
> Who can so often in his cause engage,
> The tiny Pathos of the Grecian stage,
> Whilst horrors rise, and tears spontaneous flow
> At tragic Ha! and no less tragic Oh!?
>
> (lines 156–63)[8]

Alexander Carlyle has perhaps the last word on Smollett's failure with *The Regicide*: "the Managers could not be blam'd, though it sour'd him against them, and he appeald to the Public by Printing it—But the public seem'd to take part with the Managers."[9]

None of the few commentators on *The Regicide* have had much to say about the relationship of Smollett's tragedy to the historical events that inspired it. As noted earlier, Smollett was supposed to have been stimulated to undertake his work by reading Buchanan's account of the assassination of James I. According to Buchanan, the leader of the conspiracy that killed James in 1437 was Walter, earl of Athol, the eldest son of Robert II by his first wife, Euphemia. After Euphemia's death, Robert married his mistress, Elizabeth Mure, and legitimized her three sons, the eldest of whom became Robert III, father of James I. Deprived of a crown he thought should be his, Athol secretly conspired against the throne. He eventually joined forces with Robert Graham, a brother-in-law of his niece. Graham was a longtime foe of the king because of confiscations and other injustices he claimed his family had suffered. In February 1437, the queen got wind of the conspiracy and sent word to the king, who left the field of battle against the English and joined her at Perth. There they secluded themselves in the convent of the Dominicans, near the walls of the city. In the middle of the night, a treacherous servant named John led Athol and Graham, accompanied by Athol's grandson, Robert Stewart, to the king's chambers. Once there the conspirators broke open the door and, before the eyes of the queen, stabbed the king to death.

Smollett takes great liberties with his historical data. Aside from locating the assassination in a convent in Perth and treating it as the result of conspirators bursting into the king's chambers in the middle of the night, Smollett retains in his play few events that correspond to those recorded by Buchanan. Most of the events in the play leading up to the actual slaying are pure inventions, as is the romantic triangle involving Eleanora and the two rivals for her love, Stuart and Dunbar. The opposition to James that led to his assassination was mostly a small cabal; there was no mass rebellion, as there is in Smollett's play. The attack on Perth by multitudes of rebellious clansmen early in the play—Athol mentions ten thousand in act 3, scene 8—is completely unhistorical. Robert Graham, apparently the most aggressive and implacable of the historical king's enemies, had gathered at most a few hundred supporters to his cause; they constituted a small band of would-be regicides, but certainly no army of rebels.

All the persons of the drama except Dunbar and Ramsay can be found in Buchanan, although in most cases Smollett took a hint or a name and then worked with it as he chose. The king and queen are, of course, important figures in both Buchanan's account and Smollett's play. In making James I a just and forceful monarch, one who claims to have brought peace and order to a heretofore turbulent kingdom, Smollett follows Buchanan's general assessment of the king's character and career. He similarly follows Buchanan in characterizing the queen as a somewhat timorous woman, full of fears and forebodings. Unlike the queen in Smollett's drama, however, the historical queen was not killed at the time of the regicide.

In *The Regicide* Athol is derived from his historical namesake, and, like him, he is an aging man; the historical Athol was seventy-five at the time of the assassination. Smollett's Grime is based on Robert Graham—Smollett's spelling must be a phonetic one—but similarity of name and participation in the assassination of the king are the only links connecting the two. The traitorous John of Buchanan's account has his counterpart in Smollett's Cattan. Smollett's rebel Stuart is based on the historical Robert Stewart, who is little more than mentioned by Buchanan. Smollett changes Stewart's relationship to Athol from grandson to nephew and, even more unhistorically, has him killed off before he has a chance to participate in the final tragic murder. Buchanan speaks of one William Douglas, earl of Angus, as one of James's foremost military leaders, his prowess being particularly noteworthy in the fighting against the English, who were plundering Scotland at the time. Smollett gives Angus's name to the king's chief lieutenant and makes him do double duty as the father of Eleanora. The name *Eleanora* is not found at all in Buchanan, but Smollett's character owes her origin to the most memorable incident in Buchanan's account. According to Buchanan, the traitor John had removed the bar on the door leading to the king's chambers. Upon hearing an alarm raised as the conspirators were about to break into the king's chambers, a young woman of the Douglasses (or, maybe, the Lovels), apparently in attendance on the queen, attempted to use her own arm to bar the door. As the conspirators forced the door, the brave girl's arm was broken, and the conspirators then rushed into the room to attack their victim. Smollett expands the role of the vaguely identified young woman, giving her the leading female part of Eleanora in his play, and his heroine suffers not just a broken arm, but death. That the actual woman was reported to have been a Douglas made it convenient for Smollett to tie things up by making Eleanora the daughter of Angus. For the third person of the fictional Eleanora-Stuart-Dunbar triangle, he appears to have simply borrowed the name of a leading Scottish family.

Perhaps the original version of Smollett's tragedy was closer to Buchanan's account. One can well imagine the sophisticated men of the London theater with whom Smollett was trying to gain favor advising him to improve the play by enlarging the role of the pathetic Eleanora or by making the rebel Stuart more passionate. But wherever the responsibilities for the final version lie, *The Regicide* remains poor history and ineffective drama. The action itself is fairly well structured, with conflicts well defined and changes of fortune clearly plotted and worked out. As a mechanism *The Regicide* is neither better nor worse than such models of "rebellion" drama as the two parts of Shakespeare's *Henry IV* or Thomas Otway's *Venice Preserved*, but the play never develops beyond its mechanical form. The characters are lifeless; their motives and personalities are leaden stereotypes; and—probably the greatest weakness in the play—they speak a language so forced that it could almost serve as a parody of the efforts of hundreds of adolescent playwrights to write genuine Shakespearean blank verse. Readers may find some interest in the play's thematic concern with the monstrous and unnatural consequences of rebellion against established order, a vital concern for eighteenth-century Britons still mindful of the civil upheavals of the previous century and of the ongoing threat of Jacobite insurgency. But interest in *The Regicide* will probably remain largely biographical, emphasizing what its text and its history can tell us about Smollett's early struggles to make a name for himself through the work of his imagination.

Even as Smollett was giving up on *The Regicide*, his desire for recognition in the London theatrical world was leading him to pursue new dramatic projects. Although John Rich had bluntly rejected *The Regicide*, by the beginning of 1749 Smollett found himself engaged to produce the text for one of Rich's theatrical spectacles to be entitled *Alceste*. How Rich and Smollett came to such an engagement is unknown—Moore says Smollett "was applied to by Mr. Rich"[10]—but in February 1749 Smollett announced to Alexander Carlyle: "I have wrote a sort of Tragedy on the Story of Alceste, which will (without fail) be acted at Covent Garden next Season, and appear with such Magnificence of Scenery as was never exhibited in Britain before."[11] Smollett's confidence seemed well founded. Rich, an enthusiastic theatrical entrepreneur when he wanted to be, at first pushed the project vigorously. The great George Frederick Handel was engaged to write the music, and Jean-Nicholas Servandoni, a well-known French architect, was to design the elaborate scenery.

Later in 1749, however, Smollett became something less than sanguine about developments. Writing to Carlyle on 1 October, after a summer spent traveling in the Low Countries, he complained:

> Two days Ago, I sent my Masque to Rich, that it may be put into Rehearsal immediately; but he is Such a Compound of Indolence, Worthlessness and Folly, that I cannot depend upon any thing he undertakes. . . . Tho' he has no objection to the Piece, which has been again and again approved of by the very Judges he himself appointed; tho' he has no other Prospect of being saved from Destruction than that of exhibiting it immediately; and tho' he is almost certain of uncommon Success on its Appearance, he is such an infatuated Miscreant that he has told some of his friends in Confidence that the Performance was cramm'd down his throat.[12]

By the following summer it was clear that Smollett's fears about Rich's inconstancy had been realized and that, despite what must have been a considerable outlay on Rich's part,[13] the entire project had been called off. Smollett's remarks to Carlyle make it clear that the text of *Alceste* was brought to a fairly finished form, but in the abandonment of the project all that seems to have survived are a few lyrics that were set to music by Handel.[14] Thus, for a second time in his quest for recognition in the theatrical world, Smollett felt himself victimized by unprincipled and capricious playhouse managers.

At the same time that Smollett was working on *Alceste*, he was possibly also trying to promote a comic work he had written. There is evidence that he may have undertaken a theatrical piece in the comic vein sometime during or before 1747. In a letter to Carlyle that appears to have been written in that year, he mentions a desire to send his friend "the New Play and Farce, Two Satires called Advice and Reproof . . . and . . . the Tears of Scotland."[15] The "New Play" here mentioned is probably the most recent version of *The Regicide*, but of the farce no further mention is found either in Smollett's writings or in the documents related to his theatrical activities. The farce may actually be the comedy that John Hunter, in a manuscript annotation to Samuel Foart Simmons's *Life of William Hunter* (1783), mentions as having been written by his brother James in collaboration with Smollett.[16] Since James Hunter died in 1745, any work on which he collaborated with Smollett would have been done in the early 1740s. If Hunter is correct in saying that his brother wrote an unproduced comedy with Smollett, but if that unproduced comedy is not the same work as the farce Smollett wrote about to Carlyle, then students of Smollett must conclude that there is yet another play with which he was involved in the 1740s and that it has been lost. No other allusion to this alleged collaboration is known to students of the Smollett canon.

Another possible lead to identifying the farce mentioned by Smollett is a work that emerged over thirty-five years later, in 1785, as an afterpiece to a production of John Home's *Douglas*. The newspaper announcements of this work promise "a Farce of Two Acts, taken from a piece written by Dr. Smollett, but never before published or performed, called THE ISRAELITES; or, *The Pampered Nabob*."[17] After its performance at Covent Garden on 1 April 1785, the newspapers reported that the farce was "altered from a manuscript of the late Dr. Smollett."[18] Robert Anderson, many years later, added the information that the piece was "said to have been left by Smollett, in the hands of a printer."[19] These scraps of information, if they are to be relied upon, make it appear that sometime during his career, possibly quite early, Smollett wrote a farce that was sold (or maybe just presented with the hope of being sold) to a printer, who placed it on a shelf and forgot about it. Then, in 1785, the manuscript was presumably discovered by some theatrical person who thought it promising enough for the tastes of the day to revise it, making it more topical, and to put it onto the stage at Covent Garden. Although the text of *The Israelites* is extant,[20] it is impossible on the evidence now available to substantiate fully the tradition that the work was originally by Smollett or, if the tradition is accepted, to discover how much of the text derives from the Smollett original.[21]

A short time after writing of the nameless farce of 1747, Smollett announced to Carlyle another venture in comedy. In a letter of 7 June 1748, he wrote: "I will also impart another piece of News which I believe, will surprise you no less, after having perused the Revenge I have taken on the Playhouse Managers in Roderick Random. In short, I have planned a Comedy which will be finished by next winter. Garrick who was inexpressibly galled at the Character of Marmozet, has made some advances towards an Accomodation with me."[22] Possibly this is the comedy whose name and fate show up in a 1752 "Catalogue of Books in Quires, and Copies" of one "Mr. Tho. Woodward, Deceas'd." To this catalogue is appended a list of "Books and Copies left unsold at Mr. John Osborn's 'Sale.' " Lot 7 of this list is "The Absent Man, a Comedy, wrote by Mr. T. Smollet, half the Copy-Right, and Profits in the Acting. The Copy. is in the Possession of Mr. Smollett, and the Purchaser is to run all risks of its being ever acted, or printed."[23]

This comedy is probably also the one that, according to Horace Walpole, Smollett was advised to write by Lord Lyttelton. Walpole reports that Smollett sent a tragedy (presumably *The Regicide*) to Lyttelton, and then he writes: "Lord Lyttelton, not caring to point out its defects, civilly advised him to try comedy. He wrote one, and solicited the same Lord to recommend it to the stage. The latter excused himself, but promised if it should be acted, to do all the service in his power for the author."[24]

Once again, Smollett was due for a disappointment. In a letter of 11 May 1750 to Francis Hayman, the painter and illustrator, he asks Hayman to transmit his play to David Garrick, "tho' I can forsee that I shall suffer the Mortification of a Second Refusal." In the rest of the letter Smollett bemoans his lack of success in the theater, defending himself and blaming the prejudice of others:

> It cannot be supposed that I would sit down to write a Comedy before I had endeavoured to investigate the nature of the work; or that I am so ignorant of the Stage, so incorrigible, or unqualified as to produce a dramatic piece that should deserve no favour from an audience which never discountenanced any thing that had the least pretension to Encouragement; and yet I have been frustrated in all my attempts to succeed on the Stage, not by the Publick which I have always found favourable and propitious, but by the Power of two or three Persons who (I cannot help saying) have accepted and patronized the works of others, with whom, in point of Merit, I think myself, at least, upon a par.[25]

Nothing further is to be heard of Smollett's comedy except, that is, for the sale notice mentioned above, which, by reserving half the copyright to Smollett, makes it appear that he still had some lingering hopes of its production or publication. It is to be surmised that Smollett did indeed "suffer the Mortification of a Second Refusal." Having justified his dramatic endeavors and castigated the powers of the theatrical world in his letter to Hayman, Smollett apparently forsook for the next several years his search for the laurels of the dramatic muse. Instead, he turned his full attention to prose fiction and journalism, where recognition of his endeavors seemed more easily come by.

By the mid-1750s Smollett's reputation as a man of letters was well established, but it had not yet brought him the financial security he desired. Consequently, the last years of the decade found him involved in numerous projects for the booksellers of London, some of these little better than hackwork. Early in 1756 the *Critical Review* commenced publication. To this, as editor, Smollett was to devote much of his energy during the next several years. In addition, from 1755 to 1757 he was working on his *Complete History of England*, a massive project that alone could have been full-time work for a person of less drive than Smollett. In the midst of these time-consuming labors, he still found time to revive his ambitions of writing for the theater. On 22 January 1757 he had at long last the satisfaction of hearing words he had written declaimed from an English stage when his two-act comedy, *The Reprisal; or, The Tars of Old-England*, was presented at the Drury Lane Theater as an afterpiece to a performance of Aaron Hill's *Merope*.

Smollett's first mention of this new stage work occurs in a letter dated 24 November 1756 and addressed to Dr. George Macaulay, an obstetrician and fellow Scot. Macaulay on a number of occasions helped Smollett with his financial affairs, and in a letter to him a few months earlier Smollett had detailed some of his financial difficulties and his embarrassment in the face of certain unmet obligations. In the November letter he sees promise of being relieved of some of the embarrassment by the production of his play: "I think I may now with Confidence beg your Interposition with Mr. Maclane about Hamilton's Note, as the Farce which is coming on immediately will undoubtedly enable me to discharge that obligation." [26] (Who Maclane and Hamilton were has not been clearly established.)

Evidently, then, one of Smollett's motives for turning again to the theater was the hope of a fairly quick monetary return. But he would hardly have subjected himself anew to the devious ways of playhouse managers unless he had had assurances of better treatment than he had previously received at their hands. Such assurances must have come from his improved relations with David Garrick, who had been comanager, with James Lacy, of the Drury Lane Theater since 1747. Garrick had been caricatured as Marmozet in *Roderick Random* and satirized again in the first edition of *Peregrine Pickle* because of what Smollett considered to be his blameworthy role in the misfortunes of *The Regicide*, and Smollett had probably taken further umbrage because of Garrick's part in turning down *The Absent Man*. Something, however, brought about a reconciliation, so that by 1756 a fairly pleasant relationship existed between them. Early in that year some very laudatory lines on Garrick's acting appeared in the *Critical Review*.[27] These seem to indicate some mending of the breach between the two. By the end of the year, in another letter to Macaulay bearing upon his financial affairs, Smollett could indicate the congeniality of relations between himself and Garrick by writing, "Mr. Garrick in a very civil Letter gave me to understand that it will be proper to defer the Representation of my Piece till after the Holidays."[28]

In a letter to Garrick himself, dated by Knapp around January 1757, Smollett is especially gracious: "I, in justice to myself, take the liberty to assure you that if any person accuses me of having spoken disrespectfully of Mr. Garrick, of having hinted that he solicited for my farce, or had interested views in bringing it up on the stage, he does me wrong, upon the word of a gentleman. . . . I must own you have acted in this affair of the farce with that candour, openness, and cordiality, which even mortify my pride while they lay me under the most sensible obligation."[29]

In settling upon the misadventures of men aboard a naval vessel as a subject for his new theatrical piece, Smollett must have been moved by several considerations. An important element in his success with *Roderick Random* had been its depiction of naval life. And he had enjoyed additional success with his portraits of such comic naval types as the Welshman Morgan and Lieutenant Bowling in *Roderick Random* and of Commodore Trunnion, Hatchway, and Pipes in *Peregrine Pickle*. Other possible considerations in Smollett's return to playwriting and in Garrick's acceptance of *The Reprisal* were suggested by David Hannay in his nineteenth-century study of Smollett: "Like most of Smollett's work in those years, this comedy has its touch of journalism. It was written to revive the patriotic sentiment of the nation, which had been much depressed by Byng's failure off Minorca, and the consequent loss of the island in the previous year. The *actualité* of the subject may have helped to persuade Garrick to accept the piece for Drury Lane; but he would have been a less sagacious man than he was if he had not seen that the editor of *The Critical*

David Garrick, attributed to George Dance.
(Courtesy of the National Portrait Gallery, London.)

Review was entitled to more consideration than the unknown author of the 'Regicide.' "[30]

In a letter written by Smollett to Garrick several days after the first performance of *The Reprisal*, the playwright expresses his "warmest acknowledgements" for "the friendly Care you have exerted in preparing it for the stage."[31] Thus it would seem that Garrick not only accepted the play as one of the managers of the theater but also took an active part in its staging. Smollett also must have had an opportunity to make his voice heard in the staging of the work, because Arthur Murphy tells how the actor Henry Woodward, who played the role of Block, was "made by the author to lie down, and whimper and cry, in a manner that gave no adequate idea of a British tar." Murphy further reports that the play "met with tolerable success, and the author reaped the profits of a very large benefit."[32] Murphy's remarks about a "tolerable success" seem appropriate for a play that was given for the next four nights following its opening performance and then had an additional six performances before the end of the theatrical season in May.[33] According to a brief entry in the diary of Richard Cross, the prompter at Drury Lane, the opening night performance "went off [with] great App[lause]."[34]

Smollett was particularly gratified by the results of his benefit night, the performance of 1 February. He acknowledged Garrick's generosity in a letter written a few days after the occasion: "I am still more particularly obliged by your allotting the sixth Night for my Benefit, instead of the Ninth to which only I was intitled by the Custom of the Theatre, and your acting [in the main feature, *Zara*] on my night I consider as an additional Favour." In this same letter of thanks Smollett took occasion also to urge further performances: "To crown all these Benefits, you will, I hope, order the Piece to be acted occasionally that it may have some Chance of being saved from Oblivion."[35] Just how much Smollett received from his benefit night cannot be precisely ascertained. In a letter to Smollett written several months later, in November 1757, Garrick apologized for an accounting error that had resulted in Smollett's originally receiving less than was customary. Garrick explained that, although the expense of the house each night was over ninety pounds, "yet we take no more from gentlemen, who write for the theatre, and who produce an original performance, than sixty guineas."[36] Richard Cross notes in his diary the round figure of two hundred pounds as the receipts on Smollett's benefit night;[37] that figure, minus the sixty guineas (sixty-three pounds) mentioned by Garrick, would give nearly 140 pounds as the amount realized by Smollett from the benefit performance.

Whatever the exact amount, it must have been a gratifying sum to the financially pressed Smollett as well as a partial vindication of his confidence in his playwriting abilities. Adding to his income from the production of *The Reprisal* was whatever he received from its publication, which occurred on the same day as his benefit, 1 February 1757. One thousand copies, priced at one shilling each, were printed by William Strahan for the bookseller R. Baldwin, but no record exists of how well they sold.

The "tolerable success" of *The Reprisal* with its audiences was not fully matched by the reception given it by the reviewers of the day. The *Critical Review*, as might be expected of Smollett's own journal, is the kindest. Besides giving a summary of the plot with a few excerpts from the text, the reviewer remarks, "Impartial judges, and those who have real taste, allow the author of this piece to be not only a master of genius and invention; but happily just at drawing characters." He speaks in generally admiring terms of the Irishman, the Scotchman, and the Frenchman and likes especially the character of the English sailor Block. His reservations are few: "Could this piece have been so planned as to have furnished a few more incidents; could the scenes have been shorter, and sometimes changed, the whole would have been more entertaining."[38] The *Monthly Review*, however, in a one-sentence review, dismisses *The Reprisal* as "calculated for the Meridian of Bartholomew-Fair."[39] *The Theatrical Review: for the Year 1757, and Beginning of 1758* calls Smollett's farce "this short lived child of dulness," and goes on to mention "the most glaring absurdities, such as making the theatre of Drury-lane represent the cabin of a small frigate, making the hero of the piece an English gentleman, to leave his mistress in the hands of an enemy, and a rival, in order to provide for his own safety; and introducing his mistress singing, when she has every thing to fear from the meanest of mortals. . . . No humour, no plot, no scenes, no characters, poor English, horrid French, and his own country-dialect, the Scotch as ill characterised as the Irish."[40]

Like many other plays in theatrical history, *The Reprisal* managed to survive unfavorable reviews to become a living piece for at least a generation. This is not to say that it was ever widely produced; still, it did enjoy revivals on the London stage at least three times during Smollett's lifetime (during the seasons of 1758–59, 1761–62, and 1770–71) and probably well beyond that.[41] Lewis M. Knapp has identified a production of the farce in Edinburgh in 1759, which prompted a Scottish reviewer, who was more enthusiastic than the English ones, to praise it as a "little Piece, which, although it is but a slight, easy Sketch of his Pencil, carries plain Marks of the Hand of a great Master, and convinces us, that the Doctor can make his most leisure Hours subservient to the Diversion of the Public."[42] Knapp has also found records of a number of performances on North American stages as well as the inclusion of *The Reprisal* in a 1786 anthology entitled *A Collection of the Most Esteemed Farces and Entertainments Performed on the British Stage*.[43]

If *The Reprisal* was not the theatrical masterpiece that Smollett had hoped to write in his youth, at least it gained him an entry into the list of minor playwrights who have provided a pleasant hour or so for English-speaking audiences and readers. It must have provided Smollett a fairly satisfactory ringing down of the curtain on his efforts to add the drama to his realm of literary accomplishments.

Notes

1. Moore, cviii–cx.
2. For details on theatrical activity in eighteenth-century Scotland, mostly Edinburgh, see Terence Tobin, *Plays by Scots, 1660–1800* (Iowa City: University of Iowa Press, 1974), particularly the section entitled "Scots at Home 1660–1800."
3. Allardyce Nicoll, *A History of English Drama: 1660–1900* (Cambridge: The University Press, 1955), 2:61, 96.
4. Buck, *Study*, chap. 3, thoroughly explores Smollett's two accounts of the history of his play and their relationship to one another. Knapp, 49–57, also provides a detailed analysis.
5. *Letters*, 10.
6. The complete notice reads as follows: "This Day is Publish'd Proposals for Printing by Subscription on a superfine royal paper, for the benefit of the Author, 'The Regicide, or James the First of Scotland, a Tragedy' By the author of Roderick Random. The singular way in which this performance has been excluded from both theatres (as will appear in the Preface) obliges the Author to publish it in a way otherwise not agreeable to his inclination. The Price to Subscribers will be five shillings. Subscriptions are taken and Receipts signed by the Author, deliver'd by J. Osborn in Paternoster-Row; A. Millar in the Strand; J. Brackstone at the Royal Exchange; J. Jolliffe in St. James's Street; and H. Chapelle in Grosvenor Street. N.B. Those who are willing to encourage the above subscription are desired to subscribe as soon as possible, that the Number to be printed may be ascertained."
7. *Monthly Review* 1 (May 1749): 72.
8. *The Poetical Works of Charles Churchill*, ed. Douglas Grant (Oxford: Clarendon Press, 1956), 41.
9. Carlyle, 98.
10. Moore, cxviii. Moore, however, places the *Alceste* episode sometime in 1746, a date that does not square with any of the other evidence.
11. *Letters*, 9–10.

12. *Letters*, 12.

13. Knapp, *Letters*, 10 (n. 1), provides evidence that Smollett received one hundred pounds from Rich on 1 March 1750 as partial payment of the copyright; Knapp also quotes John Home as stating that Smollett received altogether from Rich a sum of three hundred pounds.

14. See above, "Lyrics from *Alceste*," pp. 61–66.

15. *Letters*, 5.

16. For details see James G. Basker, "Another Smollett Play?" *Notes and Queries*, n.s., 28 (1980): 33–34.

17. *Morning Chronicle*, 31 March 1785; the same notice was repeated in the *Universal Daily Register*, 1 April 1785.

18. *Morning Chronicle*, 2 April 1785; also in the *Universal Daily Register*, 2 April 1785.

19. *The Miscellaneous Works of Tobias Smollett*, 6th ed. (Edinburgh, 1820), 1:107.

20. See H. R. S. Van der Veen, *Jewish Characters in Eighteenth Century English Fiction and Drama* (Groningen-Batavia: J. B. Wolters, 1935), 270–90.

21. Richard W. Bevis, "Smollett and *The Israelites*," *Philological Quarterly* 45 (1966): 387–94, provides the most thorough discussion of the play and of the likelihood of Smollett's being the original author. Bevis feels quite certain that Smollett did indeed write the original play and speculates that "the date of composition . . . should fall between 1750 and 1753, and the sale to a printer between 1753 and 1756" (p. 393). He also offers some conjectures as to what elements in the play are most likely to be additions to and revisions of the Smollett original.

22. *Letters*, 8.

23. Alan D. McKillop, "Smollett's First Comedy," *Modern Language Notes* 45 (1930): 396.

24. Walpole, *Memoirs*, 3:97.

25. *Letters*, 13.

26. *Letters*, 50.

27. *Critical Review* 1 (March 1756): 149.

28. *Letters*, 51–52.

29. *Letters*, 53.

30. David Hannay, *Life and Writings of Tobias George Smollett* (London, 1887), 144–45.

31. *Letters*, 53.

32. Arthur Murphy, *The Life of David Garrick* (London, 1801), 1:313–14.

33. The dates of performance were 22, 24, 25, 26, 27 January; 1, 3, 21 February; 25, 27 April; 5 May. See pt. 4, vol. 2, of *The London Stage: 1660–1800*, 5 pts. in 11 vols., ed. George Winchester Stone et al. (Carbondale: Southern Illinois University Press, 1960–68).

34. Quoted in *The London Stage*, pt. 4, vol. 2, p. 577.

35. *Letters*, 53–54.

36. Murphy, *Life of David Garrick*, 2:299–300.

37. *The London Stage*, pt. 4, vol. 2, p. 579.

38. *Critical Review* 3 (February 1757): 157–60.

39. *Monthly Review* 16 (February 1757): 179.

40. *The Theatrical Review: for the Year 1757, and Beginning of 1758* (London, 1758), 47.

41. See Robert Anderson, *The Life of Tobias Smollett*, 4th ed. (Edinburgh, 1803), 80, where *The Reprisal* is referred to as "still a favourite after-piece."

42. Knapp, 201. The review appeared in *A View of the Edinburgh Theatre During the Summer Season, 1759* (London, 1760), 49.

43. Knapp, 201.

THE REGICIDE

THE
REGICIDE:

O R,

JAMES the FIRST,

O F

SCOTLAND.

A

TRAGEDY.

By the Author of RODERICK RANDOM.

— Τόν δ' ὑμνοποιόν, αὐτὸς ἂν τίκτη μέλη,
Χαίροντα τίκτειν.——   Eurip. IKETIΔ.

Hunc————————
Anxietate carens animus facit, omnis acerbi
Impatiens, cupidus filvarum, apturque bibendis
Fontibus aonidum————   JUVENAL.

LONDON:
Printed by SUBSCRIPTION, for the BENEFIT
of the AUTHOR.

M DCC XLIX.

(Price Five Shillings.)

Title Page of *The Regicide*, First Edition, 1749.
(Axson Collection, Woodson Research Center, Rice University Library.)

PREFACE.

Whatever *Reluctance I have to trouble the Publick, with a Detail of the Mortifications I have suffered, in my Attempts to bring the ensuing Performance on the Stage; I think it a Duty incumbent upon me, to declare my Reasons for presenting it in this extraordinary Manner; and, if the Explanation shall be found either tedious or trifling, I hope the candid Reader will charge my Impertinence upon those who drove me to the Necessity of making such an ineffectual Appeal.*

Besides, I flatter myself, that a fair Representation of the Usage I have met with, will be as a Beacon, to caution other inexperienced Authors against the Insincerity of Managers, to which they might otherwise become egregious Dupes; and, after a cajoling Dream of good Fortune, wake in all the Aggravation of Disappointment.

Although I claim no Merit from having finished a Tragedy at the Age of Eighteen; I cannot help thinking myself intitled to some Share of Indulgence, for the Humility, Industry and Patience, I have exerted during a Period of ten Years, in which this unfortunate Production hath been exposed to the Censure of Criticks of all Degrees; and in consequence of their several Opinions, altered, and (I hope) amended, Times without Number.

Had some of those who were pleased to call themselves my Friends, been at any Pains to deserve the Character, and told me ingenuously what I had to expect in the Capacity of an Author, when I first professed myself of that venerable Fraternity, I should, in all Probability, have spared myself the incredible Labour and Chagrin I have since undergone: But, as early as the Year 1739, my Play was taken into the Protection of one of those little Fellows who are sometimes called great Men;[1] and like other Orphans, neglected accordingly.

Stung with Resentment, which I mistook for Contempt, I resolved to punish this barbarous Indifference, and actually discarded my Patron; consoling myself with the barren Praise of a few Associates, who, in the most indefatigable Manner, employed their Time and Influence, in collecting from all Quarters Observations on my Piece, which, in consequence of those Suggestions, put on a new Appearance almost every Day, until my Occasions called me out of the Kingdom.[2]

Soon after my Return, I and my Production were introduced to a late Patentee,[3] of courteous Memory, who (rest his Soul!) found Means to amuse me a whole Season,[4] and then declared it impracticable to bring it on 'till next Year; advising me to make my Application more early in the Winter, that we might have Time to concert such Alterations, as should be thought necessary for its successful Appearance on the Stage. — But I did not find my Account in following this wholesome Advice; for, to me, he was always less and less at Leisure. In short, after sundry Promises, and numberless Evasions, in the Course of which, he practised upon me the whole Art of Procras-

tination, I demanded his final Answer, with such Obstinacy and Warmth, that he could no longer resist my Importunity, and refused my Tragedy in plain Terms.— Not that he mentioned any material Objections to the Piece itself; but seemed to fear my Interest was not sufficient to support it in the Representation; affirming, that no dramatic Composition, however perfect, could succeed with an English *Audience by its own Merit only; but must entirely depend upon a Faction raised in its Behalf.— Incensed at this unexpected Declaration, I reproached him bitterly, for having trifled with me so long; and, like my Brother* Bayes, *threaten'd to carry my Performance to the other House.* [5]

This was actually my Intention, when I was given to understand by a Friend, that a Nobleman of great Weight, had expressed an Inclination to peruse it; and that, as Interest was requisite, I could not do better than gratify his Desire with all Expedition. I committed it accordingly to the Care of my Counsellor, who undertook to give me a good Account of it in less than a Fortnight: But four Months elapsed before I heard any Tidings of my Play; and then it was retrieved by pure Accident (I believe) from the most dishonourable Apartment of his Lordship's House. [6]

Enraged at the Behaviour of this supercilious Peer, and exceedingly mortified at the Miscarriage of all my Efforts, I wreaked my Resentment upon the innocent Cause of my Disgraces, and forthwith condemned it to Oblivion, where, in all Probability, it would have for ever slept, like a miserable Abortion; had not a young Gentleman of Learning and Taste waked my paternal Sense, and perswaded me not only to rescue it from the Tomb, where it had lain two whole Years; but also to new model the Plan, which was imperfect and undigested before, and mould it into a regular Tragedy, confined within the Unities of the Drama.

Thus improved, it fell into the Hands of a Gentleman who had wrote for the Stage, and happened to please him so much, that he spoke of it very cordially to a young Nobleman, [7] *since deceased, who, in the most generous Manner, charged himself with the Care of introducing it to the Publick; and, in the mean time, honour'd me with his own Remarks, in Conformity to which, it was immediately altered, and offered by his Lordship to the new Manager of* Drury-lane *Theatre.* [8] *It was about the latter End of the Season, when this candid Personage, to whom I owe many Obligations for the Exercises of patience he has set me, received the Performance, which, some Weeks after, he returned, assuring my Friend, that he was pre-ingaged to another Author, but if I could be prevailed upon to reserve it 'till the ensuing Winter, he would bring it on.—In the Interim, my noble Patron left* London, *whither he was doomed never to return; and the conscientious Manager next Season, instead of fulfilling his own Promise and my Expectation, gratified the Town with the Production of a Player,* [9] *the Fate of which every Body knows.*

I shall leave the Reader to make his Reflections on this Event, and proceed to relate

the other Particulars of Fortune, that attended my unhappy Issue, which in the suc-
ceeding Spring, had the good Luck to acquire the Approbation of an eminent Wit, [10]
who proposed a few Amendments, and recommended it to a Person, [11] *by whose Influ-*
ence, I laid my Account with seeing it appear at last, with such Advantage as should
make ample Amends for all my Disappointments.

But here too, I reckoned without my Host. [12] *The Master of* Covent-Garden
Theatre, [13] *bluntly rejected it, as a Piece altogether unfit for the Stage; even after*
he had told me, in Presence of another Gentleman, that he believed he should not
venture to find Fault with any Performance which had gained the good Opinion of
the honourable Person who approved and recommended my Play.

Baffled in every Attempt, I renounced all Hopes of its seeing the Light, when a
humane Lady of Quality, [14] *interposed so urgently in its Behalf, with my worthy*
Friend the other Manager, [15] *that he very complaisantly received it again, and had*
Recourse to the old Mystery of Protraction, which he exercised with such Success, that
the Season was almost consumed, before he could afford it a Reading. — My Patience
being by this Time quite exhausted, I desired a Gentleman, who interested himself
in my Concerns, to go and expostulate with the Vaticide: [16] *And indeed, this Piece of*
Friendship he performed with so much Zeal, upbraiding him with his evasive and
presumptuous Behaviour, that the sage Politician was enraged at his Reprimand;
and in the Mettle of his Wrath, pronounced my Play a wretched Piece, deficient in
Language, Sentiment, Character and Plan. My friend, who was surprised at the
Hardiness and Severity of this Sentence, asking how he came to change his Opinion,
which had been more favourable when the Tragedy was first put into his Hands; he
answered, that his Opinion was not altered, neither had he ever uttered an Expression
in its Favour.

This was an unlucky Assertion—For, the other immediately produced a Letter
which I had received from the young Nobleman two Years before, beginning with
these Words——

"Sir, I have received Mr. L——'s answer; who says, he thinks your Play has indu-
bitable Merit, but has prior Promises to Mr. T——n, [17] *as an honest Man, cannot*
be evaded."——And concluding thus; "As the Manager has promised me the Choice
of the Season next Year, if you'll be advised by me, rest it with me."

After having made some Remarks suitable to the Occasion, my Friend left him
to chew the Cud of Reflection, the Result of which was, a Message to my Patroness,
importing, (with many Expressions of Duty) that neither the Circumstances of his
Company, nor the advanced Season of the Year, would permit him to obey her Com-
mand, but if I would wait till next Winter, and during the Summer, make such
Alterations as I had agreed to, [18] *at a Conference with some of his principal Per-*
formers, he would assuredly put my Play in Rehearsal, and in the mean time give me

an Obligation in Writing, for my further Satisfaction. — I would have taken him at his Word, without Hesitation, but was persuaded to dispense with the proffered Security, that I might not seem to doubt the Influence or Authority of her Ladyship. — The Play (however) was altered and presented to this upright Director, [19] *who renounced his Engagement, without the least Scruple, Apology or Reason assigned. ——*

Thus have I in the most impartial Manner, (perhaps too circumstantially) displayed the Conduct of those Playhouse Managers with whom I have had any Concern, relating to my Tragedy: And whatever Disputes have happened between the Actors and me, are suppressed as frivolous Animosities unworthy of the Reader's Attention.

Had I suffered a Repulse when I first presented my Performance, I should have had Cause to complain of my being excluded from that Avenue to the public Favour, which ought to lie open to all Men of Genius; and how far I deserve that Distinction, I now leave the World to decide; after I have in Justice to my self, declared that my Hopes of Success were not derived from the partial Applause of my own Friends only, but inspired (as some of my greatest Enemies know) by the Approbation of Persons of the first Note in the Republic of Taste; whose Countenance, I vainly imagined, would have been an effectual Introduction to the Stage.

Be that as it will; I hope the unprejudiced Observer will own, with Indignation and Disdain, that every Disappointment I have endured, was an accumulated Injury; and the whole of my Adversary's Conduct, a Series of the most unjustifiable Equivocation and insolent Absurdity: For, though he may be excusable in refusing a Work of this kind, either on Account of his Ignorance or Discernment; surely, neither the one nor the other can vindicate his Dissimulation and Breach of Promise to the Author.

Abuse of Prerogative, in Matters of greater Importance, prevails so much at present, and is so generally overlooked, that it is almost ridiculous to lament the Situation of Authors, who must either, at once, forego all Opportunities of acquiring Reputation in Dramatic Poetry; or humble themselves so, as to sooth the Pride, and Humour the Petulance of a meer Goth, [20] *who by the most preposterous Delegation of Power, may become sole Arbiter of this kind of Writing.*

Nay, granting that a Bard is willing to prostitute his Talents so shamefully, perhaps he may never find an Occasion to practice this vile Condescension to Advantage: For, after he has gained Admission to a Patentee, who is often more difficult of Access than a Sovereign Prince, and even made Shift to remove all other Objections; an insurmountable Obstacle may be raised by the Manager's Avarice, which will dissuade him from hazarding a certain Expence on an uncertain Issue, when he can fill his Theatre without running any Risk, or disobliging his principal Actors, by putting them to the trouble of studying new parts. —

Besides, he will be apt to say within himself, "if I must entertain the Town with

Variety, it is but natural that I should prefer the Productions of my Friends, or of those who have any Friends worth obliging, to the Works of obscure Strangers, who have nothing to recommend them but a doubtful Superiority of Merit, which in all likelihood, will never rise in Judgment against me."

That such have been the Reflections of Patentees, I believe no Man of Intelligence and Veracity will deny; and I will venture to affirm, that on the Strength of Interest or Connection with the Stage, some People have commenced Dramatic Authors, who otherwise, would have employed their Faculties in Exercises better adapted to their Capacity.

—After what has been said, any thing by way of Application would be an Insult on the Understanding of the Public, to which I owe and acknowledge the most indelible Obligation, for former Favours as well as for the uncommon Encouragement I have received in the Publication of the following Play.

Persons of the Drama

King of *Scotland.*

Angus.

Dunbar.

Ramsay.

Athol.

Stuart.

Grime.

Cattan.

Queen.

Eleonora.

Guards, Attendants, &c.

SCENE, *A Convent in* Perth.

THE

REGICIDE:

A

TRAGEDY.

ACT I. SCENE I.
A Convent in PERTH.

ANGUS, DUNBAR.

DUNBAR.

But that my Duty calls, I would decline
Th' unwelcome Office. — Now, when Justice waves
Her flaming Sword, and loudly claims her Due,
Thus to arrest her Arm, and offer Terms
Of Peace to Traitors who avow their Crime,
Is to my Apprehension weak, and suits
But little with the Majesty of Kings. ——
Why sleeps the wonted Valour of our Prince?

ANGUS.

Not to th' ensanguin'd Field of Death alone
Is Valour limited: She sits serene
In the delib'rate Council; sagely scans
The Source of Action; weighs, prevents, provides,
And scorns to count her Glories, from the Feats
Of brutal Force alone, —
                                        — What Frenzy were it
To risk our Fortune on th' unsure Event
Of one Occurrence, naked as we are
To unforeseen Disaster, when the Terms
We proffer may retard th' impending Blow?
— Better to conquer by Delay: the Rage
Of *Athol*'s fierce Adherents, flush'd with Hope

Of Plunder and Revenge, will soon abate,
And ev'ry Hour bring Succour to our Cause.

DUNBAR.

Well ha'st thou taught me, how the piercing Eye
Of calm Sagacity, excels the Dint
Of headstrong Resolution. — Yet, my Soul
Pants for a fair Occasion to revenge
My father's Wrongs on *Athol*'s impious Head!
Yes, *Angus*, while the Blood of *March*[21] revolves
Within my Veins, the Traitor shall not find
His Perfidy forgot —— But what of this?
What are my private Injuries, compar'd
To those he meditates against the State!
Against a Prince with ev'ry Virtue grac'd
That dignifies the Throne, to whom the Ties
Of Kindred and Allegiance could not bind
His faithless Heart: Not ev'n the sacred Bond
Of Friendship unreserv'd! — For well thou know'st,
The king securely list'ned to his Voice,
As to an Oracle.

ANGUS.
'Twas there indeed
He triumph'd in his Guile! — Th' unwary Prince
Sooth'd by his false Professions, crown'd his Guilt
With boundless Confidence; and little thought
That very Confidence supply'd his Foe
With Means to shake his Throne! — While *Athol* led
His royal Kinsman thro' the dang'rous Path
Of sudden Reformation, and observ'd
What Murmurs issu'd from the giddy Croud;
Each popular Commotion he improv'd
By secret Ministers; and disavow'd
Those very Measures he himself devised!
Thus cherish'd long by his flagitious[22] Arts,
Rebellion glow'd in secret, 'till at length
His Scheme mature, and all our loyal Thanes
At their own distant Homes repos'd secure,

The Flame burst out. — Now from his native Hills,
With his Accomplice *Grime*, and youthful Heir,
Impet'ous *Stuart*, like a sounding Storm
He rushes down with five revolting Clans;
Displays a spurious Title to the Crown,[23]
Arraigns the Justice of his Monarch's Sway,
And by this sudden Torrent, means, no doubt,
To sweep him from the Throne.

DUNBAR.

       Aspiring Villain!
A fit Associate has he chose: A Wretch
Of Soul more savage breathes not vital Air,
Than *Grime:* — but *Stuart* 'till of late, maintain'd
A fairer Fame.

ANGUS.

    A cherish'd Hope expires
In his Dishonour too! — While *Stuart*'s Ear
Was deaf to vicious Counsel, and his Soul
Remained unshaken, by th' enchanting Lure
Which vain Ambition spread before his Eye,
He bloom'd the Pride of *Caledonia*'s Youth,
In Virtue, Valour, and external Grace: —
For thou sole Rival of his Fame, wa'st train'd
To martial Deeds, in Climes remote.

DUNBAR.

        O Thane!
Whatever Wreaths from Danger's Steely Crest
My Sword hath won; whatever Toils sustain'd
Beneath the sultry Noon, and cold, damp Night;
Could ne'er obtain for me one genial Smile
Of Her, who bless'd that happy Rival's Vows
With mutual Love! —— Why should I dread to own
The tender Throbbings of my captive Heart!
The melting Passion which has long inspir'd
My breast for *Eleonora*, and implore
A Parent's Sanction to support my Claim?

ANGUS.

Were she more fair and gentle than she is,
And to my partial Eye, nought e'er appear'd
So gently fair, I would approve thy Claim
To her peculiar Smiles.

DUNBAR.

           Then will I strive
With unremitted Ardour, to subdue
Her coy Reluctance; while I scorn the Threats
Of frantic Jealousy that flames unrein'd
In *Stuart*'s breast! — But see! the fair one comes,
In all the Pride of dazz'ling Charms array'd.

SCENE II.

ANGUS, DUNBAR, ELEONORA.

ELEONORA.

Something of Moment, by a fresh Dispatch
Imparted to the King, requires in Haste
The Presence of my Sire.

ANGUS.

           Forbear a while
Thy Parly with the Foe; and here attend
Our Consultation's Issue. —

                                  [Exit Angus.

SCENE III.

DUNBAR, ELEONORA.

DUNBAR.

           Ill it suits
A Soldier's Tongue, to plead the Cause of Love,
In Phrase adapted to the tender Theme:

But trust me, beauteous Wonder! when I swear
Not the keen Impulse, and impatient Hope
Of Glory, glowing in the Warrior's Breast,
With more awak'ned Transport, fill'd my Soul
When the fierce Battle rag'd, than *that* I feel
At thy Approach!——My Tongue has oft reveal'd
The Dictates of my Heart; but thou, averse
With cold Disdain, hast ever chill'd my Hopes,
And scorn'd my proffer'd Vows!—

ELEONORA.

O Youth, beware!
Let not the flow'ry Scenes of Joy and Peace,
That faithless Passion to the View presents,
Ensnare thee into Woe!—Thou little know'st
What Mischiefs lurk in each deceitful Charm;
What Griefs attend on Love.—

DUNBAR.

Keen are the Pangs
Of hapless Love, and Passion unapprov'd:
But where consenting Wishes meet, and Vows
Reciprocally breath'd, confirm the Tie,
Joy rolls on Joy, an inexhausted Stream!
And Virtue crowns the sacred Scene with Peace!

ELEONORA.
Illusion all! the Phantoms of a Mind
That o'er its present Fate repining, Courts
The vain Resource of Fancy's airy Dreams.—
War is thy Province.—War be thy Pursuit.—

DUNBAR.
O! thou would tell me, I am Savage all—
Too much estrang'd to the soft Arts of Life,
To warm thy Breast—Yes, War has been my School—
War's rough Sincerity, unskill'd in Modes
Of peaceful Commerce—Soften'd not the less
To pious Truth, Humanity and Love.

ELEONORA.

Yes:—I were envious to refuse Applause,
When ev'ry Mouth is open'd in thy Praise.—
I were ungrateful not to yield thee more,
Distinguish'd by thy Choice; and tho' my Heart
Denies thee Love, thy Virtues have acquir'd
Th' Esteem of *Eleonora*.

DUNBAR.

        O! thy Words
Would fire the hoary Hermit's languid Soul
With Extasies of Pride!—How then shall I,
Elate with ev'ry vainer Hope, that warms
Th' aspiring Thought of Youth, thy Praise sustain
With Moderation?——Cruelly benign!
Thou hast adorn'd the Victim; but, alas!
Thou likewise giv'st the Blow.—
                Tho' Nature's Hand
With so much Art has blended ev'ry Grace
In thy enchanting Form, that ev'ry Eye
With Transport views thee, and conveys unseen
The soft Infection to the vanquish'd Soul,
Yet wilt thou not the gentle Passion own,
That vindicates thy Sway!—

ELEONORA.

          O gilded curse!
More fair than rosy Morn, when first she smiles
O'er the dew-brighten'd Verdure of the Spring!
But more deceitful, tyrannous, and fell,
Than Syrens, Tempests, and devouring Flame!
May I ne'er sicken, languish and despair
Within thy dire Domain!—Listen ye Powers!
And yield your Sanction to my purpos'd Vow—
—If e'er my Breast——
                                      [*Kneeling.*

DUNBAR.

        For ever let me pine
In secret Misery, divorc'd from Hope!

But ah, forbear! nor forfeit thy own Peace
Perhaps in one rash Moment——

SCENE IV.

DUNBAR, ELEONORA, HERALD.

HERALD.
——From the Tower
That fronts the Hills, due North, a moving Host
Is now descry'd: And from the southern Gate
A Cloud of Dust is seen to roll, the Gleam
Of burnish'd Arms, oft thro' the dusky Sphere
Salutes the dazzled Eye;—a loyal Band
With valiant *Ramsay*, from the Banks of *Tweed*,
That hastens to our Aid.—The first, suppos'd
The rebel Train of *Athol*.—By Command
Of *Angus*, I attend thee, to demand
An Audience of the Foe.

DUNBAR.
I follow straight.

[*Exit Herald.*

Whate'er is amiably fair—Whate'er
Inspires the gen'rous Aim of chaste Desire,
My Soul contemplates and adores in thee!
Yet will I not with vain Complainings, vex
Thy gentle Nature.—My unblemish'd Love
Shall plead in my Behalf.

[*Exit Dunbar.*

SCENE V.

ELEONORA.
Adieu brave Youth!
Why art thou doom'd to suffer fruitless Pains!
And why, alas! am I the destin'd Wretch
That must inflict them?—Agonizing Thought!

I yielded up my fond, believing Heart
To him who basely left it, for the Charms
Of treacherous Ambition! — hapless *Stuart*!
How art thou chang'd! how lost! thy cruel Fate,
Like a false Harlot, smiles thee into Ruin!

SCENE VI.

Enter STUART *disguised like a Priest.*

STUART, ELEONORA.

STUART.

The mighty Schemes of Empire, soar too high
For your Distinction, Daughter. — Simple Woman
Is weak in Intellect, as well as Frame,
And judges often from the partial Voice
That sooths her Wishes most.   [*Discovering himself.*

ELEONORA.

                         Ha, frantic Youth!
What guilty Purpose leads thy daring Steps
To this forbidden Place? — Art thou not come
Beneath that sacred Veil, the more to brave
Th' avenging Hand of Heav'n?

STUART.

                         No — that I tread
The Paths of Danger, where each Bosom pants
With keen Revenge against me, speaks aloud
The Fervour of my Love — My Love misplac'd!
Else, would'st thou not receive the gen'rous Proof
With Anger and Disdain. —

ELEONORA.

                         Have I not Cause
To drive thee from my Heart? — Hast thou not chac'd
All Faith, and Truth, and Loyalty from thine?

Say, hast thou not conspir'd against thy Prince?
A Prince! who cherish'd thee with parent Zeal,
With Friendship honour'd thee, and ev'ry Day
With bounteous Favour crown'd thy rising Wish?

STUART.

Curse on his Arts!—his Aim was to enslave
Th' aspiring Soul, to stifle and repress
Th' emerging Dictates of my native Right,
To efface the glowing Images within,
Awak'd by Glory, and retain by Fraud
The Sceptre he usurps!

ELEONORA.
     Insidious Charge!
As feeble as unjust! for, clear as Day
In Course direct——

STUART.
     In idle Argument
Let us not now consume the precious Hour;
The middle Stream is pass'd; and the safe Shore
Invites our dauntless Footsteps—Yonder Sun
That climbs the Noon-tide Arch, already sees
Twelve thousand Vassals, marching in the Train
Of warlike *Athol*; and before the Shades
Of Ev'ning deepen, *Perth*'s devoted Walls
Will shake before them—E'er the Tempest roars,
I come to snatch thee from th' impending Storm—

ELEONORA.
O impotent of Thought!—O! dead to Shame!
Shall I for pompous Infamy forego
Th' internal Peace that Virtue calls her own!

STUART.
Or, say, thy Love inconstant as the Wave,
Another Object claims.—False—perjur'd Maid!
I mark'd thy Minion, as he charm'd thine Ear

With grov'ling Adulation. — Yes, I saw
Thy Looks, in artful Languishment, disclose
Thy yielding Soul, and heard thy Tongue proclaim
The Praises of *Dunbar.* —

ELEONORA.
                    Away — away!
I scorn thy mean Suspicion, and renounce
Thy Passion with thy Crimes. — Tho' bred in Camps,
Dunbar is gentle, gen'rous and humane;
Possess'd of ev'ry manly Grace, to win
The coyest Virgin's Heart. —

STUART.
                    Perdition whelm
The prostrate Sycophant! — may Heav'n exhaust
Its Thunder on my Head — may Hell disgorge
Infernal Plagues to blast me, if I cease
To persecute the Caitif, 'till his Blood
Assuage my parch'd Revenge! — perfidious Slave!
To steal between me and my darling Hope! —
The Traitor durst not, had I been — O Vows!
Where is your Obligation? — *Eleonora!*
O lovely Curse! restore me to myself! —

ELEONORA.
Rage on fierce Youth, more savage than the Storm
That howls on *Thule*'s Shore![24] — th' unthrifty Maid
Too credulously fond! who gave away
Her Heart so lavishly, deserves to wed
The Woes that from her Indiscretion flow! —
— Yet ev'n my Folly should, with thee, obtain
A fairer Title and a kinder Fate! —

STUART.
Ha! weep'st thou? — witness all ye sacred Pow'rs!
Her Philtres[25] have undone me! — lo, my Wrath
Subsides again to Love! — Enchantress! say,
Why hast thou robb'd me of my Reason thus?

ELEONORA.

Has *Eleonora* robb'd thee! — O recal
Those flatt'ring Arts thy own Deceit employ'd
To wreck my Peace! — recal thy fervent Vows
Of constant Faith — thy Sighs and ardent Looks!
Then whisper to thy Soul, those Vows were false —
Those Sighs unfaithful, and those Looks disguis'd!

STUART.

Thou — thou art chang'd — but *Stuart* still the same!
Ev'n while thou chid'st me, ev'ry tender Wish
Awakes anew, and in my glowing Breast
Unutterable Fondness pants again! —
— Wilt thou not smile again, as when, reclin'd
By *Tay*'s smooth-gliding Stream,²⁶ we softly breath'd
Our mutual Passion to the vernal Breeze?

ELEONORA.

Adieu — dear Scenes adieu! — ye fragrant Paths
So courted once! — ye spreading Boughs, that wave
Your Blossoms o'er the Stream! — delightful Shades!
Where the bewitching Music of thy Tongue,
First charm'd my captive Soul! — when gentle Love
Inspir'd the soothing Tale! — Love — sacred Love
That lighted up his Flame at Virtue's lamp! —

STUART.

In Time's eternal Round, shall we not hail
Another Season equally serene? ——
— To Day, in Snow array'd, stern Winter rules
The ravag'd Plain — Anon the teeming Earth
Unlocks her Stores, and Spring adorns the Year:
And shall not we — while Fate, like Winter, frowns,
Expect revolving Bliss?

ELEONORA.

           — Would'st thou return
To Loyalty and me — my faithful Heart
Would welcome thee again! —

ANGUS *Within.*
                              Guard ev'ry Gate
That none may 'scape—

ELEONORA.
                              Ha!—whither wilt thou fly?
Discover'd and beset?

STUART.
                              Let *Angus* come—
His short-liv'd Pow'r I scorn—
                              [*Throws away his Disguise.*

SCENE VII.

Enter ANGUS *with Guards,* STUART, ELEONORA.

ANGUS.
                              What dark Resolve
By gloomy *Athol* plann'd, has hither led
Thy Steps presumptuous?—*Eleonora*, hence.—
It ill befits thee—but, no more—away—
I'll brook no Answer—   [*Exit* Eleonora.
                    —Is it not enough,
To lift Rebellion's impious Brand on high,
And scorch the Face of Faith; that ye thus creep
In ruffian Ambush, seeking to perform
The Deed ye dare not trust to open War?

STUART.
Thou little know'st me—or thy rankling Hate
Defrauds my Courage.—Wherefore should I skulk
Like the dishonour'd Wretch, whose hireling Steel
In secret lifted, reeks with human Gore,
When valiant *Athol* hastens at the Head
Of warlike Thousands, to assert our Cause?

ANGUS.

The Cause of Treason never was confin'd
To Deeds of open War; but still adopts
The Stab of crouching Murder. — Thy Revolt,
The stern Contraction of thy sullen Brow,
And this Disguise, Apostate! speak thee bent
On fatal Errand. —

STUART.

That thou seest me here
Unarm'd, alone, from *Angus* might obtain
A fair interpretation — *Stuart*'s Love
Pleads not in mystic Terms; nor are my Vows
To *Eleonora*, cancell'd or unknown ——
Vows by thyself indulg'd, e'er Envy yet,
Or Folly had induc'd thee, to embrace
The Fortunes of our Foe. — Thy foul Reproach
My Soul retorts on thee! and mark, proud Lord,
Revenge will have its Turn! —

ANGUS.

Ha! must I bear
A beardless Traitor's Insults? — 'tis not mine
To wage a fruitless War of Words with thee,
Vain-glorious Stripling. — While thine Aims were just,
I seal'd thy Title to my Daughter's Love;
But now, begrim'd with Treason, as thou art,
By Heav'n! not Diadems and Thrones shall bribe
My Approbation! — but the King himself
Shall judge thy Conduct. — Guards —

SCENE VIII.

Enter ELEONORA, *who kneels.*

— O! let me thus
Implore Compassion, at a Parent's Knees,
Who ne'r refus'd —

ANGUS.
— Convey him hence. —

[Stuart *is led off.*

— Arise —

Remember, *Eleonora*, from what Source
Thine Origin is drawn. — Thy Mother's Soul
In Purity excell'd the snowy Fleece
That cloaths our northern Hills! — her youthful Charms,
Her artless Blush, her Look severely sweet,
Her Dignity of Mien and Smiles of Love
Survive in thee — Let me behold thee too
Her Honour's Heiress —

[*Exit* Angus.

SCENE IX.

ELEONORA.
— Yes — I will adhere
To this ill-omen'd Honour! sacrifice
Life's promis'd Joys to its austere Decree;
And vindicate the Glories of my Race,
At the sad Price of Peace! — If *Athol*'s Arms
(Which Heav'n avert!) to Treason add Success;
My Father's Death will join his Sov'reign's Fall!
And if the Cause of Royalty prevail,
Each languid Hope with *Stuart* must expire! —
    From Thought to Thought, perplex'd, in vain I stray,
    To pining Anguish doom'd, and fell Dismay!

END of the FIRST ACT.

ACT II. SCENE *Continues.*

ANGUS, DUNBAR.

DUNBAR.
By Heav'n it glads me, that my Sword shall find
An ample Field to Day. — The King arrous'd,
Chafes like a Lion in the Toils betray'd? [27]

ANGUS.

I mark'd his Indignation, as it rose
At *Athol*'s proud Reply, from calm Concern,
To anxious Tumult, menacing Disdain,
And overboiling Wrath.—But say, my Friend,
How move the Rebels?—Are their Ranks dispos'd
By military Skill?—Or come they on
In undistinguish'd Crouds?—

DUNBAR.

         In Concourse rude
They swarm undisciplin'd—all arm'd alike
With Sword and Target.[28]—On their first Assault
(Fearless indeed and headlong!) all their Hopes
Of Conquest, must depend.—If we, unbroke,
Sustain their Onset; little skill'd in War,
To wheel, to rally and renew the Charge,
Confusion, Havock and Dismay will seize
Th' astonish'd Rout.—

ANGUS.

      What Numbers bring they on?

DUNBAR.

Ten thousand, as I guess.—

ANGUS.

        Ours scarce amount
To half the Number: Yet, with those, we mean,
To hazard an Encounter.—Thou, mean while,
Shalt visit ev'ry Passage, sound th' Alarm,
And man the City-Walls.—Here I attend
The King—and lo! he comes.—

                                [*Exit* Dunbar.

SCENE II.

KING, ANGUS.

KING.

— The Commonweal
Has been consulted. — Tenderness and Zeal
Became the Parent. — Those have nought avail'd. —
Now, let Correction speak the King incens'd!

ANGUS.

Not without Cause, my Liege, shall dread Rebuke
Attend your royal Wrath. — What Reign shall 'scape
Rebellion's Curse, when your paternal Sway
Has hatch'd the baneful Pest?

KING.

Let Heaven decide
Between me and my Foes. — That I would spare
The guiltless Blood which must our Quarrel dye,
No other Proof requires, than my Advance
To Reconcilement — opposite perhaps
To my own Dignity. — But I will rise
In Vengeance mighty! and dispel the Clouds
That have bedimm'd my State.

ANGUS.

The Odds are great
Between the Numbers: But our Cause is just:
Our Soldiers regularly train'd to War,
And not a Breast among us, entertains
A Doubt of Victory.

KING.

O valiant Thane!
Experienc'd oft, and ever trusty found!
Thy penetrating Eye, and active Zeal
First brought this foul Conspiracy to Light;
And now thy faithful Vassals, first appear

In Arms for my Defence! — Thy Recompence
My Love shall study.

ANGUS.

Blotted be my Name
From Honour's Records, when I stand aloof,
Regardless of the Danger that surrounds
The Fortunes of my prince!

KING.

I know thee well. —
Mean time, our Care must be, to obviate
With Circumspection and preventive Skill,
Their Numbers. — In unequal Conflict joins
Th' unwieldy Spear that loads the Borderer,[29]
With the broad Targe[30] and expeditious Sword:
The loyal Band that from the Hills of *Lorn*[31]
Arriv'd, shall in our Front advance, and stand
With Targe to Targe, and Blade to Blade oppos'd;[32]
The Spears extended form the second Line,
And our light Archers hover to and fro,
To gall their Flanks. — Whatever Accident
In Battle shall befal, thy Vigilance
Will remedy. — Myself will here remain
To guard the Town, and with a small Reserve,
(If Need requires) thine Exigence supply.

ANGUS.

With Joy, the glorious Task I undertake!   [*Exeunt.*

SCENE III.

DUNBAR, RAMSAY.

RAMSAY.

They halt, and occupy the narrow Pass
Form'd by the River and th' impending Hill;
With Purpose (as I deem) to charge our Host
On the small Plain that skirts the Town. —

DUNBAR.

'Tis well. —

Thus hemm'd, their useless Numbers will involve
Themselves in Tumult, to our Arms secure
An easy Conquest, and retard their Flight. —
To *Angus* hie thee straight with this Advice. —
My Task perform'd, I wait the King's Command
In this appointed Place. —

[*Exit* Ramsay.

SCENE IV.

ELEONORA, DUNBAR.

ELEONORA.

I sought thee, Youth. —

Ere yet this dreadful Crisis shall decide
The public Fate, let us to private Woe
Devote one Moment! — Tell me, brave *Dunbar*,
Wilt thou not, from the Hurry of the Day,
One Moment snatch to hear me, and condole
The Anguish of my Soul? —

DUNBAR.

O *Eleonora*!

Sooner shall the parch'd Traveller refuse
The gelid[33] Fountain, than my raptur'd Soul
The Music of thy Tongue! — What Grief profanes
Thy spotless Bosom? — happy! far above
The Pride of Conquerors, were I to ease
Thy Sorrow's Pangs! —

ELEONORA.

Thy gen'rous Heart alone

Can brook the Enterprize —

DUNBAR.

O! task my Love;

That I more swift than Gales that sweep the Plain,
May fly to thy Relief!

ELEONORA.

                    Then summon up
Those elevated Thoughts, that lift the Soul
To Virtue's highest Pinnacle; the Boon
My Misery demands, will crave them all!—

DUNBAR.

Be it to brave the Menaces of Death
In Shape however horrid, so my Faith
And Love remain inviolate, my Heart
Beats with unusual Ardor; and demands
The Test, impatient!—

ELEONORA.

                    Friendless and forlorn,
In Fetters *Stuart* lies!—

DUNBAR.
                    Ha!

ELEONORA.

                    From the Snares
Of gloomy Fate release him.—

DUNBAR.

                    Cruel Maid!—
Nay, let me call thee barbarous! in spite
Of Adoration.—Could thy Mind suggest
No forward Slave, to set thy Lover free,
But a despairing Rival?—'Tis not giv'n
Th' impassion'd Soul of Man, to execute
A Deed so fatal to its own Repose!

ELEONORA.

I sought not—witness ye celestial Powers!
To aggravate thy Pain—my Mind, perplex'd,
Revolv'd in silent Woe, nor could unload
Her Burden to another.—Thou alone,
Hast won my fair Opinion and my Trust;

And to thy Word indebted, Honour claims
Th' Engagement all her own. —

DUNBAR.

                                Yet, with Reserve
Was that impawn'd: My Loyalty and Love
Were sacred ev'n from that: Nor can I loose
His Chains, without an Injury to Both! —

ELEONORA.

Cold — unaspiring is the Love that dwells
With tim'rous Caution; and the Breast untouch'd
By Glory's Godlike Fervour, that retains
The Scruples of Discretion. — Let the Winds
That have dispers'd thy Promise, snatch thy Vows! —

DUNBAR.

Shall I, thro' rash Enthusiasm, wed
Eternal Anguish? — Shall I burst asunder
The Bonds of awful Justice, to preserve
The Serpent that has poison'd all my Peace! —
No, *Eleonora!* — blasted be ——

ELEONORA.

                                Take heed!
Nor by an Oath precipitate, involve
Thy Fate beyond Resource: For know, *Dunbar,*
The Love of *Stuart,* with his Guilt abjur'd,
This Morn, my solemn Vow to Heav'n appeal'd,
Hath sever'd us for ever. —

DUNBAR.

                                Then, I'm still! —
Still as the gentle Calm, when the hush'd Wave
No longer foams before the rapid Storm! —
Let the young Traitor perish, and his Name
In dark Oblivion rot. —

ELEONORA.

     Shall I, alas!
Supinely savage, from my Ears exclude
The Cries of youthful Woe? — of Woe intail'd
By me too! — If my Heart denies him Love,
My Pity, sure, may flow! — Has he not Griefs
That wake ev'n thy Compassion? — Say, *Dunbar*,
Unmov'd could'st thou survey th' unhappy Youth
(Whom but this Morn beheld in Pride of Hope
And Pow'r magnificent!) stretch'd on the Ground
Of a damp Dungeon, groaning with Despair!
With not one Friend his Sorrows to divide,
And chear his lone Distress? —

DUNBAR.

     Can I resist
So fair a Motive, and so sweet a Tongue!
When thy soft Heart with kind Compassion glows,
Shall I the tender Sentiment repress? —
No! — let me rather hail the social Pang;
And ev'ry selfish Appetite subdu'd,
Indulge a Flame so gen'rous and humane! —
— Away with each Emotion that suggests
A Rival favour'd and a Traitor freed!
My Love unbounded reigns, and scorns to own
Reflection's narrow Limits. — Yes, my Fair,
This Hour he shall be free. ——   [*Exit* Dunbar.

SCENE V.

ELEONORA.

     O wond'rous Power
Of Love beneficent! — O gen'rous Youth!
What Recompence (thus bankrupt as I am!)
Shall speak my grateful Soul? — A poor Return
Cold Friendship renders to the fervid Hope
Of fond Desire! and my invidious Fate
Allows no more. — But let me not bewail,

With Avarice of Grief, my private Woe;
When pale with Fear, and harass'd with Alarm,
My royal Mistress, still benign to me,
The zealous Tender of my Duty claims.   [*Exit.*

SCENE VI.

Discovers STUART *in Chains.*

STUART.

Curse on my headstrong Passion! — I have earn'd
The Wages of my Folly! — Is it thus
My faithless Destiny requites my Hope!

SCENE VII.

STUART, DUNBAR.

STUART.

Ha! com'st thou to insult my Chains? — 'Twas well
My unpropitious Dæmon gave me up
To your Resentment, tamely. —

DUNBAR.

                                   To exult
Ev'n o'er an Enemy oppress'd, and heap
Affliction on th' afflicted, is the Mark
And the mean Triumph of a dastard Soul. —
'Tis what *Dunbar* disdains. — Perhaps, I come
To pity, not rejoice at *Stuart*'s Fate. —

STUART.

To pity! — Torture! am I fall'n so low! —
Ha! Recreant! — move thy Pity! — Hell untie
These slavish Manacles, that I may scourge
This wretched Arrogant! —

DUNBAR.

          True Courage scorns
To vent her Prowess in a Storm of Words:
And to the Valiant, Actions speak alone: —
Then let my Deeds approve me. — I am come
To give thee instant Freedom. —

STUART.

          Mean'st thou Death? —
I shall be free then. — An apt Minister
Th' Usurper has ordain'd to perpetrate
His secret Murders. —

DUNBAR.

          Why wilt thou belye
Thy own Intelligence? — Thou know'st, my Sword
Was ne'er accustom'd to the Bravo's Stab;
Nor the Designs of Him so falsely stil'd
Usurper, ever sully'd with a Stain
Of Cruelty or Guile. — My Purpose is,
To knock thy Fetters off, conduct thee safe
Without the City-Confines, and restore thee
To liberty and *Athol.* —

STUART.

          Fawning Coward!
Thou — thou restore me! — thou unbind my Chains!
Impossible! — Thy Fears that I may 'scape,
Like Vultures gnaw thee! —

DUNBAR.

          When the Battle joins,
Thou shalt be answer'd. —

STUART.

          When the Battle joins! —
— Away, Dissembler! — Sooner would'st thou beard
The Lion[34] in his Rage, than fairly meet
My Valour on the Plain!

DUNBAR.
Ha! who art thou
That I should dread thy Threats? — By Heav'n's high Throne!
I'll meet thee in a Desart, to thy Teeth
Proclaim thy Treachery, and with my Sword
Explore thy faithless Heart! — Meanwhile, my Steps
Shall guide thee to the Field.   [*Stuart is unchained, and
presented with a Sword.*]

STUART.
No! — Lightning blast me,
If I become thy Debtor, proud *Dunbar*!
Thy nauseous Benefits, shall not enslave
My freeborn Will. — Here, Captive as I am,
Thy lavish'd Obligation shall not buy
My Friendship! — No! nor stifle my Revenge!

DUNBAR.
Alike unpleasant would it be to me,
To court thy Love or deprecate thy Hate: —
What I have proffer'd, other Motives urg'd. —
The Gift is *Eleonora*'s. —

STUART.
Sacred Powers!
Let me not understand thee! — Thou hast rous'd
My Soul's full Fury! — In the Blood that warms
Thine Heart, Perfidious, I will slake mine Ire!³⁵

DUNBAR.
In all my Conduct, insolent of Heart!
What hast thou mark'd so abject and so mean,
That thy foul Tongue its Licence thus avows?
To boundless Passion subject, as thyself,
Wild Tumult oft my Reason overwhelms! —
Then tempt me not too far, lest blindfold Wrath
Transport my Soul, and headlong Ruin, crush
Thy Pride ev'n here! —

STUART.

    In this accursed Place
Let me be shackled—rivetted with Bolts,
'Till the Rust gnaw my Carcase to the Bone,
If my Heart throbs not for the Combat, here!—
Ev'n here, where thou art, Lord!—Ha! do'st thou shake?
By Heav'n, thy quiv'ring Lip and haggard Look
Confess pale Terror and Amaze!—

DUNBAR.

                    —Away!—
Away, lewd Railer!—not thy sland'rous Throat
So fruitful of Invectives, shall provoke me
To wreak unworthy Vengeance on thee, safe
In thy Captivity:—But soon as War
Shall close th' encountring Hosts, I'll find thee out—
Assert my claim to *Eleonora*'s Love,
And tell thee, what thou art.

STUART.

            I burn—I rage!
My fell Revenge consumes me!—But no more—
Thou shalt not 'scape me—Goaded by my Wrongs,
I'll hunt thee thro' the various Scenes of Death!—
Thou shalt be found!—

DUNBAR.

    I triumph in that Hope.

                                    [*Exeunt.*

SCENE VIII. *Changes.*

KING, QUEEN, *attended.*

KING.

Couragious *Angus* shall not be o'erpower'd—
Myself will bring him Aid.—

QUEEN.

Alas! my Prince!

KING.

What means the gentle Part'ner of my Heart?
Dismiss thy Fears.—This Day will dissipate
The Cause of thy Dismay.—Ev'n now, I go
To pluck the Wreath of Victory, and lay
Fresh Laurels in thy Lap.

QUEEN.

Ah! why let in
A Train of harpy[36] Sorrows to my Breast!—
—Ah! why in your own precious Life, expose
Your Kingdom's Safety, and your Consort's Peace!
—Let me restrain you from the Field to Day.—
There is no Fame—no Glory to be won
From a Revolter's Brow.—

KING.

The Public-weal
Commands to arm—Dishonour taint my Name,
When I reject the Call!—

QUEEN.

Ill-omen'd Call!
That like the Raven's Croak,[37] invades my Quiet!
O! would to Heaven, our Minutes smoothly roll'd
In humble Solitude, with meek-ey'd Peace!
Remote from Royalty, and all the Cares
That brood around the Throne!—

KING.

No, let us scorn
Unfeeling Ease, and private Bliss forego,
When public Misery implores our Aid.—
What Dignity of Transport feels the Prince,
Who, from the Fangs of fierce oppressive Power,
A People rescues?

QUEEN.
What a dreadful Host
Of Dangers 'circle him!

KING.
Disease confers
The Stamp of Value upon Health; and Glory
Is the fair Child of Peril. —— Thou thyself
My Conduct wilt applaud, soon as thy Mind
Its native Calm regains, and Reason sways
Uncheck'd by Fear. —— Secure 'till my Return
Remain within, and ev'ry Thought indulge
Foreboding my Success. —

QUEEN.
Adieu — Adieu!
Heav'n crown your Valour with a happy Wreath.
[*Exit Queen.*

KING, *to an Attendant.*
Swift, hie thee to *Dunbar*, and bid him lead
The chosen Citizens ——
Enter RAMSAY.

SCENE IX.

KING *attended*, RAMSAY.

RAMSAY.
O fatal Chance!
The Traitor *Grime*, with a selected Band,
(While *Angus*, press'd on every Side, sustains
Th' unequal Fight) a secret Path pursu'd
Around the Hills, and pouring all at once,
Surpriz'd the eastern Gate! — the Citizens
With Consternation smote, before his Arms
In Rout disorder'd fly! —

KING.

Ha! then the Wheel
Of Fate full Circle rolls to crush me down!
Nor leaves one Pause for Conduct!—Yet I'll bear
My Fortunes like a King—Haste and collect
The scattered Parties—Let us not submit
'Ere yet subdu'd—To arms.   [*Drawing.*

RAMSAY.

Alas my Prince!
The Convent is beset—Hark! while we speak
The Gates are burst—Behold—

KING.

We must prevent
The Pangs of ling'ring Misery, and fall
With Honour, as we lived—

SCENE X.

KING *attended*, RAMSAY. GRIME *with Followers bursting in.*

KING.

What bold Contempt
Of Majesty, thus rudely dares intrude
Into my private Scenes?

GRIME.

The Hour is fled,
That saw thy wanton Tyranny impose
The galling Yoke—Yes, I am come to wrest
The prostituted Sceptre from thy Hand,
And drag thee fetter'd to the royal Throne
Of *Walter*, whom I serve.

KING.

Outragious Wretch!
Grown old in Treachery! whose Soul untam'd,
No Mercy softens, and no Laws restrain!

Thy Life thrice forfeited, my Pity thrice
From Justice hath redeem'd; yet art thou found
Still turbulent — a rugged Rebel still,
Unaw'd, and unreclaim'd! —

GRIME.
                              That I yet breathe
This ambient Air, and tread this Earth at will,
Not to thy Mercy but thy Dread I owe. —
Wrong'd as I was — my old Possessions reft
By thy rapacious Power, my Limbs enchain'd
Within a loathsom Dungeon, and my Name
Thy loud Reproach thro' all the groaning Land;
Thou durst not shed my Blood! — the purple Stream
Had swell'd — a Tide of Vengeance! and o'erwhelm'd
The proud Oppressor. —

KING.
                              Traitor to thy Prince,
And Foe perverse to Truth! — how full thy Crimes,
Thy Doom how just — my Pardon how humane,
Thy conscious Malice knows — But let me not
Degrade my Name, and vindicate to thee
The Justice of my Reign.

GRIME.
                              Vain were th' Attempt
With Artifice of Words, to sooth my Rage,
More deaf to Mercy, than the famish'd Wolf
That tears the bleating Kid! — My starv'd Revenge
Thy Blood alone can satiate! — Yield thee then:
Or sink beneath mine Arm.

KING.
                              Heav'n shall not see
A Deed so abject vilify my Name —
While yet I wield this Sword, and the warm Blood
Still streams within my Veins;[38] my Courage soars
Superior to a Ruffian's Threats. —

GRIME.
>Fall on,

And hew them Piece-meal.

[King, Ramsay, and Attendants drive off Grime and his
Followers; but are afterwards overpowered and disarmed.

GRIME.
>Wilt thou yet maintain

Thy Dignity of Words? — Where are thy Slaves,
Thy Subjects, Guards and Thunder of thy Throne,
Reduc'd Usurper? — Guard these Captives hence.

[Exeunt King, Ramsay, &c. guarded.

SCENE XI.

Enter a SOLDIER *to* GRIME.

SOLDIER.
A Troop of Horsemen have possessed the Gate
By which we gain'd the City. —

GRIME.
>Blast them Hell!

We must retreat another Way, and leave
Our Aim unfinish'd! — Our victorious Swords
At least shall guard the Treasure they have won.
  When the fierce Parent-Lion bites our Chain,
  His Whelps forlorn, an easy Prey remain.

END of the SECOND ACT.

ACT III. SCENE I.

QUEEN, ELEONORA, CAPTAIN.

QUEEN.
What from the Battlements hast thou descry'd?

CAPTAIN.

Nothing distinct, my Queen—Involv'd in Clouds
Impervious to the View, the Battle long
Continu'd doubtful, 'midst the mingling Sounds
Of Trumpets, neighing Steeds, tumultuous Shouts
Of fierce Assailants, doleful Cries of Death,
And clatt'ring Armour; 'till at length, the Noise
In distant Murmurs dy'd.—O'er all the Plain,
Now a dread Stillness reigns!

QUEEN.

                    Then all is lost!—
Why pauses Ruin, and suspends the Stroke!—
Is it to lengthen out Affliction's Term,
And feed productive Woe!——Where shall the Groans
Of Innocence deserted find Redress!
Shall I exclaim to Heav'n?—Already Heav'n
Its Pity and Protection has withdrawn!
Earth yield me Refuge then!—give me to lie
Within thy cheerless Bosom!—there, put off
Th' uneasy Robe of Being—there, lay down
The Load of my Distress!

ELEONORA.

                    Alas! my Queen,
What Consolation can the Wretched bring!
How shall I from my own Despair, collect
Asswasive Balm?—Within my lonely Breast
Mute Sorrow and Despondence long have dwelt!
And while my Sire, perhaps, this Instant, bleeds,
The dim, exhausted Fountains of my Grief,
Can scarce afford a Tear!

QUEEN.

                    O Luxury
Of mutual Ill!—Let us enjoy the Feast!
To Groan re-echo Groan, in concert raise
Our Lamentation; and when Sorrow swells
Too big for Utterance, the silent Streams

Shall flow in common!—When the silent Streams
Forbear to flow, the Voice again shall wail!
O my lost Lord!—O save him—save him Powers!

ELEONORA.

Is there no gentle Remedy, to sooth
The Soul's Disorder; lull the jarring Thoughts,
And with fair Images amuse the Mind?
—Come smiling Hope—divine Illusion! come
In all thy Pride of Triumph o'er the Pangs
Of Misery and Pain!

QUEEN.
                Low—low indeed,
Have our Misfortunes plung'd us; when no Gleam
Of wand'ring Hope, how vain soe'er or false,
Our Invocation flatters!—When—O when
Will Death deliver me!—Shall I not rest
Within the peaceful Tomb, where I may sleep
In calm Oblivion, and forget the Wrecks
Of stormy Life!—No Sounds disturb the Grave,
Of murther'd Husbands!—Or the dismal Scream
Of Infants perishing.—Ha! whither leads
Imagination!—Must ye perish then,
Ye tender Blossoms!—Must the lofty Oak
That gave you Life, and shelter'd you from Harm,
Yield to the Traitor's Ax!—O Agony
Of fond Distraction!

ELEONORA.
                Ha!—behold where comes
The warlike son of *March*!—What, if he brings
The News of Victory!

QUEEN.
                My Soul alarm'd,
With Eagerness and Terror waits her doom!

SCENE II.

QUEEN, ELEONORA, DUNBAR.

QUEEN.

Say, Youth, how fares the King!

DUNBAR.

                    Fair Princess, hail!
To you my Duty and my Speed were bent—
Your royal Consort triumphs.

QUEEN.

                Lives he then!
Lives he, deliver'd from the fatal Snares
Which had enclos'd him!

DUNBAR.

             To their Hills repell'd,
The vanquish'd Rebels curse his conqu'ring Arm—
He bade me fly before him to the Queen;
With the glad Tidings chear her drooping Soul;
And bear his kindest Wishes to the Shrine
Himself will soon adore.

QUEEN.

             Will he then come
And wipe the Tear of Sorrow from my Cheek!—
Ah, no!—thy Pity flatters me in vain!

DUNBAR.

Let me not dally with my Queen's Distress.—
What were it, but to lift incumbent Woe,
That it might fall more grievous.—By the Faith
Of my Allegiance, hither speeds the King,
By Love attended, and by Conquest crown'd.

QUEEN.

O welcome Messenger!—How sweetly sounds
Thy Prelude!—Thus, the warbler of the Morn,

To the sick Wretch who moan'd the tedious Night,
Brings balmy Slumber, Ease and Hope and Health!
O wondrous Destiny!

ELEONORA.

Thus, on my Queen
May Fortune ever smile. — May Bliss to Bliss
Succeed, a tranquil Scene! — Say, noble Youth,
Returns my Sire in Safety from the Field? —

DUNBAR.

Safe as thy fondest filial Wish can form. —
In War's Variety, mine Eyes have seen
Variety of Valour and of Skill:
But such united Excellence of both —
Such Art to baffle and amuse[39] the Foe; —
Such Intrepidity to execute
Repeated Efforts, — never, save in him
My Observation trac'd! — Our Monarch's Acts
My feeble Praise would sully and profane.

ELEONORA.

Thy Words, like genial Showers to the parch'd Earth,
Refresh my languid Soul! —

QUEEN.

The Trumpet swells!
My Conqueror approaches! — Let me fly
With Extasy of Love into his Arms! —
He comes! — the Victor comes! —

SCENE III.

KING, QUEEN, ELEONORA, DUNBAR.

KING, *embracing the* Queen.

My better Part! —
My Soul's chief Residence! — my Love! my Queen!

Thou hast been tender overmuch, and mourn'd
Ev'n too profusely!

QUEEN.

Celebrate this Hour
Ye Songs of Angels! and ye Sons of Earth,
Keep Festival!—My Monarch is return'd!
I fold him in these Arms!—I hear his Voice—
His Love soft-chiding!—

KING.

O ye Powers benign!
What Words can speak the Rapture of my Soul!
Come to my Breast, where, cherish'd by my Love,
Thy fair Idea rooted, blossoms forth
And twines around my Heart!

QUEEN.

Mysterious Fate!
My Wishes are compleat!—Yet, I must ask
A thousand Things, impertinently fond!
How did you 'scape?—What Angel's Hand, my King,
Preserv'd you from Destruction?

KING.

Heav'n, indeed,
Espous'd my Cause, and sent to my Relief
The Son of *March*, who, with a chosen Few,
Deliver'd me from *Grime:*—Thence to the Field
We speeded, and accomplish'd what the Sword
Of *Angus* had well nigh atchiev'd before.

QUEEN, *To* Dunbar.
How shall Acknowledgment enough reward
Thy Worth unparallel'd?

KING.

Now, by my Throne!
Not my own Issue shall engross me, more

Than thou, heroic Youth! — Th' insulting Foe,
In spite of fresh Supplies, with Slaughter driven
To the steep Hills that bound the Plain, have sent
An Herald, in their Turn, to sue for Peace. —
An Audience have I promis'd. — Ere the Hour
Arrives, I will retire, and in the Bath
Refresh my weary'd Limbs. —

[*Exeunt* King, Queen, *Attendants.*

SCENE IV.

Dunbar, Eleonora.

Eleonora.
                          Renown, to Day
Has lavish'd all her Honours on thy Head.

Dunbar.
What boots it, that my Fortune decks me thus
With unsubstantial Plumes; when my Heart groans
Beneath the gay Caparison,[40] and Love
With unrequited Passion wounds my Soul!

Eleonora.
Is unpropitious Love unknown to me?
To me for ever doom'd (alas!) to nurse
The slow-consuming Fire. —

Dunbar.
                          Heav'ns! — what are all
The boasted Charms, that with such wond'rous Power
Attach thee to my Rival? — Far from me
Be the vain Arrogance of Pride, to vaunt
Excelling Talents; yet I fain would learn,
On what admir'd Accomplishment of *Stuart*,
Thy Preference is fix'd. —

ELEONORA.

　　　　　Alas! *Dunbar*,
My Judgment, weak and erring as it is,
Too well discerns on whom I should bestow
My Love and my Esteem:—But trust me, Youth,
Thou little know'st how hard it is to wean
The Mind from darling Habits long indulg'd!
I know that *Stuart* sinks into Reproach:
Immers'd in Guilt, and, more than once, subdu'd
By thy superior Merit and Success:
Yet even this *Stuart*,—for I would not wrong
Thine Expectation,—still retains a Part
Of my Compassion—nay, I fear, my Love!—
Would'st thou, distinguish'd by th' Applause of Kings,
Disgrace thy Qualities, and brook[41] the Prize
Of a divided Heart?—

DUNBAR.

　　　　　No!—witness Heav'n
I love not on such Terms!—Am I then doom'd,
Unfeeling Maid! for ever, to deplore
Thy unabating Rigour?—The rude Flint
Yields to th' incessant Drop;[42] but *Eleonora*,
Inflexibly severe, unchang'd remains—
Unmov'd by my Complaint!—

ELEONORA.

　　　　　My Father comes!
Let me, with pious Ravishment, embrace
His martial Knees, and bless the guardian Power
That screen'd him in the Battle!

SCENE V.

ANGUS, DUNBAR, ELEONORA.

ANGUS.

　　　　　Rise my Child,
Thou hast been always dutiful, and mild

As the soft Breeze that fanns the Summer-Eve!—
Such Innocence endearing, gently stole
Into my youthful Bosom, and awak'd
Loves tender Languishment, when to my View
Thy Mother first display'd her Virgin Bloom!

> [*Turning to* Dunbar.

Come to my Arms *Dunbar*!—To shield from Death
A Parent, is the venerable Act
Of the most pious Duty.—Thus adopted,
Henceforward be my Son!—The rebel Chiefs
Secure in my Safe-conduct, wait without
The promis'd Audience.—To the King repair,
And signify their Presence.—   [*Exit* Dunbar.

SCENE VI.

ANGUS, ELEONORA.

ANGUS.

> *Eleonora,*

Behold th' undaunted Youth, who stept between
The Stroke of Fate and me.—O'erpower'd, unhors'd,
And by the Foe surrounded, I had sunk
A Victim to Barbarity enrag'd;
If brave *Dunbar*, to his own Peril blind,
Had not that Instant, to my Rescue sprung.—
Nay, when that youthful Traitor—by whose Arm
Releas'd, I know not, headlong rush'd against me;
My vigilant Deliverer, oppos'd
The fierce Aggressor, whose aspiring Crest
Soon prostrate fell.—

ELEONORA.

> Ha! fell!—Is *Stuart* slain?

O! speak my Father!—

ANGUS.

> Wherefore this Alarm!

Let me not find thy Bosom entertain

A Sentiment unworthy of thy Name! —
The gen'rous Victor gave him back his Life;
And cry'd aloud, "This Sacrifice I make
For *Eleonora*'s Love." —

ELEONORA.
                    O matchless Youth!
His Virtues conquer'd my Esteem, before:
But now, my grateful Sentiment inflames
Ev'n to a Sister's Zeal!

ANGUS.
                    With rigid Power
I would not bridle thy reluctant Thought:
Yet, let me, with parental Care, commend
The Passion of *Dunbar*. —

ELEONORA.
                    A fairer Garb
His Title could not wear: — But when I think
What Rocks in secret lie — what Tempests rise
On Love's deceitful Voyage; my timid Soul
Recoils affrighted, and with Horror shuns
Th' inviting Calm! —

ANGUS.
                    Retire, my Child, and weigh
The diff'rent Claims. — Here, Glory, Love and Truth
Implore thy Smiles: — There, Vice with brutal Rage
Would force thee to his Wishes. — But too long
I tarry in this Place. — I must attend
My Sov'reign in his Interview with *Athol*.   [*Exeunt.*

SCENE VII. *Changes to another Apartment.*

ATHOL, GRIME.

ATHOL.
What we to Fortune ow'd, our Arms have paid:
But let us now, the Changeling Pow'r renounce. —

Unhappy those, who hazard their Designs
On her without Reserve! —

GRIME.
                    Our Plan pursu'd
A Purpose more assur'd: — With Conquest crown'd,
Our Aim indeed, a fairer Wreath had worn:
But that deny'd, on Terms of darker Hue
Our Swords shall force Success! —

ATHOL.
                              Th' approaching Scene
Demands our utmost Art! not with tame Sighs
To bend before his Throne, and supplicate
His Clemency, like Slaves; nor to provoke
With Pride of Speech, his Anger half appeas'd:
But with Submission mingle (as we speak)
A conscious Dignity of Soul, prepar'd
For all Events. —

GRIME.
                    Without the City-Walls,
The Southern Troops encamp'd, already fill
The festal Bowl, to celebrate the Day. —

ATHOL.
By Heav'n! their flush'd Intemperance will yield
Occasion undisturb'd. — For while they lie,
With Wine and Sleep o'erwhelm'd; the Clans that lurk
Behind th' adjacent Hills, shall in the Dark,
Approach the Gate when our Associate *Cattan*
Commands the Guard; then introduc'd by him,
We take, with Ease, Possession of the Town,
And hither move unmark'd. —

GRIME.
                        Here, if we fail,
May my shrunk Sinew never more unsheath
My well-try'd Dagger; nor my hungry Hate
Enjoy the sav'ry Steam of hostile Gore!

ATHOL.

How my fir'd Soul anticipates the Joy!
I see me seated in the regal Chair,
Enthron'd by *Grime*, the Partner of my Power! —
But this important Enterprize demands
More secret Conference. — The Sword of *Stuart*
Will much avail: But his unpractic'd Youth
To Doubts and Scruples subject, hitherto
Declines our last Resolve. —

GRIME.

                    It shall be mine,
To rouse his Passion to the Pitch requir'd. —
But soft! [43] — who comes? — Ten thousand Curses load
Th' ambitious Stripling!

Enter DUNBAR.
                    By the King's Command,
I come to guide you to the Throne.

ATHOL.

                              'Tis well. —   [*Exeunt.*

SCENE VIII.

Discovers the KING *seated,* ANGUS, *Attendants.*
Enter ATHOL, GRIME, *introduced by* DUNBAR.

KING.

It is not well — it is not well we meet
On Terms like these! [44] — I should have found in *Athol*
A trusty Counsellor and steady Friend:
And better would it suit thy rev'rend Age,
Thy Station, Quality, and kindred Blood,
To hush ill-judging Clamour, and cement
Divided Factions to my Throne, again,
Than thus embroil the State. —

ATHOL.

               My present Aim
Is to repair, not widen more, the Breach
That Discord made between us: This, my Liege,
Not harsh Reproaches, or severe Rebuke
Will e'er effectuate: — No — let us rather,
On Terms which equally become us both,
Our Int'rests re-unite.

KING.

            Hah! — re-unite!
By Heav'n, thy proud Demeanor more befits
A Sov'reign than a Subject! — Re-unite! —
How durst thou sever from thy Faith, old Lord!
And with an Helmet load that hoary Head
To wage rebellious War!

ATHOL.

         The Sword of *Athol*
Was never drawn but to redress the Wrongs
His Country suffer'd. —

KING.

          Dar'st thou to my Face,
Impeach my Conduct, baffled as thou art,
Ungrateful Traitor? — Is it thus, thy Guilt
My Clemency implores?

ATHOL.

         Not yet so low
Has Fate reduc'd us, that we need to crawl
Beneath your Footstool: — In our Camp remain
Ten thousand vig'rous Mountaineers, who long
Their Honours to retrieve. —

KING, *rising hastily.*

         Swift, hie thee to them,
And lead thy fugitive Adherents back! —
Away. — Now by the mighty Soul of *Bruce!*[45]

Thou shalt be met. — And if thy savage Clans
Abide us in the Plain, we soon will tread
Rebellion into Dust. — Why move ye not?
Conduct them to their Camp. —

ATHOL.

Forgive, my Prince,
If on my own Integrity of Heart
Too far presuming, I have gall'd the Wound
Too much inflam'd already. — Not with you,
But with your Measures ill-advis'd, I warr'd:
Your sacred Person, Family and Throne
My Purpose still rever'd. —

KING.

O wretched Plea!
To which thy blasted Guilt must have Recourse!
Had thy Design been laudable, thy Tongue
With honest Freedom boldly should have spoke
Thy Discontent. — Ye live not in a Reign
Where Truth, by arbitrary Pow'r depress'd,
Dares not maintain her State. — I charge thee, say
What lawless Measures has my Pow'r pursu'd?

ATHOL.

I come, to mitigate your royal Wrath
With Sorrow and Submission; not to sum
The Motives which compell'd me to the Field. —

KING.

I found your miserable State reduc'd
To Ruin and Despair: — Your Cities drench'd
In mutual Slaughter, desolate your Plains:
All Order banish'd, and all Arts decay'd: —
No Industry, save what with Hands impure
Distress'd the Commonwealth: — No Laws in Force,
To screen the Poor and check the guilty great;
While squalid Famine join'd her Sister Fiend
Devouring Pestilence, to curse the Scene! —

I came, — I toil'd, — reform'd, — redress'd the whole:[46]
And lo, my Recompence! — But I relapse. —
What is your Suit?

ATHOL.

We sue (my Liege) for Peace. —

KING.

Say, that my Lenity should grant your Prayer,
How, for the future, shall I rest assur'd
Of your Allegiance?

ATHOL.

Stuart shall be left
The Pledge of our Behaviour. —

KING.

And your Arms
Ere Noon to Morrow, shall be yielded up.

ATHOL.

This too, shall be perform'd. —

KING.

Then mark me Thane. —
Because the Loins, from whence my Father sprung,
On thee too Life bestow'd; enjoy the Gift. —
I pardon what is past. — In Peace consume
The Winter of thy Days. — But, if ye light
Th' extinguish'd Brand again, and brave my Throne
With new Commotions: — By th' eternal Power!
No future Guile, Submission, or Regard
Shall check my Indignation! — I will pour
My Vengeance in full Volley; and the Earth
Shall dread to yield you Succour or Resource!
Of this, no more. — Thy Kinsman shall remain
With us, an Hostage of thy promis'd Faith. —

So shall our Mercy with our Prudence join,
United brighten, and securely shine.

END of the THIRD ACT.

ACT IV. SCENE I.

STUART.

This Solitude but more foments Despair!
Recals — compares — and to th' incessant Pangs
Of Spite, Revenge, and Shame condemns my Soul! —
O! what a miserable Slave am I![47] —
Precipitated from the tow'ring Hope
Of eagle-ey'd Ambition, to th' Abyss
Of mutt'ring Horror, curs'd from Thought to Thought!
— Hah Jealousy! — I feel th' infernal Power!
Her hissing Snakes arrouse — her Torch inflames
My madd'ning Soul! — Yes, — if he thus permits
My Feet to range at will; my 'vengeful Hand
Will soon requite him. — [*Enter* Grime.

SCENE II.

STUART, GRIME.

GRIME.
Wherefore thus alone?
Thy noble Kinsman, who now parted hence,
Observes a sullen Cloud o'erhang thy Brow. —
Since from the Dungeon to his Wish restor'd,
A mute Aversion to his Love, secludes
Thy lonely Steps —

STUART.
Yes, — thou thyself hast nam'd
The Cause accurs'd! — ha, from the Dungeon freed! —
And freed by whom! — there's Poison in the Thought!
— Am I not Hostage of my Uncle's Shame? —

GRIME.

Thou dwell'st on that too much. — Few live exempt
From Disappointment and Disgrace, who run
Ambition's rapid Course. — Inur'd to Pain,
The hard'ned Soul, at last, forgets to feel
The Scourge of Fate; and fearless, rushes on
To Deeds advent'rous. —

STUART.

          Who shall frame th' Attempt
That *Stuart* dreads t' atchieve? — Not Pestilence,
Not raging Seas, nor livid Flames can bound
My dauntless Undertaking! — Tell me, *Grime*,
For thou wast train'd to Feats of horrid Proof,
Since, not the Voice of Heav'n itself, can lure
My Honour back again; — what Pow'r of Hell
Shall I invoke to deepen my Revenge? —

GRIME.

Ha! Did'st thou say, Revenge? — Hail, sable Pow'r,
To me more dear than Riches or Renown!
What gloomy Joy, to drench the Dagger deep
In the proud Heart of him who robb'd my Fame!
My Fortune thwarted; or essay'd by Fraud
To poison my Delights! —

STUART.

          Ha! thou hast rous'd
The Scorpion-Thought that stings me! —
          — Mark me, *Grime*, —
Our baffled Cause could not alarm me thus:
If Conquest for the Foe declar'd to Day;
Our Arms again the Vagrant might compel,
And chain her to our Side. — But know, my Love
Has been defrauded! — *Eleonora*'s Heart
That Wretch invades. — That Ravisher, who cropt
My budding Fame and sunk me to Reproach!
He, whom my Jealousy, in all its Rage,
Hath singled for Destruction! —

GRIME.

He shall die! —

STUART.

Yes, he shall die! — He shall be flea'd[48] — impal'd!
And his torn Bowels thrown to Beasts of Prey! —
My savage Hate shall on his Tortures feed!
I will have Vengeance!

GRIME.

Would'st thou have it full,
Include his Patrons. —

STUART.

Ha! — What — shall my Arm
Unsheath the secret Steel!

GRIME.

Yes. — Strike at once,
For Liberty, Ambition and Revenge. —
Let the proud Tyrant yield his haughty Soul:
And all his Offspring swell the sanguine Stream.
Let *Angus* perish too. —

STUART.

O wond'rous Plan
Of unrestrain'd Barbarity! — It suits
The Horrors of my Bosom! — All! — What all?
In slaughter'd Heaps. — The Progeny and Sire! —
To sluice[49] them in th' unguarded Hour of Rest! —
Infernal Sacrifice! — dire — ev'n too dire
For my Despair! — To me what have they done
To merit such Returns? — No, my Revenge
Demands the Blood of one, and he shall fall. —

GRIME.

It shall suffice — *Dunbar* shall bleed alone. —
But let us seize him on the Verge of Bliss;
When the fond Maid's enkind'ling Looks confess

The Flames of bashful Love: When eager Joy,
And modest Fear, by Turns exalt the Blush
To a more fervid Glow.—When *Eleonora*
Unfolds Elysium to his raptur'd View,
And smiles him to her Arms.—

STUART.

        Hah!—Light'ning scorch
Thy Tongue, Blasphemer!—Sooner may this Globe
Be hurl'd to the profound Abyss of Hell!—
But vain are Words.—This is no Place—remember,
He shall not triumph thus!—Thou hast bely'd him—
He means it not.—Nor will the Syren smile—
No, *Grime*,—she dares not smile him to her Arms!

GRIME.

Reproach, or mute Disgust, is the Reward
Of candid Friendship, that disdains to hide
Unpalatable Truth!—I tell thee, Youth,
Betroth'd by *Angus* to *Dunbar*, she yields
Her plighted Faith, this Hour.—But see!—the Maid
Moves hitherward alone!—

STUART.

        Haste,—leave me, *Grime!*
My Soul is up in Arms!—my Vengeance boils!
Love, Jealousy, implacable Despair
In Tempest's wheel.—

GRIME.

        Thou shalt not tarry here!—
Thy frantic Rage may rashly overturn
Our whole Design!—

STUART.

        Let me not urge again
Thy swift Departure!—hence—I come anon.—

                          [*Exit* Grime.

SCENE III.

Stuart, Eleonora.

Stuart.

When last we parted, Love had reconcil'd
Our mutual Jealousies; and breath'd anew
The Soul of Harmony within our Breasts. —
Hast thou not, since that Period, entertain'd
One adverse Thought to Constancy and me?

Eleonora.

Say, who invested thee with Pow'r supreme
O'er *Eleonora*'s Conduct; that thou com'st
With frowning Aspect, thus, to judge my Fame? —
Hast thou not forfeited all Claim to me?
Have I not seen thee stray from Honour's Path?
And shall my Love be to the Breast confin'd,
Where Treason in her darkest Hue presides! —
No! — let me wipe thee, blotted as thou art,
From my abhorrent Thoughts! —

Stuart.

Not all this Pride
Of mimic Virtue — not th' assembled Host
Of female Wiles, how exquisite soe'er,
Shall shelter thee, Deceiver! — What new Stain
Defiles my Bosom, since the Morning saw
Thy Tenderness o'erflow; and heard thy Tongue
Seduce me to thy faithless Arms, again?

Eleonora.

Is this the Testimony of thy Love?
This thy asserted Honour! to revile
Defenceless Innocence? — But this will aid
My Duty, to forget thee. — Do'st thou ask
What recent Outrage has estrang'd my Heart? —
There needed none. — The Measure of thy Guilt
Was full enough before. — Yet thou hast heap'd

Offences to Excess: In Battle fought
Against thy King; and sought, with lifted Arm,
My Father's Life — ungrateful as thou art!
Know then, the Honour of my Name forbids
Our Fates to join; and it shall ne'er be said,
That *Eleonora*, lost to Glory, took
A Traitor to her Bed! —

STUART.
　　　　　　　Perfidious Witch!
Thy Charms shall not avail thee; for I come
Th' avenging Minister of broken Faith!
To claim the promis'd Fruitage [50] of my Love —
Or — mark me — punish, with thy guilty Blood,
Thy Perjury and Fraud! —

ELEONORA.
　　　　　　　　Wilt thou attempt
To gain by Menaces, what the soft Sigh
Of plaintive Anguish, would implore in vain?
Here strike — and let thy ruthless Poignard drink
The Blood of *Douglas*, which has often flow'd
In Virtue's Cause; and ev'ry Soil enrich'd,
From wintry *Scania* [51] to the sacred Vale
Where *Lebanon* [52] exalts his lofty Brow. —

STUART.
Egregious Sorc'ress! — give me back my Peace —
Bid Yesterday return, that saw my Youth
Adorn'd in all its Splendor, and elate
With gen'rous Pride and Dignity of Soul! —
Ere yet thy Spells had discompos'd my Brain,
Unstrung my Arm, and laid me in the Dust,
Beneath a Rival's Feet! —

ELEONORA.
　　　　　　　Hear all ye Powers!
He claims of me, what his own conscious Guilt
Hath robb'd him of. — And do'st thou look for Peace

In my afflicted Bosom?—There, indeed,
Thine Image dwells with Solitude and Care,
Amid the Devastation thou hast made!   [*Weeps.*

STUART.

O Crocodile![53]—Curse on these faithless Drops
Which fall, but to ensnare!—Thy specious Words
Shall sooner lull the sounding Surge, than check
The Fury that impels me!—Yet—by Heav'n,
Thou art divinely fair! and thy Distress
With magic Softness ev'ry Charm improves!—
Wer't thou not false as Hell, not Paradise
Could more Perfection boast!—O! let me turn
My fainting Eyes from thy resistless Face;
And from my Sense exclude the soothing Sound
Of thy inchanting Tongue!—Yet—yet renounce
Thine Infidelity—To thine Embrace
Receive this Wanderer—this Wretch forlorn!—
Speak Peace to his distracted Soul; and ease
The Tortures of his Bosom!—

ELEONORA.

                              Hapless Youth!
My Heart bleeds for thee!—careless of her own,
Bleeds o'er thy Sorrows!—'mid the flinty Rocks
My tender Feet would tread, to bring thee Balm:
Or, unrepining, tempt the pathless Snow!—
O! could my Death recall thy banish'd Quiet!
Here would I kneel, a Suppliant to Heav'n,
In thy Behalf; and offer to the Grave
The Price of thy Repose!—Alas! I fear
Our Days of Pleasure are for ever past!

STUART.

O thou hast Joy and Horror in thy Gift!
And sway'st my Soul at Will!—bless'd in thy Love,
The Memory of Sorrow and Disgrace,
That preys upon my Youth, would soon forsake
My raptur'd Thought, and Hell should plot in vain,

To sever us again!—O! let me clasp thee,
Thou Charm ineffable!

ELEONORA.

            Forbear, fond Youth,
Our unrelenting Destiny hath rais'd
Eternal Bars between us!

STUART.

            Ha!—what Bars?

ELEONORA.
A Sacrifice demanded by my Sire—
A Vow—

STUART.
Perdition!—Say what Vow, rash Maid!

ELEONORA.
A fatal Vow! that blasts our mutual Love—

STUART.
Infernal Vipers gnaw thy Heart!—A Vow!—
A Vow that to my Rival gives thee up!—
Shall he then trample on my Soul at last.—
Mock my Revenge and laugh at my Despair!
Ha!—shall he rifle all thy Sweets, at Will,
And riot in the Transports due to me?
Th' accursed Image whirls around my Brain!—
He pants with Rapture!—Horror to my Soul!
He surfeits on Delight!—

ELEONORA.

           O gentle Heav'n!
Let thy soft Mercy on his Soul descend
In Dews of Peace!—Why roll with fiery Gleam
Thy starting Eye-Balls?—Why on thy pale Cheek
Trembles fell Rage!—and why sustains thy Frame
This universal Shock?—Is it, alas!

That I have sworn, I never will be thine? —
True, this I swore —

STUART.

Hah! — never to be mine!
Th' awaken'd Hurricane begins to rage! —
Be Witness, Heav'n, and Earth, and Hell! she means
To glad the Bosom of my Foe! — Come then
Infernal Vengeance! aid me to perform
A Deed that Fiends themselves will weep to see!   [*Draws.*
Thus, let me blast his full-bloom'd —

Enter DUNBAR, *who interposes.*

SCENE IV.

DUNBAR, STUART, ELEONORA.

DUNBAR.

Ruffian, hold
Thy desp'rate Hand! — What Fury 'scap'd from Hell,
Inspires thy Rage to wanton in the Blood
Of such excelling Goodness? —

STUART.

Infamy
Like mine, deface the Glories of thy Name!
What busy Dæmon sent thee hither, now,
My Vengeance to defeat? — The Hour is come —
The Hour is come at last, that must decide
For ever our Pretensions!

DUNBAR.

Whatsoe'er
Thy Hate could meditate against my Life,
My Nature might forgive: But this Attempt
Divests my Soul of Mercy —

STUART.

               Guide my Point
Ye Pow'rs of Darkness, to my Rival's Heart,
Then take me to yourselves.   [*They fight.*

ELEONORA.

                Restrain — restrain
Your mutual Frenzy! — Horror! — help — behold —
Behold this miserable Bosom! — plunge
Your Poignards here; and in its fatal Source
Your Enmity assuage! —

STUART *falling.*

               It will not be —
Thy Fortune hath eclips'd me: And the Shades
Of Death environ me. — Yet, what is Death
When Honour brings it, but th' eternal Seal
Of Glory, never — never to be broke! —
O thou hast slain me in a dreadful Hour!
My Vengeance frustrated — my Prospect curs'd
With thy approaching Nuptials! and my Soul
Dismiss'd in all her — *Eleonora!* — Oh!   [*Dies.*

SCENE V.

DUNBAR, ELEONORA.

DUNBAR.

Ah! wherefore dost thou wring thy tender Hands
In woeful Attitude? — ah! wherefore lift
Thy streaming Eyes to Heav'n; while the deep Groan
Dilates thy lab'ring Breast?

ELEONORA.

             This is too much —
This is too much to bear! — thou hast destroy'd
My last Remains of Peace!

DUNBAR.

       And, was thy Peace
Deposited in him? — In him who rais'd
His impious Hand to kill thee? — Is it well
To mourn his Fall, and thus accuse the Blow
That rescu'd thee from Death?

ELEONORA.

       I blame not thee,
No, Heav'n forbid! — I blame not my Protector —
Yet thy Protection has undone me quite!
And I will mourn — for ever mourn the Hour —
Th' ill-omen'd Hour, that on thy Sword conferr'd
Such terrible Success —— How pale appear
These clay-cold Cheeks where Grace and Vigour glow'd!
O dismal Spectacle! —— How humble now
Lies that Ambition which was late so proud! ——
Did he not call me with his latest Breath! —
He would have said — but cruel Fate controul'd
His fault'ring Tongue! — He would have said, "For thee,
For thee false Maid, I perish undeplor'd!"
O! hadst thou known how obstinately true
My Heart remained to thee, when thy own Guilt,
My Duty, and thy Rival's Worth, conspir'd
To banish thee from thence; thy parting Soul
Would have acquitted — nay, perhaps, bewail'd
My persecuted Truth!

DUNBAR.

     O turn thine Eyes
From the sad Object! — Turn thy melting Thoughts
From the disastrous Theme, and look on me —
On me who would with Exstasy resign
This wretched Being, to be thus embalm'd
With *Eleonora*'s Tears! — Were I to fall,
Thy Pity would not thus lament my Fate!

ELEONORA.

Thy Death, such Lamentation would not move,
More envy'd than bemoan'd; — thy Memory
Would still be cherish'd, and thy Name survive
To latest Ages, in immortal Bloom. —
Ah, 'tis not so with him! — He leaves behind
No dear Remembrance of unsully'd Fame!
No Monument of Glory, to defy
The Storms of Time! — Nought but Reproach and Shame!
Nought, but perpetual Slander, brooding o'er
His Reputation lost! — O fearful Scene
Of dire Existence, that must never close!

SCENE VI.

ANGUS *entring*, ELEONORA, DUNBAR, *Attendants.*

ANGUS.

What sound of femal Woe — Ha! *Stuart* slain!
Alas! I fear thou art the fatal Cause.   [*To* Eleonora.

ELEONORA.

Too well my Father has divin'd the Cause
Of their unhappy Strife! — Wherefore, ye Powers!
Am I to Misery deliver'd up!
What kindred Crime (alas!) am I decreed
To expiate, that Misfortunes fall so thick
On my poor Head!

ANGUS *to* Dunbar.
                How durst your lawless Rage
Profane this sacred Place with private Brawl!

DUNBAR.

By Heav'n! no Place how much soe'er rever'd,
Shall screen th' Assassin who, like him, would aim
The murd'rous Steel at *Eleonora*'s breast!

ANGUS.

Ha!—were his Aims so merciless?—Too just
The Vengeance that o'ertook him!—But th' Event
With this unstable Juncture ill accords!—
Remove the Body.—Thou meanwhile retire,
Thy Presence may awake, or aggravate
The rage of *Athol*.   [*The Body is removed.*

DUNBAR.

                Therefore I obey.—
And O thou lovely Mourner! who now droop'st
Like the Spread Rose beneath th' inclement Shower,
When next we meet, I hope to see thee bloom
With vernal Freshness, and again unfold
Thy Beauties to the Sun!   [*Exit* Dunbar.

SCENE VII.

ANGUS, ELEONORA.

ANGUS.

                Let us, my Child,
Lament with Steadiness, those Ills that flow
From our Mishap: Yet therefore not ascribe
To self Demerit, impotently griev'd,
The Guilt of Accident.—Thou hast enough
Denoted thy Concern.—Let me not think,
Thy Sorrow hath espoused a Traitor's Cause.

ELEONORA.

Ah! what avails to me, the hard won Palm
Of fruitless Virtue?—Will it lull to Rest
Internal Anguish!—Will it yield me Peace?—

ANGUS.

Thy indiscreet Affliction, shall not plead
Against thee, with me, now.—Remember this,

If thou art weak enough to harbour still
A guilty Flame; to thy Assistance call
That noble Pride and Dignity of Scorn,
Which warms, exalts and purifies the Soul. —
But I will trust thee to thyself. — Withdraw;
For *Athol* comes, and on his Visage lours
A Storm of Wrath.   [*Exit* Eleonora.

SCENE VIII.

ANGUS, ATHOL.

ATHOL.
              Are these the fair Effects
Of our Submission! — These, the promis'd Fruits
Of Amity restor'd! — To violate
The Laws of Hospitality — To guide
The midnight Murderer's inhuman Blow,
And sacrifice your Guests!

ANGUS.
                      That *Athol* mourns
This unforeseen Severity of Fate,
I marvel not. — My own paternal Sense
Is wak'd by Sympathy; and I condole
His interesting Loss. — But thus to tax
Our blameless Faith with traiterous Design,
Not with our pure Integrity conforms,
Nor with thy Duty, Thane.

ATHOL.
                      Ha! — who art thou,
That I should bear thy Censure and Reproof? —
Not Protestation, nor th' affected Air
Of Sympathy and Candour, shall amuse
My strong Conception, nor elude the Cry
Of Justice and Revenge!

ANGUS.
                    Had Justice crav'd
With rigid Voice, the Debt incurr'd by thee,
How had'st thou far'd?—Say, what hast plac'd thy Deeds
Above my Censure?—Let this Day's Event
Proclaim how far I merit thy Disdain.—
That my Humanity is misconceiv'd
Not much alarms my Wonder: Conscious Fraud
Still harbours with Suspicion.—Let me tell thee—
The Fate of *Stuart* was supremely just.
Th' untimely Stroke his savage Heart prepar'd
Against the guiltless Breast of *Eleonora*,
Avenging Heav'n retorted on himself.

ATHOL.
I thought where all thy Probity would end,
Disguis'd Accomplice!—But remember, Lord,
Should this blood-spotted Bravo 'scape, secure
In thy Protection, or th' unjust Extent
Of regal Pow'r; by all my Wrongs! I'll spread
Th' Seeds of Vengeance o'er th' affrighted Land,
And Blood shall answer Blood!

ANGUS.
                              How far thy Threats
Are to be fear'd, we know.—But see, the King!—

SCENE IX.

KING, ANGUS, ATHOL.

KING.
Tell me—proud Thanes, why are ye found oppos'd
In loud Revilings?—You, that should promote
By fair Example, Unity and Peace!

ATHOL.
Have I not Cause to murmur and complain?

Stuart, the latest Gift and dearest Pledge
Of Love fraternal, sooth'd my bending Age:
Him hath the unrelenting Dagger torn
From my parental Arms; and left (alas!)
This sapless Trunk, to stretch its wither'd Boughs
To you for Justice! — Justice then I crave.

KING.

To send the injur'd unredress'd away,
How great soe'er th' Offender, or the Wrong'd
Howe'er obscure, is wicked — weak and vile:
Degrades, defiles and should dethrone a King!
Say freely, Thane, who has aggriev'd thee thus,
And were he dear as her who shares our Throne,
Thou shalt have ample Vengeance.

ATHOL.

                              Then I charge
The son of *March* with Perfidy and Murder.

ANGUS.

Were I with mean Indifference to hear
Th' envenom'd Tongue of Calumny traduce
Defenceless Worth, I should but ill deserve
Your royal Confidence. — *Dunbar* has slain
The Kinsman of this Thane; yet fell he not
By Murder, Cowardice, or foul Design.
The Sword of *Stuart* was already drawn
To sacrifice my Daughter, when *Dunbar*,
By Heav'n directed hither, interpos'd,
Redeem'd the trembling Victim, and repell'd
His Rival's Fury on his hapless Head.

ATHOL.

Must I refer me to the partial Voice
Of an invet'rate Foe? — No, I reject
The tainted Evidence, and rather claim
The Combat Proof — Enfeebled are my Limbs
With Age that creeps along my Nerves unstrung,

Yet shall the Justice of my Cause recal
My youthful Vigour, rouse my loit'ring Blood,
Swell ev'ry Sinew, strengthen ev'ry Limb,
And crown me with Success — Behold my Gage —
I wait for Justice.

> KING.

Justice shalt thou have —
Nor shall an equitable Claim depend
On such precarious Issue. — Who shall guard
The Weak from Violence, if brutal Force
May vindicate Oppression. — Truth alone
Shall rule the fair Decision, and thy Wrongs,
If thou art wrong'd, in my unbyass'd Sway
Shall find a just Avenger. — Let *Dunbar*
Appear when urg'd, and Answer to the Charge.   [*To* Angus.
                                                    [*Exeunt King*, Angus.

SCENE X.

> ATHOL, GRIME.

> ATHOL.

Curse on the smooth Dissembler! — Welcome *Grime*.
My Soul is wrought to the sublimest Rage
Of horrible Revenge! — If aught remain'd
Of cautious Scruple, to the scatt'ring Winds
I give the Phantome. — May this Carcase rot,
A loathsome Banquet to the Fowls of Heav'n,
If e'er my Breast admit one Thought to bound
The Progress of my Hate!

> GRIME.

What means my Prince?

> ATHOL.

Th' unhappy Youth is slain!

GRIME.

                  Ha! — Hell be prais'd
He was a peevish Stripling, prone to Change.   *[Aside.*
— Vain is Condolance. — Let our Swords be swift
To sate his hov'ring Shade. — I have conferr'd
With trusty *Cattan*, our Design explain'd,
And his full Aid secur'd — To Night, he rules
The middle Watch. — The Clans already move
In Silence o'er the Plain.

ATHOL.

              Come then ye Powers
That dwell with Night, and patronize Revenge!
Attend our Invocation, and confirm
Th' exterminating Blow! — My Boughs are lopt,
But they will sprout again: my vig'rous Trunk
   Shall flourish from the Wound my Foes have made,
   And yet again, project an awful Shade.

END of the FOURTH ACT.

ACT V. SCENE I.

KING, QUEEN, DUNBAR.

QUEEN.

O! this was more than the ill-sorted Train
Of undetermin'd Fancy! — This convey'd
No loose imperfect Images: But all
Was dreadfully distinct! as if the Hand
Of Fate had wrought it. — Profit by those Signs —
Your guardian Angel dictates. — O my Prince!
Let not your blind Security disgrace
The Merit of your Prudence.

KING.

           No, my Queen,
Let us avoid the opposite Extremes

Of Negligence supine, and prostrate Fear.—
Already hath our Vigilance perform'd
What Caution justifies: And for thy Dream;
As such consider it.—The vain Effect
Of an Imagination long disturb'd.—
Life with substantial Ills, enough is curs'd:
Why should we then, with frantic Zeal, pursue
Unreal Care; and with th' illusive Form
Which our own teeming Brain produc'd, affright
Our Reason from her Throne?

QUEEN.
                              In all your Course
Of youthful Glory, when the guiding Hand
Of warlike *Henry*[54] led you to the Field;
When my Soul suffer'd the successive Pangs
Of fond Impatience and repressive Fear:
When ev'ry reeking Messenger from *France*,
Wreath'd a new Garland for *Albania*'s Prince,[55]
And shook my Bosom with the dreadful Tale
That spoke your Praise; say, did my weak Despair
Recal you from the Race?—Did not my Heart
Espouse your Fame, and patiently await
The End of your Career?—O! by the Joys
I felt at your Return, when smiling Love
Secure, with Rapture reign'd.—O! by these Tears,
Which seldom plead; indulge my boding Soul!
Arrouse your conqu'ring Troops; let *Angus* guard
The Convent with a chosen Band.—The Soul
Of Treason is abroad!—

KING.
                              Ye ruling Powers!
Let me not wield the Sceptre of this Realm,
When my degen'rate Breast becomes the Haunt
Of haggard Fear.—O! what a Wretch is he,
Whose fev'rous Life devoted to the Gloom
Of Superstition, feels th' incessant Throb

Of ghastly Pannic! — In whose startled Ear
The Knell still deepens, and the Raven croaks!

QUEEN.

Vain be my Terrors — my Presages vain —
Yet with my fond Anxiety comply,
And my Repose restore! — Not for myself —
Not to prolong the Season of my Life,
Am I thus suppliant. — Ah, no! for you —
For you whose Being gladdens and protects
A grateful People. — You, whose parent Boughs
Defend your tender Offspring[56] from the Blasts
That soon would tear them up! — For you, the Source
Of all our Happiness and Peace, I fear!   [*Kneels.*

KING.

Arise, my Queen — O! thou art all compos'd
Of melting Piety and tender Love!
Thou shalt be satisfy'd. —— Is ev'ry Guard
By *Angus* visited? —

DUNBAR.

                Ev'n now, my Liege,
With *Ramsay* and his Troop, he scours the Plain.

KING.

Still watchful o'er his Charge. — The lib'ral Hand
Of Bounty will have nothing to bestow,
'Ere *Angus* cease to merit! — Say, *Dunbar*,
Who rules the nightly Watch?

DUNBAR.

                To *Cattan*'s Care
The City Guard is subject.

KING.

                I have mark'd
Much Valour in him. — Hie thee to him, Youth,
And bid him with a chosen few, surround

The Cloisters of the Convent; and remain
'Till Morn full streaming shall relieve his Watch.   [*Exit* Dunbar.
Thus shall Repose, with glad Assurance, waft
Its balmy Blessing to thy troubled Breast.   [*Exeunt.*

SCENE II.

GRIME, CATTAN.

GRIME.

Thus far, brave *Cattan*, Fortune seems inclin'd
To recompence us for the Day's Disgrace.—
Our Band conceal'd within the Cloisters, wait
With Eagerness and Joy the auspicious Hour,
To perpetrate the Deed.——It now remains,
To regulate our Conduct, and to each
His Share of this great Enterprise assign.—
If *Angus* lives, in vain our Arms devote
The Usurper and his Progeny to Death:
His Power and Principles will still supply
Fresh Obstacles, which all our future Efforts
Can ne'er surmount.

CATTAN.
                    Then let our Swords prevent
All further Opposition, and at once
Dismiss him to the Shades.

GRIME.
                    Thine be the Task—
I know with what just Indignation burns
Thy gen'rous Hate, against the partial Thane,
Who, to thine Age and Services, preferr'd
A raw unpractis'd Stripling.

CATTAN.
                    Ha!—no more.
The bare Remembrance tortures me!—O *Grime*!
How will my Soul his mortal Groans enjoy!

GRIME.

While we within perform th' intrepid Blow,
To his Apartment thou shalt move alone;
Nor will Pretence be wanting: Say, thou bring'st
Intelligence important, that demands
His instant Ear: — Then shalt thou find thy Foe
Unarm'd and unattended. —— Need my Tongue
Instruct thee further?

CATTAN.

    No, — let my Revenge
Suggest what follows —— By the Pow'rs of Hell!
I will be drunk with Vengeance!

GRIME.

     To thy Guard
Meanwhile repair, and watch 'till he returns
With *Ramsay* from the Plain. — But see! they come,
We must avoid them, and retire unseen.   [*Exeunt.*

SCENE III. *An Apartment.*

ANGUS, RAMSAY.

ANGUS.

By Heav'n, it much alarms me! — Wide o'er all
The dusky Plain, by the Fires half extinct,
Are seen the soldiers, roll'd in Heaps confus'd,
The Slaves of brutal Appetite. — Save those
Beneath thy Discipline, scarce one remains
From the Contagion free.

RAMSAY.

     When we return'd
Fatigu'd from Battle, Numbers brought, unask'd,
Refreshments for the wounded from the Town:
Thence, the Temptation spread from Rank to Rank,
And few resisted.

ANGUS.
        But that I consult
My King's Tranquillity, and would not wake
Th' affrighted Citizens with an Alarm,
An hundred Trumpets should this instant, raise
Their brazen Throats together, and arrouse
Th' extended Sluggards.—Go, my valiant Friend,
And with thy uninfected Troop attend
To ev'ry Motion of th' incertain Night.   [*Exit* Ramsay.

SCENE IV.

ANGUS.

Now, the loud Tempest of the toilful Day
Subsides into a Calm.—And yet my Soul
Still labours thro' the Storm!—By Day or Night,
In florid Youth, or mellow Age, scarce fleets
One Hour without its Care!—Not Sleep itself
Is ever balmy; for the shadowy Dream
Oft bears substantial Woe!

SCENE V.

ANGUS, CATTAN.

CATTAN.
                My noble Lord,
Within the Portal as I kept my Watch,
Swift gliding Shadows by the glimm'ring Moon,
I could perceive in Forms of armed Men,
Possess the Space that borders on the Porch—
I question'd thrice; they yielded no Reply:
And now the Soldiers, rang'd in close Array,
Wait your Command.

ANGUS.
            Quick, lead me to the Place—
Foul Treason is at work!—

CATTAN.

It were not good
To venture forth unarm'd. — Couragious Thane,
Receive this Dagger. —   [*Attempts to stab* Angus, *who wrests the*
                                Dagger from him, and kills him.

ANGUS.

Ha, perfidious Slave!
What means this base Attempt? — Thou shalt not 'scape.

CATTAN.

Curse on my feeble Arm that fail'd to strike
The Poignard to thy Heart! — How like a Dog
I tamely fall despis'd!

ANGUS.

Fell ruffian! say,
Who set thee on? — This Treachery, I fear,
Is but the prelude to some dreadful Scene! —

CATTAN.

Just are thy Terrors. — By the infernal Gulph
That opens to receive me! I would plunge
Into the Abyss with Joy, could the Success
Of *Athol* feast my Sense!
                    [*A Noise of clashing Swords and Shrieks.*
                — Hah! — now the Sword
Of Slaughter smoaks! — Th' exulting Thane surveys
Th' imperial Scene; while grimly smiling *Grime*
With purple Honours deck'd——

ANGUS.

                    Tremend'ous Powers!

CATTAN.

O'er the faln Tyrant strides——   [*Dies.*

ANGUS.

                                   Heav'n shield us all!
Amazing Horror chills me! — Ha, *Dunbar*!
Then Treason triumphs! — O my Son! my Son!

SCENE VI.

ANGUS, DUNBAR *wounded.*

DUNBAR.

I sought thee, noble Thane, while yet my Limbs
Obey their Lord. — I sought thee, to unfold
My zealous Soul, 'ere yet she takes her Flight. —
Stretch'd on the Ground, these Eyes beheld the King
Transfix'd a lifeless Coarse! And saw this Arm
Too late to save — too feeble to avenge him! —

ANGUS.

Weep, *Caledonia*, weep! — thy Peace is slain[57] —
Thy Father and thy King! — O! this Event,
Like a vast Mountain, loads my staggring Soul,
And crushes all her Pow'rs! — But say, my Friend,
If yet thy Strength permits, how this befel.

DUNBAR.

A Band of Rebels, glean'd from the Defeat,
By *Athol*, lurk'd behind the adjacent Hills:
These, faithless *Cattan*, favour'd by the Night,
Admitted to the City, join'd their Power
With his corrupted Guard, and hither led them
Unmark'd, where soon they enter'd unoppos'd. —
Alarm'd, I strove — but strove, alas! in vain.
To the sad Scene 'ere I could force my Way,
Our Monarch was no more! Around him lay
An Heap of Traitors, whom his single Arm
Had slain before he fell. — Th' unhappy Queen,
Who, to defend her Consort's, had oppos'd

Her own defenceless Frame, expiring, pour'd
Her mingling Blood in copious Stream with his!

ANGUS.

Illustrious Victims! — O disast'rous Fate!
Unfeeling Monsters! Execrable Fiends!
To wanton thus in royal Blood!

DUNBAR.

        O Thane!
How shall I speak the Sequel of my Tale!
How will thy fond parental Heart be rent
With mortal Anguish, when my Tongue relates
The Fate of *Eleonora*!

ANGUS.

        Ha! — my Fears
Anticipate thy Words! — O say, *Dunbar*,
How fares my Child!

DUNBAR.

        The Shades of endless Night
Now settle o'er her Eyes! — heroic Maid!
She to th' assaulted Threshold bravely ran,
And with her snowy Arm, supply'd a Bolt
To bar their Entrance: — But the barb'rous Crew
Broke in impet'ous, crush'd her slender Limb,[58]
When *Grime*, his Dagger brandishing, exclaim'd,
Behold the Sorc'ress whose accursed Charms
Betray'd the Youth; and whose invet'rate Sire
This Day revers'd our Fortune in the Field! —
This for Revenge! — then plung'd it in her Breast! —

ANGUS.

Infernal Homicide!

DUNBAR.

        There — there I own
He vanquish'd me indeed! — What tho' I rush'd

Thro' many a Wound, and in th' Assassin's Heart
Imbrew'd my faithful Steel. — But see, where comes
By her Attendants led, the bleeding Fair!

SCENE VII.

ANGUS, DUNBAR, ELEONORA *wounded and supported.*

ELEONORA.
Here set me down — vain is your kind Concern. —
Ah! who, with parent Tenderness, will bless
My parting Soul, and close my beamless Eyes!
Ah! who defend me, and with pious Care
To the cold Grave commit my pale Remains!   [*Swoons.*

ANGUS.
O Misery! — look up — thy Father calls —   [*Embracing her.*

ELEONORA.
What Angel borrows that paternal Voice!
Ha! lives my Father! — Ye propitious Powers!
He folds me in his Arms — Yes, he survives
The Havock of this Night! — O let me now
Yield up my fervent Soul with raptur'd Praise!
For *Angus* lives t' avenge his murder'd Prince,
To save his Country, and protract his Blaze
Of Glory, farther still!

ANGUS.
                    And is it thus,
The melting Parent clasps his darling Child!
My Heart is torn with agonizing Pangs
Of complicated Woe!

DUNBAR.
                    The Public craves
Immediate Aid from thee — But I wax weak. —
Our Infant King[59] surrounded in the Fort,
Demands thy present Help. —

ANGUS.

Yes, loyal Youth!
Thy glorious Wounds instruct me, what I owe
To my young Sov'reign, and my Country's Peace!
But how shall I sustain the rav'nous Tribe
Of various Griefs, that gnaw me all at once?
My royal Master falls, my Country groans,
And cruel Fate has ravish'd from my Side
My dearest Daughter and my best lov'd Friend!

DUNBAR.

Thy Praise shall be thy Daughter; and thy Friend
Survive unchang'd in ev'ry honest Breast.

ANGUS.

Must we then part for ever!—What a Plan
Of peaceful Happiness, my Hope had laid
In thee and her!—alas! thou fading Flower,
How fast thy Sweets consume!—come to my Arms,
That I may taste them e're they fleet away!

[*Embracing her.*

O exquisite Distress!—

ELEONORA.

For me, my Father,
For me let not the bootless Tear distil.—
Soon shall I be with those, who rest secure
From all th' Inclemencies of stormy Life.

ANGUS.

Adieu, my Children!—never shall I hear
Thy chearing Voice again!—a long Farewell!

[*Exit* Angus.

SCENE VIII.

DUNBAR, ELEONORA.

DUNBAR.

Soon shall our short'ned Race of Life be run. —
Our Day already hastens to its Close;
And Night eternal comes. — Yet, tho' I touch
The Land of Peace, and backward view, well pleas'd,
The tossing Wave from which I shall be free:
No Rest will greet me on the silent Shore,
If *Eleonora* sends me hence unbless'd.

ELEONORA.

Distemper'd Passion (when we parted last)
Usurp'd my troubled Bosom, and *Dunbar*
With Horror was beheld: But Reason now
With genial Mildness beams upon my Soul,
And represents thee justly, as thou art,
The tend'rest Lover and the gentlest Friend.

DUNBAR.

O Transport, to my Breast unknown before!
Not the soft Breeze, upon its fragrant Wings,
Wafts such refreshing Gladness to the Heart
Of panting Pilgrims, as thy balmy Words
To my exhausted Spirits! — but alas!
Thy purple Stream of Life forsakes, apace,
Its precious Channels! — on thy polish'd Cheek
The blowing Roses fade; and o'er thine Eyes
Death sheds a misty Languor!

ELEONORA.

              Let me lean
Upon thy friendly Arm — Yet, O retire!
That guilty Arm! — Say, did it ne'er rebel
Against my Peace? — But let me not revolve
Those Sorrows now. — Were Heav'n again to raise
That once lov'd Head that lies (alas) so low!
And from the Verge of Death my Life recal;
What Joy could visit my forlorn Estate,
Self-doom'd to hopeless Woe!

DUNBAR.

                  Must I then wander
A pensive Shade, along the dreary Vale,
And groan for ever under thy Reproach!

ELEONORA.

Ah no! thou faithful Youth, shall I repay
Thy Love and Virtue with ungrateful Hate?
These Wounds that waste so lavishly thy Life,
Were they not all receiv'd in my Defence?
May no Repose embrace me in the Tomb,
If my Soul mourns not thy untimely Fall
With Sister-Woe!—thy Passion has not reap'd
The sweet Returns its Purity deserv'd.

DUNBAR.

A while forbear, pale Minister of Fate,
Forbear a while; and on my ravish'd Ear
Let the last Music of this dying Swan,
Steal in soft Blandishment, divinely sweet!
Then strike th' unerring Blow.—

ELEONORA.

                  That thus, our Hopes
Which blossom'd num'rous as the flow'ry Spring,
Are nipp'd untimely, ere the Sun of Joy
Matur'd them into Fruit; repine not, Youth.—
Life hath its various Seasons, as the Year;
And after clust'ring Autumn—but I faint—
Support me nearer—in rich Harvest's Rear
Bleak Winter must have lagg'd.—Oh! now I feel
The leaden Hand of Death lie heavy on me.—
Thine Image swims before my straining Eye.—
—And now it disappears.—Speak—bid Adieu
To the lost *Eleonora.*—Not a Word!
—Not one Farewell!—Alas! that dismal Groan
Is eloquent Distress!—Celestial Powers
Protect my Father, show'r upon his—Oh!   [*Dies.*

DUNBAR.

There fled the purest Soul that ever dwelt
In mortal Clay!—I come my Love! I come—
Where now the rosy Tincture of these Lips!
The Smile that Grace ineffable diffus'd!
The Glance that smote the Soul with silent Wonder!
The Voice that sooth'd the Anguish of Disease,
And held Attention Captive!—Let me kiss
This pale deserted Temple of my Joy!
This, Chastity, this, thy unspotted Shade
Will not refuse.—I feel the griesly King—
Thro' all my Veins he shivers like the North—
O *Eleonora!* as my flowing Blood
Is mix'd with thine.—So may our mingling Souls
To Bliss supernal wing our happy—Oh!   [*Dies.*

SCENE the Last.

ANGUS, RAMSAY. ATHOL, *&c. Prisoners.*

ANGUS.

Bright Deeds of Glory hath thine Arm atchiev'd,
Courageous *Ramsay;* and thy Name shall live
For ever in the Annals of Renown.—
—But see, where silent as the Noon of Night
These Lovers lie!—rest—rest ill-fated Pair!
Your dear Remembrance shall for ever dwell
Within the Breast of *Angus;* and his Love
Oft with paternal Tears bedew your Tomb!

RAMSAY.

O fatal Scene of Innocence destroy'd!

ANGUS, *To* Athol.

O bloody Author of this Night's Mishap!
Whose impious Hands are with the sacred Blood
Of Majesty distain'd!—Contemplate here

The Havock of thy Crimes; and then bethink thee,
What Vengeance craves. —

ATHOL.

                         With Insolence of Speech
How dares thy Tongue licentious, thus insult
Thy Sov'reign, *Angus?* — Madly hath thy Zeal
Espous'd a sinking Cause. — But thou may'st still
Deserve my future Favour. —

ANGUS.

                         O thou Stain
Of fair Nobility! — thou Bane of Faith!
Thou Woman-killing Coward, who hast crept
To the unguarded Throne, and stabb'd thy Prince!
What hath thy Treason, blasted as it is,
To bribe the Soul of *Angus* to thy Views?

ATHOL.

Soon shalt thou rue th' Indignity now thrown
On me thy lawful Prince. — Yes, talking Lord,
The Day will soon appear, when I shall rise
In Majesty and Terror, to assert
My Country's Freedom; and at last, avenge
My own peculiar Wrongs. — When thou, and all
Those grov'ling Sycophants, who bow'd the Knee
To the Usurper's arbitrary Sway,
Will fawn on me. — Ye temporizing Slaves!
Unchain your King; and teach your humble Mouths
To kiss the Dust beneath my royal Feet. —

                                             [*To the Guard.*

ANGUS.

The Day will soon appear! — Day shall not thrice
Return, before thy Carcase be cast forth
Unbury'd, to the Dogs and Beasts of Prey. —
Or, high-exalted, putrify in Air
The Monument of Treason. —

ATHOL.

Empty Threat!
Fate hath foretold that *Athol* shall be crown'd.[60]

ANGUS.

Then Hell hath cheated thee. — Thou shalt be crown'd —
An Iron Crown, intensely hot, shall gird
Thy hoary Temples; while the shouting Crowd
Acclaims thee King of Traitors.

ATHOL.

Lakes of Fire! —
Ha! said'st thou Lord! — a glowing Iron Crown
Shall gird my hoary Temples! — Now I feel
Myself awake to Misery and Shame!
Ye Sceptres, Diadems and rolling Trains
Of flatt'ring Pomp, farewell! — Curse on those Dreams
Of idle Superstition, that ensnare
Th' ambitious Soul to Wickedness and Woe!
Curse on thy Virtue, which hath overthrown
My elevated Hopes! and may Despair
Descend in Pestilence on all Mankind!

ANGUS.

Thy Curse just Heav'n retorts upon thyself!
To sep'rate Dungeons lead the Regicides. —

[*Exit Guard with the Prisoners.*

From Thirst of Rule what dire Disasters flow!
How flames that Guilt Ambition taught to glow!
Wish gains on Wish, Desire surmounts Desire;
Hope fanns the Blaze, and Envy feeds the Fire:
From Crime to Crime aspires the madd'ning Soul;
Nor Laws, nor Oaths, nor Fears its Rage controul;
'Till Heav'n at length awakes, supremely just,
And levels all its tow'ring Schemes in Dust!

FINIS.

THE REPRISAL

THE

REPRISAL:

OR, THE

TARS of Old England.

A

COMEDY

Of TWO ACTS,

As it is Performed at the

THEATRE ROYAL

IN

DRURY-LANE.

LONDON:

Printed for R. BALDWIN, in Paternoster-Row.
MDCCLVII.
(Price One Shilling.)

Title Page of *The Reprisal*, First Edition, 1757.
(Axson Collection, Woodson Research Center, Rice University Library.)

PROLOGUE.

Spoken by Mr. HAVARD.

An ancient sage, when death approach'd his bed,
Consign'd to Pluto his devoted head;
And, that no fiend might hiss, or prove uncivil,
With vows and pray'rs he fairly brib'd the Devil:
Yet neither vows nor pray'rs, nor rich oblation,
Cou'd always save the sinner—from damnation:
   Thus authors, tottering on the brink of fate,
The critick's rage with prologues deprecate;
Yet oft the trembling bard implores in vain,
The wit profess'd, turns out a dunce in grain:[1]
No plea can then avert the dreadful sentence,
He must be damn'd——in spite of all repentance.
   Here justice seems from her straight line to vary,
No guilt attends a fact involuntary;
This maxim the whole cruel charge destroys,
No Poet sure was ever dull—by choice.
   So pleads our Culprit in his own defence,
You cannot prove his dullness is—prepense.[2]
   He means to please—He owns no other view;
And now presents ye with—a Sea-ragout.[3]
A dish—howe'er you relish his endeavours,
Replete with a variety of flavours:
   A stout Hibernian, and ferocious Scot,
Together boil in our inchanted pot;
To taint these viands with the true fumet,[4]
He shreds a musty, vain, French—martinet.
This stale ingredient might our porridge marr
Without some acid juice of English tar.
To rouse the appetite the drum shall rattle,
And the desert shall be a bloodless battle.
   What heart will fail to glow, what eye to brighten,
When Britain's wrath arrous'd begins to lighten!
Her thunders roll—her fearless sons advance,

And her red ensigns wave o'er the pale flow'rs of France.
Such game our fathers play'd in days of yore,
When Edward's banners⁵ fann'd the Gallick shore;
When Howard's arm⁶ Eliza's vengeance hurl'd,
And Drake⁷ diffus'd her fame around the world:
Still shall that God-like flame your bosoms fire,
The gen'rous son shall emulate the fire;
Her ancient splendor England shall maintain,
O'er distant realms extend her genial reign,
And rise—th' unrival'd empress of the main.

PERSONS represented.⁸

HEARTLY, a young gentleman of Dorsetshire, in love with HARRIET,	Mr. *Usher.*
BRUSH,⁹ his servant,	Mr. *Palmer.*
CHAMPIGNON,¹⁰ commander of a French Frigate,	Mr. *Blakes.*
OCLABBER,¹¹ an Irish lieutenant in the French service,	Mr. *Yates.*
MACLAYMORE, a Scotch ensign in the French service,	Mr. *Johnston.*
LYON, lieutenant of an English man of war,	Mr. *Jefferson.*
HAULYARD,¹² a midshipman,	Mr. *Beard.*
BLOCK,¹³ a sailor,	Mr. *Woodward.*
HARRIET, a young lady of Dorsetshire betrothed to HEARTLY,	Miss *Macklin.*

Soldiers, Sailors, &c.

SCENE, *on board a* French *ship lying at anchor on the coast of Normandy.*

THE

REPRISAL:

OR, THE

TARS[14] of Old England.

ACT I.

SCENE I.

HEARTLY, BRUSH.

BRUSH.

Well, if this be taking diversion on the water, God send me safe on English ground! and if ever I come in sight of the Sea again, may a watry grave be my portion. — First, to be terrified with the thoughts of drowning — Secondly, to be tossed and tumbled about like a foot-ball — Thirdly, to be drenched with Sea-water — Fourthly, to be stunk to death with pitch and tar and the savoury scent of my fellow-sufferers — Fifthly, to be racked with perpetual puking ['till my guts are turned inside out] — And sixthly and lastly, to be taken prisoner and plundered by the French!

HEARTLY.

Enough — Enough —

BRUSH.

Enough! — aye, and to spare — I wish I could give part to those who envy my good fortune — But, how will the good Lady Bloomwell moralize when she finds her daughter Miss Harriet is fallen into the hands of Monsieur de Champignon?

HEARTLY.

No more — that reflection alarms me! — yet I have nothing to fear — as there is no war declared, we shall soon be released: and in the mean time the French will treat us with their usual politeness.

BRUSH.

Pox on their politeness! ah, master! commend me to the blunt sincerity of the true surly British mastiff—The rascallion that took my purse bowed so low, and paid me so many compliments, that I ventured to argue the matter in hopes of convincing him he was in the wrong—but he soon stopped my mouth with a vengeance, by clapping a cocked pistol to my ear, and telling me he should have the honour to blow my brains out—Another of those polite gentlemen begged leave to exchange hats with me—A third fell in love with my silver shoe-buckles—Nay, that very individual nice buttock of beef, which I had just begun to survey with looks of desire, after the dismal evacuation I had undergone, was ravished from my sight by two famished French wolves,[15] who beheld it with equal joy and astonishment.

HEARTLY.

I must confess they plundered us with great dexterity and dispatch; and even Monsieur de Champignon the commander did not keep his hands clear of the pillage—An instance of rapaciousness I did not expect to meet with in a gentleman and an officer.—Sure he will behave as such to Harriet!

BRUSH.

Faith! not to flatter you, Sir, I take him to be one of those fellows who owe their good fortune to nothing less than their good works—He first rifled your mistress, and then made love to her with great gallantry—but you was in the right to call yourself her brother—if he knew you were his rival you might pass your time very disagreeably.

HEARTLY.

There are two officers on board, who seem to disapprove of his conduct; they would not be concerned in robbing us, nor would they suffer their soldiers to take any share of the prey, but condoled Harriet and me on our misfortune, with marks of real concern.

BRUSH.

You mean lieutenant Oclabber and ensign Maclaymore, a couple of damn'd renegadoes!—you lean upon a broken reed if you trust to their compassion.

HEARTLY.

Oclabber I knew at Paris, when I travelled with my brother, and he then bore the character of an honest man and a brave officer—The other is an Highlander, excluded (I suppose) from his own country on account of the late rebellion;[16] for that reason, perhaps, more apt to pity the distressed. — I see them walking this way in close conference — While I go down to the cabin to visit my dear Harriet, you may lounge about and endeavour to over-hear their conversation. [*Exeunt.*

SCENE II.

OCLABBER, MACLAYMORE.

OCLABBER.

Arrah,[17] for what? — I don't value Monsieur de Champignon a rotten pota-toe; and when the ship goes ashore, I will be after asking him a shivil question, as I told him to his face, when he turned his back upon me in the cabin.

MACLAYMORE.

Weel, weel, maister Oclabber, I wonna tak upon me to say a'together ye're in the wrang — but ye ken there's a time for a'things; and we man gang hooly[18] and fairly while we're under command.

OCLABBER.

You may talk as you plaise, Mr. Maclaymore — you're a man of learning, Honey. Indeed, indeed I am always happy when you are spaiking, whether I'm asleep or awake a gra.[19] But, by my saoul I will maintain, after the breath is out of my body, that "the English pleasure boat had no right to be taken before the declaration of war;" much more the prisoners to be plundered, which you know is the prerogative of pyrates and privateers.

MACLAYMORE.

To be sure, the law of nations does na prescind[20] that privilege in actual war: for ye ken in ancient times, the victor teuk the *spolia opima;*[21] and in my country to this very day we follow the auld practice, *pecudum prædas agere.*[22] But, then, ye man tak notice, nae gentleman wad plunder a leddy — awa', awa'! — fie for shame! and a right sonsy[23] damsel too. I'm sure it made my heart wae,[24] to see the saut brine come happing o'er her winsome cheeks.

OCLABBER.

Devil burn me! but my bowels wept salt water to see her sweet face look so sorrowful! —— och! the delicate creature! — she's the very moral of[25] my own honey dear Sheelah o'Shannaghan [whom I left big with child in the county of Fermanaghan, grammachree!] [26] — Ochone [27] my dear Sheelah! — [Look here, she made me this sword-belt of the skin of a sea wolf [28] that I shot at the mouth of the Shannon — and I gave her at parting, a nun's discipline to keep her sweet flesh in order — och! "my dear honey captain, (cried she) I shall never do penance, but I will be thinking of you."] — Ah! poor Sheelah she once met with a terrible misfortune gra: we were all a merry-making at the castle of Ballyclough; [29] and so Sheelah having drank a cup too much, honey, fell down stairs out of a window. When I came to her she told me she was speechless; [and by my shoul it was tree long weeks before she got upon her legs again:] then I composed a lamentation in the Irish tongue — and sung it to the tune of *drimmendoo;* [30] but, a friend of mine of the order of St. Francis, has made a relation of it into English, and it goes very well to the words of Elen a Roon. [31]

[MACLAYMORE.

Whether is't an elegy or a ode?

OCLABBER.

How the devil can it be odd, when the verses are all even?

MACLAYMORE.

Gif it be an elegy, it must be written in the carmen elegiacum; [32] or giff it be an ode, it may be monocolos, dicolos, tetrastrophos, — or perhaps its loose iambics.

OCLABBER.

Arra, upon my conscience I believe it is simple shambrucks, [33] honey.] But if you'll hold your tongue you shall see with your own eyes.

SONG.

I.

Ye swains of the Shannon, fair Sheelah is gone,
Ye swains of the Shannon, fair Sheelah is gone,
Ochone my dear jewel;
Why was you so cruel
Amidst my companions to leave me alone?

II.

Tho' Teague[34] shut the casement in Bally-clough hall;
Tho' Teague shut the casement in Bally-clough hall;
  In the dark she was groping;
  And found it wide open;
Och! the devil himself could not stand such a fall.

III.

In beholding your charms, I can see them no more,
In beholding your charms, I can see them no more,
  If you're dead do but own it;
  Then you'll hear me bemoan it;
For in loud lamentations your fate I'll deplore.

IV.

[Devil curse this occasion with tumults and strife!
Devil curse this occasion with tumults and strife!
  O! the month of November,
  She'll have cause to remember
As a black letter day all the days of her life.]

V.

With a rope I could catch the dear creature I've lost!
With a rope I could catch the dear creature I've lost!
  But, without a dismission,
  I'd lose my commission,
And be hang'd with disgrace for deserting my post.

Shall I never see you, my lovely Sheelah, these seven long years? — An it plaised God to bring us within forty miles of each other, I would never desire to be nearer, all the days of my life.

MACLAYMORE.

Hoot-fie![35] Captain Oclabber, whare's a' your philosophy? —— did ye never read Seneca *de Consolatione*?[36] — or Volusenus,[37] my countryman, *de Tranquilitate Animi*? —— I'se warrant we have left a bonny lass too, in the braes of Lochaber[38] — my yellow hair'd deary that won't to meet me amang the hether —— Heigh sirs! how she grat[39] and cried, *waes my heart that we should sunder.* — Whisht, what's a that rippet?[40]

              [*A noise of drums.*

OCLABBER.

Arra-mon-deaul! they are beating our grenadier's march, as if the enemy was in view: but, I shall fetch them off long enough before they begin to charge; or, by St. Patrick! I'll beat their skulls to a pancake.

[MACLAYMORE.

[*To a bag piper crossing the stage.*
Whare are ye ga'ane with the moosic, Donald?

PIPER.

Guid fait! an please your honour, the commander has sent for her to play a spring[41] to the sasenach[42] damsel: but, her nain sell[43] wad na pudge the length of her tae, without your honour's order—and she'll gar[44] a' the men march before her with the Pritish flag and the rest of the plunder.

MACLAYMORE.

By my saul! he's a gowk,[45] and a gauky,[46] to ettle[47] at diverting the poor lassy with the puppet-shew of her ain misfortune — but, howsomever, Donald, ye may gang and entertain her with a pibroch of Macreeman's composition;[48] and if she has any taste for moosic, ye'll soon gar her forget her disaster.

OCLABBER.

Arrah, now since that's the caase, I would not be guilty of a rude thing to the lady; and if it be done to compose her spirits, by my saoul! the drum shall beat till she's both deaf and dumb, before I tell it to leave off — but, we'll go and see the procession.   [*Exeunt.*

SCENE III.

A Procession.

[*First the bag-pipe — then a ragged, dirty sheet for the French colours — a file of soldiers in tatters — the English prisoners — the plunder, in the midst of which is an English buttock of beef carried on the shoulders of four meagre Frenchmen.*[49] *The drum followed by a crew of French sailors.*]]

CHAMPIGNON, HARRIET.

CHAMPIGNON.

Madame, you see de fortune of de war—my fate be admirable capricieux[50]—you be de prisonier of my arm—I be de cautive[51] of your eye—by gar! my gloire turn to my disgrace!

HARRIET.

Truly, I think so too——for, nothing can be more disgraceful than what you have done.

CHAMPIGNON.

Den vat I ave done!—parbleu![52] I not understand vat you mean, madame— I ave de honor to carry off one great victoire over de Englis.

HARRIET.

You have carried off an unarmed boat contrary to the law of nations; and rifled the passengers in opposition to the dictates of justice and humanity—I should be glad to know what a common robber could do worse.

CHAMPIGNON.

Common robber!—Madam your serviteur tres humble—de charm of your esprit be as brilliant as de attraits of your personne: in one and t'oder you be parfaitement adorable—souffrez den dat I present my 'art at your altar.

HARRIET.

If you have any heart to present, it must be a very stale sacrifice——for my own part I have no taste for the *fumét;* so you had better keep it for the ladies of your own country.

CHAMPIGNON.

Ah cruelle!—de ladies en France will felicite demselves dat you renonce de tendre of monsieur de Champignon.—[Madame la duchesse——mais taisons[53]—] alte la[54]—et la belle marquise! ah quelles ames![55]—vanité apart, madam, I ave de honneur to be one man à bonnes fortunes.[56]——diable m'emporte![57] 'till I rencontre your invincible eye, I ave alway de same succès in love as in war.

HARRIET.

I dare say you have been always equally lucky and wise.

[CHAMPIGNON.

Ah ma charmante!—dat is more of your bonté den of my merite—permettez donc, dat I amuse you wid the transports of my flame.

HARRIET.

In a proper place, I believe I should find them very entertaining.]

CHAMPIGNON.

How you ravish me, my princesse!—avouez donc,[58] you 'ave de sentimens for my personne——parbleu! it is all your generosité—dere is noting extraordinary in my personne, diable m'emporte! hai, hai.   [*Cuts a caper.*

HARRIET.

Indeed, monsieur, you do yourself injustice; for, you are certainly the most extraordinary person I had ever the honour to see.

CHAMPIGNON.

Ah, ah, madame! I die under the charge of your politesse——your approbation ave dissipé de brouillard[59] dat envelope ma fantasie——your smile inspire me wid allegresse[60]——allons! vive l'amour!——la, la, la, la,——

HARRIET.

What a delicate pipe! I find, monsieur! you're alike perfect in all your accomplishments.

CHAMPIGNON.

Madame, your slave eternellement——personnes of gout[61] ave own dat me sing de chansonettes not altogether too bad, before I ave de honour to receive one ball de pistolet in my gorge, wen I board de Englis man of war, one, two, three, four, ten year ago——I take possession sabre a la main;[62] but, by gar, de ennemi be opiniatre![63]——dey refuse to submit and carry me to Plimout—— dere I apprehend your tongue, madame—dere I dance, and ave de gallanteries parmi les belles filles Angloises[64]—I teash dem to love—they teash me to sing your jolies vaudevilles.[65]—— *A coblere dere vas,[66] and he live in one stall*——Hai, hai! how you taste my talens, madame?

HARRIET.

Oh! you sing inchantingly; and so natural, one would imagine you had been a cobler all the days of your life——Ha, ha, ha!

CHAMPIGNON.

Hai, hai, hai!——if you not flatter me, madame, I be more happy dan Charlemagne——but I ave fear dat you mocquez de moi——tell a me of grace, my princesse, vat sort of lover you shoose——I vil transform myself for your plaisir.

HARRIET.

I will not say what sort of lover I like; but I'll sing what sort of lover I despise.

CHAMPIGNON. (*Aside.*)

By gar, she love me eperduement.[67]

SONG.[68]

I.

From the man whom I love, tho' my heart I disguise,
I will freely describe the wretch I despise,
And if he has sense but to ballance a straw,
He will sure take the hint from the picture I draw.

II.

A wit without sense, without fancy a beau,
Like a parrot he chatters, and struts like a crow:
A peacock in pride, in grimace a baboon,
In courage a hind, in conceit a gascoon.[69]

III.

As a vulture rapacious, in falsehood a fox,
Inconstant as waves, and unfeeling as rocks;
As a tyger ferocious, perverse as an hog,
In mischief an ape, and in fawning a dog.

IV.

In a word, to sum up all his talents together,
His heart is of lead, and his brain is of feather:
Yet, if he has sense but to ballance a straw,
He will sure take the hint from the picture I draw.

CHAMPIGNON.

Morbleu,[70] madame, you sing a merveilles——but, by gar, de figure be ver singulier.

SCENE IV.

HARRIET, CHAMPIGNON, HEARTLY.

CHAMPIGNON.

Mons. Artlie, I ave de honeur to be your most umble serviteur—— mademoiselle your sister ave des perfections of an ange; but she be cold as de albâtre.[71] You do me good office—I become of your alliance—you command my service.

HEARTLY.

I hope my sister will set a proper value upon your addresses: and you may depend upon my best endeavours to persuade her to treat your passion as it deserves.

CHAMPIGNON.

As it deserve!—mardy![72] dat is all I desire—den I treat you as one prince. [*A servant whispers and retires.*] Comment! que m'importe[73]—madame I must leave you for one moment to de garde of Mons. your broder; but I return in one twinkle.   [*Exit.*

SCENE V.

HEARTLY, HARRIET.

HEARTLY.

My dear Harriet, have you good nature enough to forgive me for having exposed you to all these dangers and misfortunes?

HARRIET.

I can't but be pleased with an event which has introduced me to the acquaintance of the accomplished Champignon, ha, ha, ha!

HEARTLY.

You can't imagine how happy I am to see you bear your misfortune with such good humour, after the terror you underwent at our being taken.

HARRIET.

I was indeed terribly alarmed when a cannon shot came whistling over our heads; and not a little dejected when I found myself a prisoner — but, I imagine all danger diminishes, or at least loses part of its terror, the nearer you approach it: and as for this Champignon, he is such a contemptible fellow, that upon recollection, I almost despise myself for having been afraid of him. — O' my conscience! I believe all courage is acquired from practice. — I don't doubt but in time I should be able to stand a battery, myself.

HEARTLY.

Well, my fair Thalestris,[74] should you ever be attacked, I hope the aggressor will fall before you. —— Champignon has certainly exceeded his orders, and we shall be released as soon as a representation can be made to the French court.

HARRIET.

I should be loth to trouble the court of France with matters of so little consequence. Don't you think it practicable to persuade the captain to set us at liberty? There is one figure in rhetoric which I believe he would hardly resist.

HEARTLY.

I guess your meaning, and the experiment shall be tried, if we fail of success from another quarter. I intend to make myself known to Oclabber, with whom I was formerly acquainted, and take his advice. He and the Scotch ensign are at variance with Champignon, and disapprove of our being made prisoners.

SCENE VI.

HEARTLY, HARRIET, BRUSH.

HEARTLY to BRUSH.

Well, sir, you have been fishing the bonny Scot: have you caught any intelligence?

BRUSH.

Sir, I have done your business—Capt. Maclaymore and I have been drinking a bottle of sour wine to the health of Miss Harriet and your worship; in a word, he is wholly devoted to your service.

[HARRIET.

Pray, Mr. Brush, what method did you take to ingratiate yourself with that proud, stalking Highlander?

BRUSH.

I won his heart with some transient encomiums on his country. I affected to admire his plaid, as an improvement on the Roman toga; swore it was a most soldierly garb; and said, I did not wonder to see it adopted by a nation equally renowned for learning and valour.

HEARTLY.

These insidious compliments could not fail to undermine his loftiness.

BRUSH.

He adjusted his bonnet, rolled his quid[75] from one cheek to the other, threw his plaid over his left shoulder with an air of importance, strutted to the farther end of the deck; then returning with his hard features unbended into a ghastly smile, "By my saul! man (says he) ye're na fule; I see ye ken foo weel how to mak proper distinctions—you and I man be better acquanted."—I bowed very low in return for the great honour he did me—hinted, that, though now I was in the station of a servant, I had some pretensions to family; and sighing, cried *tempora mutantur, et nos mutamur in illis.*[76]

HEARTLY.

That scrap of Latin was a home thrust—You see, sirrah, the benefit of a charity school.[77]

BRUSH.

Ay, little did I think, when I was flogged for neglecting my accidence, that ever my learning would turn to such account—Captain Maclaymore was surprized to hear me speak Latin: yet he found fault with my pronunciation. —He shook me by the hand, though I was a little shy of that compliment, and said he did not expact to find flowers under a nettle: but I put him in mind of the singat cat, for I was better than I was bonny[78]—then he carried me to his cabin, where we might discourse more freely; told me the captain was *a light-headed guse*, and expressed his concern at your captivity, which he said was a flagrant infraction of the treaty of *Aix la Chapelle*.[79]

HARRIET.
There I hope you backed his opinion with all your eloquence.

BRUSH.
I extolled his understanding; interested his gallantry in the cause of a distressed lady; and in order to clinch my remonstrance, told him that my master's great grandmother's aunt was a Scotchwoman of the name of Mackintosh, and that Mr. Heartly piqued himself on the Highland blood that ran in his veins.

HEARTLY.
I'm obliged to your invention for the honour of that alliance — I hope the discovery had a proper effect upon my cousin Maclaymore.

BRUSH.
He no sooner heard that particular, than he started up, crying, "What the deel say ye? Mackintosh! — swunds[80] man! that's the name of my ain mither — wha kens but mester Heartly and I may be coozens seventeen times removed:" then he gave me a full account of his pedigree for twelve generations, and hawked up[81] the names of his progenitors till they set my teeth on edge: to conclude,] he has promised to give you all the assistance in his power, and even to favour our escape; for, over and above his other motives, I find he longs to return to his own country, and thinks a piece of service done to an English gentleman may enable him to gratify that inclination.

HEARTLY.
But what scheme have you laid for our escape?

BRUSH.
The boat is along side, — our men are permitted to walk the deck — when the captain retires to rest, and the watch is relieving, nothing will be more easy than to step on board of our own galley, cut the rope, hoist the sails, and make the best of our way to Old England.

HEARTLY.

But, you don't consider that Mr. de Champignon, if alarmed, may slip his cable[82] and give us chace——nay, compliment us with a dish of sugar plumbs that may be very hard of digestion.

BRUSH.

There, the friendship of Maclaymore will be of service: for, as soon as our flight is known, he and his men, on pretence of being alert, will make such a bustle and confusion, that nothing can be done until we are out of their reach; and then we must trust to our canvas and the trim of our vessel, which is a prime sailer.

HARRIET.

The project is feasible, and may be the more practicable, if the Irish lieutenant can be brought to co-operate with the ensign.

HEARTLY.

Odso![83] there he comes——Brush go and wait upon Miss Harriet to her cabin, while I accost this Hibernian.

SCENE VII.

HEARTLY, OCLABBER.

OCLABBER.

Your humble servant, sir—I hope the lady is plaised with her accommodation——don't you begin to be refreshed with the French air blowing over the sea?—upon my conscience! now, it's so delicate and keen, that for my own part, honey, I have been as hungry as an Irish wolf dog, ever since I came to this kingdom.

HEARTLY.

Sir, I thank you for your kind inquiry—I am no stranger to the French air, nor to the politeness of Capt. Oclabber——What! have you quite forgot your old acquaintance?

OCLABBER.

Acquaintance, honey!—by my saoul! I should be proud to recollect your countenance, though I never saw you before in the days of my life.

HEARTLY.

Don't you remember two Englishmen at Paris, about three years ago, of the name of Heartly?

OCLABBER.

Ub ub oo! — by Shaint Patrick I remember you as well as nothing in the world — Arrah, now, whether is it your own self or your brother?

HEARTLY.

My brother died of a consumption soon after our return to England.

OCLABBER.

Ah! God rest his soul, poor gentleman — but it is a great comfort to a man to be after dying in his own country — I hope he was your elder brother, gra. — Oh! I remember you two made one with us at the Hotel de Bussy[84] — by my saoul! we were very merry and frolicksome; and you know I hurt my ancle, and my foot swelled as big as tree potatoes — by the same token I sent for a rogue of a surgeon, who subscribed for the cure, and wanted to make a hand of my foot. — Mr. Heartly, the devil fly away with me, but I am proud to see you, and you may command me without fear or affection, gra.

HEARTLY.

Sir, you are extremely kind; and may, I apprehend, do me a good office with Capt. Champignon, who, I cannot help saying, has treated us with very little ceremony.

OCLABBER.

I'll tell you what, Mr. Heartly, we officers don't choose to find fault with one another; because there's a discipline and subordination to be observed, you know; — therefore I shall say nothing of him as an officer, honey; but, as a man, my dear, by the mass, he's a meer baist.

HEARTLY.

I'm glad to find your opinion of him so conformable to my own. — I understand by my servant too, that Mr. Maclaymore agrees with us, in his sentiments of Monsieur de Champignon; and disapproves of his taking our boat, as an unwarrantable insult offered to the British nation.

OCLABBER.

By my saoul! I told him so before you came aboard. — As for ensign Maclaymore, there is not a prettier fellow in seven of the best counties in Ireland — as brave as a heron, my dear — arrah, the devil burn him if he fears any man that never wore a head — Ay, and a great scholar to boot — he can talk Latin and Irish as well as the archbishop of Armagh.[85] —— Did'n't you know we are sworn brothers — tho' I'm his senior officer, and spaik the French more fluid, gra.

SCENE VIII.

HEARTLY, OCLABBER, BRUSH.

BRUSH.

O Lord, sir! all the fat's in the fire.[86]

OCLABBER.

Arrah what's a fire honey?

BRUSH.

All our fine project gone to pot! —— [We may now hang up our harps among the willows, and sit down and weep by Babel's streams.][87]

HEARTLY.

What does the blockhead mean?

BRUSH.

One of our foolish fellows has blabbed that Miss Harriet is not your sister, but your mistress; and this report has been carried to Monsieur de Champignon, whom I left below in the cabin, taxing her with dissimulation, and threatening to confine her for life. —— He sings, capers, swears and storms in a breath! — I have seen Bedlam:[88] but an English lunatic at full moon, is a very sober animal when compared to a Frenchman in a passion.

HEARTLY.

I care not for his passion or his power —— By Heaven! he shall not offer the least violence to my Harriet, while a drop of blood circulates in my veins! — I'll assault him, tho' unarmed, and die in her defence ——   [*Going.*

OCLABBER.

Won't you be easy now?—your dying signifies nothing at all, honey; for, if you should be killed in the fray, what excuse would you make to the young lady's relations, for leaving her alone in the hands of the enemy?—by my saoul! you'd look very foolish.—Take no notice at all, and give yourself no trouble about the matter—and if he should ravish your mistress, by my salvation! I would take upon me to put him under arrest.

HEARTLY.

The villain dares not think of committing such an outrage!

OCLABBER.

Devil confound me! but I'd never desire a better joke——Och! then my dear, you'd see how I'd trim[89] him—you should have satisfaction to your heart's content.

HEARTLY.

Distraction!——If you will not give me your assistance, I'll fly alone to her defence.

BRUSH.

Zooks![90] sir, you're as mad as he.—You'll ruin us all past redemption.—What the deuce are you afraid of?—Ravish!—An atomy[91] like that pretend to ravish! No, no: he'll ravish nothing but our goods and chattels, and these he has disposed of already.——Besides, Miss Harriet, when his back was turned, desired me to conjure you in her name, to take care of yourself: for Champignon would have no pretence to confine her, if you was out of the way.

OCLABBER.

O'my conscience, a very sensible young woman! When there are two lovers in the caase, 'tis natural to wish one of them away.—Come along with me, honey; we'll hold a council of war with ensign Maclaymore—perhaps he may contrive mains to part you.—No man knows better how to make a soldierly retreat.

BRUSH.

Soldierly or unsoldierly, it signifies not a button—so we do but escape, I shall be glad to get away at any rate, even if I should fly like a thief from the gallows.

OCLABBER.

Devil fire you, my dear! you're a wag.—Arrah, who told you that my friend Maclaymore escaped from the gallows? —— By my saoul! 'tis all *fortune de la guerre*.[92] — Indeed, indeed, I would never desire to command a better corps than what I could form out of the honest gentlemen you have hanged in England.

HEARTLY.

I'm so confounded and perplexed in consequence of this unlucky discovery, that I can't start one distinct thought, much less contribute to any scheme that requires cool deliberation.

OCLABBER.

Arrah faith, my dear, we must leave those things to wiser heads.—For my own part, I'm a soldier, and never burden my brain with unnecessary baggage.

I won't pretend to lead, but I follow in the throng;
And as I don't think at all, I can never think wrong.

END *of the* FIRST ACT.

ACT II.

SCENE I.
[*A great noise and bustle behind the scenes.*

MACLAYMORE, CHAMPIGNON.

CHAMPIGNON *running upon the stage in a ridiculous dishabille.*
Prenez garde qu'elle ne vous echappe![93] —— aux armes! —— Mons. le Second —— contre maitre[94] —— la chaloupe![95] la chaloupe!

MACLAYMORE.
[*Overturning him as if thro' mistake.*
As I sall answar, the folks are a' gaen daft!—deel stap out your een! I'm nae sic midge[96] but ye might a seen me in your porridge.

CHAMPIGNON.

Ah meurtre! assassin! vous avez tué votre commandant![97] —— holla ho! mes gens, a moi.[98]

MACLAYMORE.

Hout, na! it canna be our commander Monsieur de Champignon, running about in the dark like a worricow![99] —— Preserve us a'! it's the vara man —— weel I wot,[100] Sir, I'm right sorry to find you in sic a pickle —— but, wha thought to meet with you playing at blind Harry[101] on deck?

CHAMPIGNON. [*Rising.*

Ventre saingris![102] my whole brain be derangée! — Traitre! you be in de complot.

MACLAYMORE.

Traiter! me nae traiter, Mester Champignon, or gude faith! you and I man ha' our kail thro' the reek.[103]

CHAMPIGNON.

Were be de prisoniers? — tell a me dat — ha! — mort de ma vie![104] de Englis vaisseau! — de prise! de prisoniers! —— sacrebleu![105] ma gloire! mes richesses! rendez moi les prisoniers — you be de enseigne, you be de officier.

MACLAYMORE.

Troth, I ken foo weel I'm an officer — I wuss some other people who haud their heeds unco high, ken'd the respact due to an officer, we should na be fashed[106] with a' this din.

CHAMPIGNON.

Tell a me au moment, were be Monsieur 'Artlie? were be de prisoniers? wat you beat my brains wid your *sottises*?[107]

MACLAYMORE.

Nay, sin ye treat me with sa little ceremony, I man tell you, Mester Heartly was na committed to my charge, and sae ye may gang and leuk after him — and as for prisoners, I ken of nae prisoners but your ain valet whom you ordered to be put in irons this morning for supping part of your *bouillon*, and if the poor fallow had na done the deed I think he must have starved for want of victuals.

CHAMPIGNON.

Morbleu! Monsieur Maclaimore, you distrait me wid your babil——I demand de Englis prisonniers——m'intendez vous? [108]

MACLAYMORE.

Monsieur de Champignon, je vous entens bien—there was nae English prisoner here——for I man tell you, Sir, that if ever you had read *Grotius de Jure Belli ac Pacis* [109]—or *Puffendorf de officio Hominis & Civis* [110]—ye wad a' seen he could na be in the predicament of a *captus in bello,* or an *obses* or *vades*—for what? ye'll say—because he was na teuk *flagrante bello*—*ergo* he was nae prisoner of war——now what says the learned *Puffendorf?* [111]

CHAMPIGNON.

Comment! you call me Puff-and-horf? ventre bleu! [112] you be one impertinent.

MACLAYMORE.

What, what!——that's a paughty [113] word, Sir—that's nae language for a gentleman—nae mair o' that, or gude faith we'll forget where we are.

CHAMPIGNON.

Morbleu! you ave forget dat I be your general—your chief.

MACLAYMORE.

By my saul man! that's strange news indeed!—You my chief! you chief of the Maclaymores!

CHAMPIGNON.

Si, moi, rustre [114]——moi qui vous parle.

MACLAYMORE.

Donna rustre me, Sir, or deel dam my saul, but I'll wrast your head aff your shoulders, if ye was the best Champignon in France.   [*They draw and fight.*

SCENE II.

OCLABBER, CHAMPIGNON, MACLAYMORE.

OCLABBER.

Devil fire you my lads! what's the maining of all this disturbance? ——
o' my conscience! there's no such thing as resting below —— a man would
lie as quiet at the bottom of the sea — I've been a bed these tree hours, but I
could not close an eye, gra; for, you waked me before I fell asleep.

[*Pretending to discover Champignon.*

Arrah, now don't I dream, honey? what is it your own self Monsieur de Cham-
pignon, going to attack my ensign? — by my saoul! that's not so shivil now,
aboard of your own ship — Gentlemen, I put you both under arrest in the
king's name —— [you shall see one another locked in your cabins with your
own hands;] and then, if you cut one another's troats, by the blessed Virgin!
you shall be brought to a court martial, and tried for your lives, agra.

MACLAYMORE.   [*Sheathing his sword.*

Weel, weel, Sir, —— ye're my commanding offisher —— *tuum est im-*
perare[115] —— but, he and I sall meet before mountains meet[116] —— that's a'.

CHAMPIGNON *to* OCLABBER.

Vat! you presume to entremettre[117] in mes affaires d'honneur —— you ave
de hardiesse[118] to dispute wid me de command of dis Vaisseau de Guerre?[119]
—— tell a me, if you know my condition, ha?

OCLABBER.

Indeed, indeed my dear, I believe your present condition is not very savoury
—— but, if ensign Maclaymore had made you shorter by the head, your con-
dition would have been still worse —— and yet upon my conscience! I have
seen a man command such a frigate as this, without any head at all.

CHAMPIGNON.

Monsieur O-claw-bear, you mocquez de moi — you not seem to know my
noblesse —— dat I descend of de bonne famille —— dat my progeniteurs ave
bear de honourable *cotte*[120] —— de *cotte* of antiquité.

OCLABBER.

By my saoul! when I knew you first, you bore a very old coat yourself, my
dear; for it was thread-bare and out at elbows.

CHAMPIGNON.

Ah! la mauvaise plaisanterie.[121] —— daignez,[122] my goot lieutenant O-claw-bear, to onderstand dat I ave de grands alliances —— du bien —— de rente[123] —— dat I ave regale des princes in my chateau.

OCLABBER.

Och! I beg your chateau's pardon, grammachree! I have had the honour to see it on the banks of the Garonne[124] —— and by my saoul! a very vener-able building it was —— aye, and very well bred to boot, honey; for, it stood always uncovered: and never refused entrance to any passenger, even tho' it were the wind and the rain, gra.

CHAMPIGNON.

You pretendez[125] to know my famille, ha?

OCLABBER.

By shaint Patrick! I know them as well as the father that bore them —— your nephew is a begging brother of the order of St. Francis[126] —— Mademoiselle, your sister, espoused an eminent *savatier*[127] in the county of *Bearne;*[128] and your own shelf, my dear, first mounted the stage as a charlatan; then served the count de *Bardasch*[129] for your diversion; and now by the king's favour, you command a frigate of twelve guns, lying at anchor within the province of Normandy.

CHAMPIGNON.

Ah quelle medisance![130] —— que vous imaginez bien Monsieur —— but, I vill represent your conduite to des Marechaux of France: and dey will con-vince you dat Monsieur de Champignon is one personne of some consider-ation —— un charlatan! —— mardy! dat be ver plaisant. — Messieurs, servi-teur —— I go to give de necessaires ordres pour r'attraper[131] de Englis chaloupe — jusque au revoir —— Charlatan! — Savatier! — Mort de ma vie.

[*Exit.*

SCENE III.

OCLABBER, MACLAYMORE.

OCLABBER.

Faith and troth! my dear, you'll see the chaloupe far enough out of sight, by this time.

MACLAYMORE.

By may saul! captain, ye sent him awa' with a flea in his bonnet——He'll no care to wrestle anither fa' with you in a hurry——he had the wrang sow by the lug.[132]

OCLABBER.

If he will be after playing at rubbers, he must expect to meet with bowls ——pooh! I main, he must look to meet with bowls, if he will be playing at rubbers——arra man deaul! that's not the thing neither——but, you know my maining, as the saying is.[133]

MACLAYMORE.

Hoot, aye—I'se warrant I ken how to gar your bools row right—and troth I canna help thinking but I played my part pretty weel for a beginner.

OCLABBER.

For a beginner!——Devil fetch me! but you played like a man that jokes in earnest——but your joke was like to cut too keen, honey, when I came to part you——and yet I came as soon as you tipped me the wink with your finger.

MACLAYMORE.

Let that flie stick i' the wa'——when the dirt's dry it will rub out[134]——but, now we man tak care of the poor waff[135] lassy that's left under our protection, and defend her from the maggots[136] of this daft Frenchman.

OCLABBER.

I will be after confining him to his cabin, if he offers to touch a hair of her beard, agra.

MACLAYMORE.

It's now break of day——donna ye see the bonny grey eyed morn blinking o'er yon mossy craig?—We'll e'en gang doun and tak a tasse[137] of whisky together, and then see what's to be done for Miss Harriet.   [*Exeunt.*

SCENE IV.

HARRIET, BRUSH.

HARRIET.

O Lord! I'm in such a flutter——What was the meaning of all that noise?——Brush, are you sure your master is out of all danger of being re-taken?

BRUSH.

Yes, yes, Madam, safe enough for this bout—The two land officers per-formed their parts to a miracle——My Master and our people slipped into the boat, without being disturbed by the centries who were tutored for the purpose; and they were almost out of sight, before Champignon was alarmed by a starved Frenchman, whose hunger kept him awake——but, now they have doubled the point of land,[138] and in four hours or so will be in sight of sweet Old England——I'm sure, I sent many a wishful look after them.

HARRIET.

What! you are sorry then for having stayed behind with me?

BRUSH.

O! by no manner of means, Ma'am——to be sure you did me an infinite deal of honour, Ma'am, in desiring that I might be left, when you spoke to my Master thro' the barricado——but, yet, Ma'am, I have such a regard for Mr. Heartly, Ma'am; that I should be glad to share all his dangers. Ma'am——tho' after all is done and said, I don't think it was very kind in him to leave his Mistress, and faithful servant in such a dilemma.

HARRIET.

Nay, don't accuse your Master unjustly——you know how unwillingly he complied with my request——we could not guess what villanous steps this fellow, Champignon, might have taken to conceal his rapine, which Mr. Heartly will now have an opportunity to represent in its true colours.

BRUSH.

Well——heaven grant him success, and that speedily——for my own part, I have been so long used to his company, that I grow quite chicken-hearted in his absence——If I had broke my leg two days ago, I should n't have been in this quandary——God forgive the man that first contrived parties of pleasure on the water.

HARRIET.

Hang fear, Brush, and pluck up your courage—I have some small skill in physiognomy, and can assure you it is not your fate to die by water [139]——Ha! I see the captain coming this way——I must bear the brunt of another storm.

BRUSH.

Odso! I'll run down to lieutenant Oclabber, and his ensign, and give them notice, in case there should be occasion to interpose.   [*Exit Brush.*

SCENE V.

CHAMPIGNON. HARRIET.

CHAMPIGNON.

Madame, you pardon my presomption, dat I pay ma devoirs [140] in dishabille—bot it be all for your service——Monsieur your amant ave decampé sans façon [141]——I take de alarm, and make all my efforts to procure you de plaisir of seeing him again——Ah! he be de gallant homme to abandon his Maitresse.

HARRIET.

Is there no possibility of bringing him back?

CHAMPIGNON.

By Gar! it be tout a fait [142] impossible——he steal comme one thief into de chaloupe, and vanish in de obscurité!

HARRIET.

I'm heartily glad to hear it!

CHAMPIGNON.

For wat you be glad, my princess, ha?

HARRIET.

That he's no longer in your power.

CHAMPIGNON.

Bon! — juste ciel![143] — how you make me happy to see you glad, Madame!
la, la, la, ra, ra —— Ventre bleu! he be one fugitif —— if we rencontre again,
Revanche![144] Revanche! la, la, la, ra, ra —— Permettez donc, Madame, dat I
ave de honeur to languisse before your feet —— ave pitie of me —— take my
sword —— plongez dans my bosom —— Ah! Larron![145] perfide! — la, la, la,
ra, ra.

[He sings, kneels, and dances by turns.

Monsieur Artlie is not in my power —— bon! —— but, by Gar! Madame,
you know who is, hah!

HARRIET.

As for me, my sex protects me —— I am here indeed, a prisoner and alone;
but you will not, you dare not treat me with indignity.

CHAMPIGNON.

Dare not! — Bravo — shew to me de man vil say I dare not —— ça[146] —
ha — hah!

[Capers about.

HARRIET.

You're in such a dancing humour, 'tis pity you should want musick ——
Shall I sing you a song?

CHAMPIGNON.

Ah cruelle! —— you gouverne wid souverain empire over my 'art — you
rouse me into one storm —— you sing me into one calm.

SONG.[147]

I.

Let the nymph still avoid, and be deaf to the swain
Who in transports of passion affects to complain;
For his rage, not his love, in that frenzy is shewn;
And the blast that blows loudest is soon overblown.

II.

But the shepherd whom Cupid has pierc'd to the heart,
Will submissive adore, and rejoice in the smart;

Or in plaintive soft murmurs, his bosom-felt woe
Like the smooth gliding current of rivers will flow.

III.

Tho' silent his tongue, he will plead with his eyes,
And his heart own your sway in a tribute of sighs;
But, when he accosts you in meadow or grove,
His tale is all tenderness, rapture, and love.

SCENE VI.

CHAMPIGNON, HARRIET, BRUSH.

BRUSH.

News! news! there's an English man of war's boat along side, with a flag of truce.

CHAMPIGNON.

Comment! [148] —— Madame, you ave de bonté [149] to retire to your cabane —
I go dress my self, and give de audience.

[*Exit Champignon.*

SCENE VII.

HARRIET, BRUSH.

HARRIET.

O Brush! Brush! how my little heart palpitates with fear and suspense! ——
What does the arrival of this boat portend?

BRUSH.

Our deliverance from the hands of the Philistines, I hope —— it could not arrive at a more seasonable juncture; for my spirits are quite flagged —— not that I'm so much concerned on my own account, Ma'am —— but, I can't be insensible to your danger, Ma'am —— I should be an ungrateful wretch if I did not feel for one that is so dear to Mr. Heartly, Ma'am.

HARRIET.

Really, Mr. Brush, you seem to have improved mightily in politeness, since you lived among these French Gentlemen.

BRUSH.

Lived, Ma'am!——I have been dying hourly since I came aboard; and that politeness which you are pleased to mention, Ma'am, is nothing but sneaking fear and henheartedness, which I believe (God forgive me) is the true source of all French politeness; a kind of poverty of spirit, or want of sincerity ——I should be very proud to be drubbed in England for my insolence and ill-breeding.

HARRIET.

Well, I hope you'll soon be drubbed to your heart's content——When we revisit our own country, you shall have all my interest towards the accomplishment of your wish——mean while do me the favour to make further inquiry about this same flag of truce, and bring an account of what shall pass, to my cabin, where I shall wait for you with the utmost impatience.

[*Exeunt.*

SCENE VIII.

BLOCK, and another Seaman.

BLOCK.

Smite my limbs, Sam, if the lieftenant do clap her aboard,[150] here is no plunder——nothing but rags and vermin, as the saying is——we shall share nothing but the guns and the head-money[151]—if you call those heads that have no bodies belonging to 'un.——Mind that there scarecrow—see how his cloth hangs in the wind——Adzooks! the fellow has got no stowage ——he's all upperwork and head-sail[152]—I'll be damn'd if the first hard squall don't blow him into the air like the peeling of an onion.

To him BRUSH.

Heh!—how!—no sure!—Yes faith but it is—Odso! cousin Block, who thought to meet with you among the French?

BLOCK.

What chear ho? —— How does mother Margery? [153] —— meet me among the French? Agad! I'd never desire better pastime than to be among 'em with a good cutlash in my hand, and a brace of pistols in my girdle —— Why look you, brother, hearing as how you and your mistress were wind-bound,[154] we are come along side to tow you into the offing.

BRUSH.

The lord reward you, cousin —— but, what if this damned Frenchman should refuse to part with us?

BLOCK.

Why then, lieftenant Lyon is a cruising to windward of that there head-land — he'll be along side in half a glass, fall under your stern, clap his helm a starboard, rake you fore and aft, and send the Frenchman and every soul on board, to the devil, in the turning of an handspike.[155]

BRUSH.

The devil, he will! —— but cousin, what must become of me then?

BLOCK.

Thereafter as it may be —— You must take your hap, I do suppose —— we sailors never mind those things — every shot has its commission, d'ye see — we must all die one time,[156] as the saying is — if you go down now, it may save your going aloft another time, brother.

BRUSH.

O! curse your comfort.

BLOCK.

Heark ye, brother, this is a cold morning —— have you picked up never a runlet [157] along shore? — What d'ye say to a slug?

BRUSH.

Slug! —— O, I understand you ——
     [*Fetches a keg of brandy, which Block sets to his head.*

BLOCK.

Right Nantz,[158] strike my topsails! [159] —— Odds heart! [160] this is the only thing in France that agrees with an Englishman's constitution. —— Let us drink out their brandy, and then knock out their brains —— This is the way to demolish the spirit of the French. — An Englishman will fight at a minute's warning, brother —— but a Frenchman's heart must be buoyed up with brandy — No more keg, no more courage.

BRUSH.

T' other pull, cousin.

BLOCK.

Avast, avast —— no more canvas than we can carry — we know the trim of our own vessel. — Smite my cross trees! [161] We begin to yaw already — Hiccup. ——

BRUSH.

Odso! our commander is coming upon deck, to give audience to your midshipman.

BLOCK.

Steady.

[*Exeunt.*

SCENE IX.

CHAMPIGNON, OCLABBER, MACLAYMORE, BRUSH, TOM HAULYARD an English midshipman.

CHAMPIGNON.

Eh bien, Monsieur, qui souhaite il? [162]

HAULYARD.

Anan —— Monseer sweat he! —— Agad! I believe, if we come along side of you, we'll make you all sweat.

MACLAYMORE.

That's mair than ye can tell, my lad —— ye may gar me sweet with fechting; but it's no in your breeks to gar me sweet with fear.[163]

OCLABBER.

You may sweat me after I'm dead, honey — but, by the blessed Virgin! you shall not sweat me alive — and so you may be after delivering your message, gra.

HAULYARD.

If it wa'n't for such as you that shew your own country the fore-top-sail, wold our enemy's cable,[164] and mann their quarters, they would never ride out the gale, or dare to shew their colours at sea — but howsomever, we'll leave that bowling i' the block,[165] as the saying is — if so be as how, that there Frenchman is commander of this here vessel, I have orders from my officer to demand an English young woman, with all her baggage and thingumbobs, that he took yesterday out of a pleasure-boat, belonging to one Mr. Heartly of Dorsetshire, who slipped the painter[166] this morning.

CHAMPIGNON.

Mardy! de commission be very peremptoire! — ecouté mon ami,[167] vat you call Monsieur your commandant?

HAULYARD.

I don't take in your palaver, not I — and may hap, you don't know my lingo; but, agad! we'll soon make you understand plain English.

OCLABBER.

Monsieur Champignon wants to know who is your commanding officer, honey.

HAULYARD.

Who should it be, but lieutenant Lyon of the Triton man of war of sixty guns? as bold a heart as ever crack'd biscuit.

CHAMPIGNON.

Bon! —— suppose dat I refuse de demand of Monsieur Lionne?

HAULYARD.

Suppose! —— if you do, he'll run you along-side, yard arm and yard arm,[168] and blow you out of the water; that's all.

CHAMPIGNON.

By Gar! he vill find himself mistaken: here is not vater for one sixty gun ship—(*aside*) Heark you me, Monsieur vat is your name, tell Monsieur Lioni dat I am called Michel, Sanson, Goluat de Champignon, Marquis de Vermisseau [169]——— dat I ave de honeur to serve de king——— dat fear be one bagatelle of wich I have de Mepris [170]——— dat I regard you ambassade as de Galimatias [171]——— dat my courage suffice to attack one whole Englis escadre; [172] and dat if Mons. Lionne be disposed to rendre moi un visite, I shall ave de gloire to chastise his presomption; so I permitte you go your way.

[MACLAYMORE.

Dissentio [173] — bide you Billy — there's nae clerk here I trow — weel, lieutenant Oclabber, I tak instruments in your haund against the proceedings of Captain Champignon, wha has incarcerate the English leddy, contrair to the law of nature and nations. [174] Now, cocky, [175] ye may gang about your business; when ye come back, I'se tauk with you in another stile.

OCLABBER.

For my own part, Honey, I shall be after shewing you some diversion in the way of my duty; but, I taake you to witness that I have no hand in detaining the lady who is plaised to favour us with her company against her own consent, gra.]

HAULYARD.

May hap you may trust to your shoal water — if you do you're taken all aback, brother: for, lieutenant Lyon commands a tender of twelve guns and fifty stout hands, that draws less than this here frigate by the streak; [176] and — heh! — agad! yonder she comes round the point with a flowing sail — b'w'ye, [177] Monseer Champignon; all hands to quarters; up with your white rag; I doubt my officer and I will taste some of your soupe meagre [178] by that time you pipe to dinner.   [*Exit.*

SCENE X.

CHAMPIGNON, OCLABBER, MACLAYMORE, BRUSH.

CHAMPIGNON.

Mort de ma vie! je ne vous attendois pas sitot, [179] a quelle coté faut il que je me tourne? [180] sacrebleu!   [*Aside.*

Messieurs, I demand your conseil; you protest against my conduite; if you tink me ave done de injustice, you vil find me tout a fait raisonable; we render Mademoiselle to de Englis; for I juge it bien mal a-propos to engage de enemi, wen de spirit of contradiction reign among ourselves.

OCLABBER.

Faith and troth! my dear, the contradiction is all over; you have nothing to do but to station your men; and as for Mr. Maclaymore and my own shelf, the English cannon may make our legs and arms play at loggerheads in the air, Honey; but we'll stand by you for the glory of France, in spite of the devil and all his works, gra.

MACLAYMORE.

Never fash your noddle [181] about me: conscience! I'se no be the first to cry *barley*. [182]

OCLABBER.

Ensign Maclaymore, I order you to go and take possession of the forecastle with your division, Honey. I wish they may stand fire 'till you're all knock'd o'the head, gra; but, I'm afraid they're no better than dunghills; for they were raised from the *Canaille* [183] of Paris. — And now I'll go and put the young lady below water, where she may laugh in her own sleeve, gra; for if the ship should be blown up in the engagement, she is no more than a passenger you know; and then she'll be released without ransom.

BRUSH.

God bless you, captain Oclabber, for your generosity to my poor lady: I was ordered by my master to give her close attendance; and tho' I have a great curiosity to see the battle, Miss Harriet must by no means be left alone.

[*Exeunt* Oclabber, Maclaymore *and* Brush.

SCENE XI.

CHAMPIGNON.

Ventre saingris! que ferai-je? Je me sens tout embrouillé — ces autre Anglois sont si precipitées! que diable les etouffe. [184] Allons! Aux armes! matelots — mes enfans? [185] chardon — chifon — ortie — fumiere — l'hibou — la faim [186] — allons — vite, vite — aux armes!

[*A crew of tatterdemalions running up and down the deck in confusion—the noise of cannon and musquetry.*

Ah mon bon dieu! ayez pitie de moi encore—qu'on m'apporte de l'eau de vie. Ah miserable pecheur!—je suis mort!—je suis enterré!——ah! voila assez mes enfans——cessez—desistez—il faut amener [187]——Monsieur O-claw-bear——lieutenant O-claw-bear——

SCENE XII.

OCLABBER.   [*Behind the scenes.*

Holloa!——

CHAMPIGNON.

Laissez——laissez——leave off your fire—de ennemi be too strong——we ave abaissée le drapeau [188]——I command you leave off——

OCLABBER.

Leave off! arrah for what?

CHAMPIGNON.

De ennemi vil accord no quartier.

OCLABBER.

Devil burn your quarter!—what signifies quarter when we're all kill'd. The men are lying along the deck like so many paise; and there is such an abominable stench, gra—by my saoul! I believe they were all rotten before they died.

[*Coming upon the stage.*

Arrah mon deaul! I believe the English have made a compact with the Devil to do such execution; for my ensign has lost all his men too but the piper, and they two have cleared the forecastle sword in hand.

BRUSH.   [*In great trepidation.*

O Lord! Mr. Oclabber, your ensign is playing the devil——hacking and hewing about him like a fury; for the love of God interpose, my master is come aboard, and if they should meet there will be murder.

OCLABBER.

By my saoul! I know he has a regard for Mr. Heartly, and if he kills him it will be in the way of friendship, Honey——howsomever, if there's any mischeif done, I'll go and prevent it. [*Exit* Oclabber.

SCENE XIII.

CHAMPIGNON, lieutenant LYON, HEARTLY, HAULYARD, BRUSH, BLOCK, and English sailors.

CHAMPIGNON.
[*Throwing himself on his knees and presenting his sword.*
Ah! misericorde,[189] Mons. Artlie, quartier——quartier, pour l'amour de Dieu!

HEARTLY.

I have no time to mind such trifles——where is my Harriet?

BRUSH.

I'll shew you the way to the poor solitary pigeon—Ah, master, this is a happy day! [*Exeunt* Heartly *and* Brush.

SCENE XIV.

OCLABBER, MACLAYMORE, lieutenant LYON, HAULYARD, CHAMPIGNON, &c.

OCLABBER.   [*Delivering his sword.*
Gentlemen, yours is the fortune of the day. You ought to be kind to us, for we have given you very little trouble. —— Our commander there, is a very shivil person, gra; he don't turst after the blood of his enemy. As for the soldiers, I shall say nothing; but upon my saoul! now they're the nimblest dead men I ever saw in the days of my life! about two minutes agone they were lying like so many slaughtered sheep, and now they are all scamper'd off about their business.

MACLAYMORE.

As I sall answar it's a black burning shame! and I hope the king will order them to be decimated, that is, every tenth man to be hanged in terrorem.[190]

OCLABBER.

By my salvation! if the king will take my advice, every single man of them shall be decimated.

SCENE the last.

To them HEARTLY, *leading in* Harriet.

HEARTLY.
[*Embracing* Oclabber *and* Maclaymore.
Gentlemen, I'm heartily glad of having an opportunity to return, in some measure, the civilities you have shewn to this young lady. Mr. Lyon, I beg you'll order their swords to be restored; they were in no shape accessary to our grievances.

OCLABBER.   [*Receiving his sword.*
Mr. Lyon, you're extraimly polite; and I hope I shall never die 'till I have an opportunity to return the compliment. Madam, I wish you joy of our misfortune, with all my saoul.

LYON.
I a'n't used to make speeches, Madam, but I'm very glad it was in my power to serve such a fine lady, especially as my old school-fellow Heartly is so much concerned in your deliverance. As for this fair weather spark, Monsieur de Champignon, if he can't shew a commission authorizing him to make depredations on the English, I shall order him to be hoisted up to the yard's arm by the neck as a pyrate; but if he can produce his orders, he shall be treated as a prisoner of war, tho' not before he has restored what he pilfer'd from you and Mr. Heartly.

HARRIET.
At that rate I'm afraid I shall lose an admirer. You see, Monsieur de Champignon, the old proverb fulfilled; hanging and marriage go by destiny:[191] yet I should be very sorry to occasion even the death of a sinner.

CHAMPIGNON.

Madame, I implore your pitie and clemence; Monsieur Artlie, I am one pauvre miserable not worth your revanche.

[*Enter* BLOCK *drunk, with a portmanteau on his shoulder.*

BLOCK.

Thus and no nearer — bear a hand my hearts —
[*Lays it down, opens it, takes out and puts on a tawdry*
suit of Champignon's *cloaths.*
By your leave, Tinsey[192] — Odds heart! these braces are so taught, I must keep my yards square,[193] as the saying is.

LYON.

Ahey! — what the Devil have we got here? how now, Block?

BLOCK.

All's fair plunder between decks — we ha'n't broke bulk,[194] I'll assure you — stand clear — I'll soon over-haul the rest of the cargo.
[*Pulls out a long leathern queue with red ribbons.*
What's here? the tiller[195] of a monkey! — s'blood the fellow has no more brains than a noddy, to leave the red ropes[196] hanging over his stern, whereby the enemy may board him on the poop.[197]
[*The next thing that appears, is a very coarse canvas shirt*
with very fine lac'd ruffles.
This here is the right trim of a Frenchman — all ginger-bread work,[198] flourish and compliment aloft, and all rags and rottenness alow.
[*Draws out a plume of feathers.*
Adzooks! this is Mounseer's vane, that like his fancy, veers with every puff to all the points of the compass — Hark'ee, Sam — the nob must needs be damnably light that's rigg'd with such a deal of feather. The French are so well fledg'd no wonder they're so ready to fly.
[*Finds a pocket glass, a paper of Rouge and Spanish*
wool,[199] with which he daubs his face.
Swing the swivel-ey'd son of a whore! he fights under false colours like a pirate — here's a lubberly dog, he dares not shew his own face to the weather.

CHAMPIGNON.

Ah! Monsieur de Belokke, ave compassion —

BLOCK.

Don't be afraid, Frenchman — you see I have hoisted your jacket, thof I struck your ensign[200] — we Englishmen never cut throats in cold blood: the best way of beating the French is to spare all their Shampinions — Odd's heart! I wou'd all their commanders were of your trim, brother; we'd soon have the French navy at Spithead.[201]

LYON.

But in the mean time I shall have you to the gangway,[202] you drunken swab.

BLOCK.

Swab! — I did swab the forecastle clear of the enemy, that I must confess.

LYON.

None of your jaw, you lubber.

BLOCK.

Lubber! — Man and boy, twenty years in the service — lubber! — Ben Block was the man that taught thee, Tom Lyon, to hand, reef, and steer[203] — so much for the service of old England — But go thy ways, Ben, thy timbers are crazy, thy planks are started, and thy bottom is foul — I have seen the day when thou would'st have shewn thy colours with the best o'un.

LYON.

Peace, porpuss.

BLOCK.

I am a porpuss; for I spout salt water, d'ye see. I'll be damn'd if grief and sorrow ha'n't set my eye-pumps a-going.

HARRIET.

Come Mr. Block, I must make you friends with lieutenant Lyon — As he has been your pupil, he must be an able navigator; and this is no time for our able seamen to fall out among themselves.

BLOCK.

Why, look ye here, mistress, I must confess, as how, he's as brisk a seaman as ever greas'd a marlinspike[204] — I'll turn 'un a drift with e'er a he that ever reefed a foresail — A will fetch up his leeway with a wet sail,[205] as the saying is — and as for my own part, d'ye see, I have stood by him with my blood — and my heart — and my liver, in all weathers —— blow high — blow low.

HARRIET.
Well, I hope you'll live to see and sail with him as an admiral.

BLOCK.
I doubt a must be hove down first, keel out of the water, Mistriss, and be well scrubbed, d'ye see —— then a may to sea when a wool, and hoist the union flag —— Stand clear, John Frenchman — "The Royal Sovereign of England will ride triumphant over the waves," as the song[206] goes.

LYON.
And now for you, Monsieur Champignon.

CHAMPIGNON.
Monsieur Lionne, I ave not altogether contradicted, but, perhaps, a littel exceeded my ordres, wich were to take one English chaloupe for intelligence.

HEARTLY.
Well — I'm persuaded Mr. Lyon will not be very severe in his scrutiny; and, to shew that we Englishmen can forgive injuries, and fight without malice, give me your hand — I can't part with my mistress; but in other respects I am Monsieur de Champignon's humble servant.

LYON.
I was once taken by the French, who used me nobly. — I'm a witness of their valour, and an instance of their politeness —— but there are Champignon's in every service — While France uses us like friends, we will return her civilities: when she breaks her treaties and grows insolent, we will drub her over to her good behaviour — Jack Haulyard, you have got a song to the purpose, that won't, I believe, be disagreeable to the company.

SONG.[207]
Behold! my brave Britons, the fair springing gale,
Fill a bumper and toss off your glasses:
Buss and part with your frolicksome lasses;
Then aboard and unfurl the wide flowing sail.

CHORUS.

While British oak beneath us rolls,
And English courage fires our souls;
To crown our toils, the fates decree
The wealth and empire of the sea.

II.

Our canvas and cares to the winds we display,
Life and fortune we cheerfully venture;
And we laugh, and we quaff, and we banter;
Nor think of to morrow while sure of to day.

CHORUS.

While British oak, &c.

III.

The streamers of France at a distance appear!
We must mind other musick than catches;
Mann our quarters, and handle our matches;
Our cannon produce, and for battle prepare.

CHORUS.

While British oak, &c.

IV.

Engender'd in smoke and deliver'd in flame,
British vengeance rolls loud as the thunder!
Let the vault of the sky burst asunder,
So victory follows with riches and fame.

CHORUS.

While British oak beneath us rolls,
And English courage fires our souls;
To crown our toils the fates decree
The wealth and empire of the sea.

FINIS.

EPILOGUE.

Spoken by Miss MACKLIN.

A ye — *now I can with pleasure look around,*
Safe as I am, thank Heaven, on English ground. —
In a dark dungeon to be stow'd away,
Midst roaring, thund'ring, danger and dismay:
Expos'd to fire and water, sword and bullet —
Might damp the heart of any Virgin pullet.[208] —
I dread to think what might have come to pass,
Had not the British Lyon quell'd the Gallic ass —
By Champignon a wretched victim led
To cloister'd cell, or more detested bed.
My days in pray'r and fasting I had spent:
As nun, or wife, alike a penitent.
His gallantry, so confident and eager,
Had prov'd a mess of delicate soupe — *maigre.*
To bootless longings I had fallen a martyr:
But, Heav'n be prais'd, the Frenchman caught a Tartar.
  Yet soft — *our author's fate you must decree:*
Shall he come safe to port, or sink at sea?
Your sentence, sweet or bitter, soft or sore,
Floats his frail bark, or runs it bump ashore. —
Ye wits above restrain your awful thunder:
In his first cruise, 'twere pity he should founder. [To the gall.
Safe from your shot he fears no other foe,
Nor gulph, but that which horrid yawns below. [To the pit.
The bravest chiefs, ev'n Hannibal and Cato,
Have here been tam'd with — *pippin and potatoe.*
Our bard embarks in a more christian cause,
He craves not mercy; but he claims applause.
His pen against the hostile French is drawn,
Who damns him, is no Antigallican.[209]
Indulg'd with fav'ring gales and smiling skies,
Hereafter he may board a richer prize.
But if this welkin[210] *angry clouds deform,*

  [Looking round the house.

And hollow groans portend the approaching storm:
Should the descending show'rs of hail redouble,
And these rough billows hiss, and boil and bubble,
He'll launch no more on such fell seas of trouble.

[To the gall.
[To the pit.

The Briton

INTRODUCTION

When George III ascended the throne of Great Britain in October 1760, his most conspicuous inheritance from his grandfather, George II, was a successful, ongoing war directed by a popular, energetic minister. The war was the Seven Years' War, in which England was struggling with France for supremacy on several battlefronts throughout the world. The minister was William Pitt, "the Great Commoner," who, taking control of the reins of government in mid-1757 after the war had begun with a series of military and naval defeats for British forces, had engineered a remarkable reversal of his nation's fortunes and brought off several spectacular campaigns that left Britain all but crowned as victor in the war. Little more than a month before George II's death, Pitt had enjoyed one of his greatest moments when France surrendered its Canadian possessions to British forces.

But the new king, only twenty-two years of age, was not particularly delighted with the state of his inheritance. From infancy he had been reared in a household where, owing to a long-standing animosity between his parents and grandparents, he had been taught to despise his predecessor as a weak king, submissive to the will of self-serving factions and infatuated with his fondness for Hanover, the small German electorate that was the family's ancestral home. A few years after the death in 1751 of his father, Frederick, Prince of Wales, George had come under the tutelage of John Stuart, earl of Bute. Bute, a Scotsman, had imbued him with an earnest desire to be a strong, devoted, and virtuous monarch, ruling justly over his people and recovering for the crown the esteem of his subjects and those proper prerogatives which, it was maintained, had been bargained away by the venality and corruption of government in the preceding two reigns.

The war, commanding much of the nation's interest and resources, was obviously a concern to which much of the new king's attention would have to be given. George came to the throne sharing with many public figures a number of sincere reservations about the course the war was taking under Pitt's bellicose and decisive direction. The war was becoming highly expensive, and many in positions to be heard were beginning to question whether the benefits of further reducing French power would be worth the costs in the long run. Moreover, the system of alliances that had been forged to pursue the war found Britain subsidizing Frederick the Great of Prussia in his attempt to establish an empire in central Europe and providing a large army on the Continent to assist Frederick and ostensibly protect Hanover. Increasingly to many Englishmen, it appeared that the continental phase of the war was a waste of English resources, resulting only in helping a German prince pursue his own policy of national aggrandizement.

Two pamphlets published in the months just preceding the death of George II broach ideas that were gaining currency and setting the stage for the political developments of the first few years of George III's reign. These were Israel Mauduit's *Considerations on the Present German War*, the popularity of which is attested by six printings in quick succession, and John Douglas's *Letter Addressed to Two Great Men, on the Prospect of Peace*. Mauduit's *Considerations*, a closely reasoned argument against England's further involvement in the land war on the Continent, laid down many of the assumptions and lines of argument about the folly of such involvement that were to be heard during the ensuing two and a half years. Douglas's *Letter* was primarily a commentary on possible peace terms, but it also urged the ministers of the day to adopt, once peace was reestablished, a "patriot" program by reducing factional power and influence and establishing the independence of Parliament. His pamphlet promoted the notion that true "patriot" leaders would be characterized by their independence from any faction and their freedom from corruption.

By labeling his platform a patriot one, Douglas was calling to his readers' minds ideas formulated by Henry St. John, Viscount Bolingbroke, in his famous political treatise written in 1739, *The Idea of a Patriot King*.[1] In this treatise, Bolingbroke, one-time Tory minister to Queen Anne and for many years the most ardent foe of Sir Robert Walpole (who served as prime minister from 1721 to 1742), had argued that England's only salvation from the corruption and political degeneracy of the long Walpole era would be the succession to the English throne of a patriot king. A patriot king, by being himself an example of virtue and by surrounding himself with disinterested ministers, would act as a father to all his people, rid the political system of contentious factions, and restore concord and public virtue to the nation.

Variations on Bolingbroke's ideas, particularly the notion that the ascendance of self-serving factions was both a cause and an effect of the degeneracy of English political life, continued to be used by the opposition to the Whig ministers of George II throughout his reign. Following George's death, it was but a matter of time until notions associated with Bolingbroke's patriot king and the presence of a new, apparently reform-minded king became commingled in the minds of many of George III's supporters. Before long they accepted as a matter of fact that their monarch had come to the throne with the solid intention of reigning as a patriot king.

Many of the king's early pronouncements demonstrated how his thoughts and intentions were suitable to the setting that the ideas published by Mauduit and Douglas had provided his reign. In addressing the privy council assembled to declare him king, he spoke of the "bloody war" in which the kingdom was engaged. Although, at Pitt's insistence, the words were changed in the published version to "expensive but just and necessary war,"[2] they clearly were clues to his sentiments and they anticipated policies based on those sentiments. And in his first address to Parliament, the king spoke words that were to become a banner for his supporters and a sure proof to them of his dedication to the idea of a patriot king reigning over a united people: "Born and educated in this country, I glory in the name of Briton, and the peculiar happiness of my life will ever consist in promoting the welfare of a people, whose loyalty and warm affection to me, I consider as the greatest and most permanent security of my throne."[3]

Immediately after his accession, George III named his mentor Bute, whom he often addressed in his correspondence as "dearest friend," to be groom of the stole and a member of his cabinet. The king relied heavily upon Bute for advice and assistance in practically every concern, and in March 1761 Bute received the more powerful office of secretary of state for the northern department. In May 1762 he became first lord of the treasury, the senior position among the king's ministers. Bute's influence and position were used in the king's council to push vigorously for a speedy conclusion of peace with France. Earlier, in 1761, French and English agents had begun discussions on possible terms for a peace treaty. But Pitt, whom the king had retained as secretary of state for the southern department, continued to press for a comprehensive war policy that would ensure Great Britain's enjoyment of the full reward of its naval and military successes whenever a peace should be concluded. The various policies and possibilities were fully scanned in the public press of London, and the "soft-liners" and the "hard-liners," the followers of Bute and the followers of Pitt, began to be clearly distinguished, both in governmental circles and in the public eye. During the summer of 1761, France concluded with Spain a Family Compact (so named because the Bourbon family possessed the thrones of both France and Spain); Spain had heretofore been uninvolved in the conflict, and the compact therefore greatly strengthened the French position and caused the French to draw back markedly from many of their positions they had earlier been willing to consider negotiable. The upshot of this development was a demand by Pitt in the fall of 1761 that Great Britain declare war on Spain. His demand was turned down by a council more inclined to end the war than enlarge it; two days later Pitt returned the seals of his office to the king. The king accepted his resignation quite willingly, although only a few months later circumstances forced him to follow Pitt's counsel and declare war on Spain. Pitt's resignation served only to raise his stock with the London populace. On the occasion of the lord mayor's dinner on 9 November, friends had arranged for him to be wildly cheered in the streets and warmly applauded at the Guildhall while the king himself received only token recognition and Bute was almost assaulted by mobs on his way to the feast. Pitt's apparent effrontery in seeming to compete with the king for popularity was to give his enemies a good deal of ammunition in the ensuing war of words.

The duke of Newcastle, the last symbol of the old regime of George II, remained in office a few more months. But he, too, was soon forced out, and Bute was free to push his own program for a conclusion to the Seven Years' War, even if it meant settling for considerably less than the complete dismemberment of the French empire and leaving Prussia to fend for itself on the Continent.

In his *Continuation of the Complete History of England*, Smollett vividly summarizes the clamor unleashed by Pitt's resignation and the king's acceptance of it:

> It divided the nation into violent factions, and deluged the public with inundations of pamphlets, papers, and pasquinades. The friends and admirers of Mr. P— exclaimed, that . . . he was ungratefully thwarted in his designs for the public good, and thrust from the helm at the most critical juncture, by a cabal of wicked and worthless men. . . . Another party were not less vehement in their invectives against the late S—y. They taxed him with inconsistency, want of principle, and the most turbulent ambition. They asserted . . . that enamoured of this new idol [the continental war], he squandered upon it immense sums, so as to impoverish his country and accumulate the load of her debts to such a degree, that she could scarce crouch under her burthen.[4]

Particularly loud in defense of Pitt and his policies were the outcries of the *Monitor*, an established weekly journal and the spokesman, by and large, for London commercial interests. Week after week the *Monitor* accused the Bute ministry of being run by favorites and aliens who ignored the public good and of being willing, in exchange for a dishonorable peace, to abandon the conquests that had signalized the last year of George II's reign.

The Earl of Bute, by Joshua Reynolds.
(Courtesy of the National Portrait Gallery, London.)

Although Bute was not inclined to pay much attention to the public clamor, which was especially loud in London, where Pitt was a great favorite, he was aware that his task of bringing about the peace the king desired would be easier if his policies could garner greater public support and if the numerous attacks made against himself as a "favorite" of the king and as a Scottish adviser could be countered. It was at this juncture that Tobias George Smollett, one of the busiest journalists in a city filled with busy journalists, was enlisted by his fellow countryman to propagandize the public in behalf of Bute's peace policy. On 29 May 1762, the London reading public saw the first number of Smollett's *Briton*. Printed for J. Coote at the King's Arms in Paternoster Row and selling for "Two-pence Halfpenny," the new sheet was designed, as it asserted, to "pluck the mask of patriotism from the front of faction, and the torch of discord from the hand of sedition."

Just how and why Tobias Smollett was chosen to become propagandist for the king's ministry is uncertain. Certainly it was not that he had no other enterprise going at the time. As he had been since its inception in 1756, Smollett was still very much involved with the *Critical Review*, a monthly review of the London publishing scene. He was also connected with the *British Magazine*, a more general journal for which he had recently written his fourth novel, *The Adventures of Sir Launcelot Greaves*, as a serial publication. He was probably still working on his *Continuation of the Complete History*, following up his *Complete History of England* (1757–58), and he was helping to edit *The Works of M. de Voltaire* in English. Although Smollett was always a hard worker, the incentives or pressures must have been strong for him to take on the additional task of putting out a weekly sheet for the ministry, particularly since he was surely aware that he would be stepping into the midst of a storm of words.

Stormy circumstances, however, were not unfamiliar to Smollett, who, in addition to being known as an energetic editor and writer, had established something of a reputation as a journalistic pugilist. Indeed, it had been less than two years since he had served a term of three months as a prisoner in the King's Bench for his libelous attack on Admiral Knowles in the *Critical Review*.[5] And this was but the most notorious of the quarrels that Smollett had at one time or another found himself engaged in because of the barbs in his printed words. Smollett's capacity for literary jousting was neatly recognized in a statement attributed to John Wilkes, soon to become his most conspicuous antagonist. According to an anecdote recorded by Smollett's friend and early biographer, John Moore, Wilkes, upon hearing that Bute had engaged Smollett to conduct a political paper, remarked, "After having distributed among his adherents all the places under Government, his Lordship is determined, it would seem, to monopolize the wit also."[6]

It is impossible to state with certainty who acted for Bute in persuading Smollett to undertake a ministerial paper. Although the ubiquitous place-hunter Bubb Dodington, who had recently managed to gain Bute's favor, has been proposed,[7] what little concrete evidence is available points most strongly to Alexander Wedderburn and his brother-in-law, Sir Harry Erskine, who were Scottish members of Parliament and intimates of Bute. (Wedderburn later became Lord Loughborough and first earl of Rosslyn; he was lord chancellor for nearly a decade at the end of the century.) According to H. V. Knox in his manuscript reminiscences, Wedderburn and Erskine tried to thrust themselves into importance when their countryman became chief minister. Knox records rather tersely that "they set up the *Briton* and *Auditor*, in defence of Lord Bute, but the conductors complained of being ill-furnished with materials, and both were dropt."[8] Erskine and Wedderburn seem not to be mentioned in any other records connected with Smollett, but since Wedderburn was a member of the Select Society of Edinburgh, many of whose members were well known to Smollett, it is likely that he and Smollett became acquainted when Wedderburn came to London in 1757. If so, he was in a good position to approach Smollett about serving their countryman as the editor of a new political sheet.

Thus Smollett's success as a hardworking journalist, as well as his Scottish origins, may have had something to do with his being commissioned to handle the *Briton*. Moreover, many of Smollett's published remarks had already identified him as one whose views were largely sympathetic to the new king and to the attempts of his most trusted minister to move speedily toward a peace treaty. In his *Complete History* Smollett had described the reigns of the first two Georges as a period when public spirit and morality in government had generally declined as a result of the corruption encouraged by Sir Robert Walpole and his successors. In a passage typical of those that might have been noticed by some of Bute's advisers, Smollett describes the general condition of England during George II's reign: "The vice, luxury, and prostitution of the age, the almost total extinction of sentiment, honour, and public spirit, had prepared the minds of men for slavery and corruption. The means were in the hands of the ministry: the public treasure was at their devotion: they multiplied places and pensions to increase the number of their dependents: they squandered away the money of the nation without taste, discernment, decency, or remorse."[9]

In his preface addressed "To the Public" at the beginning of the *Continuation*, Smollett characterizes events described in the latter part of his earlier work as "an unpleasing tissue of misconduct and miscarriage . . . a people groaning under the double pressure of internal discontent and external dishonour." But, he asserts, the scene had now been "agreeably changed": England was now ruled by a king and minister respected by the people, and it was being shown that government could operate without corruption.[10] In the *Continuation*, Smollett's editorializing on the war, and particularly on the German phase of it, is almost invariably critical and tinged with an irony that foreshadows many of the comments in the *Briton*. In reporting the king's address to Parliament at the end of 1757, he sarcastically observes that "those happy days were now approaching, that saw the commons of England pour their treasures, in support of a German prince, with such a generous hand, that posterity will be amazed at their liberality." And later, in commenting on the king's address to Parliament in November 1759, he animadverts generally on the absence of opposition to the ministry, the costliness of the war, and the turnabout of ministers who had formerly opposed the expenses of a continental war. The last two topics are among those most frequently treated in the *Briton*. Especially significant is a nearly twenty-page summary of *Considerations on the Present German War* that appears in the *Continuation* with Smollett's remark, "the sentiments of the author are exactly conformable to our own." [11]

Additional confirmation of Smollett's sympathies with Bute's peace policy, sympathies that made him a likely candidate for the editorship of a ministerial paper, may be found in the pages of the *Critical Review*. Students of Smollett have usually felt safe in assuming that, even though Smollett may not have written any particular piece in the journal (the pieces are all published anonymously), his ideas are reflected in it.[12] The *Critical Review*, like the *Continuation* (although somewhat cautiously), endorsed Mauduit's *Considerations* when reviewing it in November 1760, and the reviewers of the journal remained quite consistent, especially throughout 1761, in commenting adversely on the high costs of the German war and the belligerent attitude of those who wanted to press for further advantage against the French.[13]

Those responsible for commissioning Smollett as editor of the *Briton* might also have noticed his ambivalent attitude toward the bête noire of the ministry, William Pitt, an ambivalence he shared with a fairly important segment of public opinion. Like many others, Smollett had expressed appreciation for Pitt's honesty and integrity and for the energy with which he had managed the turnabout in Britain's fortunes of war. But also like many others, Smollett had begun to worry about the effects of Pitt's continued pursuit of the war, both because of the money and national resources expended and because of the aggressiveness, hostility, and imperial pride that the war was encouraging in the national character. Smollett had dedicated his *Complete History* to Pitt when it was published in 1757–58. This dedication was completely complimentary, speaking highly, for example, of Pitt's "shining talents." When the *British Magazine* began publication in January 1760, its first number contained another dedication to Pitt. Since Smollett was the leading figure behind this magazine during its early years, one supposes that he was responsible for this gesture or at least that he agreed with it. In this dedication Pitt is again praised for his integrity and resolution, but there is a note of restraint, even of criticism: "War, at best, is but a necessary evil: a cruel game of blood, in which even triumph is embittered with all the horrors that can shock humanity: but peace is the gentle calm, in which the virtues of benevolence are happily displayed; in which those arts which polish and benefit mankind will lift their heads, and flourish under your protection."[14] A similar expression of Smollett's abhorrence of the enormities of war appeared a few months later in a comment in the *Continuation*: "War is so dreadful in itself, and so severe in its consequences, that the exercise of generosity and compassion, by which its horrors are mitigated ought ever to be applauded, encouraged, and imitated."[15]

Such a statement as this last may reflect Smollett's memories of the brutalities and horrors of war he experienced firsthand as a young man in the British expedition to Carthagena. Remembrance of the atrocities of the Jacobite rebellion of 1745–46 (the 'Forty-Five) and of the present war may also have helped Smollett to develop the conscience of a pacifist and even to become something of an anti-imperialist. Whatever the reasons for his attitudes, his published statements obviously qualified him both philosophically and rhetorically to enter the lists against the advocates of Pitt's hard-line policies: the *Monitor*, the London populace, the mercantile interests, and many of the parliamentary survivors of the old Walpole and Pelham oligarchies—a formidable lineup, and one against which Smollett gained little ground during the paper war that was unleashed with the publication of the first *Briton* on 29 May 1762.

Smollett designed the first few numbers of the *Briton* to answer directly the charges and arguments that the *Monitor* had been printing in its previous few numbers. The *Monitor* was trying its best to discredit Bute and his ministry by charging the Scottish minister with devious proceedings in his quest for peace and with ignoring the interests of the people in his narrow-minded service to the king. Smollett took the high road in a tone of exasperated reasonableness, charging the *Monitor* with partisan distortion and suppression of facts and attributing the highest motives of loyalty and public service to the maligned Bute. The title of the new paper, which clearly referred to George III's published pronouncement that he "gloried in the name of Briton," was itself an indication of the ground Smollett wanted to occupy in defending the king and his minister: that the king was a just and generous monarch who was motivated only by his desire to promote the welfare and unity of all his subjects; and that his minister was a loyal servant who acted only to promote the wishes of his monarch and was impervious to the pressures of self-serving factions. This position sounded noble, and Smollett exerted all his rhetorical skill in giving it expression. But the nobleness of the abstraction was no match for the name-calling and innuendos that the realpolitik of the 1760s made grist for the journalistic mills.

The effect that the entrance of the *Briton* had on the political and journalistic scene is best indicated by the appearance one week later of the first number of the *North Briton*. It is something of a compliment to Smollett and the potential power of his pen that the antiministerial forces wasted no time in organizing countermeasures, and that in organizing them they turned to John Wilkes, still a relatively obscure member of Parliament but one whose wit, daring, and flair for attracting public attention were sufficiently conspicuous to make him ideally suited to fill the role of a rough-and-tumble propagandist.

With its title glancing ironically at the birthplace of both Bute and Smollett and at the claims of their newborn publication, the first number of Wilkes's *North Briton* put Bute on notice that this mordant new foe would make the task of his public relations men a more challenging battle of wits than had been expected. Although it is hard to accept the proposition of some modern commentators that within less than two weeks the Bute ministry had decided Smollett's *Briton* "was unequal to the task that the Bute ministry had assigned it,"[16] it is clear that the ministry felt reinforcements were advisable. On 10 June 1762 an additional entry into the fray made its appearance in the form of another government-sponsored sheet, the *Auditor*, edited by the Irish playwright Arthur Murphy. Although a few other short-lived journals and numerous pamphlets added to the tumult, for the next several months the conflict of words over governmental policy centered in the confrontation between the *Briton* and the *Auditor* on the side of the government, and the *North Briton* and the *Monitor* on that of the opposition.

Under Wilkes, who had considerable assistance from another expert satir-ist, Charles Churchill,[17] the *North Briton* soon seized the initiative in the war of words. As evidenced by the seven extant letters Smollett wrote to Wilkes from early 1759 to 28 March 1762, the two men had been on extremely good—one might even say intimate—terms in the few years before they found themselves editing opposing journals. Perhaps Smollett was naive enough to believe that it would be possible to restrict the controversy to the issues at hand, reasonably discussed by friendly and mutually respected opponents. But Wilkes's tactics soon dispelled any such naïveté, if Smollett ever harbored it. Unrestrained by any scruples that a sense of personal friendship or nice rules of fair debate might have suggested, Wilkes launched sustained volleys of personal abuse and invective against Bute or anyone unfortunate enough to be associated in any way with him, even against the royal family itself. Smollett was forced to reply in kind in the *Briton*, to the gain of the modern reader: such numbers of the journal as 11, 13, 15, and 38, in which he re-sorts to demeaning caricature and denigrating historical parallels, are among the liveliest and most telling of the thirty-eight numbers. But the reader is left with the impression of Wilkes and Churchill as yapping terriers, darting agilely toward and away from their target, while Smollett, bulldoglike, tries to hang on, hoping to wear down his opponents by the sheer tenacity of his efforts.

It is difficult to assess the impact or success of the *Briton*. If quieting the clamor of Bute's opponents was its aim, it was a total failure since it succeeded only in making them more vocal and—by bringing the *North Briton* onto the scene—more effective. There seems little question that, in garnering pub-lic attention, the *North Briton* far outstripped other entries in the fray. John Almon, whose evidence must be weighed against the fact that he was a strong supporter of Wilkes, says that the *North Briton* "was instantly admired and bought up, by people of all ranks."[18] Speaking of the *Briton*, Almon claims elsewhere that "the insignificant sale of the paper was a proof of its being destitute of all merit: for the number printed was but 250, which was as little as could be printed with respect to the saving of expence."[19] But occasion-ally the *Gazetteer and London Daily Advertiser* reprinted an issue of the *Briton* or summarized it, thus widening its circulation somewhat. The *Gentleman's Magazine* also provided summaries every month or so of the various political sheets, including the *Briton*. And on 19 July 1762, an enterprising publisher began publication of *The Political Controversy: or, Weekly Magazine of Minis-terial and Anti-ministerial Essays*, which contained reprints of the preceding week's essays by the four main combatants as well as related material from the newspapers, nonce publications, and some original contributions. Some-time during 1763 there also appeared a sixty-six-page pamphlet entitled *The True Flower of Brimstone: Extracted from the Briton, North Briton, and Auditor*, an anthology of some of the more striking satiric passages, both proministry and antiministry, from these three papers (and a few others), arranged under the names of the chief political figures of the day. It included such bits as excerpts from the dialogue of Aniseed (Wilkes) and Gothamstowe (Temple) in the *Briton*, number 15, and the lampoon of Newcastle in number 32.

It is clear from such reprinted material, as well as from an examination of the numerous pamphlets and prints which capitalized on the public fray, that the *Briton*, along with the *Auditor*, was recognized as a leading voice of the administration and that its views and statements were well known to all who followed public affairs with any interest. Thus the *Briton* at least gained the public notice and fame necessary to set off the rhetoric of Wilkes and Churchill and to make certain that the contentions of the ministry were, if not accepted as widely as had been hoped, at least well aired. Although for Bute it may have been a matter of making do with what was available, the *Briton* was serviceable enough to the ministry to continue until the Peace of Paris was concluded in February 1763. The last *Briton*, number 38, came out on 12 February, two days after the treaty was signed.

The main drawback for the *Briton* and the *Auditor* was that they were needed at all. Despite grumblings, the war was popular. Few ministers in English history had been more adulated than Pitt—and Smollett was in the embarrassing position of having promoted that adulation—whereas Bute was incapable of appealing to popular feeling and popular taste. Even worse, Bute was a Scotsman. Smollett had for years sampled the English prejudice against the Scots, and so it should not have come as a surprise that no amount of logic, no appeal to a sense of fairness, would overcome the uproar that the antiministerial writers could raise simply by reminding their London readers that Bute was a Scottish Stuart and that Smollett was a Scottish hireling. Moreover, the *Briton* usually found itself on the defensive, its counterattacks arising from the necessity of defending an admittedly unpopular position. Bute's willingness to give up considerable military gains in order to conclude a peace was difficult to make palatable. Smollett's contention that Britain was in danger of overreaching itself and turning its conquests into liabilities may have appealed to a few as a convincing paradox. But to most readers a statement such as "among the other evil consequences of the war, I might reckon our extraordinary success" (number 6) was bound to sound more like an absurdity.[20] Assert as he might the merits and successes of the Bute administration, Smollett was readily answered that the previous ministry had laid the groundwork for any signal accomplishment and, moreover, would have done even better. And, of course, any misstep, such as the temporary loss of Newfoundland in the summer of 1762,[21] was capital material for the antiministerial papers to flaunt before their adversaries. To add to Smollett's problems, it appears that Bute was not very helpful in providing information to his propagandists.

Smollett himself has left practically no record of his struggles in working with the *Briton*. Indeed, the only document that gives his personal reaction to the paper war is a letter that appeared in the *Gazetteer and London Daily Advertiser* for 7 October 1762, in which he defends himself against charges of inconsistency in his treatment of Pitt. The letter reads, in part:

> I am informed that I have been lately attacked in the Ledger, by some anonymous defamer,[22] who, upon the supposition that I am author of a political paper called *the Briton*, taxes me with venality and inconsistency, for having in that paper, insulted Mr Pitt, whom I had before deified in the dedication of my history of England.
>
> I shall not give this unknown aggressor the satisfaction to declare that I have no connection with *the Briton* or any other paper whatsoever, written either for, or against the ministry: but I challenge him and all the world to prove me guilty, in one single instance, of venality, prostitution, or any other species of dishonour.[23]

In the last volume of the *Continuation*, Smollett reflects upon the general circumstances of the journalistic war of 1762, if not upon his own particular troubles:

> Had the promulgators of the first defamatory libels that appeared against the k—g and his family, been apprehended and punished according to law, the faction would have found it a very difficult task, in the sequel, to engage either printer or publisher in their service: . . . but they were emboldened by impunity to proceed in their career, to confirm their calumnies by unrefuted falshoods, and to give a loose to the most audacious scurrility; until the minds of the people were so deeply and so universally tainted, that it became hazardous to call the libellers to account.[24]

For Smollett, the eight months of engagement with the *Briton* were clearly trying and exasperating. The first issues are professional, but perfunctory. Later, after the jabs of the *North Briton* began to strike home, the essays become somewhat more vigorous, pointed, and satiric, laced with the skilled rhetoric of an aroused partisan incensed by the assaults of a shameless demagogue. But the vigor is never sustained for long, and, especially toward the end of the series, repetition and a kind of rhetorical lassitude indicate how hard it had become for Smollett, despite the sincerity of his commitment, to keep his energies equal to the task at hand. That he was becoming physically exhausted and perhaps continued the chore only in hope of some future emolument is indicated by a letter he wrote at the end of 1762 to John Home, the Scottish playwright of the celebrated *Douglas* and at the time a private secretary to Bute. The letter begins: "My Flesh continues to waste, and I begin to think the best chance I have for Recovering will be a Removal into a warmer climate. As I am unwilling to eat the Bread of Idleness, and flatter myself that I might be still in some shape serviceable to my Country, I cannot help expressing my wish that, instead of the Pension, I were gratified with some moderate Consulship abroad." [25]

But neither consulship nor pension was forthcoming. Bute quickly and quietly dropped Smollett as soon as signatures were affixed to his long-desired treaty. Worn out both physically and spiritually—to intensify his woes, his only child, Elizabeth, died in April 1763—Smollett left England for warmer climes a few months after the *Briton* ceased publication, searching for some kind of regeneration. The first letter of his *Travels through France and Italy* (1766), which chronicles that search, seems to sound the last melancholy note of Smollett's venture into the abrasive world of political journalism: "You knew, and pitied my situation, traduced by malice, persecuted by faction, abandoned by false patrons . . . . You know, with what eagerness I fled from my country as a scene of illiberal dispute, and incredible infatuation, where a few worthless incendiaries had, by dint of perfidious calumnies and atrocious abuse, kindled up a flame which threatened all the horrors of civil dissension." [26]

Smollett was only too glad to try to forget the *Briton*. And the nation seemed to follow his example. John Wilkes went on to more conspicuous journalistic escapades, including the alleged defamation of the king in the notorious *North Briton*, number 45, [27] but the reading public of England seemed quite willing to let the *North Briton*'s erstwhile rival sink quietly into obscurity. [28]

Smollett and his contemporaries may have been willing to let the *Briton* be quickly forgotten, but the student of Smollett and of England in the early years of the reign of George III can find the perusal of its pages a revealing and rewarding undertaking. The contusions of the struggle continued to

The Mountebank.

Satiric print representing Bute as a mountebank cajoling the people of England, with Smollett as his zany.
(Courtesy of the British Library.)

pain Smollett; the convictions that motivated his undertaking the *Briton* continued to throb in his imagination. The time is now past when Smollett may be considered, as he once was, merely a coarse and robust storyteller. The intellectual sinews that gave tension and direction to his storytelling are beginning to be more appreciated, but are not yet fully understood. Particularly for understanding both the ideas and the rhetoric of the mature Smollett, the imaginative writer in coherent command of a ripe vision of life in *The Expedition of Humphry Clinker* (1771), the *Briton* is a revealing document.

Intimations of distinctive elements in the works of Smollett's last years can be detected in the *Briton*. Several of the numbers, for example, feature letters. Some of these may be bona fide letters and therefore not written by Smollett—there seems to be no way of establishing this point for sure; but others seem quite clearly fictional, exercises for Smollett in creating personae as well as in treating the subject at hand. The most conspicuous example of this technique, which is, of course, basic to the composition of *Humphry Clinker* and, to a lesser extent, of the *Travels through France and Italy*, is the letter of the semiliterate Winifred Bullcalf in number 11. The foreshadowing of Win Jenkins in *Humphry Clinker* seems clear. Other good examples are the letters of Richard Draff, the pugnacious trueborn Englishman, in number 14; Junius Brutus Cockney, the ironically conceived persona, in number 15; and Benjamin Hempley, the Scot-hater, in number 34.

The treatment of the ludicrous duke of Newcastle in the London scenes of *Humphry Clinker* is very much in the spirit of his belittlement in the *Briton*, and several other political personalities that appear in Smollett's last novel, though not so prominently as Newcastle, are treated there in tone and imagery similar to those of the *Briton*.[29] And the game of hiding the names of actual persons and institutions by teasing the reader with numerous dashes, sarcastic epithets, and pseudonyms looks both backward to Smollett's practice in his early verse satires and forward to many similar passages in *The History and Adventures of an Atom* (1769) and *Humphry Clinker*.

The occasional flashes of coarse fantasy-satire that blaze up in the *Briton* can be seen as preliminary to the full-length satiric allegory of the *Adventures of an Atom*. The image of Pitt as an arrogant, inconsistent demagogue playing on the ignorance and prejudice of an excitable mob carries over, and numerous tropes referring to the corruption and factionalism of ministers from preceding reigns and the stupidity of army and naval heroes have their equivalents in the bizarre political activities of the later work.[30]

The England—and especially the London—allegorized in *Adventures of an Atom* and represented in *Humphry Clinker* is largely the turbulent world of the

Briton, the historical world of the battling political factions of the early 1760s and their hireling journalists, but even more the rhetorical world limned in the alternating logic and invective, persuasion and outcry, of Smollett's sheets. This England is an England dominated by selfish commercial interests, by petty imperialists who have lost all consciousness of a worthy, humane community. It is an England where unscrupulous politicians conspire in factions to destroy the image of the king as the force from which the nation's well-being and cohesiveness should derive. Above all, it is an England in which the mob has been set free by power-hungry demagogues to break down all the fragile barriers between savagery and civilization. Lurking always in the background of the *Briton* is the dread of licentiousness, of the breakdown of decorum—the word's twentieth-century connotation of prissiness belies the eighteenth-century cultural dynamic it represents—and, ultimately, of anarchy.[31] The England of the *Briton* is strewn with seeds germinating into the blight of a new Yahooland or into the chaos of Pope's new night of Dulness. The caricatured statesmen of the *Briton* would indeed be comfortably at home among the grotesques of the *Dunciad*.

But there is a positive element to the rhetoric of the *Briton*, an image of something that could reverse the decay of public and private morals that Smollett sees embodied in the opponents of the king's ministry. This is the image of the king himself as a benevolent, devoted, and impartial patriarch. Smollett's most convincing rhetoric is brought to the defense of George III as a patriot king, cast in the mold of Bolingbroke's national savior. Many of the specific points that Smollett tries to make appear to be straws futilely clutched; many of his arguments seem hauled out in desperation. But in his appeal to his readers to support their monarch as a patriot king, he seems to have found an issue to which he could commit himself wholeheartedly.

Historians have often debated the role that the concept of the patriot king played in the actual working out of policy and political structuring in the early years of George III's reign.[32] But there is little question that, to many of the distressed moralists and politicians of the day, the image of George III as a trueborn Briton and a patriot king had the makings of a viable myth. This myth represented the reign of the young king as a chance to turn back from the corruption and factionalism of the Leaden Age of the first two Hanoverian monarchs to a Golden Age of an ordered and harmonious society, supporting and drawing support from a beneficent, equitable monarch. The idea is succinctly stated by Smollett in *Briton*, number 18: "Let us depend upon the paternal affection of a virtuous Sovereign, who can have no views distinct from the interest and happiness of his people."

It is this call for a happier England, embedded, it is true, among much niggling debate and captious name-calling, that gives the *Briton* its greatest depth as a significant look into Smollett as a political philosopher and moralist of his day. Smollett was never one to be too optimistic about the human race. And his experience with the *Briton* was, at best, distressing. But as with Swift and Pope, those sturdy pessimists of the preceding generation, his distress was the product of comparing the world that was with the world that could be.

Ultimately the *Briton* is, certainly not a great, but at least a significant document because it is one of the last—*Humphry Clinker* may well be *the* last—expressions of the nostalgic myth much cherished by many mid-eighteenth-century moralists: the myth of an ordered England free from self-seeking, petty factions, of a rational commonwealth of generous souls ruled by a monarch whose "hand is liberally opened to every appearance of merit," whose "sole aim is to augment and secure the happiness of his people with the independence of his crown" (number 1).

Notes

1. Bolingbroke wrote *The Idea of a Patriot King* in 1739. In 1740 he gave permission to Alexander Pope to print privately a small edition, but was dismayed when Pope printed far more copies than had been authorized. In 1749 an authorized edition appeared as part of a collection of Bolingbroke's writings; in this edition the work is entitled *On the Idea of a Patriot King*.
2. John Brooke, *King George III* (London: Constable, 1972), 75.
3. *Parliamentary History*, 15:982.
4. *Continuation*, 4:327–29.
5. Smollett had published a very severe review of *The Conduct of Admiral Knowles on the Late Expedition Set in a True Light* in the *Critical Review* 5 (May 1758): 438–39. Admiral Charles Knowles, who had been involved in a recent abortive expedition to attack Rochefort, claimed defamation of character and instituted legal proceedings that resulted in Smollett's being fined one hundred pounds and imprisoned in the King's Bench Prison from late November 1760 to February 1761. Smollett's quarrels in connection with the *Critical Review* are most thoroughly surveyed by Claude Jones in "Smollett and the *Critical Review*," *Smollett Studies* (Berkeley: University of California Press, 1942).
6. Moore, clxvi.
7. With no source cited, Arnold Whitridge writes that Smollett was "said to have been recommended by Bubb Dodington"; see his *Tobias Smollett* (privately printed, 1925), 60. Although deficient in documentation, Whitridge's chapter entitled

"Smollett the Political Pamphleteer" is quite helpful. Knapp, 245, repeats from Whitridge the possibility of Dodington's involvement.

8. Historical Manuscripts Commission, *Report on Manuscripts in Various Collections* 6 (Dublin: H. M. Stationery Off., 1909): 267–68.

9. *Complete History*, 4:519.

10. *Continuation*, 1:iii–iv.

11. *Continuation*, 2:187, 3:286–87, 4:155–73.

12. James G. Basker, *Tobias Smollett: Critic and Journalist* (Newark: University of Delaware Press, 1988), appendix A, compiles a lengthy list of reviews that he attributes to Smollett; the review of Mauduit is not included.

13. See *Critical Review* 10 (1760): 403–4. Robert Donald Spector, *English Literary Periodicals* (The Hague: Mouton, 1966), 124–26, gives an excellent summary of the *Critical Review*'s position toward Bute's peace policy.

14. This passage is quoted more fully in Lewis M. Knapp, "Smollett and the Elder Pitt," *Modern Language Notes* 59 (1944): 252–53, where Knapp also provides a good summary of Smollett's relations with and feelings toward Pitt.

15. *Continuation*, 2:261–62.

16. Spector, *English Literary Periodicals*, 99; see also Robert R. Rea, *The English Press in Politics, 1760–1774* (Lincoln: University of Nebraska Press, 1963), 30.

17. Charles Churchill, a clergyman turned satirist, had previously found cause to attack Smollett because of an unpleasant review of his *Rosciad* (1761) in the *Critical Review* 11 (March 1761): 209–12. Churchill turned the episode into a feud when he retorted to the review with *The Apology: Addressed to the Critical Reviewers* (1761).

18. Almon, *The History of the Late Minority* (London, 1765), 78.

19. Almon, *A Review of Lord Bute's Administration* (London, 1763), 55.

20. In number 21, Smollett also contends that "the acquisition of Mexico and Peru would serve only to hasten the ruin of Old England."

21. See *Briton*, no. 20, n. 8, and no. 33, n. 8.

22. The author of this attack has not been identified.

23. The complete letter is printed in Knapp, 245–46.

24. *Continuation*, 5:120.

25. *Letters*, 110–11.

26. Tobias Smollett, *Travels through France and Italy*, ed. Frank Felsenstein (Oxford: Oxford University Press, 1979), 2.

27. *North Briton*, no. 45 (23 April 1763), questioned a speech from the throne recently delivered to Parliament and in effect accused the king of lying. Warrants were immediately issued for the arrest of those involved in the publication of the allegedly seditious libel, and the ensuing judicial uproar became a cause célèbre.

28. One trace of the *Briton* to be found a few years later, however, is a little booklet entitled *A Collection of All the Remarkable and Personal Passages in the Briton, North Briton, and Auditor* (London, 1767). Similar to the 1763 *True Flower of Brimstone*, the booklet—under headings such as "Mr. Alderman Beckford," "The Earl of

Bute," "Mr. Pitt," and "Mr. Wilkes"—reprints fragments from the three papers and a couple of other pamphlets pertaining to the dramatis personae of the 1762 propaganda war. It includes a number of the *Briton*'s more pungent passages.

29. These similarities are discussed in Byron Gassman, "The *Briton* and *Humphry Clinker*," *Studies in English Literature* 3 (1963): 397–414. The same essay also treats the way the *Briton*'s portrait of England, mentioned subsequently in the present introduction, reappears in *Humphry Clinker*.

30. Smollett's methods and materials in the *Briton* have been helpful evidence for Robert Adams Day in his investigation into the authorship of *Adventures of an Atom*. That investigation has convincingly established Smollett's authorship of the latter work, which Day prepared for publication as a volume in the Georgia Edition of Smollett's works (1989).

31. In *Luxury: The Concept in Western Thought, Eden to Smollett* (Baltimore: Johns Hopkins University Press, 1977), John Sekora discusses most of Smollett's writings from the mid-1750s on, including the *Briton*, as part of a widespread attack during the age on luxury and its alleged corruption of English morals and politics. The image of an England being destroyed by luxury is another version of the anarchic England here described.

32. A work extremely useful in following this debate is Herbert Butterfield, *George III and the Historians* (New York: Macmillan, 1959).

THE BRITON

No. 1. Saturday, 29 May 1762.

Ego semper ea mente fui, ut, quæ utilia æquaque viderentur, consilia de republica afferrem: quod quidem hoc præsertim tempore facturus sum: in quo si concordiam, abjecta contentione & fastidio, inter nos confirmabimus, & ipsi incolumes erimus, & alios vel invitos conservare poterimus.

CICERO.[1]

The Briton thinks it unnecessary to produce himself amidst the parade of pompous professions, which serve only to excite idle curiosity, and raise expectations which may be attended with disappointment. Neither will he make any apology for thus appearing to the public view, without the ceremony of a formal introduction: his intention is not to alarm, but appease; not to puzzle, but explain; not to inflame, but to allay. His design is that which ought to be the aim, and is the undoubted privilege of every Briton, to speak his opinion freely, and offer his advice with decency and candour, on every subject that concerns the community, of which he is a member; to watch the exertions of power and prerogative; to observe the tides of popular commotion; to detect the falsehood of malice; to expose and refute the insinuations of calumny; to pluck the mask of patriotism from the front of faction, and the torch of discord from the hand of sedition.

To a merely speculative politician, it will appear scarce credible, that there should be the least occasion for a task of this nature, at a period when the Throne is filled with such exalted virtue, as the poisonous breath of envy cannot taint, as all the tongues of slander cannot charge with blemish or infirmity: at a period when the councils of the Sovereign are shared among the natural counsellors of the Crown, a set of noblemen whose abilities are unquestionable, whose probity is unimpeached: at a period when the administration is conducted with such integrity as defies reproach; with such vigour and success as, one would think, might silence the most inveterate malice: at a period when the whole kingdom echoes with the sound of triumph and festivity; and the consummation of national happiness depends, in an especial manner, upon the continuation of national concord.

But as the sun that ripens the peach, and renovates all nature, is also known to exalt the poison of the viper, and hatch every species of vermin that annoys mankind; so extraordinary merit, while it adorns and sustains the common

THE
B R I T O N.

NUMBER I.

To be continued every SATURDAY. *Price Two-pence Halfpenny.*

" *Ego semper ea mente fui, ut, quæ utilia æquaque viderentur, consilia de*
" *republica afferrem : quod quidem hoc præsertim tempore facturus sum :*
" *in quo si concordiam, abjecta contentione & fastidio, inter nos confirma-*
" *bimus, & ipsi incolumes erimus, & alios vel invitos conservare pote-*
" *rimus.*" CICERO.

SATURDAY, *May 29th.*

HE BRITON thinks it unneceffary to produce
himfelf amidſt the parade of pompous profeſ-
ſions, which ferve only to excite idle curiofity,
and raife expectations which may be attended
with difappointment. Neither will he make any
apology for thus appearing to the public view,
without the ceremony of a formal introduction :
his intention is not to alarm, but appeafe; not to puzzle, but ex-
plain; not to inflame, but to allay. His defign is that which
ought to be the aim, and is the undoubted privilege of every
Briton, to fpeak his opinion freely, and offer his advice with de-
cency and candour, on every fubject that concerns the communi-
ty, of which he is a member; to watch the exertions of power and
prerogative; to obferve the tides of popular commotion; to detect
the falfehood of malice; to expofe and refute the infinuations of
calumny; to pluck the mafk of patriotifm from the front of fac-
tion, and the torch of difcord from the hand of fedition.

A   To

The Briton, Recto of First Leaf, First Number, 29 May 1762.
(Special Collections and Rare Books, University of Minnesota Library.)

weal, has the particular faculty of generating and inflaming the virulence of envy, and all her rancorous attendants.

I was led to this reflection by perusing the last number of a weekly paper, called the Monitor;[2] a paper so devoid of all merit in the execution, that the author, conscious of his own unimportance and incapacity, seems to have had recourse, in despair, to the only expedient which he thought would give him any chance for engaging the attention of the public; to insinuation against the Th——ne, and abuse on the M——y. He knew that calumny was a weed which throve in every soil: that where credulity, and a propensity to scandal prevailed, fiction would make proselytes, and scurrility be heard with pleasure. Full of this idea, he has undertaken the vilest work of the worst incendiary: he has scattered his fire-arrows with a rash and desperate hand; he has not only directed them against a M——y without blame, but even dared to aim them at the bosom of a Sovereign that never knew dishonour.

It can hardly be supposed, that a meer attention to self-interest, even in the most sordid and illiberal mind, should instigate a man to bid defiance thus to truth and common honesty, to stifle the suggestions of conscience, and broach those calumnies with his hand, to which his heart must have given the Lie. No, his malice must have been pointed by personal hatred; his pen must have been guided by implacable revenge. This conjecture will appear to have the greater force, if we consider, that in feigning facts his passion has hurried him beyond the bounds of probability; and that in following the *ignis fatuus*[3] of his resentment, he has lost sight of all regard to his own safety. Though he has turned his abuse into the channel of insinuation, his violation of truth is so flagrant as to stand self-refuted, and his calumny so atrocious, as to subject him to the correction of the law. This being the case, he might be left to the fate of his own rancour and absurdity; to incur the contempt of all honest men, and be indulged with scope, until he hath strangled himself with the tether of his own malice. But as there is no slander so bare-faced, as not to produce some effect, and no argument so frail, as not to persuade some wellmeaning individuals, whom it may be worth while to undeceive; I shall take the trouble to examine the particulars of this honest essay, and, I doubt not, shall be able to convict the author, not barely of fallacy, but of fraud, not of a weakness only, but of wickedness also.

The motto he has chosen, by way of text, is a quotation from Tacitus,[4] implying, that Sejanus, by various arts, gained such ascendency over the mind of Tiberius, as rendered that prince dark and reserved to all others, but undisguised and uncautious to him alone. The motto serves not only as a text to be descanted upon by this candid Monitor, but as the hand on scandal's dial, to point out the real objects of his obloquy and abuse: for, every reader knows that Sejanus was a minister and favourite, and that Tiberius was the sovereign of Rome. Every reader likewise knows, that Sejanus was the most wicked minister of one of the most execrable tyrants that ever disturbed the peace of mankind; and every reader of common penetration must know, that if the Monitor had any meaning at all, it must have been to insinuate, that there was some resemblance between Tiberius and the r——g Prince; between Sejanus and the present M——r. But is it possible that any man should be so abandoned to all sense of honour, and of shame, so infatuated by rage and malevolence, as to hint a comparison so void of all propriety, so injurious to virtue, and so scandalously opposite to truth, that the falsehood and rancour of it glare in the face of the whole nation! Let this political firebrand step forth, and, armed with all his effrontery, point out one circumstance of similitude between the characters of Tiberius and his own S——n. Can he produce one instance of insolence, cruelty, profligacy, or oppression, chargeable on the King of Great B——n? Can he discover one circumstance that arraigns his prudence? Can he fix the least imputation on his morals? He cannot, he dare not descend to particulars which would answer his purpose, and therefore he restrains himself to a general charge, conveyed in the most insidious insinuation, hoping that it may have some effect among those who have no opportunity, nor capacity, nor inclination, to examine the truth.

If he has presumed to lift his irreverent pen, in order to blacken the conduct of his Sovereign, it is not to be wondered at, that he should pour forth the foulest stream of his calumny to disguise and defile the character of his servants. Having in this candid essay premised, that it is dangerous for a Prince to have a *Favourite*, he proceeds to describe what he calls the *Favourite* of a crowned head; and in this description, unites all the bad qualities that can be conceived to center in the breast of one man. "Without merit or service, he acquires a great and almost exclusive influence and power over the mind of his Royal Master: By an early admission to his presence, conversation, and private recreations, he seizes every opportunity, to discover his weaknesses, to mark his foibles, and to ingratiate himself, till he gains an entire ascendant over his will, and governs him without controul. Having succeeded thus far during a minority, by meer professions of duty, and a diligent attention to gratify his passions, he attempts to maintain his own influence and power, by destroying and preventing the growth of great and royal sentiments in his mind, and to usurp the whole authority and management of the state, by filling his Master's head with pleasures and unprofitable amusements.—He guards against every means to detect his usurpation; he permits none but such as are devoted to his interest, to approach the Prince; and those he disposes about the Royal Presence, in such a manner as to make them his spies, to keep out men of merit, to degrade patriotism with a mortal hatred, to assist him in the sacrifice of public interest to his private views, and to share with him the fruits and advantages of the Royal Favour—His conduct is founded upon flattery—he loves none but himself, and sacrificeth honour, gratitude, and justice, to his private interest."[5]

Waving the inaccuracy and inelegance of stile in these curious periods, we shall point out the absurdity, and detect the malice they contain. Because bad men have been the favourites of weak and worthless princes, does it follow, that every individual, distinguished by the favour of his sovereign, must be such a caitiff as you have described? In what school of logic did you learn to make this wise inference? because some weak princes have given themselves up wholly to the guidance of wicked favourites, and followed their pernicious counsels, to the ruin of themselves, and the damage of their subjects, does it follow that all princes are weak, and that all favourites are wicked? If you would insinuate this is the present case in your own country, you may be answered in one word: every reflection that occurs, every honest man you meet, even your own conscience will tell you, it is an infamous untruth.

In any court of judicature, a general charge, unsupported by evidence, is answered and refuted by a general negation. Even where there is a suspicion of guilt; unless that guilt is made manifest by circumstantial proof, the culprit is of course acquitted. Shall the privilege granted to the meanest subject, be refused to the Prince? Shall we upon your unfounded insinuations condemn our So——n, against whom your inventive malice has not been able to collect the least grounds for suspicion? or, would you deprive him of the prerogative, which every prince and every private man enjoys, of forming friendships, of rewarding services, of distinguishing merit? Have you exhibited any specimens of his weakness, of his tyranny, of his having given himself up implicitly to the pernicious counsels of any favourite? Have you adduced one circumstance to render it probable, that any individual has crept into his favour by the vile arts of flattery and vicious complaisance; or to prove, that any favourite has maintained his influence, by discouraging patriotism, rejecting merit, planting the throne with spies, excluding truth from the Royal ear, and sacrificing the good of the public to his own private advantage? If no such circumstances are to be found—if on the contrary, our Sovereign's character is in all respects so amiable as to engage the affection of every one not blasted with envy, not inflamed with rancour: if his heart benevolently sympathises with all the children of distress: if his hand is liberally opened to every appearance of merit: if his sole aim is to augment and secure the happiness of his people with the independence of his crown; and he has invariably pursued that aim with prudence, dignity, and resolution: if he has communicated his councils and diffused his confidence among the nobles of the land; among men distinguished by their virtue, capacity and experience, without partiality of favour, without distinction of party: if the person whose character you have defamed and traduced by implication, under the odious title of *favourite*, be a nobleman of unblemished integrity,[6] who attached himself to his Sovereign in his tender years, who helped to form his young mind to virtue, who infused into his heart the principles of a patriot king, directing him to pursuits which were truly royal; if he has ever scorned, and taught his Prince to scorn the vile arts of a sycophant; if, in the execution of his office, he hath ever avoided the least appearance of usurpation, and stood forth among the other servants of the crown, the open steady honest counsellor of his Sovereign, undisturbed by prejudice, undismayed by clamour. — If all these suppositions are true; and that they are literally true your own heart will declare; what character must you maintain in the opinion of all good men; let me add, in your own opinion? the character of a desperate incendiary, perhaps the partisan and tool of disappointed ambition, endeavouring to depreciate one of the best princes that ever reigned, to defame one of the most upright ministers that ever lived; to embroil a virtuous prince with an affectionate people; to clog the wheels of government at a juncture which is truly critical; and finally, to ruin that commonwealth, which it could not rule.

No. 2. Saturday, 5 June 1762.

Adversarios in odium rapiemus, si quid eorum spurce, superbe, perfidiose, crudeliter, confidenter, maliciose, flagitiose factum, vel dictum proseremus.

CICERO de PACE.[1]

I know not whether it should most excite mirth or indignation, to observe the author of the last letter in the Monitor, pouring forth the epithets of abuse upon the writer of a pamphlet, intitled, "A full exposition of the observations on the papers relative to the rupture with Spain."[2] The truth is, he appears to be sore from the stripes of detection, and twists and twines like an eel on a grid-iron, endeavouring to find some subterfuge through which he may escape with some appearance of credit. For this purpose he has recourse to the art of prevarication, which, however, will not avail.

The Observator, in his inflammatory production, had endeavoured to possess the public with a notion, that the present ministry had garbled and mutilated some, and concealed others, of the papers relating to the rupture with Spain; and Mr. Monitor, like a faithful echo, repeated these terms of garbling, mutilation, and concealment, with a view to keep up the clatter which his fellow labourers, in the forge of faction, had raised. Unluckily for both, the author of the Exposition unmasked their pretences, refuted their sophistry, pointed out their misrepresentations, and shewed *how a plain tale could put them down*.[3] He proved, that all the material papers relative to that rupture had been laid before the parliament: he affirmed, that if the late m——r, or his adherents, had really thought otherwise, they would have closed with the proposal made by a right honourable gentleman,[4] who declared, that if any other paper were thought necessary, it should be produced, upon a motion made for that purpose: but, it was not their intention, it was not their interest to make this demand; their clamour was not to be raised upon any thing that could be shewn; but on the presumption of something that was concealed.

This obstinate fact the Monitor endeavours to evade, by giving an artful turn to the proposal of the right honourable gentleman, who (he affirms) declared only, *that if any particular paper, necessary to the vindication of certain persons, be specifically moved for, it might be given.* "This (says he) was a fallacious offer; as the right honourable gentleman very well knew the late minister could not mark out, nor call, in a parliamentary way, for a specific paper, with the contents of which he had been intrusted before, by his S——n, under the seal of secrecy!"[5]

I shall allow him, (as he seems to be in distress) the benefit of this interpretation, as far as it will go: but, I must also observe, for the sake of truth, that a certain noble lord promised to apply to the crown for a dispensation from the oath of secrecy, with full liberty to lord T——,[6] or any other, to lay before the house all he knew concerning this subject; nay, he twice afterwards repeated the offer, which, however, the friends and patrons of the Monitor were wise enough to decline, well knowing how little the exposure of those papers would conduce to their reputation.

What therefore must we think of the modesty of this Monitor, who still rings the changes upon garbling, mutilating, and concealment, after he is thus fairly convicted, of knowing that his friends might have commanded, and may still command *any*, or *all* of the papers, about which they have made such a noise, and endeavoured to excite a spirit of dissatisfaction against the K——g and his ministers? Will not the unprejudiced part of mankind look upon him and his coadjutors as the tools of faction, who have seared their own consciences; who have left honour and veracity on their left hand; sat down to write against their own conviction; bedaubed their leader with undeserved encomiums; and blackened his successor with unmerited abuse?

Nay, this consistent penman, the professed admirer and beef-eater[7] of the m — r, who avowedly patronized the German war, attempts to defend him from the imputation of these German measures, by ascribing the first Prussian treaty,[8] to his immediate predecessor in the secretary of state's office. This remark, which seems to have escaped him in the hurry and agitation of his spirits, is at least an implied acknowledgment, that very little honour is due to the authors of the negotiation; and if this be the case, how did that measure, which was so scandalous in the beginning, become so honourable in the sequel? Did it change its nature in being adopted by Mr. P — ? Was his administration so holy as to consecrate the sin of his predecessor?

You say, so far as he was concerned, the publication of those sacred records, would tend only to increase his honour, and the good opinion in which he stands with his country. Let it be recorded then, for his honour, that if he was not the first proposer, he adopted and executed the project of an hitherto unheard-of alliance, by which he subjected his country to the payment of an annual tribute equally enormous and disgraceful, without stipulating one reciprocal advantage for such humiliating condescension; that after he had declaimed for a series of years, with peculiar vehemence against foreign connections; after he had refused to reinforce his sovereign's son with one British regiment, when he was out-numbered, and almost surrounded by the foe on the banks of the Weser;[9] after he had publicly denounced vengeance against that minister who should presume to send a single man to that continent; he all at once renounced these maxims; precipitated himself into foreign measures, with an impetuosity of zeal that transcends belief; involved his country in a G — n war, as opposite to her interest, as ineffectual for the purpose intended: a war in which her blood and treasure have been lavished with a wasteful hand: a war in which she hath been produced upon the stage like a prize-fighter[10] by her own mercenaries, and undergone every species of indignity and imposition.

The Expositor had said, that all the papers relating to the rupture with Spain were actually produced; and that the other transactions with the court of Madrid had no relation to the said rupture. "Ridiculous! (cries the Monitor) did not the concealed papers contain three claims made by Spain, relating to the present rupture with that nation? Were not those claims declared by France to be the seed of a new war, in which she would be obliged to take a share with Spain? Was it possible to make a good peace by granting those claims? Was there any way to secure ourselves from the bad consequences of those claims, but by a due exertion of our strength? — well then, all the papers relative to those claims, ought to have been produced."

This indeed is such a rhapsody, as truly characterises the candour and capacity of our sage politician. To your first interrogation I answer No; the three claims made by Spain had certainly no relation to the rupture with that crown — What were those claims? I will refresh your memory — The court of Madrid claimed our evacuation of their territory, upon which we had encroached in America, declaring at the same time it would, in case of our compliance, settle in our favour the long contested right of cutting logwood on that coast. — It claimed a share of the cod-fishery on the banks of Newfoundland, founded upon an old pretension, which, by the treaty of Utrecht,[11] it was authorised to ascertain. — It claimed the restitution of some ships which were taken under Spanish colours by the English cruisers since the beginning of the present war. Now I will ask any man of common honesty and common sense, whether these claims, asserted in the course of a long negotiation afford a sufficient cause for England to break with Spain? whether they do not rather imply the sense of an injury received on the part of that crown, and constitute the cause of dissatisfaction with the m — y of Great Britain?[12] If a neighbour accosting you in a civil manner, puts you in mind of an old claim he has upon your estate, and begs the matter may be compromised in an amicable manner; would you, instead of discussing the subject calmly, lift up your cane and knock him down, without further ceremony or intimation? This might be Robin-hood law; but certainly it would be deemed by all the sober and honest part of mankind, an outrageous insult upon the law of nature and of nations,[13] upon the principles of eternal justice.

But if these claims were thought adequate provocation to war and hostility, why did Mr. P— so long refrain, as they certainly were repeated during the whole course of his administration? why did he tamely acquiesce in the only transaction that could be deemed an insult on the part of Spain, I mean the seizure and detention of the Antigallican privateer and her prize,[14] which undoubtedly was a shameful instance of partiality in favour of our enemies? why did he truckle on this occasion to the court of Madrid, contrary to the general sense of his fellow-subjects, contrary to the honour of his country? why did he condescend to protract the negotiation upon the disputes already mentioned; to suggest reconciling memorials, and instruct our embassador to deal mildly and gently in his remonstrances to the ministers of his Catholic Majesty? If the claims were so injurious as to justify an immediate rupture; why did he pursue this pacific plan, even after that step of the Spanish ministry, against which he and his partizans have so loudly declaimed as an additional affront, that never could be forgiven; I mean the memorial presented to him by M. de Bussy,[15] in favour of the Spanish pretensions? because he knew, in his own heart, that the old claims had nothing in them of an inflammatory nature, and might have been easily adjusted by a friendly communication: because he was convinced that Spain had no hostile intention in mingling her concerns with the negotiation for peace between Great-Britain and France.

To ask, were not these claims declared by France to be the seed of a new war is a question truly ridiculous. Every dispute whatever may be inflamed into a war. The late m——r has shewn, that the most trivial disputes may be blown up into a dangerous and expensive war, by the turbulence and ambition of either party. But, is it for the interest or honour of any nation to cherish those petty seeds into a war, which may be destroyed or removed by pacific intercourse and friendly mediation? Neither is the Monitor more fortunate in his other interrogations. To say it was impossible to make a good peace by granting those claims is begging the question—it is taking for granted, that no peace could be made but by admitting those claims; a conclusion that has no relation to the premises. The Court of Spain itself had pointed out a healing expedient, which might have been made the basis of a solid and lasting pacification. "Withdraw your settlers from the *Rio Tinto*[16] (says the Spanish ministry) and his Catholic Majesty promises, on the word of a King, that the English shall be admitted to the privilege of logwood-cutting on the coast of New Spain." What was this, but asking us to make some slight reparation to the honour of his crown, for having invaded and occupied his territories in the time of profound peace; and declaring he would confirm that right or privilege which hath been the main source of all our late contests with the Spanish monarchy? Had this material point been settled, the other relating to the fishery might, and undoubtedly would have remained undetermined, as it has been for a great length of time, and as much neglected as the obsolete claim of his Britannic Majesty to the crown and dominions of France. Here then is a plain and easy way found to secure ourselves from the bad consequences of those claims, without any exertion of our strength, which indeed we could not have exerted solely on account of those claims, consistent with any sound maxim of policy, or with any law divine or human.

This being the case, nothing can be more absurd than the Monitor's deduction, "that all the papers relative to those claims ought to have been produced." The house was almost unanimously of opinion, that the examination of such a heap of papers relating to a negotiation of many years, on a subject altogether foreign to the purpose, would be a tedious and a needless task. Had the patrons and prompters of the Monitor thought otherwise;

had they known any paper, the perusal of which would either have gratified their spleen or conduced to the glorification of their conduct; they would have urged the noble lord to the performance of what he proposed; namely to obtain of the king an absolution from the obligation to secrecy; that any particular paper may be called for specifically in parliament: or had they declined his application, they might have had recourse to a motion, in consequence of which, the whole cargo would have been submitted to public inspection.

But if neither of these offers are accepted, and their emissaries still persist in rebellowing the terms, *garbling, mutilation,* and *concealment,* like Othello raging about the handkerchief;[17] if they, in defiance of common sense, proceed to clamour about the expulsion of the immaculate P——, while his own modest appeal to the public bears testimony to his *voluntary and head-strong resignation,* even against the express request of his S——n: if they swell their bill of imaginary grievances, with the patriotic abdication of his noble friend, who, with a spirit of sagacity peculiar to himself, gave up all his gay prospects of R——l favour, all his importance in the council, all his consequence in the state, for a place in the triumphal car of his political pattern, while he rode in procession, through the hired acclamations of a venal and ignorant multitude; they may make some proselytes among the dupes of hypocrisy and the slaves of prejudice; but the sensible and candid part of their fellow-subjects must suppose that these demagogues want to search for the lost arcanum of m——l power, by the light of national flames kindled for that purpose; that in the horrors of disappointed ambition, they have engaged their adherents to blacken the present ministry, by the most insidious misrepresentations; that they have retained by the week, a callous hard-mouthed drudge, to discharge a periodical issue of foul invectives against the characters of honest men; to circulate the ensnaring oracles of a false deity called mock-patriotism; and to blow the scorching furnace of discord and sedition.

No. 3. Saturday, 12 June 1762.

— Aliusque et idem
nasuris.
HORACE.[1]

The Monitor has found a coadjutor, who appears under the name of North Briton;[2] and now this brace of honest politicians vouch for one another's integrity, like the crazy watchman and his goose;[3] the one proclaimed the hours at noon-day, and the other cackled approbation. I shrewdly suspect, however, that these seemingly distinct personages are one and the same individual, under different disguises, by means of which, he may have an opportunity of extolling in one mask, the trash he obtrudes upon the world in the other. By this contrivance too, he hammers out his metal into a more extended plate of brass leaf, to adorn the character of his patron: at any rate, it will afford room to hedge and to shift, to explain away meanings by which he dare not abide, and to practise more at ease, the art of evasion, in which he seems to be an adept.

Accordingly we find him at that work in the very first page of his lucubration. He denies that the Monitor, in his paper of May 22d, even squinted at the character of his S — n, in the candid parallel he drew; and affirms, there is no mention of Tiberius through the whole of that paper, excepting only in the motto from Tacitus.[4] This is really such a plea, as, we believe, no person upon earth but the Monitor, and his advocate, would have thought of urging. If a man was to be tried for a libel against the government, and would plead in his own defence, that the government was not mentioned, excepting *only in one line*, would not the court laugh at the folly, and be astonished at the effrontery of the culprit? Will not the unprejudiced public be affected in the same manner, by the declaration of this sensible, honest, modest writer, when he affirms that a minister may, in all points, resemble Sejanus, and yet the Sovereign may be a Trajan or a Titus?[5] In other words, the minister may be a corruptor, an oppressor, a poisoner, an assassin, and the Prince who employs this minister, remain one of the best Kings that ever sat on any throne. If this inference were to be distilled with all the art of sophistry, in twenty different alembics, it would in every trial come over stark nonsense and contradiction.

Though the Monitor may now think it convenient to use this subterfuge, he would have been sorry to find his readers such fools as to mistake his meaning, when the paper was first published. Nay, that there might be no doubt about this subject, he took care, in express terms, to treat with contempt the character of the Prince, whose minister he has branded with the odious name of Favourite. "He improved (says he) every opportunity to discover *his weaknesses*, to mark *his foibles* — he filled his Master's head with pleasures and unprofitable amusements. — When a Prince has once given himself up to the management of such a Favourite, he may be carried as far as the ambition of his Favourite pleaseth, in *tyranny*, in *profusion*, in *pleasures*, in the *neglect of his just rights and national interest*."[6] If therefore his abuse was directed against the person of a B — sh M — r, and he himself does not deny this was the case; is there a reader of common sense that does not see, is there one of common honesty who will not own, that it reflected the most flagitious reproach upon the character of the Prince by whom that M — r was patronised? Who will not say, that this shameless dauber is not endeavouring to varnish the most hideous part of the picture which himself or his friend had presumed to draw, and labouring to screen his malice behind the thin curtain of prevarication.

I said, in my first paper, the administration is conducted with such integrity as defies reproach; and this wretched trifler replies, "The king of Prussia, *still our ally*, tells the world the contrary."[7]—In what manner, and upon what occasion, has the king of Prussia impeached the integrity of the British administration?—until this is declared, we shall number this assertion among the other infamous calumnies which have dropped from the pens of a faction in despair. If the K— of P— was so unreasonable as to complain, that a stop has been put to the annual tribute,[8] in the payment of which, the honour and the interest of the nation were so scandalously prostituted; the rectitude of that measure would not be the less obvious. All Europe would have cause to wonder, not that the subsidy has ceased, but that it was ever granted on such inglorious conditions; and the people of Great Britain would have reason to rejoice, in having a ministry endued with honesty and resolution, to disengage their necks from such a vile subjection.

But I am challenged by this umbra of the Monitor, to name the success which hath attended the measures of the present administration.——What he has so fairly mentioned as a reproach upon their integrity, I insist upon as a proof of their vigour and success. They have broken the shackles of this dishonourable G——n connection, and in that single article saved near a million annually to the nation; they have contributed in a great measure to deliver that boasted ally from the most formidable of all his enemies; and by the wisdom of their negotiations, prevented a new war from breaking out in the North of Europe. If we turn our eyes to the steps they have taken, more immediately relating to the interest of Great Britain, we shall find they have reinforced Sir Charles Saunders[9] so powerfully, as to enable him to maintain the empire of the Mediterranean; to annihilate the commerce and navigation of the enemy in that sea, to insult the coasts, and block up the harbours of France and Spain: they have, with uncommon diligence and dispatch, equipped and forwarded a gallant expedition, by which the important conquest of Martinique, Granada, and all the neutral islands in the West-Indies,[10] hath been atchieved. They have, at the same juncture of time, sent forth another powerful armament against the chief settlements of Spain[11] in that part of the world; and in all probability, by this time, the object of their enterprise is accomplished; at least, if any unforeseen accident may have frustrated the design, the miscarriage cannot with any justice be imputed to the indolence or neglect of the administration.

I have now named the *time when*, and the *place where*, and leave it to the world to decide upon the candour and veracity of this writer. I leave it to the judicious reader to compare the transactions of this year with those of 1760, when the Monitor's patron was in the zenith of M——l power; when our fleets and armies lingered in the harbours of Great Britain, a whole summer, and not one stroke was struck against the enemy, on our own element, although twenty millions had been exacted from the people for the service of the year.

With respect to underhand offers made to the court of Vienna,[12] I should be glad to know in what manner this author was made privy to such offers: did the M——y consult with him or his employers on the subject? or did the court of Vienna communicate the secret to the Monitor and his worthy collegue in the work of defamation? Considering how their characters stand in point of veracity, we shall beg leave to look upon this as another oblique shaft of malice, until the author thinks proper to be more particular in his information. But if it should appear in the issue, that those underhand offers were no more than fair and honourable proposals, to terminate by a just and equitable peace, a war which hath been attended with such misery and desolation; a war kindled by ambition and rapacity, fomented by a B——sh M——r in servile compliance with the prejudices and predilection of a weak S——n, and maintained by the blood and treasure of the B——sh nation; the honest part of that nation in particular, and of mankind in general, will think themselves obliged to the M——y for taking steps so suitable to the distressed circumstances of their country; so conformable to the interests of religion and humanity: but, what will they think of those audacious emissaries, who with a virulence of rancour peculiar to themselves, attempt to poison the best qualities, and pervert what ought to be the theme of universal approbation, into a subject of censure and reproach?

Like a wretch in danger of drowning, that catches at every straw, this indefatigable emissary lays hold on the most trivial circumstances to alarm the public. What a clamour has he raised about the innocent head-piece that appears in the first page of the Briton! "He has displayed the Royal Arms at the head of his papers; (cries he in an affected surprise) does he mean to intimidate? does he mean to insinuate, that his paper comes forth with the authority of a Gazette; and that he fights under the banners of the administration?"[13] No, Sir, he means nothing less. Had you made an excursion to Pater-noster-Row,[14] you might have seen, with half an eye, that the King's Arms make the sign of my publisher; and, I apprehend, he has a right to use them as such, without giving offence. Had he displayed an Orator's head, or a Negro's head, or a Hog's head,[15] it would have been of the same consequence to the writer, who arrogates to himself no authority, but that which is derived from a strict regard to truth and morality; and these are the only banners under which he presumes to write.

As to the precious stuff this babbler has thrown out about the words *Briton*, and *Free Briton*, and *Foolish Briton*, *Alliterations*, *Scotticisms*, *Language*, and *Sentiments*, I shall treat it with the scorn it deserves, as the vulgar recrimination of an illiberal mind, which hath received its first and most lasting impressions, *Non in aula, sed in caula;* not in a hall, but in a hog's-stye.[16] Nothing is so easy as to retort the epithets of fool, dunce, coxcomb, and venal scribbler; they naturally offer their assistance to bad authors, when they are at a loss for matter and argument. Had any writer of character taxed me with venality, I should have been mortified: but I laugh to hear myself accused as venal, by a scribe who, in defiance of his own conscience, has inlisted himself in the dirty work of propagating slander, and circulating false surmises, to raise a combustion in the commonwealth. What interested motives he may have in pursuing this honourable occupation, I shall not give myself the trouble to inquire: but with respect to the M — y, I will venture to affirm, whatever his inclinations may be, it is not in his power to be venal; for, his talents are too contemptible to bear any price.

The national sting in the tail of his essay, relating to pensioned Scotchmen, is a most unfortunate sarcasm for the author. His patron[17] will not thank him for touching upon this string: it is like talking of halters in the house of a man whose father was hanged. — A pension is a thing not to be joked with; it is a temptation to which, in all probability, our author's virtue will not be exposed: but if it should, we presume he would follow the example of his Great Archetype —, that phœnix of ministers, that mirror of disinterested patriotism. — Having set him up as a pattern of all earthly perfections, he would moreover be apt to imitate him in point of gratitude, in receiving the bounty, and then kicking his heels in the face of his benefactor.

No. 4. Saturday, 19 June 1762.

— Surgis tu pallidus Ajax
Dicturus dubiâ pro libertate, Bubulco
Judice — rumpe miser tensum jecur, ut tibi lasso
Figantur virides scalarum gloria Palmæ.
JUVENAL.[1]

To the BRITON.

SIR,

I shall not enquire whether you are a North Briton, a South Briton, or an Antient Briton, but I shall venture to pronounce with your antagonist, that you are little better than a *Foolish Briton*, for having undertaken a task at once so odious and impracticable. Had you stood forth the champion of any particular minister however respectable he might be in point of real character, I should consider you as a sort of Don Quixote in humanity, going to encounter the wind-mills of popular clamour and abuse, which it is the passion and privilege of an English mob to raise and discharge at all administrations. But in taking up the cudgels for a minister who happened to be born on the north-side of the Tweed, I know not whether you most excite my pity or indignation. All you can say, Sir, in his justification, may be answered in one word, and that word shall be unanswerable: it shall have more efficacy than the ABRACADABRA,[2] or any talisman that ever necromancy contrived.

Should you assert that L——d B—te is a man of worth and probity, and challenge his bitterest enemies to produce one instance to the prejudice of his moral character; should you declare that his abilities are equal to his integrity; should you defy the Monitor, and his crew of associates, to point out one error or neglect, or mark of timidity in his administration, to trace the least sign of corruption in his heart, rapacity in his disposition, or partiality in the distribution of his favours; should you affirm, that his loyalty and attachment have been proved in a long course of the most faithful and important services; that as the sovereign can have no interest independent of the happiness of his people, and as he has owned and evinced a heart that is truly British,[3] the minister who implanted, will endeavour to cultivate these sentiments; that his duty and interest will coincide in exerting his best endeavours for the service and welfare of England, where he possesses an ample fortune, and is intimately allied with the best families of the kingdom; for, where his chief substance is, there his heart ought to be. I answer, "All this may be very true, but I will silence you with one word; he is a—*Scotchman*." This is a term which implies every thing that is vile and detestable.

I remember a contest between two physicians who made interest for being elected to the service of a certain hospital in the city; an honest fish-monger accosting one of the candidates, expressed his satisfaction, that the doctor's opponent was a man of a worse character than himself. The candidate, surprised at this declaration, eagerly desired to know in what particular; when the citizen gravely replied, "The worst they can say of you is, that you are an Atheist, and a S——te, but your competitor is a *Scotchman*." If a player introduces in a farce, a very great scoundrel in the character of a Scotchman,

you see with what eagerness the good people of England croud to the per-
formance; you hear with what shouts they applaud the piece. Whether this
be the character of the Scots in general, they care not to reflect, but chuckle
with particular pleasure over the national indignity; and in this particular
alone, countenance and encourage the defamer, whom they hold to be equally
stupid and infamous in every other respect. If a foreigner of no extraordi-
nary character, should undertake a public work, he is permitted to finish his
undertaking in peace; but if a native of North Briton, who has distinguished
himself by his ingenuity, should be employed upon a subsequent task of the
same nature, all the mouths of clamour are immediately opened. Pamphlets
are written, and prints cast off to revile and ridicule his character, and every
ale-house rings with his reproach. What has this miserable artist done? is any
doubt made of his capacity? is any exception taken to his morals? No: what
then? he is a *Scotchman*, and that includes *reprobation*.

Should you plead against the prescription, that the Scots and we are fellow-
subjects, incorporated by a solemn and constitutional treaty of union, intitling
them to every right and privilege which any other Briton enjoys: that for
more than a century past, they have been indiscriminately employed in the
army, in the navy, and in the state: that they have borne the first offices in
the cabinet, and in the field, and generally executed their respective trusts
with diligence and fidelity. To these hints I reply, that you may as well lull a
tempest with a whisper, as influence the mob with the dictates of equity, or
remove with argument the barriers of popular prejudice.

You will be apt to insinuate, that such an attempt to blow up jealousies,
and foment animosity between the people that inhabit different parts of the
British dominions, at a juncture too, when we are involved in an expensive
and dangerous war, is the office of an unprincipled wretch, who hath sold
himself as an emissary to the enemies of his country, and consequently as
such, must be detested by every one who retains the least sentiment of patrio-
tism. — Lack-a-day! how childishly you argue! It is not to people who exercise
their reason, that such appeals are made; you are not weak enough to imagine,
that any man who gives his reason fair play, could, upon reading the general
tropes of abuse, so plentifully discharged by the Monitor and his confederates
against the Earl of B—te, be inspired with any emotion but that of contempt
for the worthless authors. No, they apply to the million; to the base illiberal
herd who have neither sense to attain conviction, nor sentiment to own the
force of truth, who fatten upon the spoils of reputation, and greedily snuff up
the fumes of scandal, even to intoxication.

This is the last resource of a gasping faction; and it has this advantage over all others, that it can be enjoyed without talents, decency, or discretion. Cast your eyes upon the *North Briton* of last Saturday, and you will see what sort of understrappers are used to sound the horn of sedition. Never were such recruits enlisted by any former officer in the trained bands of slander; never before was such a babbler admitted into the pack of defamation:—qualified, I own, to keep up the cry, and that is all his employers require: "we expect from your endeavours, (say they) neither argument nor fact, neither wit nor veracity: all we desire is, that you will exalt your throat in general invectives against B—te, and plentifully bespatter the whole Scotch nation." He has fully answered their purpose.

Having stirred the fire, prepared the cauldron, and invoked the demon of discord, like the witch in Macbeth, he howls aloud, "Beware the thane of B—te,[4] beware the first lord commissioner of the treasury![5] He will build bridges over the Tweed, and bring in a deluge of his countrymen." If you ask what this minister has done to incur these suspicions? Has he squandred away the national treasure among the natives of North Briton? Has he thrust them into places or pensions over the bellies of better men? Has he discovered the least partiality in their favour? No, nothing of this kind has been alledged; but then he is a member of the Scottish nation, and therefore unfit for the office of a British minister; unqualified both in principle and capacity. Scotland has given birth to two dangerous rebellions[6]—But was the Earl of B—te, or any of his family engaged in either? No, they were principally concerned in extinguishing both; and if we condemn a whole nation for the crime of a few insurgents, I doubt we must look for a m——r in some other country than in England, which hath been as fruitful in insurrections as any kingdom in Europe.—If Scotland is to be upbraided with the last rebellion, let it also be remembered, that not one hundredth part of the Scottish nation was embarked in that desperate scheme: that not one native of Scotland, employed in the service of the government, shrunk from his duty, or betrayed his trust on that occasion; that his Majesty, convinced of their fidelity, entrusted the chief command of the forces in South Britain, at that ticklish conjuncture, to a Scotchman;[7] that the Duke of Cumberland led the Scots by whole regiments against the rebels at Culloden; that the number of Scotchmen in his army on that auspicious day, was at least equal to that of their southern brethren, and every officer that fell on his side in the battle, was a native of North Britain. Let it be moreover remembered, that many of those delinquents were cut off by the sword; that some were offered up as necessary victims to public justice; and that the survivors have since literally washed away their offences with their blood; witness their bones now bleaching in almost every quarter of the globe, — at Cape Breton, Ticonderoga, Fort du Quesne, and Quebec, in Guadaloupe and Martinique, before the walls of Pondicherry, and in the plains of Westphalia;[8] witness those swarms of miserable maimed Highlanders, who are daily seen crawling about with scarce any vestige of the human form, in the skirts of this metropolis: but, the great objection still remains, and that is insurmountable; "Though Mr. Horace Walpole has paid a national compliment to the understanding of Scotchmen,[9] yet Mr. Walpole, with all his partiality to that people, will not say that the Scots have any humour: now Lord B—te being a Scotchman, can have no humour; and if he has no humour, how can he pretend to rule the English, who are a nation of humorists?"

This is truly a diverting specimen of the sense and sagacity of those curious penmen, who are hired to rail at the administration: it puts me in mind of an inference made by the ever-memorable Orator Henley,[10] when he was once called upon in public as an umpire, to decide a dispute between the facetious Mr. Foote, and the renowned Opthalmiater,[11] who complained that the other had injured his character, by *taking him off* for the entertainment of the town. Mr. Foote alledged that he had a particular respect for the chevalier as an oculist; but that he ridiculed him only as an orator, in which character he appeared ridiculous and *unnatural*. Orator Henley being desired by the audience to decide upon the merits of those two gentlemen, passed sentence against Mr. Foote, "because, (says he) as he imitates the unnatural parts of the doctor's character, he is an *unnatural* imitator."

If you ask who this Henley was, I will endeavour to give you satisfaction. He was a tall brawny rustic who had made shift to obtain holy orders, and for a little time enjoyed a small curacy; his time was chiefly spent at Hockley in the Hole,[12] at the Bear-garden, in skittle-grounds, in ale cellars, booths, and low b——dy houses, where he distinguished himself occasionally as a boxer, cudgel-player, and hector.[13] From threshing cobblers, he took to threshing his own scull, and commenced author. He attacked all cotemporary writers, lampooned his Ordinary,[14] and supplying the want of genius with impudence and scurrility, acquired a few admirers among the wits of Butcher-row:[15] the irregularities of his life having brought upon him the censure of his bishop, he was deprived of his cure, and turned free-thinker in despair. He offered his talents as a political writer to the minister for the time being, and meeting with a repulse, set up a paper against the government, which, though equally replete with virulence and dulness, soon sunk into contempt. Thus rejected both by church and state, he opened, what he called, an oratory, among his friends, the butchers of Clare-market: there he acted the buffoon in canonicals every Sunday, and for some time subsisted, by regaling his hearers with a strange olio[16] of blasphemy, treason, and nonsense. Poor Henley was in hopes of attaining the pillory, or of being brought to the cart's-tail;[17] events which would have given him consequence among the multitude on whom he depended; but the ministry and the bishops were so cruel as to take no notice of his demerits. The mob grew tired of his harrangues; even his friends of Clare-market fell off: his oratory was deserted: he had recourse to dram-drinking, and died in great want and obscurity. The chapel is now to be let, and perhaps the North Briton may know some parson militant,[18] who will prove a worthy successor to the defunct.

No. 5. Saturday, 26 June 1762.

Turno tempus erit, magno cum optaverit emptum
Intactum Pallanta.

VIRGIL.[1]

To the BRITON.

SIR,

I was one of those who thought you had undertaken a task which you would never be able to perform. I could not conceive it was possible that the conduct of any minister could be justified, excepting still the patriot-minister, the minister of the people, who appears in this our hemisphere, like a white elephant in the kingdom of Pegu,[2] once in two or three centuries. I am now undeceived in my opinion.

The tools of faction are fairly convicted of the vilest calumny levelled at the present adm——n, and glanced at the S——n himself. Detected in this worst species of detraction, they have shuffled and evaded: they have endeavored to explain away their own meaning: they have pleaded insanity in excuse of sedition, and floundered from one absurdity into another, until they have ex-cited the compassion, even of those who detest their malice. You challenged them to produce one fact to the prejudice of the m——r's character, which they had so liberally reviled. Could they afford one instance of his corrup-tion, misconduct, or partiality? Here then is a phœnomenon which, I believe, never appeared in England before: an administration that defies the censure of prying envy, and unwearied faction!

What a dust they raised about the papers relating to the negotiation with

Spain,[3] endeavouring to propagate a belief that some of them were suppressed for sinister purposes! You and others explained this affair: their allegations were refuted, and they thought proper to drop the subject. They challenged you in their turn, to name any instance of activity or address in the present administration. You enumerated a greater number of particulars than, I am persuaded, they desired to see; and as they thought it incumbent upon them to say something in extenuation of the praise so justly due to the ministry on the score of those transactions, the Monitor of last Saturday[4] has performed this office in such a manner, that I know not whether most to admire his understanding or integrity.

I shall pass by his flowers of abuse; his recrimination of malice, falsehood, and detraction, which come with a good grace from a writer, the detected minister of obloquy, the professed retailer of reproach, who exists entirely dependant on his talent for defamation: and here I must beg leave to disapprove of your engaging in any altercation of this nature—Leave all personalities and national reflections to this honest politician, and the low buffoons who squirt their illiberal sarcasms in that despicable paper the North Briton; convinced that these are themes with which the public will soon be cloyed, and consoling yourself in the mean time with the charitable reflection, that such authors are in some sort excuseable, as they seem altogether unqualified to gain a livelihood by any other species of writing.

But, to return from this digression, the Monitor seems to be mightily scandalized at your calling the treaty with P——a, an inglorious connection, in which the honour and advantage of the nation have been prostituted; and labours hard to bring you in guilty of a libel upon K——g and parliament, for this political blasphemy against one of the capital measures of his patron's administration. He then launches out into a rhapsody in favour of the G——n war; expatiates upon the old hackneyed expressions of the ballance of power, the protestant religion, and the liberties of Europe; and professes astonishment that you should dare to hint at the weakness and predilection of his deceased M——y. I must inform this wise Monitor, that every Briton has a right to speak and write freely on the grievances of his country; that it is no breach of privilege to blame the bad measures of former P——ts; nor treason to mention the weakness of any deceased S——n.

That the G——n war was pernicious to the concerns of Great Britain, as well as to the liberties of Europe, and the interests of humanity; that the protestant religion was entirely out of the question, and only used as a juggling term to dazzle the eye, and puzzle the understanding of the vulgar; that the treaty of P——a was an inglorious connection, by which we entailed upon ourselves the certainty of an enormous expence, without the possibility of receiving any advantage; that the subsidy granted was, in effect, a scandalous tribute, given in consideration of forbearance; that the nation has been drained of above six millions annually, and the British successes in America have been impeded, by maintaining a needless and ineffectual war on the continent of Germany, are truths which have been so often demonstrated beyond all contradiction, and are now become so glaringly self-evident, that every Briton, whose soul is not wholly g — nized, or actuated by worse principles, must assent to them with indignation and chagrin.

But, who is this mild creature, this mirror of decorum; overflowing with the milk of human kindness,[5] who takes offence at your hinting any imperfections in the character of the late K — g; and at your condemning a German war, which hath lavished away our best blood, and added at least thirty millions to the national debt? Pray, mark; it is the worthy Monitor, he, who but the other day, ventured to diffuse the basest insinuations against the character of his living S — n. He, good man, could not bear to be put in mind of a late monarch's prejudices and predilection, against which his patron had so many years declaimed, which all Europe saw, all England felt, and every honest Briton lamented; but he has dared, for the worst purposes of faction, to plant unfounded jealousies around the th — ne, to scatter implied calumnies even upon the character of his P — ce; to depreciate him in the eyes of his people, by implied favouritism; by taxing him with puerile attachments, and weaknesses which had no existence, but in his own vicious invention. This egregious moralist, so delicate with respect to the memory of the late K — g, is, or pretends to be, the implicit admirer of the man, who, even in the face of the senate, on sundry occasions, presumed to stigmatize the conduct and person of that Pr — ce, then his sovereign, with such abusive epithets, that the hearers were struck with astonishment, and the K — himself was so incensed at the unmannerly freedoms he had taken, that all the servility of his m — l compliance, when he afterwards forced himself into the c – b — t, could not overcome the disgust he had occasioned by his former virulence.

This justificator of the G — n war, so free of his subsidies, so warm in his attachments to the P — n monarch, is the professed champion of him who raised himself into a colossal idol of popularity, by no other means but those of inveighing against continental connections, and reviling our Westphalian allies. Let us hear how he expatiated on those topics[6] in the house of C — s, and with what respect he mentioned the character of the late K — g, about the beginning of the last war, before his mouth was padlocked with a place. "It is now too apparent, that this great, this powerful, this formidable kingdom, is considered only as a province to a *despicable electorate;* and that in consequence of a scheme formed long ago, and invariably pursued, these troops are hired only to drain this unhappy nation of its money: that they have hitherto been of no use to Great Britain, or to Austria, is evident beyond controversy; and therefore it is plain, they are retained only for the purposes of Hanover. How much reason the transactions of almost every year, have given for suspecting this *ridiculous, ungrateful,* and *perfidious partiality,* it is not necessary to mention. I doubt not but most of those who sit in this house, can recollect a great number of instances, from the purchase of part of the Swedish dominions, to the *contract which we are now called upon to ratify.* I hope few have forgotten the memorable *stipulation for the Hessian troops; for the forces of the Duke of Wolfenbuttle, which we were scarcely to march beyond the verge of their own country;* or the *ever-memorable treaty,*[7] of which the tendency is discovered in the name: *The treaty by which we disunited ourselves from Austria; destroyed that building which we may, perhaps, now endeavour, without success, to raise again, and weakened the only power which it was our interest to strengthen.* To dwell upon all the instances of *partiality* which have been shewn; to remark the yearly visits that have been made to *that delightful country;* to reckon up all the *sums* that have been spent to aggrandize and enrich it, would be at once invidious and tiresome; tiresome to those who are afraid to hear the truth, and to those who are unwilling to mention facts *dishonourable* or *injurious* to their country; nor shall I dwell any longer on this unpleasing subject, than to express *my hopes, that we shall no more suffer ourselves to be deceived and oppressed."* The application is so obvious it need not be pointed out. I shall leave it to the sagacity, the common sense of every reader, who is not blind to conviction, who is not abandoned by every sentiment of honesty and patriotism.

The Monitor not only exclaims against you, for the little regard you pay to G——n connections, but he affirms, that the present m——y had no concern in the peace concluded between the Czar and the K——g of P——a, unless you can prove that death was employed as a British messenger; for the accommodation was the natural consequence of the Czarina's decease.[8] As the Monitor does not deal much in jokes, I shall give him credit for this attempt to be facetious, tho', God knows, it is no more than a ghastly grin; but I must inform him, that altho' the death of the Czarina was a favourable incident, it was the British ministry who first made use of that favourable incident, to propose, mediate, promote, and hasten the accommodation; and therefore it is no very honest part in Mr. Monitor, to filch away from them the credit of this transaction.

Neither will he allow that Sir Charles Saunders[9] hath been enabled to maintain the empire of the Mediterranean, "because," says he, "if report may be credited, the French and Spanish squadrons are joined." Here a vague report is brought in, to over-ballance an established fact. But, let us grant the report is true; how will it invalidate your assertion, that Sir Charles Saunders does not ride triumphant in the Mediterranean, and interrupt the commerce of the enemy? Has he quitted the open sea, and retired to any harbour for safety, against the attempts of the united squadrons? Has he left off cruising along their coasts, or in any shape declined an engagement; or have they, confiding in their superior strength, come forth to give him battle? Nothing of this kind has happened; therefore the insinuation is equally idle and impertinent.

To conclude, our politician would rob the adm — n of the honour resulting from the conquest of Martinique,[10] by declaring this expedition was the plan of the late m — r. This is begging honour for his patron with a witness. The plan of attacking the French in America, was adopted as a national maxim self-evident, before Mr. P — tt, or any one of his emissaries was born. A man must have been a genius at cross-purposes, who could have mistaken the object. The French had little else to lose, which it would have been worth while to conquer, except Louisiana, and that Mr. P — tt, with a sagacity peculiar to himself, over-looked during the whole course of his ad — n. True it is, he sent an armament to make a descent upon Martinique; but, this was so injudiciously contrived, as to be found inadequate to the purpose. The honour due to the present m — y arises, not from their inventing the plan, which required no conjuration; but from proportioning the means to the desired success; from equipping the armament with vigour and expedition, and sending it out at a proper season, under the conduct of officers of approved ability. And here I take my leave for the present, of the sage, modest, and conscientious Monitor, who, perhaps, may deserve some future strictures from,

SIR,

Your humble servant,

MILO[11]

No. 6. Saturday, 3 July 1762

Virtus, repulsæ nescia sordidæ, in-
contaminatis fulget honoribus;
Nec sumit aut ponit secures
Arbitrio popularis auræ.

HOR.[1]

To the Right Honourable the Earl of B——.

MY LORD,

As I have suffered in your cause, I think myself in some measure en-
titled to your attention. Fired with honest indignation at the shameless
emissaries of a rancorous faction, whose calumny did not even respect the
Th——e itself, and whose revenge overflowed with unprovoked abuse upon
the present administration; I seized the pen in order to vindicate the honour
of my P——ce, which had been so invidiously aspersed, and to justify the con-
duct of a ministry which had been irreproachable. I no sooner brandished my
weapon, like a political knight-errant, in defence of innocence traduced, than
the whole caitiff crew exalted their throats with redoubled clamour; the mon-
sters, the giants, and the dwarfs of falshood, malice and misrepresentation.
New sluices of slander were opened; new defamers retained: your Lordship
was bespattered from every dark alley of scandalous insinuation; while the
poor Briton was reproached as a fool, a dunce, and the venal prostitute of a
minister.

Whether I deserve that epithet, your Lordship already knows, and the pub-
lic will judge in the course of these my lucubrations. When they see me
disgrace the character of a true Briton, in attempting to justify bad measures,
to varnish over the practices of corruption, to palliate the least encroach-
ment upon the honour and the liberties of my country, they may then justly
brand me with the name of venal scribbler. In the mean time, the honest and
judicious part of the nation will detest as the worst of hirelings, him who
prostitutes his own conscience, by enlisting under the banners of faction, to
forge calumnies, hint reproach, circulate falsehood, traduce virtue, insinuate
treason, and sow the seeds of sedition.

I flatter myself I have, by refuting their allegations, and detecting their
malice, been in some measure instrumental in rendering their schemes abor-
tive. This indeed was no difficult task, considering the little art they used to
conceal their real aims, and the palpable absurdities they mixed in the cup of
delusion which they offered to the public. Determined virtue, my Lord, will
generally be too hard for all the arts of the most subtle malice. Secure in her
conscious strength, she holds on her course rejoicing; and tho', like the sun,
she may be obscured for a season by the clouds of envy and detraction; like
him she will triumph at the last, disperse those gloomy vapours, and break
forth with redoubled lustre.

Your enemies, finding your character proof against every infamous weapon
they could wield, have changed their object, and directed their batteries
against your country: there let them discharge that spleen, and welcome.

They will not be able to make a breach so wide as to cut off all communi-
cation between the northern and southern parts of his majesty's dominions;
and I hope your Lordship is too good a Briton to interest yourself in such
national distractions. If you have any such partialities, (and the best hearts
are not always exempt from these weaknesses) I doubt not but your good
sense, your philosophy, and the consideration of the conspicuous place you
now fill, will enable you to restrain them so effectually, that no Englishman
shall perceive in your conduct, the least marks of your having been born on
the other side of the Tweed. The English people are humoursome, blunt, and
even boisterous, my Lord, but they are at bottom just, generous, and dis-
cerning. They will murmur from prejudice; and a small ingredient of artful
misrepresentation will set their passions in a ferment: but these prejudices
and passions will soon subside; then they will see with accuracy, and reflect
with coolness. They will ever honour true patriotism, and be grateful to that
minister, under whose administration they find themselves quiet, happy, and
secure.

By the English people, I do not mean the base, unthinking rabble of this
metropolis, without principle, sentiment, or understanding; the undistin-
guishing babblers that open[2] on every scent with equal clamour; the vilest
stubble of faction, supplying fuel to every incendiary. To the abandoned, the
idle, and the profligate, scenes of tumult and dissention will always be agree-
able. The English people, considered as a respectable community, are the
honest, the sober, the thriving sons of industry, who have an interest in the
country they inhabit; who have sense to value the blessings they enjoy. They
compose the strength and riches of the nation; consequently their ease and
happiness ought to be the great object of every administration.

But, this object cannot be properly consulted while our country is involved
in a cruel and destructive war, which hath shed her best blood, exhausted her
treasure, and strained every sinew to bear the loads it hath imposed. War is a
misfortune to every kingdom, but peculiarly fatal to a nation which depends
upon commerce, and this fatality hath been terribly aggravated by the in-
judicious manner in which the war has been carried on. That this hath been
the case, will appear to every man who reflects, that in the prosecution of
a G——n war so foreign to our interests, that all the world looks upon it as
an astonishing instance of infatuation; Great Britain now expends annually,
more than the amount of the whole yearly supply, which was granted in the
reign of Queen Anne, when we subsidised almost all the princes of Germany,
brought above two hundred thousand men into the field, and maintained a
mighty war against Lewis XIV.[3] in the zenith of his power and glory. The

mismanagement will appear in still more glaring colours, when we consider that near double of the annual supply then granted, is now added yearly to the national debt; and that the national debt is accumulated to the enormous burden of one hundred and thirty-six millions.[4]

After mentioning these particulars, it may seem necessary to enumerate the other grievances that attend the prosecution of the war, such as the depopulation of the country, the want of hands for agriculture and manufacture, the price of labour so much enhanced by the continual addition of fresh duties and taxes, that it will be found impossible to maintain our interest at foreign markets, whenever there is the least competition. Our very existence as a powerful nation, seems to be at stake. Whatever may be urged by a set of infamous usurers, who prey upon the necessities of their country, I insist upon it, the public credit is drawn so fine as to threaten cracking at the very next stretch. We all remember the difficulties of last year, when the high premiums granted by the g——t, tempted every individual who could command a sum of ready money, to leave his just debts undischarged, that he might embrace the proffered advantage. Thus all the cash in the kingdom centered in the capital, and the extreme parts were left almost entirely without circulation. The disaster would have been the lighter, had it been immediately distributed again from the exchequer, through the canals that would have diffused it over the extremities of the nation; but, great part of it was conveyed to Germany, from whence it never can return; and considerable sums were remitted to America, from whence it must one day return, tho' perhaps too late to save the credit of the nation.

Among the other evil consequences of the war, I might reckon our extraordinary success, which hath elevated us to a pitch of enthusiasm, and inspired a rage of conquest, that will, in all probability, prove one of the greatest obstacles to a peace. This is the more dangerous, as it is unlimited; one conquest will suggest another, and we shall dance after the *ignis fatuus* of glory, until we are weakened, exhausted, and unable to proceed. I will venture to say, we have already made more conquests than it is our interest to retain. Our motive for engaging in this war was to defend and secure our colonies in North America. This end is fully—, at least, in a great measure, accomplished, by the entire conquest of Canada, Acadia,[5] and Cape Breton. Nothing remains to render the work complete, but the reduction of Louisiana, without which, I will be bold to affirm the task is left unfinished and imperfect.

Louisiana is the last stake the French have on the continent of America, and they husband it accordingly. They are now, by single vessels, pouring in troops to the rivers Mississippi and Mobile: they are fortifying their towns, extending their settlements, and decoying their former subjects from the countries lately annexed to the British dominions. The country of Louisiana is infinitely more fertile, and the climate more benign, than the soil and seasons of Canada. The river Mississippi has been traced near three thousand miles up the country, thro' innumerable nations and tribes of Indians, the very names of which we do not know. The French, by means of their missionaries, who are equally intrepid and indefatigable, as well as by their natural powers of insinuation, which they possess above all other people, will not fail to ingratiate themselves with those savages. They will supply them with European commodities, and by dint of this correspondence, divide the fur-trade with the English. If this was all the grievance, it might be endured: but they will have recourse to their former arts of debauching the other Indians from their dependance on the crown of Great Britain; they will clandestinely excite them as before, to invade, plunder, and destroy the English settlements, and perpetrate the most inhuman barbarities on our defenceless colonists.

These inevitable mischiefs might have been effectually prevented, and all possibility of disturbance from the savages entirely removed, by sending a few regiments to take New Orleans, a few years ago, when it could have made no resistance, when the whole number of souls settled on the Mississippi, including man, woman, child, and negro-slaves, did not exceed ten thousand. That this object, so important in itself, so essential to the completion of our American plan, was neglected or over-looked by the late m — r, reflects but little honour on his vigilance or sagacity: It is not yet too late to rectify his error of omission. It is to be hoped, that some part of the force under lord Albemarle, and sir George Pococke[6] will, after having fulfilled our expectations at the Havannah, be detached to the Mississippi for this purpose. At any rate we may for this infant settlement exchange some other conquest at the peace. I say at the peace, because I flatter myself your lordship will contribute your influence towards putting an immediate stop to the ravages of war. This your own humanity will suggest: this the true interest of your country demands. From this salutary end, I am persuaded your lordship will not be diverted by any difficulties you have to encounter before it is attained; by the murmurs of those who find their private account in the calamity of the public; by the clamour of an ignorant licentious multitude; by the secret machinations and open virulence of a baffled party.

Should those pseudo-patriots continue to carp, to cavil, and equivocate; should they set the trumpet of their mouths, and sound a fresh alarm to fright away the harbingers of peace; should they presume to exclaim against the terms of pacification, how equitable and advantageous soever they may be;

should they, like the obscene harpies in Virgil,[7] squall and squirt, utter false predictions, disturb and defile those whom they have not power to wound; let them be confronted with the Gorgon's head[8] of the articles so lately embraced by their all-perfect minister: he, who left our American colonies unsecured; who admitted the enemy to a share of the Newfoundland fishery; who resigned our conquests in Africa and the West Indies, in consideration of their evacuating the dominions of our German allies; who, rather than repay about two or three hundred thousand pounds for prizes taken before the declaration of war, from private merchants trading under the faith of treaties; I say, who rather than repay that sum, which, if I mistake not, was deposited on purpose to be restored at the peace, chose to protract the annual expence of twenty millions, and expose his country to the uncertain vicissitudes, and the certain calamities of a dreadful war, unexampled in the history of former ages: or, to give him all the credit which his best friends can claim on his behalf, let us allow that this impediment was reinforced by another; that the French refused to evacuate a town or two which had belonged to the K——g of P——a, who, by-the-bye, had voluntarily withdrawn his garrisons from those towns at the beginning of the war, not without suspicion of having purposely left the door open into Germany, that the English m——y might be intimidated into an immediate compliance with his demands; or, if Mr P—tt was induced to break off the late negotiation, because the French king declared he could not restore those places without the consent of the Empress Queen,[9] in whose name they were secured; which of his partisans will have effrontery enough to deny, that in this instance, the concerns of Great Britain, were shamefully sacrificed to the interest of a G——n ally, whose bootless friendship we had before purchased with torrents of blood and heaps of treasure![10]

That your Lordship, in adjusting the terms of accommodation between us and our enemies, will cherish a more tender regard for the lives of your fellow-subjects, and the dearest interests of your country, is the darling hope and established expectation of,

My Lord,

Pater-noster-Row,
   July 1, 1762.

Your Lordship's most obedient humble servant,
The BRITON.

No. 7. Saturday, 10 July 1762.

The Briton, when he made his first appearance, undertook to refute the false reasonings, and expose the misrepresentations of those writers who make it their business to deceive and mislead the public. They have now fallen upon a method of evading the force of argument, and screening themselves from the danger of refutation. The North Briton in particular, is become a new Atalantis,[1] and deals, not in politics, but in scandal; scandal the most atrocious that malice could conceive, or impudence promulgate. His last week's paper[2] is such a shocking composition, that it is impossible to comment upon it, without sharing the criminality of its author, and becoming in some sort an accomplice of that abandoned scribbler, whom every gentleman, every honest mind, and every loyal subject must hold in abhorrence and detestation.

And here I cannot help vindicating myself from an aspersion thrown upon me by the author of a letter in last Tuesday's Gazetteer,[3] who taking upon him the task of characterising public writers, says, "The sum of the Briton's doctrine is irreconcileable to common sense, as he will not suffer it to be believed that Mr. P—tt ever did any service to the nation, or that he ever was actuated by any other principles than those of ambition and avarice." How far this author is a judge of what is reconcileable to common sense, I shall not give myself the trouble to enquire: but, he will find it difficult to reconcile his assertions to common veracity. The sum of the Briton's doctrine was to vindicate his S——n, and his S——n's faithful servant, from the infamous calumnies with which they had been traduced; and Mr. P—tt was never mentioned but as he was inseparably connected with the subject: but, I will defy this letter-writer to produce one passage in any paper of the Briton, inculcating a belief that Mr. P—tt never did any service to the nation, or that he was actuated by motives of avarice, which indeed I never took to be part of his character, and therefore I was the more surprised when he accepted of a pension.

Jam fides, et pax, et honor, pudorque
Priscus, et neglecta redire virtus
Audet——
                                    Hor.[4]

To the BRITON.

SIR,

The only objections which the enemies of peace have started, in order to impede and frustrate the endeavours of those who wish to put an end to the war, may be reduced to these two propositions. We are bound by treaty with the K——g of P——a, to continue the war until he shall agree to the terms of pacification; so that by making a separate peace, we shall disoblige that illustrious ally, and violate the good faith of the nation.

The finances of the French king, and all his resources are exhausted, and another campaign will reduce him so low, that he will be glad to sue for peace, and accept it on any terms we may think proper to impose.

With regard to the first of these arguments, I know of no engagements with P——ssia, or any other power, by which this nation is obliged to truckle to the ambition or caprice of any ally whatsoever. It is a maxim adopted by all civilians,[5] that no state can be bound by any treaty, which shall turn out manifestly prejudicial to its interest, because it is always supposed, that every engagement of this nature, is contracted with a view to self-preservation, or public advantage; therefore every treaty in which these ends are shamefully sacrificed, must be *ipso facto* void and of no effect: for, it is a self-evident absurdity to suppose that any community can knowingly betray its own concerns. That our treaty with P——a, had neither our preservation, our interest, or honour in view, but, was indeed destructive of all three, hath been so often demonstrated, that every thinking man is now convinced on the subject; therefore the nation has a right to renounce, nay, it is our duty to withdraw ourselves from such a pernicious alliance. This is a right which hath been exercised by all states, and in all ages, and without which, every federal connection might be converted into a shameful bond of perpetual slavery. For example, if a weak or wicked minister should entangle his country in the trammels of an alliance, by which she is bound to support at an immoderate expence, a foreign prince of boundless ambition and insatiable rapacity; a royal free-booter, whose triumphs are attended with horror and distress; whose progress is marked by misery and desolation. Suppose it is stipulated in the treaty, that neither of the contracting parties shall make peace without the consent of the other; should this ambitious prince, finding his account in protracting a war, of which his ally bears the whole burden, while he reaps the whole profit, reject every overture of peace, and refuse the most equitable terms of accommodation; would it not be the height of folly, madness, and injustice, in that ally to persist in draining its treasures, stretching its credit, and accumulating its own burdens, to support him in his career of cruelty and usurpation?

It would be quite superfluous to confirm what I have said, by instances drawn from history and experience, because there is scarce one example on record, of a confederacy formed of different powers, in which particular states have not separated themselves from the general alliance. The K——g of P——a himself, has shewn how little he thought himself bound by treaties in some particular emergencies: witness his conduct during the last troubles of Germany, when in the very bosom of peace, he, without any previous intimation, made a sudden irruption into Saxony, and took possession of Dresden.[6] If he is really author of the examen of Machiavel's Prince,[7] it is his own maxim, that there are some melancholy and disagreeable occasions, which oblige a prince to infringe his treaties and alliances: but this should be done in an honourable manner, by giving his allies timely notice, that he intends to separate himself from them: and never proceed to such extremities, unless compelled to them by his attention to his people's safety. And here I cannot help mentioning another remark which occurs in the same performance, and may be turned upon his P——n M——y, like one of his own cannon in the field of battle. "Princes (says he) sometimes explain the natures of their proceedings in a manifesto, and presently after, act in direct contradiction to their own declarations; but such hazardous strokes soon destroy all trust and dependance; and the earlier they happen, the more shameless does their prevarication appear." The application will be obvious to those who read the P——n monarch's manifesto,[8] published the very day on which he invaded S——y, at the beginning of the present war, and compare it with his subsequent conduct.

To return from this digression, the *salus populi*, is certainly the *suprema lex*,[9] which must supercede all other ties and considerations; and this, I apprehend, may be adduced as one reason to detach us from the P——n alliance, if that alliance cannot be retained without our consenting to perpetuate the war. But if this reason did not exist in its full force, there is another gate open, through which we may make a very honourable retreat. The engagement with P——a was contracted in a former reign, in consequence of a plan, which perhaps his present M——y does not approve, and therefore is not bound to pursue. Nothing can be more absurd, than to affirm, that the rash or partial connections of a deceased prince are binding upon his successor; or that the national faith is engaged for the observance of a treaty, in which the national honour and interest were equally sacrificed.

The only question that deserves consideration is, whether we have more to apprehend from that ally's resentment, than we have to suffer by his friendship. Should he seize H——r as he has already taken possession of S——y; it is the duty, the interest of the Germanic body to see justice done to any of its constituent members that shall be oppressed: but should they neglect their duty and interest on such an occasion, I hope the elector of H——r will never again have influence enough with the K——g of G——t B——n, to engage him in a war for retrieving it, that shall cost his kingdom annually, for a series of years, more than double the value of the country in dispute. Should he, on the other hand, disarm the B——sh troops in Westphalia, or, as he dealt with the S——ns, dissolve the English regiments, and incorporate the men by compulsion in his own army; we may, for this disgrace, thank that m——r who sent the flower of the English soldiery to serve as an auxiliary corps to their own mercenaries, under the conduct of a foreigner,[10] who is known to be the creature of his P——n M——y, a soldier of fortune, whose interest it is to husband the war; who, unless he is restrained by principle, has it in his power to insult, to oppress, to embezzle, without being called to account, without being amenable to any British jurisdiction.

Having thus explained the nature of our national obligations to P——a, I shall now consider the other objection to a peace, which is founded on the supposed distress of the French government. That the French king's treasury was exhausted to the last livre, his revenue anticipated, and the credit of his government bankrupt, we heard repeated and re-echoed every season, since the close of the second campaign; but every succeeding summer has proved the falsehood of this clamour. Certain it is, the marine and navigation of France have been for some time ruined, consequently their naval commerce must be greatly impaired; though perhaps, even in this particular, the war has not been so fatal to her as is generally supposed. She has continued to manage a considerable traffic in neutral bottoms;[11] and it is a melancholy truth, that many of her sea-ports have been enriched, and thrive exceedingly, by the success of their privateers, against which we can have no effectual remedy. Over and above this external commerce, every body knows that France has a very considerable internal trade by virtue of her wines, her manufactures, hats, laces, silks, stuffs, toys,[12] and a great number of articles of luxury and convenience, which are purchased in large quantities all over the continent. By these means they lay all their neighbours, and even England itself under contribution: for the British money expended in Westphalia and Brandenburg, circulates through all Germany, and great part of it centers at Hamburgh, and other cities where French modes prevail, and French commodities are vendible.

It cannot be denied, that Lewis XIV. maintained a war of ten years against all Europe, and produced four (sometimes five) armies in the field at one time, before his kingdom reaped the least advantage from one external colony. The same sinews remain in full vigour, though the burden is much more easily borne. It may seem a paradox, (but it is true) that their burdens have been lightened by their disasters. They are now eased of the heavy expence incurred by maintaining a numerous fleet, and strong garrisons in those colonies which we have subdued; and our expence multiplies in the same proportion. They no longer pay subsidies to Russia and Sweden; but, on the contrary, receive continual pecuniary supplies from the court of Madrid. Their great, and almost their whole expence then is limited to the war in Germany, which, I insist upon it, they are able to maintain without contracting one shilling of debt, or laying any heavy additional imposition on their people. The army of France, in time of peace, falls very little short of two hundred thousand men; a number, more than sufficient to afford such armies as we cannot over-match in Westphalia. Her standing revenue, clear of all anticipation or mortgage, amounts to seven millions sterling, which, considering the smalness of their military appointments, the low price of labour among them, and the œconomy with which their affairs are managed, will go very near as far as double the sum in the English service. The extraordinary charge incurred by marching their army with a train of artillery into Westphalia, will be more than over-balanced by these savings; and every person of common sense will foresee the consequence. France will be enabled to protract the war in that country, without devising new taxes, borrowing on remote funds, or adding to her national incumbrances; while Great Britain will run every year in debt, more than the whole amount of the French revenue, until all her resources are drained, and her credit utterly extinguished. How soon this will be the case, heaven alone can tell. Public credit is delicate and fugitive: it often depends upon the breath of a capricious multitude; and hath hitherto flourished and expanded beneath the warm sun of uninterrupted triumph and success: but, the least reverse of fortune, the softest whisper of national miscarriage or defeat, may shrivel it up at once, and blast it beyond all hope of recovery.— But this is a disagreeable theme. The anarchy and horror that would ensue, will, I hope, be effectually prevented by a speedy, safe, and honourable peace. In this hope, I am,

> SIR,
> *Your very humble servant,*
> ATTICUS.[13]

No. 8. Saturday, 17 July 1762.

Obtrectatio et livor pronis auribus accipiuntur; quippe adulationi fœdum crimen servitutis, malignitati falsa species libertatis inest.

TACITUS.[1]

As a Briton, I should be sorry to see this kingdom ruled by a Scotch administration. How far the natives of North Briton have a right to share in the ministry, is another question: but surely the King has an indubitable right to chuse his ministers from among any department of his own subjects, whether born in Scotland, Ireland, Wales, or America.

As I wish that England may never be governed by a Scotch cabal, so I hope I shall never live to see again the administration of Great Britain totally engrossed by one person, or one party. It is impossible that any one minister can properly manage the vast variety and complication of affairs that constitute the external and internal policy of this great and important nation. It is scarce possible to find one man whom the possession of such power and influence would not intoxicate to a very dangerous degree of pride, insolence, and intractability.

We all remember a very extraordinary transaction[2] in the late reign, when a fierce rebellion had broke out in the extremity of the island; when the insurgents, headed by a pretender to the crown, had defeated a body of regular forces, and penetrated into the very bowels of South Britain; when the whole nation was overwhelmed with fear, and the public credit seemed to depend upon nothing so much as upon the unanimity and vigour of the King's councils. At that very delicate and hazardous conjuncture, when the Sovereign presented the seals to a nobleman of distinguished ability, upon whose fidelity and attachment he had the most perfect reliance; the two brothers[3] who had hitherto engrossed the whole machine of government, being averse to this associate, whose superior talents they dreaded, and enraged that the K——g should pretend to encroach upon their monopoly of administration, came, attended by all their adherents, and offered such an insult to their Prince, as, I believe, stands unparalelled in the records of this history. They threw up their places in disdain, leaving the business of the nation at a stand, and distressing the hands of government in such a manner, by their defection, that the K—— was fain to sacrifice his favourite servant to their animosity, and receive them again upon their own terms. I should be glad to know in what manner they could have more effectually assisted the cause of the Pretender, unless they had declared for him openly, and enlisted themselves under his banners. Had they joined him personally, they could not have served him so well; for, in that case, they would have embarrassed his councils, and hastened on his final ruin, by their blundering and timidity.

It was but the other day, that a m——r, in the midst of a ruinous G——n war, which he had rashly entailed upon his country, when the prospect from that quarter appeared dark and gloomy, and the eyes of the people began to be opened, so as to perceive the dreadful precipice, to the brink of which they were driven — It was this very ticklish occasion which he pitched upon to manifest the plenitude of his power, even in opposition to his S — n, and to establish an uncontroulable tyranny on the neck of competition. He suddenly proposed in C — l, that we should, without adequate provocation, or further enquiry, run headlong into another expensive war. When he found himself almost single in this opinion, and the K — g himself condescended to signify his disapprobation of such a precipitate and dangerous measure; he treated his fellow c — rs with the most supercilious contempt: he paid no regard to the mild and sensible remonstrances of his S — n; but dashed the s — ls from him with all the insolence of indignation; and after having accepted of a pension from the P — ce he had so scandalously deserted, had the presumption to declare in public, that he resigned his place, because he could not rule the nation with absolute authority.[4]

He imagined the crown would, as in the case of his predecessor, truckle to the petulance of his humour, and compliment him with a *carte blanche* for his future administration; that his R — l and indulgent Master should

> Bend low, and in a bondman's key
> With bated breath, and whisp'ring humbleness,
> Say this, — Fair Sir,[5] 'tis true I am your K — g;
> What then? no reason sure that I should use
> The senses heaven hath lent me, or presume
> To argue 'gainst the opinion you espouse,
> Ev'n tho' my kingdom were at stake — pray, pardon
> This rash attempt — resume the reins — henceforth
> I am a Thing of wax which you, fair Sir,
> Shall mould at pleasure — all my counsellors
> Shall sit like dumb dogs in your worship's presence,
> Or open in your cry — .

He thought, perhaps, when he quitted the council-chamber, that all the officers of state would have followed at his heels; that all the different departments of government would be left in confusion; that popular clamour would be raised to a higher pitch than ever; and that, as it happened on a former occasion,[6] he would be brought back in triumph to the cabinet. But, he did not consider that times were greatly altered since his last exaltation; that the Prince who now wields the scepter, is a native Briton, with a true British heart, whose throne is established in the affections of his people; a

Prince who disdains to rule by corruption or cabal; who has no partialities to bias him, no foreign prejudices to gratify; who understands the true interest of his kingdom, and will pursue it invariably; who has sense to distinguish with his own eyes, and vigour of mind to act according to his own judgment; who, conscious of his own internal rectitude, fears no faction, and heeds no slander; whose spirit will not brook the peevishness of those servants who grumble in the execution of their duty, nor suffer any insolent plebeian to erect a dictatorial chair upon the basis of his throne.

These circumstances seem to have been overlooked by our political alchymist, in the article of projection.[7] He withdrew as quietly as a lord mayor, when his year of magistracy is expired. Not a sigh was uttered, nor a tear shed at his retreat: the wheels of government continued to move, and the operations of war proceeded with unabated vigour. Instead of making an irrepairable breach or chasm in the council, he was followed but by one solitary peer,[8] who threw many a long look behind, in hopes of an invitation to return. He, indeed, had not the same cause of comfort that fell to the s — y's share. He had not secured a pension for himself and family; nor had he enjoyed the sweets of ministerial omnipotence. On the contrary, he had the mortification to find he had rashly excluded himself from the court and confidence of a young Prince endowed with uncommon discernment, upon whose favour he might have raised the fairest superstructure of honour and advantage.

Hence his disappointment was attended with rage and distraction. He inveighed in private and in public against those who presumed to take in hand the helm which his illustrious b — r had abandoned. He employed emissaries, who have not failed to misrepresent their conduct, and revile their characters; to circulate the vilest insinuations against the person of his S — n, and those whom his S — n most esteemed; to draw infamous parallels, consisting of

Figures ill-pair'd, and similies unlike;[9]

to feign incidents, start jealousies, and practise every art of faction to whet the sword of civil dissention.

After all these pains taken to light the torch of national discord, he may repair to his villa, and from his temple warehouse, select a new structure to be dedicated to the *concordia civium*.[10] There it is to be hoped he will find a place for the head of the writer who calls himself *North Briton*, (I do not mean his real head, as that and his body may be destined to another fate) I mean a bust of him, to represent the united virtues of decency and candour.

This delicate penman, in his last Saturday's essay, has, with his usual consistency and regard to truth, endeavoured to frighten the mob with the bugbear of a Scottish administration; and in the very same page, laboured to prove that the two corner-stones of this Scottish administration are natives of South Briton. Two gentleman, namely, Mr. F—x and Mr. G—— G—lle,[11] upon whom he has exercised his irony with great success. With respect to Mr. F—x, I never before heard it insinuated, that he had any partial affection for the Scottish nation. His abilities as a minister have been generally acknowledged; and his political conduct was never called in question, except by the partizans of Mr. P—tt, during his contest for power with that prodigious luminary. That he has taken care of his own family, will not be denied; but, all those reversions, about which so great a clamour was raised, will be found short of that pension which hath been so glibly swallowed by his great political rival. If then, he has unquestionable abilities; if he has sense to see his own interest, and perseverance to consult it without flinching, he will always find it his interest to act as a faithful servant to a Prince who has no interest distinct from the happiness of his subjects.

As to Mr. G—— G—lle, his morals, I apprehend, are unimpeached: that he refused to resign, his own discernment, his respect to his Sovereign, and his regard to his country, for any private views of family-advantage, will ever redound to his honour in the opinion of every unprejudiced Briton. Mr. G—lle does not set up for a first rate orator: but he is a man of business, who understands the nature and proceedings of a house of commons, as well as any other member of that assembly, and is perfectly well acquainted with the detail of government. If I could wonder at any absurdity that drops from the pen of the *North Briton*, I should be surprised at his effrontery in attempting to ridicule this gentleman as the author of *the Act for the Encouragement of Seamen.*[12] The bill was indeed brought in by Mr. G—lle, and supposed to be extremely well calculated for the purposes intended; but, this bill which the North Briton condemns by the lump, without pretending to specify its defects, was patronized, supported, and carried through the house, by the great Colossus P—tt, for whom he expresses such implicit veneration. With the like honesty of intention, he might have stigmatized Mr. G—lle, for having planned and promoted the late act for laying an additional duty on spirituous liquors;[13] an act which was opposed by the all-perfect m——r, who, biassed by his personal attachment to that eminent patriot of the plantations, so much admired for his eloquence, so warmly beloved for his liberality, wanted to suppress the British distillery by a total prohibition. Yes, to the private advantage of that wise, respectable A——n,[14] who deals in rum and molasses; he would have sacrificed one of the most important manufactures of Great Britain, the duty upon which, as it was devised and established by the sagacity and influence of Mr. G——lle, produces a clear annual revenue of four hundred thousand pounds.

This, at least, was an instance of merit, which would not have passed un-honoured, even by the *North Briton*, if he had retained the smallest regard for his *patria*,[15] or revered in any shape the *patrias artes*.[16] But, this accursed Scotch administration has thrown down all distinctions; and the extremes of party have united for their common safety. I would therefore, upon second thoughts, humbly propose to the right honourable personage, who admits his friends into the temple of immortality; that in his new *Ædes concordiæ*,[17] he would represent the coalition of the sugar and malt distillery, under the figures of the *Monitor* and the *North Briton*, mixing up a drench of rum and geneva,[18] to animate their understrappers to a more inflammatory pitch of defamation; and this union may be distinguished by an inscription to the fol-lowing effect; part of which I have borrowed from the front of Mr. Ashley's punch-house upon Ludgate-hill:[19] COTAMUS PRO BONO PUBLICO.[20]

The conscientious *North Briton* must think the good people of England already as blind and undiscerning as he would wish to make them, if he imag-ines they will swallow his insinuation, that the present M——r is supported by none but Mr. F—x and Mr. G——lle, or that these three engross the whole administration. No doubt, they will severely feel the loss of the d—— of N——e, whose superlative wisdom had so long sustained the Majesty of the British throne, given vigour to the conduct, and reputation to the councils of his S——n; whose exceeding merit is so pathetically celebrated by the chief emissary of his grace's quondam rival: but, neither the illustrious P——t, the serene T——le, nor the stupendous N——le, has swept away one of his fellow-counsellors in his retreat. Not a single member followed their fortunes: no convulsion attended their removal. The two kings of Brentford[21] were not more quietly deposed. The throne is still surrounded, and the councils of his Majesty are upheld by the nobles of the realm; the great officers of state; by the ability and integrity of a Henley,[22] the genius, knowledge and experience of a Granville, the extensive capacity and untainted probity of an Halifax; the sense and spirit of a Talbot; the *acumen ingenii*,[23] penetration, and fire of a Townshend. I might swell the list of friends to the present administration, with all the most illustrious names of the British peerage——let me add of the British senate, and challenge the North Briton to confront it, with the catalogue of those who adhere to his boasted patrons; but, this would afford a diverting contrast, with which, I dare say, he will never gratify the public.

---

* * The Tale is come to hand, and will be inserted in the next Number.[24]

No. 9. Saturday, 24 July 1762.

Solve senescentem mature sanus equum, ne
Peccat ad extremum ridendus, et ilia ducat.
                                HORACE.[1]

I t was a custom among the ancients to discharge the superannuated gladia-
tor, by giving him a rod or cudgel, hence he was called *rude donatus*,[2] or
rudiarius. I would recommend this practice to the employers of the Monitor,
who seems to be quite exhausted in the service. His invention and his mem-
ory have failed at the same time. Having poured out his calumny and abuse
to the very dregs, he begins to decant it over again,[3] not considering that it
is now become vapid; not remembering, that when it was first offered to the
public, the pernicious contents of it were annalized and diluted.

Tho' his wretched system of politics has been exposed, and his perfidious
slander refuted, he still continues to repeat the same note, like a magpye in a
cobler's stall, which has learned to call *cuckold*. He still harps upon the neces-
sity of supporting our G——n allies—his cry is still "the Protestant Religion
is in danger;" and he still charges the *Briton* with want of respect to his P——n
M——y. With respect to the G——n war, if I thought he spoke the real dic-
tates of his heart, I should pity his infatuation. The nature and tendency of
our G——n connections, have been so clearly explained, and so often dem-
onstrated beyond all controversy, that it is impossible they should be now
justified by any thinking being, who is not actuated by some sinister motive,
or rendered so callous by prejudice, as to be insensible to the force of truth.

The writer who persists in jarring upon this discordant string, I have
already pronounced, and, I think, fairly proved to be a venal fool, as void of
principle as of talent, who, like a mercenary Swiss,[4] would draw his pen on
either side of any dispute as he happened to be listed, without the least regard
to the merits of the cause in which he embarks. I may venture to extend my
censure, and affirm that he is worse than any common mercenary, inasmuch
as he undertakes the assassination of character, and performs this honour-
able service, skulking all the while behind the traverse of distant parallel and
juggling equivocation.

I know not whether it ought to raise our mirth or our indignation, to see
the interests of the protestant religion so warmly espoused by an author, who
never could find any other avenue to the public attention, but the dirtiest
common sewer of slander, whose invention hath been employed in coining

falsehood to disparage his P——e, to defame his P——ce's nearest and dearest relations, and to soil the reputation of his neighbour. I should be glad to know by what religion these duties are inculcated; I should be glad to know in what other country, or under what other government but the present administration, as remarkable for lenity as for uprightness, such a vile incendiary would be suffered to escape unpunished. Yet, this detected calumniator, with religion in his mouth, and rancour in his bosom, has the effrontery, even in the article of conviction, to tax the Briton with malice, falsehood, and detraction, the very crimes of which he himself is so notoriously guilty. Does he think then that the public has forgot the occasion upon which the Briton made his first appearance; that instead of professing scandal, he assumed the pen on purpose to vindicate the characters of his sovereign, and the chief servant of the crown, from the false, wicked, and atrocious aspersions which had been so infamously thrown upon them by the writer who takes the name of Monitor? or does he imagine it so blind or biassed, as not to perceive, that every base insinuation he dropped against his Prince, has been refuted, and every fact he alledged against the M——y, disproved? Does he suppose that mankind will justify him, for having blown the coals of civil dissention in his country, and falsely reviled his own S——n; and condemn me for having presumed to censure the public conduct of a foreign Prince, to whom I owe neither obligation nor allegiance? Let him repeat the terms in which I mentioned his P——n Majesty. Have I treated his person with disrespect? Have I searched into his private character with a view to expose his secret vices and infirmities; and finding neither, have I had recourse to fiction, and propagated forged calumnies in order to depreciate him in the eyes of his people, and fill his court with domestic disgust? No, I leave these honest practices to the Monitor and his coadjutors, whose writings are a reproach to literature, and a disgrace to humanity.

Now we are on the subject of the P——n monarch, whom those people have celebrated as the great patron and prop of the protestant religion, as the most important ally and unshaken friend of Great Britain; I would ask them what became of the protestant interest in the last war, when Great Britain supported the house of Austria, and his Prussian Majesty was strictly attached to the French King then at war with England? How did this K——g's good faith triumph, when on the back of the treaty of Breslaw,[5] by which he engaged to observe a strict neutrality during the war, he suddenly entered Bohemia then destitute of troops, reduced the defenceless cities of Prague, Tabor, Budweis, and several other places, before the Austrian army came up and drove him out of that kingdom? How did his regard to treaty shine with peculiar lustre, when after a second accommodation, by which England became guaranty of his possessions in Silesia, as ceded to him by the treaty of Breslau, he made a sudden irruption into Lusatia, took possession of Gorlitz, ravaged Saxony, took Dresden, expelled the King of Poland from his hereditary dominions,[6] and afterwards gave him peace, on condition that he himself should retain all his contributions, and receive a million of German crowns, to be paid by his Polish Majesty at the next fair of Leipsic? How conspicuous did his friendship for Great Britain appear, by making a diversion in favour of her enemies the French, and thus overturning all her schemes of conquest, when her army, amounting to near one hundred thousand effective men, was encamped on the plains of Lisle, when Count Saxe, at the head of no more than thirty thousand, was fain to intrench himself to the teeth, so that there was nothing to obstruct our march to the gates of Paris; and Prince Charles of Lorrain, with a powerful body of Austrians had passed the Rhine, and penetrated into Alsace? Then it was that the K——g of P——a, the great ally of England, who had engaged to observe a strict neutrality, and leave the Queen of H——y[7] unmolested, in consequence of that part of Silesia which she had ceded to him; — then it was, I say, that without any fresh provocation, he invaded Bohemia, by way of diversion, in favour of France; by which step, Prince Charles was obliged to repass the Rhine, and advance against the invader; the French King was enabled to reinforce his army in Flanders; and thus the hopes of Great Britain proved abortive.

His conduct in the present war is so fresh in every man's memory, that it needs not to be recapitulated; but, it requires a better memory than I have, to recollect any one circumstance by which the protestant religion appeared to be in danger. It is therefore incumbent upon the Monitor, who has so often made use of this plea, to shew that any design was formed against the protestant religion; or that the K——g of P——a ever distinguished himself at the head of this interest. On the contrary, it is as clear as day, that the dreadful war which he kindled in the bowels of his country, hath divided, weakened, and threatened the total ruin of the protestant interest; that far from being the acknowledged chief of that confederacy, he, in his late contests, counted among his declared enemies, a much greater number of protestant powers, than ever appeared in arms, as his allies; and that not one protestant in Germany (his own subjects excepted) would have drawn a sword in his defence, if he had not been paid for so doing, with the money of Great Britain.

I am weary of foiling this contemptible antagonist, otherwise I might expatiate upon the absurdity of his clamouring against the terms of a peace supposed to be upon the carpet,[8] without pretending to specify, or even to know the articles of the future treaty: an absurdity of the same stamp with that of an old woman, who envying the poetical reputation of Mr. Pope, wrote a lampoon upon his translation of the Iliad, before one line of the said translation appeared.[9] I might insist upon the folly and assurance of the man, in affirming, that the subsidies granted to Russia, &c. for the preservation of the peace of Germany, before the commencement of this German war, were greater than those given to the K——g of P——a, as the price of his alliance. I might observe, that supposing this had been the case, two blacks would not make one white: one absurdity could never justify another: but, the fact is glaringly false. The subsidy stipulated to the Russians, was little more than half of what has been given to the K——g of P——a; and that connected with the express condition of the Czarina's sending a powerful army to act in favour of the Elector of H——r, in case his electoral dominions should be attacked:[10] but, this is not all. His P——n M——y has, for some time received a subsidy of seven hundred thousand pounds *per annum*, not surely for preserving the peace of the empire—not for the defence of H——r, which he does not even pretend to protect. That herculean task we ourselves have undertaken to perform, at the annual expence of six millions sterling, over and above the P——n tribute.

I am also accused, by this polite author of falsehood, in having hinted, that his M——y did not approve of our late treaty with P——a. In answer to which charge, I shall only observe, that his M——y's having discontinued the subsidy, is no great sign of his approving the treaty by which it was given; and now the public may judge whether I am guilty of insinuating a false fact, or the Monitor of bearing false witness. This is not the only quarter from which I have been bespattered. The author of a letter in the Gazetteer,[11] who seems to lie in wait, like a village-cur, to snap at the heels of travellers, has, on the faith of a paragraph in a Dutch paper, boldly charged me with having magnified the national debt, with a view to discourage and dispirit my fellow subjects; and in consequence of this pretended detection, he compares the Briton to Maubert,[12] whom he mentions (I suppose) as an emblem of falsehood and venality. I should treat this obscure scribler with the contempt he deserves, if his malice rested upon matter of opinion: but as his calumny is founded on matter of fact, it may be necessary to undeceive the public, by way of formal refutation. The Briton has said the national debt amounts to one hundred and thirty-six millions. The Dutchman (it seems) affirms, that it does not much exceed one hundred and twenty millions. Now it appears, that the national debt, as it stood 11 Jan. 1760, according to the state thereof made up at the exchequer, in order to be presented to parliament, amounted to

	90365586	8	2¼
New debts contracted by the Resolutions of Dec. 1759,	8240000	0	0
Ditto contracted by the resolutions of May 13 1760,	5102706	9	9
Navy debt as it stood Dec. 31 1759,	3784861	17	0
	107493154	14	11¼
Debt charged upon the civil list revenue, and provided for by a tax upon salaries, &c.	1000000	00	00
	108493154	00	00
Debt contracted in 1761 by the resolutions in parliament,	12000000	00	00
Ditto 1762,	12000000	00	00
	132493154	00	00¼

To this,[13] if we add the vote of credit granted to his Majesty last month, the navy-debt contracted since Dec. 1759, and other deficiencies, we shall see that the sum total of the national debt amounts to above one hundred and thirty-six millions sterling; and now the candid reader may determine whether the charge of misleading the public ought to be with me, or with my anonymous accuser.

N.B. For want of room, the Tale[14] must be postponed till our next.

No. 10. Saturday, 31 July 1762.

Tu ne cede malis, sed contra audentior ito.
Virgil.[1]

I have been reproached as an advocate for the present ministry, and as a panegyrist of Lord B—te. I own it gives me particular pleasure to see the administration of my country conducted in such a manner, as will stand the test of the severest enquiry; and there is no task I would more chearfully embrace than that of paying the just tribute of applause to extraordinary virtue. This, however, is a task which, I apprehend, any man has a right to decline, without any imputation upon his character, should it clash with his interest, or interfere with other more necessary occupations: but, when a good man is vilely slandered, it becomes a duty of humanity to undertake his defence. This consideration, and this only induced the Briton to interpose, when the hounds of faction began to mangle the reputation of a M——r whom I knew to be without blame. How far I have succeeded, I leave the public to judge.

People of the most upright intentions may differ in political opinions, with respect to the rectitude or expediency of certain measures; and these subjects may be canvassed with temper, decency, and candour; but, the present outcry against the Earl of B—— was not founded on any supposed difference of sentiment. It issued immediately from the foul throat of calumny, and scandal. A series of falsities was urged against his ministerial conduct; a succession of the most infamous slanders was forged to blacken his moral character. The imputed criminality in his public conduct, I have proved to be no other than the rancorous misrepresentation of malice. I have challenged his adversaries to particularize one blemish in his private life. Conscious of their own iniquity, they have avoided all such explanations; they have had recourse to the last and lowest shifts of scurrility and defamation. They have discharged a torrent of general abuse upon his country; and finding this too illiberal to interest the public, too contemptible even to provoke a reply; they have, with such licentious rage as, I believe, stands without example, broke through every restraint of truth, decorum, and humanity. They have trumped up pretended parallels, replete with the most gross, indelicate, and treacherous insinuations, against the first and most respectable personages in the kingdom; such insinuations, that we will venture to say, the authors of them would be universally held as infamous in every other civilized nation of Europe! They have indeed rendered themselves so impure, by this exercise of scattering their filth, that no man can enter the lists with them, but at the hazard of contamination.

The Monitor, who began this decent method of soiling the reputation of his betters, is sometimes pleased to intersperse among his calumnies, a species of argumentation, which proves how well he is qualified to instruct the public. Among other curious deductions, he has laboured to establish a similarity of circumstances between the present period, and that æra in Queen Ann's reign, when the negotiations for the peace were brought upon the carpet; especially in the particular of deserting our allies; a circumstance upon which he dwells with peculiar self-complacency. He has wisely chosen for his motto, a sentence in the Queen's speech,[2] implying, "That nothing can be more evident, than if the French King continues master of the Spanish monarchy, the ballance of power in Europe, is utterly destroyed, and he will be able, in a short time, to engross the trade and wealth of the world—". Sensible writers,

in their choice of mottoes, generally select such pertinent maxims as are con-
firmed by the experience and observation of mankind: but, the Monitor is
one of the few who pitches upon apothegms, the absurdity of which he him-
self hath seen demonstrated; tho' in this particular, he may be compared to
the right reverend historian of his own times,[3] who declared to Queen Anne
in private, that any treaty by which Spain and the West Indies were left in
the hands of King Philip, must in a little time deliver all Europe into the
hands of France: that if any such peace was made, the Queen was betrayed,
and her people ruined: that in less than three years, she would be murdered,
and the fires would blaze again in Smithfield.[4] The good bishop lived to see
his prognostic disappointed; but, nevertheless, he transmitted this anecdote
to the public, as a specimen of his own patriotism and sagacity.

In the year 1705, when the speech quoted by the Monitor was made, the
French King could not with any propriety be termed the master of the Span-
ish monarchy, which was powerfully contested with his grandson, by Charles
at the head of a very formidable army, supported by a strong party in that
kingdom.[5] In the sequel, indeed, he became master of it, and it has remained
in his family ever since, without the French King's being able to destroy the
ballance of power in Europe, or to engross the trade and wealth of the world:
the prognostic, therefore, appears to have been erroneous, and the Moni-
tor's quoting it as an established maxim, is ridiculously absurd. But, as he
has endeavoured to strike out a likeness between this war and that of 1702,
and to draw from that pretended resemblance, consequences unfavourable to
the present administration, I shall, in my turn, attempt to draw a parallel, in
which there shall be neither falshood nor scurrility.

The continental war[6] that distinguished the reign of Queen Anne, was the
result of an illustrious confederacy of almost all the European states united, to
bridle the boundless ambition, and restrain the growing power of the French
monarch, who had too plainly shewn, that his aim was universal empire; in
this case the continent of Europe was the natural scene of action. The present
war arose from an American quarrel between Great Britain and France, and
America was the proper scene of operation; nor could it possibly be trans-
ferred to the continent of Europe, without offering violence to the interests of
this nation. One great end of Queen Anne's war, was to preserve the ballance
of power between the houses of Austria and Bourbon: but, the present war in
Germany has absolutely destroyed that ballance, and driven those two formi-
dable powers into a conjunction, which undoubtedly threatens the liberties
of Europe. In the former contest, England engaged in the continental war, as
one of a great number of confederates, who contributed to the general alli-

ance, their several proportions of troops and money. Great Britain embarked in the present G——n war as a principal, without one ally, but such as she purchased with enormous subsidies. In the year 1706, the whole expence of the land-army, including all the subsidies paid by Great Britain, and her quota of troops employed in the common cause, did not exceed two millions, eight hundred fourteen thousand, five hundred and eighty-three pounds, fifteen shillings and nine-pence; in return for this expence incurred by England, the allies brought about two hundred thousand effective men into the field. The French were opposed by them, in Portugal, Spain, Italy, Savoy, Germany, and Flanders. Lewis XIV. lost twenty thousand men at the battle of Ramillies; and a whole army, with half a million of treasure, at the siege and battle of Turin.[7] The present G——n war costs this nation near seven millions annually; and our troops can hardly keep their ground in Westphalia; and not one man is contributed by one ally, unless we bestow that specious title on our own mercenaries. In 1706, we paid a subsidy of fifty thousand pounds to the King of P——a, in consideration of which he furnished a considerable body of forces to act in the common cause: in 1760, we paid a subsidy of fourteen times that sum to the King of P——a, in consideration of which, our army was, I think, reinforced at one time with a single regiment of black hussars;[8] and, at another time, we reinforced this subsidiary with a body of twelve thousand men, to protect him from the vengeance of his own enemies, against whom we had no cause of quarrel. In the war of Queen Anne, the annual expence of the nation seldom exceeded six millions; in the present war, it amounts yearly to more than three times that sum. At the death of that Princess, the public debt stood at fifty millions; at this hour, it does not fall short of one hundred and thirty-six millions. Immediately before the treaty of Utrecht,[9] the bulk of the people, distressed by those burdens, and perceiving that the great object of the war had ceased in consequence of the death of the Emperor Joseph,[10] expressed an uneasiness at the continuance of it, and longed eagerly for peace. There was a set of people who found their own private interest in protracting the calamities of their country, such as contractors, stock-jobbers, and public usurers: they were animated by the influence of a mercenary general,[11] who fattened upon the blood and spoils of Great Britain; they were inflamed with all the animosity of party-rage against the ministry; and instigated by the emissaries of selfish allies, who thought Britain had not yet sacrificed herself enough for their interests. Actuated by these concurring motives, they raised a hideous clamour in the nation. They opened all the sluices of calumny; they branded the ministry with Jacobitism, and accused them of deserting their allies: they affirmed there was a design against the succession: they exclaimed that the Protestant Religion was in danger. In a word, they did the French King's work so effectually, by raising and fomenting jealousies, distrusts and dissensions, among the people, that he would not acquiesce in terms, to which he certainly would have subscribed, had not he seen the nation weakened by intestine divisions: and the ministry, whether swayed by motives of resentment or self-preservation, rashly concluded a disadvantageous peace, which afterwards proved their own ruin. With respect to the present times, as the nation is loaded with much heavier burdens, so the people's desire of peace is much more eager. There is indeed, a much more iniquitous clamour raised against a much honester ministry: but I have too good an opinion of the penetration, good sense, and candour of the public, to believe it will produce any effect that can possibly disturb the measures of the administration, or in any shape impede their efforts to terminate the miseries and horrors of a destructive war. At any rate, I am sure they will not be provoked into a bad peace; and I hope, the rancour and detraction of a few obscure individuals, operating upon the refuse of the vulgar, will never have power to deter them from embracing such terms of accommodation, as may suit the honour and advantage of their country.

To the Author of the BRITON.

If it be not contrary to the design of your paper, you will oblige, by admitting the following little Tale into it,

Your humble servant,
CURIOSUS NON CURATUS.[12]

The MODERN PATRIOT, a TALE.

> A Butcher's dog right English stuff,
> With heart of oak, and hide of buff,
> Was wont to carry, day by day,
> Well fill'd with meat his master's tray.
> Was ever dog more wise, and just,
> More brave, and faithful to his trust?
> He'd spend his life's blood drop by drop,
> Rather than lose a single chop,
> And die with hunger, starveling elf,
> Sooner than pick one bone himself.

By chance, as thro' a public road,
He bore along the tempting load,
A hundred dogs, from neighb'ring village
Rush'd in at once, intent on pillage;
Dutch mastiffs, lurchers, fox-hounds, harriers,
With spaniels, water-dogs, and tarriers.
What could he do? — 'midst such a fray,
How shall he guard the fleshful tray?
Astride he stood in furious fit,
And bit, and bark'd, and bark'd and bit:
No patriot bent on all that's good,
By lucre's filthy sons withstood,
Ere play'd his part with nobler zeal,
Or roar'd, and bullied half so well.
Poor dog in vain! — by foes surrounded,
O'ermatch'd, out-clamour'd, and confounded,
He saw, with such a tribe opprest,
'Twas downright madness to contest:
No mortal force, no mortal wit,
For such an arduous task was fit:
And would the rulers of the sky
Come from their silver bow'rs on high,
Leave yon imperial realms of day,
As seconds to so vile a fray,
And here on earth shew churlish breeding,
By hind'ring hungry dogs from feeding?
Whate'er in Homer's days was done,
When gods would fight and scold for fun,
Would aid a rogue's or harlot's cause,
And quarrel ev'n for barley straws,
The times alas! are altered since,
For now, like some proud eastern Prince,
They keep remote from mortal sight,
Tho' dogs, or men, or monarchs fight. —
    Fatigu'd at length, and sore with pain,
The dog found all resistance vain;
Then thus, with patriot speech burst out——
"Ye wretches, ye voracious rout,
Pox on your grumbling, and your growling,
Here take the meat, and stop your howling! —
But soft — 'tis only just and fair,
That patriot Shock should have his share:

Have I not all your rage withstood,
And wrestled for my master's good?
Not * Heav'n-born Clive, with sword in hand,
Could make a braver, bolder stand; —
Then give me, honest friends, my due,
This stake for me — and those for you."
The dogs agreed, and gave him way:

MORAL.

For every dog should have his day.

*The dog in this place, and indeed thro' his whole speech, imitates our *Modern Orator*, who, with a *curious felicity*,[13] peculiar to himself, called Lord Clive, in the house of Commons, the Heav'n-born Clive.[14]

No. 11. Saturday, 7 August 1762.

I shall dedicate this paper to my correspondents, and the more earnestly wish their letters may prove agreeable to the reader, as their future interposition may afford me a comfortable respite from my own labours.

To the BRITON.

SIR,
The man who calls himself the North Briton, has hinted more than once that you are my countryman, and affirmed that you cannot write English; as a proof of this assertion, he hath twice twitted you in the teeth with the word *glorification*[1] printed in *italics*. Now, although I don't pretend to be a connoisseur in the English language, I will affirm, in my turn, that *glorification* is an *English* word, to be found in all the common dictionaries, and to be met with more than once in scripture: his criticism therefore, is a little unfortunate, and the more extraordinary, as the author of it is said to be a clergyman,[2] who ought to be better acquainted with his bible, than to fall into such a palpable blunder. On the other hand, I could wish he would settle the authenticity of the word *vouchsafements*,[3] used as a substantive in the same page; a word which I don't remember to have seen in any dictionary or writer of reputation. With respect to his national favours, which he hath so liberally dispensed, I have little to say, but repeat the words of honest parson Adams: "I would much rather be the subject than the author of his delicate satire."[4] He seems to

have the true spirit of the village-cock that crows couragiously on his own dunghill, and puts me in mind of the hero in the romance of *Perceforest*,[5] who was so animated with the fire and enthusiasm of true chivalry, that he attacked the trees of the first wood he encountered on his road, and hacked and hewed with incredible prowess; not one of the said trees daring to lift a bough in opposition to this formidable assailant. I hope, while he proceeds in the same career of glory, he will ever meet with the same success. I rejoice in the happy coolness with which you have declined the contention; and should be much mortified to see any of my countrymen enter the lists in order to combat him with his own weapons, in the management of which, I believe in my conscience, he far excels all champions that Scotland ever produced. — But I am wandering from my purpose, which was to inform you, that though I am not much conversant with the English tongue, I pretend to be a perfect connoisseur in the *Erse* or ancient *Gaelic*, and can enjoy the poems of Ossian[6] in the original. I have also a smattering in classical knowledge, and think I have found in Virgil one of the most remarkable prophecies that ever oracle delivered. I need not tell you, that among the antients, a prophet and a poet was distinguished by the same appellation, *vates;* and that some learned critics have displayed much erudition to prove, that one of Virgil's eclogues was a prophecy of our Saviour.[7] For my own part, I think the subject is too serious and sacred to be handled in a critique on any profane author: but certainly there is no harm in trying for diversion, the *sortes Virgilianæ*, which are said to have proved ominous to King Charles I. and the Lord Falkland.[8] You must know, that tho' I am a native of North Britain, I have spent the greater part of my life in England, where I married young; and by dint of industry, without reproach, I have obtained a comfortable settlement. I have a boy at school, who has made some progress in learning, and with him in Holy-day-time, I sometimes engage in classical amusements. Among others, we frequently consult Virgil by way of sortilege,[9] not only for ourselves, but also in favour of our friends and benefactors. The other day I desired Dick to open for the King, and was not a little surprised to see him turn up the following passage in the Æneid, relating to the young prince Ascanius:

> *Macte nova virtute, puer. Sic itur ad astra;* —
> —— *formam tum vertitur oris*
> *Antiquum in* BUTEN. —
> *Tum comitem Ascanio pater addidit.* —
> *Atque his ardentem dictis adfatur Iulum:*
> *Sit satis, Æneide* —
> —— *primam hanc tibi magnus Apollo*

Concedit laudem, et paribus non invidet armis
Cetera, parce, puer, bello — [10]

Such a wonderful assemblage of circumstances, including the very name of *Bute* literally specified, could not fail to make an impression upon a man born on the hills of Morven, early tinctured with the romantic superstition of the Highland Shenachies,[11] accustomed to repeat the songs of Ossian and Caryl,[12] and attached by love and veneration to the family of the noble Lord, thus (as it were foretold by name) in the works of a pagan author, above seventeen hundred years ago. I fairly own my weakness in exclaiming when I made this discovery; "By the spirit of Ossian, Virgil had the second sight!" But, to be serious, Mr. Briton, are not you astonished at reading this passage, when you reflect upon the strange affinity it has to the circumstances of our present situation? A young Prince of the most amiable character, left to sustain the weight of a dangerous war, distinguishing the beginning of his government by acts of uncommon virtue; assisted by the councils of *Bute*, a chief of antient and of noble pedigree, whom the Prince's father had appointed as the companion of his youth; the glorious success of his first essays in war; and (I hope I may add) the sentiments of his ministers and council with respect to peace, so conformable to the interest and desire of the nation in general. I have nothing further to say, but to beg pardon for these trifling and whimsical conceits, which I hope will be found, at least as excusable and entertaining as the wretched Greek pun that lately made its appearance in the front of the paper called the North Briton.[13] You will also excuse the Scotticisms which the pretended North Briton will, by dint of his exceeding penetration, discover in this epistle; and allow me to assure you, that I am a hearty well-wisher to South Britain, altho' a native of Argyle.

To the BRITON.

SIR,

A wise man will scorn alike the censure and applause of the multitude; the first as an impotent attack which virtue cannot avoid, and innocence has no cause to fear; the last as a contemptible bubble, without solidity or duration. There are some examples on record, of good men and great patriots sacrificed by popular frenzy: but I could fill a whole volume with instances, both from antient and modern history, of men without real merit, whom the mob, without reason, has raised into idols, worshipped for a season; and then their adoration changing into disgust, abandoned to contempt and oblivion.

William Pitt, after Richard Brompton.
(Courtesy of the National Portrait Gallery, London.)

Reverses of this nature might be found in the annals of this country, even within my own remembrance: but as such a review might be displeasing to some persons still living, whom I have no intention to offend, I shall select one remarkable instance from a foreign republic, the case of a famous demagogue in Florence, called *Luca Pitti*,[14] who flourished, and fell in the fifteenth century. He was a plebeian of a bold and turbulent spirit, who sought to gratify the most aspiring ambition, by courting the favour of the populace. This, he found no difficulty in acquiring, possessed as he was of a natural flow of eloquence, perfectly adapted to the taste and understanding of the vulgar. By dint of exerting this talent in the council of the state, and espousing the cause of the multitude on all occasions, he raised himself into such consideration among the lower class of citizens, that nothing was heard but the praise of *Pitti*. When he appeared in public, the mob rent the air with acclamations; and every mechanic[15] of any substance, presented him with some valuable token of his esteem. Cosmo de Medicis the first, the wealthiest and the best subject of the republic, who knew his disposition, and was well acquainted with his aim, imployed his influence in such a manner, that *Pitti* was chosen gonfalonier of justice;[16] and then his real temper appeared without restraint. He no longer kept any measures with his fellow-citizens. He treated his superiors with insolence, and his equals with contempt: he fleeced the people without mercy: he granted protection and encouragement to the most abandoned profligates, who were endued with any art or talent which could be turned to his private advantage; and the multitude, which he had formerly courted and caressed, he now held in the most mortifying subjection. Afterwards, when the family of Medici was supposed to aspire to sovereign power; when the people were alarmed for their liberty; when opposite factions were on the point of drawing the sword, and his country was threatened with the horrors of a civil war: in this emergency, when certain patriots entreated him to interpose his influence towards an accommodation, or declare himself in favour of those who wished well to the constitution; he shrunk from the service of his country in the day of danger and distress. He lent a deaf ear to all their solicitations; and wrapt himself in the shades of inglorious retirement, at a critical juncture, when public freedom was at stake, and his country in an especial manner demanded the full exercise of his faculties and interest. His behaviour on this delicate occasion, though palliated by a few hireling emissaries, provoked his former adherents to such a degree, that their attachment was changed into hatred; their applause into reproach. The gifts they had formerly bestowed with rapture, they now recalled with disdain: not one gold box or trinket was left as a testimony of his former credit! Their indignation, however, gradually subsided into contempt. *Luca Pitti*, who had appeared like a comet in politics, now set, never to rise again. He passed the evening of his life in disgraceful solitude, and died in utter oblivion. It must be owned, however, in behalf of this man, that when he quitted the helm, he was quiet. He did not attempt to disturb the operation of that machine which he would no longer manage; and if he did not exert himself to the utmost of his power, for the service and advantage of the public; so neither did he employ or countenance a set of desperate incendiaries, to kindle the flames of civil dissension in the bowels of his country. If any turbulent *Pitti* is living at this day, he will do well to take warning from the fate of this Florentine; or should such infamous partizans be at work, I hope every good man will think it a duty incumbent upon him to detect and expose them to the detestation of their fellow-subjects,

I am, SIR,
Your humble servant,
CURIO.[17]

To the BRITON.

Mr. BRITTIN,

Althof my neighbour Firkin says you can't rite English, therefore must be a Scotchman; and being a Scotchman, you have no right to call yourself a Brittin; and as how you are a vagabond people, that come over in shoals with every fair wind, like locusts to devour us; yet I knows what's what. There are good and bad of all countries, and mayhap your Lord B — e may behave as honourable as some who hold their heads very high in the city of London. There is Sir Dogberry Verges[18] of our ward, who was made a knight for speechifying, and subscribes himself the dear friend of the great orator P — : I remembers well is the time, when he was no more than — but no matter for that. You must know, Mr. Brittin, that he bespoke my husband to hollow among the mob at Temple-Bar and Guild-Hall, as having a special good counter-tenor voice; and I'll assure you he did not spare it, as we have many witnesses to prove. Sir Dogberry promised him his own vote, and the interest of Mr. Alderman Grog,[19] to make him clerk of the parish when there should be a vacancy: but, the old man's dead, and another chosen; and all that my husband got for tearing his pipes to pieces, was poor five shillings and half a gallon of new rum. Now, I knows as how they want voices to rail at your countryman; to swear he has sold Newfoundland to the French, and is going to bring in Popery and the Pretender: but I am resolved they shall no

more dance to his pipe, unless he is better paid for his music——My husband
can hollow bass as well as treble.——A word to the wise, Mr. Brittin, and so
I remain hereafter, as it may be,

> *Your humble servant,*

Portsoken-Ward, Aug. 1.

> WINIFRED BULLCALF.[20]

No. 12. Saturday, 14 August 1762.

> *This fellow's of exceeding honesty,*
> *And knows all qualities, with a learned spirit*
> *Of human dealings.*
> SHAKESPEAR.[1]

As my good friend the North Briton has taken some pains to settle arrears[2]
with me in his last paper but one, he will give me leave, in my turn, to
except against some articles of the account; and as I am overpaid, return the
ballance, tho' not in his own coin. I will neither call him knave, nor fool, nor
dunce, nor declare that his writings are equally replete with nonsense and
scurrility: for whatever energy these epithets and censures may have, I take it
for granted, that the public will not implicitly acquiesce in the characters we
may bestow upon each other; but assert the privilege of judging for itself. All
that I shall say of the compliments with which I am so liberally indulged is,
that the North Briton, like the lion, seems to have lashed himself into a rage
with his own tail;[3] and this is the only circumstance in which I shall pretend
to compare him to that generous savage. In the delicacy of his utterance, he
resembles another long-ear'd animal that shall be nameless. Tho' I decline
all contest with him in respect to the literary merit of our lucubrations, I find
it a duty incumbent upon me to wipe off the aspersion of having promul-
gated falshood, in order to deck with borrowed plumes, the reputation of the
present ministry. He says I have filched from Mr. P——tt, the honour of having
planned the expedition to Martinique:[4] he proceeds to demonstrate, that the
said expedition was concerted before the resignation of that minister: then,
by way of inference, reviles the Briton as a venal prostitute for ascribing the
plan to the new ministry; and affirms, that all the merit the present ad——n
can claim from the success of the armament, is their having suffered it to
be carried into execution. Now, this is precisely what the Briton contended

for; and therefore this precious politician has done no more, than combated a shadow of his own making.

If the successor of Mr. P—tt had been the fearful, vacilating, or wrong-headed minister he has been represented by the North Briton and his honest confederates, he might have suspended the execution of the scheme upon various pretences: he might have detained the armament a whole season without any pretence at all, as his predecessor acted the preceding year.[5] He might, in lieu of General Monckton, have substituted another commander,[6] without skill to understand the nature of the service, without spirit to seize the advantages which his strength and opportunities afforded, who would have made an ineffectual landing, and, without the least shew of opposition, given up the project in despair, at the very time when the principal inhabitants were assembled to treat of a surrender. He might, in imitation of the illustrious pensioner, have changed the object, and sent that powerful armament against some barren rock without consequence, where the blood and treasure of his country would have been wantonly sacrificed without any prospect of advantage; or he might have wasted it in petty excursions along the coast of France,[7] in breaking glass-windows, and alarming fishermen, under the direction of great officers who, at the approach of the enemy, would have wisely declined a battle, without having taken any precautions for a retreat, and left the whole rear of his army to be cut in pieces, or carried into captivity.

I am also accused of having falsely and traiterously alledged, that the plan of carrying on the war in America was ever espoused in this, or any former dispute, previous to the reign of W— IV.[8] And here I cannot but admire the extensive knowledge and egregious modesty of my sage antagonist. Is it possible he can be so ignorant, as not to know, that ever since the Revolution, and even before that period, the continent and islands of America have been always considered as the most tender parts in which both France and Spain can be affected? Did he never hear of two successive, tho' unsuccessful expeditions to Quebec,[9] in the reigns of King William III. and Queen Anne? Does not he remember the powerful armament equipped in the last war, and sent to the West Indies under the command of Admiral Vernon?[10] An armament sufficient, if properly managed, to have subdued all the settlements of Spain in that part of the world? Has he forgot that our colonies in North America, raised of themselves a body of troops, which actually conquered the important island of Cape Breton,[11] and took the strong town of Louisbourg by a regular siege: that they had planned the reduction of Quebec, and raised companies for that purpose, which were to be reinforced by an armament from England, which tho' really embarked at a very great expence to the nation, never proceeded on the voyage, but was, by the weakness of the reigning ministry, the remnant of which the North Briton has very lately extolled, perverted to a most ridiculous purpose? [12]

If his intelligence, or his memory does not reach so far back, he could not but know, that in the beginning of the present war, America was chosen as the chief scene of action, previous to Mr. P—tt's administration; that a considerable body of regular troops was sent thither under the command of Mr. Braddock,[13] whose misfortune did not at all detract from the merit of the design, which even at that time extended to the conquest of Cape Breton, and all Canada. With what face then, can this author assert that no effectual steps were taken for prosecuting hostilities in America, either in the last or present war, before the ad—n of his boasted patron? What a degree of assurance and intrepidity must he possess, in openly charging me with rancour and falsehood, for having affirmed that there was no penetration required in adopting a plan which could not have been overlooked with any pretensions to common sagacity. But, indeed, I ought not to be surprised at this instance of effrontery in a writer, who, rolled in all the infamy of scandal, raked together by forgery and malice, in order to defile the character of his P—ce and his family, steps forth, and audaciously retorts the charge of calumny and abuse, upon those whose sole endeavour has been to vindicate that innocence which he had so foully aspersed, to detect his iniquity, and refute his slander.

After having discharged his virulence against the Briton, he makes a transition to a subject, upon which both he and his prototype the Monitor expatiate with peculiar self-complacency, as a fresh source of detraction; I mean the late expedition of the French to Newfoundland,[14] where it seems they have done some damage to the fishery of Great Britain. Whatever the enemy's success in this attempt may have been, I question whether there is one native of France, to whom it gives such exquisite pleasure, as it has afforded to the political scandal-mongers of London and Westminster. They have been for some time hovering and croaking like birds of ill omen, in hope and expectation of a national calamity; and now Providence has gratified their spleen, by permitting a disaster to befall their country. The French have stoln out of their own harbour, and surprised some fishing vessels on the banks of Newfoundland, where they are also said to have destroyed a few old wooden stages, and taken one or two inconsiderable places which never were thought tenable, under any administration. This is the dreadful calamity upon which the Monitor and North Briton have extended their throats, and made as much noise, as if the enemy were in possession of the Tower of London. This, they

cry, is such a misfortune as could not have happened under the late adminis-
tration; and therefore it is owing to the neglect or incapacity of the present
M——r. Pray heaven, it is not deducible from something worse than inca-
pacity! Who knows but the earl of B——e has weakened the defence of the
place, on purpose that it might fall an easy prey to the French squadron? This
is just such an inference as might be expected from the honesty and candour
of those writers, who are hackneyed in the most infamous ways of scandal
and abuse: but, I believe, they pray much more fervently that the French may
not have already abandoned the important conquest they had made; and that
they may not be expelled from it, until they have more effectually conduced
to excite the spirit of discontent in the British nation.

It would be doing too much honour to the talents of these revilers, to
suspect they are employed by the French King as incendiaries, to raise a com-
bustion in the bowels of their country; but, it cannot be deemed unfair to
charge them with having engaged as volunteers in this honourable service.
With respect to the affair of Newfoundland, it may be thought superfluous
to observe, that our loss is in itself inconsiderable, when weighed against the
advantages we have gained in the course of the war: that the French have,
in all probability, by this time quitted the coast; or if they have not, that
their whole armament will run the most imminent risk of falling into the
hands of the squadron appointed to recover the places they may have taken:
that if the misfortune had been much greater, it could not be imputed to the
present, more than to the past administration, inasmuch as the same force
which had been judged necessary by the last M——r, for the protection of
the fishery on that coast, was continued by his successor without diminution:
that the same attempt must have met with the same success, had it been made
when Mr. P—tt stood at the helm; and therefore, the comparison made by
the North Briton upon this subject, is founded upon falsehood and absurdity;
two principles to which he has invariably adhered ever since he made his first
appearance in public.

It must be owned, however, that as no honour can possibly redound to
Mr. P—tt's ad——n from our fisheries having been carried on without mo-
lestation, because the enemy never attempted to disturb it; so neither could it
have reflected any disgrace upon his conduct, had the French then executed
the enterprise which they have now atchieved. He must be ignorant indeed,
who does not know that the British settlements and possessions abroad, are
infinitely too extensive to be secured in every part, by any land or naval
force we can exert: that in the prosecution of an active war, small consider-
ations must sometimes give way to objects of great importance; and that if

the defence of Newfoundland had been weakened, in order to strengthen the armament destined against the Spanish settlements in the West Indies, the ministry would have been excusable, and even praise-worthy, for hazarding a little to gain a great deal: but the truth is, no such risk was run; no force was recalled from Newfoundland; the fishery was guarded by the usual convoy; not a French man of war was to be seen upon the Atlantic; and the harbour of Brest was blocked up by an English squadron. The enemy made a desperate push. They had the good fortune to give our squadron the slip. Their destination was uncertain. They fell upon the defenceless coast of Newfoundland. They might have insulted the greatest part of North America. They might have made a descent upon the island of Barbadoes. They might have scoured the whole coast of Africa, and made themselves masters of all the English settlements in that part of the world: our forts in Guinea would make but a poor defence. The Af——n company sollicited an augmentation of five thousand pounds *per annum* to keep them in repair: but this paultry sum, necessary for the maintenance of castles, upon which that valuable commerce entirely depends, was thought too exorbitant by the late M——r, at a time when as many millions were yearly expended for the interests of P——a and H——r.

Let me now appeal to the impartial reader, whether or not Lord B——e stands acquitted of all guilt and misconduct; whether every fact alledged against him, either as a M——r or a man, has not been fairly proved false or frivolous; the suggestions of malice and perfidy; the vile forgeries of desperate tools, endeavouring to raise dangerous commotions in the commonwealth?

As to my own particular, I am content to be abused with my betters. The discharge of calumny is habitual to the North Briton. His mouth no sooner opens, than the foul stream of scandal issues forth. I would not willingly offer violence to his excessive modesty, by owning how much I stand in awe of his formidable pen; how much I envy the honours of his literary reputation. I can however, as a christian declare, that I heartily forgive his resentment, and even with compassion hear him exclaiming about a pension—Alas! as Polonius says, "Still harping on my daughter!"[15] *Hinc illæ lachrymæ.*[16] A pension is, to be sure, an interesting subject to a political adventurer; and very different methods have been used to obtain such a comfortable establishment. We have seen some writers acquire it by flattering weak ministers, and varnishing over the practices of corruption. Other furious drawcansirs[17] have extorted it by menacing clamour and virulent reproach. I need not mention which of these roads to a pension the North Briton has thought fit to pursue; but time will discover whether the desirable sop will be thrown to this triple-headed Cerberus[18] that guards the cave of defamation: yet, he will do well to consider, that there is some small difference between the past and present times. Former oppositions were founded upon melancholy truths, which could not be disproved. The present arises from palpable falsehoods, which have been again and again detected: former ministers have trembled from a sense of guilt: the present stands secure in conscious innocence.

As to his wise remark, that I have dignified the persons concerned in the late rebellion,[19] with the name of insurgents, out of tenderness to the cause in which they were embarked; it deserves no answer: it is a piteous indication of malice and imbecillity; of a piece with his precious comment upon my pre-sumption in assuming the name of Briton; in using the sign of my publisher as a headpiece to my paper, and hazarding the word *glorify* as an English ex-pression. It is impossible I should be angry with such an antagonist, any more than I should be at the howling of a chop-fallen[20] beagle without teeth or discernment, that in attempting to bite, can only discharge a nauseous stream of ineffectual slaver.

With regard to the matter which these my papers contain, I put myself on my country, to be scrutinized with severity, and judged with candour. I pre-tend not to infallibility. I may be betrayed into small mistakes by inadvertency or misinformation: but if it shall appear, that I have wilfully misrepresented any fact from malice or prostitution; that I have forged the most inconsid-erable article, or strained the smallest circumstance to depreciate virtue, or adorn vice; to traduce any character, or justify any administration; let me find no favour with the public, but be consigned to that scorn and detestation, which ought to be the fate of every venal tool, of every base calumniator.

No. 13. Saturday, 21 August 1762.

—— Dabit in laqueum vestigia noster
Perfidus——

JUVENAL.[1]

I have often heard it observed by men of sense and candour, that the friends of his M——y and his m——rs, in condescending to refute the scurrili-ties that have been published against them, have done too much honour to an opposition, the most unfounded and contemptible that ever appeared in any age or nation; that its slanders were so wretchedly contrived, as to stand self-convicted of malice and stupidity; and that silence and neglect would prove the most infallible means to hasten their progress to oblivion. "Should a gentleman (say they) in passing along the street, be abused by a drunken chimney-sweeper, he would be in the wrong to degrade himself so far as to enter into altercation with such a dirty antagonist: his better way would be to proceed without stopping, and leave the sooty reviler to the cognizance of the next constable." This advice, I apprehend, is to be taken with some limitation. If the said chimney-sweeper contents himself with the exercise of his humour, and cracks his jokes upon any supposed peculiarity in my appearance, I should leave him to the triumphs of his wit, and perhaps laugh with the rest of his audience: but, if with malice prepense,[2] he endeavours to obstruct my passage, and rancorously throws his smut upon my coat, or character, I then sustain a real injury; and it becomes a duty to the public, as well as to myself, to bring the miscreant to condign punishment; at least, it may be necessary to clear myself from the dirt with which I am so foully bespattered. Before the venerable tribunal of the mob, a chimney-sweeper is as much respected as the first peer of the realm; and such is the depravity of human nature, that scandal is generally welcome to the populace, from whatever infamous source it may have flowed. It must be owned, indeed, there is a species of abuse, so low, so gross, so void of all spirit and entertainment, that even the mob itself will surfeit on it; and such precisely is the precious mess which the authors of the North Briton have presented to their customers, in one dull course of repetition. From their stile and manner, one would imagine they belonged to the vociferous tribe of draggled-tail'd females who stroll about with bundles of brown paper, vending the lucubrations of Grub-street. Half a dozen of these vagrants, assembling in some paved court or blind alley, are capable of raising such an outcry as will alarm a whole neighbourhood. Their text is some mysterious hint of scandal, and they run about in the utmost agitation, bawling aloud, "Buy my Rosemary — A Word to the Wise — Keep your own Council!"[3] The curiosity of the populace being thus arroused, they lay out their halfpence, read the performance; but, finding it utterly destitute of sense, amusement, and information, they condemn it to the jakes,[4] and fairly wish the whole noisy crew that hawked it, at the devil.

To the BRITON.

Sir,

Since the first æra of the British history, the spirit of faction, (if at all awakened) never wore so contemptible an aspect as at present. It was formerly our misfortune to see men of the greatest influence and ability hurried away by self-interest, pride, or resentment, and for a time lost to every principle of public virtue. Shaftesbury and Bolingbroke,[5] at certain seasons, were very dangerous persons; nay, Swift and Addison,[6] more than once, have thrown conscience to the left, for the sake of their different parties. The usual consequence ensued. The nation was perplexed; parties were formed, and animosities contracted; while the public service was either neglected, or at best retarded.

But, thanks to providence, those days are over. Every man hath seen and felt the absurdity and mischief of sacrificing the general interest to private pique and particular connection. To this universal spirit of union we owe the rapidity and number of our conquests; and that this national union sprung from a national conviction of party-inconvenience, no man in his senses will deny.

I know there is a hum-drum fellow, who would insinuate, that this coalition was effected by a man whom he bedaubs as his patron, or rather worships as his deity. Long may they enjoy each other! — But, surely, were he worth an answer, there is scarce a school-boy who, from his own recollection of facts, could not easily point out his absurdity — Can this Solomon forget how we stood immediately after the commencement of this war? — Let him recollect, if he is able: — let him even assert, with his usual veracity, that all public virtue was dead; yet, still he must confess, that our public danger was such as would have *united* any people, not entirely lost to all sense of self-preservation.

We saw our flag insulted, and the strong hold of Minorca wrested from us — We saw the enemy greatly superior in India — We saw America on the verge of ruin; Braddock and his army lost, and many fortresses taken. We saw a mighty armament on the coast of France; and were alarmed daily with the reports of a triple invasion —— And could not all this wed us to the common interest? —— No — till the great orator (like doctor Squintum in the farce[7]) stept in with his *saving* grace, and said, *be ye one!*

But, Mr. Monitor, this doctrine is more thread-bare than your cassock: you must take it to Rag-fair,[8] or go without a purchaser. Politicians of your size will scarcely persuade men to swallow an alligator. The *Nobility* and *Commons* not only approve, but applaud his M — y's choice of a M — r, unexceptionable in his public and private capacity. The present chief magistrate[9] and council of this loyal *metropolis* are equally thankful for so fresh an instance of his paternal regard. They are sensible of his mild and happy government; nor can a *paltry individual* divide their affections with the best of S — ns. No, notwithstanding that audacious forged report of their blind attachment to a certain frothy declaimer, the imperial city of *London* will not surely suffer any bear-leader to clap a ring in her nose, and drag her about at pleasure.

But, if the *Lords*, the *Commons*, and the city, are fast friends to the present ministry; it may be asked whence flow these tides of scurrility and treason, these deluges of filth and sedition that drown our daily papers, and stink in the nostrils of mankind? — From a fourth estate distinguished by the name of *Rabble*, which I divide into three corporations, *viz.* Hedge coffee-house politicians, bankrupt mechanics soured by their losses, and splenetic sots, who change their no-opinions oftener than their linen. These illustrious tribes are led by an equal number of chiefs, *viz. Jacky-Dandy*, *Pædagogus Latro*, and *Bruin*.[10] Jacky is what the world calls a *buck* and a *smart:* his father was a painstaking man, and having scraped together some money (the Lord knows how) left this spark a *gentleman*. Jacky no sooner fingered the cash, than he felt a strange ambition to become a wit, made himself master of *Joe Miller*, and the *Vade Mecum*,[11] frequented the greenroom,[12] cracked jokes in all companies; and finally procured an introduction to Bruin and Pædagogus. Here all parties found what they sought for. — He could treat; they could scribble; and though Jacky's friends are not of the highest order, they will probably procure him an *elevation*, that may cause an increase in the dimensions of his Perriwig.

Pædagogus is a melancholy instance of merit unrewarded. In his halcyon days, he enjoyed the important post of deputy usher to an academy, whence being driven, for reasons best known to himself, he now keeps a shred of existence together by begging subscriptions, and spunging on school-boys. Sometimes he feeds on Bruin's offal, whom he frequently follows, and helps out with scraps of blasphemy, ribaldry and treason.

As to Bruin himself, *O Dii boni!*[13] What language can do him justice! but, as a sketch of him has been given in a former paper, I shall pass him over for the present. However, before I take my leave, I would advise him to ask his friend lawyer *Small*[14] for the act of parliament that united these kingdoms: but, lest the lawyer should not be furnished with the book of statutes, I shall beg leave to quote a few abstracts from that law. By these the reader may partly perceive how far the legislature intended to proscribe Scotchmen as aliens and inferiors.

Statute 5th of Q. Anne, c. 8.[15] Article I. enacts, "That the said kingdoms (England and Scotland) the first of May 1707, and for ever, shall be united into one kingdom, by the name of Great Britain: and that the ensigns armorial be such as her Majesty shall appoint, and the cross of St. George and St. Andrew be conjoined."

ART. VI. All parts of the united kingdom to have the same allowances and encouragements, and be under the same regulations of trade, *&c.*

BRUISER, C. CHURCHILL (once the Rev.ᵈ) in the Character of a *Russian* Hercules, Regaling
himself after having Kill'd the Monster Caricatura that so lovely Gall'd his Virtuous friend the Heaven born WILKES
— But he had a *Club* this Dragon to Drub. Or he had ne'er don't I warrant ye. Dragon of Won.

The Bruiser, C. Churchill, by William Hogarth.
(Reproduced by permission of the Huntington Library, San Marino, California.)

ART. XXIII. After reciting the privileges of the sixteen peers, proceeds, "And all peers of Scotland, and their successors, shall be peers of Great Britain, and have rank and precedence next after the peers of the like orders and degrees in England, and before all peers of Great Britain of the like orders and degrees created after the union; and shall enjoy all privileges as fully as the peers of England, except sitting in the house of Lords, and voting on trials of peers."

ART. XXIV. "That there be one great seal for the united kingdom, different from the great seal used in either kingdom; and the quartering the arms, and the *precedence* of Lyon king of arms of Scotland left to her Majesty."

These hints may serve to shew the iniquity of that clamour which has been raised against our fellow-subjects of North Britain, as well as to determine whether the laws of England would not construe such virulent and outragious abuse, into a false, scandalous, malicious, and seditious libel. I am,

SIR,

Your humble servant,

MILO.[16]

No. 14. Saturday, 28 August 1762.

Haterius invisior fuit, quia somno aut libidinosis vigiliis marcidus, illustribus viris perniciem, inter Ganeam et stupra meditabatur.

TACITUS.[1]

Human misery is not so apt to excite compassion, as superior virtue is to generate envy and detraction.

When the celebrated Caliph *Haroun Rachid*[2] governed the Arabian empire, and diffused the blessings of beneficence thro' all his extensive dominions; when his name went forth like a Sabean odour,[3] chearing the hearts, and inspiring the songs of his happy subjects; when every corner of the imperial city of Bagdad resounded with the praise of his Vizir, *Giafar* of the race of *Baramak*, the most uncorrupt minister, the most liberal encourager of merit that ever executed the orders, and supported the dignity of the Caliphat; who had superintended the education of *Haroun*, the instructor of his youth, the companion of his solitude, ere yet he approached the throne which he was destined one day to ascend. In this season of general felicity, there was a remnant of miserable wretches, who, from disappointed ambition, or inveterate envy, repined at the success of merit, and like so many dæmons, damned without all prospect of redemption, derived fresh torments from the happiness which their fellow-creatures seemed to enjoy.

Of these children of perdition, the most wicked and abandoned was *Jahia Ben Israil Ginn*,*[5] a being of such an unhappy disposition, that it was commonly believed his soul was confined to its present prison, in order to do penance for some atrocious crime, unexpiated in its former state of existence. His external form was such as happily expressed the deformity of his mind. His face was meagre, sallow, and forbidding, as if he looked pale and haggard from the consciousness of guilt. His eyes were distorted, with such an hideous obliquity of vision,[6] that the sight of him alone had frightened some matrons into miscarriage, and made such an unfortunate impression on the imaginations of others, that instead of children, they brought gogle-eyed monsters into the world. His chin was long and incurvated, like the moon in her first quarter. His jaw was furnished with large irregular tushes;[7] and when he spoke, his mouth overflowed with a plentiful discharge of slaver.

With respect to his mental qualifications, he was totally destitute of principle, and never felt the influence of one liberal sentiment. Deaf to every suggestion of virtue, and dead to all the feelings of humanity, his heart afforded a receptacle to pride, malice, cruelty and slander. These were the passions that took the lead in regulating his conduct; though upon some occasions he was actuated by a kind of caprice that was not reducible to any determinate motive, and appeared equally absurd and fantastical. His capacity was more than sufficient to comprehend and retain the first elements of erudition: tho' like an unclean cask, it communicated a disagreeable flavour to every doctrine which it received. He imbibed a smattering in several branches of learning. The tropes and figures of obloquy he studied with peculiar eagerness; and his tongue wagged with such incessant rotation, that he seemed to labour under an involuntary emission of words.

He was more obliged to fortune than to nature: for, though his birth was obscure, his parents were wealthy, and took pride in training him up for a higher sphere of life, than that to which they themselves had been allotted by the dispensations of providence. *Jahia Ginn,* instead of feeding his father's goats, appeared by times in the gay world; exhibited himself to the public in gorgeous apparel; contracted acquaintance with the young Emirs of Bagdat; gave sumptuous entertainments; enlisted parasites; commenced rake and voluptuary, and, by dint of perpetual talking, sneering, laughing, shrugging,

---

*According to the doctrine of the Alcoran, the *Ginn* or *Ginni* was a malignant spirit, created from intense fire, not empyrean, but empyreumatic.[4]

John Wilkes Esqr., by William Hogarth.
(Reproduced by permission of the Huntington Library, San Marino, California.)

and slabbering, acquired some reputation as a satirist and buffoon. The opin-
ion of his father's wealth paved his way to an advantageous match of interest,
by which he became master of such a sum as seemed to intoxicate his brain,
and impel him to gratify all his passions without distinction or restraint. He
now affected the man of wit and pleasure; scoffed in public at religion; ridi-
culed morality; reviled merit; plunged headlong into riot and debauchery;
squandered away his means without taste; treated his wife like a true Arab,
and even repudiated her after the manner of the mussulmen.

Finding his constitution decayed, his character tainted, and his fortune
greatly impaired, he had recourse to the art of corruption, by which he ob-
tained a seat in the council of the *Schieks*,[8] flattering himself, that his extraor-
dinary talents would make such a figure in that assembly, as should entitle him
to preferment in the state: but *Jahia* had greatly over-rated his own genius.
He attempted to speak on several subjects, but was always heard with disgust
or derision. Enraged at this disappointment, he gave a loose to his malice and
misanthropy, not without hope, that how inconsiderable soever he might be
in the council, he should shine distinguished in the province of calumny and
abuse, because these were subjects the best suited to the malevolence of his
disposition.

The Caliph had, by public edict, indulged all his people with liberty of
speech concerning his person and government: his whole aim was to make
them happy; and thought, that from this indulgence, he might draw such in-
formation as would enable him to prosecute this aim the more effectually.
Jahia being thus secured against corporeal correction, went and offered his
talents to a discarded courtier, who took him forthwith into his protection;
and he began his probation with a libel against the government. He took post
in one of the most conspicuous parts of the city, and poured forth invectives
against the accomplished Caliph. He depreciated the character, he censured
the morals of his sovereign. He poured forth the most audacious slanders
against his mother, a venerable Princess,[9] universally revered for virtue and
benevolence: nor did the beloved consort of *Haroun* escape the lash of his
licentious tongue. The populace were at first confounded at the audacity of
this insolent plebeian: but, their astonishment was soon succeeded by in-
dignation, and, notwithstanding the edict of the Caliph, they would have
sacrificed this son of calumny to their resentment, had not his life been saved
by an Iman,[10] who, chancing to be on the spot, declared he was mad, conse-
quently held sacred by the law of the Prophet. The multitude immediately
dispersed; *Jahia* found himself alone in the streets of Bagdad. He then turned

his battery against the whole race of *Baramack*, whom he abused with all the licence of scurrility. The race of *Baramack* heard him in silent disdain.

Mortified at this mark of their contempt, he made a large collection of filth, and chusing his station near the precincts of the palace, began to pelt the Vizir as he passed and repassed to and from the court of the Caliph: but, whether he was too blind to take a proper aim at his object, or too unskilful to throw his dirt with any effect, certain it is, he never once hit the mark; and every effort he made served only to betray himself, and raise an intolerable odour, until he became such a public nuisance, that he was universally avoided: this was the only way in which he had it in his power to offend. — The Genii that protected this district, taking compassion on the inhabitants, exerted his power for their relief. *Jahia Ginn* going to the common sewer of the city, for a supply of soil, was suddenly petrified in the very act of stooping, and converted into a grotesque image, his mouth standing wide open as a spout for the discharge of filth: but it required the invention of a Genii to render *Jahia Ginn* in any shape serviceable to society. His Patron the Emir *Timour Basch*, (a title equivalent to that of Lord Chuckle-head[11] in *English*) insisted upon burying this petrefaction, alledging that images were forbid by the law of Mahomet: but, this motion was over-ruled, as it appeared, that although the spout retained every feature of *Jahia Ginn*, it could not be deemed the likeness of any ordinary production of nature.

To the BRITON.

SIR,

As I profess myself downright Swiss,[12] it will be unnecessary to use farther preamble. The *North Briton* affirms you are very dull, and as a Scotchman incapable of writing either sense or English. Being myself partly of his opinion, I humbly offer my services to your supposed patron Lord B——, declaring myself a *true born Englishman*,[13] perfectly well acquainted with all the familiar idioms of my mother tongue. My father dealt in hog's-flesh, and brought his pigs to a very good market: but I have been always conversant with animals of a more fashionable species; with hounds, horses, and whores. I have wore a laced coat from my infancy; frequented brothels and taverns, and displayed myself in the united characters of a gentleman, scholar, wit, and atheist. Having wasted my constitution and my means among rooks[14] and harlots, I made interest for a post in the militia: but all the places were filled except that of drill-serjeant, which required more knowledge and industry than I was master of. No body ever doubted my courage, or could suppose that I, who had been so many years known by the name of *blaspheming Dick*, and always set my Maker at defiance, would now shrink at the distant prospect of bodily danger. He needs not surely be afraid of temporal death, who hath resolution enough to brave eternal damnation. I think myself peculiarly qualified to enter the lists with the *North Briton*, and even to foil him at his own weapons; for, I have intrigued with oyster-wenches, and diligently attended the lectures of Billingsgate:[15] besides, I am provided with two staunch understrappers, one of them a reverend deacon in a laced hat and leather breeches; the other a learned pedagogue,[16] without any breeches at all. Their appetites are very keen; their teeth very sharp: they are coupled together, and crouch for employment, eager to bite, and tear, and taint, and havock. Backed by these twin terriers, I'll engage to attack any set of men or measures; to dash thro' thick and thin; to swear and forswear, forge calumny, detract and retract, affirm and deny, bespatter and bedaub, without any scruple of conscience, or any stings of compunction. Should the M——r decline inlisting us in the service of the commonwealth, we must even prey upon her, and then we may chance to attain a certain degree of exaltation. In that case, we shall not want companions to keep us in countenance, and I hope we shall all behave like *true born Englishmen*, proud to the last of that happy distinction, which we enjoy in common with so many honourable fraternities in this great metropolis. At any rate, it will be a great consolation to me in my last moments, to reflect, that tho' I may be chargeable with fraud, felony, sacrilege and treason; the world cannot with any justice impute to me, the indelible disgrace and unpardonable crime of being born on the North-side of the Tweed. I have no more to say, but to desire you will communicate these hints to the M——r, from yours, as you use me,

RICHARD DRAFF.[17]

No. 15. Saturday, 4 September 1762.

——*Mihique posthac bonos potius defendere liceat,*
Quam improbos accusare necesse sit. —— [1]

It is of little consequence to the public, to know in what manner the following dialogue fell into my hands. The sensible reader will perceive it has all the external marks of being genuine; and as it is truly dramatic, the anxious politician will rejoice in perusing such an unquestionable proof of the virtue and abilities which distinguish those illustrious patriots, who have charged themselves with the task of vindicating their country from the disgrace of a Scottish administration.

Lord GOTHAMSTOWE, and Capt. IAGO ANISEED.[2]

Lord GOTH.

My dear Aniseed! come to my arms, thou cordial to my drooping spirits.'Tis thou and thou alone that can'st dispel those carking cares that rankle in my bosom. Say, what tidings dost thou bring?

ANISEED.

Misfortune on misfortune! that cursed Scottish Earl——

Lord GOTH.

Ha! what has he done?—has he retaken Newfoundland? has he concluded a just and advantageous peace?——those hideous looks of thine——they harrow up my soul with fear and wonder![3]

ANISEED.

Things are not yet so desperate as your Lordship's apprehension preconceives: but, our lands are overgrown with thistles—insatiate B——e, not content with having filled our army, navy, treasury, and pension-list with his countrymen, has even planted one of them as a scullion in the Royal kitchen.

Lord GOTH.

Oh horrible!—in time that scullion will rise into a cook, and then the Caledonian haggish[4] will smoak beneath the nostrils of a British King—Foh! the very prospect turns my stomach.

ANISEED.

That caudle[5]—that caudle, good my Lord, which the aldermen and common-council, so lately swilled, was made—(*animus meminisse horret!*[6]) ——was made of Scottish oatmeal!——The customs and the manners of those northern free-booters, gain ground apace——I hear the piper of Inverary is to be appointed master of his Majesty's band of music——I expect to see the nobles of this land appearing at court without breeches, like so many Highland chiefs; and I suppose, in half a century, there will not be one temple of Cloacina[7] left in England, except perchance, one single fane[8] among your Lordship's collection of rarities.

Lord GOTH.

Good heaven avert the dire calamity!

ANISEED.

Methinks I see the mighty Earl Gothamstowe wrapped in a chequered plaid: these delicate thighs exposed to the bleak winds of winter; that head —— that comely head ——

Lord GOTH.

No more! my friend ——

ANISEED.

That ample head, the magazine of wit—

Lord GOTH.

Nay, prithee, honest Aniseed—

ANISEED.

The repository of science ——

Lord GOTH.

Dear captain! truce ——

ANISEED.

The favourite residence of wisdom ——

Lord GOTH.

For heaven's sake! —

ANISEED.

The sacred temple of taste ——

Lord GOTH.

Spare me, good Iago ——

ANISEED.

The ever-springing fountain of political sagacity; —— that peerless head disgraced with a blue-bonnet:[9] a rusty iron-hilted ferrara[10] depending from these puissant loins; and these elegant limbs cased in woollen buskins striped with green and yellow.[11]

Lord GOTH.

O monstrous! monstrous! shroud me from the frightful portrait thou hast drawn! — but, say my friend, did these same aldermen swallow their draughts of caudle with marks of satisfaction? or did they seem (like Pistol) to drink in token of revenge.[12]

ANISEED.

They drank in seeming extasy, like veteran gossips used to christenings.

Lord GOTH.

Degenerate brutes! yet I console myself by reflecting, that our friend Mr. Alderman Rumford [13] would not be present at that hateful ceremony.

ANISEED.

That Alderman, my Lord, is no true British spirit — he will not be found proof — already he capitulates with the foe — a title brings him over to the c — t ——

Lord GOTH.

Ha! will he then apostatize? what right has such a caitiff to renounce the principles he professed, and veer about with every wind of interest or ambition? This is the privilege of superior spirits, like my brother and myself — I mean my brother of adoption.[14] He who changed his party as often as he changed his cloaths; who, like some of our G — n allies, appeared in the front of opposite armies in the course of one campaign; who pocketted the reward of patriotism, and then openly received the wages of a c — t; who, without any reason assigned, espoused with all a lover's ardour to day, those very measures which he yesterday condemned to reprobation; who by turns reviled, and truckled to a weak and corrupt ad — n; who successively deserted three royal and indulgent masters at their time of need, and retreated with a pension,[15] in order to insult his benefactor; who could thus confound all the ordinary distinctions of right and wrong; adopt every known form of contradiction and inconsistency; and defy every decision of common sense, without forfeiting the esteem and worship of the multitude. ——

ANISEED.

These are undoubted marks of a transcendant genius. Your Lordship too, has given some shining specimens of the same egregious conduct. — We all remember the figure you made, and the orations you delivered among the independent electors of Westminster, when you inveighed with such force of eloquence and argument, against the brothers who then directed the helm of g——t;[16] when the cocoa-tree[17] was revered as the temple of true patriotism; when the Th——e itself was ridiculed as the seat of sordid avarice, and the Lord of Cl——em——t,[18] as the minister of folly and corruption. With what dignity of transition do we now behold your Lordship, beaming in the opposite extreme! upbraiding the present m——y, with favouring the men who sat under the shadow of that very tree, which your Lordship now stigmatizes as the notorious rendezvous of Jacobitish disaffection. With what peculiar grace, does your Lordship now extol the wisdom and the virtue of that consummate statesman lately set aside,[19] whom your raillery and rhetoric had so often represented as the shameless broker of venality; as the ludicrous ape of politics, that from the summit of greatness, exposed his naked posteriors to the contempt and laughter of mankind!——

Lord GOTH.

These, my friend Aniseed, are the peculiarities of mighty minds, that in their revolutions are not restricted by the laws which influence inferior planets. Our seeming irregularities and eccentricity, serve only to increase the wonder and the reverence of those who mark our course. But for a wretch like Rumford, a thing produced by some low negro-driver; reared among sugar-canes in one of our plantations; nourished with molasses, and sent hither in a puncheon[20] of rum; he to pretend to motion retrograde! he to presume to fall off from his engagements, and to enter into a separate treaty;—— 'tis preternatural and portentous!—there is no faith in man—and now I do remember—Thou, Aniseed,—even thou art said to row one way and look another, with war and vengeance on thy tongue, but peace and pension in thy heart.

ANISEED.

My Lord, I have not merited this keen reproach—The scripture saith, a man must leave father and mother and cleave unto his wife:[21] but, I have forsaken father, mother, family, and friends, nay, wife and all, and cleaved unto your Lordship. I have inlisted myself under the banner of your resentment, and prosecuted all your views in spite of conscience, loyalty and truth—In your cause I have encountered detection and disgrace, and with a countenance unabashed, reproduced the lie three times refuted—I have run the risk of *pumpings, purgings, blankettings, and blows.*[22]

Lord GOTH.

—— *Thou shouldst be honest* —

ANISEED.

I should be wise[23] — honesty is out of the question. — True, I have been tampered with; but, my attachment to your Lordship enabled me to withstand the temptation — even now I might be appointed scavenger to the palace, on the easy terms of clearing away the filth which I have there discharged ——

Lord GOTH.

No easy task, God-wot — the Augean stable[24] was not more befouled; and that required the strength of Hercules — but see — who comes?

ANISEED.

It is our setter[25] Peto;[26] a trusty varlet — how now Peto —

PETO.

Preliminaries of the peace undoubtedly are signed —

Lord GOTH.

Ha! what! how! where? when? —— heaven and earth —— haste Aniseed, again adore the powers of Calumny — dip thy pen in gall — let loose thy dogs of rancour — feign, fib, and forge — decry the terms, altho' thou knowest them not, as shameful, infamous, and ruinous — annihilate the council, and transfer the entire blame of this pernicious peace, upon the Scotchman's shoulders — O for a dash of treason to inflame the account — Had ye but courage to incur the smart of pains and penalties — how should I rejoice to see my Aniseed exalted to the pillory! to behold our parson Brawn[27] shorn of his ears! to hear the scourge resounding from the back of Birch the pædagogue![28] *that were a consummation devoutly to be wish'd!*[29] — away. ——

No. 16. Saturday, 11 September 1762.

Sit fur, sit sacrilegus, sit flagitiorum omnium vitiorumque princeps; at est bonus legislator, et ad dubia reipublicæ tempora reservandus —— [1]

Every kingdom, and every age, for a series of centuries, has produced a set of speculative philosophers, who have endeavoured to refine upon the constitution of their country; and almost all of these projectors, have either affected, or actually felt, an enthusiastic attachment to the democracies of ancient Greece. Some have commenced advocates for the liberty of the people, merely from the pride of classical knowledge, and have extolled the laws of Solon, for no other reason but because they were written in Greek. Others have conceived republican principles from envy to their superiors in wealth and affluence. A third sort of reformers have espoused the plebeian interests, from an innate aversion to all order and restraint. And it is to be hoped, for the honour of human nature, that some few of those theoretical legislators have been actuated by motives of humanity and benevolence. This, however, I take to be a mistaken philanthropy, which, conceiving every individual to be equally free by nature, draws this erroneous inference, that every individual has an equal right to intermedle in the administration of public affairs; a principle subversive of all government, magistracy and subordination; a principle destructive to all industry and national quiet, as well as repugnant to every fundamental maxim of society.

To give us a just idea of a mob-ruled commonwealth, we need only peruse the histories of Athens and of Rome, during those periods at which their government was purely republican. There we shall meet with nothing but faction, animosity, persecution, ingratitude and disquiet. We shall find the people of Athens led about by every turbulent orator in their turns, like an ill-tamed monster, from vanity to vice, from folly to caprice, from the lowest depth of despondence, to the most giddy height of elation. All was violence, tumult, injustice, and presumption. They banished Æschines, in order to gratify his rival orator; and then drove Demosthenes[2] himself into exile, after they had crowned him in the theatre of Bacchus, as the first patriot of the commonwealth. The same ingratitude did they manifest towards Aristides, who, for his extraordinary virtue had acquired the surname of *just*; and this was the reward of Themistocles,[3] who saved their country, and defeated the Persian fleet at Salamis, when that formidable power threatened destruction to all the free states of Greece. The internal state of Rome, from the expulsion of the kings, to the final extinction of their liberty, what was it but an uninterrupted scene of tumult and sedition, excited by the illiberal envy, insolence, and profligacy of the vulgar, cloaked under the specious name of freedom. Witness their secession to the *Mons sacer*,[4] and their shocking cruelty and ingratitude to Manlius Coriolanus[5] under Scipio Africanus.[6]

If such was the disposition and conduct of the Athenian and Roman people, so celebrated for their sensibility, penetration, and patriotism; what but the most savage brutality could be expected from the populace of a Gothic nation;

uninspired by sentiment, unenlightened by science, and unrestrained by laws; instigated by sedition, and inflamed by intoxication. Such were the mob-reformers which have appeared at different times, in almost every kingdom of Christendom, offering their sage counsel on the points of their swords, and endeavouring to new-model the constitution of their country. Such were those venerable legislators, Wat Tyler and Jack Straw,[7] who unfolded the banners of ignorance, barbarity, and rebellion; who, in all the pride of refor-mation, promulgated a plan for rectifying the errors of the state; who visited the metropolis with one hundred thousand armed peasants at their heels, de-nouncing vengeance against all rank, order, learning, and ingenuity. All the world knows in what manner all his laudable schemes were defeated by a very extraordinary instance of courage, exerted by a Mayor of London.[8]

It will no doubt give great satisfaction to the sect of republican philoso-phers, to see that this rectifying spirit has revived at the end of so many centuries, in the very same scene, the city of London, among the same class of men; kindled by the same means, and fed with the same sort of fuel. When I say the same scene, and the same class of people, I ought to specify some necessary distinctions: for, that ancient plan of reformation began among the peasants of Kent and Essex, tho' they were afterwards joined by a set of patriots whom venal historians have stigmatised as debauched, profligate, and desperate villains, and reinforced by the populace of London. Now, it is well known, that those peasants were in a state of actual slavery, denomi-nated villenage; whereas the present Reformers pique themselves upon being free-born Englishmen: but, like their predecessors, they are headed by their Wat Tyler and Jack Straw, and animated by a reverend apostle of equal virtue and capacity with the celebrated John Bull,[9] the honest priest of those days, who acted as principal incendiary, spiriting up the multitude to mischief and rebellion by inflammatory sermons, quaint rhimes, and treasonable papers, dispersed among the leaders of the people. What a loss it was to mankind, and a disgrace to the government of England, that this worthy reformer, in canonicals, should have been hanged as a sower of sedition!

True it is, the malcontents of our days have not yet proceeded to open insurrection; perhaps their courage is not sufficiently roused, nor their cause sufficiently strengthened for such an attempt; but, it must be owned, they have exactly followed the footsteps of their ancestors in those circumstances we have already mentioned, as well as in divers other particulars. They have taken public exceptions to the proceedings of government, and boldly in-trenched upon the King's prerogative. They have not indeed assembled, and sent a message, giving him to understand they were come to speak with him about certain important affairs: but, they have freely condemned his conduct, and insisted upon a change of measures. They have steadily kept in view the example of Mr. Tyler's followers, in directing their chief animosity against the treasurer, and in treating the K——g's mother with the most outrageous indignity.

In some other respects, their virtue hath soared a pitch above the patriotism of former times. Their interposing in state-affairs is not the effect of oppression and despair, which were the avowed motives of Tyler's insurrection; but, the spontaneous working of public spirit. They groan under no species of tyranny. They complain of no taxation. On the contrary, they strenuously contend for a prosecution of such measures as must accumulate the public burden; and reject with scorn all thoughts of a pacification, until they themselves shall have an opportunity of sending deputies to the congress. In another particular, their spirit seems to transcend that magnanimity which Tyler's bands displayed. Without having recourse to arms for their defence; without taking any measures for securing themselves from the penalties of the law; they have had the courage to scatter the seeds of sedition in public; to practice every species of defamation; to insult the government, and belie the ministry; to laugh at Bridewell[10] and flagellation; despise and brave the pillory, and even set the gallows at defiance. But, their courage is not more admirable than their penetration. Other malcontents have complained only of such grievances as they pretended to feel, and condemned such measures as were already known to the public: but, our Reformers are too quick in their apprehension to wait for events in the ordinary course of production: they penetrate into the womb of time, and, by a peculiar sagacity, anticipate the birth of incidents.

Let us hear with what energy of argument, with what a tide of elocution, those consummate politicians inveigh against the peace which is supposed to be upon the carpet. Have they considered the horrors of war? —— They never thought upon the subject. — Do they understand the true interest of their country? — They have no interest in their country. —— Do they know the terms of peace which the enemy has offered? They do not even pretend to guess. — But, the spirit of patriotism whispers them in the ear, that it is their duty, and their birth-right, as free-born Englishmen, to revile their P——ce, defame his friends, and oppose his g——t: Jacky Straw assures them, it is their privilege to be insolent and refractory; and Bull the parson[11] declares, that *Vox populi est vox Dei:*[12] the voice of the people is the voice of God.

As these Reformers have, upon all occasions, assumed the title of free-born Englishmen, and denominated themselves *the good people of England;* it will not be amiss to enquire who the individuals are that compose this respectable community. Are they persons of wealth, property, or credit? — No. —— Have they distinguished themselves as valuable members of the commonwealth, by their industry, probity, or learning? — No such matter. — Do they contribute to the necessities of the public, or of the poor, by paying scot or lot,[13] King's-tax, or parish-tax? — Not a farthing. They reverence no King: they submit to no law: they belong to no parish. Have they a right to give their voice in any sort of election, or their advice in any assembly of the people? They have no such right established by law; and therefore they deduce a right from nature, inconsistent with all law, incompatible with every form of government. They consist of that class which our neighbours distinguish by the name of *Canaille*,[14] forlorn Grubs and Garetteers, desperate gamblers, trades-men thrice bankrupt, prentices to journeymen, understrappers to porters, hungry pettifoggers, bailiffs-followers, discarded draymen, hostlers out of place, and felons returned from transportation. These are the people who proclaim themselves free-born Englishmen, and, transported with a laudable spirit of patriotism, insist upon having a spoke in the wheel of government; who distribute infamy among the great; calumniate their S — n, asperse his family; condemn his ministers, criticise his conduct, and publicly declaim upon politics, in coffee-houses, ale-houses, in cellars, stalls, in prisons, and the public streets. And indeed, if we reflect, that this division of the species among us, are neither electing nor elected, neither representing nor represented in any national, provincial, municipal or parochial assembly: it is proper they should enjoy some extraordinary privilege to ascertain their title of free-born Englishmen.

I have no sort of objection to their being confirmed in the liberties they have lately taken with the characters and conduct of Princes, ministers, magis-trates, and others unjustly denominated their superiors and betters. Every plebeian among the Athenians, who attended the assembly of the people, spending his time, and exerting his wisdom for the good of his country, was entitled to a provision of three oboli[15] or halfpence *per diem*, to be paid out of the public treasury. If they were thus considered for speaking their minds, how much better are the *Canaille* of London entitled to speak on af-fairs of importance, when instead of demanding three halfpence for opening their mouths; each individual generally pays that price for an opportunity of holding forth in places of public resort.

I am well aware of the expedients which some of those Reformers have fallen upon to make their public spirit, and their private interest, coincide; by disposing of their lucubrations for hire, and exposing to sale their satires in emblematical prints,[16] exhibited to the view of passengers in the public streets of this metropolis. But, as this practice may be attended with some inconvenience to the persons of those worthy patriots, I shall first describe the risk they run, and then point out an easy and effectual method to screen them from all jeopardy and vexation. Some of the essays which they have lately published, may, I apprehend, from the iniquity of the laws now in force, be construed into high-treason; and all of them may subject their authors to dangerous prosecutions for libels and sedition. The ingenious and significant hieroglyphics, displayed in all the print-shops, from Temple-Bar to the Royal-Exchange; tho' immortal monuments of genius, taste, and humour, may fall under the cognizance of Gothic magistrates, who are no judges of their merit, and out of meer hatred to the arts which they do not understand, will be apt to persecute the inventors and venders of these witty conceits. Some future ministers, not quite so passive as the present government, may think it necessary to support their authority by making a proper number of examples; and a Lord Mayor of London[17] may arise, who will not suffer the windows of printshops to be lined at noon-day, with figures which are an outrage upon decency, a scandal upon the nation, and a reproach upon police.[18] Who knows but some officious Bishop of London[19] may interpose in behalf of what is called christian charity and decorum?

Should such an unfortunate æra cast up, pains and penalties will ensue; and those venerable patriots be exposed to a variety of persecutions. Some perhaps will fall martyrs to their patriotism at Tyburn; others be pelted in the pillory, scourged at the cart's-tail, deprived of their ears, fined, imprisoned, or transported. The examples of our Stubs's, Lilburn's, Prynne's, Burton's, and Bastwick's,[20] will be revived; and perhaps, the noble spirit of Reformation, be entirely exterminated.

In order to prevent such a national calamity, I would humbly propose, that in these days of patience and philosophy, the P——t would take this affair into consideration, and by an express statute, exempt these illustrious guardians of the public, from the penalties of every law that ever was enacted for the support of the Royal Authority, the punishment of sedition, the suppression of calumny and slander, and the maintainance of good order. Every person qualified to take the benefit of this statute, may be registered *gratis* at an office established for this purpose, and be distinguished on the back by the letter C! which will stand either for counsellor or canaille. Every person wearing this badge, from Jack Straw, down to Jack Ketch,[21] shall be sacred from correction, insult, or reproof. He may write and publish treason by the sheet, preach sedition by the hour, slander the most unexceptionable characters from the rising of the sun to the setting thereof, and exhibit the most indecent prints which obscenity and impudence can contrive, in every place of public resort in London and Westminster, and through the whole extent of the bills of mortality.[22]

No. 17. Saturday, 18 September 1762.

——Honores, quos quieta republica, desperant, perturbata, consequi se posse arbitrantur.
CICERO in L. Catilinam.[1]

To the BRITON.

SIR,

I t has generally been supposed that war was a misfortune to every country, particularly to a trading nation; but, if we were to judge from the clamour which has been raised, and the papers which have been lately published,[2] in order to obstruct the progress of a negotiation for peace, we should conclude, that a state of perpetual hostility, was the greatest blessing which could happen to these kingdoms. To justify this conclusion, we should take it for granted, that Great Britain overflowed with a superfluity of wealth, which threatened a total corruption of manners; and that war was the only effectual drain to carry off this dangerous superabundance; we should be persuaded that our lands, manufactures, and commerce, were over-stocked with labourers, which must be thinned and weeded by the sword; or that the people were grown too wanton and mutinous for the restraints of civil government, and a copious bleeding[3] was required for the benefit of the constitution.

Whether this was our situation at the beginning of the war, it will be needless to enquire. Those who conducted it, seemed to be of that opinion, by the large evacuations they prescribed. Our political doctors have proceeded upon the principles of Sangrado.[4] They have had recourse to repeated bleedings, as if the plethora[5] had been inexhaustible; and now (to use the physician's phrase) our disease is no longer repletion, but inanition. We began the war with a national debt of eighty millions, which, in the latter end of the last century, was supposed to be double of what our commerce and industry could bear; and in about seven or eight years we have made shift to contract an additional incumbrance, to the amount of fifty-five millions, besides having expended the standing revenue of the nation, including the land and malt-tax, as well as the produce of the sinking-fund;[6] all which, at a moderate computation, might be equal to the annual sum of five millions; the total of our expence therefore, in eight years, falls not short of ninety-five millions; a sum so enormous and discouraging to the lovers of their country, that one can hardly refrain from exclaiming with King Henry in the play,

> *O Lord! take from them now*
> *The sense of reck'ning.* —— [7]

It pretty plainly appears then, that at the commencement of the war, we had no great overflow of riches; or, if this had been the case, the inundation is now effectually restrained within its former channel, and the stream sunk to such a low ebb, as never was known in this country. Before this period, neither the commerce of this, nor of any other country under the sun, was ever able to bear a load of taxes sufficient to defray the interest of one hundred and thirty-five millions; much less support itself under any considerable addition to this intolerable burthen, which must be the consequence of the war's being prolonged. With respect to the diminution of our numbers, I shall appeal to the common observation of every individual, whether some parts of the country are not almost depopulated, in order to recruit the army, the navy, and the militia. I appeal to those few who have taken pains to investigate the subject, whether the number of people in Great Britain,[8] had not been continually decreasing since the beginning of this century, even while the nation enjoyed a profound peace; so that any body may judge in what proportion this deficiency must have increased since the beginning of hostilities, and the prosecution of one of the most bloody wars that ever raged among the powers of Europe; a war which cannot have added less than forty thousand to our annual expence of serviceable men. Indeed, the necessary and unavoidable calamities of war, are so obvious and shocking, that we can hardly believe the sensible and honest part of any nation, would hesitate in embracing the first opportunity of putting a stop to such inhuman violence.

It may be worth while therefore, to enquire who those people are who so industriously blow the coals of discord. This is an office that cannot be imputed to the landholders, who, of all others, sustain the more immediate, and most grievous pressure of the war, in being subject to a heavy land-tax; the bankruptcy of tenants, and an increasing poor's-rate, owing to a want of serviceable hands, and a relaxation of industry. Accordingly, the landed interest in general, from the peer to the peasant, makes no scruple of declaring their sentiments unanimously in favour of peace. We cannot suppose this clamour is raised by the stock-holders, or creditors of the nation; because the continuance of the war, must augment the debts of the public; and all the world knows, that the value of the mortgage, or strength of security, diminishes in proportion to the increase of the debt for which that mortgage or security is given. The truth of this assertion is proved by the daily fluctuation of the stocks, which now continue to rise and fall, as the prospect of peace is brought nearer, or removed to a greater distance. Surely the merchants and traders of the kingdom cannot be advocates for the protraction of war, which throws such a variety of restraints, clogs, and trammels upon commerce; subjecting them to the imposition of severe duties, the grievance of pressing, the delay of convoy, the risk of capture, and the exorbitancy of insurance. Nor can we imagine that this cry is raised or propagated by those who have any regard to the interests of humanity; who sympathise with the distress of the widows and the orphans whom this war hath made; who feel the loss of their relations, friends, and fellow-citizens; and cannot without shuddering reflect, that there are five or six hundred thousand of their fellow-creatures butchering one another, in different parts of Europe and America.

If this aversion to peace does not prevail among the land-holders, the stock-holders, the merchants, and manufacturers, upon whom all the industrious and valuable part of the common people depend; nor finds a place in the hearts of those who retain the least regard to religion and humanity: we must search for it among the idle and the profligate, who have neither diligence nor virtue to earn a subsistence in any calm, pacific course of life; among a set of selfish people who find their account in the war; an iniquitous band of money-brokers, usurers, contractors, and stock-jobbers, who prey upon the necessity of their country, and fatten on her spoils. These are joined by certain individuals in the public service, who sacrifice every patriotic sentiment to the desire of preferment: but those who raise their voices the highest in this discordant cry, are the vile hackneyed retainers to a desperate faction, actuated by implacable malice, rancorous envy, and guilty ambition. It is equal to them, whether this country enjoys the blessings of peace, or groans under the calamities of war. They have no objection to the peace, but to the peace-makers, whom they have aspersed with every species of defamation: but rather than the present m — y should have the honour to give peace to the nation, they would wish to see it not only prostrate beneath the victorious sword of external foes, but also involved in all the miseries of civil dissention, which they have endeavoured by the most flagitious arts to excite. This they dare not — they cannot deny — the public have seen the repeated efforts of their unexampled malice and effrontery, leveled against their S — n, his family and servants — The public has seen them convicted of repeated falshood; has seen their scurrility despised, and their slanders refuted; and if their names and characters should be preserved beyond the present time, posterity, uninfluenced by prejudice or faction, will unanimously declare that this, of all oppositions, is the most unreasonable, and they, of all opposers, are the most illiberal and unworthy.

They will no doubt exclaim, that they are no enemies to a good peace; but think it incumbent upon them to oppose such terms as may be disadvantageous or dishonourable to the nation. I pretend not to know the state of the negotiation which is now upon the carpet: but, I take it for granted, that their intelligence is as limited and imperfect as mine; and that they found their objections on certain conjectural conditions, which have been handed about among the private politicians of this metropolis. By these then it appears, that the French have not only granted every thing which the late M——r demanded in the last negotiation, but even enlarged their condescension beyond what he required. What then, shall one M——r be extolled for prescribing articles which the enemy rejected, and for redoubling the horrors of war; and another be reviled for compelling the enemy to accept those very terms they had before refused, and even to make further concessions; for quenching the dreadful flames of war, and retrieving to his fellow-subjects the blessings of security and peace? for shame! Let not such an instance of ingratitude, prejudice, and infatuation, rise up against us, lest we become a reproach among the nations, and discourage future M——rs from exerting their endeavours for the benefit of the commonwealth.

I know it is alledged, that since the period I have mentioned, we have made a conquest of Martinique,[9] which gives us a right to rise in our demands: but, we ought also to consider, that since the last negotiation, we have added considerably to the public debt; we have two powerful nations instead of one, to cope with; and we are saddled with the protection of Portugal,[10] which makes a very considerable addition to the expence of the war. Notwithstanding these circumstances, which so strongly preponderate against us, we have risen in our demands, and acquired substantial advantages by the treaty: we have retained the fruitful island of Granada and the Granadilloes; we have secured three out of the four neutral islands; we have retained Senegal on the coast of Africa, and extended our possessions in America to the banks of the river Mississippi. Had we expelled the French from Louisiana, the peace, no doubt, would have been more advantageous, durable and secure; and that we have not carried our success to this happy issue, is entirely owing to the conduct of that M——r, who shamefully neglected that important object, at a time when it might have been easily accomplished, and this whole country subdued without resistance; who diverted the principle channel of the war to the plains of Westphalia, and filled it so profusely in favour of aliens, that we can no longer supply the other streams that ought to flow for our own benefit.

The presumption of our having taken the Havanna, affords another source of exclamation against the peace; and indeed, if our design were to conquer the whole Spanish West-Indies, the possession of Cuba would be a considerable step towards the execution of that scheme. But, this is an idea too ridiculously chimerical: and all that we can expect in return for restoring this conquest, are certain commercial advantages which may be equivalent to such a sacrifice. Even these, it seems, are already stipulated. Spain will relinquish all title to the fishery on the banks of Newfoundland: she will confirm our privilege of cutting logwood in the bay of Honduras, and acquiesce in our trading to the Musqueto shore:[11] points which have formed a perpetual bone of contention between the two nations; about which we have negotiated and quarrelled alternately above a whole century, to the great interruption of commerce, and the grievous annoyance of our navigators in the seas of America.

On the whole, I earnestly exhort my fellow-subjects to lay aside pique and prejudice, and before they join in this cabal against the peace, seriously revolve the following considerations. Let them reflect that the kingdom is already exhausted of men and money, chiefly by the misconduct of a M——r who hath wantonly plunged us into a G——n war, that costs us above six millions yearly, remitted in specie to a country from whence it never returns; a sum considerably greater than that which results from the annual profits of our whole commerce: that, over and above this fatal sluice, which of itself, would infallibly drain us to the bottom, we are obliged to pay the interest of one hundred and thirty-six millions, an enormous burden which is daily increasing: we are moreover subject to the incredible expence of a land and sea war, maintained against the two most formidable powers in Europe; and under the necessity of supporting our allies of Portugal, altho' the loss of our trade with Spain hath considerably diminished our resources. These circumstances being duly considered, it will appear, that the continuance of the war must be attended with misery and distress to the nation in general, even tho' we should proceed from one conquest to another, until we are undone by our success.

An indifferent peace therefore, would seem to be a necessary respite from calamities that can scarce be borne; then, how much more eligible must an honourable accommodation appear! That the terms supposed to be stipulated are honourable, safe, and advantageous, I believe no honest and intelligent Briton will deny, when he considers, that the original intent of the war, the security of our American colonies is, if not wholly, at least in a great measure, accomplished by the entire conquest of Canada, and the demolition of Louisbourg in the island of Cape Breton; that by these conquests, Great Britain has gained a valuable and immense acquisition of territory, and engrossed the whole Indian trade of that vast continent, which may, if properly managed, open inexhaustible sources of wealth to these kingdoms: that by retaining Senegal, she remains mistress of the gum trade,[12] by which she lays under contribution other nations, to whom she formerly paid considerable sums for this commodity: that she acquires peaceable possession of divers fruitful islands; establishes a right to a free traffic in the bay of Honduras, and all along the Musquito shore; retrieves the important island of Minorca; obliges the enemy to withdraw their armies from Germany; to evacuate Cleves, demolish the fortifications of Dunkirk, and to abandon Nieuport and Ostend:[13] that as the French marine cannot be re-established for a great length of time, that restless nation will find it their interest to be quiet for a good number of years, during which we may cultivate every branch of commerce with peculiar advantages, and establish some salutary system for diminishing the national debt; or, if our ambitious neighbours should be rash enough to give us any disquiet, before they are in a condition to abide the consequences, we may resume the rod of chastisement, unencumbered by that intolerable G——n connexion, which now hangs like a dead weight about the neck of our country.

These premises being duly considered, I would ask my sober fellow-citizen whether he thinks it more eligible to prosecute the trade of death and desolation, at the hazard of bankruptcy and ruin to his country; or put a stop to the miseries of mankind, and enjoy the benefits of such an equitable peace; a peace which is not suggested by any favourite, or imposed by any dictator in the state; but planned by a patriot-king, whose chief aim is the happiness of his people; fairly and openly proposed, freely and fully examined; and unanimously approved by the members of a C——l, composed of the first, the best, the wealthiest, and the wisest men of the nation. I am, Sir,

Your humble servant,
MILO.[14]

No. 18. Saturday, 25 September 1762.

Quis est enim, cui non hæc templa, aspectus urbis, possessio libertatis, lux denique hæc ipsa, et hoc commune patriæ solum, cum sit carum, tum vero dulce atque jucundum?

CICERO.[1]

The politicians who daily and weekly oblige the world, with their ideas touching the present posture of affairs, and particularly the negotiation for the peace, which is supposed to be upon the carpet, put me in mind of the fable of the prayers preferred to Jupiter.[2] One petitioned for rain, and another for dry weather; a third for the continuation of frost; a fourth for a speedy thaw; a fifth for a southerly wind; and a sixth for a northerly gale, according as the particular interest of each suggested the supplication; so that it was impossible to comply with all their requests, without reconciling contradictions, and unhinging the whole order of things.

Similar is the case of those who, at this juncture, publish their remonstrances to the ministry, with one considerable difference, however; instead of praying, they protest; instead of offering their opinions, they convey instructions; and far from acquiescing in the measures of government, claim it as a right to controul the administration. Some of these wise and worthy patriots declaim against the peace, out of hatred to the peace-makers, without pretending to know the cessions that have been offered, or the terms which are imposed. Others insist upon our prosecuting the war, until our allies have received entire satisfaction, and Great Britain is indemnified for the monstrous expence she has undergone.

One gentleman proposes that we should leave the Wolf in Germany,[3] withdraw our forces from that continent, hold fast the conquests we have made, and exclude our enemies from all future benefit of navigation. For my own part, I so far adhere to this opinion, that if we could put an honourable end to the enormous charge incurred by a fruitless war in Germany, I would freely give my vote for retaining as many of our conquests in the West Indies, and other parts of the globe, as we could possibly keep with any prospect of advantage to the nation, even tho' we should be obliged to prosecute hostilities for seven years longer: but if our M——s should embrace this proposal of leaving the Wolf in Germany; how shall they be screened from the resentment, the howling, and the teeth of fiercer wolves at home, which have already opened against them, on the supposition that our G——n connections may be possibly renounced? In what manner will they silence the clamour raised by the partisans of that mighty statesman, who brightened and strengthened that glorious chain; that chain which he had so long endeavoured to depreciate and disunite?

Should we leave the Wolf in Germany, and shake the annual burden of six or seven millions from our shoulders, how will those guardians of our honour exclaim against the baseness, the perfidy, the infamy of abandoning such precious allies? And here it may not be amiss to vindicate myself from an imputation which has been thrown upon me by a set of writers, whose calumny has appeared in every shape of malice and of falshood. It was affirmed in one of the papers of the Briton,[4] that no nation was supposed capable of entering into a treaty repugnant to its own interest and preservation; and that every nation had a natural right to withdraw itself from an alliance, when the purpose of that engagement was fulfilled or frustrated; when the ally reaped all the profit, and sustained none of the loss resulting from the confederacy, and proudly rejected all equitable terms of accommodation. These are the assertions for which the Briton has been branded as a violater of the most sacred ties, as an encourager of perfidy, and a professed enemy of good faith. Howsoever I may despise the rancour of these malignant scribblers, who are hackneyed in the ways of obloquy and abuse, it may be necessary to clear myself in the opinion of other well-meaning people, not conversant with subjects of this nature, who have suffered themselves to be prepossessed by misrepresentation. With this view, I shall only observe, that the maxims in question, are adopted by all the authors that ever wrote upon the law of nature and nations; and that they are founded on the basis of eternal equity and truth. If a man should give an estate of five hundred pounds a year for a child's rattle, or engage to pay twenty thousand pounds for a hog's-stye not worth ten shillings, and his heir refuse to execute the contract, would not any court of equity uphold him in his refusal, and declare the bargain null and of no effect, taking it for granted, that the contractor must have been *non compos mentis*,[5] otherwise he could not possibly have subscribed to an agreement so detrimental to himself and his family? If this consideration prevails in the case of an individual, how much more strongly ought it to operate, when the interest and preservation of a whole kingdom are at stake? If a weak Prince should be so far over-reached as to bind himself by treaty, to pay an exorbitant tribute or subsidy, to an ambitious neighbour, and maintain an army of one hundred thousand men for his convenience, without stipulating any advantage in return for his own people, who are to bear the load of this unnecessary expence, would not the successor of that weak Prince have an undoubted right to withdraw himself from this treaty, as a fraudulent engagement, dishonourable to his throne, and destructive to his kingdom, of itself null and of no effect, because totally destitute of that reciprocality of inter-est which ought to be the cement of every alliance, and directly tending to the disgrace, detriment, and ruin of one of the contracting parties? If every state has not this internal right, to consult its own safety and preservation, what would be the consequence? The ambitious ally finding his account in the war, would reject all equitable terms of pacification, and prosecute his conquests from one acquisition to another, at the expence of his confederate, until that confederate should be entirely exhausted, both of wealth and credit, and left naked, as a prey to the first enemy that should take the advantage of his distress. This is the sum of the doctrine broached by the Briton, which hath attracted so much contumely and abuse, from those who have proved themselves adversaries to loyalty, decency, truth, and sound argument; and I leave it to the few who judge with accuracy, and decide with candour, to pronounce whether my assertions were subversive of all political honesty and good faith, or salutary maxims dictated by the law of nature, and established by the consent of all civilized nations.

If these deductions therefore are consonant to reason, we have an indubi-table right, not only to separate ourselves from the engagement with P——a, but even to recal our forces from Westphalia: but this right is to be exerted so as to preserve the honour of the nation, and consult the safety of our troops. Towards the first consideration, some sacrifice ought no doubt to be made in favour of those allies, whom a former ad——n hath hung round the neck of Great Britain: accordingly it may be taken for granted, that their interests will not be neglected in the negotiation for peace: but should we abruptly aban-don those G——n allies; should we throw away the scabbard, declare eternal war against France, and attempt to withdraw our troops from W——ph——a; any person of common discernment, may perceive the imminent hazard they must run, by retreating in the face of an enemy five times their number, by separating from the army of their allies, exasperated to see themselves thus abandoned and exposed to the rage and resentment of a victorious foe. Would not they be tempted to repeat the manœuvre of his P——n Majesty,[6] who first disarmed the S——ns, and then pressed them into the service? Would not they be under the necessity of accepting terms from the French King at a minute's warning, and even declare themselves his good friends and allies, as they did immediately after the convention of Closter-Severn?[7] In that case, would not they naturally concur with him in harrassing, attacking, and de-stroying the British forces? In order to prevent this damage and disgrace, to disentangle our country from the labyrinth of G——n connections, with credit and deliberation, it hath been found necessary to put an end to the calamities of war, by a general pacification, in which the utmost attention will be paid to our own interest, as well as to that of all our allies; in which the original design of the war will be effectually answered, many valuable conquests annexed to the dominion, and a number of advantages stipulated for the commerce of Great Britain.

With respect to the scheme of universal conquest, either by sea or land, nothing could be more preposterous in any trading nation, and nothing more impracticable for this in particular: I will even venture to affirm, that we cannot keep all the acquisitions we have made, with any regard to the true interest of our country. The number of people in Great Britain and Ireland,[8] by the best, and latest computations, does not exceed eight millions, and this number had been gradually, tho' very perceptibly decreasing from the beginning of this century, even during a period of profound peace. One third of the land in these kingdoms lies waste and uncultivated; so that if agriculture and commerce were carried to that extent, of which they are capable, they would maintain more than double the present number of inhabitants. It is an eternal truth, that the strength and riches of every nation, increase in proportion to the number of industrious hands, until the different branches of husbandry, trade, and manufacture, shall be over-stocked. If therefore there was a vast deficiency of people before the war; if the waste was greater than the increase, from the loss sustained by navigation, and migration in times of peace and plenty; what additional havock must have been made in the course of a long and sanguinary war, prosecuted at one time in the four quarters of the globe? and how is it possible, that thus reduced in point of number, we can, consistent with the true interest of our country, afford such considerable supplies of men, as would be sufficient to maintain all the countries and islands which we have wrested from the enemy? When we consider the extent of our conquests in North America, stretching above twelve hundred leagues from the banks of the St. Laurence to the Mississippi, peopled by new subjects, indisposed to our dominion from national as well as religious aversion, and surrounded by innumerable nations of fierce Indians, whom it will be absolutely necessary to over-awe and restrain by a chain of strong forts and garrisons: when we reflect upon the great expence of men that will be required for retaining Martinique, Guadaloupe, Senegal, and Goree;[9] and remember the shocking mortality that rages among Europeans in those unhealthy climates; we must surely own, that the retention of all our conquests, tho' perhaps attended with some immediate advantage in point of wealth, would, in a great measure, conduce to the depopulation of our mother-country, and of consequence turn out a very grievous misfortune.

In favour of the scheme for conquest, I have heard the examples of the Carthaginians and the Romans alledged. But these are unfortunate examples: for all the world knows, that those two flourishing nations were ruined by their thirst of dominion. The Romans, sensible that great acquisitions were not to be made and retained without vast supplies of people, took every method to augment the number of their citizens. They naturalized all the states of Italy; they admitted to the same privilege the Grecian commonwealth, with great part of Spain, Gaul, and Germany, where they settled colonies, built trading cities, established the Roman laws, and introduced the Latin language. By these means they had infinite resources of men, which enabled them to extend and aggrandize their empire, until it sunk by its own weight. Their governors of remote provinces affected independence; and all their resources of men proved ineffectual to resist the torrent of their enemies, tho' these enemies were barbarians, so much inferior to them in arts and military discipline. But how is Great Britain qualified to make or retain extensive conquests? She has no such reservoir of men—She has but an handful of people, daily diminishing; and instead of strengthening our numbers by naturalizing foreigners, we seem rather inclined to weaken our own hands still further, by affecting a disunion with a whole nation of our fellow-subjects, whom, some among us, have spared no sarcasms, no abuse, no falshood, to provoke and exasperate. Besides, we have not to do with barbarous nations, without art, policy, riches, or connection. We number among our enemies the most formidable powers in Europe, and we are watched with jealous eyes by the rest, as a proud encroaching people, intoxicated with success, and aspiring at commercial despotism, impatient of rivalship and competition.

We will therefore do well to consider, whether it is most eligible to protract the miseries of mankind, to keep conquests which we have not hands to retain; to prosecute the war by which we are already exhausted; to tempt the inconstancy of success; to excite the jealousy and distrust of all our neighbours; perhaps, to hazard a confederacy against us by all the maritime states of Europe; or to put a stop to the effusion of human blood; to ease ourselves of the load of a ruinous war, which we can no longer bear without the most imminent danger of being entirely crushed; to sacrifice a little of our superfluity to this important consideration; to turn our swords into plough-shares and pruning-hooks,[10] to enjoy the ease, the dignity, the comforts of a safe, honourable, and advantageous peace—There is no room for hesitation——Let us lay all prejudice, all party aside: let us unite as Britons, as fellow-subjects, and fellow-citizens. Let us despise and detest those parricides who have endeavoured to kindle the flames of civil discord in the bowels of their country.

Let us depend upon the paternal affection of a virtuous Sovereign, who can have no views distinct from the interest and happiness of his people. Let us depend upon the care and fidelity of an honest minister, who is engaged by every tie of loyalty, of honour, and of interest, to promote the patriot designs of his Master, to consult the glory and welfare of the nation. Finally, let us acquiesce in the deliberations and determinations of a Council, composed of men eminent for their wisdom and integrity, who by their rank and understanding, are qualified for the office of advising their Prince, and by their extensive property, unalienably attached to the interest and concerns of the people.

No. 19. Saturday, 2 October 1762.

To the Author of the NORTH BRITON.

Sir,

The charge you have brought against a certain right honourable personage, rolls upon two capital principles, both of them attrocious in their kinds, and such as he must plead guilty to. The first is that he is a Scotchman, and the next that he is a Stuart.[1]

Every one knows what a shallow-pated Prince Henry the Seventh of England was, when he imagined, that he could not preserve the independency of his crown so effectually, as by giving his eldest daughter in marriage to a Scotchman.[2] What a glorious figure must England have made at this time, had she been the pupil of French power and French policy, and annually received a viceroy from Versailles to collect her tribute, and to teach us politeness. To swell the charge against his Lordship, it is to be remarked, that the Scots have at all times manifested a most obstinate spirit of independency; and, notwithstanding the superior power of England; they have dared to assert their privileges as free-born subjects.

Their claims to independency have at times carried them to the most extravagant lengths, and they were even insolent enough to pretend to treat with England upon an equal footing. If there was any difference amongst themselves concerning the union, it was, who should carry their claims of independency the highest; and they were seconded by the whigs and the great patriots to whom the present Royal Family owes its accession to the crown.

Let us therefore revive the Egyptian custom of bringing the dead into judgment.[3] Let us arraign the *manes*[4] of Sommers, Godolphin, Cowper,[5] and the whole band of whig patriots, who were so degenerate as to court, in the most abject manner, the Scots to a union, and who thought that, without such an union, the protestant succession in the house of Hanover never could be safe. Let us wish with Caligula, that those whigs had but one neck, that their heads might be cut off at a single blow.[6] Above all, let us detest the memory of the great Duke of Marlborough, as he is called, who, before he was made an English peer, took his seat in a Scots parliament,[7] a precedent that gives too great a countenance to our considering the Great Man in question, as being no alien, especially, if I have been rightly informed, as his Lordship was actually born since the conclusion of the treaty of union, and must be considered as much a Briton as any man in England, unless we have a mind to weaken the right which the present Royal Family has to the crown. I am therefore afraid, that a repeal of the treaty of union is absolutely necessary, and that some other expedient should be devised for our safety.

Let us likewise stigmatise the memories of John Duke of Argyle, John Earl of Stair,[8] and about twenty or thirty more Scotch noblemen whom I could name, and who were eminently instrumental in fighting the cause of England against the French, and who received the highest honours and rewards from the crown, and even the people of England.

As to the second part of the charge against his Lordship, it is in itself so fundamental, as to imply a radical, and indeed a total alteration in the whole system of our civil government. That his name is Stuart, is undeniable, and that he is descended of a legitimate branch (so much the worse) of that Royal Family; his ancestor being Sir John Stuart, son to King Robert the Second, before he came to the crown of Scotland, and inheriting part of the patrimonial estate of that family in the isle of Bute, from which he now derives his title. All this appears in full charge against him by several authentic charters, particularly one granted to him by his brother Robert the Third, 362 years ago.

It would be in vain for his Lordship, or his advocates, to pretend to deny the facts here brought against him; for their criminality appears from many additional circumstances and confirmations of the original charters; nay, in the year 1340, one of his predecessors was presumptuous enough to serve as a privy-counsellor to James the Second, and his son obtained the hereditary constabulary of the castle of Rothsay, a royal seat, and which gives to the Prince of Wales the first Scotch title he possesses. All which facts and allegations can be fully made out by an action of trover,[9] for searching into the muniments of his Lordship's family. I have however too good an opinion of his modesty, to suppose that he will put the public to that trouble, and I shall therefore proceed upon the charge as taken for granted.

Perseverance in criminality aggravates the guilt. You see, Mr. North Briton, what old offenders this family have been, but this is not all; for so inveterate was their enmity to the English, that three uncles of the Sir John Stuart I have already mentioned, were killed in one battle, *viz.* that of Berwick, fighting against the English; nor does it appear that the descendants of the family, thro' all the wars their country waged with us, ever abated in the same barbarous bloody-minded principles. Shall we then, who are born and bred Englishmen, degenerate from our ancestors, by admitting an hereditary traitor to have power over us? Is the *Ni fallat fatum* [10] to extend to all the branches of the Stuart family; and shall its descendants avenge themselves of the blood their forefathers lost in battle by the swords of the English?

I know, Sir, there are some little objections to what I am now about to propose; but they are so trifling, that I should not mention them, were it not to stop the mouth of clamour, and to seal up the lips of contradiction.

The first is, that the present Royal Family are now sitting on the throne of England in right of a Stuart,[11] descended from the same ancestors from whom the Earl of B — draws his original; and therefore the execrations you pour out against all the family of Stuart, are somewhat indecent with regard to his present Majesty.

But, Sir, allowing the fact to be so, what is that to principles? If the people of England called a Stuart to their crown; if he was nominated to it by the greatest Princess that ever swayed a scepter, we are to remember that the English were then over-run with prejudices, and had but just got clear of the errors of popery. They were not at that time free-thinkers, either in religion or politics; nor had they yet learned to put a King of the name of Stuart to death on a scaffold.

As to Queen Elisabeth's nomination, nothing is more easy than to account for it; for, it is plain, that she was then in her dotage, and had but a few years before put to death Mary Stuart, the mother of that very King whom she appointed to be her successor. Thus, Sir, I think, I have irrefragably proved, that no reflections upon the name of Stuart can possibly affect his Majesty's title to our allegiance.

The remaining part of the objection I have started, is still less worth the answering. It is true that King William the Third was the son and the husband of a Stuart; and that, had it not been for his wife, he never could have swayed the British scepter. But, Sir, it will not, I hope, be pretended, that

K. William's name was Stuart; and were five hundred ladies of that name to arise, I have nothing to say to any of them. My charge is against the men. But admitting all those ridiculous objections to have their full weight, how does it affect the present question? If our forefathers proceeded upon wrong principles and false suppositions, are we to do the same?

It is true, that when the act of settlement[12] was made, the limitations in it to the family of Hanover, immediately respected the Princess Sophia and her descendants, as being born of a Stuart; and it is generally supposed, that the right which the parliament gave to the present family in filling up the throne, was in consideration of its being the next protestant heirs to the family of Stuart. But, in order to destroy all such ridiculous suggestions, we need but appeal to a Scotch authority, I mean Burnet bishop of Salisbury, who wrote a pamphlet, to prove that King William had a right by conquest to the crown of England.[13] I know it may be objected, that this pamphlet was burnt by order of the house of commons; but we are to consider that the house of commons is but one half of the parliament; and therefore it cannot properly be said to have been done by act of parliament, because it does not appear that either the King, or the house of peers gave their consent.

The history of England is full of instances of the jealousy our Kings entertained of the most distant pretenders. Edward the Fourth put to death an ale-house man, only for saying that he would make his son heir to the crown, which, it seems, was his sign.[14] Innumerable are the sacrifices made to this state-jealousy, during the reigns of Richard the Third, Henry the Seventh, and Henry the Eighth. It is well known that Henry the Seventh put to death a poor Prince of the blood-royal, tho' he was so ignorant as not to know the difference between a cock and a goose.[15] In the succeeding reign, not to mention other instances, the gallant Earl of Surry had his head cut off, only for quartering his arms with those of Edward the Confessor; and his father must have followed him, had the old King lived but a day or two longer.[16] Even the mild Edward the Sixth took off the heads of the two only uncles he had,[17] because it was thought they aspired to sovereignty. All the innocency of lady Jane Grey,[18] could not protect her from sharing the same fate in the succeeding reign; and the case of Mary Queen of Scots, under Elizabeth, has been already mentioned. If we are to believe history, even the Stuarts themselves were not void of state-jealousy; witness the fates of the Earl of Gowry, the lady Arabella, and the Duke of Monmouth.[19]

But supposing all of them to have been criminal, what can their guilt amount to, compared to a Stuart, who is said to have assumed as an inscription upon his house, *We are not from Kings, but Kings are from us?*[20] I know it may be answered, that this inscription alludes to the original owner of the house, who was the ancestor of the Royal Family of Stuart, (if I must use that hated expression) and that the fact is true. This apology makes the case still worse. It is well known, that by the English law, *truth does not justify a libel;* nay, in some cases, as in the present, it makes it still more libellous. What does this inscription imply, but that his Lordship is waiting only for a proper opportunity to assert his hereditary right to the crown of these realms. Who knows, at this distance of time, whether his Lordship may not take it in his head to pretend, that his predecessor was the elder brother of Robert the Third. In the transcript of the family-charters, remaining in the British museum, I can find no expression that can ascertain this moot point; The words are *sciatis nos dedisse et hac presenti charta nostra confirmasse dilecto fratri nostro Johanni Senescallo de Bute officium vice-comitatus de Bute & Arran datum,* 11th Nov. 1400.[21] Here we see nothing by which we can gather, that this same John was a younger brother, and what dreadful consequences must happen to this devoted country, should such a family-claim be insisted on.

I propose a remedy for all this, an absolute, entire, and irrevocable dissolution of the treaty of union between Scotland and England.

If it should here be objected, that the union cannot be dissolved without manifest injustice and breach of national faith, I absolutely deny the fact; for, I do not think that there is, at this time, one man alive who was a party in the treaty. Therefore no man can be perjured, in agreeing to its being dissolved. This being the case, how advantageous must such a dissolution be to the English, who have scarce any thing to lose in Scotland, while the Scots must be ruined in England.

It may, I know, be urged, that his Majesty may not be very fond of seeing a civil war break out in his kingdoms, which may be attended with very dangerous consequences to his crown; and that it is more than probable, he would employ force to prevent it. But, Mr. North Briton, what force could he employ? The standing army in case of peace must be reduced, and I make no question, that we should be able to find a sufficient number of such friends as you amongst the militia, who would be ready to fight *pro aris et socis,*[22] provided you were properly tutored; but the whole, my dear Sir, depends upon this circumstance, and therefore I shall give you a word or two of advice on that head.

In the first place, lay your foundation in your zeal for your king and country, and be sure never to divide those two terms; for the one will catch, if the other should miss; but most commonly both of them will hook. Never fail to pretend that you espouse them, to rescue both out of the hands of a faction, headed by a Scotchman; and that your only aim is to make his Majesty the greatest, the most independent, and the richest king on the face of the earth; that old England shall give law to all the world. If you meet with a squeamish soul, who shall boggle at rebellion, blood and murder, you are to bait the hook, and tell him, that you take the only way to prevent all three; that the militia is the natural, the constitutional strength of this country, and that the only way to preserve its peace, is to unite as one man against the ministry, and force them to continue the war.

Perhaps it may be objected, that victory is precarious; that even our conquests impoverish us; that tho' we can force towns, we cannot force trade, which no sooner deviates from its natural channel, than it runs to waste; that by comparing our exports and imports for these twenty years past, the increase of the national stock bears no kind of proportion to the expences of the public; and that hands will be wanting soon, equally for war and commerce. To those who reason in this manner, recapitulate all the victories we have gained, from the battle of Poictiers down to that of Minden;[23] and be sure to conclude with an observation, that we are a match for all the world, both by sea and land. As to the want of hands, fetch a walk with your friends in holiday-time through the streets, and round the neighbourhood of this great metropolis, and then ask him whether he thinks there is any danger of our wanting hands; bid him observe the crowds that every where abound.

In reply to all those arguments, it will, I know, be urged, that our officers of the militia, being either men of property, or supposed to be such, will never consent to plunge their country in a civil war. I am of the same opinion, and therefore that thing must be done by degrees; for which reason, I would humbly propose to take for a pattern the proceedings of the year 1641. The gentlemen and noblemen who contributed the most to the civil distractions at that period, were the men in England, who had the greatest reason to wish for tranquillity; had the least intention to involve the nation in the miseries that followed, and repented the most heartily of them. Had they seen all at once the whole extent of the schemes that were laid, they must have been struck with horror; but they were brought on by degrees, till the ice broke under them, and till they had nothing left but either to swim a shore, (which many of them were not able to do) to sink in this general wreck, or ride upon the ruins of their country.

We have a finer game to play at present, than either the republicans or Cromwell had. Our cause is far more plausible than theirs, and more interesting to Englishmen. We not only have domestic considerations, equally powerful with what they had, but foreign ones, of which they had none. The new acquisition of the Havannah,[24] gives us the Spanish as well as the French trade; and let it be declared to be high-treason, in the same manner as the Romans did when Hannibal was at their gates, so much as to talk of peace. I am, Sir, yours,

A SOUTH BRITON.

No. 20. Saturday, 9 October 1762.

—*velut Sylvis, ubi passim*
Palantes error certo de tramite pellit,
Ille sinistrorsum, hic dextrorsum abit: unus utrique
Error, sed variis illudit partibus.

HORACE.[1]

We have heard much clamour uttered against the treaty of Utrecht;[2] which, undoubtedly, might have been more favourable to the interest of Great Britain, had the reigning ministry used all the advantage which the success of the war afforded. Why they did not make use of those advantages is a question, which, perhaps, hath never been candidly discussed. To say they were bribed by the French King to desert their allies; or that they formed a scheme for bringing in the Pretender, which could not be executed in time of war, are assertions that savour much of party, and stand unsupported by any positive proof. Though the enquiry into the conduct of that ministry, which took place in the beginning of the ensuing reign, was carried on with all the eagerness of inveterate rancour, no discovery was made, which could fix upon them the imputation of any such correspondence or design. On the contrary, had any plan been formed by them in favour of the Pretender, it was more likely to have succeeded in time of war, when they could have sent abroad those troops which they could not trust at home, and might have paved the way for a French invasion, in order to facilitate the projected succession: but it is now well known, that the rival ministers of Queen Anne[3] were, at this very time, each separately endeavouring to ingratiate himself with the house of Hanover; and some persons of honour at that time, principally concerned in the schemes and deliberations of the Tory party, are still living to bear witness, that nothing was ever intended by that party to the prejudice of the Protestant Succession, which, indeed, they themselves had established by act of parliament.

We must, therefore, find out some more adequate reasons that should induce the ministry of those days, first to negotiate with France, and then conclude such an exceptionable treaty. That it was high time for the English to think of peace, will scarce be denied by those who reflect, that the political circumstances of Europe, which gave rise to the alliance against France, were entirely changed by the death of the Emperor Joseph.[4] The business was to curb the ambition of the French monarch, and prevent the kingdom of Spain from being united in his family, lest the ballance of power between the houses of Bourbon and Austria should be destroyed, and the liberties of Europe be endangered from the encroachments of the preponderating competitor for universal dominion. By the time King Charles was called to the imperial throne, the power and insolence of Lewis were humbled in the dust. He had felt the most mortifying reverses of fortune: his kingdom was exhausted; and his remaining subjects were reduced to misery and despair. With respect to the ballance of power, his scale now kicked the beam;[5] and if any danger threatened the liberties of Europe at this juncture, it was natural to look for it in the quarter of Austria, an house notorious for rapacity and usurpation, which, considering the low state of France, would have become too formidable, from the possession of Spain, and the West Indies, vested in the person of one individual.

The original aim of the war, was therefore frustrated; and the prosecution of it would have been productive of that very evil, which it was meant to prevent. Besides, England bore a great deal more than her share of the burden, without the possibility of reaping advantage from any conquests that might be made on the continent of Europe, to which the endeavours of the confederacy, were in a peculiar measure confined. A continuation of the war, would have served only to waste the blood and treasure, and augment the burdens of Great Britain, to oblige our thankless and mercenary allies, who never honestly paid their proportion of the expence, though they were enriched by the war; to increase the dominion of the Emperor, and by crushing the house of Bourbon, destroy that very equilibrium, which it was the professed intention of the confederacy to preserve.

These motives, tho' of themselves sufficient to influence an honest ministry to embrace the first opportunity of concluding an honourable and advantageous peace, were, in all probability, reinforced by others of a factious nature; but, I am persuaded, that the treaty was precipitated by the virulent opposition which was made to the measures of the administration; and that France owed all the favour which she found in this treaty, much more to the emissaries of the Whig Party, than to the indulgence of the Tory Ministers. Great Britain was divided into two powerful factions; and the contest was for power.

The Tories had engrossed the administration; and the Whigs eagerly seized every occasion to bring their adversaries into disgrace with the people. It was not the good of their country, but the interest of their faction, which they had at heart. They certainly had no attachment to the house of Austria, which had ever been greedy and ungrateful; unpropitious to the liberties of Europe, and averse to the Protestant Religion: neither had they any affection for our Dutch allies, our insidious rivals in commerce, whose conduct had been ever selfish and sordid; who had shuffled and evaded furnishing their quota of troops and money, and made a scandalous jobb of the war, by maintaining a clandestine trade with the common enemy. They were not actuated by any regard for the liberties of Europe, because their desire of protracting the war manifestly tended to destroy the ballance of power, which they affected to establish. All these therefore, were no other than pretences, furnished by the occasion, to throw dust in the Eyes of the public, and exasperate the bulk of the people against those ministers, whom they wished and endeavoured to supplant.

Accordingly, the cry was raised to a hideous pitch of seditious clamour. The Queen was scandalized in her private character; she was represented as a woman of weak intellects; as a contemptible puppet, moved by worthless favourites; and privy to a design in favour of the Pretender. Her ministers were reviled as the authors and instigators of this infamous scheme; as the panders of arbitrary power; the abettors of Romish superstition; the enemies of good faith; the betrayers of the honour and interest of the nation; who had shamefully abandoned their allies; relinquished and renounced the patriot views of the grand alliance; and concluded with the house of Bourbon a separate treaty, in which the advantages of the war, the dignity, the security, and commerce of their country, were scandalously and treacherously sacrificed.

The cry began while the treaty was in agitation. No abuse was spared: no source of calumny was left unexhausted. The partisans of the opposition railed and reproached in public and in private, in writing and conversation. They started a thousand objections, and damned the treaty by anticipation. They feigned circumstances, and argued upon them as facts. When the peace was concluded, every article of it passed the fiery ordeal of their censure: they pretended to demonstrate the absurdity, the dishonour, the pernicious tendency of every stipulation. They set the seal of reprobation on the whole; they did not scruple to declare, that such a peace could be of no duration; that the war would break out with redoubled violence, in less than twelve months; or, (which was worse) the Pretender would be brought in, popery re-established, and the fires of Smithfield[6] be lighted up to burn the Protestants, before three years should be elapsed. Such are the inflammatory notes which have always been uttered to awake the spirit of civil discord and sedition. These were swelled into a loud chorus by a variety of instruments, by the ministers of our German allies; the emissaries of our Dutch allies; the friends and adherents of a mercenary, enriched by contracts, connivance, and every species of military peculation; finally, by all those who found their private account in the continuation of the war, and might be said to fatten on the blood of the nation.

One may easily judge what an outcry must have been raised by such a numerous and eager pack of adversaries, heated by faction, stimulated by avarice, and unrestrained by principle; and what effect it must have had on the minds of a populace, incapable of thinking for themselves, sudden, suspicious, and impatient, greedily devouring every doubt, and easily fermented by artful insinuation. The situation of the ministry was truly perplexing. The humanity of their sovereign, the true interest of their country, declared for peace: the multitude clamoured for war, while those who influenced the moneyed corporations, threatened to distress the hands of government, in the article of supplies, by which only the war could be maintained. The French King was well informed of these transactions; and did not fail to take advantage of the intestine troubles, which perhaps, his emissaries had helped to foment in the bowels of this kingdom. He knew that peace was the only method by which the ministry could extricate themselves and their country from the difficulties in which they were involved: he therefore declined accepting such terms as he must have been obliged to receive, had the British nation been unanimous and determined.

Even after the treaty was signed, and confirmed by the sanction of parliamentary approbation, the ferment among the people did not subside. The indefatigable demagogues continued to speak, to write, to preach, and to prophecy against the infamous peace of Utrecht. They had artfully insinuated themselves into the good graces of the Prince destined to the succession; and he no sooner ascended the throne, than they seized the opportunity of gratifying their revenge. The individuals concerned in negotiating and ratifying the treaty, were persecuted, impeached, imprisoned, and some of them obliged to abandon their country.[7] But as soon as their adversaries had overwhelmed them with ruin, and established their own influence about the throne, beyond all possibility of reverse, the treaty of Utrecht, which they had branded as infamous and pernicious, they left unaltered and undisturbed; and instead of producing a fresh rupture in less than one year, it remained in full force very near thirty, a period of tranquillity almost unexampled in the annals of England, during which, she enjoyed, without interruption, every blessing which opulence and security could bestow.

The same arts that were used to embarrass the ministry, and retard the peace of Utrecht, have been lately revived with redoubled rancour; and, as the emissaries of faction have proceeded with less artifice, their endeavours have met with success from a greater fund of infatuation. As for those honest partizans, who now labour in the vineyard of sedition, their misrepresentations have been so gross, their aspersions so brutal, and their falshood so often refuted, that it is scarce credible they should meet with the least degree of credit or attention, from a people who had not resigned all regard for decency and virtue, and all pretensions to human reason. It is not expected, that men of weak understandings should enter into subtle discussions on points of political speculation; far less is it imagined, that candour can reside among the devotees of faction: but one would naturally hope, that those who have reason would exercise it; that they would enquire, distinguish and determine for themselves, rather than yield implicit faith to every assertion, even the most infamous, that drops from the pens consecrated to faction, obloquy, and defamation: that they could consider objects in every point of view, and endeavour to examine every circumstance, so as to judge from the general effect of the whole, instead of rashly deciding from a superficial glance of one particular part, exhibited in a false, fallacious light, by the hands of men repeatedly convicted of imposture.

I am led into this reflection by a remarkable instance of prejudice, which lately fell under my own observation. A very honest man, at a certain coffee-house, taking up a paper, which, for some time past, has been the hackneyed vehicle of scurrility and slander, read a paragraph, importing, that Lord B——e had weakened the squadron destined for the defence of our fishery on the banks of Newfoundland; and that instead of two ships, half a dozen had been appropriated for that service, during the ministry of his predecessor.[8] On this foundation, which was a notorious falshood, the author had raised a superstructure of the vilest calumny and abuse. The gentleman, without giving himself the trouble to enquire whether the premises were true, swallowed the deduction with peculiar eagerness, and exclaimed: "These are stubborn facts, which the friends of Lord B——e will never get over." A person who sat by him, without making any reply, took care to supply him with another paper,[9] in which the falshood of this very imputation was detected; and this he perused in silence, without having candour enough to own the injustice of the charge, and the effrontery of the accuser. If a man of sentiment and education could be thus warped by the most palpable slanders;

what effect must they have upon the illiterate and illiberal dregs of the people, who ferment with every leaven, and are never better pleased, than when their spleen is gratified with some calumny, which tends to the disgrace of their superiors!

All I contend for is this: That those whom heaven hath blessed with rational faculties, would employ these faculties with temper and deliberation, in their enquiries after truth; that they would be upon their guard against prejudice and partiality, that they would vindicate themselves from the inglorious fetters, which any set of men would hang upon their understanding, and receive with proper caution, and laudable distrust, every defamatory hint, every insidious insinuation, whether relating to private character, or public conduct, which may be circulated by a vile crew of incendiaries, the professed enemies of their Prince and his government, the prostitutes of a desperate faction, and, as far as in them lies, the parricides of their country.

No. 21. Saturday, 16 October 1762.

Virtus recludens immeritis mori
Cœlum, negata tentat iter viâ:
Cœtusque vulgares et udam
Spernit humum fugiente pennâ.
HORACE.[1]

The malevolence of party is at length disappointed. The Havanna is reduced by the forces of Great Britain.[2] The militia of faction were already drawn out. They had pointed their artillery, and double-charged it with abuse, waiting with the most eager impatience for the news of our miscarriage, that they might pour the whole thunder of reproach upon the head of the devoted[3] minister.

Never did a flight of hungry carrion-crows more greedily snuff up the steams of animal putrefaction, than did those unnatural vultures long to feast upon the disaster of their country. They were prepared to have inveighed against the design upon the Havanna, as chimerical; to have demonstrated the absurdity of the steps taken for the execution of the scheme; to shew that the armament was sent abroad at an improper season of the year; that the troops were exposed to numberless hardships in an unhealthy climate; that they were deficient in number, short of provisions, destitute of proper refreshment, and ill supplied with stores and implements of battle, battery, or siege. All these errors and defects they were to have loaded on the shoulders of the unfortunate Minister, as the projector of this iniquitous plan; and to have overwhelmed him with the tropes of obloquy and exaggeration. Such censures they had actually circulated in private conversation, and their goose-quills, dipped in rancour, were already drawn to transmit them to the public view; when all their hopes were crushed, and all their purposes defeated, by the arrival of those who brought the happy tidings of our success. They drooped amidst the general joy; they repined at the glory of their countrymen; they sickened at the triumphs of the nation. It were a reproach upon Providence, if such parricides should escape with impunity: but, Heaven already vindicates its justice on their heads. Like those guilty dæmons, whom the divine vengeance incessantly pursues, they carry their hell about with them. By the nature of their own dispositions, they are rendered the most miserable of all mortals. They feel the pangs of the damned at every effort of virtue which they cannot emulate; at every glimpse of happiness which they cannot partake.

True to these diabolical principles, indeed incapable of any other, and dead to every generous emotion of the heart; they have used their first recollection to poison the cup of public joy, and pervert that which was a source of approbation and honour to a foul sewer of slander and disgrace. I remember to have seen a mountebank in Germany, who swallowed different kinds of liquors successively, and afterwards brought up any particular species which the spectators desired him to disgorge: but, these empirics[4] in politics, whatever they may swallow, reproduce nothing but one virulent discharge. The venom of their malignant hearts communicates itself to every idea they imbibe; and what they receive as applause, they return as invective.

They will now attempt to filch from the present administration the credit of the plan, which they were prepared to decry: they will deduce from our success, arguments to obstruct the negotiation for peace, which is become so indispensably necessary to the kingdom. They will dazzle the eyes of the ignorant with the illusions of false glory. They will inflame a pernicious spirit of conquest, which hath lain hold of the lower class of people. They will exclaim, that the reduction of the Havanna intitles us to rise in our demands; and that this acquisition, which hath cost so many lives and such a world of treasure, is not to be returned without a valuable consideration.

This, it must be owned, is a specious doctrine, but at the same time unsolid and fallacious. The articles in dispute between Great Britain and Spain, with respect to our commerce are, it is to be hoped, already adjusted; and therefore, our success at the Havanna ought not to retard one moment the negotiation for the peace. We have nothing farther to ask of Spain. We want none of her possessions in the West Indies. The acquisition of Mexico and Peru would serve only to hasten the ruin of Old England. It would enervate our minds, debauch our morals, destroy our industry, and depopulate our country. Spain herself has declined in strength and importance, ever since she depended upon the treasures of America. At present, her subjects may be considered as our drudges, who labour in the mines under an unhealthy climate, to find gold and silver for our benefit. They sustain the danger and the toil, and we reap the greatest part of the advantage.

By wresting from them the dominions they possess on the north and south-side of the Isthmus of Darien,[5] we should excite jealousy of all our neighbours; while, at the same time, we should in reality become objects of compassion or contempt. Every fresh conquest would be a new grave opened for our fellow-subjects; who, tempted by the prospect of wealth, would flock thither from all quarters, until all our other settlements would be abandoned, and even Great Britain itself be robbed of the best part of its inhabitants.—— Besides, though it were really our interest to hold what we have got, and extend our conquests in the West Indies, we ought to consider, that we have neither men to retain and prosecute such advantages, nor funds to support the war. Another year of hostilities, would, in all probability, prove fatal to our national credit; and it might be productive of other unfavourable events. Fortune is inconstant and capricious. She hath showered her favours upon us with a lavish hand. We ought to distrust the extraordinary indulgence, so far as to realise the advantages she offers; and now that all the purposes of the war are fully answered, put it out of her power to surprise us with any untoward reverse.

Should it be asked, "What then have we gained by the wealth we have expended, the blood we have shed, the valour which we have displayed, and the conquests we have made, in the expedition to the island of Cuba?" I answer, "The immediate objects of this war, were to punish the arrogance of Spain, and prevent her giving law to us in the peace." These are now accomplished. We have chastised her insolence, and humbled her pride: we have destroyed her navy, and fully indemnified ourselves at her expence, for the charges of the expedition. We have convinced her, feelingly, of our being able, at any time, to reduce her strongest fortresses in that part of the world; to vindicate our empire in the gulph of Florida, and thus effectually stop the channel of her American supplies: a circumstance which will, in a special manner, tend to render the pacification durable and secure; as it will much more powerfully restrain her from incurring our future resentment, than our bereaving her of any part of her dominions, which would act as a thorn in her side, perpetually irritating her to renounce the conditions of an oppressive peace.

But were we actually resolved to hold the Havanna, which we have taken; it is not to be supposed that Spain would purchase peace with such a sacrifice. There are certain points, which, rather than give up, she would risque the consequences of prolonging the war; and this is one of them: the possession of the Havanna is essential to her American interests; and she could not cede the one, without betraying the other. She knows that West-Indian conquests would infallibly prove fatal to the conquerors; and we know, that the expence of the war would, in a very little time, totally ruin our finances.

The reduction of the Havanna is an event which nobly crowns the successes of a glorious war. It is an heroic atchievement, which ascertains beyond all possibility of doubt, the superior power and prowess of Great Britain; and enables her in a distinguished manner, to display her superior wisdom and generosity. What man, who feels for the honour and advantage of his country, would not, rather than protract the miseries of war; rather than tempt the vicissitudes of fortune; rather than increase the public burdens, which are already intolerable; rather than run the hazard of a national bankruptcy, upon the brink of which we totter; — what Briton, I say, rather than expose his country to such calamity and disgrace, would not eagerly seize the present opportunity of giving peace to his fellow-creatures, of putting a stop to the slaughter of his fellow-subjects and friends; to the reign also of rapine, cruelty, and desolation; of giving permanency to the glory and advantages we have gained; and of adding to the renown of victory, the more amiable praise of moderation?

No. 22. Saturday, 23 October 1762.

—— *nunc accipe quare*
Desipiant omnes. ——
HORACE.[1]

One would imagine the people of this metropolis *had eaten of the insane root, that takes the reason prisoner;*[2] or that like those who have been bit by the tarantula,[3] they have suffered from the stings of certain mischievous insects, which have the power of infusing such virulent poison in the wounds they give, as produces a temporary delirium, during which they act a thousand extravagancies.

When we hear the present ministry reproached in every coffee-house, in every ale-house, and almost in every private house within the city of London: when we hear the plebeian politician accuse them of want of capacity, of want of spirit and activity; and exclaim with an air of contempt, "What have they done since Mr. P—tt was driven from the administration?" When we revolve the great and important conquests they have made, first of Martinique, and its appendages; and then of the Havanna, with its dependencies; and compare the operations of the last campaign with those of the year that closed the former ad — n; we cannot help exclaiming in our turn, "What have they not done? What have they neglected, which they could possibly have undertaken for the honour and advantage of their country?"

When we hear the same candid politicians inveighing against the peace which is said to be upon the carpet, as dishonourable, treacherous, and infamous; when we examine such supposed articles as they are pleased to specify; and collate them with the terms in which their immaculate m — r acquiesced in the late negotiation;[4] when we find them much more favourable for Great Britain than were those which he had adopted; when we recollect with what silent approbation his propositions were received; and hear with what outragious clamour, a much more honourable and advantageous peace is now rejected by the multitude; what can we think, but that heaven hath actually deprived the people of their senses; or that they are blinded by the most absurd prejudices, and transported by the most ungenerous and unjustifiable resentment?

Is it possible, that rational beings should be so weak, so humble, as to resign all their own ideas and reflections, and listen with implicit faith, to the idle declamation of a few worthless incendiaries, who do not even take the trouble to amuse them with the faintest shadows of reason; but seem to overbear their intellects with a foul torrent of general abuse, totally devoid of truth, argument, and probability?

To these abandoned wretches, who have devoted their talents, such as they are, to the propagation of slander and sedition, and perpetually ring the changes upon *venal pens, ministerial hirelings, and mercenary writers, attempting to defend an infamous peace;* what should I oppose but ineffable contempt, and silent disdain? I might retort their scurrility with interest: I might drag them from their obscurity, and exhibit them in their proper colours to the astonished public, many individuals of which would be ashamed of the leaders, under whose banners they had enlisted: I might prove that he is the vilest of all mercenaries, who prostitutes his conscience for hire, and engages to do the worst drudgery of faction; to traduce character, hint slander, inculcate falshood, scatter the seeds of disloyalty, and kindle the flames of civil dissension in the bowels of his country.

But, this is a task as unnecessary as it is disagreeable. The business is, not to asperse, but to justify; not to recriminate, but to refute; particularly to demonstrate the folly of those who clamour, that we are going to give up tamely the advantages we have gained, without proper considerations, without securing to ourselves an indemnification for the expence of the war; whereas, we ought to retain the French sugar-islands,[5] and the Havanna, and exclude both French and Spaniards from any share of the fishery on the banks of Newfoundland.

I shall not pretend to argue from motives of humanity, as they seem to be entirely out of the question; nor mention it as a circumstance worth notice, that we might be justly taxed with cruelty and oppression, should we interdict, or exclude even a vanquished enemy from the common benefits of nature: sentiments of generosity and compassion are, it seems, not to be indulged when the fate of empires is at stake; we must then listen to nothing but the dictates of ambition, interest and convenience. Be it so—I will proceed upon that foundation—I have, on a former occasion,[6] proved that extensive conquests must be fatal to Great Britain, by their own weight; that she would be in the condition of a waggon loaded, until the axle-tree cracks in the center; that she would resemble an emaciated body with dropsical members: the vitals would be exhausted, and the limbs would mortify for want of circulation from the heart—I will now endeavour to prove, that insisting upon rigorous terms of peace, especially on an utter exclusion of the French from the fishery on the banks of Newfoundland, would, in all probability, be attended with the ruin of these kingdoms.

The French will, no doubt, remonstrate to this effect. "Were we compelled by necessity to acquiesce in the rigorous terms you want to impose, you could not hope that the peace would be lasting; you must take it for granted, that we would seize every opportunity to vindicate ourselves from the oppression you exercise, and employ all our engines to interest the other powers of Europe in our behalf. Ours would then become a common cause; and it would be the interest of every other maritime power to unite in a confederacy, to retard the progress of England towards absolute dominion and despotism by sea. If you are determined to keep possession of Canada, to deprive us of our fishery, and withhold our sugar islands, you must also determine to continue the war; because, in that case, our navigation being entirely ruined, it will not be worth our while to accept of peace. We shall make shift, by the help of our privateers, to interrupt your commerce, alarm your coast, and bring part of your wealth into the harbours of France: we shall be able to find you an annual vent for six or seven millions in Germany, and put you to the yearly expence of twice as much more in prosecuting your hostilities in other quarters. We ourselves, in the mean time, may be hampered in the article of finances; but you will be pleased to consider that France maintained five numerous armies in different parts of Europe, for a series of ten years, before she had any colonies at all from which she reaped the least advantage; that she has still the same resources within herself; that her subjects are numerous, and devoted to the glory of their Prince; that she abounds with corn, wine, and oil; that she carries on a prodigious inland traffick with all the most considerable powers on the continent; that she even touches a considerable part of the money which England lavishes away in Germany; that she can maintain the war in Westphalia with little or no addition to her ordinary expence in time of peace; and that, while she proceeds in her career, without contracting new incumbrances, Great Britain is adding yearly twelve millions sterling to her national debt, already so oppressive, that she can hardly stagger under the enormous burden. You demand an indemnification for the expences of the war; 'tis already in your hands. We are content to cede for ever the immense dominions of Canada, a country very near as extensive as all Europe taken together. We leave you in full possession of the whole American fur-trade, which, in time, may open new sources of commerce. If you have squandered away your treasures in G—y, upon objects that were foreign to the true interest of your country, you cannot expect that we should refund what you have so wantonly and unwisely sacrificed. Your late K—g was offered a neutrality for his E—te, which he rejected with disdain. We afterwards granted a capitulation to his troops when they were at our mercy, which naturally terminated the war in W—ph—a; but, this capitulation was broke, and those troops recommenced hostilities at the requisition of another Prince, who pretended that the El—r of H—r had instigated him to attack his neighbours; and therefore he insisted upon being supported by the troops and treasure of Great B—n. The expence you have incurred in G—y, therefore, was either to support an unnecessary ally, from whose success you could reap no advantage; or to protect the Electorate of H—r, which would have needed no protection, had your M—h accepted of the proffered neutrality, or adhered to the capitulation of Closter-Severn:[7] nay, had Great B—n, and the Germanic Body, allowed us to take peaceable possession of that El—te, at the beginning of the war, the people would have lived happy and secure under the mild administration of France, and we should have been glad to restore it at the peace for less than one fifth of the sum which is annually expended in its defence. In that case, your fellow-subjects of H——r, and all your Westphalian allies, would have rejoiced in the blessings of peace and plenty; whereas they now see their cities ruined, their palaces destroyed, and their country laid waste. One half of them has already perished by the calamities of war; and the survivors, reduced to beggary, imprecate the vengeance of heaven upon G——t B——n, by whose boasted alliance and protection, they are undone. You ought not therefore to charge the expence of the G——n war upon France; but place it to the account of your own rashness and indiscretion!"

Without all doubt, France has reason to make such a remonstrance; and those who demand of her an indemnification for the whole expence of the war, argue in the stile which was lately adopted by the panegyrists of a noble D—ke,[8] remarkable for political sagacity. When he was removed from the T——y, they observed that this was but an ungrateful return for having spent above half a million of his own money in the service of the government. With a parity of reason, I once heard a decayed subaltern damn the army, because, while he received no more from the G——t, than the wretched pay of a lieutenant, he had spent ten thousand pounds of his own money in debauchery and extravagance.

But, let us grant we are intitled to a full indemnification from France: in what manner is this indemnification to be obtained? If we gain by retaining Guadaloupe, Martinique, and all the other acquisitions we have made in the course of the war, an addition of three or four millions to our annual revenue; and in consequence of retaining these conquests be obliged to maintain the war at the expence of six times the sum; where is the man so lost to common sense, who will not own, that our protracting the war would be equally pernicious and absurd? If any person would undertake to fill a cask that leaked six gallons in an hour, with a pipe that runs no more than two in the same time, would not every hearer perceive at once, and own the folly of the undertaker? Yet such a project would not be more preposterous than that of prosecuting the war, until we indemnify ourselves with our conquests. Instead of supplying what is already wasted, we should only drain ourselves to the bottom; and when once our public credit is cracked, all Europe will rejoice at our bankruptcy; for, there is not a power in Christendom, which does not, at this very hour, look upon our success with an evil eye; nor do I believe, there is one state in Christendom which, without particular views to its own interest, would assist us with one regiment to save us from ruin.

The truth is, we have become too formidable to our neighbours: we have used our success in such an imperious manner, as to excite the disgust, as well as the jealousy of the other maritime states of Europe; and, were it possible to continue the war, until our rage of conquest could be satiated, I should expect to see this nation exposed to the hostilities of a grand alliance, formed on purpose to set bounds to our ambition. I should be glad to know upon what power we could depend for assistance in that day of distress?

Such a day will, I hope, never break upon Great Britain. It is high time to give peace to the panting nations of the earth. It is from peace alone, from an equitable peace, dictated by the spirit of humanity and moderation, that we are to derive those advantages which will indemnify us for the expences of the war; from an immediate cessation of those grievous exactions, which are yearly augmenting the public distress; from a due encouragement of art and industry; from a particular attention to trade, which ought to be freed from certain restrictions, tenderly cherished, extended and improved, so as to enjoy its advantages, without competition, at this period, when no power is in a condition to rival us in foreign markets; from a more equal distribution of the public burdens, which are, in some respects, at present, partially imposed; from a well-digested system of police for abolishing idleness, restraining rapine, punishing profligacy, and maintaining order; from a proper regulation of the finances, a scrupulous regard to national oeconomy; and a practicable plan for gradually discharging the incumbrances of the public. These, I hope, are the salutary aims of a patriot king, and a virtuous ministry; and if they are accomplished, many people who now, from prejudice or misapprehension, join the cry against the peace, will bless heaven for having favoured them with an administration, which had benevolence and courage enough to make them happy, even in their own despite.

No. 23. Saturday, 30 October 1762.

To the Author of the BRITON.

SIR,

A s I seldom of late have dipt into political papers, my motive for chusing you to be my correspondent, is the result of prepossession, rather than of partiality; and the motive of that prepossession is, perhaps, too trifling to mention, as it is no other than the preference I give to the title of your paper, which I take to be more comprehensive, and consequently more suited to my sentiments than that of your antagonist. You are therefore not to expect from me any high encomiums, either upon the plan or execution of your work, because, to say the truth, I am a stranger to both, and this letter is so entirely impartial, that it may be addressed to the North Briton, with as much propriety as it is to the Briton.

The differences between Great Britain and France have hitherto employed the heads of our politicians; those between us and Spain, tho' perhaps, of equal consequence, have lain dormant, from a presumption that the Spaniards are no other than the bully-backs[1] of the French, and will follow their principals. How far they were so in the beginning of the war, I shall not pretend to dispute, but in the progress of it, they are certainly become, properly speaking, as much principals as the French themselves.

It is to the honour of the late minister I mention it, that he brought the differences between us and France into a very practicable accommodation; and, to say the truth, I am of myself so dull, as not to comprehend the reason, after the concessions that were made on both sides, why so many millions of money, not to mention the lives that have been lost, have not been saved to Great Britain since the first of May 1761.[2]

Having said this much in favour of the late minister, I cannot help thinking that his system of politics was somewhat deficient, in disregarding, as he did, the claims of Spain. They might be improperly urged; but it is certain, that they were materially cognoscible[3] before the tribunal of reason and equity. His conduct therefore, in one respect, is unaccountable, by his *swallowing the cow, and choaking on the rump;*[4] for I must say, that at the time of the late negotiation, our differences with Spain were no more than the *rump* of our difficulties; tho' they are now become, what we may call the *head* and *body*, as well as the *tail*.

We have taken the Havanna, and it is possible, that the Spaniards have taken Portugal. I shall not pretend to decide in that case, *who has the better bargain;* but I must be of opinion, that a little, and a very little pliancy in our late minister, might have prevented both events; nay, I can scarce call it *pliancy;* perhaps it ought to be termed rather *good manners:* but *what is done, cannot,* as the saying is, *be undone;*[5] we are therefore to look forward, and make the best of our bargain, be it good or bad. I cannot, however, help thinking, that the good people of this country are too much swayed by semblances and sounds. The taking the Havanna, looks as big, and sounds as pompously as the conquest of Peru and Mexico; nay, I shall even admit it in reality, and in its consequences.

But here old Esop comes in my way. "A covetous fellow," says he, "had a goose, which every day laid him a golden egg, and he imagined, that if the animal was killed, he would find in her belly the source of all this wealth, and so become rich all of a sudden. The poor goose was killed, and her inside was no other than that of the rest of her species." The application of this fable can scarcely be mistaken. The Spanish America has laid us many a golden egg, and it is a dangerous experiment to put a knife to its throat, and to dig in its bowels for the treasure.

I cannot help thinking, that our forefathers, with all their *crassa Minerva*,[6] had as much sound judgment as their posterity have hitherto displayed. Nothing was held more sacred with them, than that the Spanish West Indies should belong to Spain, and to Spain only. Any person who reads the history of Queen Elizabeth, must be sensible, that it was in her power to have broken into this maxim. She was sometimes in a fit of passion inclined to have done it; but upon recollection, she with-held the knife from the throat of the goose, and was contented with the golden egg, which enriched her people, and prompted their industry; a mine richer by far than any the bowels of the earth can afford.

The earl of Salisbury,[7] who is said to have been the last good minister, and the first bad one that England has since had, was termed so, not from any defect of his wisdom, but from the depravity of his politics, which led him into compliances with a prodigal spendthrift master. Those compliances, however, were confined to England, without affecting foreign affairs; for all the false steps which James made in his transactions with the rest of Europe, happened after Salisbury's death. He was the first English minister who, after the making the famous treaty, that has been since held so sacred, under the name of the *Golden Compact*, concluded a formal treaty with Spain:[8] but that treaty held the indivisibility of the Spanish America to be sacred. No farther treaty, or indeed negotiation between us and Spain, happened till the time of Cromwell.

If there is a point, in which all historians are agreed, it is, that that usurper failed in his politics, by attempting to kill the goose, I mean, by destroying the indivisibility of the Spanish America. He was led to this by the perpetual opposition he met with at home, which required perpetual supplies of money. He failed, happily for this nation, in his attempt. The goose continued to lay the golden egg, and we found the mine that supplied it in the perpetual current of our industry. England, it is true, was originally no party in the treaty of Munster,[9] which gave Cromwell a handle to pretend that he was not bound by it; but the principles of the indivisibility of the Spanish monarchy were so self-evidently rational, and calculated for the interest of England, as well as the rest of Europe, that his not succeeding in his claims upon Spain, has been universally acknowledged to be a lucky miss to this nation.

The next æra to which we steer, is that of 1667. If I designed this paper to be the squib[10] of a party, it would be easy for me to prove how parallel the circumstances of 1667, are to those of 1762. To rescue Portugal from falling a prey to Spain, was the original intention of the treaty of 1667.[11] We succeeded in our attempt, tho', it is certain, at that time, the weakness of the Spanish monarchy was deplorable, and nothing would have been more easy, than for us to have cut off the head of the goose. We however chose, that she should continue to lay, and we found an annual advantage in it.

A very few years brought about a revolution in our politics. It was perceived, that the treaty of 1667, was not sufficiently precise and clear with regard to the Spanish West-Indies. Another treaty, which was concluded in 1670,[12] accordingly took place, and was formed upon the principles of the peace of Munster, establishing the indivisibility of the Spanish West-Indies, and the balance which their American possessions ought to hold both in Europe and America.

Having said thus much, my reader may perhaps ask, how are we to resent an insult, or an injury from Spain, but by putting the knife to the throat of the goose? I answer, let us do it by all means; nay, if she shall prove invincibly refractory, that is, if she should be mad, and persist in being *felo de se*,[13] let us even apply the steel, with whatever reluctance we may do it. Nay, I will go farther, and insist, that we ought not to put up the knife till we have received indemnification for the past, and security for the future; and that, in all subsequent negotiations, *the turn of the scale*,[14] as it is called, should be in our favour.

The young students in mathematics, have a particular proposition in Euclid, which they call the *Pons asinorum*,[15] and they think, that the mastering it leads them more than half-way to perfection. The Havanna has for many years been the *Pons asinorum* of the English. We have passed it, and the ball lies now at our foot. How are we to dispose of it? Shall we endeavour to put an end to the game, or shall we continue it? Which is for the interest of Great Britain?

We cannot put an end to the game, but by making ourselves masters of all the Spanish West-Indies, which would effectually give them the *coup de grace*. But what would be the consequence? are we sure that the fate of Midas would not be ours? Like us, he asked from heaven the childish boon, that every thing he touched should turn to gold. The effect was, that gold became to him of no value, and like honest Baucis and his wife,[16] he clubbed[17] another wish, to *get the ladle out again*.[18] But supposing that not to be the case, are we sure that the Spanish West-Indies, when in our possession, would bring us in as much money as they do at present; or that they can be of equal value to us as they now are? For my own part, I cannot a moment hesitate in pronouncing in the negative; and there are not, perhaps, five thinking men in England, who can doubt, that such an acquisition would effectually undo her.

But, setting this political consideration aside, let us examine how such an acquisition would stand in point of prudence. I can make no manner of doubt in saying, that Europe would be divided into two parties; of which the one would be England, and all the other kingdoms and states would form the other. It would then be nonsense to talk of separate interests. All would be consolidated into one. The French, the Spaniards, the Germans, the Italians, the Dutch, the Northern,[19] and all other nations would lose their several denominations, and be known by no other than that of enemies to Great Britain. The case would be the same at present, were the West-Indian Spaniards of any other character than what they now are; that is, were they to change indolence for industry, and the habits of idleness for a life of activity. It is their uninterprising spirit, that has so long given peace to that half of the globe.

As I set out in this paper with professions of strict impartiality, I think myself obliged to keep them up, even towards our enemies. I shall not here enter into a disquisition, how far the Spaniards have, or have not an original right to what they possess in America; they certainly have a prescriptive[20] one. It has been recognised by the most solemn treaties; and prescriptive right is perhaps the best that we ourselves can shew for many of our own possessions there. It has, I know, been urged, that we have a prescriptive right to the cutting logwood in the bay of Campeachy.[21] Nothing, however, can be worse founded than this allegation; for tho', in the year 1717 or 18, our board of trade at London, did make a report, in favour of an original right of the English to this logwood trade; yet it is certain, that about the time the treaty of 1667 was concluded, the Spaniards were in full and undisturbed possession of that trade; nor does it appear, that either the Earl of Sandwich, Sir Richard Fanshaw, Sir William Godolphin, or Lord Sunderland,[22] who all of them negotiated our affairs about that time at the court of Spain, ever pretended that the English had an original, or even a prescriptive right to that trade. It is true, we had a right of indulgence;[23] but the principles of that right are widely different from those of prescription; tho' in reality their effects are the same. For my own part, I am so short-sighted a politician, as to doubt very much, whether the difference of the claim, that was urged by our minister at the court of Spain, and that which the Spanish minister was willing to have granted, was of so much consequence, as to hazard a rupture between two nations, whose welfare consists in a mutual good correspondence with each other.

While I am on this subject, I shall just mention a word or two with regard to the celebrated family compact.[24] This treaty has been represented in the most hideous and infernal colours, and the discoverer of it has had as much honour paid him upon it, as any of the discoverers of America ever had. I have been at great pains to investigate the grounds of the clamour against this formidable family-compact; but can find in it only certain harmless precautions against the spirit of conquest, that seems to threaten the Spanish, as well as the French interest in America, as well as in Europe. I am,

SIR,

Your humble Servant,
AMERICANUS.

No. 24. Saturday, 6 November 1762.

Ego omnibus meis opibus, omnibus conciliis, omnibus dictis atque factis repugnarim et restiterim crudelitati——

CICERO.[1]

An honest minister of state, in England, is a great rarity. Indeed one would imagine, to hear the opinions of men in general, that an upright minister was like the phœnix, a creature of the imagination, which never existed in reality. Even those who pique themselves upon their candour and reflection, seem to consider the phenomenon as portentous; and when they hear such a character tainted by the breath of slander, observe that the abuse and censure of the multitude is a kind of artillery, which hath been levelled at all ministers; and that the management of this artillery, is one of the dearest privileges of the English people. I am of a different sentiment; and if I can prove from the British annals, that a mild government, and upright administration, were seldom or never exposed to popular abuse; it must be owned, that those who so scandalously revile the present ministry, mingling every species of falshood with their reproach, have basely degenerated from the honesty of their ancestors. This inference will appear the more uncontrovertible, if I demonstrate, that all the clamour against kings and ministers, (except where religion interposed to foment disaffection) which hath flowed thro' history from the conquest[2] to the present reign, was the effect of tyranny and oppression.

We are not to look for written libels against the government, in the early ages of our empire, before our civil and religious liberties were established; when men's minds were contracted by ignorance, and their lips were padlocked by arbitrary power. Even when liberty first degenerated into license, and the subjects flew in the face of their sovereign, the opposition did not arise among artisans, inferior tradesmen, and the lower class of plebeians, such as those who now presume to direct the wheels of government. Not a ray of liberty beamed on these degrees of the people. They were considered as slaves, and overwhelmed under the pressure of the most despotic dominion. Resistance to arbitrary power, was a natural right claimed by the great Barons only; and this they asserted in the field, by the prowess of their knights or military tenants.

The reign of William the Conqueror was a tissue of despotism and revolt. He parcelled out the lands of England among his chieftains, and each of these may be considered as a minister whom he employed in breaking his new subjects to his yoke. When he first revisited his own country, he left the regency of England in the hands of his own half-brother Odo bishop of Bayeux, and William Fitzosborne, two rapacious ministers, who seized all opportunities of fleecing the people, and at length provoked them into a revolt. They were joined in the exercise of their rapine, by Geoffrey bishop of Coutance, who possessed two hundred and eighty manours, usurped from the lawful proprietors.[3] As for Odo, he amassed so much treasure, that he resolved to purchase the papacy; but was prevented by the vigilance of the Conqueror, who having received intimation of his design, surprized him in the very act of embarking; apprehended him with his own hands, seized his treasure, and imprisoned him in the castle of Rouen in Normandy, where he remained till William's death.[4]

That prince's son and successor, William Rufus, reposed his chief confidence in a minister of a still more odious character, Ralf Flambard, son of a presbyter of Bayeux, who had ingratiated himself with his sovereign, by projecting schemes of oppression to fill the King's coffers.[5] It was by his advice, that Rufus caused a new survey to be taken of all the lands and property of the kingdom; and wherever he found them undervalued in the Doomsday-book, he raised the proportion of the taxes accordingly.[6] These arbitrary exactions gave rise to a conspiracy against the life of Flambard, who was actually kidnapped on board of a vessel to be assassinated; but, he had the address to gain over the assassins, and lived to be promoted to the see of Durham; tho', in the beginning of the next reign, he was committed prisoner to the Tower of London. From thence, however, he was released in the sequel, and restored to his bishopric, of which he had been deprived.

Henry I. generally managed the reins of his own government, tho' he sometimes delegated his power to ministers, who sacrificed every idea of justice to the arbitrary views of their master. We know that his judges were barbarous and venal: that Roger bishop of Salisbury caused a considerable number of persons, accused of coining, to be deprived of their eyes, and castrated, without form of trial; and the tenants of the crown were so oppressed with taxes, that they took all opportunities of meeting the king in his progress, and presenting their plough-shares as useless implements.[7] Roger bishop of Sarum,[8] at certain periods, governed the whole kingdom, and acquired vast wealth and influence, which he afterwards employed against the daughter and heir of his benefactor, in favour of the usurper Stephen, by whom he was so ill requited, that he died of grief and vexation.[9]

The usurpation of Stephen was rendered insupportable by the insolence, cruelty, and exactions of his favourite William d'Ypres.[10] Under the ministry of this stranger, every species of oppression was exercised by a body of foreign mercenaries whom he had introduced. They plundered and burned the towns and villages, imprisoned, tortured, and even murdered the wretched people with impunity. Nothing could exceed the misery of the English at this period: they were driven to despair, and actually formed a conspiracy to massacre all the foreigners in the kingdom.[11]

Henry II. was his own minister, and indeed his unwillingness to part with any share of the administration, was the chief cause that induced not only the principal noblemen of his kingdom, but even his own wife and children, to engage in various conspiracies against his government and life.[12] He maintained his prerogative with amazing fortitude, against all the artillery of Rome, and all the machinations of treason: but this exertion of the prerogative never interfered with the liberties of his people, which he intrenched with many excellent laws and regulations.[13]

While Richard Cœur de Lion distinguished himself in Palestine, his kingdom was exposed to every kind of peculation, by the rapacity of William Longchamp bishop of Ely, a Frenchman of low extract, to whom he had entrusted the guardianship of the realm.[14] This insolent foreigner behaved with the most insufferable arrogance, and set every thing to sale with the most shameful venality. He had not discretion enough to bear with moderation the civil authority and legatine[15] power which were united in his person, but proceeded in such a career of extravagance and oppression, that it was generally supposed his brain was disordered.[16]

John had many favourites, chiefly foreigners; but no ministers that acted upon fixed principles.[17] His conduct was influenced by the caprice of his own temper, in consequence of which he was overtaken with disgrace, discomfiture, and ruin.

Henry III. was one of those weak Princes, who never govern in their own persons.[18] As they have neither maxims, knowledge, nor resolution, by which they can manage the helm of government, they necessarily become a prey to insinuating, ambitious individuals, who rule them and their realms in the characters of favourites and ministers. Hubert de Burgh, in this capacity, rendered his sovereign odious to the nation, and brought himself to the brink of destruction. He was superseded in his authority and influence, by Peter de Roches bishop of Winchester, and his nephew Peter de Rivaux, who filled the principal posts in the kingdom with their own countrymen from Gascony and Poictiers, and provoked the English barons to revolt, by their insolence and oppression. These Poitevins were no sooner removed from the King's councils, than this weak Prince fell into the hands of another foreigner, William de Savourie, bishop elect of Valence, and uncle to queen Eleanor, a prelate who insinuated himself so artfully into the confidence of Henry, that he resigned himself wholly to his direction; and these ministers did not fail to entail upon him by their conduct, the contempt and detestation of his subjects.[19]

In the reigns of wise and resolute Princes, we hear of no bad ministers. Edward I. stood by his own helm, and conducted the state-machine with equal wisdom and success:[20] but his son was the very emblem of imbecillity, and therefore dupe to a succession of worthless favourites; first to Piers Gaveston, and afterwards to the two d'Espensers, all of whom were sacrificed to the resentment of the barons.[21] This was also the fate of Mortimer, who, in conjunction with the Queen-mother, engrossed the administration during the minority of Edward III. Even this great Prince outlived all his vigour, and magnanimity. In his old age, he was so infatuated with the personal charms of his concubine Alice Pierce, that he gave himself wholly up to her guidance, and connived at certain corrupt practices, in order to gratify the avarice of this infamous woman. His son John Duke of Lancaster was contented to govern the kingdom under the shadow of her influence, and engaged in some scandalous practices, which drew upon him and his accomplices, the hatred and vengeance of the people.[22]

All the world has heard of the weakness, levity, and misconduct of Richard II. and of his ministers and favourites, Michael de la Pole Earl of Suffolk, Robert Vere Duke of Ireland, the Earl of Wiltshire, Sir John Bussy, Sir Henry Green, and Sir William Bagot, by whose pernicious counsels, he forfeited the affections of his people, was deprived of his crown, and afterwards of his life.[23]

The two succeeding Princes, the fourth and fifth Henrys,[24] had too much spirit to delegate the administration among favourites: but, this weakness proved fatal to the sixth of that name, whose affairs were egregiously mismanaged; first by his two uncles, the Duke of Gloucester and the Cardinal of Winchester, and afterwards by his Queen Margaret, with her ministers, the Dukes of Suffolk and Somerset.[25]

Edward IV. exposed himself to the resentment of his most powerful nobles, by allowing Earl Rivers, and the other relations of the Queen, to engross the whole administration, to govern the kingdom in an arbitrary manner, and to subject the most faithful servants of the crown to such mortifications as provoked them into rebellion.[26]

Every body has heard of Crookback's three infamous ministers, Lovel, Radcliff, and Catesby; tho' far from governing the state, they were no more than tools of their master's tyranny.[27]

Nor is any historical fact better known than the extortion of Henry VII. which he practised by means of two ministers, called Empson and Dudley, who followed the profession of the law, and employed all its subterfuges in oppressing the subjects with false accusations and imprisonment, until they were obliged to purchase a mitigation with the best part of their substance.[28]

The pride, vanity, ambition and arbitrary genius of Wolsey, who directed the councils of the Eighth Henry, are themes upon which every historian has expatiated.[29]

The Duke of Somerset, protector of the realm under Edward VI. was far from being a bad man, tho' he was a weak minister, and fell a sacrifice to the intrigues of a powerful rival who suffered in his turn, under all the weight of popular detestation.[30]

The administration of Mary was disgraced by the knavery of Gardiner and the brutality of Bonner.[31]

Elizabeth distinguished between her minions and her ministers. Her ministers were not exempt from censure, tho' generally revered by the people; because, while they acted as the servants of the crown, they shewed themselves the friends of the public.[32]

The administration of James I. was justly stigmatized as a ridiculous system of arbitrary power, influenced by insolent favourites whom their sovereign had distinguished for no other merit than personal beauty.[33]

In the reign of Charles I. Buckingham was detested for his pride, arrogance and contempt of the Commons, and Strafford for his haughty disposition.[34]

After the restoration Clarendon was respected for his virtue and integrity; while those infamous ministers who constituted the cabal, became the objects of popular execration.[35]

It was not without reason that the nation exclaimed against the ministers of James II. the Earl of Sunderland, Tyrconnel, Jeffries and other evil counsellors, by whom he was encouraged in his despotic principles and bigotry, which ended in his expulsion and ruin.[36]

One happy consequence of the Revolution was the liberty of the press,[37] which produced a plentiful crop of altercation and scurrility, in the partizans of two inveterate factions, which disputed the administration with each other during the whole reigns of William and his successor;[38] and yet the censures and recriminations that mutually passed between the Whig and Tory ministers were generally founded on facts which could not be controverted.

As to the system of corruption which succeeded these disputes, and prevailed for the greater part of the two last reigns, it was so flagrant and pernicious, that I believe there is hardly an individual now alive who will venture to say that the clamour which it occasioned was frivolous or ill-founded. In justice to the late minister, it must be owned that the system expired when he assumed the reins of government; and as soon as corruption was exploded, all clamour immediately ceased.

From this rude sketch then it appears, that the people of England, at almost every period of the common-wealth, have had but too much reason to inveigh against the conduct of the ministers by whom they have been governed; that every upright administration of former times hath passed uncensured, and been remembered with respect; and that the present, is the first æra in the annals of Great Britain, distinguished by a torrent of the foulest slander and abuse, poured upon the character of a Prince, who deserves to be the darling of his people; upon the reputation of a minister, whose conduct has defied the severest scrutiny of malice.

No. 25. Saturday, 13 November 1762.

O civem natum reipublicæ, memorem fui nominis, imitatoremque majorum! —

Cicero.[1]

To the BRITON.

Sir,

Howsoever you may disguise your real sentiments from venal motives, it is not unknown to you that this nation is brought to the very brink of destruction, by the pernicious counsels of your patron Lord B——, whose want of principle, and want of capacity, are so flagrant, that the writers in the opposition have thought it altogether unnecessary to specify one instance of either. That the spirit of the war has flagged ever since he assumed the reins of government, needs no other proof than the observation of every man who is capable of reflecting upon the operations of this and the last campaign, and comparing them with the events which distinguished the two last years of the preceding administration.

As he is unequal to the task of carrying on the war, so he seems still less qualified to negotiate the peace; witness those preliminaries, concerning which, a worthy grey-headed patriot, in a late public address to the Lord Mayor, the worshipful aldermen, and common-council of the city of London, has, with all the outward marks of inspiration, already prophesied, that *they will blow us up in a trice!*[2] What then does that minister deserve, who has charged the mine, and now stands with his dark lanthorn and match,[3] ready to kindle the train, which is to send us all up in the air in a moment!

The prospect of our situation is truly tremendous! – Brief let me be[4] – perhaps it is yet not too late to save himself and his country. I will propose a scheme, in which, if he should acquiesce – *myself will mount the rostrum in his favour, and strive to gain his pardon from the people.*[5] Let him break off the negotiation for peace, and procure an act of p——t, constituting the Lord M——r of L——n, for the time being, prime minister of G——t B——n. This is a mark of consideration which we certainly owe to the importance and dignity of the capital, that great emporium of trade, that center of wealth, patriotism, and political knowledge.

The free states of Greece generally derived their appellations from their chief cities, such as Athens, Lacedemon,[6] and Thebes; and Rome conferred her name upon that vast empire which embraced the greatest part of Europe, Asia, and Africa. Even the Carthaginians, our great prototypes, as a trading people, owed their denomination to a single city, the remains of which are still to be seen in the neighbourhood of Tunis on the Barbary shore. In imitation of these great examples, why should not the same honour be decreed to the metropolis of this kingdom, which hath produced greater orators than Athens, greater generals than Lacedemon, greater poets than Thebes, greater patriots than Rome, and greater merchants than Carthage? Why should not Augusta[7] bear the same preheminence in Britain, that Rome bore in Italy, and the *London Empire* be substituted in the room of *the kingdom of Great Britain!* For my part, I cannot help thinking, that the corporation of London was modelled after the constitution of Rome. The Lord Mayor's person, and office, are sure as venerable as those of any Roman consul. The sheriffs, with their furred gowns, and golden chains, may be compared to a couple of pretors;[8] and the Cripplegate grenadiers[9] to the pretorian cohorts: *Alderman*

is synonimous with *Senator:* those among them who have been honoured with
the order of knighthood, are equivalent to the Roman *Equites*[10] in rank, if not
in activity. The deputies and common-councilmen represent the *Curiones* and
the *Decuriones;*[11] and the separate tribes were no other than types of the wor-
shipful mob of liverymen and their dependants, who constitute the populace
of London.

Every body knows, that the plebeians in Rome, in the purest age of the re-
public, reserved to themselves the greatest share of the government; and that
no resolution for peace or war was taken but in their assemblies. We now see
the same privileges claimed by the right worshipful mobility of London; and
I hope to see these privileges established by the sanction of the legislature.

This great point can never be settled at a more interesting æra than the
present juncture, when the fate of this mighty empire depends upon the peace
which is said to be upon the carpet; and the chief magistrate of the metropo-
lis[12] is so exquisitely qualified to conduct and manage the deliberations of a
congress. That great man seems indeed to have been formed by the hands
of Providence, on purpose to effect extraordinary reformations, and shine
with peculiar lustre as the first prime minister of the *London Empire!* It is well
known he was born to empire; to immense property, acquired without fraud
or extortion, and handed down to him from a long line of illustrious progeni-
tors: that he sucked ideas of government from the breast of his nurse, who
was a blackamoor Princess, the daughter of an African Caboceiro,[13] and along
with these a disposition to benevolence and humanity: that from his tender
years, he hath been accustomed to the exercise of absolute dominion, over
some thousands of his fellow-creatures; and that, by dint of experience, he
hath learned that form of rule which is best calculated to restrain the enormi-
ties of human nature. Who can be better qualified to perform the functions
of a civil magistrate among the free people of L——n, than he who hath so
long exerted absolute power over a community of negro-slaves? He who hath
exercised that power without rigour, without reproach, without incurring the
slightest imputation of cruelty or oppression: he who was never suspected
of pride, insolence, or rapacity; but hath approved himself on all occasions
the liberal patron, the kind master, the quiet neighbour, and obliging friend!
Who can so worthily fill the place of p——e m——r, as he who knows so
well how to mediate between the prerogative of the King, and the rights of
the people? who has himself acted in the different spheres of sovereign and
subject; who hath exhibited such shining specimens of loyalty, reverence and
respect towards the person and family of the Prince to whom his allegiance is
due; who hath, with such dignity, supported the character of a good citizen,

and set so many bright examples of filial and paternal virtue; whose capacity is so extensive, as to comprehend the whole circle of science; who perfectly understands all the tropes and figures of rhetorick, and in particular, the art of adducing arguments *from facts, à priori;* whose accomplishments and virtues have been the theme of the modern Demosthenes,[14] who hath publicly extolled him for his learning, ingenuity, eloquence, urbanity, and above all things, recommended him as a most excellent physician.

Let him therefore be employed to cast the water[15] of this land, which is sick of a Scotch administration. Let him act, not only as L — d-Mayor of L — n, but also as mayor of the palace:[16] let him transfer the burden of g — t from the shoulders of his P — e; and, instead of troubling the antient counsellors of the th — ne, let him submit the deliberations of state to the worshipful the common-council of the city of London. On particular occasions, that require an extraordinary exertion of human sagacity, he may assemble the people *tributim,* or *centuriatim;*[17] and for the dernier resort, a college may be instituted of those geniuses who belong to neither ward, livery, hundred, nor tything,[18] that they may be also consulted in case of emergency. These may be considered as the *proletarii* of the Roman people, the confused multitude, who were exempt from taxes, and excused from going to war, and served the common-wealth no other way but by stocking it with children, whence their denomination was derived. The same class of the London people will serve for politicians, as well as for the purpose of propagating the species; and over and above the ordinary fruits of their labour, may have an allowance from the chamber of London, for animating the citizens by their occasional writings and harrangues.

Should the execution of this salutary scheme excite any disturbance, the dictatorial power may be safely lodged, for a certain period of time, in the hands of the Lord-M — r, minister elect of the *London Empire;* and he, no doubt, will chuse for his *magister equitum,*[19] that unblemished hero Colonel Jack,[20] that modern Lilburn[21] in war and patriotism, who hath so often ventured his ears for the good of his country. The present town-clerk,[22] whose virtues reflect exceeding lustre on the knightly order, may, with great propriety, be elevated to the office of censor; and the auspices will be skilfully conducted by the two reverend augurs,[23] who have so eminently distinguished themselves in opposition to the ministry of B — e.

You may be surprized, that in this sketch of reformation, I have scarce mentioned the k — ly name; but, the truth is, I would consider it as a name only, a *vox et præterea nihil.*[24] I would have the K — of E — d like the last Caliphs of Bagdat, or the Dairo of Japan,[25] or that race of sovereigns, known in France by the epithet *Faineans*.[26] They enjoyed the nominal honours, the personal veneration of the subjects, the form, the pomp, the trappings and geugaws of royalty; but, the substance of empire, the power, the influence and authority resided in the sultan, the cubay,[27] and the mayor of the palace.

In like manner, let the first personage of the *London Empire* possess the name, the rank, the splendour of a sovereign Prince: let him eat, drink, and be merry[28] at the public cost, and make a couch or settee of the throne, upon which he may slumber at his ease: but let the prerogative of making peace and war, of contracting engagements with foreign powers, of appointing the great officers of state, in a word, of conducting the whole machine of government, be vested in the Lord-Mayor of London, with the assistance of the worshipful aldermen, common-council, and common mob of that great metropolis.

If you are honest and wise enough to print this letter, I will undertake to recommend you to his Lordship for some kind of provision; and as you are not qualified to live among free-men, I make no doubt but you may be appointed negro-driver on one of his plantations in Jamaica. In the mean time, I am yours, as you may deserve,

Junius Brutus Cockney.[29]

As to my own particular, I think myself obliged to this zealous reformer for his promised recommendation; but, with regard to the public, I am afraid his project comes too late, for, we are assured, the preliminaries of the peace are actually signed;[30] not but that another crisis may happen, when his proposal will deserve the attention of the legislature: mean while, let me advise him to acquiesce in the measure which cannot now be recalled, and endeavour, with his fellow-citizens, to make the most of a bad bargain: but, I shall have occasion to hazard my sentiments more at large upon this subject, if Mr. H——'s prediction[31] should not be literally fulfilled before next Saturday.

No. 26. Saturday, 20 November 1762.

To the BRITON.

Sir,

If the following is worth your while, you will do me a favour in publishing it; if not, throw it aside.

Res prosperæ insolentiam pariunt.[1]

SIR,

The sauciness of servants is now become an epidemical evil. Go where you will, you hear nothing but complaints of them: but methinks, the case of one Mr. Fitz-George[2] deserves particular notice and commiseration. This young gentleman, it seems, came to the possession of a plentiful estate, about two years ago, by the death of his grandfather. Being a humane, generous, good-natured man, he suffered most of the servants who were in the house in his grandfather's time to continue; and as for the few whom he found it prudent to part with, he gave them pensions for life. Mr. Fitz-George enjoyed his house and family with great peace and comfort for about a twelvemonth, when one Will Pitot[3] (for so I think they called him by way of nick-name) gave his master warning in a great passion. People were very much surprised at this, as they knew Will had had a very good place of it. But Will himself soon unfolded the mystery, by publishing a letter,[4] in which he told us, that he had given his master warning, because he was not allowed to rule his master and the whole house. Many of the tenants of the manor were not sorry for Will's leaving his place; for they say, that though he had been very zealous in maintaining the rights of the manor, yet he had such a number of over-sea acquaintances, to whom he sent presents out of the manor, that he some years laid out the whole rents upon them, which were about six millions. This the tenants murmured at very much; for in consequence of this, their Lord was obliged to raise their rents every year to maintain his house, and supply the exigencies of the manor, even to the amount, they say, of twelve millions a year sometimes. This they reckoned very hard, as they had nothing to do with, nor received any advantage by, these acquaintances of Will's. And this they looked upon as the more unaccountable still, because Will, when he was an out-door servant, had exclaimed most bitterly against the servants before him, who had followed these practices, though they had never spent the half of the money upon their foreign acquaintances, that Will did upon his. But what provoked them most of all was, that they had helped Will to the place, merely with a view that he might break the neck of these things; and when they found, that instead of this, he increased them, they did not scruple to say aloud, that he had betrayed them. But Will was a strange sort of fellow, and had got some peculiar notions of œconomicks; for what was wrong when done by another, he thought right when done by himself. Nay, when he heard some whispers through the manor with respect to these things, after he left his place, he told the tenants in the letter already mentioned, that indeed he should give himself no trouble to sollicit the return of their favour. This they considered as worse than all the rest, first to deceive them, and then to bid them defiance; but Will knew what he was saying, for, he had some how or other, got an annuity for three lives.

Things continued in this posture about half a year, when another servant, who had lived long in the house, and been kindly used, I think his name was Tom Give-place, or Buy-vote,[5] I don't know which, took it into his head to give his master warning also, unless he would double his wages. This was thought to be a very odd proposal, as Tom was now far advanced in years, and almost past his labour. The case, it seems, was this; money was wanted in the office to which Tom belonged; application was made to Mr. Fitz-George for it. He asked how much would do for such a time. Tom answered two millions. Mr. Fitz-George (as the money was to be raised upon his tenants) was willing to be as gentle to them as possible; he therefore asked some of his other servants, whether a less sum would not suffice; they replied, that, considering the burden the tenants had lain under for a great while, they thought one million was as much as they could in conscience demand of them, and that, with good management, would do very well; or if it would not hold out till the time proposed, their Lord might make a second demand when it was found necessary. Tom, taking this much amiss, left his place.[6] Upon this, a great many of the out-door servants, raised a clamour, as they had done in Will's case before. The reason was, that as Will had often cajoled some of them, by saying, he liked their livery, *viz.* an alderman's-gown, better than his own, tho' he only played on them; so Tom had often employed others of them in jobbs about the house, for which he had every now and then given them a bit or a sop. This they were afraid they would now lose, and therefore mouth'd very undeservedly both against the master and the new servant he put in Tom's place. They objected that he was a stranger, though both he and his progenitors had belonged to the manor for several centuries; and long before some of themselves were so much as heard of in it. When this could not be denied, they then urged that he was however born on the northern part of the manor, and themselves in the southern or the western; to this it was rationally enough answered, that the northern part belonged to the manor as well as the southern; and to prevent all objections of that kind for the future, proposed that the manor-house should be built exactly in the middle of the estate, and then the tenants would be all equally near it, according to their respective divisions. When they found therefore that these objections were treated only with ridicule by the opposite party, and people who had taken no side, they then trumped up a story, that he was not qualified for the place, because he did not know the way of the house. To this it was replied, If they meant the former way of it, they were undoubtedly right; for it was allowed, that formerly there had been a great deal of waste and profusion in it; but if they meant a way which would be most advantageous, both to the master and the tenants, they were mistaken, for he understood that as well as any man; and as a proof of it, they urged, that it was now plain from fact, that he had done the same service for one million, for which Tom (as mentioned above) had demanded two. This new servant's name, I find, was Jack Scot,[7] and related, they say, to Mr. Fitz-George's family. This fellow, it seems, had been much addicted to reading, which gave him something of the college, together with the court air. However, it made him master of a good deal of polite and useful literature, which afforded a handle to some to upbraid him with learned disquisitions upon cockle-shells, plants and flowers:[8] and others, whose genius could not soar so high as this happy flight, came nevertheless very near it, by the curious invention of the name Jack-a-boot,[9] which, it seems, they struck out by an uncommon effort of wit, from a titular name his family had long borne.

All these objections operated wonderfully upon many sensible people, both without and within the house; for one Harry Chamberman[10] soon after gave his master warning likewise. Harry, we hear, had absented himself from his service for some time past; his master advertised him twice, but to no effect. However, whether of his own accord, or in consequence of a third advertisement, is not material, Harry did return; but it appears it was not to ask his master's pardon, or to apologise for what he had done, but to let him know he would serve him no longer. So Harry gave up his livery, and after dining with an old acquaintance, viz. Tom Give-place, went down to his friends in the country. In consequence of this, one Charley Check,[11] whose business in the house was to see that the cooks, and other servants, put nothing to waste, gave Mr. Fitz-George warning also; the reason, they say, was not want of victuals, ill-paid wages, or being overwrought, but that, being a relation of Harry Chamberman's, he would not stay in the house after he was gone. The same, we hear, was the case of one Peter Post-boy.[12] His office was to carry his master's letters to and fro; but tho' his master paid him very liberally for it, kept him always in good livery, and never made him go in dark nights, yet he has given him warning too. Such is the way this young gentleman has been used by his servants; so that people of lower rank need not wonder if they are ill-used by theirs. Which of them have taken the example from the other, I cannot tell; but as to the designs of Mr. Fitz-George's servants in acting so, people seem to be universally agreed, that they want to force every body else out of the house, and to have the whole of it to themselves, and such as they shall put in. Whether Mr. Fitz-George will thus give up his house to them or no, no body as yet pretends to say. Many of the tenants heartily wish he would not; for they think it is a shame they should be so presumptuous: but however these things may be, there are two or three foolish curs, commonly called Monitor, North-Briton, Patriot,[13] &c. but I understand their true name is Yelper, and all of one litter, who post themselves in dark corners, and snarl in an angry manner, both at Mr. Fitz-George, and his new servants, whenever they pass by; but when any of the old ones happen to come in their way, they fawn, and lick their feet most wishfully, particularly Will Pitot's, tho' he has been longest out of the house. Whether Will had been kind to them while he was in it, by throwing them a little bone now and then, or whether they wanted to bespeak his favour beforehand, in case he should chance to come into it again, or whether they had something of an inbred antipathy against Scot, can't be certainly determined. Some are of opinion that there is a mixture of all three: be that as it will, Mr. Fitz-George and his servants, have hitherto gone out and in about their business, without taking any notice of them, because, I suppose, they don't think them worth their while.

This is the best and fullest account I can give you of this matter at present; but if you want further information about it, perhaps one Charles Say,[14] a news-man, or his eldest brother, may be able to satisfy you. These gentlemen have generally very early intelligence, with respect to what passes in Mr. Fitz-George's family, and one of them let us know the other day, that there is a talk of seventeen more of that gentleman's servants going to give him warning. Whether this is true or false, time only can discover. But it is thought, if they should do so, Mr. Fitz-George will be in no difficulty to supply their places, as there are many in all parts of the manor who would be glad to serve him. I am,

SIR,

Hammersmith, Nov. 9th.

Your very humble servant.

No. 27. Saturday, 27 November 1762.

—*garrit aniles*
Ex re fabellas.
HORACE.[1]

To the BRITON.

Sir,

I have lately met with a pamphlet[2] entitled, "A Letter to the Right Hon. the Lord Mayor, the worshipful aldermen, and common-council, the merchants, citizens, and inhabitants of the city of London, from *an old servant*"; and indeed, to put the most charitable construction on the contents of it, this servant seems to be so old, that, I think, it is high time he were released from his labour. I don't intend to enter into a minute description of every palpable blunder that occurs in every page of this performance: but I beg leave to animadvert upon a few particulars; and when I have done, perhaps, the reader may say I have been very ill employed in refuting the reveries of a disturbed imagination.

With respect to the peace now upon the carpet, the letter-writer, after having branded the preliminaries as shameful, pernicious, and unnecessary, and prognosticated in plain terms, that a peace founded on them, would blow us up in a trice; proceeds to shew, what I believe, no man ever doubted, that before the war, France carried on a greater trade in sugar and cod-fish than England, consequently maintained a greater number of hands in these branches of traffick, which made greater returns of bullion to their native country. In stating the profits of our Newfoundland-trade, at 300,000 *l. per annum*, I apprehend he is considerably under the mark; but, granting them to be no more than 300,000 *l.* I look upon the deductions he has drawn to be palpably erroneous.

"As the returns of France (says he) are above four times that sum, we make them a present of above twelve hundred thousand pounds annually, by allowing them to fish on the banks of Newfoundland, and our own fishery will be annihilated." If the French employ a greater number of hands in this fishery, it is because they have a much greater number of hands to employ: if they make greater returns, these returns are diffused among a greater number of people. If we have a great number of idle hands, which might be profitably employed in the fishery; why are they not so employed? Are the shoals of fish diminished? that is not pretended—what then is the rub? They now fish with manifest advantage over those dangerous rivals; they have the whole coast of Acadia, or Nova-Scotia to themselves; they have Cape Breton and the neighbouring islands, the whole gulph and river of St. Lawrence, to which, before this period, they had no access. These are acquisitions added to the banks of Newfoundland, added at the expence of the French who formerly possessed them; who are now excluded from all these shores; who have even, on the banks of Newfoundland, no harbour, shelter, or security, but two little islands at one particular part of the coast; and these under the inspection of an English commissary. Instead of giving them back the whole American fishery, we have deprived them of a great part of it; and with respect to the rest, have laid them under severe restrictions; it will therefore be the fault of the British subjects, if they do not greatly improve this valuable branch of traffick: it will be a disgrace to our fishers, if they do not cut out the French by dint of industry, possessed as they are of such superior advantages.

To prove that we run any risk of seeing our Newfoundland fishery annihilated by the French, our author ought to have shewn, that in proportion as the French fishery increased, the English fishery declined; but this, we know, is not to be done; for our fishery has been increasing for a century past, even while our rivals were in possession of those advantages, of which they are now deprived; and instead of employing three hundred ships on that trade, we might have employed three thousand, provided we could have spared hands for that purpose; so that our author's deductions are evidently erroneous.

What follows is, perhaps, the most extraordinary part of this performance. The author exclaims with extraordinary vehemence and indignation against H——n interests, and G——n connections; and almost in the same breath launches out in the most extravagant encomiums on that m——r who drew those connexions so close; who tied this nation to G——y at such an expence, as now renders a peace absolutely necessary to effect a separation. The contents of these few pages, in which the reprobation of H——r-connections, and the praises of Mr. P—— are jumbled together, I cannot help looking upon with an eye of pity, as the most melancholy instance of infatuation, which the prejudice of this day hath brought forth.

If, as the letter-writer affirms, the late m——r condemned those G——n connections in private, while in public he cherished them as the apple of his eye, why have his professed friends, admirers, and emissaries, in a continued series of public papers and pamphlets, abused and reviled his successor at the helm, on the supposition that he was inclined to withdraw the neck of his country from those ruinous connections? Have they not branded him as a man devoid of good faith; as an enemy to the true interest and honour of the nation, who could even think of abandoning such precious allies? Have not these invectives, mingled with menaces and scurrility, been repeated and re-echoed by all the weekly vehicles of slander and sedition? Are not the patrons and instigators of all those revilers, perfectly well known? The circumstance is extraordinary enough. Mr. P—— and his emissaries have denounced vengeance, and levelled all the shafts of obloquy against the present m——y, for having discovered the least coldness to our G—— connections; and this letter-writer, who talks in raptures of the said Mr. P——, who extols him as the greatest statesman, the most uncorrupt patriot, the most perfect m——r that ever existed, who recommends him with all the enthusiasm of love to the esteem, the confidence of his fellow-citizens; yet, nevertheless, consigns his favourite measure to political damnation, as a system pernicious to this country; and invokes axes, halters, confiscation, and *ex-post-facto*-laws on the head of that ministry who shall pursue the footsteps of his unerring pattern.— Good heaven! Is it possible that this way of arguing should excite any passion but that of pity for the author?

Alas! the inconsistency does not end here—If the giving up Guadaloupe, and allowing the French to fish on the banks of Newfoundland, must be necessarily attended with the ruin and slavery of this poor country, as our author expressly affirms; how came his all-perfect minister to acquiesce in those very terms; in the negotiation of last year? Was that *infallible* minister so blind as not to foresee, that these concessions would be attended with the ruin of his country? Was he so wicked as to subscribe, with his eyes open, to the ruin of his country? Was his situation so embarrassed, that he was fain to shut his eyes on the consequences? Or are those cessions pernicious under the m——y of B——e, which would have been salutary in a P——'s administration? Let every honest man, laying his hand upon his heart, ask himself these questions, and then determine what regard is to be paid to the exhortations and maxims of this letter-writer.

Among these, I shall take notice of a few other particulars, equally astonishing as those I have already mentioned. He affirms that Great Britain has been jostled by the French, out of two of the most valuable branches of her commerce, the sugars and her fishery; that we see her naval power daily declining, and that of France augmenting, *&c.* To shew that we have been jostled out of the sugar-trade and the fishery, he ought to have proved that our colonies produce less sugar than they formerly did; and that we send fewer fish to market than we have formerly done: but in both these instances, the facts, we all know, would turn out diametrically opposite to his position. As to the decline of our naval power; the assertion is so truly ridiculous, that I might be justly taxed with folly for attempting to refute it. I will challenge him, and all the world, to instance one period of time, at which the naval power of Great Britain, or indeed of any other state, had ever risen to such a pitch as it is at present.

Neither will it avail him to say, he meant the state of our naval power before the war—The state of our navy and commerce, even at that juncture, was such as enabled us, at a minute's warning, to equip squadrons sufficient to sweep the seas of the enemy; and that enemy, whose naval power and commerce are so dreadful to the letter-writer, as having daily augmented while our's daily declined, has been obliged to abandon the seas in all the four quarters of the globe, and lay up his ships for want of hands to navigate and work them.

With the same precision this author asserts, that the French appear to be possessed of fourteen times more of the African-trade, than we are; and consequently import from it fourteen times more bullion, and grow fourteen times more in naval strength than we do. At this rate, France should export from the coast of Africa, fourteen times the number of slaves, that are exported by the subjects of Great Britain. Now we know, from the examination of African-traders, taken at the bar of the house of commons during the last peace, when it was under consideration to dissolve the old African company,[3] that the subjects of Great Britain had, in the course of one year, exported forty thousand black slaves from the coast of Guinea; so that, according to the pamphleteer's calculation, the French must have exported fourteen times that number, which amounts to five hundred and sixty thousand; an assertion so extravagant, that it needs no refutation: otherwise I might add, that during the same enquiry, it appeared, that instead of fourteen times the number, the French had never exported three times the number of slaves purchased by the British-traders on the coast of Africa. Is it possible that Mr. H——[4] could be ignorant of these particulars? and if he was not, to what principle must we ascribe such a wide alteration from the truth?

The same fallacy is observable in his manner of stating the ballance of naval power between us and the French nation, in the article of British sugars. He fixes the number of hogsheads for foreign markets at 5211, and argues upon that number in such a manner, that persons unacquainted with the subject would imagine our colonies raise no more than that number; or at least, that what they produce over and above that number, was of no advantage to the nation: but, the truth is, our islands of Jamaica, Barbadoes, St. Christopher's, Antigua, Nevis, and Montserrat, produce a greater quantity of sugar, than all the French islands together, excepting their settlements on Hispaniola; besides great quantities of coffee, cacoa, pimento, cotton, and other valuable commodities, over and above molasses and rum, which last is not manufactured in the French islands; that they employ near a thousand sail of ships, and a great many thousands of seamen; give bread to an infinite number of tradesmen and labourers of all kinds, and consume an immense quantity of British manufactures. Now, all these circumstances, the candid letter-writer has industriously sunk on the side of Great Britain; while the benefits of internal traffic and circulation are ostentatiously displayed in favour of France, and the advantage of home-consumption is confirmed by the old observation, that a *penny saved, is a penny got.*[5]

He has likewise carefully avoided informing those for whom he writes, that the French, notwithstanding the vast number of slaves purchased by them on the coast of Guinea, amounting, according to his reasoning, to above five hundred thousand head *per annum*, are obliged to deal at their islands with British-traders, for a considerable number, in order to stock their plantations. If then the English, by their moderate exportation of thirty or forty thousand slaves from the coast of Africa, can supply their own islands, which employ a thousand sail of ships, and yet spare a considerable overplus to Portugal, Spain, and France; and the French, who export five hundred thousand, find that number insufficient for their sugar-plantations, the number of their ships employed in this single branch of traffic must exceed fourteen thousand; which is near double the number belonging to Great Britain and Ireland, and all her settlements and plantations in different parts of Europe, Asia, Africa, and America. To this number, if we add the thirteen hundred and fifty sail employed by them on the North-American fishery, and those by which all the other branches of the French commerce are carried on, to the East-Indies, Turky, Italy, Barbary, Spain, Portugal, Holland, Denmark, Sweden, Russia, and in the coasting-trade, the whole cannot fall short of twenty thousand sail of ships; and allowing twelve men to each at an average, the number of sailors will amount to two hundred and forty thousand, exclusive of those employed in the King's navy. — This, indeed, is a dreadful reckoning, concerning which, I shall not make one reflection, but leave it to the reader's own consideration, who then will settle with himself the credit and attention which is due to this stupendous performance.

In the same strain does this wise politician argue about the cession of Goree,[6] and the retention of Senegal. "Senegal, therefore, without Goree (says he) will be an useless expence to this nation." Is it possible, that a man bred a merchant in the city of London, should be so ignorant of commerce, as not to know that the whole trade of Gum Senega[7] is confined to the river Senegal and that neighbourhood; that we expended, for this gum, a yearly sum not less than one hundred thousand pounds, before we made ourselves masters of this settlement; that during the war, this money, thro' the medium of the Dutch, was paid to our enemies; that by retaining Senegal we not only save this annual sum, but in our turn lay France under contribution; and that Goree is of no other service but as a harbour and factory for other branches of the African-trade, which do not interfere with the gum-trade of Senegal. But the possession of Senegal, moreover, opens us an avenue to the inland parts of Africa, to regions hitherto unexplored by European merchants, abounding with gold, ivory, and drugs, and, in all probability, with many other rich sources of commerce, which industry and adventure will discover.

In the mean time, I do not pretend to exhibit an exact account of the trade of Senegal; that is a task which very few are qualified to execute with precision; all I contend for is, that the possession of this settlement is a point of national importance, which was amply explained to the satisfaction of the late m——r, otherwise that great genius, to which the letter-writer looks up with awe and admiration, would not (it is to be hoped) have employed so much of the national money in its reduction; that the advantages resulting from the possession of it are not only considerable, but such as we cannot enjoy without retaining it in our own hands; that the benefits of Senegal are independent of Goree; and therefore the letter-writer's assertion, that *Senegal, without Goree, will be an useless expence to the nation*, is equally untrue and absurd.

Perhaps I may take another opportunity of considering the sequel of this curious letter, and of shewing with what consistency the author flounders on to the end of the chapter.——Mean while, I am yours,

CRITO.[8]

Hackney, Nov. 20, 1762.

No. 28. Saturday, 4 December 1762.

Populo Romano usitata ac prope jam obsolita ex victoria gaudia esse, ac plus parcendo victis, quam vincendo imperium auxisse.

LIV.[1]

To the BRITON.

SIR,

I happened the other day to call in at a noted coffee-house in the city, where I found a certain person surrounded by a croud of political pupils, declaiming against those preliminary articles of the peace, which have been published without authority, in some of the daily papers;[2] and he concluded his harrangue with this question, "If these preliminaries are genuine, I should be glad to know what we have got in return for the millions we have spent, and the blood we have shed in the course of the war?" As no other person present seemed able or willing to answer this question, on the spot; and as the orator threw out this interrogation with an air of triumph, as a challenge to the friends of the government, I will venture to take up the glove, and shew what we have got by the war, supposing these preliminaries to be genuine.

In the first place then, we have accomplished the original aim of the war, which was to ascertain the limits of Nova Scotia, and to secure our North-American colonies, on which the commerce of this kingdom, in a great measure depends, from the encroachments and depredations of the French in Canada, and their Indian allies. That these were objects of the utmost difficulty and importance, must be allowed by every man who reflects upon the perplexities occasioned between the two nations for above a whole century, in their endeavours to adjust the boundaries of Acadia; who is acquainted with the advantages resulting to Great Britain, from her traffic with these colonies, which are indeed the main pillars of her commerce; and who knows with what indefatigable pains, dexterity, and perseverance, our restless neighbours had hemmed them in with a formidable chain of fortifications, thro' an extent of country, reaching above twelve hundred miles, and seduced many Indian nations from their attachment to, and their dependance upon Great Britain.

These great objects are fully accomplished. The limits of Acadia are now settled beyond any possibility of doubt. There is no occasion for commissaries to dispute; there is no room for ministers to cavil, equivocate, and misinterpret. The whole country in litigation is solemnly ceded to Great Britain. Their chain of forts is destroyed; their forces are not only repelled, but they are driven away beyond the power of returning; and their Indian allies now sue to us for protection: yet, these are not all the advantages we have obtained by the peace. We have gained an immense territory; the whole country of New-France; not a wide extended desart, as it hath been insidiously represented;[3] but, a country smiling with cultivation, with populous cities, towns, and plantations; watered with mighty navigable rivers, and prodigious lakes affording a vast extent of inland navigation; a country abounding with excellent furs, timber, fish, and doubtless with many other valuable productions of the animal, vegetable, and mineral kingdoms; a country extending many thousand leagues to the North-West, even to the coasts of the Pacific Ocean, comprehending unnumbered tribes of savages, who may in time be civilized, and employed advantageously in behalf of the British Commerce. With this country we have gained an accession of many thousand industrious subjects, by whose means, those savages may be cultivated and civilized, as the Canadians are already intermingled with the native Indians, understand their language, and can conform to their customs. Nothing, therefore, can be more absurd, than to form comparisons of the value of Canada, and the French sugar-islands, upon the present revenue derived from both.

The possession of Canada secures our colonies, and, in this particular view, is of more consequence to England, than all the French sugar-islands thrown together. The immediate produce of Guadaloupe and Martinique may be five times the value of what Canada affords; but Canada, in point of profit, is a field scarce opened. We know the Hudson's-Bay company has been enriched by the trade, which is confined to one of the most inhospitable corners of that great continent. We know from the inquiries made by a committee of the house of commons, in the year 1748,[4] that the company purchased no more than the refuse of the American furs, the best of which were ingrossed by the French dealers of Canada. If then this company has been enriched by the refuse of this trade; what advantages must flow from its being wholly in our possession? Now, all these advantages in trade, which may at present, or hereafter, be derived from the possession of that immense country, are additional benefits to the accomplishment of the first aim of the war, which was to defend and secure our colonies in North-America.

We have to the Southward enlarged our boundaries as far as the Mississippi, and secured a free navigation on this river, to which, before this treaty, we never had access. Thus our American empire is bounded on the North and South by two noble rivers, above fifteen hundred miles asunder; and stretches Westward through countries, nations, and languages unknown. With respect to the fishery, we have restricted our restless rivals in such a manner, that they can never rival us again, except thro' our own sloth or want of œconomy: for, he must be weak indeed, who thinks, the French confined to the inconsiderable rocks of St. Peter and Miquelon,[5] will ever be able to cure one fifth part of the fish which they manufactured while they possessed the island of Cape Breton, and the coasts of the gulph of St. Lawrence, from whence they are now expelled.

We have gained the three (formerly neutral) islands of Tobago, St. Vincent, and Dominica,[6] which, tho' affectedly under-valued at this juncture, by the partisans of faction, have been deemed of such consequence, that attempts to settle them have excited jealousies, produced negotiations and remonstrances, and had very near kindled war between the two nations, even in our own remembrance. So lately as the year 1748, information having been received, that the French intended to settle these neutral islands, the nation took the alarm, and it was deemed such a parliamentary concern, that a motion was made in the house of commons to address the King, that he would be graciously pleased to give directions for laying before the house copies of the instructions given to the governor of Barbadoes, for ten years past, so far as they related to these neutral islands. Nor is this alarm to be wondered at, if we consider that they are naturally fertile, well supplied with wood and water; so capable of cultivation, that in a little time, their produce might exceed in value that of all our sugar-islands, Jamaica and Barbadoes excepted; and so intermingled with the French islands, as to be effectual checks upon their enterprising inhabitants. We have moreover gained the large and fruitful island of Grenada, already settled and fortified to our hands, adorned with beautiful sugar-plantations, and affording one of the best harbours in the West-Indies.

We have gained the important settlement of Senegal in Africa, which leaves us in possession of the gum-trade, and masters of one of the finest rivers in the world; an acquisition which was magnified with all the pomp of hyperbole among the atchievements of Mr. P——'s ministry; but now shrunk and diminished, as beheld thro' the medium of party and prejudice. We have obliged the French to evacuate Ostend and Nieuport, to demolish the fortifications of Dunkirk, to deliver Cleves to the King of Prussia, to renounce their claim to the restitution of the prizes taken from their subjects before the declaration of war; and to withdraw their armies from Germany, by which single article, Great Britain saves above six millions annually. We lay them under such restrictions in their trade to the river Ganges in the East-Indies, as must leave them always at the mercy of our company's officers in that part of the world; and we have retrieved the island of Minorca, concerning the importance of which, so many pamphlets, papers, and prints, were written and published immediately after it fell into the hands of the enemy, tho' the enemies of the government, including many of those very encomiasts, have now the effrontery to talk of it as a matter of little or no consequence to this nation.

Such are the benefits acquired by our war with France: now, let us see what we have got by our hostilities with Spain, in the course of one year. We have taken great part of their navy, with a considerable treasure in bullion. We have got the whole country of Florida, including the towns and fortifications of St. Matheo and St. Augustin, extending from the confines of Georgia to the mouth of the Mississippi, a country valuable from its own natural fertility; but more valuable as it rounds off the dominions of Great Britain in that continent, shutting, as it were, the back-door into her colonies, and renders us, in a great measure, masters of the Gulph of Florida, thro' which all the Spanish plate-fleet[7] passes from the Havanna homeward-bound. We have at last obtained the long disputed privilege of cutting logwood in the Bay of Honduras, and of sailing without search in the seas of America, which have been, for above a century, the great, and indeed the only objection to a perfect reconciliation between the Kings of England and Spain; and we have obliged his Catholic Majesty to relinquish his old claim of fishing on the banks of Newfoundland. But, what is of more immediate consequence than all these, we have retrieved our trade with Portugal, which was lost by the Spanish war, a trade which is supposed to bring in a clear annual ballance of one million sterling to Great Britain. We have retrieved our trade with Spain herself, which, tho' not an object of such consequence as it formerly was, must be owned is still very considerable. We have disengaged ourselves in the most honourable manner from our fatal G——n connections, so that we shall be enabled to maintain any future war on British principles only, and at half the expence which this hath occasioned. We have put a stop to bloodshed and depopulation; to the accumulation of the public debt, and the augmentation of grievous taxes, big with bankruptcy and ruin; from the brink of which we are snatched by this seasonable peace.

Every lover of his country, who fairly and candidly considers these circumstances; who reflects, that he and his fellow-creatures are pressed with a public debt of one hundred and thirty-six millions, one third of the interest of which is paid to foreigners: that every convenience, and even necessary of life, is already loaded with severe impositions, to defray the interest of this enormous sum: that, during every year of the war, this nation raised above two and twenty millions, a sum, (I fully believe) exceeding the revenues of all the Kings of Europe, great part of which was added to the public burden: that if the war had continued, we should have had two powerful nations to cope with, though our debts were increased, and two of our resources stopt in the loss of our trade to Portugal and Spain; I say, if he will reflect seriously and candidly on these particulars, and then weigh the advantages we have gained, he will own that peace was absolutely necessary, for the preservation of our public credit, which had been stretched even to bursting; that the peace we have made is salutary, definitive, and promises to be permanent, as founded on the two rocks of precision and good faith; that the treaty is in all respects glorious for England, and more advantageous respecting her commercial interests, than any she hath subscribed, since her being first numbered among the kingdoms of Christendom.

Moved by this conviction, he will do justice to those who have laboured so effectually in the cause of his country. He will take it for granted, that they have exerted their best endeavours to procure national advantages adequate to the success of our arms; and that they have retained all the conquests which they thought it was the interest of the kingdom to possess; or at least, all of them which our enemies would relinquish, without prosecuting the war, which it would have been impossible for us to maintain, without the most imminent risk of bankruptcy and ruin. He will think it his duty to pluck the mask of patriotism from the front of faction; to undeceive the well-meaning among his fellow-citizens, who are misled by prejudice, and exasperated by sedition; to soothe the minds which have been irritated by calumny and misrepresentation, and to the utmost of his power and influence, dispose the people to enjoy the blessings that are brought within their reach.

And here I cannot help freely telling you, Sir, that you yourself have sometimes lost your temper, in the course of that political altercation in which you are engaged, and dropped some expressions of asperity against certain individuals, and even communities, which had been much better omitted. Nevertheless, as you have honestly adhered to the laudable aims of defending innocence, and asserting truth, in opposition to malice and abusive clamour, I think you are entitled to the thanks and approbation of,

SIR,

Your humble servant,

CURIO.[8]

No. 29. Saturday, 11 December 1762.

Nos manet Oceanus, circumvagus: arva, beata
Petamus arva, divites et insulas,
Reddit ubi Cererem tellus inarata quotannis.
HORACE.[1]

To the BRITON.

SIR,

In all disputes, I ever looked on abuse and recrimination, as circumstances entirely foreign to the subject, which, instead of promoting the investigation of truth, serve only to irritate the parties, and give disgust to the public. I am pleased to find, in the small circle of my acquaintance, that the most sensible and candid men, are the best satisfied with the preliminaries of the peace, which have been just published by authority.

But there is a set of partisans who make it their business to declaim against them in public places, with a view to mislead those who cannot, or will not think for themselves; and I observe, that all these general declaimers insist upon two propositions: that Mr. P——, whom they profess to admire as a perfect minister and unshaken patriot, has declared the preliminaries are dishonourable, and the cessions of France inadequate to the success of the British arms: and that the places recovered, or retained by Great Britain, are of little or no consequence to the commerce of this kingdom. They affect to treat the neutral islands as objects of contempt; to undervalue Minorca as an useless burden to the community; to hold Senegal in derision; to despise the acquisition of Canada, and the expulsion of the French from Cape Breton. They consider the cession of Florida with St. Augustin, as of no use: they mention the liberty granted to cut logwood in the Bay of Honduras, as a trifling privilege; and exclame, that the article of *no search* is still left undecided.

With respect to Mr. P——'s abilities, character and consistency, I shall say nothing at present: but fairly mention a few uncontrovertible facts, and leave them to speak for themselves to the conviction of all my countrymen, who have virtue enough to wish themselves undeceived. And first, for the neutral islands; without specifying the disputes and negotiations between the two crowns, to which they have given rise before the beginning of this century, I shall only enumerate a few circumstances that will evince, of what consequence they were in the opinion of our g——t and legislature, and the nation in general, even since the peace of Aix-la-Chapelle.[2] In the year 1748, information being received, that the French intended to settle the neutral islands of St. Lucia, Dominica, St. Vincent, and Tobago, the whole nation took the alarm. A motion was made in the house of commons, to address his Majesty, that he would be graciously pleased to give directions for laying before the house, copies of the instructions given to the governors of Barbadoes for ten years last past, so far as they related to those neutral islands—The governor of Barbadoes having received intelligence, that the French had actually begun to settle Tobago, sent thither Capt. Tyrrel in a frigate, who found above three hundred men already landed, secured by two batteries, and two ships of war, and in daily expectation of a further reinforcement from the governor of Martinique—These particulars shew, that both we and the French thought this island of importance.[3] It was in consequence of a spirited remonstrance, by the British ambassadors at the court of Versailles, that the French King disowned the proceedings of M. de Caylus, governor of Martinique, and sent orders to the settlers to abandon the island.

In regard to the opinion generally entertained of Minorca, it might be sufficiently demonstrated, by recalling to remembrance the noise, the clamour, the ferment which the loss of it produced:[4] but as this might be supposed the effect of vulgar prejudice; let us see in what manner it is mentioned by those who certainly ought to have been best acquainted with its consequence. In the year 1756, the Lord Mayor, the aldermen, and common-council of the

city of London, presented an address to the King,[5] in which they expressed
their apprehension, "That the loss of the *important* fortress of St. Philip, and
island of Minorca, *possessions of the utmost consequence to the commerce and naval
strength of Great Britain*, &c. would be an indelible reproach on the honour
of the British nation."

In considering the national importance of Senegal, we must take notice,
that the whole gum-trade, from Cape Blanco, to the river Gambia, an ex-
tent of five hundred miles, had been engrossed by the French, who built fort
Louis, within the mouth of the river Senegal, and extended their factories
above three hundred miles up the river: that the gum Senega, of which a
great quantity is used by the manufacturers of England, being wholly in the
hands of the enemy, the English dealers were obliged to buy it at second-
hand from the French, who exacted an exorbitant price for that commodity:
that, over and above the gum, this coast produces many other valuable articles
of commerce, such as gold-dust, elephants-teeth, hides, cotton, bees-wax,
slaves, ostrich-feathers, indigo, ambergrease, and civet; and that if Mr. P——,
in whose ministry it was conquered, had not been fully convinced of its im-
portance, he would not surely have put his country to such expence in its
reduction.

But how the island of Cape Breton, and the whole country of Canada have
so lately shrunk in their consequence, it is not easy to conceive. The conquest
of Cape Breton and Louisburg in the last war, was projected by a gentleman,
at that time judge-advocate of the court of admiralty in New-England.[6] He
demonstrated, that the reduction of Cape Breton, would put the English in
possession of the whole fishery of North America, which would annually re-
turn to Great Britain two millions sterling for the manufactures used in the
plantations: that it would remove from the English fishers on the banks of
Newfoundland, all apprehension of rivalship or competition; that it would
cut off all communication between France and Canada, so that Quebec would
fall of course into the hands of the English, who might expel the French
from America, open a correspondence with the remote Indians, and render
themselves masters of the fur-trade, which the enemy then engrossed. All
these consequences are now realized: yet still our politicians exclaim, "our
conquests in North America are good for nothing."

Very different was the opinion of the Lord Mayor, aldermen, and commons
of the city of London, who, in their address of congratulation to the King,[7]
on the series of victories gained in the course of the year 1759, expressed
themselves in these words, "The reduction of Fort du Quesne on the Ohio;
of the island of Goree in Africa; and of Guadaloupe with its dependencies, in

the West-Indies; the repulse and defeat of the whole French army by a hand-ful of infantry in the plains of Minden; the taking of Niagara, Ticonderago, and Crown Point, the naval victory off Cape Lagos; the advantages gained over the French nation in the East-Indies; and *above all*, the conquest of Que-bec (the capital of the French empire in America) in a manner so glorious to your Majesty's arms, against every advantage of situation, and superior numbers, are such events, as will for ever render your Majesty's auspicious reign, the favourite æra in the history of Great Britain." Now, if I understand English, the city of London, in the most solemn manner, by the mouths of their magistrates and representatives, thus declared, the reduction of Que-bec of more consequence and value to this kingdom, than the conquest of Goree and Guadaloupe; and the victory of Minden, by which the electorate of Hanover was secured from a French invasion. Shall we suspect, that the first citizens of the capital of England, were at that time ignorant of the true commercial interests of their country? or shall we conclude, that the present decriers of that conquest, speak the language of prejudice and faction?

Florida has been disparaged as a sandy desart, without any other inhabi-tants but a few straggling savages, distinguished by such a barbarous ferocity, as no art or example can civilize. Granting this to be really the case, we must, at the same time allow, that it contained the Spanish settlement and fortress of St. Augustin, which was a continual thorn in the sides of our southern colo-nies. It was a door that opened access to them for every armament from the Havanna. It was a city of refuge, that presented an asylum to all the negroes of South Carolina, who were tired of servitude, disgusted with their masters, or obnoxious to the law by crimes and misdemeanours. This was found such an inconvenience, that the settlers of Georgia were obliged to preclude them-selves entirely from the service of negroes, knowing how impossible it would be to retain them in the neighbourhood of St. Augustin. That the conquest of this place was deemed an object of importance, appears from the armament that was equipped against it in the last war; that the neighbourhood of it was dangerous to our colonies, may be gathered from the invasion which was made thro' it upon Georgia by the Spaniards in the late war, who were re-pulsed by the gallantry and conduct of General Oglethorpe.[8] The possession of St. Augustin, therefore, stops up an ugly gap in our southern colonies, pre-vents the desertion of our negro-slaves, and by the help of row-gallies, such as the Spaniards now maintain at this place, on account of shallow water, enables us in a great measure to command the channel of the Gulph, thro' which every Spanish ship must pass from the Havanna in her return to Europe.

But, it is still more surprising to hear the enemies of the peace depreciate the liberty we have obtained of cutting logwood in the Bay of Honduras. A point which has been the grand source of all our disputes with Spain since the middle of the last century: a point which they tenaciously refused to give up, even when they seemed the most pacifically inclined towards this nation. In the treaty of 1750, in which the King of Spain engaged to indemnify the South-sea company for all their claims, by virtue of the Assiento contract;[9] when he agreed, that the English should be treated in all the ports of Spain, on the footing of the most favoured nations, and enjoy the privilege of taking in salt at the island of Tortuga, there is not a word mentioned of the cutting of logwood, which Spain always considered, not only as an act of violence and rapine, but also as a dangerous traffick, under colour of which, the British traders carried on a clandestine contraband-trade with her West-Indian subjects. This great point she has now ceded; and the uses that may be made of her concession, are such as need no explanation to those who are ever so little acquainted with the commerce of those seas.

The last complaint which I shall consider, is that relating to the article of *no search*, which has been obtained upon this occasion. Immediately after the peace of Aix-la-Chapelle, Sir John Hynd Cotton, in the house of commons, observed, that the peace could not be properly stiled compleat, as nothing had been stipulated with respect to the article of *no search*, without which, both houses of parliament had formerly voted, that there should be no peace with Spain. Mr. Pelham answered, that a parliament of Great Britain had once voted "no peace, while any part of the West-Indies should remain in possession of the Spanish King;" but a train of incidents, which they could not then foresee, rendered it necessary afterwards to conclude a peace, without insisting upon this condition.[10]

When the last treaty with Spain was inveighed against in the house of commons, as defective in the article of *no search*, Mr. P— justified the treaty,[11] and answered all objections. He said, the article of *no search*, was a stipulation which it would have been ridiculous to insist upon. He owned, that he had formerly strenuously contended for an address, that no treaty of peace with Spain should be admitted, unless such a stipulation was first obtained as a preliminary, because, being then very young and sanguine, he thought it right and reasonable; but now, being ten years older, he had considered matters more coolly, and was convinced, that the privilege of *no search*, with respect to British vessels sailing near the American shore, would never be obtained, unless Spain should be brought so low, as to acquiesce in any terms we, as victors, might impose. — He moreover declared himself convinced, that all addresses from the house of commons, for prescribing terms of peace, were in themselves ridiculous; and that even such address was an encroachment upon the King's prerogative, which had always been attended with unlucky consequences.

Concerning this demanded privilege of sailing along the coasts of South-America, without being subject to examination, his remarks were certainly just. The Spaniards knew, that no English ships could be upon those coasts, except with a view to carry on an illicit trade with the subjects of Spain, and the commanders of their guard-ships stationed along that coast, in order to prevent this illicit trade, have undoubtedly a natural right, and it is certainly their duty, to examine all ships that fall under the suspicion of such a traffick.

If the French traders made a practice of smuggling wool from Ireland, they might, with the same justice, claim the freedom of navigating their ships along the coasts of that kingdom, without being subject to examination, by the captains of those vessels which are expressly appointed to prevent this clandestine exportation.

Should the Spanish commanders in the West-Indies exceed their commissions, and exercise any acts of cruelty, oppression, or injustice, the fair and natural method of proceeding, is to demand signal reparation of the Catholic King; and should this be refused, recourse must be had to reprisal and hostility. I am,

SIR,

Your humble servant,

MILO.[12]

No. 30. Saturday, 18 December 1762.

Infelix, que tanta animum dementia cepit?
Non vires alias, conversaq; numina sentis?
Cede Deo.

VIRGIL.[1]

The transmutation of sexes has been so well attested by grave and learned authors, that it would be but spending the reader's time to attempt any farther proof of it. I must however observe, that the transmutation of the male to the feminine sex, is by far the rarest; and yet there is a passage in Quintilian, which seems to hint, that the Romans were no strangers to this phœnomenon: *Petuita*, says he, *anilitatem generat et inde matronisatio;*[2] that is to say, the petuita (which is a phlegmatic substance) begets anility or old womanhood, and from thence proceeds matronisation. As to the last expression, some critics have thought, that it was a form or ceremony which the Romans had of admitting into the order of matrons, such of their countrymen as grew to be old women.

For my own part, I own I am by no means satisfied with this opinion, and the matter is of such importance to learning, that I humbly recommend it to those noble Mecœnates[3] who reward literature, as a subject for the next prize-medals. In the mean while, as a politician scorns to be outdone by a naturalist, I have ordered, in imitation of a doctor, who is well known,[4] my publisher, Mr. Coote,[5] to present the author of the best essay on that head, with a compleat set of Britons, bound, gilt, and lettered. A curiosity that has lately fallen into my hands, has given rise to the enquiry. It is no less than a letter from the Magdalen Monitors (for so they sign themselves) to myself. By which denomination, I suppose, they confess themselves to be the penitent prostitutes of the pen. But I shall fairly lay this curiosity before my reader.[6]

There are two maxims which are equally laudable; the one applicable to public, the other to private life. The one is, that government ought always to revert to first principles; and the second, that no man should be ashamed to acknowledge himself not infallible. The first principles of this paper undoubtedly were anticontinental. We proceeded upon those principles for some months, if not years, and so far we are intitled to favour from the public. How we came to deviate from them, we cannot better express, than by telling the following story, which we hope will, at least, put the reader in good humour, and incline him to give us a fair hearing as to what we have farther to offer.

A certain head of a college at Oxford, who never spent one farthing that he could decently save, lived to his fiftieth year without having once seen London. Perceiving that this lessened his importance in company, who often jeered him for his not having seen the world, he secretly resolved to set out for London; but not knowing the way, and unwilling to be at expences, he thought his best method would be to set out with the stage-coach, and always keep his eye upon Will the coachman,[7] who was a very civil fellow, and an excellent driver. The Doctor accordingly ordered his nag to be saddled by four next morning, and still keeping his eye on Will the coachman, he proceeded with great comfort and tranquillity, till they came to High-Wycomb,[8] where they stopt and dined, as the Doctor did, but in a separate apartment. Having drank his half pint of wine, and smoaked his pipe, he was told, according to his orders, that the coach was ready to set out; and the Doctor had but just time to pay his reckoning, when he saw Will the coachman upon the box. Will set out; the Doctor jogged after. About six o'clock, he began to have some very odd notions that the neighbourhood of London was very like that of Oxford, but still keeping his eye on Will the coachman, all his doubts vanished, till about seven, he fairly found himself at Oxford again. This was owing to the honest Doctor's not knowing that Will the coachman had changed coaches, as he always did with the stage that came from London, and drove it on to Oxford the same day.

We are not ashamed to own, that our mistake was owing to the same cause with that of the Doctor, for we still kept our eye upon WILL the coachman, without knowing that he had altered the direction of his driving, and thereby, instead of Old England, before we were aware, we found ourselves in Germany; and, like men of spirit, we still ate the wrong end of the asparagus;[9] because eating the right end of it, would have shewn, that once in our lifetime, we had been mistaken.

But, not to lay the blame entirely on Will the coachman, we had many inducements for opposing the present administration; nay, such as, (if any allowance is to be made to human infirmity) must acquit us in the eyes of the impartial public.

In the first place, who could have imagined, ever since the time of Alexander's mounting Bucephalus,[10] that John,[11] who never had been noted for horsemanship, could have reined a steed, that had overthrown the ablest jockeys in the world; but to speak without metaphors, I shall appeal to the breast of every candid reader, whether at the time that we began to Germanize, he thought that matters would have possibly taken the turn they have since done. As every malefactor has a right to make himself no worse than he is, so we must make use of that right, to shew, that if we were mistaken, it was only, as has been already hinted, because we were not infallible.

When the honourable gentleman, on whom we fixed our eyes, took into his hands the reins of government, did not all Britain believe, that he never could drive to Germany? Did not all the people of England, as well as ourselves, place an implicit confidence in him? Were they not warmed with that enthusiastic anticontinentalism that seemed to fire him? Did not they make even a merit of resigning all their senses to him; and did he not mount the pontifical chair of politics, before ten men in the nation reflected, that it was possible he might be frail or fallible?

Candour does not judge from events. Had it been your own case, gentle reader, you would have sworn, had you not been landed at Hanover, that Will the coachman was driving you to London: but indeed, we had many other inducements, besides the undoubted abilities of our guide, to act and write as we did; and we shall here lay some of them before the public, in hopes, not of vindicating ourselves, but of alleviating the censure fallen upon us, for having departed from our original plan.

Did not all the world allow, that the just and necessary war we were engaged in with France, was gloriously conducted; and that no hand, but that of our patron, was equal to the management of it? Did any man, at the time the battle of Minden was fought, and Quebec was taken, speak a single word about frugality, or the prodigious expences that attended the war? What therefore did we in continuing our paper, but second the voice of the people? Could we imagine, that when OUR minister retired, the war would be carried on with redoubled success? that Martinico would be subdued? that the Havannah, that Palladium [12] of the Spanish monarchy, would be taken? and that the product of the richest capture that ever was made by Briton, would grace the birth-day of a Prince of Wales, and renew the union between Plutus and Lucina? [13]

We shall never forget it, that our patron, upon the conclusion of the peace of Aix-la-Chapelle, was himself brought into the ministry, by a strain of interest, which was very unusual with Mr. Pelham, in order chiefly to defend that treaty; and we ourselves heard him declare, in the house of commons, that he did not believe there was a man in England, so ridiculously absurd, as to imagine, that the Spanish claim of searching our ships was attainable; or that they ever would give us by treaty, a right to cut logwood in the Bay of Honduras. [14] For the truth of this fact, we can appeal to the memory of many members now living.

Reader, if thou hast the least compassion for human weakness, consider what we have to plead in excuse for our infirmities. How was it possible for us to think, after those averrments of our political oracle, that a minister would arise, who, without violating one branch of our constitution, without betraying a friend, without courting an enemy, and without injuring the honour of his Sovereign, should bring one half of that to pass which infallibility itself (for so we thought it) had pronounced to be impossible? How could we imagine, that the war, when our patron desisted from *guiding* [15] it, could be carried on at less expence, and with greater success?

We have been accused of insolence and abuse against the present minister. What we have to say in mitigation of that, if the charge is true, is, that upon the surprisal of Newfoundland by the French, [16] the temptation for abuse was as irresistible as the event was certain; and such incidents have always been held by political writers, to be fair hits at a minister, and esteemed the lawful plunder of his power. If we were deceived as to the consequences, you, reader, was so likewise. You never dreamed, that the boasted success of France; a success that resounded in the chapels of Versailles and the churches of Paris, should add a fresh wreath to the present minister's political garland. When we abused him for that surprisal, you, as well as we, were ignorant, that the same attention had, during the then short time of his administration, been paid to the coasts of Newfoundland, as had been observed during the administration of our patron: but even if that had not been the case, how natural was it for us to triumph on the occasion? We could not imagine, that an unpractised minister should, almost in the twinkling of an eye, have recovered, without expence to the nation, without effusion of blood, that important settlement, to the loss, disgrace, and confusion of our enemies, in such a manner, that the loss was scarcely felt before it was repaired.

Having made the above full and ample concessions, the reader will not be surprised, when we tell him, that after taking great pains, we discovered from history, and experience of every kind, that no wise Prince or nation, that entered into treaty with a people they were at war with, ever made demands upon their enemy that were strictly adequate to their successes. But unfortunately for us, the present minister has pursued a plan of politics, of which the execution has been as destructive of our scheme of opposition, as we observe, taking shame to ourselves, it has been of advantage to this nation. He has followed maxims that have, in every period of our history, contributed to our glory. The great lines he has chalked out by the present peace, have given us scope for improving those former plans of industry, that have made us a great and a powerful people. To deviate from them must be our ruin, as the possession of the mines of Mexico and Peru was that of Spain.

Having made this plain and ingenuous confession, and having vindicated ourselves from every imputation but that of human infirmity, we are now to inform our readers, that as our intentions upon our first setting out were good, we are now determined to pursue them in a constitutional manner; and let no advertisements, paragraphs, or insinuations of those underlings, who are good for nothing, but to be exposed as Timariots[17] are amongst the Turks, to the front of prosecution, and to serve as *food* for its *powder*,[18] induce the good people of this nation to suspect, that this paper is carried on by hands different from those of its original plan.

Our endeavours shall be to court the attention of the public upon our original plan, which was that of rendering Great Britain happy within herself; of cultivating a continual good correspondence between the best of Kings, and the happiest of people; to improve the blessings of the best peace, if we are not unfaithful to ourselves, that ever was made for Great Britain. Unanimity is, what every man who wishes well to his country ought to make his only object; and let the good of the whole prevail over every little captious exception, that may hurt the general good, or again disturb its tranquillity.

The MAGDALEN MONITORS.

No. 31. Saturday, 25 December 1762.

Tros Tyriusque mihi nullo discrimine habetur.
VIRGIL.[1]

ENGLISHED.

Be this thy interest, George, and this thy glory.
To know no difference between Whig and Tory.

It is unmanly to deform the brow of triumph with the frown of resentment. To bear success modestly, is the compleatest character of a conqueror. Never was a more compleat, a more constitutional, a more indisputed victory gained, than what now lies on the side of the minister for whom I own myself to be a professed advocate; and far be it from me, to blast the wreaths he has gained, by adding insult to conquest.

Amongst all parties, railing ought now to give place to reasoning, and the spirit of exasperated presumption to that of dispassionate enquiry. The heads of Hydra faction[2] are now cut off, all but one, and it bears a name which is so intimately connected with the vitals of a protestant government, that it ought to be handled at once with decency and tenderness. Notwithstanding this, I hope to make it appear, that it is *but a name*, that it takes its rise from mistaken ideas, and is adopted to temporary purposes: the word I mean is *Toryism*, which is pretended to be the favourite principle of the present administration. This doctrine has been long nibbled at (if we can admit length of time in this case) by the present opposition, and is now openly espoused.

A pamphlet, it seems, some time ago, (for I have never seen it) has been published, which is supposed to contain an address from the Cocoa-tree; and another pamphlet has been published in answer to it,[3] by which we are to understand, that this same Cocoa-Tree, which, I am told, is no other than the sign of a coffee-house, is in fact an assemblage of Tories, who are determined to support a particular minister, who is there described in no very favourable colours, either as to his country, or his importance.

If the Tories were accessary to the publication of the first named pamphlet, I am sorry for it, because, I think, whatever its contents may be, it exhibits no favourable idea of their judgment; but the answer gives us a very pleasant reason, for believing the said pamphlet to be an authentic act and deed of the Tories; "I shall presume," says he, addressing himself to them, "the letter, which is dated from your head-quarters, to be yours, it having hitherto not been disavowed by you." [4]

This reason plainly supposes, that all the Tories in the kingdom, in their representative if not collective capacity, are scepterly [5] conveened under the umbrageous shade of this same Cocoa-Tree. But how they were to disavow the letter published under their name, is a puzzling question. Were they, like Macbeth, to start from their seats, and staring at the ghost of Faction, pointing at the wounds it has lately received, cry out, *Thou can'st not say I did it.* [6] Were they like the lady, who forgot she was speaking of a third person, and in describing a particular situation, say, *Here lay* HER *head, and there lay* MY *feet.* [7] But to speak without allusion, can any thing be more absurd, than to suppose the gentlemen who frequent that coffee-house, to be wrong-headed enough to publish their names to an advertisement, disclaiming the pamphlet in question? But an advertisement without any name might have done it.— Yes, Mr. Answerer, and such an advertisement might have come from you or me, or the barley-broth woman at Pye-corner, [8] if we paid three shillings to the public papers for inserting it.

In short, I neither believe, that the letter from the Cocoa-Tree speaks the sentiments of all the Tories; nor that the address to the Cocoa-Tree speaks those of all the Whigs. I am the more led to believe the latter, because you appear to be either totally ignorant of the principles of the Whigs, as well as Tories, or to have most egregiously misrepresented them. You have charged the Tories with calumniating three very great names, [9] whom you place by way of anticlimax. As to the first, the lowest you have mentioned, you and I may not differ much as to the opinion the Tories might have of it. With regard to the second, it ought to be respectable, not only on account of his moderation, and his long disinterested conduct in government, but because he is too good a friend to the family of Hanover, to be dissatisfied with the present minister; and I will venture to say, you endeavour to palm an untruth upon the world, when you assert, that he was banished from court. As to the third name, it ought to be held sacred, and it is highly disrespectful in any writer, to suppose it to be attached to any cause but that of liberty and the constitution, and the uninfluenced sentiments of his royal n — w. [10]

You accuse the Tories, Sir, with the doctrine, "That the King, having a right to appoint his ministers, the people have no right to oppose them." [11] Before I close up this matter, it is necessary to detect a few fallacies that run thro' all the argumentative part (if any such there is) of your address. An Officer of state holds his employment under the constitution. The ministry of state is no Office under the constitution. I am not sure if even a secretaryship of state is; if it is, it is but of a modern standing. But were the Tories at any time ever so wrong-headed, as to say, that the people had no right to oppose a minister? I will venture to say, that the addresser, and all his party, can extract no such doctrine from the writings, speeches, or even conversation of any sober Tory that ever existed; for there are madmen of all parties.

The addresser having mistaken the doctrine of the Tories, proceeds to blunder as to those of the Whigs; and it is surprising, that one who has a tolerable knack at writing, should be so miserably deficient in what Cicero calls the *sylva rerum;* [12] that is, arguments and facts, in which we may be said, to be almost bewildered thro' the course of the English history.

The Whigs, and indeed the spirit of this constitution, never supposed the people of England to have any voice in matters of state, but thro' their constituents in parliament assembled; and this on an analogous principle pervades the whole system of our government. But the addresser totally deserts the true principles of Whiggism; and instead of the representative, he substitutes the collective body of the people. Thus, in consequence of his doctrine, while the names of High-church, Ormond and Sacheverel [13] were echoing through all the streets of London and Westminster, I may say through half the towns of England, those respectable names, according to our addresser, were the true characteristics of Whiggism, and Ormond and Sacheverel were the greatest Whigs in the nation.

That the name of the people of England, even in a collective capacity, ought to be regarded, honoured, and reverenced by ministers, I admit; but here our addresser is guilty of another no small blunder, for he confounds the people with the vulgar of England. If generals, politicians, and preachers, according to the true maxims of Whiggism, and they right ones, acquire no credit by having the vulgar for them, ought a minister to acquire discredit by having them against him?

I know our addresser and his friends, in all their speeches and writings, take it for granted, that the people of England, in their collective capacity, are disaffected towards the present minister. I deny the supposition; I am under no difficulty of admitting, that the vulgar of London are; but, I am certain, so far as any fact of that kind can be ascertained, that the majority of the people of England, at this very instant, is greatly in his favour. But we are now to return to principles; a way of reasoning which our addresser greatly affects; but how well he understands them, I shall endeavour to shew.

"We," says he, (meaning the Whigs) "apprehended, that the pretensions of a minister to his power, should be *natural, constitutional, gently asserted,* and *generally admitted.*" [14] It unfortunately happens for our addresser, that the first of those characteristicks makes directly against him; that the second strikes at the very root of Whiggism; and that the last two, if they have a meaning, it must be strongly, nay experimentally, in favour of the present minister.

Tho' a subject had connexions with all the greatest families in England, and had as much property as all of them put together, yet he can have no natural pretension to be a minister. That appointment is personal to the King, and to the King only; and under a wise Prince, it will fall upon that subject, of whose abilities, integrity, and affection to his person, he has the best opinion, from a long course of experience, if possible from his cradle. Such a minister was Pope Adrian to Charles the Fifth; Cardinal de Fleury to Lewis the Fifteenth; Sully to Henry the Fourth of France, and Clarendon to Charles the Second of England; [15] I need therefore say no more on this head, but leave the application to the breast of my reader. I therefore proceed to the second characteristic our addresser lays down.

A constitutional pretence to be a minister, I mean a first minister, is incompatible, not only with Whiggism, but with every principle of the constitution; if by that, we suppose a minister is to have the sole, or even the chief direction of government. Constitutionally speaking, the first minister in England is the Lord High Chancellor, because he puts the great seal to the great acts of state. This is talking like a Whig, and Whig governments have been known to punish those who taught, spoke, or wrote otherwise.

The *gently asserted* pretension of a minister to his power, is a characteristic I do not well understand; but if I can collect any thing from it, our author means, that a minister should not, like a draw-cansir, [16] kick every body off the stage that stands in his way. But it would be as absurd in a minister to drag an actor again upon the stage, when he wants to retire from its business. Both would be equally tyrannical. Till instances, therefore, are given of the present minister's harsh exercise of power, this characteristic must stand for nothing, or must go in our minister's favour.

The last characteristic of a minister's pretension to power, being *generally admitted,* I believe never did exist, even in the most tranquil periods of our history, from the Gavestons and Spencers, [17] to the W——es and P——s. If we are to form our ideas of a minister's pretensions to power being *generally admitted,* it must be from the representative voice of the people; and I will venture to say, that no minister, for these two hundred years past, if we are to number voices, has had that so strongly for him as the present.

"We cannot," says our addresser, "trace a single drop of English blood in his famous genealogy." [18] Why really, reader, I am not sure that this objection is not a libel upon two thirds of the noble families of England, whose ancestors, properly speaking, tho' much longer settled here than the noble Lord has been, had not, to speak in our addresser's phrase, a single drop of English blood in their veins. Notwithstanding that, they were employed by our Kings as officers, as well as ministers of state; they commanded our armies, and directed our councils. For my own part, I am not genealogist enough to contradict our author's assertion; nor am I sufficiently conversant in antiquity to maintain, that the story of Fleance,[19] the ancestor of the Stuart family is true; but if it is, our minister has in his genealogy a great many drops of Welch blood.

No. 32. Saturday, 1 January 1763.

Ita omnia in duas partes abstracta sunt. Respublica, quæ media fuerat, delacerata.

SALLUST.[1]

To the BRITON.

SIR,

I congratulate you upon the turn of the tide. Factious clamour, is at low ebb, and the refluent streams of truth and loyalty begin to visit the channels of public communication. The people at last wake from their dream of discontent, and stand astonished at their own infatuation. Party hath shrunk in the day of trial. Mock patriotism, when brought to the test, like Satan at the touch of Ithuriel's spear,[2] started up in its own hideous form, wreathed with poisonous snakes of pride and envy, rancour, and revenge. Universal detestation or contempt ensued.

The leaders of the opposition made such a wretched figure, as might even have excited compassion in the hearts of those who did not remember, that the discomfited crew were blackened with the foulest stains of malice and ingratitude: that they were the very persons who had kicked their heels in the face of the best of Sovereigns; who had endeavoured to distress the hands of government; who had employed infamous hirelings to traduce the most respectable characters of his family, to revile his servants, and to scatter the seeds of discord in the bowels of their country. Such were the demagogues, whose families, upon a certain late occasion, heaven, in its judgment, seemed to confound.

One superannuated original,[3] a quondam St——n floundered on as usual in a sea of absurdity, and was saved from sinking by nothing but his want of weight. His folly had formerly been productive of laughter, but now it was heard with silent disdain. Since that period, he is said to have been incessantly haunted, like the famous Conde d'Olivarez,[4] the discarded minister of Philip IV. with the ghost of his departed greatness. Sometimes it appears in Motley with a cap and bells; sometimes in the shape of a borough-elector hanging upon a gibbet, with a purse of money about his neck; sometimes it multiplies itself into a whole Mughouse-mob,[5] drinking d——n to the Tories; sometimes it assumes the form of a Westphalian rat[6] with long whiskers; and sometimes it takes the figure of public credit, with a consumptive look, sailing down the wind on blown bags of paper. Such are the horrid spectacles that discompose the brain of this venerable patrician, and overwhelm him with fits of melancholy despondence, from which nothing can rouse him but the sound of marrow-bones and cleavers.[7] This has nearly the same effect upon him, as the fiddle has upon those who are bit by the Tarantula.[8] He begins to wag his head and shake his heels, to utter incoherent jargon, while he dances himself into a profuse sweat, which affords him a temporary relief until the cause of his malady returns.

The subordinates of this great veteran, were still more discomposed than their leader. They gazed at one another with looks of consternation. Their conscience flew in their faces: their intellects seemed to fail, and they underwent a momentary emotion of shame and remorse, sensations which they had never felt before.

When they beheld the N——n against whom all their dark and dirty machinations had been formed, secure in conscious innocence, and firmly established on the rock of public virtue; when they heard that M——r,[9] whose integrity they threatened to impeach, whose capacity they affected to undervalue, explain the nature of the preliminaries, and refute all the objections which they and their emissaries had started to the peace; when they heard him expatiate on the contested articles, with that modest confidence which internal virtue inspires, with that candour which had power to disarm prejudice; with that strength of reason which ensured conviction, and evinced a masterly knowledge of the subject in debate; when they heard him speak on a variety of topics with ease, fluency, and precision, and answer the fiery ebullitions of personal abuse, with temper, dignity, and moderation, they were disconcerted, confounded and abashed. Their flow of altercation suddenly stopped; their tongues denied their office; they faltered in their utterance; they hesitated censure; they drawled out the disjointed tropes and figures of discontent; they stood amazed like so many shaking monuments of God's revenge against faction.

Nor did party appear in more respectable colours in the neighbouring scene, when the great methodist[10] of mock patriotism mounted the rostrum, like a candidate of ancient Rome, solliciting the mob, in a flannel gown, the frowzy badge of courted popularity.[11] In vain he looked about inviting the attention of his audience. In vain he recollected all those flowers that formed the nose-gays of his quondam oratory; they were grown stale and nauseous, as sprigs of Rosemary which had been used to sweeten the air of a charnel-house. He attempted to refute his own maxims, and to set the seal of reprobation upon the terms which he himself had approved. But, his demon had forsaken him: he no longer fascinated the judgment of his hearers: they were sick of imposition, and contradiction appeared too glaring to deceive. Even the torrent of his elocution was immediately exhausted. He bewildered himself in a wood of inconsistency, thro' which he wandered forlorn and perplexed, without being able to find the path from which he had deviated. He ballanced his hands, he changed his attitude, he lifted up his eyes, *that witnessed huge dismay;*[12] he declaimed and exclaimed; he wearied Heaven with petitions, and his auditors with repetitions; he endeavoured to melt the heart, yet he raised no passion but contempt: he had the mortification to see every individual yawning around him, and to hear his voice drowned by the murmurs of disapprobation. Nevertheless, if we may be allowed to use a wretched pun upon such a wretched subject, he made a moving speech, for, almost all his hearers moved away. In a word, the once worshipped idol is fallen to rise no more; and if the present M——r had procured him another p——n to betray his party, he could not have more effectually brought it into disgrace. All his partisans seemed planet-struck,[13] and hung their heads in manifest despondence. Ringwood,[14] the most noisy beagle of his pack, opened his mouth, but was suddenly overawed, and in a moment ceased to babble. In a word, the triumph of the M——r was compleat, and malignant faction was hooted from that place which ought to be sacred to loyalty and patriotism.

It is not however so totally extinguished, but that its clamour still is heard among the dregs of the populace. The shameless scribbler,[15] like the village-idiot, when the clock was silent,[16] still continues to strike sedition from the force of habit, even though the springs that first moved him have ceased to operate. The weekly libel[17] still appears replete with nonsense, falshood and scurrility, and tho' banished with disgrace from every creditable society, finds readers among the vulgar herd of ale-house politicians. The most shocking exhibitions of infamous scandal and stupid obscenity, are publicly vended in the shops of this metropolis, to the reproach of government, and the disgrace of the nation, as if our people delighted in malice and indecency, and there was no law in the kingdom to punish the most brutal licentiousness.

With respect to those delicate pictures[18] which are set up to the view of every passenger, if the civil magistrate so far neglects his duty, as to suffer the publishers of them to pass with impunity, and even to advertise them in the daily papers; it might be hoped, that the B——p of L——n would exert himself in the interests of religion and morality, by taking cognizance of such notorious breaches of charity and decorum. I will venture to say, that the venders and publishers of such scandalous trash, would, under any other government, even the mildest in Christendom, be punished with the loss of ears, or scourged, or branded, and afterwards expelled with infamy from their country as common nuisances.

We want not laws to punish such audacious incendiaries; and it is the duty of the government to see these laws properly executed. It is a duty which the government owes itself, because, without such execution, its authority must grow into contempt. It is a duty to the community, because, if these miscreants escape, their success will encourage other vermin of the same species to raise disturbances in the common-wealth, where a few examples, *in terrorem*,[19] would awe the whole dastardly tribe into silence and submission.

When I talk of examples, I do not mean that the government should exert any power unknown to the constitution. I do not mean that any new trammels should be hung upon the liberty of the press. Thank Heaven, there is no Star-chamber to intimidate the free-born citizen of these days. No, I would have the delinquents left to the authority of the law; to the equity of a fair trial; to the verdict of a British jury.

The law is so tender of the subject's reputation, that in some cases, it interprets truth itself into a libel. If a man is therefore subject to pains and penalties, to fine and imprisonment, for uttering unreasonable truths, for stigmatising a private character, already known to be infamous; what punishment does the malicious wretch deserve, who, prompted by envy and revenge, or actuated by the still more sordid motives of hire, lifts the murderous quill to stab the reputation of innocence, to sully the fair fame of the most shining merit, and unite the most treacherous disloyalty, with the most rancorous defamation!

I would ask, if common honesty can reside within the breast, which is con-

The Scotch Butt Or the English Archers.

Satiric print showing Smollett defending a jack boot, emblem of Bute, against Bute's political enemies.

(Courtesy of the British Library.)

secrated to falshood and dissimulation; if one virtue of humanity can warm
the heart that swells with perfidy, with hatred, and unprovoked revenge; or if
the duties of a good citizen can ever be performed by the hired, or voluntary
instrument of sedition? No; such a caitiff should not escape unpunished. He
does not deserve to enjoy the protection of the law, far less the privileges of
a native Briton: he does not deserve to breathe the free air of Heaven, but
ought to be exiled from every civilized society.

Of this stamp are those envenomed scribblers, without principle or talent,
whose libels have buzzed so long in the ears of the deluded multitude. Let
them be summoned before the tribunal of their country, whether they are the
refuse of the senate, the pulpit, or the bar; whether they are the disgrace of
magistracy, the reproach of wealth, or the outcasts of fortune. When the mask
of patriotism is plucked from their faces, they will stand forth in their natural
features, recreants to loyalty, apostates from truth, and enemies professed of
virtue and religion. They would soon be sensible, that their remaining un-
noticed, was not owing either to lack of matter for accusation, or to a want
of legal power to punish their delinquency; but that the rod of correction has
been with-held by an indulgent S——n, slow to anger, and by a mild ad——n,
whose vengeance all their malice hath not been able to provoke.

I should be sorry to see even the worst criminals offered up as victims to
resentment; but there are certain sacrifices to justice, which order, decency,
good morals, and public tranquillity require. Those audacious wretches who,
by dint of nauseous obscene sketches, or rather scratches, which they de-
nominate political prints, have endeavoured to debauch the morals, loyalty,
and taste of their fellow-creatures, may be indicted as common nusances, or
committed to the house of correction by any acting justice of the peace. As
for those who have, with equal malice and effrontery, published the weekly
mess of slander and sedition, they may be prosecuted either by indictment
or information. Almost every page of their elegant lucubrations, exhibits a
fresh libel against the g——t, exclusive of paragraphs replete with the most
malicious defamation; and he must be very little acquainted with the laws of
his country, who cannot point out in those writings, divers and sundry pas-
sages, which the law would probably interpret into a crime, even of a more
capital nature. We know it hath been adjudged, that an attempt, *forcibly to
prescribe laws to the K——g, and to restrain him of his power, implies a design to
deprive him of his crown and life; that words spoken to draw away the affection of
the people from the K——g, and to stir them up against him, tend to his death and
destruction, and are T——n;*[20] and we know that SCRIBERE EST AGERE.[21] So
little caution was observed by those emissaries of party and sedition; that

some individuals among them, have, in public coffee-houses, surrounded by a circle of hearers, harangued by the hour upon such dangerous topics, mingling the most attrocious calumny with the most audacious T——n, as if they had intended to declare open war against decency, and set the laws of their country at defiance.

These hints I communicate, not from any private pique or interested view, but from a sincere regard to religion and morality; a warm attachment to the best of Kings, and a profound respect to the civil regulations of society. I am,

SIR,

Your very humble servant,
CURIO.[22]

No. 33. Saturday, 8 January 1763.

The author of the following letter, has taken a great deal of pains to refute some late assertions of a writer, who has been detected in so many malicious falshoods, and has rendered himself so notorious for rancour, scurrility, and nonsense, that I have long thought him unworthy of a particular reply; and I give a place to this letter for no other reason, but to shew my regard to a worthy correspondent, who seems to have at heart the cause of innocence and truth.

To the BRITON.

Pallescit invidiâ, & livor præcordia edit.[1]

SIR,

If you think the following is of any use to support the cause of truth, 'tis at your service: if not, throw it aside, and excuse the trouble.

It is pleasant enough to observe the miserable shifts which sedition is now put to, in order to maintain its ground. Ever since the commencement of the present administration, till the meeting of the parliament, its emissaries seemed to triumph in the fond persuasion, that almost the whole nation was on their side. They endeavoured, by all possible arts, to instill a belief into the people, that as soon as that august body should meet, they would overturn all the measures the ministry had taken, disgrace their persons, and bring some of them, at least to a ——: we have read long ago in their papers, of "crushing the aspiring wretch who mounts to power by such means; of dragging him from behind the throne, if he should take shelter there; and of carrying him to Tyburn, to receive the punishment due to his crimes." I wrong them not, for they are the identical words of the North Briton and Monitor.[2] But by the late proceedings of the representatives of the nation, they seem to have received a severe mortification, and to be put to an absolute stand, both as to what they should say and do. They now find they have reduced themselves both to the state and name (in the proper sense of the word) of a faction, as they still continue in a fixed opposition to the legal constitution of this realm, vested in the King, Nobles, and Commons. Beset with difficulties in this situation, as they are not insensible it breaks the neck of the favourite cause, which it would seem they are resolved to adhere to, right or wrong, they are now labouring hard, by a curious slight of hand, to wriggle themselves out of disgrace, and to shift the load of contempt from their own shoulders to the backs of their antagonists.

What led me to these reflections, was the perusal of the North Briton of last Saturday.[3] In that paper, the author more than insinuates, that he and his associates are not a faction, but that the K——g, L——ds, and C——ns, with their abettors, really are. In order to prove this modest assertion, he says, that "a few, if they have justice upon their side, are the true representatives of the nation, and that the opposite party, tho' they are much more numerous, are a faction." Unanswerable argument! but who is to determine which of the parties have justice on their side; the Few, or the Many, that is, the legal representatives of the nation, or a handful who differ from them? The North Briton declaring for the Few, his cause is reduced low enough, when he must reverse the constitution in order to support it. This is just the plight in which every lover of his country would wish to see it. But it is to be hoped, he'll make but few proselytes to this pernicious doctrine, which must lead to absolute anarchy and destruction. No state ever was formed, so far as I know, or could subsist upon such principles. If this doctrine is orthodox, all the treasons and rebellions that have ever been set on foot by a minor party may be justified. What then will become of the patriots who figured, in the years fifteen and forty-five,[4] in an opposition, which this same author could so commendably descant upon, with a view to blacken a minister, and some hundred thousands of innocent people who were no way concerned in those oppositions; nay, who did all in their power to quell them? Tho' I take it for granted, this North Briton will, for his own sake, keep clear of overt-acts of rebellion, yet these are the very principles upon which avowed rebels proceed.

Farther, it was the fashionable doctrine not long ago, that *vox populi* is *vox*

Dei;[5] that a minister, if he is but only unacceptable to the people, tho' no other objection can be laid against him, ought to give way. Now, tho' I could never see either the sense or reason of this doctrine, *viz.* that the Sovereign should lose his prerogative, and a subject his right, merely because the people took it into their heads to dislike him, without assigning any ground for their dislike; yet it is plain, that according to this doctrine, and consequently their own principles, a minister ought to be continued when the *vox populi* is for him. Now, if this is the case, and sure they won't deny it, after they have inculcated this tenet so long upon us, how comes it that they still persist in their opposition against the present m — r, since it now appears, by the only way in which the people, according to our constitution, can give their voice, *viz.* by their representatives, that he has the *vox populi* in his favour? Such a bundle of absurdities and contradictions I never met with in any writer, who had the smallest claim to honesty and good sense. A minister should be discarded, if he has not the voice of the people, and discarded too, tho' he has the voice of the people, *à qua parte hunc Proteum capiemus?*[6] We see he can shift and shuffle, and change his principles just as it serves his turn. This is always held as a good proof in the case of other men, that they have no principles at all; that they have arrived at that happy facility of conscience, which permits them to veer and wheel about as their humour, caprice, or interest inclines them. They feel it is a troublesome thing to be obliged to be always consistent with one's self, and tied down by the stiff and formal rules of right and wrong, truth and falshood: they know that these things are well enough adapted to the lower class of mortals, but that noble and elevated minds must always regard such infamous conduct with scorn and detestation.

Ay, but, they will say, the people differ from their representatives. I may fairly ask, how do they know that? They had once as sanguine hopes the parliament would think as they did; they find they deceived themselves. It is probable they take an estimate of the sentiments of the people from their own wishes, or the few they converse with; but the general body of the nation may be of a very different mind from these. They may not have the same interest in the continuance of war, and in extending our conquests farther, that a particular set of men in the metropolis has. They know they are sure to bear the greatest part of the expence, but are not sure they shall ever receive one penny profit by it. They find, and they say, they have not bought sugars a farthing cheaper; but more than that, dearer, since they have been at the charge of conquering the French islands; and they suspect also they would have had but a poor chance of coming at this commodity at an easier rate even after the peace, if the whole of that trade had been engrossed by this nation, whereby the few that were concerned in it must have served the greatest part of all the quarters of the globe, and so had it in their power to set what price upon it they pleased to their fellow-subjects. They know but too well already the effects of particular monopolies, and what must have been the consequence of almost an universal one. People should be a little modest, and for mere decency's sake, content themselves with such profits by the war, as are not destructive of the interests of those who chiefly support it. It cannot be very grateful to the landed gentlemen, those whose livings are in the stocks, or dependent on yearly salaries, to the artificers, farmers, &c. to be carrying on a war in this manner, while a few are sweeping the gains of it into their own pockets. But still less can it be agreeable to them to find themselves abused and reviled, because they are not disposed to ruin themselves for the sake of a few worthless jobbers, brokers, and contractors, added to the seditious gleanings of a baffled party.

If the voices of the collective body of the people must be had in this, and all other cases, then we must, in order to gratify this egregious politician and his partizans, new-model our constitution. Parliaments must be laid aside; for they are useless, when the people come to judge and decide in their own persons. Some other little contingencies too must be provided for and insured, which, I hope, these gentlemen will take care of; and these are, first, a forum sufficient to receive the *concio populi*,[7] and a rostrum for any demagogue who is disposed to mount it, in order to harrangue them. It is certain we have nothing of this kind as yet capacious enough; for the Royal Exchange would not hold the ten thousandth part of them. Secondly, it ought to be provided, that none should be admitted to harrangue, but such as are capable of debating upon, and deciding in the matter in question; for, to admit others, would not only be unnecessary, but prejudicial. Thirdly, it ought to be provided also, that some should be working for the families of the poor members in the country, while these are attending the assembly here, perhaps at the distance of 500 miles. And lastly, some expedient should be thought of to secure unanimity; for otherwise we shall only make bad worse; that is to say, that some, as seems to be the case just now, shall not be for giving up North America as good for nothing, and keeping Guadaloupe, &c. as good for all things. Without this, we shan't mend ourselves by the change one jot.

I proceed now to another argument which this author advances in the same paper, to prove, that the K—g, M—ry, P—l—t, and their abettors, are a faction, and that is drawn from the observation you lately made, that the recovery of Newfoundland added a fresh wreath to the minister's temples.[8] This he asserts to be a falshood; and, as he supposes, that you herein speak the sentiments of the side you have espoused, he therefore infers they are a faction, because they have uttered a falshood: for he maintains that the minister had no hand in the recovery of that place; on the contrary, that it was re-conquered before any ships arrived there from Europe for that end, nay, before any orders reached any commander by sea or land for that purpose: in a word, that it was lost by the negligence of the ministry, and recovered by the vigilance of the American officers. Now, all this, I'll be bold enough to say, is a most deceitful and disingenuous account of the matter: for it appears, from Lord Colville's letter to the admiralty, that he had received orders,[9] dated the 7th of June, to endeavour to defeat the designs of Ternay's squadron, which appears to be then going against that place, having given our fleets the slip. And the reason why Lord Colville had not received these orders was, because he had left Halifax, (to which place they were directed) in order to watch the French. It is also true, that these orders were issued out exactly nine days after Lord Bute came into the treasury, for that was on the 29th of May. This, I think, may be reckoned as soon as the minister got into his seat; for the noble Duke, his predecessor, was supposed to be the minister before. Besides, commanding officers are not to expect or wait for particular orders in the places where they are posted and stationed; for their commissions bear, that they are to attack and repel the enemy wherever they find them, as discretion shall direct them; and the reason is plain, for a government at home cannot be supposed to know the motions of an enemy abroad: thus these officers had orders for what they did. I shall conclude this point with the question, Who it was that gave Mr. Elliot his particular and immediate orders to go in pursuit of Thurot, whose little squadron he took?[10] Not Mr. Pitt, the then supposed minister, but the lieutenancy of Ireland; and yet this very author reckons it among the glories of that gentleman's administration. Does no body see from this instance, as well as from a hundred others, that there is in this writer a personal rancour against the first of these ministers, and a blind attachment, either affected or absurd to the other?

And this leads me to a short animadversion upon another assertion of his in the same paper, viz. that Mr. Pitt, a fortnight before his resignation, insisted, that four ships of the line should be sent to Newfoundland. The expression insisted, is, I suppose, to be understood in the softest sense, as the gentleman who used it knew the respect that was due to Majesty; otherwise it may be thought to be of the same stile with Guide,[11] which gave some squeamish people offence about the same time. Farther, it would seem by this, that Newfoundland lay some time unregarded, even in Mr. Pitt's administration. 'Tis pity the author has not told us how long. If it was from the time that a correspondent of his informs us that he saw the troops from it landed at New York, it was a pretty while indeed: and it is to be regreted Mr. P— did not send these ships in that time. July and August were much more seasonable months for that purpose, than the beginning of October, which was the time of his resignation. I am,

SIR,

Hammersmith, Dec. 28.

Yours, &c.

No. 34. Saturday, 15 January 1763.

Tros Tyriusque mihi nullo discrimine agitur.
VIRGIL.[1]

To the BRITON.

SIR,

To the arguments you have used for proving we were under an absolute necessity to conclude a peace at this juncture, you might have added some important facts which I now communicate, for the information of those who have been misled by the indefatigable emissaries of a rancorous faction.

No fewer than three and thirty thousand men were wanted to recruit the army, the mortality still raging among the troops in the West Indies, and on the coast of Africa; and the kingdom of Great Britain so much drained, that in the whole course of last year, the officers of the army did not raise above six hundred recruits, and every one of these cost the nation an incredible sum.

Forty sail of the line, are so harrassed and shattered with long and hard service, that they must be broke up immediately; and there is not a ship in commission, exclusive of flag-ships, that is not greatly deficient in her compliment of hands.[2]

With respect to Germany, the counties of Hesse and Hanover, belonging to our allies, whom we undertook to protect, are desolated in such a manner by the ravages of war, that the people are starving by whole families, with cold and hunger, and he must have a hard heart indeed, who can travel at present without emotion, thro' the ruined fields and villages of Westphalia, where he is encountered every hour by the miserable monuments of famine, feeble old men, helpless women, and naked children, imploring charity, crying *Brodt! Brodt!* Bread! Bread! and perishing under his eye for want of food and raiment.

It were a Godlike office in our legislature, to take compassion upon those poor objects, who have been reduced to this distress by their connexion with Great Britain. It would become that humane community, the public of England, which cloathed and cherished even their enemies, languishing in captivity,[3] to extend the same benevolence and generosity to our friends and fellow-subjects of Hesse and Hanover, exposed to every species of indigence and distress, and even destitute of habitation, in an exhausted country, and a rigorous climate, during all the horrors of a severe winter.

I am persuaded, if a subscription was set on foot for the relief of those unhappy people, during this severe weather,[4] when every individual must, in a particular manner, sympathise with the wants of his fellow-creatures; it would fill a-pace, and the money thus raised, might, under the direction of a committee, chosen for the purpose, be laid out in provision and cloathing to be transported by sea to the mouth of the Weser, and afterwards distributed among proper objects, by the regency of Hanover, and the magistracy of Hesse. In submitting these well-intended hints to the public, you will oblige

Your humble servant,

COSMOPOLITE.[5]

To the BRITON.

SIR,

While I read in the public papers,[6] that four or five men are all that remain of one of the Highland battalions, which has been expended in the service of the war abroad, I cannot, without a secret satisfaction, acknowledge the justice of a reproach thrown upon the Scots in general, that they come abroad in shoals, but never return to their own country. To a true-born Englishman, who knows in what manner these interlopers swarm among us, it must be some comfort to reflect, that above thirty thousand of these vagabonds have perished in the land-service of this kingdom since the beginning of the war, exclusive of the consumption of them on board the navy, privateers, and merchant-ships, which may amount to very near the same number, and that every one of those, filled up the place of an English subject, so we may fairly infer, that the valuable lives of threescore thousand Englishmen have been saved by the use of those vermin.

If there had been no other reason for protracting the war, I should have given my voice for a continuation of hostilities, in hopes they might have been the means of extirpating this pernicious race, whose former animosity, according to a certain infallible political sage,[7] was a thorn in our sides, and whose present friendship is an intolerable plague to this nation: It was not without indignation, that I lately heard a person who calls himself an Englishman, undertake in public the defence of those northern caterpillars, who, with all their boasted shrewdness, have not had the effrontery to open their own lips, in answer to all the crimes which have been laid to their charge.

This pseudo-Englishman affirmed, it was a maxim universally established, that an accession of people, was an addition of wealth to every country not already over-stocked, provided those people brought health and industry along with them; that as population had been for many years decreasing in England, and the war occasioned an extraordinary expence of men, we were obliged to the Scotch for leaving their own country to settle among us; that all the world allowed them to be generally sensible, industrious and sober; that the magistrates of this metropolis would bear witness, they were infinitely less concerned in felonies, riots, and breaches of order, than any other subjects of his majesty; therefore, they were peculiarly adapted for the purposes of society and commerce: that the money they earned was spent in the kingdom where they settled; and that the children which they procreated were natives of England, and Englishmen to all intents and purposes, consequently nothing could be more absurd, than to charge it as a crime upon them, that they never returned to their own country. He said, if this was true in fact, they ought to be encouraged for that very purpose; for, if it was criminal at all, it argued a want of affection for their *natale solum*;[8] an inference which could not possibly be reconciled with another reproach they lie under, that of hanging together in the most partial manner, and assisting one another in all the occurrences of life. He asserted therefore, that these two articles of impeachment were contradictory; that one of them must needs be false; and that both were ridiculous. Nay, this advocate for the Scots, was transported to such a degree of zeal in their favour, as to insist, that granting they acquired fortunes in England, and conveyed their wealth to their own country, that wealth contributed as much to the advantage of the nation in general, as if the circulation of it had been confined within the boundaries of South Britain. "The money (said he) which circulates in the remotest parts of Scotland, can no more stagnate there, than the blood which flows from the heart, can be detained in the extremities of the animal machine. It returns immediately in a thousand refluent streams to the center of trade, which every body knows must be the center of South Britain, in as much as the ballance of traffic, between the two united kingdoms, is always greatly in favour of England, from whence the Scots import all their luxuries, and many of the conveniencies of life." He asked, "where we thought the noblemen, gentlemen, and adventurers of North Britain, who attended the parliament, or sollicited preferment, spent their estates and money? where, but in London? Where," said he, "does the whole Scotch nation purchase their tea and coffee, their porcelain, spices, and other East Indian commodities; their silks, brocades, and gold and silver lace, their broad-cloth, hats, toys, and hard-ware; their houshold-furniture, chairs, tables, mirrors, cabinets, bureaus, carpets, stoves, and plate? Where, but in London, and other parts of South Britain? These were the vitals which this circulation continually revisited with a perpetual motion; and it was as palpable a contradiction to common sense, to advance, that a temporary transfer of money from this kingdom to Scotland, can in any shape diminish the wealth of England, as it would be to affirm, that the ocean is impoverished by the sun's exhaling from it those vapours, which are so faithfully refunded to it, by every river and stream that waters the surface of the earth." He added, "that the Scots were our fellow-subjects, and fellow-protestants, who used the same language which we speak, who obey the same laws by which we are governed, who being surrounded by the same common barrier, seem designed by nature to be the same people with the English; who are rendered such by the constitution of Great Britain, which knows no difference between an Englishman and a Scotchman; and who cannot be disjoined from our community, without endangering, if not the immediate dissolution of the whole, at least the separate existence of each people." He concluded, "that those who endeavoured to excite animosities between the Southern and Northern inhabitants of this island, to establish a belief, that the Scots, as a people, could have any interest distinct from the English, or to induce the public to discourage the natives of North Britain to settle among us; were either secret enemies to their own country, or grossly ignorant of her true interest, and even unacquainted with the first principles of society, commerce, and population."

Such were the doctrines broached by this degenerate Englishman, in a public coffee-house, where, I am sorry to say it, he was heard with too much attention. For my own part, I shrugged up my shoulders in silence, and could not help reflecting upon that paragraph lately transcribed from an Evening Paper, by that worthy and candid compiler of the Gazetteer,[9] who hath conducted himself with such moderation and impartiality in our late political disputes: I mean the paragraph relating to a supposed Scotchman, who frequents a certain coffee-house, and is supposed to purloin all the papers that contain strictures upon his countryman who presides at the T——y B——d. If that nobleman (as the news-monger sagaciously remarks) is capable of stooping so low, as to countenance such doings, I do not wonder that he should employ emissaries to harrangue in public places, in favour of his countrymen, who, like rats, have over-run the whole nation, and slily crept into the best offices of the church, the law, the state, the army, and the navy. When I said *slily*, I might have said by the force of fascination; for, notwithstanding all that their panegyrist could urge in their behalf, I will venture to assert, that it is not to their merit, they are indebted for the good things they enjoy.

As for their boasted sobriety, it is owing to their servile disposition, and the parsimonious manner in which they are brought up. They never eat a meal of good victuals, nor drank a chearful glass in their own country, consequently their blood is poor, and they have no idea of elevation: they have not spirit enough to be insolent to their superiors; nor courage sufficient to run the risk of hanging; but they inherit a low cunning, that teaches them to keep on the lee-side of the law, and to rise in their several stations, to a sort of eminence and respect. The same legerdemain they have practised for several hundred years in other countries of Europe, in France, Spain, Italy, Holland, Sweden, and Russia; nay, one of our own travellers declares, that even in Asia, there is hardly a kingdom, state, or city, where you do not find a Scotchman in some eminent station.

This being the case, will any man tell me it is for the advantage of this kingdom, that such dangerous interlopers should be encouraged to settle among us? I am credibly informed, that fifty thousand Scots have wriggled themselves within the bills of mortality; that above twice that number have taken root in our different plantations, factories, and settlements abroad; that our army cannot be recruited, nor our navy manned, nor our manufactures proceed, nor our navigation be carried on, without employing that generation of vipers.[10] Who is so deaf, but he can hear this storm sing in the wind?[11]

I will give my vote for naturalizing the Jews,[12] the Turks, and the Gentiles; for inviting over the Corsairs of Barbary, the Hottentots of Afric, or the *Anthropophagi that one another do eat*;[13] but, I would keep the Scots, as I would keep the Devil, at arm's-length; and if I thought any North Britain would ever either mingle with my blood, or touch a penny of my substance, I would immediately hang myself like a free-born Englishman, with a cord of my own twisting.

I guess how the wind of your inclination sits; but, I challenge you to make this declaration public, and am, as you may deserve, your friend, or enemy,

BENJAMIN HEMPLEY.[14]

Limehouse, Jan. 4, 1763.

No. 35. Saturday, 22 January 1763.

To the BRITON.

S IR,

W hen Peter, in the Tale of a Tub,[1] damns and curses all who will not believe a luncheon of bread to be a leg of mutton, he is neither so ridiculous nor unreasonable as mother Monitor, and the rest of the scribblers, who pretend that the present administration is disagreeable to this nation. I shall make as great a concession as any subject of Great Britain, who is not either a Jacobite or Republican, can require, That ministers have been known by the mere dint of pensions, posts, and places, to carry questions against the public interest, and the common sense of mankind; and that such questions so carried, can only be considered as so many ministerial pills rammed down the throats of a free people.

Without having recourse to the treaty of Utrecht,[2] which was first approved of, and then damned in parliament, and both, by the force of ministerial power, we shall come to a case, which, if the abovementioned good old lady retains her intellectual as well as she does her Billingsgate faculties,[3] must be within her own memory, and cannot be unknown to her coadjutor the North Briton likewise.

The case, I mean, is the famous one of the Convention;[4] and I pitch upon it as being the only one since the time of the treaty of Utrecht, that bears any similarity to the late debate and division upon the preliminaries of the present peace. We are, however, to observe, that a place-act[5] or two have been made since that time, and consequently the numbers of place-men in the house of commons, are not so considerable now as then. The opposition at that time was composed of conscience-led members, Whigs as well as Tories, who complained with great justice, that their antagonists were all place-led, and therefore the majority that was against them, which was no more than 28, was no proof of the sense of the nation, the latter having a visible bias of interest to influence their suffrages. Their numbers standing as follows, the place-led 262, the conscience-led 234. Thus, it appears, that 234 voices in the house of commons, may be absolutely free from any bias upon their minds in giving their votes. But this is a number much superior to 65, the minority against the present minister;[6] and it is fair, by all the rules of reasoning, to infer, that in the division upon the preliminaries, the present minister had upon his side proportionably to the numbers in the house, 169 more conscience-led members for him than were against him, even supposing those against him to be under no influence, or to have no connexions that could warp their judgments.

We have of late heard mighty parades upon the merit of Whiggism, and the most sarcastic invectives against Toryism, though perhaps no principle for these 30 years past, has been better understood, than that they were terms invented by knaves, and adopted by fools.[7] In a long and fruitless opposition to Sir Robert Walpole's measures, both denominations concurred, and both were sunk in the terms of court and country-party.[8] Both travelled to a certain stage together, and there the roads divided. Some went one way, some another. Under a subsequent administration they met again;[9] and if those distinctions were kept up, or are now revived, it is certainly owing to the Whigs: for my own part, I know no difference in the principle, tho' there is in the exercise of their administrations. The Whig ministers have always been known to plume themselves in the feathers they plucked from the prerogative; and have added to their own persons, that importance which they filched from the crown. What Tory subject since the revolution, has been equal in self-importance to Sir Robert Walpole? When in power, did he not Out-herod Herod,[10] and Out-tory Toryism? When applied to for favours, that ought to have been the immediate gift of the Sovereign, he never took the royal name in his lips, but spoke in the first person, I will, or I will not, do so and so. Yet Walpole was an honourable man,[11] that is, he was a known Whig-minister; and the addresser to the Cocoa-tree[12] tells us, page 5, that a known Whig will of course enjoy popularity. Pray, Sir, was Sir Robert Walpole a popular minister? Were any of his successors in power so, till Mr. Pelham found it necessary to break into the ridiculous party-paté, which the Whigs held before them; and to widen the bottom of government, which was still farther widened by the late minister,[13] who thereby acquired the popularity he once boasted of in defiance of his fellow-counsellors?

The addresser tells us, very paradoxically, that "Whiggism is a popular principle;" a proposition *cujus contrarium est verum.*[14] All experience, and all history informs us, that the genius of the people of England inclines them to monarchy; and tho' they cannot bear to be fleeced by their Sovereign, they can far less bear to be flead[15] by his minister. They abhor to see a fellow-subject strutting in the spoils of prerogative, and usurping the attributes of sovereignty.

It is this, and this alone, that has rendered ministerial power, for above half a century, so extremely unpopular in England. The nation, once within that time, saw a Tory government, but I doubt much whether a Tory minister was at the head of it, for the Earl of Oxford[16] was not only born and bred a dissenter, but had acted all along in close conjunction with the Whigs, till he found an opportunity of undermining them. This, however, was so far from constituting him a Tory, that no fact is more certain, than that King George the I. notwithstanding all the prepossessions with which he came to the crown against the Tories, stopt the shameful prosecution carried on against him, and thereby saved the Whigs from blushing at their own Proceedings.

Till the accession of his present Majesty, there was a plain and an evident reason why the Whigs kept up the distinction between them and their antagonists. After the act of succession [17] passed, the family of Hanover kept a correspondence in England with none but Whigs, who told his present Majesty's grand-father, and great grand-father, that the Tories had all cloven feet, and that they could trust none but themselves for their continuance upon the throne. Unacquainted, as they were, with the state of parties in England, they were believed; but his late Majesty lived long enough to be undeceived, and to learn by experience, that the people of this nation, are not to be ruled under an exclusion of three-fourths of the men of natural property [18] in their country, equal at least to their antagonists in integrity and abilities, from all posts of power and trust in the government. If the present minister has cut through the isthmus that formerly prevented the flow of Royal favour through all ranks of people; if he has thrown down those paper-party walls that divided the two denominations, so often to the disgrace and distress of this nation; he has acted nobly, and to the eternal honour both of his Sovereign and himself.

But, in the mean while, I am of Sir Roger de Coverley's opinion, that much may be said on both sides,[19] were one to be asked whether the present is a Whig or a Tory administration. When I see so many great places under his Majesty, filled by the descendants of the Russels, the Campbells, the Churchills, and Spencers, the Douglasses, the Montagues, the Percivals, the Percies, the Manners,[20] and many other illustrious names that figured in the days of recovered liberty, and whom the Whigs were always proud to call their own, I cannot have the least idea of any danger of our relapsing into Toryism.

On the other hand, when I see our Sovereign restored to the highest of all his prerogatives, that of extending his favour personally to every kind of merit; of conferring honours where honours are due; of patronizing and encouraging genius, of rewarding the worthy, and relieving the needy, and shedding the dews of royalty over a whole happy land without distinction of party; I am almost sure that we are not under a Whig administration. Thus, tho' I cannot pronounce our present government to be either Whig or Tory;

yet I am not under the least difficulty in affirming that it is constitutional, and that his present Majesty, at the close of a long and happy reign, will have somewhat more to boast of, than that he has made one bishop, one admiral, and one judge.

The addresser to the Cocoa-tree, is not only mistaken, but so confined in his notions of government, especially British government, that he seems to have been taught by a Whig horn-book. He accuses the minister and his friends, of maintaining that monarchy is independent, which, says he, is only another word for unlimited. God forbid that the British monarchy should be ever other than independent: but, because it is independent, does it follow, that it is unlimited? I am afraid, the expression itself is little better than nonsense. British monarchy, however independent, must be limited by the constitution; if it is not, it is no longer British monarchy, but despotism. As to independency, unless it is independent within itself, if it is subject to the controul either of foreign power or domestic insolence, it equally ceases to be British monarchy. A man may have a small estate, that is independent, but is it for that reason unlimited, or is it the less independent, because it is possessed according to the laws of this country?

Our addresser (page 9) says, that the reason why they dislike the present minister is, because they do not know him; and, as I should be extremely fond of knowing more of him, especially as to his person, (for I think his politics are no secrets) I shall submit a few queries to the public, the solution of which will give us a farther insight into his character.

Did he ever, when in the administration, ridicule or condemn the declarations he made when he was in the opposition? — Was he ever mean as a dependent, and insolent as a superior? Did he ever sacrifice the principles that led him to popularity, on the altar of those prejudices that raised him to power? — Did he ever attempt to be eloquent in defiance of grammar, and affect the airs of an orator, while he forgot the manners of a gentleman?

Did he ever presume to guide the helm of state, while he was mean enough to forsake the post of danger? — Did he ever dictate to the crown, and bully its counsellors? — Did he ever practise the meanest arts to revive a dying popularity? — Has he courted those whom he declared he hated; and flattered others whom he professed to despise? — Has he lived long enough to survive that character that first rendered him considerable, and to break the engagements he was unable to fulfil? — Does he glory in an open contempt of all literary merit; and cloak his disregard to writers, with the pretence of his disliking their flattery? — To conclude, has any one real objection to his administration been unanswered, or the most sanguine expectation of his virtues remained unsatisfied? [21]

A full and candid solution of the above queries would go far with me towards a decisive judgment of the present minister's merits. Till then, I never can be brought to take any proposition for granted, be it ever so bold or presuming, that contradicts every evidence of common sense and common experience. But I shall close this paper with a short story,[22] that may entertain, though not instruct your readers.

Charles the II. observing the prodigious obsequiousness paid by his court-iers to his person and power, one day asked them the reason, why, when two buckets full of an equal quantity of water were suspended, one with a live carp in it, the other without one, both weighed alike? The obsequious circle, without questioning the veracity of the experiment, gave their several opinions upon the reasons. The King at last asked that of an old courtier who had remained silent. *By G—d, Sir*, answered he, *I doubt the fact.*

I am,
Your very humble servant and reader,
PHOCION.[23]

No. 36. Saturday, 29 January 1763.

Latet anguis in herba.[1]

A short ADDRESS to the Gentlemen who now distinguish themselves by the name of WHIGS.[2]

GENTLEMEN,

If you are Whigs, you need fear nothing from me, for I profess myself one in the true sense of the word. I mean not therefore to insult, but, if I can, to reform you. As individuals, you have a right to any place or office under the government, but none as a party to rule the whole. You seem not to be contented to live upon an equality with your fellow-subjects; but to strut and tower above them at your pleasure. You must either have all power or no power, all posts or no posts; that is, you must have the persons, properties, and liberties of the nation wholly at your command. In word, nothing will satisfy you, but making the one half of the people a set of specious slaves, and Royalty itself a splendid phantom.

You'll no doubt ask a proof of all this. I shall give it you; and, as I would not tire you with the length of it, I shall trace you no farther back than to about the year forty: for, I never chuse to load the memory of those whose lips are sealed by death, and who can't therefore answer for themselves. You remember, very well, gentlemen, that the administration about that time,[3] threw the nation into a flame. Some of you were nearly connected with the obnoxious minister, but you were either not able, or not willing to support him. A broad-bottomed plan[4] was formed for the extinction of parties, and admitting all without discrimination to the service and honours of their country. Allow me to ask you, whether you did not concur in, and agree to this plan? But tell us, at the same time, how it was executed? Did you not take care to place yourselves in the center of this broad-bottom, and only admit so many of the other denomination upon the edges of it, as were just sufficient to keep you in a safe ballance, and who could be shoved off when you needed them no more? Did you not amuse one with a title, and another with a place, which nevertheless you reserved still in your own power, and could resume again when you pleased? The consequence of all which was, that according to your own design, you got in a short time the whole broad-bottom to yourselves: for who was made treasurer and chancellor of the exchequer? who secretary of state,[5] &c. 'Tis needless to specify: the facts are too obvious to be disputed.

Again, gentlemen, at that period, did not you undertake to correct all the errors of your predecessor, for which he was turned out? Allow me modestly to ask the question, How many of them you did correct and avoid in your own conduct? A committee was appointed to examine his accounts:[6] under whose auspices was it, that he came off blameless? Were thanks due to his own honesty, or your favour? If to the former, methinks, he should have been restored to his place again: if to the latter, it becomes me to impute it to meer humanity; for you yourselves could dread nothing from his condemnation: or rather you were willing, it may be, to let him die in peace, as you had got what you wanted; for what good would his life do to you?

When you were thus settled, what methods did you take in order to maintain and establish yourselves? Did you renounce his maxims of government, as the nation, from a change of hands, had ground to expect? or rather, did not some of you, on whom all the rest depended, openly adopt and defend one of his first principles; That he is a pitiful fellow of a minister, who can't keep out any one that opposes his measures? Did not you, gentlemen, practise this doctrine in its full latitude? for when a certain nobleman, lately deceased, was like to take the lead from you, did you not come in a body to resign, unless his late Majesty would turn him out?[7] And at what time did you act this dutiful part to that Prince whose memory you now pretend is so dear to you? Why, when a war was raging far and wide; a rebellion in the bowels of the nation; and he knew not where to oppose his enemies first. This step shewed not only your respect to him; but also your concern for the safety of your country. But there was something, it seems which you had a greater respect to than either of these, and that was a jealous anxiety for your own power. You were resolved, it seems, that become of King or country what would, the wheels of government should not move unless you guided them: that neither Sovereign nor subject should be protected, unless you had the honour to take them under your own wings.

Besides, you know, gentlemen, that when any man of the opposite party became troublesome, you took care, as the phrase is, to take him off: witness a certain Right Hon. gentleman, to whom you gave a place in the treasury in Ireland about that time.[8] This expedient, you thought, no doubt, you might use without any danger to your own power; for this gentleman had given so many offences and disgust to his Majesty, as made you firmly hope, he would never have either the heart, or the ear of his Sovereign. He belonged originally to another party, and had spoken so very freely of a certain Electorate, that he could not be very acceptable to the person of the E — r. However, he was not so much attached to that party, as not to leave it when a better offer was made by you. With you, therefore, he always continued till a new vacancy opened, which, he thought, he might very well fill. As often as he found you not disposed to indulge him at once, he left you, and returned to the other side, till by proper ways and means he could bring you to terms. This course you and he continued, till, perhaps, you were tired of employing, and the other side of trusting him, after he had so often jockeyed you both. You know, gentlemen, I could adduce a great many more instances of all denominations, who have been taken in and turned out by you, as it appeared they were necessary, or otherwise to the support of your interest. The city of London, as well as different parts of the country, can vouch for this assertion.

Permit me, farther, gentlemen, to put you in mind, that in the preceding administration, bribery and corruption were said to be useful engines to preserve the minister in his power: and the world does much belie you, if you did not confirm their utility by practice; and, I believe, that no body can doubt, that the public money was often squandered away in carrying on elections and purchasing votes. Such practices convey to me a strange notion of a Whig; for I had always been taught to assign to him the idea of an honest man. One thing is certain, gentlemen, a deluge of perjury hath overflowed the land; and it is generally imputed to the infamous art of debauching people's consciences at these elections; for those who will swear falsely in one case, will not scruple to forswear themselves in another. The consequence of which is, that no man's property is now safe. This vice is one of the greatest plagues of this kingdom. That power had better never been earned, which was earned at such expence; and that place, however honourable, better re-signed than kept with such offence to God, and prejudice to man. Politicians may laugh at these reflections, while they are reveling in the plenitude of their uncontrouled might; but, the minister, who either permits or practices such iniquitous expedients, takes the most effectual way to dissolve all government, and is the worst minister a country can acquire. It has been said, to your praise, that you patronized liberty of conscience; but the art of bribing, is teaching conscience to take too great Liberty.

As I am upon this point, gentlemen, you'll not be offended, if I tell you, that some ascribe the rise of the rebellion in Forty-five to such proceedings as these: for a certain nobleman, who had been very serviceable in quelling that of Fifteen, being turned out of his place, because he would not vote with some of you, conceived such resentment (of which he was but too susceptible) at this usage, that he began immediately to sow the seeds of the last insurrection.[9] You may remember too, at least I have heard, that another had raised a body of his vassals for the service of the government, and only asked the favour of you, which you had granted to others, *viz.* that his son, who was to be their colonel, might be allowed to name the inferior officers; you thought fit to deny his request; and this denial provoked him to turn his arms against his country, to his own and family's destruction.[10] All such insurrections are to be held in the utmost detestation by every friend of Britain; but perhaps, they may not be altogether guiltless who give unnecessary handles[11] for popular commotion. A good minister will be upon his guard against giving any just cause of offence; for tho' the injured person may feel the effects of it first, it seldom fails at last to recoil back upon the aggressor's own head.

About that period also, gentlemen, we entered into a war with Spain,[12] principally on the account of their searching our ships. That war was conducted by some of you; and after a course of seven or eight years, you thought fit to terminate it by the peace of Aix-la-Chapelle. At that peace, you gave up the very thing for which we had commenced hostilities, after laying out 30 or 40 millions upon the war. A certain gentleman, whom you can name, had declaimed with great warmth against this injustice and insolence of the Spaniards in searching our ships. But when the peace was made, and you had yielded it to them, he harrangued as eloquently on the justification of what you had done.[13] Eight or ten years was a great while, and had afforded many new lights: and indeed he acknowledged it himself, and made use of this argument to reconcile his then compliance with his former inflexibility. Permit me, by the way, gentlemen, just to hint to you, that the present ministry recovered in half a year, what you had waged war for eight years without effect, to obtain. But, how shall I account for your conduct? You seem now to despise the article of *no search*, for which you then carried on an eight years war. There is some mystery in this matter, which you can best unfold.

After having reminded you of these particulars, allow us, gentlemen, to hope that we shall hear no more of the present minister's having no natural interest; that is, as you explain it, no popularity in the South; for you know, that on the account of the measures just now mentioned, some of those who are now your leaders, and whom you seem disposed *commiscere cœlum & terram*,[14] in order to restore, had not the least shadow of popularity, either in the South or North, for 40 years together. We expect also, that you'll never mention more the minister's, not being recommended by long services; for if one should ask what services these your leaders have done, some profane people would swear they never were capable of serving either themselves or the public. There is one indeed, who is said to have done essential service to the nation; but then you know it is a problem with many, whether he did not lose all the merit of it, by plunging us so deep into continental connections, by which means, he was wounding with one hand, while he was healing with the other. Those who adhere to this opinion, have his own formerly-avowed judgment on their side; for he had always declared, that these connections were, and would be, the bane of this country. Besides, gentlemen, you are not sure that you don't count too fast, when you reckon him of your side, for you know, that his principles are of the motley kind, *nunc inter hos, nunc inter illos. Vir omnium partium, & pars omnium virorum*.[15] So far as we can judge from this gentleman's publick conduct, he seems never to have had any set of fixed principles at all; but that, on the contrary, he left himself at the convenient liberty of veering about as his occasions required. These objections, therefore, gentlemen, against the minister, are the very worst you could possibly have chosen, as the whole infamy of them redounds upon your own heads. As to the place of his birth, which even the most modest of you seem willing to nibble at, while yet their consciences appear to smite them for so doing; you know, gentlemen, that if he was born in any part of Great Britain, he has the same right to any post or office under the government as you have. Some ignorant persons might not know this when he first entered upon his present office, and therefore might raise a clamour about a Scotchman's being at the head of the English treasury, as some expressed it to deceive the people; but you knew better, and should have informed them, it was neither the treasury of England, nor of Scotland, but of Great Britain. As to the want of experience, which you charge upon him; if he has done, and can do his duty, it is no matter how he learned it, whether from theory or practice. Some of you had been in the school of experience for more than 40 years, and yet many think you are far from being compleat statesmen at this very day.

To conclude these points, gentlemen, I suppose you have heard, that 35 millions have already been offered for the supplies of the current year. Is this a proof that the minister has no interest in the nation, or that the people have no confidence in him, as some of you have often scurrilously given out? When was such a sum ever offered before? or rather, when was the half of such a sum ever offered before? You seem, gentlemen, to have taken a wrong estimate of this minister from the beginning, which may have led you to hurt yourselves as individuals: for as to the cause which you profess to espouse, I firmly believe it will never be hurt by the present administration. His Majesty, I hope, is both too wise, and too good, to make the cause itself suffer for the faults of some pretended friends to it, who have been wanting in their duty to him. I say, some who have been wanting in their duty to him; for I am far from charging you all; but it is but too notorious, that some have been egregiously so, who call themselves of your party.

You must not now be angry, gentlemen, if I take the liberty to affirm, you are no Whigs, tho' you assume the name; for, it is the first Article of the Whig's creed, and indeed the sum of all the rest, That the King has a right to chuse his servants, and that all his loyal subjects should enjoy equal liberties and privileges. Thus it was settled at the Revolution, and confirmed again by the succession of the present Royal Family: but both these articles you re-nounced, and violated, in a late reign, as well as in the present: for then, and now, you would allow the King to have no servants, but such as you thought fit to impose upon him, nor any subject a post or place, but such as you chose to promote. By which means, the one half of the nation were robbed of their natural privileges, under the odious name of Tories, tho' all the while they contribute to the support of government equally with you. There might be some colour for a proceeding of this kind some years ago, when prejudices and party-principles ran too high in the minds of many; but now, there is not so much as a shadow of a pretence for it: for yourselves not only own, but boast, (and you'll certainly admit your own testimony) that such an una-nimity was never known in the nation, as there has been for six or seven years past. Is not this a plain declaration from your own mouths, that the Tories, as you call them, were reconciled? Was not the last parliament, and likewise the present, chosen under your auspices? Did you not reckon them equally loyal subjects then with yourselves, and that therefore they had a right to the same posts and offices with you? Are they not the same now as they were then? and yet you now exclaim against giving them any, nay, brand them with the name of Jacobites. Be not deceived, gentlemen, we are not so short-sighted, as not to see through this disguise. We think, that some of you, (for others are doubtless very respectable) hang out these opprobrious names, to invite weak tho' well-meaning people to join you in overturning the present administration, and so help you into your despotism again: but I believe, no clear-sighted Whig will ever enlist under your banners.

Lastly, excuse me when I tell you, that I think the present administration is the only one I ever remember to have proceeded upon true and genuine Whig-principles; for they allow the crown its due prerogative, and the subjects their just liberties; and they admit into places of trust, without discrimination, every man of ability who is loyal to his King and country, and qualified according to law. These are truly revolutional and constitutional measures, while those, which you are now pursuing, are in the strictest sense of the word factious and jacobitical, as those you have formerly pursued, were tyrannical and oppressive. I am, Gentlemen, yours, &c.

A WHIG.

Hammersmith, Dec. 20.

No. 37. Saturday, 5 February 1763.

Nihil tam æquandæ libertatis esse, quam potentissimum quemque posse dicere causam.

Liv.[1]

I have seen myself more than once accused in the public papers, of having practised the very same abuse against the character of Mr. P——, which I have condemned so loudly in the writings of those who weekly defame the K——g and his M——rs. I should certainly have over-looked, with silent contempt, the insinuations of all such obscure calumniators: but, as a r——t r——d P——te has, in an advertisement to a late performance,[2] condescended to interfere in this dispute, and flourish the weapons in defiance of those who presume to censure Mr. P——'s ad——n; I shall, in this paper, endeavour to shew, with what propriety the B—— has tucked up his canonicals, to mount the stage as a political prize-fighter; and with what dexterity he has managed the single faulchion[3] of his wit, in dazzling the eyes of his spectators.

Having acknowledged his duty to two masters, his God and his King, he gives us to understand, that there was no truth in a report which had been industriously circulated, that he was concerned in writing the vindication of a late M——r: he observes, that if the conduct of the said M——r, required any vindication, his own pen was more than equal to the task: but, that far from being a subject for censure, it was, and ever would be a theme of admiration and applause. I do not pretend to recollect the precise words; but this is the purport of his declaration. — Finally, he compares W — P — Esq; to Scipio, surnamed Africanus, who being abused by a low plebeian called *Nevius*,[4] who impeached him of divers misdemeanours, instead of answering the particulars of the charge, told the people assembled in the Forum, that this was the anniversary of the decisive victory which he had obtained over Hannibal and the inveterate enemies of the commonwealth, and exhorted them to follow him to church, that he might return thanks to God for these inestimable benefits.

Whether an ecclesiastic, advancing thus in the front of faction, and professing himself the champion of a demagogue, under whose banners, and in whose name, the abandoned mercenaries of sedition have raised the cry against their S — n and his g — t, and endeavoured to excite a civil war in the bowels of their country, approves himself a faithful servant either to his God, or to his King, I shall leave the impartial public to determine. But, before I proceed to consider the propriety of his comparison, I must observe, that he seems to be a little mistaken in his historical fact. Livy says, the writers of those days were not agreed about the person of the accuser, whether Scipio Africanus was impeached by the two *Pestilii*, or by *Nævius*;[5] but, there is no doubt concerning the quality of *Nævius*, who, far from being a low plebeian, was a tribune of the people. True it is, like some modern tribunes, he was not the less a rascal for his rank and influence among the multitude. He envied the virtue and the reputation of Scipio, who was a patrician of unblemished character. The prosecution was founded on malice; and his charge was equally false and frivolous; therefore he was justly branded with the names *Nebulo* and *Nugator*.[6]

I would not do his L — p the injustice to suppose, that he meant to convey a reproach in the term *Plebeian*; he who professes himself the servant of him who has no respect of persons; who owes his own importance, in a great measure, to the favour of one whom fortune once numbered among the lowest of the plebeians; who owes his own elevation from the plebeian order, to the interest and power of a plebeian M — r, even to the man before whose character he now throws the broad-buckler[7] of his defiance.

Indeed, if I was not afraid of shocking the known modesty and self-denial of this venerable P — te,[8] I should not scruple to declare, that his promotion in the Ch — , was one of the most meritorious efforts of Mr. P — 's ad — n. What ineffable blessings has he conferred on the hierarchy for procuring the

M—tre for a P——te of his speculative virtue! for a pious ecclesiastic, who hath so happily imitated the meekness, humility, and moderation of his divine Master! so eminently possessed of genius without arrogance, of learning without ostentation; whose charity is so liberal, as to embrace all mankind; who can argue with decency, refute with tenderness, and retract with candour; who never advanced a dogma which he himself did not implicitly believe; nor started a paradox for the gratification of polemical pride; nor endeavoured to puzzle with subtilty, rather than to convince with reason; nor sought to hide the nakedness of error with the multiplied folds of sophistry and supposition. Such an ecclesiastic, is, no doubt, an ornament to the Protestant Church, and a shining light among the nations; and we can never enough applaud the judgment and equity of Mr. P——, who, without being actuated or influenced by motives of private connexion, or worldly interest, added this great luminary to the episcopal sphere.

His L——p may likewise be commendable (for aught I know) in ranging on the side of his old patron, even when he heads an opposition against his P——ce: but still, I apprehend he will find it difficult to sustain his comparison of W. P——, Esq; with Scipio, surnamed *Africanus*. That illustrious Roman did not raise himself into consideration by turbulence and abuse: he was not a double apostate from the principles he originally professed: he never deserted his friends, his party, or his master. His merit did not consist in mouthing against the princes and ministers of the commonwealth; nor did he climb upon the shoulders of the mob to the first offices of the state. He did not plunge his country into a ruinous and unnecessary war, nor wantonly fleece the people, and augment the public burdens for its support; nor planned expeditions equally ridiculous and fatal; nor arrogated to himself the honour of successful expeditions, which he neither planned nor executed; nor quit the reins of g——t which he was no longer able to manage; nor insult his benefactor, by whose bounty he was raised above indigence and dependence; nor use the lowest arts of popularity to play upon the passions of the vulgar, and raise the most dangerous spirit of discontent among his fellow-citizens.

Scipio was remarkable for his sweetness of disposition, his affability, his liberality, and moderation. Tho' possessed of eloquence in an eminent degree, he scorned to use it for the purposes of faction. At the age of eighteen, he saved his father's life in battle. By his spirit and elocution, he prevented the Patricians from abandoning Rome after the defeat of *Cannæ*. Before he had attained the age of thirty, he conquered all Spain from the Carthaginians, not in his closet, but at the head of his army. He, in one day, took the strong city of New Carthage by assault, and finished that war with a battle, in which above 50,000 of the enemy were slain. Then he transferred the war to Africa, where he defeated Asdrubal and Syphax in two pitched battles, and in the following year overcame the great Hannibal in person at Zama. In a word, he besieged Carthage by sea and land, and obliged that haughty rival of Rome to submit to such conditions as he thought proper to impose.[9] It was in consequence of these important services that he rose to the highest honours of the common-wealth, and not by caballing among the mob, which he ever despised. No wonder then that he attracted the envy and hatred of the illiberal plebeians. His transcendent virtue and great reputation, were disagreeable, even to his dear son-in-law, Tiberius Gracchus,[10] the idolized orator of the populace, who would not be at rest, until he had raised a commotion that ended in his own ruin.

I cannot therefore perceive any point of view, in which our modern Gracchus resembles the character of Scipio Africanus; there is not the faintest shadow of similitude, even in the circumstance which our r — t r — d champion has thought proper to record. Scipio's enemies were plebeians; whereas the only friends and admirers that Mr. P— can boast, are of that order, except his own brother-in-law,[11] and this r — d D — ne, so lately sublimed above his native sphere. He might as well therefore compare Col. W — kes to Julius Cæsar, Ch — ll[12] to Dean Swift, or Jacob Henriquez to the Duke de Sully,[13] as to pretend to demonstrate any sort of resemblance between W — P — and Scipio Africanus.

I know the emissaries and panegyrists of a late M — r, have often repeated this assertion, That when he placed himself at the helm, the honour of the nation was tarnished by successive disgraces; and the people in general overwhelmed with despondence: that he no sooner took charge of the steerage, than the gale of fortune became prosperous: the success of the war began to change in our favour: our operations were carried on with redoubled vigour; and the spirits of the people, which had been so wofully depressed, were raised to an uncommon pitch of elevation: from these premises, they inferred, that Mr. P— alone had caused the prosperous gale to blow; that he alone had invigorated our councils, animated our efforts, and raised the dejected spirits of his fellow-citizens. With the same propriety, a peasant may claim the merit of a plentiful crop, tho' the land was manured, and the seed sown before he had possession of the farm, or a haberdasher of the city of London, might affirm, that the Lord-Mayor caused the harvest-moon to shine, because he may have happened to enter upon office in the month of September.

At the beginning of the war, our councils were weak, wavering, and distracted; our measures ill-concerted, and our plans wretchedly executed: but, experience, adversity, and a common sense of danger, had already improved and united our councils, and an animating spirit had been diffusing itself thro' every department of the civil and military administration, when it was the good fortune of Mr. P— to be lifted into the m—l chair. The tide of success must then have turned, tho' Mr. P—, had been unborn; and as Hotspur in the play replies to Glendower, who boasted, that at his birth,

> The frame, and the foundation of the earth,
> Shook like a coward.
>   So it would have done
> At the same season, if your mother's cat
> Had kitten'd, though yourself had ne'er been born.[14]

As the professed admirers of Mr. P— insist upon his having solely changed the fortune of the war, it is incumbent upon them to shew what changes he made in the plan of operations; and what officers he appointed to the command of the different expeditions. Were not both army and navy increased to a very formidable degree of power before he was concerned in the ad—n? Were not the admirals, Hawke, who so often triumphed over the enemy; Osborne, who destroyed part of the French fleet in the Mediterranean; Boscawen, who besieged Louisbourg in America, and defeated de la Clue off Lagos; Watson, who reduced Geriah and Chaudenagore in the East Indies; Pococke, who obtained three successive victories over the French Commander in that country, and has lately so gloriously contributed to the reduction of the Havanna;—— Were not all these, I say, employed under a former M—?[15] Was not North America pitched upon as the principal seat of the war, a large army assembled on that continent, and the plan of operations settled before Mr. P— took possession of his place? Was it he that sent over the gallant Wolfe who conquered Quebec, or intrusted Sir William Johnston, who twice defeated the enemy among the woods of America? Did he discover or employ the military talents of a Clive, a Lawrence, and a Coote, to which all our conquests in the East Indies are owing?[16] Let me only ask the prejudiced part of my countrymen, whether they think, that any of these brave officers exerted himself the more, for Mr. P—'s being in the m—y? whether they do not believe, that all of them would have done their duty with the same spirit, if Mr. P— had never existed; and whether his arrogating to himself the merit of conquests atchieved by their valour and their blood, is not in fact endeavouring to depreciate the characters of the living, and to defraud the memory of the dead? If any general by land, or admiral by sea, conquered under his immediate auspices, let his partisans stand forth, and tell their names and exploits. The commanders who were honoured by his choice, are well known. We all remember the gentleman who declined landing at Fouras;[17] and him who quietly withdrew from Martinique, when the islanders were assembling, in order to demand a capitulation; and him who made such a glorious retreat from the bay of St. Cas.[18] Neither have we forgot the success and importance of those expeditions which can properly be called his own. These are fruitful themes, which may hereafter engage my attention.

At present, I must be indulged with a short hearing, while I speak a few words in my own defence. I am accused of throwing out abuse upon Mr. P——'s character and Ad——n. I plead not guilty. I have freely spoken my sentiments of both; but I have neither treated him with scurrility, nor have I, in one instance, deviated one tittle from the truth, at least knowingly, and this I solemnly declare in the sight of Heaven. The charge is therefore absolutely false and malicious. The reader will remember, that I did not lift the pen in this dispute, till I saw my S——n, whom I am bound to honour, and his M——r whose virtues I had cause to respect, aspersed with such falshood, and reviled with such rancour, as must have roused the indignation of every honest man, and interested the attention of every loyal subject. The authors of those audacious calumnies have proceeded to propagate their infamous slanders against the most respectable characters of the nation, to such a degree of malice and abuse, as no age can parallel. They profess themselves the partisans of the late M——r, in opposition to the present ad——n. They are generally supposed to be his creatures; and he has never yet disowned their persons or their principles. Shall it then be lawful for his infamous tools of faction to promulgate the falsest aspersions that malice ever forged against their King, his family, his friends, and government; and be held a crime in me, to question, from undoubted facts, the pretended merit of their patron? Shall he, anointed with the dregs of popularity, believe himself invulnerable, and direct his emissaries to squirt their poison at the T——ne, secure against censure and rebuke? No, I will not dive into the recesses of his domestic concerns in search of scandal, and finding there no subject of reproach, consult the powers of fallacy and fiction. I will neither traduce the character of his mother, whom I do not know, nor question the virtue of his wife, which is truly respectable; nor treacherously feign circumstances in his private conduct, to bring him in disgrace with those who are strangers to his life and conversation: yet, such are the arts which his partizans have practised against his P——ce. But, I shall always exert the privilege of a free-born Briton, in discussing openly such parts of his public character, as, in my opinion, affect the peace and welfare of the community.

No. 38. Saturday, 12 February 1763.

Non hydra secto corpore firmior
Vinci dolentem crevit in Herculem.
HORACE.[1]

To the BRITON.

SIR,

T he letter, of which the following is a copy, was lately dropped in a public house, by a person who goes by the name of Doctor, but has been long suspected by a few individuals, of being in reality a Roman Catholic priest. The numbers, and other marks that occur in the letter, I have not art enough to decypher: but it requires not much sagacity to discover their meaning from the context. You are to take notice, that it has neither date, subscription, nor superscription, and happens to have been inclosed in a cover.

*
†Reverend Father,[2]
I received your packet by 34, and communicated the contents together with the list of Neophytes, to 48, who desires me to signify his approbation of your zeal, and his hope, that it will be always governed with discretion. He says, he could have wished to see more respectable names in your catalogue of converts, the generality of whom, if he may be allowed to judge from their designations, will (he is afraid) do little credit or service to the religion they have embraced: but, in times of dearth, the coarsest grain is better than no harvest.

With respect to 18, his opinion is, that you should in no shape intermeddle in the dispute. Too much hath been said and written about that worthless impostor. It is for the interest of the society, that all enquiries of this nature should be carefully avoided. He makes no scruple to declare his disapprobation of xxx, and father┼, and others of our persuasion for their forwardness in procuring materials for his detection.

48 has perused the periodical papers with unspeakable satisfaction. They have gone a great way towards consoling him in the affliction under which

he and all our society now groan, from the triumph and cruelty of our ene-
mies. They have opened up a prospect (which, it is to be hoped, Heaven will
in its infinite mercy consummate) of a glorious restoration—a restoration of
the church to her patrimony: a restoration of our poor persecuted order, to
that dignity and influence which it formerly maintained. Nothing, under the
miraculous interposition of Providence, can so much contribute to that re-
establishment, which we all so fervently desire, as a constant and prudent
endeavour to divide and weaken those accursed heretic tribes, which have
deprived us of our birth-right, and fatten on our spoils; and this holy pur-
pose, will undoubtedly be best accomplished by reviving ancient animosities,
and awaking that spirit of discord, which their common interest, and mutual
security had so effectually laid asleep.

I would not have you too curiously enquire into the motives which actuate
those who employ their talents so much to our advantage. Some of them are
staunch friends to our cause, and others are as clay in the hands of the potter.
They are rendered serviceable to our interest, without being conscious of
their own utility. Heaven has often made use of the vilest instruments for the
manifestation of its own glory. Much praise is certainly due to the projectors
and patrons of the M——, for having first sown the seeds of dissatisfaction,
which, I hope, by the Grace of God, will produce a plentiful crop of disaf-
fection to the reigning U——r. The methods used in this process, of surmise,
hint, parallel, supposition, and slander, are means sanctified by the use for
which they are intended. They are only criminal when employed for wicked
purposes: but become meritorious when practised for the benefit of our holy
religion.

The authors of the other Antim——l weekly productions have improved
upon the plan of their seniors. They have not only exercised their invention
for bringing the U——r into contempt, and his M——r into detestation with
the people; but they have artfully attempted by general reproach, to provoke
the whole S——sh nation into revolt—glorious design! worthy of a Campian,
a Parsons, and a Garnet![3] How did my heart palpitate with joy and won-
der, when I read those animated invectives! How did my bowels yearn with
love towards those pious labourers in the vineyard of sedition! my spirits
were flattered with the most replenishing hopes! Nay, I verily believed myself
under the influence of divine illumination. Methought I saw 13[4] stripped of
his gown, and subjected to the pains and penalties of the land; exalted on
the pillory, and abridged of his ears; tied to the cart's-tail roaring under the
scourge, and appealing to the mob from the tyranny of a S——h Ad——n. I
saw in spirit the intrepid and indefatigable 14,[5] grinning hideous in his last

agonies under the repeated application of a C—l—d——ian cudgel! I saw him expire; and could not help considering him as a martyr: I exclaimed in a rapture of devotion, *O sancte* 14! *O sit anima mea, (non corpus, Domine, sed anima) O sit anima mea cum sancto* 14![6] I have particular reasons, reverend father, for exempting 14 from the curse pronounced upon heresy. I know his principles: I am no stranger to his person—I have seen him—I have administered to him in extraordinary acts of devotion. Individuals, you know, are sometimes indulged with extraordinary privileges for the good of the church. I have known divers true sons of the beatified Loyola, cloak their pious zeal under the profession of atheism, and signally promote the interest of the church, by affecting to scoff at every form of religious worship.

But to return to my vision—Methought I saw a state persecutor arise. I beheld a L—— M——[7] hanged for sedition: I beheld an old pilot[8] conveyed through the public streets upon an ass, his face turned to the tail, with a cap and bells upon his head, a slavering-bib under his chin, and a rattle in his hand. I beheld a plebeian orator[9] in a woollen night-cap, beating hemp in Bridewell, and a B——[10] feeding him with flummery.[11] I beheld the torch of discord blazing to the utmost corners of the island; the sword of civil fury drawn; the g——t unhinged; the kingdom drenched in slaughter; heretical apostacy trodden under foot, and the holy Catholic Church riding triumphant in the midst of blood and desolation. But, alas! that fulness of time is not yet arrived. The tribes of the North are too cold to kindle. They have bore the arrows of reproach with the most mortifying indifference. They seem to me to have enjoyed in secret the calumny of their revilers, on the supposition that they were instigated by malice and envy, that never fail to torment the bosoms in which they are entertained. They have returned nothing but emanations of the most chilling contempt.

Blessed be the Lord! our friends have not been discouraged by this disappointment. They have wisely changed their battery, and pointed their artillery where, it is hoped, the breach will be found more practicable. They have industriously ripped up old sores in the South, and, as I am informed, the wounds which had been so long cicatrised,[12] begin to fester. They have conjured up the ghosts of two parties which had been damned to oblivion; and these false spectres glare at one another. They have furbished up and reared the tattered banners of faction, and revived the war-words *Whig* and *Tory*, which like *Guelph* and *Ghibelline*,[13] or like the cabalistical terms *Abraxas* and *Abracadabra*,[14] will, I hope, be the more efficacious, the less they are understood. O! that Heaven would prosper the endeavours of our zealous missionaries, the undaunted C——, and the unabashed W——! that they may be able to infuse the spirit of animosity, virulence and rancour, in the breasts of their infatuated countrymen! that they may prompt them to range themselves under one or other of the obsolete ensigns they have now reproduced. While they remained divided, our interest continued to rise; it was their union that proved fatal to our cause. It was the union of Whigs and Tories, that drove our royal brother from the throne: it was their dissention which revived our hopes in the beginning of the century: it was their subsequent coalition that drove us to despair. As for you, my reverend father, your conduct will require the utmost circumspection.

It will be your business to soothe the partisans of either party upon proper occasions: to praise this for his loyalty, and that for his independent spirit; to smile, and shrug, and shake the head, with proper significance; to hint doubts, start difficulties, and hesitate dislike:[15] in a word, to blow the flame of discord under the mask of moderation. May your heart be warmed with the ardour of St. Ignatius; may your spirit be strengthened by the perseverance of the blessed Xavier,[16] and conducted by the temper of the beatified Borgia.[17] May the blessed Virgin and all the saints have you in their holy keeping——So fervently prays your brother in the bowels of the Lord.

To the BRITON.

SIR,

I am a plain man, and shall use few words, tho' the subject of my letter is complaint. You must know I am part-owner of the good Ship Britannia, and generally sail on board as supercargo, so that tho' I be not a professed seaman, I know enough to distinguish when we go at large or close-hauled,[18] and can lend a hand upon occasion, to haul forward the main-top-bowling.[19]

In my first voyage, our Master[20] was a timorous, trifling old fellow, that would be always creeping along shore, and taking in our sails when it blowed but a capful of wind. The men used to call him an old bumboat woman, and swore he always sweated at sight of Mother Shipton's chickens.[21] I could have put up with his caution; but I found the poor old fellow's brain was but very ill-timbered. Instead of steering in a direct course to the Westward before the wind, he always insisted on going North-about, and had a particular pleasure in loitering away our time, with the expence of wear and tear, victualling, and mens Wages, in tacking to and fro in the German ocean.

At first, I was so unskilled in navigation, that I did not know we were on a wrong track, until I was undeceived by Will Timoneer,[22] one of our hands aboard, who coming upon the quarter-deck, began to abuse the master by the name of Goody Tripe, and declared, that if we did not alter our course, we should in less than two glasses[23] be bump ashore at the mouth of the Weser.[24] This Will Timoneer was never counted a thorough seaman, though he was rated able, and at this juncture acted as one of the boatswain's drivers. He could hollow so loud as to hail at the distance of half a league: he was well stowed with gum, and would hold you jaw with e'er a fisher-woman at Billingsgate. Besides, he had got the trim of all the scrappers and scrubbers on board, who danced to his whistle whenever he piped, and now followed in his wake to prefer his complaint against the master.

I consulted the officers, who acknowledged that the complaint was justly founded; and removing old Tripe from the helm, I put it into the hands of Will Timoneer, who was immediately saluted with three cheers by the crew at his back. Well, Sir, our new pilot immediately clapped the helm a lee,[25] put about ship, and hoisting all our canvas, began to spank it away to the Westward with a flowing sail. We got happily down the channel, took our departure from the lizard,[26] and losing sight of land, proceeded, as I thought, in a fair way to the coast of North America. In ten days we made land, to my great astonishment. I thought surely we had discovered some unknown island, or at least committed some great mistake in our reckoning. I ordered our mate to prepare his quadrant, to take an observation at noon; I set people at work to overhaul the logline, and desired that the lead might be hove[27] with all expedition.

All this time, Will Timoneer betrayed no symptom of surprize, but kept the head of the Ship to the land, whistling all the while with great indifference. In an hour's sail, I could plainly perceive the treading of the coast, and running up to the wheel, "Will Timoneer (cried I) Lord let me never see an end of the voyage, if that there land does not look for all the world like the mouth of the Weser!" Will shifting his quid from one cheek to the other, replied with great deliberation, "The mouth of the Weser it is, sure enough." I then began to upbraid him for deceiving me, and reminded him of his abusing Goody Tripe, as well as of his engaging to steer another course. "Damn your eyes (said he) did not you see as how I changed the course? Tripe steered to the North-east, and I steered to the North-west; and both reached the mouth of the Weser. He crept along shore like a smuggler, and I kept the open sea with all our canvas spread like a man of war. Here we are, and here we shall come to an anchor." — So saying, he ordered the sails to be taken in, and let go our best bower[28] in a very dangerous riding. The Officers, and all the old seamen stood with their arms a-kimbo, and the rest of the crew obeyed his orders without further question. For my own part, I lost all authority on board, and became a cypher in my own ship.[29]

Well, Sir, here we continued tilting among rocks, mispending our time, consuming our provision, making ducks and drakes of our broad pieces, and expending our ammunition in shooting sea-mews. At length, Will one day took it in his head to slip our cable, and run further in shore, till we found ourselves embayed. As the safety of our ship and all our lives were now at stake, I ventured to remonstrate against his proceedings, and asked him in the name of God, what he intended to do? "Why, look you, (said he, pointing to a narrow channel between two rocks) I propose to steer thro' that strait, and then we shall be able to weather the head-land." I begged him for the love of God, to desist from such a rash undertaking; and offered to treble his wages, if he would order the sails to be backed, and let go the stream-anchor. All the officers and old mariners joined in the same supplication. "I'll be damn'd if I do! (cried the inflexible barbarian) I'll either go my own way to work, or the devil may take the helm for me." [30]

By this time our danger was grown so imminent, that I looked for nothing but shipwreck, and began to prepare for the worst, while Timoneer quitting the helm, thrust his hands in his side-pockets, and whistled the Black-joke,[31] as if he had been at a hop in Rotherhithe.[32] At this juncture, one of the quarter-masters, a quiet sober fellow, whose name was Jack North,[33] leped upon the quarter-deck, and seized the tiller. The ship was now too far advanced either to wear or tack, so that he was obliged to steer directly into the strait, thro' which he brought her safe into the open sea, without the least danger to her walls or bottom. He did more — Under his Pilotage the ship performed her voyage happily, and is now brought to her moorings in a safe harbour — I forgave Will Timoneer for the injury he had done me; and as the fellow began to fail in his constitution, procured a pension for him from the chest at Chatham.[34] He relished the pension, but instead of thanking his benefactor, he once had the impudence to spit in my face, and ever since, he and all the ragamuffins of the ship, the lubbers, the scrubbers, and the scrappers, headed by Captain Swabber, and Jack i'the bread-room,[35] have been constantly employed in throwing dirt at me and Jack North, as often as we appear in public. Such is the gratitude of Will Timoneer the pensioner. — I leave the public to judge between me and him, and am,

SIR,
Your sincere friend,
AUGUSTUS ALBION.[36]

APPENDIX
DOUBTFUL ATTRIBUTIONS

ODE ADDRESSED TO THE LATE GEN. WOLFE, WRITTEN AFTER THE REDUCTION OF LOUISBOURG.[1]

I.

Sprung from an ancient, honour'd race,
Whom courage, fame and candor grace,
Accept, O Wolfe! th' exulting lay,
That hails thy valour's dawning ray.
When such atchievements gild thy morn,
What trophies shall thy noon adorn?

II.

Some deaf to the shrill trump of fame,
In sloth exhaust their youthful flame:
Some, rous'd at morn, the stag pursue;
And from the thicket sweep the dew;
While others tempt for wealth alone,
The frozen and the fervid zone.

III.

A fairer meed thy virtue charms:
A nobler flame thy bosom warms:
To wake again the British soul;
Thy country's bolts again to roll;
With vengeance whelm her haughty foe;
And with fresh conquests wreathe her brow.

IV.

Convuls'd by the tremend'ous shock,
Th' embattled tow'r and rifted rock
Shook on America's affrighted strand,
When havock rag'd at thy command;

When on the Gaul destruction broke
In horrid peals from fire and smoke.

V.

May triumphs still attend thine arm,
And Britain's cause thy genius warm;
While Drake's or Howard's mighty soul
Guides thy career to glory's goal;
The Muse shall them on bolder wing,
Essay thy bright exploits to sing.

THE JUNTO.[1]

A Council was lately assembled at Marli,
Of war and of peace to debate and to parley:
The nymph *Pompadour* took the uppermost seat,
And *Lewis the Gentle* sat down at her feet.
There was hoary *Belleisle*, grave, solemn and slow,
Soubize the polite, and pert *Richlieu* the beau;
Silhouette, in resources of cash a dear jewel,
The wary *Contades*, the choleric *Choiseuil:*
In order to season this politic olio,
They added the pepper of hot-headed *Broglio.*
Old Nestor declar'd for a congress and peace,
And the hint was espous'd by *Contades* and *Soubize:*
Silhouette frankly own'd his budget exhausted:
But *Choiseuil* still rav'd, and *Richlieu* still boasted.
Said *Lewis*, "My Lords, we would willingly learn
What funds you can fix, or what prospects discern
For maintaining or bringing this war to conclusion,
So productive of misery, shame, and confusion.
Our commerce is ruin'd; our money is flown;
Our armies are routed; our settlements gone.
Our fleets have sustain'd a most terrible blow,
In the rout of *Conflans*, and the fate of *Thurot:*
Our troops will no longer their leaders obey,
When divested of cloathing, provision, and pay:
What motive, then say, will their courage excite,

Against those who have beat them so often, to fight?"
"A motive (cry'd *Broglio*) I'd cherish with care:
Starv'd, naked, and beaten, they'll fight in despair."

MORNING, IN SPRING, A FRAGMENT.[1]

Grey morn ascends the eastern vault of Heav'n
With feather'd foot. Led by the jolly hours
That circling dance around his golden car,
See Phœbus rise, and warm effulgence spread.
The mountain top now shines with orient gold.
The face of Nature feels the kindling heat,
And laughing landscapes own the fertile god.
The dew-drop glitters through the verdant plain
With short liv'd radiance—soon to be exhal'd.
Hence grandeur learn, how fugitive thy pomp!
The garden's blossoms scent the vernal air:
On ev'ry spray the feather'd choir exult
In the soft blessings of the blooming spring;
And the sweet song from ecchoing hill and dale,
From dale to hill resounds the Deity's praise;
That power which spoke creation into life.
Now labour bursting from the bands of sleep,
Hies to the field with industry the boor,
And ploughs the stubborn glebe.

A PASTORAL BALLAD.[1]

1.

Where the elm-trees form a grove,
Sacred to the god of love;
Where the linnets chearful strain
Hails me to my lovely *Anne:*

2.

There the lonely day I mourn,
Waiting for my Love's return;

Where noon's heat the Zephyrs fan,
There I sing of lovely *Anne*.

3.
On yonder knole I oft recline,
Where spring the wood-rose and the bine;
There I sigh! Assist me *Pan*,
While I sing of lovely *Anne*.

4.
Or along the river's side,
Where the silver fishes glide,
There, Oh Cupid! first began
My passion for the lovely *Anne*.

5.
My fair's approach afar I see,
She bends her willing steps to me;
With love's swiftest foot I ran,
Joyful to meet my lovely *Anne*.

ON SIGNIOR TENDUCCI'S SINGING JUBAL'S LYRE.
BY A PRISONER IN THE KING'S BENCH.[1]

ORPHEUS, as fools believe and bards invent,
Taught rocks to dance, and Pluto to relent.
But sure as JUBAL'S LYRE Tenducci sings,
And wakes to symphony the trembling strings;
As the sweet notes now rise, now die away,
A PLAINTIFF might ev'n hear his rage away!
A voice so strong, yet soft, so soft, yet clear,
With magic pow'r would charm his savage ear;
Calm all his angry passions into rest,
And into pity melt his frozen breast!

NOTES TO THE TEXTS

Poems

A NEW SONG
Set by Mr. Oswald, the Words by Mr. Smollet

1. Title: This poem, Smollett's earliest printed work, appeared in a collection of songs entitled *Universal Harmony*, published by John Newbery in 1745, with music by the Scottish composer James Oswald, who also set *The Tears of Scotland* (and others of Smollett's poems) to music. Another setting of "A New Song" was published by Philip Hayes, Professor of Music at Oxford, in 1795. See Otto Erich Deutsch, "Poetry Preserved in Music: Bibliographical Notes on Smollett and Oswald, Handel, and Haydn," *Modern Language Notes* 63 (1948): 74–75; see also Lewis M. Knapp, "Smollett's Verses and Their Musical Settings in the Eighteenth Century," *Modern Language Notes* 46 (1931): 224–32. A three-stanza version of this poem appears in *Roderick Random*, chapter 40, under the title "On Celia playing on the harpsichord and singing"; this version is reprinted below, in the textual commentary, pp. 553–54.

2. "Sappho": Sappho, the Greek poet (fl. c. 600 B.C.), renowned since antiquity for her simple but passionate verses.

3. "To dash on rocks the tender breast": Unsupported tradition holds that, because her love for the youth Phaon was unrequited, Sappho drowned herself by leaping into the sea from a cliff on the Isle of Leucas. The best-known version of the tradition is Ovid's "Sappho to Phaon" in his *Heroides*. Smollett may be alluding to this work in the preceding lines.

THE TEARS OF SCOTLAND

1. "Mourn, hapless CALEDONIA, mourn / Thy banish'd peace": A similar expression is uttered by Angus when he hears of the king's murder in Smollett's *The Regicide*: "Weep, *Caledonia*, weep! — thy Peace is slain" (5.6, p. 163). Both utterances (and the contexts in which they occur) may have been influenced by Smollett's memory of Macduff's lament over the sufferings of his native land in *Macbeth*, and by such outcries from Macduff as "Bleed, bleed poor country" (4.3.31) or "O Scotland, Scotland!" (4.3.100). In succeeding stanzas of Smollett's poem (particularly stanza 2), one may hear echoes in imagery, tone, and situation of two other passages in Macduff's lament: "Each new morn, / New widows howl, new orphans cry, new sorrows / Strike heaven on the face" (4.3.4–6), and "Alas poor country, / . . . Where sighs, and groans, and shrieks that rent the air / Are made, not marked" (4.3.164, 168–69).

2. "hospitable roofs": One of the more favorable qualities attributed to the Scots was their hospitality. Defoe, in his *Tour*, assured his readers that "they would always meet with good Treatment and great Hospitality" among the Highland chiefs (*Tour Thro' the Whole Island of Great Britain*, ed. G. D. H. Cole [London: Cass, 1968], 1:828). In *Present State*, 1:432, Smollett says of the people of the Hebrides that they were "remarkably hospitable to strangers, whom they cultivate even with a religious veneration." In *Humphry Clinker*, Matthew Bramble praises the Scots for extending to him "more kindness, hospitality, and rational entertainment, in a few weeks, than ever I received in any other country during the whole course of my life" (Matthew Bramble to Dr. Lewis, Edinburgh, August 8, p. 225).

3. "wanton": Johnson, *Dictionary*, defines *wanton* as "frolicksome; gay; sportive; airy." *OED* observes that this denotation, usually applied to young animals, is chiefly poetic, and quotes the phrase "wanton flocks" both from *The Tears of Scotland* and from line 74 of Addison's translation (1694) of the third ode of the third book of Horace's odes. In a passage of this ode bearing some similarity to Smollett's description of the ravaging of Scotland, Horace describes the desolation of Troy.

4. "phantoms of the slain": Smollett's imagery and rhyme are both reminiscent of John Dryden's *Alexander's Feast* (1697), lines 138–40:

> These are Grecian ghosts, that in battle were slain,
> And unburied remain
> Inglorious on the plain.

Smollett says nothing of unburied Scottish warriors, but his lines, like those of Dryden, may allude to the Grecian belief that the ghosts of the dead could not rest while their corpses remained unburied.

5. "sons, against their fathers stood": No specific incidents of fathers fighting against sons seem to have found their way into the printed accounts of the battle of Culloden, but there are several examples of clans whose loyalty was split by the conflict, and one of Prince Charles's problems was the wavering loyalties and individual defections of those whom he counted on. Renegade Scots were among Cumberland's forces engaging in the brutal aftermath of the battle. Probably Smollett is using these lines to remark on the division of loyalties that did wrench Scotland apart during the 'Forty-Five.

ADVICE: A SATIRE

1. Epigraph: Juvenal *Satires* 2.12–13, 121:

> To see't [the podex] so sleek and trimm'd the Surgeon smiles
> And scarcely can for laughing launce the Piles.
>
> . . . .
>
> O Peers of Rome! need these stupendious Times
> A Censer or Aruspex for such Crimes?
>
> Trans. Nahum Tate (1693)

2. "Enough, enough": This abrupt beginning, with its tone of exasperation, recalls the opening line of Alexander Pope's *Epistle to Dr. Arbuthnot* (1735): "Shut, shut the door, good *John*! fatigu'd I said."

3. "*H*——": In first edition, H——me, suggesting perhaps Holme or Hulme, but the exact person remains unidentified.

4. "Not *C—pe* fly swifter": Sir John Cope (d. 1760) had been commander in chief in Scotland when Prince Charles Edward Stuart landed there in 1745. An early-morning attack by the rebels at Prestonpans on 21 September 1745 had routed Cope's troops and opened the way for Charles's invasion of England. About the time *Advice* was published (August 1746), a military board was examining the charges of cowardice and incompetence leveled at Cope because of the Preston-pans defeat. See below, n. 12, and *Reproof*, n. 5. The satiric print reproduced here, "A Race from Preston Pans to Berwick," mocks Cope for his flight and alleged cowardice. Smollett's frequent practice in both *Advice* and *Reproof* is to "gut" the names of actual people by substituting dashes for letters, as he does here with the name of Cope; the practice was common among satirists and political writers of the day. The posthumous collected edition of *Plays and Poems Written by T. Smollett, M.D.* (London, 1777) fills in the dashes to many of the gutted names in *Advice* and *Reproof*; this edition, the very first such collection of works by Smollett, has been used as a source by the present editor.

5. "sage *N——c——tle*": Thomas Pelham-Holles, duke of Newcastle (1693–1768), was one of the best-known political figures of the day. He held various offices throughout the tenure of Sir Robert Walpole as first minister, 1721–42. After Walpole's downfall in 1742, Newcastle and his brother, Henry Pelham, had increased their power and were in 1746 leaders of the administration. Pompous and ever maneuvering for power and place, Newcastle was well known for the lavishness of his entertainments. He appears, clinging to his fading importance, in the London scenes of *Humphry Clinker* (Jery Melford to Sir Watkin Phillips, London, June 2, pp. 96–97, and London, June 5, pp. 107–11).

6. "*Gr—ft—n* . . . throne": Charles Fitzroy, second duke of Grafton (1690-1757), was appointed lord chamberlain of the household in 1724, a position that was not administratively important but that kept him in the inner circles of court life and permitted him to nominate the poet laureate. He served both George I and George II until his death. The ironic allusion to Atlas, the Titan of Greek mythology who held the heavens on his shoulders, emphasizes Grafton's insignificance. His contemporary reputation is indicated by Lord Waldegrave's remark: "Grafton usually turned politics into ridicule, had never applied himself to business, and as to books was totally illiterate; yet from long observation and great natural sagacity he became the ablest courtier of his time"; see *The Complete Peerage* (London: St Catherine Press, 1926), 6:45.

7. "*C—lly C—bb—r*, Esq": Colley Cibber (1671–1757) became poet laureate in 1730, near the end of his highly successful career as actor, playwright, and theatrical manager. His uninspired official poetry and the publication of his lively but brash

and disorganized *Apology for the Life of Colley Cibber* (1740) occasioned a good deal of witty and malicious comment on his tastelessness and opportunism. The best-known sneers at Cibber are Fielding's various comments in *Joseph Andrews* (1742) and Pope's enthronement of him as monarch of the kingdom of Dulness in the final version of *The Dunciad* (1743).

8. "*Gr—nv—le* and *B—th*": John Carteret, Earl Granville (1690–1763), and William Pulteney, earl of Bath (1684–1764), had tried to form an administration in February 1746. The failure of this administration to last more than four days had brought much public scorn upon them. Both men had been active in the opposition to Walpole, but Pulteney had lost prestige by his acceptance of a title and Carteret had become unpopular because of his arrogance while leader of the "Drunken Administration" that followed Walpole's downfall. The phrase "sober dignity" in Smollett's next line may allude to the nickname of the Carteret administration. In *Complete History*, 4:620, Smollett again speaks very harshly of Bath's dereliction: "the sensible part of mankind will always reflect with amazement upon the conduct of a man, who seeing himself idolized by his fellow-citizens, as the first and firmest patriot of the kingdom, . . . could give up all his popularity and incur the contempt or detestation of mankind, for the wretched consideration of an empty title."

9. "Or *P—t* . . . unsung": William Pitt (1708–78) was an active mover in the shifting of administrations following Walpole's downfall. Pitt had long resisted support of the king's Hanoverian interests, but in February 1746, after his appointment as vice-treasurer of Ireland, he defended appropriations for Hanoverian troops, declaring in Parliament that he did so with an "unembarrassed countenance." This phrase and his altered position immediately raised a spate of lampoons against him, of which Smollett's "unshaken *Abdiel*" is an ironic echo. On the other hand, as paymaster general of the forces, an office he received in May 1746, Pitt refused to follow the customary practice of using the official monies at his disposal for personal financial gain. Although *Advice* was written before Pitt's policy was likely to have been fully recognized, this preservation of his integrity in the midst of corruption may lend a tinge of ambiguity to Smollett's footnote for this line. The passage quoted in the footnote, not quite verbatim, is from *Paradise Lost* 5.898–99. For Smollett's later attitudes toward Pitt, sometimes approving and sometimes critical, see Lewis M. Knapp, "Smollett and the Elder Pitt," *Modern Language Notes* 59 (1944): 250–57; see also below, introduction to the *Briton*, (pp. 228–29).

10. "*Ch—ly*": George Cholmondeley, third earl of Cholmondeley (1703–70), owed his obtaining a succession of military and political positions chiefly to the fact that he married Mary Walpole, Sir Robert's daughter, in 1723. His brother-in-law, Horace Walpole, wrote that he was "a vain, empty man, shoved up too high by his father-in-law Sir Robert Walpole, and fallen into contempt and obscurity by his own extravagance and insufficiency"; see Walpole, *Memoirs*, 1:114–15. Cholmondeley appears as one of the admirers of the narrator of "The Memoirs of

a Lady of Quality" in *Peregrine Pickle*, chapter 88, where he provides an elegant entertainment for her and a small group of friends.

11. "*Y——nge*": Sir William Yonge (1693–1775), a consistent follower of Sir Robert Walpole, incurred one of the worst reputations among the place-hunters associated with the powerful first minister. Lord Hervey gives the clue to Smollett's treatment of him: "Without having done anything I know of remarkably profligate . . . his name was proverbially used to express anything pitiful, corrupt, and contemptible. It is true he was a great liar, but rather a mean than a vicious one" (*Memoirs of the Reign of George II*, ed. J. W. Croker [London, 1884], 1:47–48). Pope comments satirically on Yonge in *An Epistle to Dr. Arbuthnot* (line 280) and *Epilogue to the Satires I* (lines 13, 68); Sir Billy, in *An Essay on Man* (4.278), may also be intended to represent Yonge. Yonge appears briefly as a "man of professed gallantry" in "The Memoirs of a Lady of Quality" in *Peregrine Pickle*, chapter 88.

12. "The person here meant": The phenomenon mentioned in Smollett's footnote remains unidentified. But C—— is very likely Sir John Cope, already mentioned disparagingly in line 8. The meter of line 29 calls for a one-syllable word; the first edition includes a couplet after line 112 (deleted in subsequent printings) naming C—pe last in a trio of pederasts—the name is certain, as it must rhyme with *grope*: "Such is the fate of F—nt—n, Sh—lly, C—pe; / For swinish bliss the filthy jakes to grope." There can be little doubt that Smollett wanted to blacken Cope's name with a charge of homosexuality. Smollett may have believed that Cope's imputed cowardice at Prestonpans suggested an effeminacy that supported the charge. The public outcry against Cope encouraged accusations that he was more courtier than warrior. Indeed, one pamphlet concluded "that he who neglects his Business, to wait on Nods and Smiles, is fitter to be Pimp to a Bawdy-House, than to command Fleets and Armies" (*An Enquiry into the Conduct of G——l C—pe* [London, 1745], 24). Smollett may easily have extended such defamatory statements to provide an unsavory explanation of why Cope had achieved a position that he had now allegedly shown himself unfit to hold. Smollett's imagination on other occasions dwelled on the idea that homosexuality might be a key to unwarranted promotion. He raised this issue twice in *Roderick Random* through his portraits of Captain Whiffle (chapters 34–35) and Earl Strutwell (chapter 51); Whiffle, in a phrase echoing the final words of this footnote to *Advice*, is accused of sexual practices "not fit to be named" (chapter 35).

13. "Th' Hesperian dragon": Ladon, the hundred-headed serpent set by Hera to guard the golden apples of the Hesperides. Securing some of the closely guarded fruit was one of the labors of Hercules.

14. "fell": "Fierce, savage; cruel, ruthless" (*OED*). "Fierce and fell" appears to have been a common alliterative pairing.

15. "the gaunt, growling janitor of hell": Cerberus, the many-headed dog who guarded the entrance to the realm of Hades.

16. "*Atticus*": One of Pope's best-known satiric portraits is that of Atticus in *An Epistle*

to Dr. Arbuthnot, lines 193–214. Using lines that Pope had originally applied to Joseph Addison, the portrait limns a jealously arrogant literary monarch. Smollett uses the name for its connotation of a proud, rarely accessible, and secretly malicious patron of struggling literary merit.

17. "in clouded Majesty": Pope, *The Dunciad* 1.45: "In clouded Majesty here Dulness shone." Pope's line, in turn, echoes Milton, *Paradise Lost* 4.605–6: "The Moon / Rising in clouded Majesty." The image may be intended also to suggest the figure of Milton's Satan and his lost brightness.

18. "the venal tribe": Pope's epithet, in *Epilogue to the Satires I*, line 31, for those whom Walpole bribed to win their support.

19. "L—*km*—*n*'s fate": John Lockman (1698–1771), a minor translator, had also tried his hand at occasional poetry, but without much success; see *Reproof*, line 108 and n. 13.

20. "The lower still . . . the higher": Perhaps echoing and reversing Alexander Pope, *The Dunciad* 2.290: "Who but to sink the deeper, rose the higher."

21. "Th' ascent is easy": Milton, *Paradise Lost* 2.81: Moloch's assertion that "The ascent is easy then." Perhaps both Milton and Smollett echo Virgil's "*facilis decensus Averno*," *Aeneid* 6.126, rendered in Dryden's translation (1697) as "Smooth the descent, and easy is the way."

22. "pathic": "A man or boy upon whom sodomy is practised" (*OED*).

23. "a truncheon and a star": The truncheon here is the staff or baton symbolic of high military office; the star is part of the insignia of knighthood, particularly the Order of the Garter.

24. "a L—*d*": Evidently *Lloyd*, in order to rhyme with *pride*, but not further identified.

25. "This child of dirt": Pope uses the expression "This painted Child of Dirt" at the beginning of his portrait of Sporus in *An Epistle to Dr. Arbuthnot*, line 310.

26. "kennels": As used here, *kennel* denotes "the surface drain of a street; the gutter" (*OED*), although there may be wordplay with the term for a doghouse.

27. "Accomplish'd W—*n*": Not identified. The 1777 collected edition of Smollett's *Plays and Poems* adds new information or commentary to several of Smollett's notes for *Advice* and *Reproof*, and in this instance observes that Warren was "commonly called Brush Warren, from having been a shoeblack: it is said he was kept by both sexes at one time." The additional material from the 1777 edition has been omitted from the present texts because it is not authorial, but it is cited and quoted, as here, in annotations.

28. "Eternal infamy . . . manhood stains": These four lines are quoted by Roderick to Earl Strutwell, his would-be seducer, in chapter 51 of *Roderick Random*.

29. "*Pollio*": Perhaps used here as merely a convenient classical name with no further connotation. Gaius Asinius Pollio (76 B.C.–A.D. 4), the best-known bearer of the name in antiquity, was a statesman, orator, rather stern critic, and patron at one time of Horace and Virgil. There is a tradition that he is Iollas of Virgil's

second pastoral and thus Corydon's (Virgil's) rival for the love of the youth Alexis. Smollett's name may also have connection with the Pollio of book 4 of *The Dunciad*. Pope's Pollio is the host of the antiquary Annius, who dines with Pollio to help promote the evacuation of the coins he has swallowed. Smollett may have found homosexual implications in lines 347–50 and 387–96.

30. "indecent grotto . . . dome": The word *dome*, meaning "a house, a home; a stately building" (*OED*), here seems to refer to particular places known as resorts for homosexual activity, but their identity has not been established. See below, n. 37. Smollett may also have been creating a double entendre, using the words *grotto* and *dome* as anatomical metaphors.

31. "Caitiff's": The word *caitiff* is defined by *OED* as "Expressing contempt, and often involving strong moral disapprobation: A base, mean, despicable 'wretch,' a villain."

32. "*Ch——n*": Possibly an allusion to Sir John Chardin (1643–1712), a French traveler and well-to-do jeweler who took up residence in England and was knighted by Charles II in 1681. No evidence has been found to connect him with the practice of pederasty. *DNB* mentions a bachelor son, also named John, who was created a baronet in 1720.

33. "The taste of *Maro* and *Anacreon*": The tradition of Maro's (*i.e.*, Virgil's) pederasty can be traced to Suetonius *De Poetis* "Vita Vergili" 9 (c. A.D. 120), which mentions two special favorites, Cebes and Alexander. Alexis, the beautiful youth whom Corydon longs for in Virgil's second pastoral, is supposedly Alexander, and Corydon's passion is thus thought to express Virgil's own. An epigram in the *Greek Anthology* 7.24, attributed (probably wrongly) to Simonides, names Megisteus and Smerdies as two youths beloved of Anacreon, the Greek lyric poet of the sixth century B.C. Both names occur in the fragments of Anacreon's verse.

34. "*Flaccus*": Flaccus is the cognomen of Horace. The only possible allusion to pederasty in Horace occurs in the first ode of book 4 of his *Odes*, where the poet speaks in amorous terms of the youth Ligurinus. The youth is apostrophized also in the tenth ode of book 4, but not necessarily with any homosexual implications.

35. "appetence": "The action of seeking for or longing after" (*OED*).

36. "*Isis*": A name for the Thames in the vicinity of Oxford.

37. "particularly at one place": The place alluded to in this note may be Parson's Pleasure, in earlier times also called Patten's Pleasure, a spot on the Cherwell (tributary to the Thames near Oxford) long known as a resort for male nude swimming and bathing.

38. "While Dullness . . . the church": The personification of Dulness suggests the mighty goddess of that name in *The Dunciad*, who, by promoting and protecting her dunces, extends her realm throughout the world. The incident of Shem and Japheth's covering their father Noah's nakedness, alluded to in Smollett's note for this line, is recorded in Genesis 9:23.

39. "*Bubo*": Pope used *Bubo*, Latin for owl, as the name for a dunce or tasteless rogue

in at least four different works during the latter part of his career: *An Epistle to Dr. Arbuthnot, Epistle to Burlington, The Second Satire of the Second Book of Horace,* and *Epilogue to the Satires I. Bubo* was also a medical term for a swelling in the groin or armpits. Although recognized as a symptom of the bubonic plague, it may also have been associated with venereal disease. Pope, and probably Smollett, seem to have intended Bubo to represent George Bubb Dodington, created Baron Melcombe in 1761 (1691–1762). As a member of Parliament and occasional minister, Dodington switched his political allegiance a number of times in currying the favor of the great, displaying the kind of sycophancy that was especially grating to Smollett. Dodington had also assumed the role of a Maecenas, patronizing a number of important literary figures such as Edward Young, James Thomson, and Henry Fielding, as well as several hacks. He had a reputation for undiscriminating taste and, at times, coarseness. His wife had been regarded as his mistress until he revealed in 1742 that they had been married for seventeen years.

40. "catamite": "A boy kept for unnatural purposes" (*OED*).

41. "no mortal credits *Curio's* word": Caius Scribonius Curio was said to have been bribed to support Julius Caesar. Mark Akenside, in his *Epistle to Curio* (1744), had attacked William Pulteney by likening his acceptance of a peerage to Curio's betrayal of liberty. Smollett probably also intended to represent Pulteney; his charge of deceitfulness echoes Akenside's lines 317–18:

> Till own'd their Guide and trusted with their Pow'r
> He mock'd their Hopes in one decisive Hour.

42. "He counts . . . stains he bears": Smollett echoes line 221 of Pope's *Epilogue to the Satires II*: "That counts your Beauties only by your Stains."

43. "An hundred footsteps . . . his hall": This and the several lines following are reminiscent of the ostentation and false taste found at Timon's villa as described in Pope's *Epistle to Burlington* (1731). One may note in particular the verbal echoes from lines 151–52, 155–56:

> But hark! the chiming Clocks to dinner call;
> A hundred footsteps scrape the marble Hall:
>
> . . . .
>
> Is this a dinner? this a Genial room?
> No, 'tis a Temple, and a Hecatomb.

44. "Hecatombs": A hecatomb is "a great sacrifice (properly a hundred oxen) among the ancient Greeks and Romans" (*OED*).

45. "those who languish . . . shade": The notion of merit neglected aroused Smollett to indignation throughout his life. The issue was very personal, as is clear from a letter to his friend John Moore, written in 1755: "I live in the shade of obscurity, neglecting and neglected, and spend my vacant hours among a Set of honest, phlegmatic Englishmen whom I cultivate for their Integrity of Heart and Simplicity of Manners" (*Letters*, 42).

46. "sharp": "To play the sharper," that is, to be a cheat or fraudulent gamester (*OED*).

47. *"Dea Bona"*: Dea Bona, the Good Goddess (also known as Fauna), was a Roman goddess of fertility worshiped exclusively by women. Juvenal, in *Satires* 6.314–41, gives a graphic depiction of the lewdness into which her worship had supposedly degenerated in his day.

48. "Again shall *Handel* . . . laurel'd brow": The years from 1744 to 1746 marked one of the low periods in the career and popularity of George Frederick Handel (1685–1759). Performances of various oratorios during this period had been poorly received and had even been the occasion of noisy demonstrations, and Handel suffered from both ill health and financial embarrassment. Smollett's forecast of better days for the musician was realized in 1747, when the production of *Judas Maccabeus*, commemorating Culloden, helped to turn the tide of Handel's fortunes. A year or two later, Smollett began his collaboration with Handel on *Alceste*, the musical stage piece that John Rich engaged them to write but that was never produced.

49. *"Frasi's"*: Giulia Frasi was an Italian opera singer who began her London career around 1742. Her name appears regularly in the casts of the operas produced at the King's Opera House during 1746; thus Smollett could easily have heard her perform.

50. "R——*l* . . . his dream": A reference to one Russell, who, in the spring of 1745, had presented a puppet show, burlesquing Italian opera, as subscription entertainment. Soon afterward he was confined for debt in Newgate and allegedly died sometime later in the Fleet Prison. Horace Walpole's comments on the reported dullness of Russell's entertainment can be found in his letter to Sir Horace Mann of 29 March 1745 (Walpole, *Correspondence*, 19:28). The expanded note in the 1777 *Plays and Poems* begins by identifying Russell as "A famous mimic and singer" and ends with the information that he "died in the utmost misery."

51. "Rather in garret . . . town alarm": It is to such Grub Street productions, suited to the taste of the mob, that the neglected talent of Melopoyn must turn in *Roderick Random*: "I have made many a good meal upon a monster; a rape has often afforded me great satisfaction; but a murder, well-timed, was my never-failing resource" (chapter 62).

52. "G——*ie*": William Guthrie (1708–70), a Scotsman who settled in London in 1730 and by the 1740s was doing well for himself as a political writer. In the first years following the downfall of Sir Robert Walpole he conducted a newspaper, *Old England; or, the Constitutional Journal*, which the government found serviceable enough to justify granting him, in 1745, a pension of two hundred pounds a year.

53. "the envious adder . . . file": One of Aesop's fables tells of the snake who began licking a file. When his own blood appeared on the file, he thought he had wounded it and licked it more vigorously than ever.

54. *"cent. per cent."*: One hundred percent interest.

55. "quack": As a trained surgeon, Smollett was always alert to possible medical quackery and liked to take swipes at pretentious physicians. See *Reproof*, n. 41.

56. "mumbling": The act of biting "softly, as with toothless gums" (*OED*).

57. "General . . . heat of the day": In the 1777 *Plays and Poems*, this note is expanded at the very end to include reference to "the Hanoverian general, in the battle of Dettingen." Smollett seems clearly to have had in mind the controversy that arose in published accounts of the Battle of Dettingen (27 June 1743), some of which catered to English prejudice by implying that the king's Hanoverian troops, led by Baron Ilten, had not contributed their share to the victory. M. Dorothy George, *English Political Caricature to 1792* (Oxford: Clarendon Press, 1959), 94, discusses two satiric prints of the day whose subject is *The H——v——n Confectioner General* and whose theme is: "the English fight, and fast—Hanoverians rest, and feast." George identifies the satiric figure of these prints as Ilten, "who was accused of preventing the Guards from following up the victory."

58. "ribbon": "The badge of an order of knighthood" (*OED*).

59. "quit th' unhospitable shore": Smollett alludes to the satiric commonplace of longing—or deciding—to leave the corrupt, inhospitable city. Its locus classicus is Juvenal's third satire, which Samuel Johnson imitated in *London* (1738).

REPROOF: A SATIRE

1. Epigraph: Juvenal, *Satires* 13.240–42.
   > What Sinners finish where they first begin?
   > And with one Crime content their Lust to Sin?
   > Trans. Thomas Creech (1693)

2. "what Dæmon thunders at the gate?": Like the opening lines of *Advice*, these lines are reminiscent of the exasperated tone at the beginning of Pope's *Epistle to Dr. Arbuthnot*. One may note in particular lines 7–8 of Pope's poem:
   > What Walls can guard me, or what Shades can hide?
   > They pierce my Thickets, thro' my Grot they glide.

3. "bubbled": Fooled or cheated (*OED*).

4. "W——ms—n": A reference to one Williamson, a deputy lieutenant governor of the Tower of London. When Lord Balmerino, one of the rebel Scottish lords, was brought to execution on 18 August 1746, he complained particularly of Williamson's ill usage of him.

5. "The vanquish'd knight": Sir John Cope. See *Advice*, nn. 4, 12. A board of general officers was appointed in September 1746 to inquire into the conduct of Cope and others during the battle of Prestonpans. The board's report cleared Cope of any blame in the English defeat, concluding that "the misfortune on the day of action was owing to the shameful behaviour of the private men, and not to any misconduct or misbehaviour of Sir John Cope" (*Gentleman's Magazine* 16 [November 1746]: 592–93).

6. "pug": A "*quasi*-proper name of an ape" (*OED*).

7. "the horned race": In this reference to horned creatures, Smollett may be playing on the old joke of horns as a sign of the cuckold.

8. "wether": A male sheep, or ram; used specifically with reference to a castrated ram (*OED*).

9. "a grave, hoary stag": The board that inquired into the conduct of Cope consisted of four generals plus Field Marshal George Wade (1673–1748) as president. Wade, in his seventies at the time, had himself commanded an army that sought to engage the Scottish rebels, but before the decisive battle at Culloden he had yielded command to Cumberland.

10. "*Certes*": L. Of a truth, assuredly.

11. "Th' *Aonian* grove": Aonia is the region of ancient Greece where Mount Helicon, home of Apollo and the Muses, was located.

12. "To crop . . . WILLIAM's head": George II's younger son, William, duke of Cumberland (1721–65), became a national hero after his victory over the Jacobite rebels at Culloden in April 1746. As is clear from *The Tears of Scotland*, Smollett was appalled by the slaughter of the battle and its aftermath and shared the minority opinion that considered Cumberland to be the butcher of the Scots. See also the apparently ironic treatment of Cumberland in *Humphry Clinker*, Jery Melford to Sir Watkin Phillips, London, June 2, p. 95.

13. "*L—ck—n*'s ode and *H—b—y*'s song": John Lockman (see *Advice*, n. 19) had written *An Ode, on the Crushing of the Rebellion . . . To His Royal Highness the Duke* (1746), in which William, "Chieftain in Freedom's Cause," is highly extolled. Another piece occasioned by the victory at Culloden was Sir Charles Hanbury Williams's *Ode to the Right Honourable Stephen Poyntz, Esq.* (1746), which praised Poyntz, Cumberland's governor and advisor, and hailed "Culloden's field, my glorious theme." Williams (1708–59) was a member of Parliament and a diplomat well known for his wit and satirical light verse. The Latin in Smollett's note to this line is from Horace *Ars Poetica*, line 375: "an unguent that is thick, and poppy-seeds served with Sardinian honey."

14. "*Stanhope*'s worth": Philip Stanhope, fourth earl of Chesterfield (1694–1773), became secretary of state in October 1746. He had been a leader of the opposition to Walpole in the House of Lords. A passage in *Peregrine Pickle*, chapter 94, appears to be a fictionalized account of Smollett's relations with Chesterfield and suggests that Smollett's acquaintance was courted by the nobleman "in consequence of a production which he had ushered into the world." Possibly this production was *Advice*. At any rate, in 1746 Smollett was encouraged to present the manuscript of *The Regicide* to Chesterfield, who read it and passed it on approvingly to Garrick, a bit of patronage which, although unproductive, must have influenced Smollett's favorable mention of Chesterfield here. (See Smollett's preface to *The Regicide*, p. 91 and n. 10).

15. "*Pope*'s immortal strain": Besides a passing reference in *The Dunciad*, only two brief passages in Pope's poetry mention Chesterfield: *Epilogue to the Satires II*, lines 84–85, "How can I Pult'ney, Chesterfield forget, / While *Roman* Spirit charms, and *Attic* wit"; and *One Thousand Seven Hundred and Forty*, line 25, "And C—d who speaks so well and writes." Perhaps Smollett is suggesting that the moral

excellence and taste for which he praises Chesterfield had already been fully and eloquently admired in Pope's poetry.

16. "*Barnard*'s praise": A reference to Sir John Barnard (1685–1764), respected alderman and member of Parliament, noted for his interest in humanitarian programs. In 1745 Barnard had helped to promote measures to restore confidence in the Bank of England; this was the immediate occasion of a plan to erect a statue of him on the Royal Exchange, a project completed in May 1747.

17. "a sinking land": See Pope, *An Essay on Man* 4.265: "Truths would you teach, or save a sinking land?"

18. "soaring *Cobham*": Sir Richard Temple, Viscount Cobham (1669?–1749), military leader and Whig politician, was active in the opposition to Walpole during Walpole's last years in power. Cobham was also well known for his estate at Stowe, with its elaborate gardens. Pope, in his *Epistle to Cobham* (1734), praised Cobham's love of his native country.

19. "the melting *Scot*": Daniel Mackercher, a Scottish lawyer resident in London, had championed the claim of James Annesley to be the legitimate heir of Lord Altham and therefore the legitimate earl of Angelsey. The claim, tried in 1743, created one of the most famous and controversial cases of the period. The celebrity of the case may explain why Smollett did not bother to mention Annesley in his note to this line. The note as expanded in the 1777 *Plays and Poems*, however, directly identifies the "brother in distress" as "Mr. Annesley, who claimed the Anglesea title and estate." Mackercher and the Annesley case are the basis of a long narrative in chapter 98 of *Peregrine Pickle*. See also Lillian de la Torre, "The Melting Scot: A Postscript to *Peregrine Pickle*," *English Language Notes* 10 (1972): 20–27.

20. "the scripture-injunction": Matthew 5:40: "And if any man will sue thee at the law, and take away thy coat, let him have *thy* cloak also."

21. "*G—d—n . . . L—sc—s . . . V—n—k*": Sampson Gideon (1699–1762) was a Jewish financier often called upon as an advisor in governmental financial operations. At the time of the 'Forty-Five he helped raise a loan of nearly two million pounds for the government. He was also accused of profiting greatly from the rebellion by purchasing stock during the panic that followed the Jacobite invasion. "L—sc—s" probably refers to Henry Lascelles (d. 1754) and his brother Edward, who had both been collectors of the custom in Barbados. Charges of fraudulent practices were brought against them around 1744 by Robert Dinwiddie, inspector general of customs; see Louis K. Koontz, *Robert Dinwiddie* (Glendale, Calif.: Arthur H. Clarke, 1941), 67–94. Henry Lascelles was elected to Parliament in 1745 as a supporter of the Pelhams, a fact that probably helps to explain why the inquiry into the charges never produced any clear-cut conclusion. Gerard Vanneck (d. 1750) and Joshua Vanneck (d. 1777) were brothers of Dutch origin who amassed huge fortunes and were much involved in governmental financing, underwriting government loans and placing government contracts. Pope probably was mocking Joshua as "vile Van-muck" in his *Second Epistle of the Second Book of Horace, Imitated* (1737), line 229.

22. "griping *J—p—r*": The reference is clearly to a person named Jasper, whose identity has not been traced. Knapp, 65, calls attention to an obituary notice of one "Edw. Jasper of Tower Hill, Esq; and Agent," in *Gentleman's Magazine* 19 (August 1749): 380. The expanded note to this line in the 1777 *Plays and Poems* describes the person referred to as "A man famous for buying poor seamen's tickets."

23. "the leering belle": The identity of this person has not been established.

24. "the titled whore": The preceding lines bear several similarities to the personification of vice in Pope's *Epilogue to the Satires I*, lines 141–64. Like Smollett's figure of Corruption, Pope's Vice travels in a "Triumphal car" (line 151). Pope also observes:

> But 'tis the *Fall* degrades her to a Whore;
> Let *Greatness* own her, and she's mean no more:
> Her Birth, her Beauty, Crowds and Courts confess,
> Chaste Matrons praise her, and grave Bishops bless.
> (lines 143–46)

25. "*Peter*'s obsequies": The name of Peter Walter (1664?–1746), a notorious usurer and member of Parliament, had become a virtual byword for unscrupulous accumulation of wealth. Pope alludes to Walter several times in his satiric and moral works; Swift had also helped to blacken his reputation, and he is said to have been the original of the miserly Peter Pounce in Henry Fielding's *Joseph Andrews*.

26. "bites": Sharpers or swindlers (*OED*).

27. "*Jonathan*'s": Jonathan's coffeehouse, near the Royal Exchange, had been a gathering place for brokers and speculators since the late 1660s. Sampson Gideon (see above, n. 21) was one of the leaders among those who resorted there.

28. "*White*'s": A fashionable and prestigious eighteenth-century club, located in Saint James's Street. At the beginning of the century it had been a public chocolate house, but by the 1740s it was a private social club best known for its gambling activities. Among its members were Cholmondeley, Chesterfield, Sir John Cope, Bubb Dodington, and Colley Cibber.

29. "*Codrus*": Codrus appears as a foolish and imperturbable poetaster in Pope's *Epistle to Dr. Arbuthnot* (line 85), the name apparently having been borrowed from a vaguely identified poet in Virgil's seventh pastoral. Smollett may be alluding more directly to a miserable pauper (but not necessarily a miser) named Codrus in Juvenal *Satires* 3.203–11. Pope also alluded to Juvenal's Codrus (who by some critics is identified with Virgil's poet) in *The Dunciad* 2.144.

30. "His party-coloured tutor": *Party-coloured* figuratively means "varied, diversified, 'chequered'" (*OED*). The term as used here can be taken to describe not only the footman-tutor's multicolored livery but also his muddled mind.

31. "Safe from the rod . . . her heir": These lines (161–66) may owe something to the account of the bad education given a young nobleman in Pope's *Dunciad* 4.282–334. In presenting the young nobleman to Dulness, his governor says:

> Thine from the birth, and sacred from the rod,

> A dauntless infant! never scar'd with God.
> The Sire saw, one by one, his Virtues wake:
> The Mother begg'd the blessing of a Rake.
>
> (lines 283–86)

32. "*R—ch*": John Rich (1682?–1761), pantomimist and theatrical manager, producer of John Gay's *Beggar's Opera*, but also well known and often satirized for his spectacular vaudevilles. At the time when he was writing *Reproof*, Smollett held a particular grudge against Rich because Rich had turned down *The Regicide* sometime during 1746; see introduction to the plays, p. 71.

33. "While his brain . . . the croud": The quotation in Smollett's note to this line is from *The Dunciad* 3.233–40, where Pope ridicules some of the spectacles that had been shown on the London stage.

34. "vaticide": The killer of a prophet or poet (the Latin word *vates* was used for both prophets and inspired poets). *OED* gives only three citations for *vaticide*: one from Pope, who used (or perhaps even coined) the term in *The Dunciad* 2.78; and two from Smollett, one of them from this line in *Reproof* and the other from the preface to *The Regicide* (see below, p. 91).

35. "hell-denouncing priest . . . whore": Knapp, 69, identifies the hell-denouncing priest as a Methodist evangelist and the sovereign whore as John Rich's tyrannical wife, whose Methodism intoxicated her husband. Knapp confirms this reading of the line by citing a passage from chapter 63 of *Roderick Random* in which Rich is caricatured as Vandal: "I have since been informed, that the poor man's head, which was not naturally very clear, had been disordered with superstition, and that he laboured under the tyranny of a wife, and the terrors of hell-fire, at the same time."

36. "the social chair": A reference to the fashionable sedan, a box seating a single person and attached to two poles by which porters carried it from place to place.

37. "lewd *T—w—y*'s face": James O'Hara, second Lord Tyrawley (1690–1773), ambassador to Portugal from 1728 to 1741, had some reputation as a soldier and diplomat. But he was best known in London for his wit, imperiousness, and profligacy. Horace Walpole wrote in 1742, "My Lord Tyrawley is come from Portugal, and has brought three wives and fourteen children" (Walpole, *Correspondence*, 18:104). Pope had written in *The Sixth Epistle of the First Book of Horace, Imitated* (1738), lines 120–21: "in each Vice out-do / K[innoul]l's lewd Cargo, or Ty[rawle]y's Crew."

38. "*H—ly*": Henry Hawley (1679?–1759) was commander in chief of English forces in Scotland in December 1745. He was known as a severe disciplinarian who was hated by his troops. In January 1746 his forces had been defeated by the rebel clans on Falkirk Muir, an episode for which he, like Cope, suffered considerable public derision. Later he was one of Cumberland's lieutenants at the battle of Culloden.

39. "*In—d—by*": Richard Ingoldsby (d. 1759) failed at the battle of Fontenoy (11 May 1745) to capture a French redoubt he had been ordered to take. Subsequently he was found guilty by court-martial of not obeying the orders of Cumberland

during the unsuccessful attack. Ingoldsby, justly or unjustly, was a convenient scapegoat in the eye of the public, and he left the army in late 1745.

40. *"Mead"*: Richard Mead (1673–1754), a leading physician of London from the second decade of the eighteenth century until his death. Cultured and learned (he was said to have one of the largest book collections of the day), wealthy and benevolent, he seems to have been above the many medical feuds in which his minor colleagues sometimes engaged. Smollett speaks of him in his *Continuation*, 4:124, as "the elegant Mead."

41. *"Th——p——n"*: Thomas Thompson, M.D. (d. 1763), made news in the spring of 1746 when accusations were leveled against him of mishandling the treatment of Thomas Winnington, paymaster general, who had died under his care. He defended himself with a full account of his diagnosis and treatment, *The Case of the Right Honourable Thomas Winnington, Esq.* (1746), in which he also advertised himself as physician to the household of the Prince of Wales. He was promptly attacked by several pamphleteers and defended by others in a minor medical squabble of which Smollett would certainly have been aware and in which he may even have participated. See Robert Adams Day, "When Doctors Disagree: Smollett and Thomas Thompson," *Etudes Anglaises* 32 (1979): 312–24. Day suggests that Dr. Wagtail in chapter 45 of *Roderick Random* may represent Thompson and that there are several allusions to Thompson and his medical practice in other works by Smollett.

42. *"C——k, B——ks, B——wby, and C——ty"*: The names are Clark, Banks, Barrowby, and Chitty. The most likely Clark for this context is Alured Clarke (1696–1742), dean of Exeter Cathedral, who in 1738 published *An Essay Towards the Character of Her Late Majesty Caroline*. The forty-six pages of this essay gave high, if not extravagant, praise to Caroline. The *DNB* quotes the duchess of Marlborough on the essay; her remarks suggest the reaction to it that led Smollett to include Clarke in his fraternity of wits: "there is [a nauseous panegyric] very remarkable, from a Dr. Clarke, in order to have the first bishoprick that falls, and I dare say he will have it, though there is something extremely ridiculous in the panegyric." Banks is doubtless John Banks (1709–51), who had gained some literary fame in 1738 when he published his *Miscellaneous Works in Verse and Prose* by subscription. Barrowby is probably William Barrowby (1682–1751), who was supposedly one of the authors of *A Letter to the Real and Genuine Pierce Dod*, a satirical piece published in 1746 abusively attacking a pompous pamphlet written by one Dr. Dod on the subject of inoculation. Chitty remains unidentified.

43. "Alike averse to censure or commend": See Pope's *Epistle to Dr. Arbuthnot*, line 205: "Alike reserv'd to blame, or to commend." Smollett echoes the thought again in a letter (1758?) to John Moore: "I am equally averse to the Praise and Censure that belong to other men" (*Letters*, 73).

44. "invocated": Invoked. *OED* gives Smollett's line as the only eighteenth-century citation exemplifying *invocated* as a participial adjective.

45. "to fill the cry": The phrase refers to "the yelping of hounds in the chase," *full cry*

meaning *full pursuit* (*OED*). Smollett must have liked the imagery of the phrase, because he used it again in chapter 103 of *Peregrine Pickle*: "A babbler, tho' he cannot run upon the scent, may spring the game, and by his yelping help to fill up the cry." The expression appears also in Smollett's review of Joseph Warton's *Essay on the Writings and Genius of Pope*, *Critical Review* 1 (April 1756): 227.

THUS HAVE I SENT THE SIMPLE KING TO HELL

1. Title: This poem appears in *Roderick Random*, chapter 40, as the composition of Narcissa's aunt, the eccentric virtuoso lady who provides a refuge for Roderick when he is abandoned on his return to England from Carthagena. The first words he hears her speak are the last lines of this poem. Later she favors him with an audition of the whole piece, explaining, "I have planned a tragedy, the subject of which shall be the murder of a prince before the altar, where he is busy at his devotions.—After the deed is perpetrated, the regicide will harangue the people, with the bloody dagger in his hand; and I have already composed a speech, which I think will suit the character extremely." Buck has noted that the mention of "regicide" and "murder of a prince before the altar" suggests, if not a burlesque of Smollett's own *The Regicide*, at least a humorous treatment of similar material (*Poet*, 44). The lines of the poem itself are a pastiche of the heroic rant, most generally associated with such characters in John Dryden's plays as Almanzor in *The Conquest of Granada* (1670) and Maximin in *Tyrannick Love* (1669). The classic parody of such ranting heroes is the character Drawcansir in *The Rehearsal* (1671), generally attributed to the duke of Buckingham. Smollett's theatergoing readers would have readily detected a typical Drawcansir in the regicide's claim to be a law unto himself, intimidating even the gods. The use of the closed couplet rather than blank verse also recalls dramas of Dryden's day, rather than more recent heroic models.

THY FATAL SHAFTS UNERRING MOVE

1. Title: In *Roderick Random*, chapter 40, these verses are presented by the hero to Narcissa along with a copy of "On Celia," Smollett's adaptation of his earlier lyric, "A New Song" (see above, "A New Song," n. 1).

TRAVESTY

1. Title: These lines appear (untitled) in chapter 53 of *Roderick Random*; an unnamed lieutenant sings them to an assembly during the episode of Roderick's courtship of Miss Snapper. Smollett's verse parodies the opening stanza of John Dalton's popular adaptation (1738) of Milton's *Comus*; the music for the adaptation was composed by Henry Lawes. See Paul-Gabriel Boucé, ed., *The Adventures of Roderick Random* (Oxford: Oxford University Press, 1979), 325, n. 5; and see Knapp, "Smollett's Verses and Their Musical Settings."

LOVE ELEGY
In Imitation of Tibullus

1. Title: In the Marshalsea Prison, Roderick Random meets the unfortunate poet-playwright Melopoyn, who entertains him with some of his poetry. Roderick inserts these verses into chapter 61 of his narrative, saying, "I was particularly pleased with some elegies, in imitation of Tibullus; one of which I beg leave to submit to the reader." Smollett's elegy is not based on any particular work of the Latin poet Tibullus (c. 50–19 B.C.), although the last stanza echoes somewhat lines 61–62 of Tibullus's Elegy 1.1: "*flebis et arsuro positum me, Delia, lecto, / tristibus et lacrimis oscula mixta dabis*" ("Thou wilt weep for me, Delia, when I am laid on the bed that is to burn; thou wilt give me kisses mingled with bitter tears"). Their general atmosphere of melancholy retirement and the thoughts of death make Smollett's lines imitative of Tibullus. In commenting on Smollett's poem, Moore says that the last stanza should have been omitted, because "the thought . . . has been often used" (p. clxxi). Buck notes that this elegy "was a favorite in anthologies, appearing more frequently than any of Smollett's other verses, except *The Tears of Scotland*" (*Poet*, 45).

2. "Monimia": Name of the pathetic heroine of Thomas Otway's *The Orphan* (1680). Smollett used the name again for the heroine of *Ferdinand Count Fathom*, one famous scene of which is the midnight pilgrimage of Renaldo, Monimia's beloved, to the churchyard where he believes her to be buried (chapter 62). The Gothic trappings and sentiments of that scene are reminiscent of stanzas 4 and 5 of this earlier work addressed to Monimia.

ADIEU, YE STREAMS THAT SMOOTHLY FLOW

1. Title: These verses appear in chapter 21 of *Peregrine Pickle*. Inspired by his first acquaintance with Emilia Gauntlet, Peregrine produces these stanzas and sends them to her.

COME, LISTEN YE STUDENTS OF EV'RY DEGREE

1. Title: In chapter 25 of *Peregrine Pickle*, Peregrine's tutor, Mr. Jumble, orders him to compose a paraphrase upon two lines from Virgil as part of a penance for nonattendance at chapel. The lines are *Aeneid* 11.715–16:

> Vane ligur, frustraque animis elate superbis,
> Necquicquam, patrias, tentasti lubricus, artes.
> (Foolish Ligurian, vainly puffed up in pride of heart,
> naught hast thou tried thy slippery native tricks.)

Peregrine is exasperated at such a reflection upon himself and his family. Learning that his tutor's father was a bricklayer and his mother a seller of pies, "he composed the following ballad in doggerel rhymes, and next day presented it as a gloss upon the text which the tutor had chosen." When other students get hold of copies, they sing the words to the tune of "A Cobler There Was," a tune better known as "Derry Down." Smollett alludes to "A Cobler There Was" again in *The Reprisal* 1.3; see below, p. 470.

BURLESQUE ODE

1. Title: These lines appear (untitled) toward the end of chapter 102 of *Peregrine Pickle*. The chapter presents the proceedings of a society of authors that Peregrine has joined. Several contemporary authors and theater personalities are satirized during the proceedings, including Henry Fielding and his patron, George, Lord Lyttelton. These lines, spoken by one of the poets present, are a rough parody of Lyttelton's *To the Memory of a Lady Lately Deceased* (1747), a nineteen-stanza monody written in memory of Lyttelton's first wife, Lucy. Lyttelton's poem was quite intimate in tone, especially for the eighteenth century, and it was probably this public exposure of personal feelings that Smollett felt to be an appropriate matter for mockery. But Smollett also held grudges against Lyttelton, whose help he had sought both with *The Regicide* and a later comic piece, only to be politely put off (see introduction to the plays, p. 78). Perhaps Smollett's jealousy of Fielding, who had dedicated *Tom Jones* to Lyttelton, also played a part in his wish to ridicule Lyttelton. Smollett's animosity subsequently softened, and he omitted almost the last third of this particular chapter, including these verses, in the second edition of *Peregrine Pickle* (where the chapter is renumbered 94). Continued improvement of relations between Smollett and Lyttelton may be inferred from a brief comment in Samuel Johnson's life of Lyttelton. Johnson comments on a note from Lyttelton to the writers of the *Critical Review* thanking them for a favorable review of his *Dialogues of the Dead*; see *Lives of the English Poets*, ed. G. B. Hill (Oxford: Clarendon Press, 1905), 3:452. Although Smollett's parody is only a fraction of the length of Lyttelton's poem, it does follow closely a number of lines of the original. Compare, for example, the entire first stanza with the seventh stanza of Lyttelton's monody:

> Where were ye, Muses, when relentless Fate
> From these fond Arms your fair Disciple tore;
>   From these fond arms that vainly strove
>   With hapless ineffectual Love
> To guard her Bosom from the mortal Blow?
> Could not your fav'ring Power, *Aonian* Maids,
> Could not, alas! Your Power prolong her Date,
> For whom so oft in these inspiring Shades,
> Or under *Campden*'s Moss-clad Mountains Hoar,
>   You open'd all your sacred Store,
>   Whate'er your ancient Sages taught,
>   Your ancient Bards sublimely thought,
> And bade her raptur'd Breast with all your Spirit Glow?

2. "wittol Ward": A satirical reference to Joshua Ward (1685–1761), a highly successful quack doctor whom Smollett here characterizes (by his use of the word *wittol*) as half-witted, senseless, and a cuckold. Ward's pill and drop were widely advertised nostrums, endorsed by many well-known persons. He was naturally also the object of much controversy and frequent attacks, especially from trained physicians.

3. "Marybone": Marybone, or Marylebone, was a somewhat disreputable section of London associated with animal fights, boxing matches, duels, gambling, and other such entertainments.

4. "Oil-dropping Twick'nham": Sometime around 1749, Joshua Ward established a manufactory for sulphuric acid (oil of vitriol) at Twickenham. Several other names in this stanza are associated with Ward's activities: he established small hospitals in Pimlico and near the Exchange, and George II granted him a room in the almonry at Whitehall. Drury Lane, notorious for its prostitutes, and the Mint, known for the debtors who sought legal sanctuary within its boundaries, are mentioned probably because they were unsavory places. Snowhill was a steep hill in the general area of Saint Paul's Cathedral. Throughout the opening of his second stanza (lines 9–22), Smollett closely parodies the eighth stanza of Lyttelton's monody, which reads:

> Nor then did *Pindus* or *Castalia*'s Plain
> Or *Aganippe*'s Fount your Steps detain,
> Nor in the *Thespian* Vallies did you play;
>   Nor then on *Mincio*'s Bank
>   Beset with Osiers dank,
> Nor where *Clitumnus* rolls his gentle Stream
>   Nor where through hanging Woods,
>   Steep *Anio* pours his Floods,
> Nor yet where *Meles*, or *Ilissus* stray.
>   Ill does it now beseem
>   That of your Guardian Care bereft
> To dire Disease and Death your Darling should be left.

5. "Cambrian": Welsh. It is not clear what connection Welsh maids might have had with Ward or with Twickenham, although the context seems to imply something salacious.

6. "kennel": The surface drain or gutter of a street.

7. "Her lib'ral hand . . . common mother were of all": These lines (23–34) perhaps originated in lines 20–24 of Lyttelton's eleventh stanza:

> Ev'n for the Kid or Lamb that pour'd its Life
>   Beneath the bloody Knife,
>   Her gentle Tears would fall,
> As She the common Mother were of all.

8. "For my . . . comfort can I find": Compare these lines (35–36) with the first two lines of Lyttelton's seventeenth stanza:

> For my distracted Mind
> What Succour can I find?

9. "O best of grannams!": Lyttelton's sixteenth stanza begins: "O Best of Wives!"

SONG "While with Fond Rapture"

1. Title: These verses appear in chapter 104 of *Peregrine Pickle*, where the Lady of Quality reappears to comfort Peregrine in one of his final distresses. To prove the passion he has long had for her, he presents her "with the following song, which he had written in her praise, immediately after he was made acquainted with the particulars of her story."

A DECLARATION IN LOVE.
ODE TO BLUE-EY'D ANN

1. Title: This work was first published in the *British Magazine* 1 (April 1760): 213. Students of Smollett have traditionally considered the verses a love poem addressed to his wife, Ann (or Anne) Lassells, a Jamaican heiress whom he married sometime in the early 1740s.

2. "Lybian sands": Lybia was the Greek name for all of North Africa except Egypt and Ethiopia. It was proverbially associated with burning sands, as in Dryden's translation of Virgil's third georgic (1697):

> Then woe to him that in the desert land
> Of Libya travels, o'er the burning sand!
> (lines 389–90)

3. "Nova-Zembla's": Nova Zembla (Russian Novaya Zemlya, or New Land), an archipelago off the northern coast of Russia, had been vaguely known to Europeans since the sixteenth century, but was not seriously explored until the last half of the eighteenth century. Smollett would have known something of it from the seventeenth-century "A Voyage to the North of Europe," included in his *Compendium of Authentic and Entertaining Voyages* (London, 1756), 5:131–97. Pope commented on the mad world of Dulness's kingdom by having Description give "to Zembla fruits" (*The Dunciad* 1.74), ironically emphasizing, as does Smollett, the idea that Nova Zembla is a place of enduring, inevitable cold.

4. "the dog-star": Sirius, the predawn rising of which, in July and August, is traditionally the sign of the dog days, the most oppressively hot season of the year.

5. "When Nature from her sphere shall start": This line gives a philosophical and typically eighteenth-century cast to the list of unnatural circumstances that are as likely to happen as the poet's ceasing to love his Ann. The moral and metaphysical connotations of *sphere* are suggested by Joseph Addison in his *Spectator*, no. 404 (13 June 1712): "Nature does nothing in vain; the Creator of the Universe has appointed every thing to a certain Use and Purpose, and determined it to a settled Course and Sphere of Action, from which, if it in the least deviates, it becomes

unfit to answer those Ends for which it was designed." Were the poet to cease loving, he would be as unnatural and defiant of universal order as Pope's proud men, who "All quit their sphere, and rush into the skies" (*Essay on Man* 1.124).

ODE TO SLEEP.
INTENDED AS A CHORUS IN A TRAGEDY

1. Title: This poem was first published in the *British Magazine* 1 (June 1760): 379.

AN ODE TO MIRTH

1. Title: This poem first appeared in the *British Magazine* 1 (August 1760): 494. Knapp discovered an Italian translation of the poem in a collection entitled *Scelta Di Poesi Inglesi, Recate In Italiano* (Torino, 1818); see Lewis M. Knapp, "Rare and Unrecorded Publications of Smollett's Works," *Notes and Queries*, n.s., 18 (1971): 338. This is perhaps the only one of Smollett's poems to be distinguished by translation into another language—except, of course, those included in translated novels.
2. "obscene": "Ill-omened, inauspicious (a Latinism)" (*OED*).

A NEW SONG "To Fix Her"

1. Title: This song first appeared in the *British Magazine* 1 (September 1760): 549.
2. "toil": According to Johnson, *Dictionary*, a toil is "any net or snare woven or meshed."

ODE TO LEVEN-WATER

1. Title: In *Humphry Clinker*, Matthew Bramble sends to Dr. Lewis an enthusiastic description of Loch Lomond and the surrounding countryside as the Arcadia of Scotland. He concludes: "Inclosed I send you the copy of a little ode to the river Leven, by Dr. Smollett, who was born on the banks of it. . . . It is at least picturesque and accurately descriptive, if it has no other merit." The poem is printed after Bramble's complimentary close and signature (Matthew Bramble to Dr. Lewis, Cameron, August 28, pp. 241–42). Smollett was born on the family estate of Dalquhurn, which overlooked the river Leven, and spent much of his childhood and youth in its neighborhood. The river, only about six miles long, flows through the vale of Leven from the south end of Loch Lomond to the Firth of Clyde.
2. "motled par": A par, or parr, is "a young salmon before it becomes a smolt [ready to migrate to the sea]; distinguished by the parallel bands on its side" (*OED*). A smelt, mentioned in Smollett's footnote, is "a small fish . . . allied to the salmon" (*OED*).

ODE TO INDEPENDENCE

1. Title: *Ode to Independence* was first published posthumously in Glasgow in 1773. See introduction to the poems, p. 17.

2. "baptized with blood": The Massacre of Verden occurred in 782 near the river Weser in western Germany. Charlemagne ordered the slaying of a large group of Saxon prisoners—the number usually given is forty-five hundred—in retaliation for the raids of the Saxons, "the sons of Woden," upon the northern borders of Charlemagne's realm and for their breach of earlier treaties. The Vitikind named in Smollett's footnote was the chief Saxon leader, who had escaped Charlemagne's roundup by drawing back into Denmark. Smollett's views on the episode are similar to those of Voltaire as described in chapter 8 of *Ancient and Modern History*, the English translation of *Essai sur les Moeurs et l'Esprit des Nations*: "Had these prisoners been really subjects in rebellion, this punishment would have been horribly severe; but, to treat in this manner men who fought for their liberty and laws, was the action of a robber" (Voltaire, 1:97).

3. "Curlieu": The curlew is a long-billed bird often found near the seashore. Its name is supposedly derived from the sound of its cry.

4. "Tritons": In Greek mythology, Triton was originally the name given to a son of the sea-god Poseidon, but the name came to be used for a class of minor sea deities often represented as holding shell trumpets.

5. "Philomel": The nightingale, so called after Philomela, a figure in Greek mythology who, according to Ovid *Metamorphoses* 6, was changed into a nightingale after being raped by her brother-in-law.

6. "Dryads": A dryad, in classical mythology, is "a nymph supposed to inhabit trees" (*OED*).

7. "The Doric muse": Most Greek pastoral poetry was written in the Doric dialect; hence the term *Doric* connoted a kind of unsophisticated and uncorrupted strength.

8. "On desart isles": Voltaire traces the growth of the Venetian republic from an inhospitable marshland first inhabited in the fifth century, to its emergence as an independent republic with the election of the first doge in 709, and then into a flourishing state by the tenth century (Voltaire, 1:277–79). Voltaire generally admired the polity of Venice, remarking in another place that "Venice is the only one of these states that has constantly preserved her liberty" (1:260).

9. "Batavian's": *Batavian*, an epithet for the Dutch, is derived from the ancient Batavi who dwelt on a Rhenish island in what is now the Netherlands.

10. "the Iberian's double chain": In 1565 Philip II of Spain attempted to establish the Inquisition in Brussels. Voltaire describes this attempt, as well as Philip's plans to impose new taxes, as important causes of the rebellion of the Low Countries. This rebellion resulted in the establishment in 1579 of the independent Seven United Provinces. Voltaire is greatly impressed by the manner in which this unpromising

land raised itself into a significant power, and compares the United Provinces to Venice: "Venice had not more noble beginnings. The greatest empires were first raised from hamlets, and the maritime powers from a few private fishing boats" (Voltaire, 4:284). Smollett's pairing of Venice and the Netherlands as examples of flourishing independent states may be a recollection from his work as editor of Voltaire.

11. "On Uri's rocks in close divan": A divan, according to Johnson, *Dictionary*, is "any council assembled." Johnson cites Pope's *Odyssey* 4.983, where Penelope "heard the consult of the dire Divan." Uri is the name both of William Tell's Swiss canton and of the lake on whose shores, according to legend, Tell and his associates held the council of Rütli in 1307. At this council they secretly swore to rid their cantons of the tyrannies of their Austrian governor, Gessler. Some time after Gessler had forced Tell to shoot an apple off his son's head, the tyrant was slain by an arrow from Tell's bow. Modern historians have discredited practically all of the Tell story, even questioning whether such figures as Tell and Gessler ever lived, but the story was generally accepted in the eighteenth century.

12. "adust": "Dried up with heat, parched" (*OED*).

13. "adamantine": Like a diamond, for which the word *adamant* was sometimes supposed to be another name; something deemed "incapable of being broken, dissolved, or penetrated" (*OED*).

14. "Timur-Bec": Another name for Tamerlane.

15. "Calvi's rocky shore": Calvi is a seaport in northwest Corsica.

16. "Corsica": During the 1760s, the struggle of the Corsicans to free themselves from Genoese and French domination gained wide attention in England. James Boswell, following his visit to Corsica in 1765, had enthusiastically spread the fame of the Corsican leader, General Pasquale Paoli. In the journal of his tour, published in 1765, he wrote of finding "what was to be seen no where else, a people actually fighting for liberty, and forming themselves from a poor inconsiderable oppressed nation, into a flourishing and independent state" (*Journal of a Tour to Corsica*, ed. S. C. Roberts [Cambridge: The University Press, 1923], 1).

17. "In Fortune's car . . . minion ride": Robert Chambers, in *Smollett: His Life and a Selection from His Writings* (London: W. and R. Chambers, 1867), 169, suggests that the minion of this strophe should be identified with the ingrate Paunceford, one of "those minions of fortune" in the Bath section of *Humphry Clinker* (see Jery Melford to Sir Watkin Phillips, Bath, May 10, pp. 65–67). Paunceford was modeled after one Alexander Campbell, a sometime acquaintance of Smollett who made a fortune in India, returned to England in 1768, and thereafter treated Smollett and other former benefactors with contempt.

18. "sumpter-mule": *OED* defines *sumpter* as "a beast of burden" and cites Smollett's line as an example of the word's usage.

LYRICS FROM *ALCESTE*

1. "*ALCESTE*": Only the vaguest outlines of the plot of Smollett's *Alceste* can be inferred from the surviving lyrics. However, it seems to follow fairly closely the traditional legend, best known in the dramatic form Euripides gave it in his *Alcestis*. Admetus, king of Thessaly, wins the hand of Alceste (or Alcestis) with the aid of Apollo, who had become a servant in his household as a punishment for having killed the Cyclopes. Soon afterward Admetus becomes mortally ill, and Apollo arranges with the Fates that he may recover if a substitute victim is found. After a widespread but futile search for a substitute, Alceste offers herself. As soon as she is taken in death, Hercules arrives and, hearing of the sad situation, vows that he will defeat Death. He overcomes Death in a wrestling match and is thus enabled to return the noble Alceste to the arms of her bereaved husband. For discussion of Smollett's collaboration with Handel on *Alceste*, see introduction to the poems, pp. 16–17; see also Deutsch, "Poetry Preserved in Music."

2. "Hymenean verse": The first act of the opera, with its several numbers alluding to Hymen, god of weddings, clearly was a spectacle depicting the wedding feast of Alceste and Admetus.

3. "Brave the one, the other fair": In his oratorio *Alexander Balus* (1751), Handel reused the words and music of these first two songs from *Alceste*, substituting the names Balus and Cleopatra for Admetus and Alceste.

4. "*Calliope's Song*": Calliope was the muse of epic poetry. Her song was probably to be sung at the point where Admetus is to recover from his illness.

5. "Ye fleeting shades": The next three lyrics were apparently parts of a scene in the underworld or the Elysian Fields, where the shade of Alceste comes, soon to be rescued by the efforts of Hercules.

6. "Enjoy the sweet Elysian grove": Handel used the words and music of the first four lines of this aria again in his interlude *The Choice of Hercules* (1750).

7. "*Calliope sings to Admetus*": Calliope's song of consolation to Admetus appears to be a kind of interlude in the action.

8. "He comes, he rises from below": The last series of lyrics celebrates the triumphant return of Hercules to restore Alceste to Admetus.

Plays

The Regicide

1. "*those little Fellows . . . great Men*": In his preface, Smollett mentions in passing a number of potential patrons, friends, and acquaintances. In the absence of any clear identifying characteristics or any helpful remarks made elsewhere by Smollett or others, most of these persons remain unidentified. For detailed studies of the numerous encounters mentioned in the preface, the continuing

quarrels that many of these provoked, and the references to them in other works by Smollett, especially in the tale of Melopoyn in chapters 62 and 63 of *Roderick Random*, see Buck, *Study*, chap. 3, and Knapp, 49–57.

2. *"my Occasions called me out of the Kingdom"*: Smollett received his warrant as a surgeon's second mate on 10 March 1740, but his ship, the *Chichester*, did not leave England until October. He returned to England early in 1742.

3. *"a late Patentee"*: Charles Fleetwood was the patentee of Drury Lane Theater from 1734 to 1744. He was a person of great personal charm, but careless in his management of the theater and deceptive in his dealings with others.

4. *"a whole Season"*: The season of 1742–43. Buck, *Study*, 57–62, was the first to deduce the chronology of Smollett's narrative in the preface, most of the events having occurred between 1742 and 1747.

5. *"the other House"*: At the conclusion of the duke of Buckingham's famous theatrical parody, *The Rehearsal* (1671), the playwright Bayes, a takeoff on Dryden, is disappointed with the response his play receives during its rehearsal. He vows, " 'Y gad, I'll be revenged on 'em; I'll sell this play to the other house."

6. *"the most dishonourable Apartment . . . House"*: Perhaps the import of this passage is based on the common joke that an unwanted manuscript or book would end up being used in a privy.

7. *"a young Nobleman"*: Lord George Graham (1715–47), son of the first duke of Montrose. In an undated letter, probably written sometime in 1747, Smollett wrote to Alexander Carlyle, "I am vain of your Approbation with regard to my Tragedy, which, as you imagine, suffered by the much lamented Death of Lord George Graham" (*Letters*, 4).

8. *"the new Manager of Drury-lane Theatre"*: James Lacy obtained the patent of Drury Lane Theater near the end of 1744. *The Regicide* was apparently first presented to him about May 1745.

9. *"the production of a Player"*: *King Henry VII; or the Popish Imposter* by the actor Charles Macklin. Attempting to capitalize on anti-Jacobite feelings, Lacy presented this play at Drury Lane on 18 January 1746, but it ran for only three nights.

10. *"an eminent Wit"*: Philip Stanhope, fourth earl of Chesterfield, the famous wit, letter writer, and statesman. A narrative by a member of the college of authors in *Peregrine Pickle* appears to be a fictionalized account of Smollett's encounter with Chesterfield and suggests that Chesterfield, "in consequence of a production [possibly *Advice*] which this gentleman [Smollett] has ushered into the world, with universal applause, not only desired, but even eagerly courted his acquaintance" (chapter 102).

11. *"a Person"*: David Garrick, the famous actor who was rapidly becoming the most celebrated theatrical personality of the eighteenth century. In the spring of 1746, Garrick returned to London after a successful season in Dublin and was immediately engaged by John Rich for the ensuing season at Covent Garden. Chesterfield

returned to England from Dublin about the same time after having served there as lord lieutenant. In a letter to the Reverend John Hoadly dated 14 September 1746, Garrick wrote, "I have a Play now with Me, sent to Me by my Lord Chesterfield & wrote by One Smollett; it is a Scotch Story, but it won't do, & yet recommended by his Lordship & patroniz'd by Ladies of Quality" (*The Letters of David Garrick*, ed. David M. Little and George M. Kahrl [Cambridge: Harvard University Press, 1963], 1:86). The episode involving Chesterfield, Garrick, and Rich, here touched on rather lightly, is given much more scope in the fictionalized version of Smollett's difficulties in chapters 62 and 63 of *Roderick Random*, where Marmozet (the fictionalized Garrick) receives more blame than almost anyone else for Melopoyn's disappointments. Writing to Alexander Carlyle about this time, Smollett complained, "I little thought my Attempt to bring my tragedy on this Season could have been baffled by the Pitifull Intrigues of that little Rascal Garrick, who, at the time he gave me all the Incouragement I could desire, in assuring me he would contribute as much as in him lay, not only to bring it on, but also to act in it with all the ability he was master of, found means to prevail on Rich to reject it" (*Letters*, 4).

12. "*I reckoned without my Host*": Expression based on a common proverb, "He that reckons without his host must reckon again." The proverb is traceable back at least to its appearance in 1489 in William Caxton's *Blanchardyn and Eglantine*.

13. "*The Master of* Covent-Garden *Theatre*": John Rich, best known as a producer of highly popular pantomimes, had been the successful manager of Covent Garden since its opening in 1732. See *Reproof*, n. 32.

14. "*a humane Lady of Quality*": Possibly, as suggested by Buck, *Study*, 26–27, Lady Anne Vane, who may have begun her acquaintance with Smollett at about this time. Their acquaintance eventually led to the insertion of her sensational memoirs into the text of *Peregrine Pickle*.

15. "*the other Manager*": James Lacy.

16. "*Vaticide*": The killer of a poet. See *Reproof*, n. 34.

17. "*Mr. T——n*": James Thomson, author of *The Seasons*, whose tragedy *Tancred and Sigismunda* was first presented at Drury Lane in March 1745.

18. "*such Alterations as I had agreed to*": In the letter to Carlyle cited above, n. 11, Smollett wrote, "Meanwhile, I have just finished the Alterations of my Play, as they were agreed upon by the Manager of Drury Lane, who has given his Word and Honour to a Person of Quality that it shall be acted next Winter, at any time before Christmass, that I desire" (*Letters*, 5).

19. "*this upright Director*": By the middle of 1747, when the final rejection of *The Regicide* took place, Lacy had sold half his interest in the patent of Drury Lane to Garrick, who was thereafter comanager of the theater and who, Smollett appears to have believed, shared with Lacy the blame for this final rejection.

20. "*Goth*": "One who behaves like a barbarian, esp. in the destruction or neglect of works of art" (*OED*).

21. "the Blood of *March*": Although the character of Dunbar is apparently a product of Smollett's imagination, the earldom of March had been held by Dunbars since its creation in 1290. The earl of March in the time of James I was George Dunbar, who had his title forfeited in 1435 and whose son and heir was Patrick Dunbar. But it seems unlikely that Smollett could have had these persons specifically in mind in working up the character of Dunbar.

22. "flagitious": "Extremely wicked or criminal" (*OED*).

23. "Displays a spurious Title to the Crown": The rebels against James I claimed he was a usurper because his father, Robert III, had received the throne instead of Walter, earl of Athol, upon the death of their father Robert II. Athol was the son of Robert's first wife, Euphemia, but after her death Robert married his mistress, Elizabeth, and legitimized her three sons, the eldest of whom displaced Athol as heir to the throne.

24. "*Thule*'s Shore": Thule was the ancient designation for the most remote northern regions. Camden's *Britannia* (1586) states that one of the Shetland Islands is the ancient Thule. In one of Jery Melford's Scottish letters in *Humphry Clinker*, he questions whether the Hebrides or Orkneys be not the *Ultima Thule* (Jery Melford to Sir Watkin Phillips, Argyleshire, September 3, p. 229).

25. "Philtres": Potions or drugs "supposed to be capable of exciting sexual love" (*OED*).

26. "*Tay*'s smooth-gliding Stream": The Tay is Scotland's longest river. Most of its course is through Perthshire.

27. "a Lion in the Toils betray'd": Toils are "a net or nets set so as to enclose a space into which the quarry is driven" (*OED*). See *Julius Caesar* 2.1.206: "Lions [may be betrayed] with toils."

28. "Target": "A light round shield or buckler" (*OED*).

29. "Borderer": "One who dwells near the border of England and Scotland" (*OED*).

30. "Targe": A light shield or buckler (*OED*); its diminutive is *target* (see above, n. 28).

31. "*Lorn*": Mountainous district of West Argyll, adjoining Perthshire on the west.

32. "Blade to Blade oppos'd": An allusion to a famous battle description in the *Iliad* 4.446–49, which Pope had rendered as follows in his translation:

     Now Shield with Shield, with Helmet Helmet clos'd,
     To Armour Armour, Lance to Lance oppos'd.
                                             (4.508–9)

     In his footnote to these lines, Pope observed that they "are perhaps excell'd by none in Homer."

33. "gelid": "Refreshingly cold" (*OED*). *OED* cites a line from Smollett's 1755 translation of *Don Quixote*: "Drinking liquid chrystal from the gelid springs."

34. "beard The Lion": To beard is "to oppose openly and resolutely," partly from the idea of taking a lion by the beard (*OED*). *OED* cites Smollett's line as an example.

35. "slake mine Ire": An altered echo of *3 Henry VI* 1.3.29: "It could not slake mine ire nor ease my heart."

36. "harpy": The harpy, part woman and part bird, was a creature of vengeance or plunder in ancient mythology. *OED* cites Smollett's line as an example of the word used attributively.

37. "the Raven's Croak": The croak of the raven as an omen of misfortune is alluded to in *Macbeth* 1.5.38–39: "The raven himself is hoarse / That croaks the fatal entrance of Duncan."

38. "the warm Blood Still streams within my Veins": See *The Tears of Scotland*, line 49: "While the warm blood bedews my veins."

39. "amuse": "To beguile, delude, cheat, deceive" (*OED*).

40. "Caparison": A caparison is "a cloth or covering spread over the saddle or harness of a horse, often gaily ornamented" (*OED*).

41. "brook": "To put up with, bear with, endure, tolerate" (*OED*).

42. "The rude Flint . . . incessant Drop": The proverbial idea that "constant dropping will wear the stone" is found widely and in various forms from antiquity to modern times. See, for example, Job 14:19, "The waters wear the stones"; and *3 Henry VI* 3.2.50, "Much rain wears the marble."

43. "But soft": An idiom very common in Shakespeare for enjoining silence or quiet, usually spoken by one character upon the arrival of another. See, for example, *Hamlet* 1.1.126, 1.5.58, 4.2.3.

44. "it is not well . . . Terms like these": In *1 Henry IV* 5.1.9–11, King Henry rebukes the rebel Worcester: " 'tis not well / That you and I should meet upon such terms / As now we meet."

45. "*Bruce*": Robert Bruce (1274–1329), king of Scotland from 1306 to 1329. He is among the most revered of Scottish monarchs because of his successful struggles for Scottish independence from the English. His most celebrated feat was the victory of Bannockburn in 1314. George Buchanan, the reading of whose *Rerum Scoticarum Historia* (1579) inspired Smollett to undertake his tragedy, praises Bruce highly in that book as "a most Illustrious Person, every way, and he can hardly be paralleled for his Virtues and Valour." See the first English translation of Buchanan's work, *The History of Scotland* (London, 1690), 281.

46. "redress'd the whole": This speech of the king, though poetically effusive, substantially describes the accomplishments of James I as Buchanan had characterized them. Buchanan's view that James, during his reign from 1424 to 1437, helped to bring law, order, civilized arts, and humane practices to Scotland—at least temporarily—is still supported by modern historians. In summarizing James's reign and character, Buchanan remarks how "in a few Years, he Govern'd so, that the turbulent State of the Kingdom was chang'd in [*sic*] a Calm and Serene One" and how he was slain "in the midst of his intended Course, to settle good Laws and Customs, in his Kingdom" (Buchanan, *History*, 356).

47. "O! what a miserable Slave am I!": Perhaps a recollection of Hamlet's soliloquy: "O, what a rogue and peasant slave am I!" (*Hamlet* 2.2.550).

48. "flea'd": Flayed. See *Briton*, no. 35, n. 15.

49. "sluice": "To drain of blood, to kill" (*OED*). Smollett's line is the sole quotation exemplifying this meaning in *OED*.

50. "Fruitage": "A crop of fruit" (*OED*). This line by Smollett is the only eighteenth-century example of this meaning recorded in *OED*.

51. "*Scania*": Latinate form of Skane, a province in southern Sweden; apparently used as a poetic designation for Sweden.

52. "*Lebanon*": Mount Lebanon, a celebrated prominence on the northern borders of the Holy Land.

53. "Crocodile": "A person who weeps or makes a show of sorrow hypocritically or with malicious purpose" (*OED*). This meaning derives from the proverbial belief that the crocodile weeps to entice its victims or to feign sorrow while devouring them.

54. "warlike *Henry*": James I had been a prisoner of the English from 1406, when he was seven years old, until 1424. Henry V took James to France with him to participate in the siege of Melun in 1420, and James remained in France, involved in the English campaigns, until after Henry's death in 1422. If Joan, James's queen, supported him with her love, as Smollett has her assert, it was before they were wed, since the marriage did not occur until 1424.

55. "*Albania*'s Prince": Albania is an obscure variant of Albany, cognate with Alba, the name of the first united Scot-Pict kingdom in the ninth century.

56. "tender Offspring": The queen had borne eight children to her husband, seven of whom were living at their father's death. The eldest, Margaret, was about twelve years old; she had already been sent to France to become the wife of the future Louis XI.

57. "Weep, *Caledonia*, weep!—thy Peace is slain": See the opening lines of *The Tears of Scotland*:

> Mourn, hapless Caledonia, mourn,
> Thy banish'd peace . . . .

58. "crush'd her slender Limb": One of the dramatic touches in Buchanan's narrative of James I's murder is his account of how a treacherous servant had removed the bar from the door of the king's bedchamber. When an alarm was raised at the discovery of the assassins' approach, a young woman (Buchanan says she was a Douglas or a Lovel; other accounts identify her as one Catherine Douglas) tried to use her own arm to bolt the door, but it was broken as the murderers forced their way into the king's chamber. See Buchanan, *History*, 356.

59. "Our Infant King": James II, six years old at the time of his father's assassination.

60. "*Athol* shall be crown'd": In describing the grisly end of Athol, Buchanan mentions a prophecy, supposedly made earlier to him by witches, that he should be crowned in a concourse of people. Athol was subjected to three days of torture, on the first of which he was placed in the pillory and had a red-hot iron crown placed on his head. Finally he was disemboweled, beheaded, and quartered. See Buchanan, *History*, 357–58.

The Reprisal

1. "*a dunce in grain*": A thorough dunce or a dunce by nature; metaphorically derived from the common phrase referring to cloth, "dyed in grain," that is, fast dyed.

2. "*prepense*": Premeditated. The word is almost always used as part of the legal phrase *malice prepense;* thus Smollett's use here involves a kind of wordplay.

3. "*a Sea-ragout*": A ragout is a highly seasoned meat-and-vegetable dish. An obvious metaphorical usage applied the term to any lively conglomeration.

4. "*fumet*": Johnson, *Dictionary:* "*fumette*, a word introduced by cooks . . . for the stink of meat." Of French origin, the word refers specifically to the scent given off by the meat of certain animals, especially wild ones. Smollett has in mind the practice of allowing some meats to sit long enough to begin spoiling before they are cooked. The same word appears again in act 1, scene 3. In *Ferdinand Count Fathom*, chapter 24, Sir Stentor Stile is given great disturbance by a "roasted leveret very strong of the fumet" (p. 103).

5. "*Edward's banners*": In June 1340 an English fleet was victorious over the French navy in a famous naval battle off Sluis on the southwest coast of the Netherlands. Edward III was present with the victorious English.

6. "*Howard's arm*": Charles Howard, first earl of Nottingham (1536–1624), was Elizabeth I's lord high admiral and commander of the fleet that defeated the Spanish Armada.

7. "*Drake*": Sir Francis Drake (d. 1596), one of Howard's lieutenants at the time of the defeat of the Spanish Armada in 1588; earlier, from 1577 to 1580, Drake had commanded the first English expedition to circumnavigate the earth.

8. "PERSONS represented": The identities of the performers named in the first edition of *The Reprisal*, so far as they can be established, are as indicated below. Unless otherwise noted, this information is drawn from *A Biographical Dictionary of Actors, Actresses, Musicians, Dancers, Managers & Other Stage Personnel in London, 1660–1800*, ed. Philip H. Highfill, Jr., Kalman A. Burnim, and Edward A. Lanhams (Carbondale: Southern Illinois University Press, 1973–).

   "Mr. HAVARD": William Havard (1710–78), who spoke the prologue, had a long acting career extending from 1730 to 1769, much of it spent in supporting roles and most of it at Drury Lane.

   "Mr. *Usher*": One Usher (first name not mentioned) appears in the playbills of Drury Lane for over a decade beginning in 1739, but the name appears in those of Covent Garden for four seasons beginning in 1750 and then reappears in those of Drury Lane for another four seasons. See Ben Ross Schneider, Jr., *Index to the London Stage: 1660–1800* (Carbondale: Southern Illinois University Press, 1979), 860.

   "Mr. *Palmer*": John Palmer (1728–68), known as "Gentleman" Palmer, was employed at Drury Lane by David Garrick in 1749 and remained with the company for the next twenty years. Brush in *The Reprisal* may have been a rather uncharacteristic role for him, for he usually played parts suitable to his nickname.

"Mr. *Blakes*": Charles Blakes was regularly employed in the winter season at Drury Lane from 1743 almost until his death in 1763. He played a great variety of comic characters and seems to have been the house specialist in the roles of Frenchmen.

"Mr. *Yates*": Richard Yates (1706?–96). For a period of twenty-five years (1742–67), Yates was one of the busiest and most highly regarded actors of comic roles in the company at Drury Lane. See *DNB* 21:1216–18.

"Mr. *Johnston*": The name of John Johnston (d. c. 1781) begins to appear in the records of Drury Lane in the early 1750s and continues to appear at intervals for some twenty-five years, but Johnston apparently never received much promotion or public notice.

"Mr. *Jefferson*": Thomas Jefferson (1732–1807) played numerous roles in both comedy and tragedy at Drury Lane from 1753 to 1758. He returned in 1767 for eleven more seasons.

"Mr. *Beard*": John Beard (1716?–91) became a London favorite singing tenor roles in the operas and oratorios of Handel. He also had a long association with Garrick and Drury Lane. His appearance in *The Reprisal* to sing "Behold, My Brave Britons" at the final curtain can be explained by his great popularity as a singer of sea chanteys and patriotic ballads such as "Rule Brittania."

"Mr. *Woodward*": Harry Woodward (1717–77), a comedian and pantomimist renowned as Harlequin, played at Drury Lane for twenty seasons beginning in 1738. See Phyllis Hartnoll, *The Oxford Companion to the Theatre*, 3d ed. (London: Oxford University Press, 1967), 1015.

"Miss *Macklin*": Maria Macklin (c. 1733–81), known both as a singer and as an actress, played many leading roles; beginning in 1753, she was employed by Garrick at Drury Lane.

9. "BRUSH": In *Roderick Random*, the valet of Captain Whiffle is named Vergette, French for "clothes brush."

10. "CHAMPIGNON": Fr. Mushroom or fungus; here, the name may carry some phallic or aphrodisiac connotations.

11. "OCLABBER": *Clabber* was a dialectal word for mud, borrowed from Irish.

12. "HAULYARD": Halyard, "a rope or tackle used for raising or lowering a sail, yard, spar or flag" (*OED*).

13. "BLOCK": See below, n. 165. A sailor by the name of Ben Block is mentioned in chapter 24 of *Roderick Random*.

14. "TARS": Probably an abbreviation of *tarpaulin*. According to *OED*, the word *tar* as a label for a sailor appears to have come into popular use toward the end of the seventeenth century.

15. "individual nice buttock . . . famished French wolves": See below, n. 49. Throughout the play, Smollett makes a number of references to the half-starved condition of the French.

16. "on account of the late rebellion": Many Scotsmen found haven in France with Charles Edward after the defeat of the Jacobite rebels at Culloden in 1746. In

Complete History, 4:674–75, Smollett narrates the escape of some rebel chiefs in two French frigates and the successful flight of Charles Edward to the friendly shores of France accompanied by a small band of exiles.

17. "Arrah": An Irish interjection, apparently useful to Smollett in stereotyping his Irishman. Rourk Oregan in chapter 49 of *Roderick Random* confirms his nationality with this interjection, as does Major Macleaver in chapter 39 of *Ferdinand Count Fathom*.

18. "hooly": Slowly, cautiously.

19. "a gra": This exclamation, or simply "gra," is a variant of *arrah*. In his initial conversation in *Humphry Clinker*, Sir Ulic Mackilligut uses the same exclamation, as well as the vocative "honey," to help give his speech the "true Hibernian accent" (Jery Melford to Sir Watkin Phillips, Bath, April 24, p. 30).

20. "the law of nations . . . prescind": As is evident from the play's later references to Grotius and Pufendorf (see below, p. 196 and nn. 109, 110), Smollett's wide reading had familiarized him with the basic concepts and elementary jargon of seventeenth- and eighteenth-century international law; he turns his familiarity to comic purposes in the mock legal discourses of Oclabber and Maclaymore. To prescind is "To cut off, detach, or separate *from*" (*OED*).

21. "*spolia opima*": A common Latin phrase used to describe the choicest spoils, those taken by a commander from a slain enemy. Smollett uses the phrase also in *Sir Launcelot Greaves*, chapter 19.

22. "*pecudum prædas agere*": To carry off booty of cattle. Apparently derived from Livy 7.30.15, "*prædas hominum atque pecudum actas.*"

23. "sonsy": Buxom; cheerful.

24. "wae": Woeful.

25. "the very moral of": "*Vulgarly.* Counterpart, likeness. Chiefly in phr. *the very moral of*" (*OED*). Smollett's line is one of three examples given in *OED*.

26. "grammachree": Gramercy; many thanks.

27. "Ochone": Scottish and Irish: Alas!

28. "sea wolf": Sea lion.

29. "the castle of Ballyclough": Ballyclough is a parish in the county of Cork. Close to the parish village is a structure known as Ballyclough Castle.

30. "*drimmendoo*": Drimmin Dhu (Black Back), "Dear Black Cow," an old Irish song, the plaintive melody of which may be found in Edward Bunting, *The Ancient Music of Ireland* (Dublin, 1840), 32. The song is mentioned also by Lismahago in *Humphry Clinker* (Jery Melford to Sir Watkin Phillips, Morpeth, July 13, p. 188).

31. "Elen a Roon": Eibhlin a Ruin, "Ellen Aroon" or "Eileen, My Secret Love," another old Irish song; its apparently much-admired melody may be found in Bunting, *Ancient Music*, 94.

32. "carmen elegiacum": Elegiac song or poem; the succeeding terms in Maclaymore's speech are all obscure Latin (originally Greek) words intended to give the effect of pedantic nonsense: *monocolos*, one unit or member; *dicolos*, two units or members; *tetrastrophos*, four strophes.

33. "shambrucks": Shamrocks.
34. "Teague": Common nickname for an Irishman.
35. "Hoot-fie": An exclamation of contempt or doubt.
36. "Seneca *de Consolatione*": A collective title for three of Seneca's essays, written at various times during his life (4 B.C.–A.D. 65) and addressing Stoic sentiments to those who have suffered loss or misfortune.
37. "Volusenus": Florence Volusene (1504?–47?), Scottish humanist and one of the Latin masters of his day, whose best-known work was *De Animi Tranquillitate*, which was written in the traditional vein of the consolation.
38. "the braes of Lochaber": A brae is a hill or hillside. Lochaber is a district in the southern part of the county of Inverness.
39. "grat": Lamented.
40. "rippet": Uproar.
41. "spring": A lively dance often played on the bagpipe.
42. "sasenach": Saxon, that is, English. See *Humphry Clinker*, Jery Melford to Sir Watkin Phillips, Argyleshire, September 3, p. 233: "The Highlanders have no other name for the people of the Low-country, but Sassenagh, or Saxons . . . ."
43. "nain sell": Own self.
44. "gar": Cause.
45. "gowk": Clumsy person.
46. "gauky": Simpleton. One of Roderick Random's schoolmates, a fellow guilty of treachery against his friend, is named Gawky (*Roderick Random*, chapters 6, 21).
47. "ettle": Make an attempt.
48. "a pibroch of Macreeman's composition": This allusion has not been traced; the composition referred to may be fictional.
49. "*buttock of beef . . . four meagre Frenchmen*": Smollett's stage picture may have been partially influenced by William Hogarth's engraving, *The Gate of Calais, or The Roast Beef of Old England* (1749), in which Hogarth intended to show how impoverished and underfed the French lower classes were in contrast with the English. One of Hogarth's central figures is a meager French cook struggling to carry a large beef loin he is delivering to a hotel for Englishmen. A Scottish mercenary and an Irish one, Jacobite fugitives, are also part of Hogarth's scene.
50. "capricieux": Capricious.
51. "cautive": Captive.
52. "parbleu": Of course. Literally the word is a mild oath, "by God," *bleu* being a French euphemism for *Dieu* that appears in many of Champignon's subsequent minced oaths.
53. "mais taisons": Let's stop talking.
54. "alte la": Stop.
55. "ah quelles ames!": What beautiful souls!
56. "man à bonnes fortunes": A lady-killer.
57. "diable m'emporte!": Devil take me!
58. "avouez donc": Admit then.

59. "dissipé de brouillard": Dissipated the fog.

60. "allegresse": Jubilation.

61. "gout": Taste.

62. "sabre a la main": Sabre in hand.

63. "opiniatre": Stubborn.

64. "parmi les belles filles Angloises": Among the beautiful English girls.

65. "jolies vaudevilles": Pretty comic songs.

66. *"A coblere dere vas"*: A ballad beginning "A cobbler there was," sung to a tune often known as "Derry Down"; the melody was printed along with a seven-stanza lyric for "A Cobler There Was," or "The Cobler's End," in *The Musical Miscellany* (London, 1729), 2:170–71.

67. "eperduement": To distraction, desperately.

68. "SONG": The musical setting for this song was composed by James Oswald, a Scotsman who probably also wrote the music for the two later songs in *The Reprisal*, "Let the Nymph Still Avoid" and "The Tars of Old England (Behold, My Brave Britons)." The association of Oswald and Smollett must have been fairly close, since Oswald had also written music for *The Tears of Scotland* and some others of Smollett's lyrics. See Deutsch, "Poetry Preserved in Music."

69. "gascoon": Unusual variant of *gascon*, a braggart. The term derives from the name of the inhabitants of Gascony, in southwestern France, who were supposed to be braggarts. In *Roderick Random*, Roderick loses a sword fight with a braggart Gascon, but soon defeats him in a second encounter (chapters 43, 44).

70. "Morbleu": Minced oath: by God's death.

71. "albâtre": Alabaster.

72. "mardy!": A variant, supposedly spoken by peasants, of the oath *mordieu* (God's death).

73. "Comment! que m'importe": But what difference does that make?

74. "Thalestris": A queen of the Amazons. The label was often applied to a ferocious woman. In chapter 4 of *Ferdinand Count Fathom*, Fathom's pillaging mother is described by Smollett as an Amazon, not inferior to Thalestris (p. 19).

75. "quid": "A piece of something (usu. of tobacco), suitable to be held in the mouth and chewed" (*OED*).

76. *"tempora mutantur, et nos mutamur in illis"*: Medieval Latin proverb: "Times change, and we change with them."

77. "charity school": In the early years of the eighteenth century, there had been a vigorous movement for the establishment of charity schools that would provide an elementary education for poor children and that would be supported by private benefactions. Many questioned the advisability of thus educating the poor; the best-known expression of such opposition was Bernard Mandeville's "Essay on Charity and Charity-Schools," added to the 1723 edition of his *Fable of the Bees*.

78. "I was better than I was bonny": The expression is based on a Scottish proverb, identified by Alexander Hislop, *The Proverbs of Scotland* (Edinburgh, 1868), in the form, "Ye're like a singed cat—better than ye're bonny."

79. "the treaty of *Aix la Chapelle*": The treaty of 1748 bringing an end to the long War of the Austrian Succession (1740–48) and establishing a temporary peace in the confused eighteenth-century struggles for power in western Europe. England and France were two of the principal signatories.

80. "swunds": Mild oath: God's wounds.

81. "hawked up": *OED* defines *hawk up* as "to bring *up* with a strong effort of clearing the throat," citing Smollett's use in *Peregrine Pickle*, chapter 14: "He hawked up, with incredible straining, the interjection ah!"

82. "slip his cable": For this phrase, *OED* cites William Falconer, *An Universal Dictionary of the Marine* (1769): "They may be ready to cut or slip the cables [attached to the anchor] when they shall be too much hurried to weigh their anchors."

83. "Odso!": Mild oath: God's soul!

84. "Hotel de Bussy": No building of this name has been identified.

85. "Armagh": Religious center of northern Ireland, seat of both Roman Catholic and Protestant archbishops and a traditional seat of learning.

86. "all the fat's in the fire": An old proverb meaning that an explosion of some sort is soon expected.

87. "hang up our harps . . . Babel's streams": Brush's version of Psalms 137:1–2: "By the rivers of Babylon, there we sat down, yea, we wept, when we remembered Zion. We hanged our harps upon the willows in the midst thereof."

88. "Bedlam": Common name for the Hospital of Saint Mary of Bethlehem, a famous asylum for the insane located in Moorfields, London.

89. "trim": "To beat, thrash, trounce" (*OED*).

90. "Zooks!": An abbreviated form of the oath *Gadzooks*, the exact origin of which is uncertain.

91. "atomy": "An emaciated or withered living body" (*OED*).

92. "*fortune de la guerre*": Fortune of war.

93. "Prenez garde . . . echappe": Be careful that she doesn't escape.

94. "Mons. le Second —— contre maitre": Subordinate naval officers.

95. "chaloupe": Fr. Cognate with the English *shallop*; used here to identify the longboat, the largest boat carried on a ship.

96. "midge": A small insect; an insignificant person.

97. "vous avez tué votre commandant": You have killed your commander.

98. "mes gens, a moi": My people, come to me.

99. "worricow": Hobgoblin.

100. "weel I wot": Assuredly.

101. "blind Harry": A Scottish name for the game of blindman's buff.

102. "Ventre saingris!": By God's bowels!

103. "kail thro' the reek": *OED* identifies the expression "To give one his kale [cabbage] through the reek [smoke]" as a Scotch phrase or proverb meaning "to treat one in some unpleasant fashion, to let one 'have it.' "

104. "mort de ma vie!": By the death of my life! This innocuous oath appears also in the speech of the Frenchman Lavement in chapter 19 of *Roderick Random*.

105. "sacrebleu!": Another mild oath, comparable to "good God!"

106. "fashed": Vexed.

107. "*sottises*": Stupid tricks.

108. "m'intendez vous?": Do you hear me?

109. "*Grotius de Jure Belli ac Pacis*": *De Jure Belli et Pacis* (1625), by the Dutch jurist Hugo Grotius (1583–1645), is considered the foundation treatise in the development of modern international law.

110. "*Puffendorf de officio Hominis & Civis*": Another important early treatise on international law was *De Officio Hominis et Civis* (1673), by the German jurist and historian Samuel Pufendorf (1632–94).

111. "*captus in bello* . . . the learned *Puffendorf*": It is difficult to know what precise point of law the pedantic Maclaymore is trying to suggest. *Captus in bello* (prisoner of war), *obses* (hostage), and *vades* (security, bail) are terms that cannot be placed in any particular context. *Flagrante bello* is a fairly common phrase in classical Latin for open war, but does not seem to be associated specifically with Pufendorf. Maclaymore is apparently echoing Pufendorf's distinction (2:14) between formal, declared war (*bellum solemne*) and informal war, waged against private citizens (*bellum minus solemne*).

112. "ventre bleu!": God's belly! This minced oath is used also by Lavement in chapter 19 of *Roderick Random*.

113. "paughty": Insolent.

114. "rustre": Lout.

115. "*tuum est imperare*": A Latin schoolbook formula: "It's your duty (or privilege) to command."

116. "meet before mountains meet": A proverbial idea expressed in many forms, such as that found in Benjamin Franklin's *Poor Richard's Almanack* (1742): "Men meet, mountains never."

117. "entremettre": Interfere.

118. "hardiesse": Audacity.

119. "Vaisseau de Guerre": War vessel.

120. "*cotte*": Coat, tunic.

121. "mauvaise plaisanterie": Bad joke.

122. "Daignez": Deign, be pleased.

123. "du bien——de rente": Property, income.

124. "the Garonne": River flowing from the Pyrenees to Bordeaux in southwestern France.

125. "pretendez": Claim.

126. "a begging brother of the order of St. Francis": A Franciscan friar; a member of one of the orders tracing back to the founding of the Friars Minor by St. Francis of Assisi in 1209.

127. "*savatier*": Cobbler.

128. "county of *Bearne*": Located in southwest France in the Pyrenees.

129. "count de *Bardasch*": *Bardash* is a rare term (from Fr. *bardache*) for a catamite, thus making this passage another example of Smollett's notion that homosexual practices were often a useful means of advancement. See introduction to the poems, pp. 12–13.

130. "medisance": Scandalmongering.

131. "r'attraper": Recapture.

132. "the wrang sow by the lug": "The wrong sow by the ear," a proverbial expression recorded as early as 1546 by John Heywood in his *Proverbs*.

133. "playing at rubbers . . . as the saying is": The saying that Oclabber cannot get straight is, "He who plays at bowls must expect to meet with rubbers." The proverb was apparently quite a favorite with Smollett; he used it in the heading for chapter 10 of *Sir Launcelot Greaves* and again in *Humphry Clinker*, Jery Melford to Sir Watkin Phillips, October 3, p. 292.

134. "Let that flie . . . rub out": Scottish proverb. Smollett's lines seem to mark one of the first appearances of the expression in print. Sir Walter Scott used the proverb with almost identical wording in chapter 23 of *Rob Roy* (1817).

135. "waff": Solitary.

136. "maggots": A maggot is "a whimsical or perverse fancy" (*OED*).

137. "tasse": Cup (as in French); in English, usually *tass*.

138. "doubled the point of land": To double is to "sail or pass round or to the other side of (a cape or point), so that the ship's course is, as it were, doubled or bent upon itself" (*OED*).

139. "it is not your fate to die by water": An allusion to the proverb, "He that's born to be hanged shall never be drowned." In *The Tempest*, Gonzalo alludes similarly to the same proverb when he remarks, of an outspoken boatswain, "Methinks he hath no drowning mark upon him, his complexion is perfect gallows" (1.1.28–30).

140. "devoirs": Respects.

141. "decampé sans façon": Departed without ceremony.

142. "tout a fait": Entirely.

143. "juste ciel!": Kind heaven!

144. "Revanche": Revenge.

145. "Larron": Thief.

146. "ça": So there.

147. "SONG": The music for these words was probably also written by James Oswald. See above, n. 68.

148. "Comment!": What!

149. "bonté": Goodness.

150. "clap her aboard": Either to come side by side (as two ships) or to come on board (as a party from one ship boarding another); in this case the latter meaning seems the appropriate one.

151. "nothing but rags and vermin . . . head-money": Block's saying about "rags and vermin" expresses a common eighteenth-century view of the sailor's sorry lot and

may have been part of contemporary seaman's lingo; however, no recorded version of it has been traced. Head money is a sum paid for each prisoner taken at sea, as a reward, not as a ransom.

152. "all upperwork and head-sail": Upperwork: "That part of a vessel which is above water-level when it is ready or laden for a voyage" (*OED*). Headsail: "A general name for any of the sails belonging to the foremast and bowsprit [the spar extending out from the bow of a vessel to which foremast stays are attached]" (*OED*).

153. "How does mother Margery?": This phrase, which seems to be a proverb or allusion, has not been traced.

154. "wind-bound": "Detained by contrary or stormy winds" (*OED*).

155. "half a glass . . . handspike": An expression such as "half a glass" usually referred to the half-hour glass. The phrase "under your stern" refers to the overhanging part at the rear of the ship. The helm was a steering apparatus; therefore, "clap his helm a starboard" means to turn the helm toward the starboard, or the right; see also above, n. 150, the expression "clap her aboard." A handspike was a wooden bar, sometimes ironshod, used as a lever; here, perhaps a bar to turn the apparatus raising an anchor.

156. "we must all die one time": A common proverbial idea, found in numerous forms. In *Roderick Random*, chapter 24, Jack Rattlin expatiates on it: "Well, well, we must all die, that's certain,—we must all come to port sooner or later,—at sea or on shore;—we must be fast moored one day,—death's like the best bower anchor as the saying is, it will bring us all up."

157. "runlet": "A cask or vessel of varying capacity" (*OED*).

158. "Nantz": Brandy produced in Nantes, France. The term was frequently compounded, as here, into *Right Nantz*.

159. "strike my topsails": A ship lowering its topsails to half-mast indicated by that action submission or respect to another.

160. "Odds heart!": Mild oath: God's heart!

161. "cross trees": Horizontal timbers at the head of a mast; among other purposes, they provided a place where sailors could stand aloft.

162. "qui souhaite il?": Whom do you want?

163. "ye may gar me . . . with fear": Scottish dialect, and possibly proverbial, but no source has been traced. Maclaymore is saying: "you may make me sweat with fighting, but it's not in your breeches to make me sweat with fear."

164. "shew your own country . . . enemy's cable": Hayward accuses Oclabber of betraying his country. The fore-topsail was above the foresail, which was the main sail on the foremast; to show the fore-topsail indicated an intention to attack. To wold, or woold, was to wind a rope or chain (or, as here, a cable) around a mast so as to strengthen it when it was broken (*OED*).

165. "that bowling i' the block": Bowling or bowline: a rope attached to the edge of a sail and to a ship's bow to keep the sail steady. Block: a pulley or pulleys through which a rope (such as a bowling) could be run.

166. "slipped the painter": To slip the painter is "to clear off"; a painter is "a rope attached to the bow of a boat, for making it fast to a ship, a stake, etc." (*OED*).

167. "ecouté mon ami": Listen, my friend.

168. "yard arm": Either end of a long spar "serving to support and extend a square sail, which is bent to it" (*OED*).

169. "Michel . . . de Vermisseau": *Vermisseau* is French for a small worm. Smollett creates a similar joke in chapter 23 of *Ferdinand Count Fathom* by giving an abbé a string of noble Christian names but a surname (de Fumier) that is a French word for dung (p. 99).

170. "Mepris": Scorn.

171. "Galimatias": Gibberish.

172. "escadre": Squadron.

173. "*Dissentio*": L. I dissent.

174. "the law of nature and nations": Alluding to a concept of international law embodied in the title of Pufendorf's *De Jure Naturæ et Gentium* (1672).

175. "cocky": A diminutive of *cock*, often used as a term of endearment; see, for example, William Congreve, *The Old Bachelor* (1687), 4.4.

176. "streak": A streak, or strake, is one of "the several continuous lines of planking or plates, of uniform breadth, in the side of a vessel, extending from stem to stern" (*OED*).

177. "b'w'ye": One of the many historical and dialectal variants of "God be with you," that is, "Good-bye."

178. "soupe meagre": Soup maigre is a "thin soup, made chiefly from vegetables or fish" (*OED*).

179. "je ne vous attendois pas sitot": I was not expecting you so soon.

180. "a quelle coté faut il que je me tourne?": Which side shall I turn to?

181. "fash your noddle": Trouble your head (used contemptuously).

182. "cry *barley*": An expression used in games by Scotch children when asking for a truce or for quarter, as in a parley.

183. "*Canaille*": Rabble.

184. "que ferai-je? . . . etouffe": What shall I do? I feel confused. These English are so precipitate. May the devil choke them.

185. "matelots—mes enfans": Sailors—my lads.

186. "chardon . . . la faim": Thistle, rag, nettle, manure, owl, hunger. Presumably these derogatory words, although not capitalized, are the names of Champignon's crewmen.

187. "Ah mon bon dieu! . . . il faut amener": Ah my dear god! have pity on me still—may the water of life be brought to me. Ah miserable sinner!—I am dead!—I am buried!—ah! enough my lads—stop—desist—we must strike our colors.

188. "abaissée le drapeau": Lowered the ensign (as a sign of surrender). See above, n. 159.

189. "misericorde": Mercy.

190. "every tenth man . . . in terrorem": A standard legal phrase used to threaten or warn of dire consequences.

191. "hanging and marriage go by destiny": A common proverb dating back at least to the sixteenth century.

192. "Tinsey": A common term used derisively in reference to a Frenchman, derived from the sparkling ornamentation ("tinsel") of fashionable or foppish dress. Smollett used the same term earlier in *Ferdinand Count Fathom*, chapter 28 (p. 130). The half-literate Win Jenkins applies it more broadly in *Humphry Clinker*; see Winfred Jenkins to Mary Jones, Bath, May 15, p. 68.

193. "braces are so taught . . . keep my yards square": A brace is "a rope attached to the yard of a vessel for the purpose of 'trimming'" (*OED*). *Taught* is a fairly common eighteenth-century variant spelling for *taut*. For *yards*, see above, n. 168.

194. "broke bulk": To break bulk is "to open the hold and take out goods thence" (*OED*, citing Captain John Smith's *The Seaman's Grammar* [1692]).

195. "tiller": A bar to turn a boat's rudder; here used figuratively as a monkey's tail.

196. "red ropes": Ropes covered with red baize, placed along either side of a gangway or ladder. Smollett uses the phrase similarly in chapter 24 of *Roderick Random*.

197. "poop": Structure at the stern of a ship.

198. "ginger-bread work": "Orig. applied by sailors to the carved and gilded decorations of a ship; hence to architectural or other ornament of a gaudy and tasteless kind" (*OED*). The earliest citation of the term in *OED* is from *Roderick Random*, chapter 3.

199. "*Spanish wool*": Wool that has been impregnated with rouge.

200. "struck your ensign": To strike an ensign would be to yield or cause to yield. See above, n. 188.

201. "Spithead": Part of the channel lying between Portsmouth, on the south coast of England, and the Isle of Wight. Spithead had long been an anchorage for the English navy.

202. "have you to the gangway": Take you to the gangway to be flogged.

203. "to hand, reef, and steer": These are basic sailship operations. In *Roderick Random*, Ben Block is praised as "the first man that taught [Tom Bowling] to hand, reef and steer" (chapter 24). To hand is "to take in, furl (a sail)"; to reef is "to reduce the extent of (a sail) by taking in or rolling up a part and securing it" (*OED*).

204. "marlinspike": A tool used for various jobs with ropes. This line is cited in the *OED* entry for "Marlinspike."

205. "fetch up his leeway with a wet sail": "To come with a wet sail" is "to make swift progress to victory, like a ship with sails wetted in order to keep close to the wind" (*OED*).

206. "the song": Unidentified.

207. "SONG": The music for these words was probably also written by James Oswald. See above, n. 68.

208. "*pullet*": A young hen.

209. *"Antigallican"*: An English privateer that in December 1756 had taken the French *Duc de Penthièvre* as a prize.
210. *"welkin"*: Sky.

The Briton

No. 1. Saturday, 29 May 1762

1. Motto: Despite the attribution, the lines are not to be found in modern editions of Cicero. They may be translated thus: "I have always intended to bring forth policies for the republic that would seem just and useful; this I will do especially at this time when if we establish harmony among us, having cast off strife and contempt, we shall both be safe ourselves and be able to save others despite themselves."
2. "the Monitor": *Briton*, no. 1, is largely a response to *Monitor*, no. 357 (22 May 1762), which had considered the dangers of a favorite as one who acts for "private interest" and had clearly insinuated that Bute was a dangerous favorite and a Sejanus-like minister. For Sejanus, see below, n. 4.
3. *"ignis fatuus"*: Med. L. Foolish light. Like the English *will-o'-the-wisp*, the phrase identifies the phenomenon of a phosphorescent light sometimes seen hovering over marshes. Both phrases are most often used figuratively in reference to a delusive notion.
4. "a quotation from Tacitus": The motto for *Monitor*, no. 357, is a quotation from Tacitus *Annals* 4.1: "Tiberium variis artibus devinxit adeo Sejanus, ut obscurum adversum alios, sibi uni incautum, intectumque efficeret." Smollett translates the quotation in the last part of his sentence. Tiberius was emperor of Rome from A.D. 14 to 37. Sejanus, although executed in A.D. 31, was for several years Tiberius's confidant and chief aide. His name became proverbial for an unscrupulous and sinister favorite.
5. "Without merit . . . private interest": The material here repeated from the *Monitor* is more faithful to the original than a paraphrase, but it is not a verbatim quotation. Smollett omits some phrases and makes changes in wording to patch up omissions and to effect a summary of them. There is no substantial distortion of the original. The practice of the *Briton* is often to put in quotation marks paraphrased or otherwise not quite verbatim passages from other papers.
6. "a nobleman of unblemished integrity": John Stuart, earl of Bute (1713–92), had become associated with the household of George III's father, Frederick, Prince of Wales, in 1750, when George was only twelve. After Frederick's death in 1751, Bute became an influential companion and mentor of the future king. There is, however, no solid evidence that Bolingbroke's *On the Idea of a Patriot King* (1749) was a text for their studies, as later historians have sometimes asserted and as Smollett goes on to imply. A pamphlet by John Douglas entitled *A Letter Addressed*

to Two Great Men on the Prospect of Peace (1760) had suggested that the government follow "patriot" principles. The idea seemed to pick up circulation quickly as George began his reign, and once he had been hopefully labeled a "patriot king," it was easy for his supporters to suggest that this was a role for which he had long been educated.

No. 2. Saturday, 5 June 1762

1. Motto: *Rhetorica Ad Herennium* 1.4: "We shall force hatred upon [our adversaries] by adducing some base, high-handed, treacherous, cruel, impudent, malicious, or shameful act of theirs." The *Rhetorica* is no longer attributed by scholars to Cicero; the author is probably Cornificius.
2. "A full exposition . . . rupture with Spain": Smollett alludes to one of the main controversies featured in the *Monitor* during the weeks before the *Briton* began. The controversy went back to the previous September when Pitt, then secretary of state, had insisted on England's declaring war against Spain in rejection of three claims that Spain had made against England earlier in the summer. (The claims are itemized by Smollett later in this number of the *Briton*.) When his proposal was turned down, Pitt resigned, making his famous declaration that he could not be responsible where he could not direct. A few months later, in January 1762, England was indeed forced to declare war on Spain, a move that seemed to Pitt's supporters to vindicate their leader. In the subsequent parliamentary debates, the papers detailing the deterioration of relations between Spain and England had been called for and shortly thereafter were published as *Papers Relative to the Rupture with Spain*. The Pitt forces were not satisfied that the full story had been told, and in March 1762 there appeared *Observations on the Papers Relative to the Rupture with Spain*, probably authored by John Wilkes. This work insists that Pitt's advice would have been even more fully vindicated had earlier papers also been published. It accuses the present administration of garbling and suppressing papers to justify the delay in declaring war. A few weeks later the ministry replied with *A Full Exposition of a Pamphlet Entitled, Observations on the Papers Relative to the Rupture with Spain*. This exposition argues that the earlier papers were irrelevant and that, in any case, their publication could have been moved for had not the anti-ministerial forces preferred to have them remain unpublished so that there would be something to make a noise about. *Monitor*, no. 358 (29 May 1762), had replied to *A Full Exposition*, and then *Briton*, no. 2, got in the next word by replying to the *Monitor*. Once the positions had been stated, subsequent entries into the fray were not much more than a rehash of what had gone before. Thus *Briton*, no. 2, does little but recapitulate in its own words the argument of *A Full Exposition*. Later in this number, Smollett refers to the anonymous authors of the quarreling pamphlets as the Observator and the Expositor.
3. "*how a plain tale could put them down*": 1 *Henry IV* 2.4.255–56: "Mark now, how a plain tale shall put you down."

4. "a right honourable gentleman": This gentleman is not identified in any of the accounts of the parliamentary proceedings.

5. "This obstinate fact . . . under the seal of secrecy!": Again, the quotations from the *Monitor* throughout this issue are slightly altered, but are essentially faithful to the original.

6. "lord T——": Apparently Richard Grenville-Temple, Earl Temple (1711–79), Pitt's brother-in-law and his close ally during the political ups and downs of this period. The "certain noble lord" of this passage has not been identified.

7. "beef-eater": "A well-fed menial" (*OED*).

8. "the first Prussian treaty": The Convention (or Treaty) of Westminster, by which George II of England and Frederick the Great of Prussia united to resist foreign invasion of Germany. The pact was signed early in 1756, when Henry Fox was secretary of state; Fox was replaced by Pitt in December 1756, and in April 1758 agreement was reached upon the annually renewable subsidies offered to the Prussians in exchange for their alliance; the amount in the first year was £670,000, and the subsidy was renewed three times. See Robert B. Asprey, *Frederick the Great: The Magnificent Enigma* (New York: Ticknor and Fields, 1986), 414–16.

9. "he had refused . . . the banks of the Weser": In the spring and summer of 1755, George II had sent his son, the duke of Cumberland, to the Continent to command an army of Hanoverians, Hessians, and Brunswickers in defending Hanover against the French. Pitt, concerned with manning other military expeditions, opposed sending any British troops to Hanover, although Cumberland's army was heavily outnumbered.

10. "prize-fighter": "One who engaged in a public fighting match" (*OED*).

11. "the treaty of Utrecht": The treaty of 1713, concluding the War of the Spanish Succession, in which France and England had fought each other. See *Briton*, no. 20, n. 2.

12. "the m——y of Great Britain": The argument in the preceding passage, stressing the reasonableness and legality of the Spanish claims, is very similar to that of *A Full Exposition*, pp. 20–23.

13. "the law of nature and of nations": English rendering of the title of one of the basic works on international law, Samuel Pufendorf's *De Jure Naturæ et Gentium* (1672).

14. "I mean . . . the Antigallican privateer and her prize": An English privateer, the *Antigallican*, had seized the French *Duc de Penthièvre* as a prize in Spanish waters in December 1756. The ship was taken to the port of Cadiz, where, after some confusing negotiations, two Spanish men-of-war forced the English crew to give it up and return it to the French.

15. "the memorial . . . M. de Bussy": The memorial was one of the documents printed in *Papers Relative to the Rupture with Spain*. In July 1761 de Bussy, a French emissary in London, presented it to Pitt in support of Spain's three claims. In effect, the memorial threatened to make the claims a part of the French cause, a threat that Pitt had angrily rejected.

16. *"Rio Tinto"*: A river (also known as the Rio Negro) in eastern Honduras, arising in the Sierra de Agalta and flowing some 150 miles to the Caribbean.

17. "Othello . . . the handkerchief": An allusion to *Othello* 3.4.89–96. When Desdemona evades Othello's questions about her lost handkerchief, he keeps demanding, "The handkerchief."

No. 3. Saturday, 12 June 1762

1. Motto: Horace *Carmen Saeculare*, lines 10–11: "reborn another and yet the same." The last word in the Latin quotation should be *nasceris*.

2. "North Briton": The first number of the *North Briton* appeared on 5 June 1762. This periodical and its editor, John Wilkes (1727–97), became the chief antagonists of Smollett during the lifetime of the *Briton*.

3. "the crazy watchman and his goose": This expression probably derived from some fable or proverb, but the source, if one exists, has not been identified.

4. "the motto from Tacitus": See *Briton*, no. 1, n. 4.

5. "a Trajan or a Titus": Trajan (ruled A.D. 98–117) and Titus (ruled A.D. 79–81) were two of the more humane Roman emperors. In *Humphry Clinker*, Smollett applies Suetonius's praise of Titus, *"delici humani generis"* (delight of the human race), to George III and speaks of him as "Titus Vespasian in generosity; Trajan in beneficence" (Jery Melford to Sir Watkin Phillips, London, June 2, p. 95).

6. "He improved . . . *national interest"*: Quoted, with a number of excisions, from *Monitor*, no. 357 (22 May 1762).

7. "The king of Prussia . . . the contrary": Quoted from *North Briton*, no. 1 (5 June 1762).

8. "the annual tribute": The subsidies paid to Frederick of Prussia had been stopped at the beginning of 1762, when Frederick made an ally of Russia, a former enemy, after the death of the Czarina Elizabeth. See *Briton*, no. 2, n. 8.

9. "Sir Charles Saunders": Sir Charles Saunders (1713?–75) was the naval hero of the battle of Quebec in 1759; in 1760 he became commander in chief of the British fleet in the Mediterranean, where he maintained British dominance until the Peace of Paris in 1763.

10. "conquest of Martinique . . . the West-Indies": Martinique had fallen to British forces early in 1762, followed soon by Grenada and all the Windward Islands. See *Briton*, no. 5, n. 10.

11. "sent forth . . . settlements of Spain": Successful expeditions against Havana and Manila were being conducted in the summer of 1762.

12. "underhand offers . . . court of Vienna": *North Briton*, no. 1 (5 June 1762), in answering Briton's charge that "the administration is conducted with such integrity as defies reproach," had remarked, "Sure you dare not allude to the unfair and underhand offers to the court of Vienna for an immediate accommodation in consequence of cessions to be made to them in Italy, *or elsewhere*." This re-

mark perhaps alludes to some of Bute's attempts, early in 1762, to effect a general peace, attempts that Frederick had resented because he might have had to give way on some of his territorial desires. Much mistrust existed between England and Prussia during 1762.

13. "He has displayed . . . administration?": More a paraphrase than a quotation from *North Briton*, no. 1 (5 June 1762).

14. "Pater-noster-Row": Adjacent to Saint Paul's Cathedral, Paternoster Row was the address for numerous booksellers. The *Briton*'s publisher, J. Coote, had his shop there, identified by the sign of the King's Arms.

15. "an Orator's head, or a Negro's head, or a Hog's head": Pitt was well known for his oratorical abilities. In *Adventures of an Atom* he is represented as Orator Taycho. The other two allusions probably are veiled sneers at Pitt's staunch supporter, William Beckford (see *Briton*, no. 8, n. 14), whose Jamaican connections associated him with slavery and the trade in rum, which was transported in hogsheads.

16. "*Non in aula* . . . hog's-stye": The source of the Latin quotation has not been traced. The ironically named *North Briton* threw out frequent sarcastic comments on the Scottish connections and language of the *Briton* and on the Scotsmen who were being given places and pensions under Bute.

17. "His patron": Smollett alludes sarcastically to Pitt, who accepted a pension of three thousand pounds per year after he gave up his ministerial post late in 1761; his wife received the title Baroness Chatham. In 1766 Pitt was named earl of Chatham. These awards remained chief targets in Smollett's attacks on Pitt, carrying over even into *Humphry Clinker*, where he is referred to as "the grand pensionary" (Jery Melford to Sir Watkin Phillips, London, June 2, p. 95).

No. 4. Saturday, 19 June 1762

1. Motto: Juvenal *Satires* 7.115–18: "You rise, a pale-faced Ajax, to declaim before a bumpkin judge in a case of contested liberty. Strain your lungs, poor fool, until they burst, that when exhausted by your labours some green palm-branches may be put up to adorn your garret."

2. "ABRACADABRA": See *Briton*, no. 38, n. 14.

3. "truly British": In his first address to Parliament, George III had implied a contrast between himself and his two predecessors (with their German connections) by saying, "Born and educated in this country, I glory in the name of Briton." His propagandists picked up this theme by frequently insisting that the new king was "truly British." See introduction to the *Briton*, p. 223.

4. "Beware the thane of B—e": Echoing *Macbeth* 4.1.72: "Beware the thane of Fife."

5. "the first lord commissioner of the treasury": Bute took over this office, usually considered the office held by the leader of the king's administration, in May 1762, when Newcastle resigned it.

6. "two dangerous rebellions": The Jacobite uprisings of 1715 and 1745.

7. "a Scotchman": John Dalrymple, second earl of Stair (1673–1747), was made "commander-in-chief of all the forces in South Britain" in 1744 (*DNB*), but he played no significant role in the military operations of the 1745 rebellion.

8. "Cape Breton . . . Westphalia": Most of the places mentioned in this passage identify battlegrounds where Pitt and his commanders had engineered significant British victories over the French. The British took control of Cape Breton with the surrender of Louisburg in July 1758. The French successfully defended Fort Ticonderoga in 1758, but the British took it in July 1759. Fort Duquesne was the object of the disastrous Braddock expedition in the summer of 1755, but was taken in the fall of 1758. The Quebec expedition under James Wolfe climaxed with the celebrated defeat of the French on the Plains of Abraham on 13 September 1759. In the West Indies, the British unsuccessfully attacked Martinique in January 1759, but finally overcame it in February 1762; Guadeloupe surrendered in April 1759. The fall of Pondicherry to British forces in January 1761 marked the end of French colonial hopes in India. During the war, there were a number of campaigns and battles in Westphalia in northwestern Germany. One of the most celebrated was the defeat of the French at Minden on 1 August 1759 by an Anglo-Hanoverian force under Ferdinand of Brunswick.

9. "the great objection . . . of Scotchmen": Horace Walpole, in a prefatory note to the section entitled "Scots Authors" in his *Catalogue of the Royal and Noble Authors of England* (1759), wrote of Scotland as "the most accomplished Nation in Europe; the Nation to which, if any one Country is endowed with a superior partition of sense, I should be inclined to give the preference in that particular." *North Briton*, no. 2 (12 June 1762), ironically referred to Walpole's compliment on the taste and accomplishment of the Scots.

10. "Orator Henley": John Henley (1692–1756) was one of the most famous eccentrics of eighteenth-century London. By a combination of religious preaching and bizarre entertainment, he captured the attention of the city and the scorn of Pope and Fielding, among others. His famed Oratory, where he held forth from 1739 until his death, was at Clare Market, in or near Lincoln's Inn Fields. The incident mentioned subsequently by Smollett may have occurred in 1747, when Henley appeared on the stage of the Haymarket Theatre with Samuel Foote (1720–77), the popular mimic, comic actor, and playwright. Robert Adams Day has suggested to me that some of the details in the concluding paragraph of this number of the *Briton* (e.g., "turned free-thinker in despair") seem really to be aimed at Charles Churchill and Robert Lloyd, two of Wilkes's henchmen. See *Briton*, no. 13, n. 10.

11. "Mr. Foote, and the renowned Opthalmiater": In 1747 Foote had appeared in *The Diversions of the Morning*, in which he had imitated a number of well-known persons, including John Taylor (1703–72), a quack eye-doctor whose oddities of speech and appearance had garnered him considerable notoriety. In 1761 Taylor published in three volumes *The History of the Travels and Adventures of the Cheva-*

lier John Taylor, Ophthalmiator. In essence this work was a huge self-advertisement telling of, among other things, the famous people Taylor had treated and the wondrous cures of distempered eyes he had effected.

12. "Hockley in the Hole": On the outskirts of London, near Clerkenwell Green; well known for its bear garden, its bulldog fights, and its wrestling and boxing matches. The name was virtually a byword in the eighteenth century for low-class entertainment, and the locale itself was a resort of the underworld. Allusions to it as such can be found in chapter 27 of *Roderick Random* as well as in the *Tatler* and *Spectator*, in Gay's *Trivia* and *The Beggar's Opera*, in Fielding's *Jonathan Wild*, and in Pope's *Dunciad*.

13. "hector": "A braggart, blusterer, bully" (*OED*).

14. "Ordinary": "One who has . . . immediate jurisdiction in ecclesiastical cases" (*OED*); in this case probably a bishop.

15. "Butcher-row": Apparently not a specific locale, but, according to *OED*, a term for a meat market or shambles. A line in *The Dunciad* (1.326) suggests that butchers may have been associated with Hockley in the Hole: "And 'Coll!' each Butcher roars at Hockley-hole." See Henry B. Wheatley, *London Past and Present: Its History, Associations, and Traditions* (London: John Murray, 1891): 2:218: "The feuds of the butchers of Clare Market, Newgate Market, and Leadenhall Market . . . were generally determined at Hockley in the Hole . . . ."

16. "olio": Originally a highly spiced Spanish or Portuguese dish with many ingredients; figuratively the word means "any mixture of heterogeneous things" (*OED*).

17. "the cart's-tail": One long-practiced form of legal punishment was to tie an offender to the back of a cart and whip him through the streets.

18. "parson militant": Probably an allusion to Charles Churchill (1731–64), an erstwhile clergyman, and his participation with John Wilkes in producing the *North Briton*. See *Briton*, no. 13, n. 10.

No. 5. Saturday, 26 June 1762

1. Motto: Virgil *Aeneid* 10.503–4: "To Turnus shall come the hour when for a great price will he long to have bought an unscathed Pallas."

2. "the kingdom of Pegu": In Burma, where the white elephant was often considered a sacred animal.

3. "papers relating to the negotiation with Spain": See *Briton*, no. 2, n. 2.

4. "the Monitor of last Saturday": *Monitor*, no. 361 (19 June 1762), replied directly to *Briton*, no. 3, and was the first issue of that sheet to take note of the *Briton*'s recent entry into the political arena.

5. "the milk of human kindness": *Macbeth* 1.5.17.

6. "how he expatiated on those topics": On 10 December 1742, Pitt had delivered a speech in which he attacked the king on the subject of Hanoverian troops. A version of the speech appeared in the *Gentleman's Magazine* 14 (February and March

1744): 76–77, 119, as part of the series of "Debates in the Senate of Lilliput." The quotation that follows in Smollett's text is almost verbatim from this version; most of the changes are typographical or consist in the substitution of real names for fictitious ones. George II had taken a great dislike to Pitt because of such out-spokenness, as is exemplified in the passage quoted by Smollett wherein Pitt calls Hanover "a *despicable electorate*" and sarcastically remarks on "the yearly visits that have been made to *that delightful country.*"

7. "the *ever-memorable treaty*": The treaty of Hanover, September 1725, by which France, Prussia, and Great Britain agreed to resist certain threats posed by treaties signed earlier that year between Austria and Spain.

8. "the Czarina's decease": See *Briton*, no. 3, n. 8.

9. "Sir Charles Saunders": See *Briton*, no. 3, n. 9.

10. "the conquest of Martinique": Admiral George Rodney and General Robert Monckton captured Martinique for the British on 12 February 1762. One of the few unsuccessful British operations in 1759 had been an earlier attempt at its capture.

11. "MILO": Titus Annius Milo (d. 48 B.C.) led an unruly mob of gladiators in fighting an equally unruly mob led by Clodius during the years of the power struggle between Julius Caesar and Pompey. Although the head of a mob, Milo supported the more aristocratic party of Pompey. When he was exiled in 52 B.C., Cicero wrote *Pro Milone* in his defense. The classical names affixed to various letters in the *Briton* do not seem particularly significant, except as they may allude in a general way to persons known for their involvement in political squabbles. Letters signed by "Milo" also appear in numbers 13, 17, and 29.

No. 6. Saturday, 3 July 1762

1. Motto: Horace *Odes* 3.2.17–20: "True worth, that never knows ignoble defeat, shines with undimmed glory, nor takes up nor lays aside the axes at the fickle mob's behest." Axes were symbols of public office in classical Rome.

2. "open": "Of hounds: . . . to begin to cry when in pursuit on a scent" (*OED*).

3. "a mighty war against Lewis XIV.": The War of the Spanish Succession, in which England was involved from 1702 until the Peace of Utrecht in 1713. See *Briton*, no. 10, n. 5, and no. 20, n. 2.

4. "one hundred and thirty-six millions": For Smollett's justification of this figure, see the last two paragraphs of *Briton*, no. 9.

5. "Acadia": Acadia was the French name for the American possessions it claimed along the North Atlantic seaboard. The name applied primarily to present-day Nova Scotia, but Smollett seems to use it also for other parts of the region, since mainland Nova Scotia had been in possession of the British since the Treaty of Utrecht in 1713.

6. "lord Albemarle, and sir George Pococke": Lieutenant General George Keppel,

third earl of Albemarle (1724–72), was commander in chief of the ten thousand troops sent against Havana. Sir George Pocock (1706–92) was commander in chief of the naval fleet which set sail from Spithead on 5 March 1762.

7. "the obscene harpies in Virgil": Aeneas encounters the half-woman, half-bird harpies of classical mythology in *Aeneid* 3.209–67. As used here by Smollett, *obscene* probably retains some of its Latin sense of ill-omened.

8. "the Gorgon's head": Medusa, one of the three Gorgons, whose hair was made of writhing snakes and the sight of whom turned men to stone. The story of the slaying of Medusa by Perseus is retold or alluded to frequently in Greek and Roman literature.

9. "the Empress Queen": Maria Theresa (1717–80), Holy Roman Empress and queen of Hungary, allied with France and opposed by Prussia in the Seven Years' War.

10. "treasure": The paragraph ending here is at best a rather warped review of the negotiations for peace during the summer of 1761. The various points hardly represent Pitt's position, but only some possibilities that were scanned and problems that were confronted. For example, Pitt strongly demanded that England retain exclusive rights around Newfoundland, but had at one time been brought to concede that the matter might be an item for negotiation. One of the most difficult features of the negotiations had been the attempt to separate the issues involved in the direct French-English confrontation from those involving England's Prussian allies and France's Austrian ones. The negotiations had broken down, at least as far as Pitt was concerned, when Spain had intervened with related demands of its own and Pitt had asked for a declaration of war against Spain rather than further pursuit of an immediate peace.

No. 7. Saturday, 10 July 1762

1. "a new Atalantis": *Secret Memoirs and Manners of Several Persons of Quality*, more commonly known as *The New Atalantis*, was a secret history, or scandalous roman à clef, published in 1709 by Delarivière Manley. Manley, writing as a Tory propagandist, defamed a number of Whig ministers in fictional guise.

2. "His last week's paper": *North Briton*, no. 5 (3 July 1762), had focused on the subject of favorites, pointing to the havoc they wrought in the reign of Edward II.

3. "last Tuesday's Gazetteer": *The Gazetteer and London Daily Advertiser* for Tuesday, 6 July 1762, had printed an article "From the Westminster Journal" disapproving of the tone and arguments of both the *Briton* and the *Monitor*.

4. Motto: Horace *Carmen Saeculare*, lines 57–59: "Already Faith and Peace and Honour and ancient Modesty and neglected Virtue have courage to come back."

5. "civilians": A civilian is "a writer or authority on the Civil Law" (*OED*).

6. "a sudden irruption into Saxony . . . Dresden": On 29 August 1756, early in the Seven Years' War, Frederick invaded Saxony and in less than two weeks captured Dresden.

7. "the examen of Machiavel's Prince": In 1740, in The Hague, Voltaire published Frederick's *Examen du Prince de Machiavel*; the work is often referred to as *The Antimachiavel*. The remarks of Frederick summarized in the succeeding lines occur in his observations on chapter 18 of *The Prince* ("How Far Princes Ought to Fulfill Their Engagements").

8. "the P——n monarch's manifesto": At the time he invaded Saxony, Frederick issued a statement justifying his actions and intentions. A copy of the French text with an English translation was soon available to the English public under the title *Motives, Which Have Obliged His Majesty the King of Prussia to Prevent the Designs of the Court of Vienna* (London, 1756).

9. "*salus populi . . . suprema lex*": A statement from the XII Tables, the first code of Roman law (fifth century B.C.), quoted by Cicero in *De Legibus* 3.3: "Let the good of the people be the highest law."

10. "under the conduct of a foreigner": The twenty-five thousand British troops serving on the Continent were attached to the armies of Prince Ferdinand of Brunswick-Wolfenbüttel.

11. "neutral bottoms": *Bottom* was a common term for the hull of a ship; it was used synecdochically for a whole ship, particularly one carrying cargo.

12. "toys": Knickknacks or trinkets.

13. "ATTICUS": Titus Pomponius Atticus (109–32 B.C.) was a correspondent of Cicero who managed to keep aloof from the civil strifes of his day and remain on good terms with all parties. Pope used the name in his satiric portrait of Addison in *An Epistle to Dr. Arbuthnot*.

No. 8. Saturday, 17 July 1762

1. Motto: Tacitus *Histories* 1.1: "[Men] listen with ready ears to calumny and spite; for flattery is subject to the shameful charge of servility, but malignity makes a false show of independence."

2. "a very extraordinary transaction": In February 1746, in the midst of the Jacobite Rebellion, the Pelhams (see below, n. 3) and their ministerial associates had shown their resentment of the king's treatment of them, and his increasing display of confidence in others, by resigning their offices. The king had thereupon offered the seals of the secretaries of state to Granville. Unable to find others willing to join the new ministry, the king had to recall the Pelhams, who were then able to demand and receive his compliance with their terms, including an office for Pitt. See *Briton*, no. 36, n. 7.

3. "the two brothers": Henry Pelham (1696–1754) and his brother, Thomas Pelham Holles, the duke of Newcastle (1693–1768), were principals in the administrations of England for more than a decade after the forced resignation of Sir Robert Walpole in 1742. Following the death of Henry in 1754, Newcastle continued to be a figure of prime importance in almost every administration until forced out of office by Bute.

4. "absolute authority": Pitt's words, often referred to in subsequent quarrels by his opponents, were: "Being responsible I *will* direct, and will be responsible for nothing I do not direct." See introduction to the *Briton*, p. 224.

5. "Fair Sir": To this point the speech is quoted from *The Merchant of Venice* 1.3.123–26, where Shylock ironically protests the ill usage of him as a Jew. The rest of the speech is apparently original, maintaining something of the Shakespearean tone but introducing diction applicable to the *Briton*'s view of the plight of George III.

6. "a former occasion": Pitt was dismissed after four months as secretary of state in April 1757, but public opinion forced George II to reinstate him in June.

7. "projection": Transmutation, as in alchemy, when base metal is changed to gold.

8. "one solitary peer": Earl Temple (see *Briton*, no. 2, n. 6), who became the patron of Wilkes and Churchill in their antiministerial labors.

9. "Figures ill-pair'd, and similies unlike": Pope, *The Dunciad* 1.66.

10. "*concordia civium*": Livy *History* 2.32.7: "Harmony amongst the citizens."

11. "F—x . . . G——lle": Henry Fox (1705–74), paymaster general of the forces, and George Grenville (1712–70), secretary of state (northern department), had been ridiculed in *North Briton*, no. 6 (10 July 1762). Grenville was Temple's younger brother and thus also Pitt's brother-in-law.

12. "*the Act for the Encouragement of Seamen*": One of Grenville's significant parliamentary contributions, the act (31 Geo. II, c. 10), passed in 1758, provided for punctual payment of seamen's wages. At the time, Grenville was treasurer of the navy.

13. "the late act . . . spirituous liquors": Probably 2 Geo. III, c. 5, "An Act for more effectually preventing the excessive use of spirituous liquors for home consumption, by laying additional duties upon spirits made in Great Britain . . . ." The act passed in the House of Commons in December 1761. Several acts relating to the excise on spirits were passed during the war years.

14. "that wise, respectable A——n": William Beckford (1709–70), wealthy alderman and, in 1762, lord mayor of London. His income, of which he was very lavish, was principally derived from his West Indies sugar plantations and the trade in rum. He was one of Pitt's staunchest supporters, a friend of Wilkes, and a sponsor of the *Monitor*.

15. "*patria*": L. Fatherland.

16. "*patrias artes*": L. Established practices.

17. "*Ædes concordiæ*": L. Temple of Concord, near the Roman Forum.

18. "geneva": Gin; a spirit originally made in Holland, flavored with juniper berries, and variously called Hollands Geneva, Hollands, or Geneva (*OED*).

19. "Mr. Ashley's punch-house upon Ludgate-hill": Ashley's, a London coffeehouse established by James Ashley probably in 1731, stood next to Saint Martin's Church on Ludgate Hill, just to the west of Saint Paul's Cathedral. See *The London Encyclopedia*, ed. Ben Weinreb and Christopher Hibbert (London: Macmillan, 1983), 471.

20. "COTAMUS PRO BONO PUBLICO": L. Let us brew for the public good.

21. "The two kings of Brentford": A famous mock spectacle in *The Rehearsal* (1671) has the two kings of Brentford "descend in the clouds, singing in white garments" (5.1). The burlesque is traditionally attributed to George Villiers, second duke of Buckingham, but apparently several persons were involved in its composition.

22. "Henley": Sir Robert Henley (1708?–72), lord chancellor; others mentioned subsequently in this passage are John Carteret, Earl Granville (1690–1763), lord president of the council; George Montagu Dunk, second earl of Halifax (1716–71), first lord of the admiralty; William Talbot, Earl Talbot (1710–82), lord steward; Charles Townshend (1725–67), secretary of war.

23. "*acumen ingenii*": Cicero *Pro Flacco* 4, speaking of the Greeks: "Non adimo . . . ingeniorum acumen" ("I do not deny . . . the keenness of their intellects").

24. "The Tale is come to hand . . . next Number": Apparently a message to the contributor of the verse tale that appears later, in *Briton*, no. 10, that the tale has been received and is scheduled to appear in the next issue. Actually it is postponed for two issues.

No. 9. Saturday, 24 July 1762

1. Motto: Horace *Epistles* 1.1.8–9: "Wisely dismiss in time the aged courser, lest, derided, he miscarry at last, and break his wind" (*Political Controversy*).

2. "*rude donatus*": Horace *Epistles* 1.1.2, in reference to the practice of giving a gladiator his sword (*rudis*) to signify that he could no longer be compelled to fight.

3. "employers of the Monitor . . . over again": *Monitor*, no. 366 (17 July 1762), deals only tangentially with the matters that the *Briton* goes on to say its author is still harping on. The *Briton* is not mentioned by name in the number. Smollett seems to be replying still to *Monitor*, no. 361 (19 June 1762), which treats of the necessity of continuing to support the war in Germany.

4. "mercenary Swiss": The Swiss were famous for providing mercenaries to the military forces of other powers. Especially well known was the Swiss guard maintained by the king of France and that employed by the pope in the Vatican.

5. "the treaty of Breslaw": The treaty of Breslau ended the First Silesian War in June 1742. Most of the events subsequently described here were part of the Second Silesian War, beginning with Frederick's invasion of Bohemia in August 1744 and ending with his capture of Dresden in December 1745. At the beginning of the second war, Britain and Austria were preparing to attack the French in Flanders, but Frederick's action caused the Austrians, under Charles of Lorraine, to return to the East, a turn of events that laid the groundwork for the British defeat at Fontenoy the following spring. Smollett narrates most of these events in *Complete History*, volume 4, book 9, chapters 7 and 8.

6. "the King of Poland . . . dominions": Augustus III, king of Poland from 1733 to 1763, was also the hereditary elector of Saxony. Upon Frederick's invasion of Saxony in 1756 at the beginning of the Third Silesian War (see *Briton*, no. 7, n. 6), Augustus quickly capitulated and was forced to leave Saxony for Poland.

7. "the Queen of H——y": Maria Theresa. See *Briton*, no. 6, n. 9.

8. "upon the carpet": Under consideration or discussion, as at a council table covered by a cloth or carpet (*OED*).

9. "an absurdity . . . translation appeared": Pope's translation of *The Iliad*, first announced in 1714, involved him in several squabbles, but the anecdote referred to here seems not to have been recorded in print elsewhere.

10. "The subsidy stipulated . . . attacked": Under the terms of an agreement signed in September 1755, England promised the Czarina Elizabeth an annual subsidy of £100,000 in return for Russian protection of Hanover; in the event of war the subsidy would increase to £500,000 per year. See *Continuation*, 1:280–82. The first of the renewable subsidies granted to Frederick the Great under terms of the Convention of Westminster came to £670,000. See *Briton*, no. 2, n. 8.

11. "a letter in the Gazetteer": *The Gazetteer and London Daily Advertiser* for 15 July 1762 printed a letter signed "John Love-Truth" that quotes an article in the latest *Hague Gazette* giving the total national debt of Britain as £122,603,836.8.2. The *Gazetteer* letter says that this figure exposes the falsehood of *Briton*, no. 6, where the debt is said to be £135 million.

12. "Maubert": Jean Henri Maubert de Gauvest (1721–67), a French writer and adventurer who began his career as a Capuchin priest in France. After leaving his order, he served in the Saxon army but was imprisoned in Germany for expressing dangerous ideas. Around 1750 he made his way to Geneva, where he became a Protestant and a journalist. He began publication of a work entitled *L'Histoire Politique du Siècle*, but the remonstrances of French authorities forced him to discontinue the project. He may have spent some time in England in the mid-1750s, and he seems to have been accused at one time or another of being an Austrian agent or some sort of foreign spy. He spent the last decade of his life moving about the Low Countries, Germany, and Denmark.

13. "To this": In calculating the total just given, Smollett made an error in arithmetic when adding in the debt charged upon the civil list. The final total should be given as 132493154 14 11¼.

14. "the Tale": See *Briton*, no. 8, n. 24.

No. 10. Saturday, 31 July 1762

1. Motto: Virgil *Aeneid* 6.95–96: "Yield not thou to the depraved; but, on the contrary, be more firm and irresistable" (*Political Controversy*).

2. "his motto . . . Queen's speech": The motto of *Monitor*, no. 365 (17 July 1762), was a quotation from Queen Anne's speech of 1 November 1705.

3. "the right reverend historian of his own times": Late in 1711, Bishop Gilbert Burnet (1643–1715) recorded the statement subsequently referred to. It was published posthumously in 1734 in *History of His Own Time* (2:83). The statement as given here is not quite verbatim but in no way distorts the sense of the original.

4. "Smithfield": The slaughterhouse section of London, famous as a site for pub-

lic executions by burning, particularly during the religious strife of the English Reformation.

5. "the French King . . . that kingdom": Louis XIV had attempted to bring Spain under French control by placing his grandson Philip on the Spanish throne; it was this move that precipitated the War of the Spanish Succession (see *Briton*, no. 6, n. 3). Charles, brother to Joseph I, Holy Roman Emperor, was the empire's claimant to the throne of Spain. In England at least, the ambitions of both France and the empire with respect to Spain were considered dangerous to the balance of power in Europe.

6. "The continental war": The War of the Spanish Succession.

7. "Lewis XIV. . . . battle of Turin": Allied forces, commanded by the duke of Marlborough, thoroughly defeated a French army at Ramillies on 12 May 1706, thus giving the allies full control of Flanders. Marlborough's triumph was one of his most celebrated. On 7 September 1706, Marlborough's fellow commander, Eugene of Savoy, defeated French forces that had besieged Turin, thus securing Italy for the allies for the balance of the war.

8. "black hussars": Hussars, or light cavalrymen (in this instance probably mercenaries), dressed in black uniforms. The subsidy Smollett refers to was one of those granted under the Convention of Westminster; see *Briton*, no. 2, n. 8.

9. "the treaty of Utrecht": In *Complete History*, 4:387–88, Smollett notes the rancorous arguments preceding the peace: "Pamphlets, libels, and lampoons, were to-day published by one faction, and to-morrow answered by the other. They contained all the insinuations of malice and contempt, all the bitterness of reproach, and all the rancour of recrimination." See also *Briton*, no. 20, n. 2.

10. "death of the Emperor Joseph": Joseph I (1678–1711), Holy Roman Emperor from 1705 until his death in 1711. His death helped speed the Peace of Utrecht in 1713. See above, n. 5.

11. "a mercenary general": John Churchill, duke of Marlborough (1650–1722), a favorite target of Tory satirists because of the profits he was alleged to have made as commander in chief during the war.

12. "CURIOSUS NON CURATUS": L. Careful but not cared for.

13. "a *curious felicity*": An English rendering of a familiar Latin tag, *curiosa felicitas* (studied felicity), used by Petronius in praising Horace (*Satyricon* 118).

14. "Heav'n-born Clive": Alluding to a speech of Pitt delivered 14 December 1757. Pitt had extolled Robert Clive as "that heaven-born general" for the decisive campaigns Clive had led in 1757 to secure control over Bengal for the English East India Company.

No. 11. Saturday, 7 August 1762

1. "the word *glorification*": *North Briton*, no. 2 (12 June 1762), and no. 8 (24 July 1762), had mockingly remarked on the *Briton*'s use of the word in its second number.

2. "a clergyman": Charles Churchill had a brief career as a clergyman before finding more congenial pursuits as a satirist and political journalist.

3. "the word *vouchsafements*": *North Briton*, no. 8, had used the phrase "wanton vouchsafements of royal favor."

4. "honest parson Adams . . . delicate satire' ": A reference to Henry Fielding, *Joseph Andrews*. Parson Abraham Adams says, "One Gentleman hath thought proper to produce some Poetry upon me, of which I shall only say, that I had rather be the Subject than the Composer" (*The History of Joseph Andrews*, ed. Martin C. Battestin [Middletown, Conn.: Wesleyan University Press, 1967], bk. 3, chap. 7, p. 247).

5. "the village-cock . . . *Perceforest*": The image of the cock crowing upon his dunghill is a proverbial joke about cowardice; Smollett uses the same joke later in *Humphry Clinker* (Jery Melford to Sir Watkin Phillips, Bath, April 30, p. 52). *Perceforest*, a romance first printed in Paris in 1528, tells the story of a legendary hero crowned king of Britain by a shipwrecked Alexander the Great; he was called Perceforest because he bravely "pierced" an enchanted forest to rescue women and children being cruelly treated there.

6. "the poems of Ossian": *Fragments of Ancient Poetry*, the first of James Macpherson's Ossianic works, had appeared in 1760, followed by *Fingal* in 1762. Support of Macpherson's fraudulent claim that the books represented translations from Gaelic originals became something of a patriotic obligation for Scotsmen. Smollett's *Critical Review* was enthusiastic about the works and wholeheartedly accepted their authenticity; see *Critical Review* 12 (December 1761): 405–18; 13 (January 1762): 45–53; 15 (March 1763): 200–209.

7. "*vates* . . . a prophecy of our Saviour": Virgil's fourth eclogue refers to a child whose birth should bring back the Golden Age; it had been interpreted since the time of the early Fathers as a prophecy of the birth of Christ. *Vates* is Latin for both a poet and a prophet.

8. "ominous to King Charles I. and the Lord Falkland": The story is told that during the civil wars Charles went to the library during a stay at Oxford. There he was shown a beautiful Virgil, and Lord Falkland suggested the *Sortes Virgilianae*, that is, fortune-telling by opening the pages of the book at random. The king turned first to the passage where Dido curses Aeneas and wishes him an untimely fall. Seeing the king disturbed, Falkland turned to another, equally ominous passage, Evander's lament for the death of his son. See James Welwood, *Memoirs of the Most Material Transactions in England* (London: 1700), 100–101.

9. "sortilege": Divination, fortune-telling (*OED*); here, by means of the *Sortes Virgilianae*.

10. "*Macte nova . . . puer, bello—*": The passage is from *Aeneid* 9.641–56, with several omissions. It gives Apollo's words approving the skill in battle of Aeneas' son, Ascanius. Apollo appears in the guise of Butes, the aged armor-bearer of Ascanius. His last words tell Ascanius to refrain from further battle.

11. "the hills of Morven . . .the Highland Shenachies": Morven was the name of Fingal's kingdom (see above, n. 6) in northwestern Scotland. Shenachies were professional clan historians or genealogists, or, more generally, tellers of traditional stories. In *Humphry Clinker*, Jery Melford reports his attendance at a Highland burial where "the orator, or *senachie*, pronounced the panegyric of the defunct" (Jery Melford to Sir Watkin Phillips, Argyleshire, September 3, p. 235).

12. "Caryl": Not identified, but the context suggests that Caryl, like Ossian, was a bardic poet, and that he was Scottish.

13. "the wretched Greek pun . . . North Briton": *North Briton*, no. 4 (26 June 1762), carried as its motto a Greek epigram punning on Bute's name:

Θαυμάζειν μοι ἔπεισιν, ὅπως Βύτος ἐστὶ σοφιστής,
μήτε λόγον κοινόν, μήτε λογισμὸν ἔχων.

The epigram, which is from *The Greek Anthology* 11.435, is translated as follows in the Loeb edition: "It strikes me as wonderful how Bytus is a sophist, since he has neither common speech nor reason."

14. "*Luca Pitti*": Luca Pitti (1394–1472), scion of a prominent, wealthy Florentine family, maneuvered himself into power as gonfalonier (chief magistrate) during the last years of the rule of Cosimo de' Medici, who died in 1464. In 1466, Luca was a leader in an unsuccessful conspiracy against Piero de' Medici. When the conspiracy was discovered and Luca abandoned his fellow conspirators, he was condemned to death, but Piero allowed him to continue living in disgrace in Florence until he died a few years later. (Luca was also the founder of the famous Pitti Palace.)

15. "mechanic": Figurative for a low or vulgar person (*OED*).

16. "gonfalonier of justice": A judicial officer whose authority was recognized by his carrying in state processions the gonfalon, a banner attached to a crossbar at the top of a pole.

17. "CURIO": The name of a famous Roman family of statesmen and generals. The name perhaps also reflects the word *curioso*, "one who is curious in matters of science and art . . . a connoisseur, virtuoso" (*OED*). Letters signed by "Curio" also appear in *Briton*, nos. 28 and 32.

18. "Sir Dogberry Verges": In *Much Ado about Nothing*, Dogberry is the comic constable and Verges is his associate. If the name Sir Dogberry Verges is intended to poke fun at a real person, that person's identity has not been discovered.

19. "Mr. Alderman Grog": Probably another jab at William Beckford and his interests in the rum trade. See *Briton*, no. 8, n. 14.

20. "WINIFRED BULLCALF": This Winifred and her malapropisms may be the germ from which grew the character of Winifred Jenkins in *Humphry Clinker*.

No. 12. Saturday, 14 August 1762

1. Motto: *Othello* 3.3.258–60.

2. "to settle arrears": *North Briton*, no. 9 (31 July 1762), began, "I have a considerable arrear to settle with the Briton."

3. "lashed himself into a rage with his own tail": John Dryden, "Astraea Redux" (1660), lines 117–18: "Rous'd by the lash of his own stubborn tail, / Our Lion now will foreign foes assail." The idea traces back to Pliny *Natural History* 8.19, which records the belief that when the lion is calm, its tail is motionless, but when it is angered, it lashes itself with its tail to incite its own rage.

4. "the expedition to Martinique": See *Briton*, no. 3, n. 10.

5. "detained the armament . . . preceding year": Pitt, in 1761, had delayed the sailing of the expedition to Martinique until the end of summer.

6. "in lieu of General Monckton . . . another commander": General Robert Monckton (1726–82) commanded the army that conquered Martinique in February 1762, an action contrasting with Pitt's alleged indecisiveness of the preceding summer. Here and in the following lines, Smollett supports his defense of Bute as a decisive minister by pointing to other supposedly inconclusive or wasteful actions undertaken while Pitt was in office. The allusion to the substitution of another commander is possibly to Pitt's replacement of Lord Loudon with General James Abercromby as commander in chief of British forces in America. Abercromby's first campaign ended in his failure to take Ticonderoga in July 1758; critics blamed his failure on lack of determination. But the last clause of Smollett's sentence sounds like his later comment, in *Continuation*, 3:134, on the failure of British troops under General Thomas Peregrine Hopson to capture Martinique in 1759, when the "principal individuals" among the enemy officers "were actually assembled at the public hall in Port Royal, to send deputies to the English general with proposals of capitulation and surrender." The sentence following may refer to the subsequent substitution of Guadeloupe as the object of attack at that time, although Guadeloupe was hardly a "barren rock." It is more likely that Smollett, by juxtaposing discrete events, alludes to one of Pitt's favorite schemes, the capture of Belle Isle off the coast of Brittany in 1761. In *Continuation*, 4:261–62, Smollett's comment is: "Thus, at the expence of an exorbitant sum, and about two thousand choice troops . . . the English atchieved the conquest of a barren rock."

7. "petty excursions along the coast of France": During 1758, British forces under General Thomas Bligh made several forays along the French coast. Smollett is probably alluding specifically to the unsuccessful excursion against Saint Cas in September. In *Continuation*, 2:264, Smollett editorializes on this failure: "a descent ought never to be hazarded in an enemy's country, without having taken proper precautions to secure a retreat."

8. "W— IV": Another ironic thrust at William Pitt's alleged insubordination. The joke here is that Pitt has usurped the authority of a monarch; hence the title William IV. William III died in 1702.

9. "unsuccessful expeditions to Quebec": In 1690 and again in 1711, unsuccessful attempts to capture Quebec had been launched from New England. The 1711 attempt was characterized by Smollett in *Complete History*, 4:384, as a "paultry expedition."

10. "Admiral Vernon": Admiral Edward Vernon (1684–1757) had led a British naval

fleet against Spanish possessions in the West Indies in the fall of 1739. Smollett was a participant in the expedition, which ended disastrously with an unsuccessful attack on Carthagena. He gave a vivid satirical version of the expedition in *Roderick Random*, chapters 24–37. He also composed a more factual, but still critical, version in "An Account of the Expedition Against Carthagena," published in his *Compendium of Authentic and Entertaining Voyages*.

11. "Cape Breton": Louisburg, a key French fortress on the east coast of Cape Breton, had been captured by an American colonial expedition in June 1745. Smollett gives an account of this praiseworthy feat in *Complete History*, 4:659–60.

12. "a most ridiculous purpose": In the summer of 1746 the Pelham ministry (headed by Henry Pelham and his brother, the duke of Newcastle) assembled a squadron at Portsmouth to sail to America in support of an attack on Quebec. But the squadron was delayed in getting underway and eventually, to satisfy public opinion, was diverted to an expedition against Lorient in Brittany that achieved very little.

13. "Mr. Braddock": On 9 July 1755, French and Indian forces routed the troops of General Edward Braddock (1695–1755), which were advancing toward Fort Duquesne. This celebrated encounter was one of the first during the Seven Years' War between English and French forces in America.

14. "the late expedition . . . to Newfoundland": In June 1762 the French took Saint John's, Newfoundland, but the British quickly recaptured it later in the summer. See *Briton*, no. 20, n. 8, and no. 33, n. 8.

15. "Still harping on my daughter": *Hamlet* 2.2.187–88.

16. "*Hinc illæ lachrymæ*": A proverbial Latin expression, originating in Terence *Andria* 1.1.99: "Hence were those tears."

17. "drawcansirs": In *The Rehearsal* (see *Briton*, no. 8, n. 21), Drawcansir was a character designed to parody the ranting Almanzor, hero of John Dryden's tragedy *The Conquest of Granada* (1670); the name became a common noun to denote any blustering person, particularly a military one.

18. "Cerberus": The three-headed dog that in Greek mythology was assigned to guard the entrance to Hades. In *Aeneid* 6, the sibyl leading Aeneas to the underworld throws a drugged cake to Cerberus that lulls him and allows them to pass by; hence a sop for Cerberus is proverbial for a means of pacifying an antagonist.

19. "the late rebellion": The Jacobite rebellion of 1745–46, toward which Smollett, as a Scot, might have been supposed to be sympathetic.

20. "chop-fallen": "With the lower jaw fallen, hanging down . . . dejected, dispirited" (*OED*).

No. 13. Saturday, 21 August 1762

1. Motto: Juvenal *Satires* 13.244–45: "Our subtilty will, if you don't take care, assuredly ensnare you" (*Political Controversy*).

2. "malice prepense": Legal term for premeditated malice.

3. "Buy my Rosemary . . . your own Council!": The first of these expressions is a street vendor's cry. "A word to the wise is enough" is a proverb that can be traced

back to Plautus *Persa*, line 729: "Dictum sapienti sat est." In *Spectator*, no. 12 (14 March 1711), Mr. Spectator writes, "I am the best Man in the World to keep my own Counsel," but the proverbial idea can be traced back, in various forms, at least as far as Chaucer.

4. "jakes": A privy. It was a common joke to condemn a publication by finding it suitable only for use in a jakes.

5. "Shaftesbury and Bolingbroke": Anthony Ashley Cooper, first earl of Shaftesbury (1621–83), was the leader of the attempt in 1680–81 to thwart Charles II's will by excluding the duke of York (later James II) from his right to the throne because he was a Roman Catholic. Henry St. John, Viscount Bolingbroke (1678–1751), one of Anne's chief ministers from 1710 to 1714, was believed to have engaged in maneuvers to bring back the Jacobite pretender to the throne after the queen's death.

6. "Swift and Addison": Jonathan Swift (1667–1745) was, in effect, the public relations man for the Tory ministry in office during the last years of Queen Anne's reign. Joseph Addison (1672–1719), in addition to pursuing his literary and journalistic efforts, served as a member of Parliament and a Whig officeholder during the turbulent last years of Queen Anne's reign and the early years of George I's.

7. "doctor Squintum in the farce": A character in Samuel Foote's *The Minor* (1760), written to ridicule the Methodist George Whitefield. Mrs. Cole, the Methodist bawd in the play, quotes Scripture and religious cant, always with the tag, "as Mr. Squintum says."

8. "Rag-fair": "A market for the sale of old clothes, held at Houndsditch in London" (*OED*).

9. "The present chief magistrate": Sir Samuel Fludyer (1705–68), who was lord mayor until William Beckford was elected to succeed him late in 1762.

10. "*Jacky-Dandy, Pædagogus Latro,* and *Bruin*": The persons satirized by these pseudonyms were identified by *Political Controversy* in its reprint of this number of the *Briton*. Jacky-Dandy is, of course, John Wilkes. Pædagogus Latro (*latro* is Latin for "robber") is Robert Lloyd (1733–64), an obscure writer and friend of Charles Churchill. Bruin is Churchill himself; Hogarth similarly caricatured him in a satirical print of 1763 entitled *The Bruiser*, in which he is represented as a bear in priest's clothing.

11. "*Joe Miller,* and the *Vade Mecum*": *Joe Miller's Jests: or, the Wit's Vade-Mecum*, a famous collection of jokes and repartee, was first published in 1739 by John Mottley. It had gone through at least fifteen editions by 1760.

12. "greenroom": A room in a theater where the players could gather with friends when they were not required on stage.

13. "*O Dii boni*": Latin exclamation, "O good gods," found, for example, in Terence *Andria* 2.2.1 and *Eunuchus* 2.1.19.

14. "lawyer *Small*": Small, according to *Political Controversy*, is George Colman (1732–94), a barrister, a minor playwright, and an "inseparable companion of Bruin and Pædagogus."

15. "Statute 5th of Q. Anne, c. 8": See *Articles of the Treaty of Union* (London, 1706).

As given by Smollett, the material from the statute is not quite verbatim; some connectives are elided, but otherwise the quotations are accurate.

16. "MILO": See *Briton*, no. 5, n. 11.

No. 14. Saturday, 28 August 1762

1. Motto: Tacitus *Annals* 6.6: "Haterius was far more odious; because he was a nasty libidinous fellow; who practised debauchery and incest, to the greatest degree; and rendered himself pernicious to men of illustrious rank and good morals" (*Political Controversy*).

2. "Caliph *Haroun Rachid*": Haroun (or Harun) al Raschid (d. A.D. 809), the most famous caliph of Baghdad, who figures in many of *The Arabian Nights* with his vizier Giafor of the noble family of Barmakids, or Barmecides. *The Arabian Nights* first appeared in English in 1707 in a translation based on the collection that Antoine Galland began publishing in French in 1704; other editions appeared at frequent intervals throughout the eighteenth century.

3. "a Sabean odour": Saba is a region in southern Arabia, also known as Sheba. The phrase is from Milton, *Paradise Lost* 4.161–63: "North-East winds blow / *Sabean* Odours from the spicy shore / Of *Araby*."

4. "empyreumatic": "Tasting or smelling of burnt organic matter" (*OED*).

5. "*Jahia Ben Israil Ginn*": Although one of the enemies of the historical Haroun was named Yahya, the character of Jahia Ginn and his story are apparently invented by Smollett to serve the purpose of an allegory satirizing Wilkes for his attacks on the king. The name Smollett contrived for his satiric figure alludes to the fact that John Wilkes's father was Israel Wilkes, owner of a profitable distillery. (In *Adventures of an Atom*, Smollett gives Wilkes a somewhat similar name, Jan-ki-dtzin.) In continuing the story, Smollett takes advantage of the fact that there were complaints made to Haroun about the power of the Barmakids similar to the complaints voiced about Scottish influence in the councils of George III.

6. "an hideous obliquity of vision": John Wilkes had a well-known squint; Hogarth immortalized it in his famous print of Wilkes published in May 1763.

7. "tushes": *Tush* is a variant form of *tusk*, often used for a sharp, pointed tooth, such as a canine tooth. Hogarth also emphasized Wilkes's prominent teeth in his 1763 print.

8. "*Schieks*": Schiek is a variant spelling for sheikh, an Arab chief; in Smollett's allegory, it would signify a member of Parliament.

9. "the most audacious slanders . . . a venerable Princess": The opponents of Bute made frequent salacious use of the rumor that he was the lover of the king's mother, Augusta, the dowager princess of Wales. Some of the satiric prints of the period are particularly daring in this regard. See, for example, "The Scotch Broomstick & the French Besom, A German Tale, by Sawney Gesner," included (print no. 3852) in the Georgia Edition of Smollett's *Adventures of an Atom*. There

is no evidence that such slanders as the *Briton* seems to suggest in the succeeding lines were directed against Queen Charlotte.

10. "Iman": A Mohammedan priest or leader.

11. "Lord Chuckle-head": Earl Temple. See *Briton*, no. 2, n. 6.

12. "downright Swiss": A mercenary. See *Briton*, no. 9, n. 4.

13. "a *true born Englishman*": A phrase made famous in the title of Daniel Defoe's *True-Born Englishman* (1701), in which Defoe had satirized attacks on William III as a foreigner by pointing out that most Englishmen were descendants of foreign invaders and usurpers. Defoe also satirized the English for their heavy drinking and their political fickleness.

14. "rooks": A rook is "a cheat, swindler, or sharper, *spec.* in gaming" (*OED*).

15. "the lectures of Billingsgate": Billingsgate was the fish-market of London. The foul, abusive language of the vendors there had long been proverbial.

16. "a reverend deacon . . . a learned pedagogue": *Political Controversy* identifies the "reverend deacon" as Charles Churchill and the "learned pedagogue" as Robert Lloyd. See *Briton*, no. 13, n. 10.

17. "DRAFF": Refuse, dregs (*OED*).

No. 15. Saturday, 4 September 1762

1. Motto: Source not identified, but translated by *Political Controversy* as "Hereafter, however, I shall engage myself rather in defending the honest party, than accusing the dishonest one."

2. "Lord GOTHAMSTOWE, and Capt. IAGO ANISEED": The context of the ensuing dialogue makes it evident that Iago Aniseed is intended for John Wilkes. The allusion to Shakespeare's Iago would remind readers of Wilkes's alleged malice and treachery. Aniseed is an aromatic seed used medicinally to expel wind from the bowels. Since Aniseed is clearly Wilkes, the identification of Gothamstowe as Earl Temple, the nobleman who was Wilkes's main sponsor in the enterprise of the *North Briton*, seems equally evident. Stowe was the name of the celebrated country seat of the Temple family in Buckinghamshire; Gotham may allude to the proverbial stupidity of the "Wise Men of Gotham." Temple had had a rather erratic political career since entering Parliament in 1734; he was distinguished mainly by following the line set down by Pitt, his brother-in-law.

3. "they harrow up my soul with fear and wonder": *Hamlet* 1.1.44: "It harrows me with fear and wonder."

4. "Caledonian haggish": Haggish, or, more commonly, haggis, is a dish made of various minced organ meats mixed with oatmeal, seasoned, stuffed into the stomach of a slaughtered sheep or calf, and boiled like a pudding. During the Bramble party's stay in Scotland in *Humphry Clinker*, Jery Melford reports, "I am not yet Scotchman enough to relish their singed sheep's-head and haggice" (Jery Melford to Sir Watkin Phillips, Edinburgh, August 8, p. 214).

5. "caudle": "A warm drink consisting of thin gruel, mixed with wine or ale, sweetened and spiced, given chiefly to sick people, esp. women in childbed" (*OED*).

6. "*animus meminisse horret*": Virgil *Aeneid* 2.12; translated in *Political Controversy* as "I shudder at the recollection."

7. "Cloacina": A very obscure Roman goddess of the sewers who had been revived by Gay (*Trivia* 2.115) and Pope (*The Dunciad* 2.93) for humorously scatological purposes. In *The Dunciad Variorum*, Pope's footnote identifies her as "the *Roman* Goddess of the Common-shores."

8. "fane": A temple.

9. "blue-bonnet": "A broad round horizontally flattened bonnet or cap of blue woolen material, formerly in general use in Scotland" (*OED*).

10. "ferrara": A broadsword (*OED*).

11. "woollen buskins striped with green and yellow": Buskins were half boots reaching to the calf or the knee. Originally the buskin was the high, thick-soled boot worn by the actors in Greek tragedy; figuratively, it was often opposed to the sock, or low shoe, worn in comedy. The word *woollen* as used here emphasizes Bute's Scottishness. Bute, a Stuart, was the nephew of the duke of Argyll and was further related to the Argyll family by the marriage of the first earl to Ann, the eldest daughter of the first duke of Argyll; the Argylls were Campbells, and all Campbell tartans featured the colors green and yellow. See Sir Thomas Innes, *The Tartans of the Clans and Families of Scotland*, 8th ed. (Edinburgh and London: Johnston and Bacon, 1971), "Campbell of Argyll."

12. "to drink in token of revenge": Probably the reference is to *Henry V* 5.1.47. Pistol, having been forced to eat a leek by Fluellen, vows, "By this leek, I will most horribly revenge."

13. "Mr. Alderman Rumford": William Beckford; see *Briton*, no. 8, n. 14. *Rumford* would remind readers that Beckford's wealth came from his sugar-cane plantations, a source of molasses and rum.

14. "my brother of adoption": Temple's brother-in-law, William Pitt. The charge of inconsistency was frequently used by Pitt's detractors, who called attention to his denunciation of continental connections in his famous "Rhone-Saône" speech of November 1755 and his subsequent turnabout in committing his ministry to continental measures to pursue his military campaigns.

15. "retreated with a pension": Another allusion to Pitt's notorious pension. See *Briton*, no. 3, n. 17.

16. "the brothers who then directed the helm of g——t": Henry Pelham and his brother, the duke of Newcastle. See *Briton*, no. 8, n. 3.

17. "the cocoa-tree": Since the reign of Queen Anne, the Cocoa-Tree (at first a chocolate house, later a club located on Pall Mall) had been known as the resort of Tory politicians.

18. "the Lord of Cl——em——t": The duke of Newcastle. Claremont was the name of one of Newcastle's residences; Newcastle held a subsidiary title as earl of Clare.

19. "that consummate statesman lately set aside": Newcastle left office on 26 May 1762.
20. "puncheon": A large cask.
21. "a man must . . . his wife": Genesis 2:24.
22. "*pumpings, purgings, blankettings, and blows*": Pope, *The Dunciad* 2.154. The order of the first two words has been reversed from Pope's original.
23. "*Thou . . . be wise*": *Othello* 3.3.381–82. Smollett echoes an exchange between Othello and Iago.
24. "the Augean stable": One of the labors of Hercules was to clean the stables of Augeas. The stables, housing three thousand oxen, had not been cleaned for thirty years. The task has become proverbial for any virtually impossible labor.
25. "setter": A spy in the employ of murderers or robbers (*OED*).
26. "Peto": One of Falstaff's gang of petty crooks in *2 Henry IV*. The name, of course, suggests Pitt.
27. "our parson Brawn": Charles Churchill; see *Briton*, no. 13, n. 10.
28. "Birch the pædagogue": Robert Lloyd; see *Briton*, no. 13, n. 10.
29. "*that were a consummation devoutly to be wish'd*": *Hamlet* 3.1.62–63.

No. 16. Saturday, 11 September 1762

1. Motto: Source not identified, but translated in *Political Controversy* as "He may be a villain, a sacriligious villain; the ring leader of every atrocious crime; yet he is an excellent legislator, and very reserved [*i.e.*, held in reserve] with regard to the critical affairs of the commonwealth."
2. "Æschines . . . Demosthenes": Aeschines and Demosthenes were rivals during the period 346–330 B.C., when Athens was coming under Macedonian control. Aeschines, overpowered by Demosthenes' rhetoric and popularity, retired from Athens in 330 B.C. Changes in Athenian policy resulted in Demosthenes' exile less than a decade later.
3. "Aristides . . . Themistocles": Aristides and Themistocles were rival statesmen and military leaders during the Persian Wars in the fifth century B.C. Both were subject at one time or another to enforced exile. The battle of Salamis, to which Smollett alludes in this same sentence, was fought in 480 B.C.
4. "*Mons sacer*": A hill about three miles from Rome where Roman plebeians resorted and fortified themselves during a quarrel with the senate in 494 B.C. A similar revolt occurred a generation later in 449 B.C. The incidents are reported in Livy *Ab Urbe Condita* 2.32 and 3.52.
5. "Manlius Coriolanus": Apparently the Manlius who was a consul and who, in 189 B.C., led a successful military campaign in Galatia. Rivals attacked and denounced him in the senate two years later, although he was eventually cleared of charges made against him.
6. "Scipio Africanus: Roman general who defeated Hannibal of Carthage in the Sec-

ond Punic War (218–201 B.C.). Scipio was accused of bribery but acquitted in 187 B.C. See *Briton*, no. 37, n. 9.

7. "Wat Tyler and Jack Straw": Two of the leaders of the Peasants' Revolt in 1381. The revolt began in Kent and Essex with the rebels' demands for the abolition of serfdom and the poll tax, for a limit on rents, and for revocation of the Statute of Labourers of 1351. In *Complete History*, 2:142–46, Smollett grants the harshness of conditions provoking the revolt but is severe toward the rebels who created "those commotions which had like to have destroyed the English constitution"; he uses such terms as *insolence, ministers of sedition, debauched, profligate*, and *desperate villains* to characterize the rebels.

8. "a Mayor of London": Sir William Walworth (d. 1385) vigorously defended London when Tyler's Kentish mob descended on the city. When King Richard II was confronted by Tyler and his mob at Smithfield, Walworth, in defending the king, slew Tyler with his sword.

9. "the celebrated John Bull": John Bull or John Ball, a participant in the Peasants' Revolt, characterized by Smollett in *Complete History*, 2:146–47, as "a fanatic priest, who acted as principal incendiary," and as "this wretched fanatic." A few weeks after the revolt was quelled, Ball was hanged, drawn, and quartered.

10. "Bridewell": Bride's Well was, in the sixteenth century, a London hospital turned into a house of correction. By the seventeenth century, *Bridewell* was a generic term for any jail.

11. "Jacky Straw . . . and Bull the parson": Once again, John Wilkes and Charles Churchill.

12. "*Vox populi est vox Dei*": A well-known Latin maxim apparently first found in Alcuin's *Admonitio ad Carolum Magnum* (c. A.D. 800).

13. "scot or lot": Usually *scot and lot*, a municipal or borough tax, roughly equivalent to the modern rates.

14. "*Canaille*": Fr. Rabble, mob.

15. "oboli": Plural form of *obolus*, a small silver or bronze coin of ancient Greece. In England the word was sometimes used for a halfpenny.

16. "emblematical prints": As is evident from the listings of 1762 in *Catalogue of Prints and Drawings in the British Museum, Division I, Political and Personal Satires*, vol. 4 (1883), the printmakers of London kept busy satirizing Bute, his journalistic hirelings, and others connected with him. The catalogue lists occasional advertisements of some of these prints in the daily papers. Versions of many of them are to be found in cheap print collections, such as *The British Antidote to Caledonian Poison*, 2 vols. (London, 1763, 1764). These make a fascinating visual companion to the written polemics. See also Byron Gassman, "Smollett's *Briton* and the Art of Political Cartooning," *Studies in Eighteenth-Century Culture*, vol. 14, ed. O M Brack, Jr. (Madison: University of Wisconsin Press, 1984): 243–58. See *Adventures of an Atom*, pp. 269–323, for reproductions of many of the prints Smollett refers to

here. The present volume includes two such prints, "The Mountebank" (p. 235) and "The Scotch Butt" (p. 399).

17. "a Lord Mayor of London": The *Briton*'s reference may be to the office itself rather than to the particular officeholder at this time, Sir Samuel Fludyer. See *Briton*, no. 13, n. 9.

18. "who will not suffer . . . a reproach upon police": It was a common practice among printers and booksellers to display satirical prints and broadsides in their shop windows as a way of attracting customers. There was no established police force in London in the mid-eighteenth century (only a relatively ineffectual constabulary); many satirical prints were violently libelous, even to the point of threatening to incite civil disruption, and Smollett seems to have seen them as a genuine danger against which there was little public protection. He may also have simultaneously intended to suggest a familiar alternative meaning of the term *police* as the name for civil organization itself (*OED*).

19. "officious Bishop of London": The passage may be a glance at Richard Osbaldeston (1690–1764), who became bishop of London early in 1762; he seems to have been somewhat ill-tempered and a rather mediocre ecclesiastic.

20. "Stubs's, Lilburn's, Prynne's, Burton's, and Bastwick's": A reference to five men associated with puritan and antiroyalist pamphlets of the seventeenth century. Henry Stubbs was imprisoned in 1673 for denouncing the marriage of the duke of York (later James II) to Mary of Modena. John Lilburne was pilloried, imprisoned, and exiled for his political agitation. In pre–Civil War days, William Prynne, Henry Burton, and John Bastwick were charged with libel in a common indictment; all three were pilloried and had their ears cut off. In *Complete History*, 3:225–27, Smollett mentions several of these same men, referring to Prynne, for example, as "a sour insolent puritan" and accusing Burton and Bastwick of "having published seditious and schismatic libels."

21. "Jack Ketch": The public executioner, so named from an actual executioner who held the office from about 1663 to 1686.

22. "the bills of mortality": Lists (or "bills") of baptisms and deaths were regularly compiled by parish clerks for the metropolitan area of London; they did not include the parishes of Marylebone, Saint Pancras, Paddington, Kensington, and Chelsea. See M. Dorothy George, *London Life in the Eighteenth Century* (1925; reprint, New York: Harper Torchbooks, 1965), 21–28.

No. 17. Saturday, 18 September 1762

1. Motto: Cicero *In Catilinam* 2.9: "A crazy republic imagines, that she can attain to honours which a wise and quiet nation despairs of obtaining" (*Political Controversy*).

2. "the papers which have been lately published": In midsummer 1762, the Bute

ministry was pressing toward ending the war by appointing the duke of Bedford to travel to Paris to negotiate a peace treaty, some possible terms of which had already been exchanged between representatives of the combatants. Many rumors flew around London about preliminary peace terms that had been or were about to be agreed upon. The *Gazetteer and London Daily Advertiser* had printed on 1 September a brief list of eight items reported to be in the preliminaries to peace being negotiated. *Auditor*, no. 15 (16 September 1762), had compared "Mr. Pitt's Peace" with "Mr. Say's Peace" (Charles Green Say was the printer and publisher of the *Gazetteer*) in side-by-side columns to show that the recently published terms were similar in demands and concessions to those that Pitt had been willing to negotiate in the summer of 1761, before the trouble with Spain put off the possibilities for peace. This number of the *Briton* proceeds to defend the terms with similar arguments.

3. "a copious bleeding": Phlebotomy (taking blood from a patient by opening a vein on the supposition that the body suffered from an oversupply of blood) was still one of the most common surgical practices of the eighteenth century. As such, it readily supplied metaphors for conditions in which a supposed superfluity might need to be reduced.

4. "Sangrado": In Lesage's *Gil Blas*, Sangrado is the quack doctor who bleeds his patients as a cure for all ailments. Smollett's English translation of *Gil Blas* first appeared in 1748.

5. "plethora": An overabundance of any bodily humor, particularly of blood, the remedy for which was bleeding.

6. "sinking-fund": A fund created by the periodic setting aside of sums from public revenues and allowing them to accumulate interest for the purpose of reducing the principal of the national debt (*OED*). Smollett here complains that the fund had been plundered to pay expenses of the war, thus seriously threatening the economic welfare of the nation.

7. "*O Lord! . . . reck'ning.*——": *Henry V* 4.1.289–91. The *Briton* deletes two phrases. Shakespeare's vocative is "O God of battles."

8. "the number of people in Great Britain": Since the first census of England was not undertaken until 1801, modern demographers are not at all in agreement about details of population figures before that time. However, there does seem to be a fairly general agreement that the population of England was somewhat below six million in 1700, that it grew at such a small pace for the first half of the century as to be almost static (perhaps six and a quarter million by 1750), and that it then accelerated to reach over nine million by the census of 1801. In 1780, Dr. Richard Price, in *An Essay on the Population of England, from the Revolution to the Present Time*, estimated that England then had one and one-half million fewer persons than in 1688, so the *Briton* was not alone in interpreting population conditions of the time as indicating a decline during the preceding decades. See George, *London Life*, 37.

9. "a conquest of Martinique": See *Briton*, no. 5, n. 10.

10. "the protection of Portugal": After declaring war against Spain at the beginning of 1762, Great Britain had to send several thousand troops and a large subsidy to Portugal to help defend it against a Spanish invasion.

11. "the Musqueto shore": An area lying mostly along what is today the eastern coast of Nicaragua. Now it is usually called the Mosquito coast, named for the Indian tribe (the name of which is variously spelled) originally inhabiting it.

12. "the gum trade": See *Briton*, no. 27, n. 7.

13. "Cleves . . . Ostend": The duchy of Cleves, a hereditary possession of the house of Brandenburg along the Rhine, was controlled by the French during most of the war. Dunkirk (in France), Nieuport, and Ostend (both in Belgium) were important channel ports.

14. "MILO": See *Briton*, no. 5, n. 11.

No. 18. Saturday, 25 September 1762

1. Motto: Cicero *In Catilinam* 4.7: "Where lives the man to whom these temples, the view of this city, the possession of liberty, the sky, the soil of our native country are not truly dear, agreeable and delightful?" (*Political Controversy*).

2. "the fable of the prayers preferred to Jupiter": Although this fable would seem to be almost proverbial, no printed source for it has been found. Smollett may be echoing (inaccurately) the Fable of "Jupiter and a Farmer," no. 435 in Sir Roger L'Estrange's often reprinted *Fables* of Aesop (1692); or the similar "Jupiter and the Tenant Farmer," no. 4 in book 6 of Jean de la Fontaine's *Fables* (1668–94), which had been popular in England since the first translation in 1734.

3. "the Wolf in Germany": In *A Letter to a Gentleman in the City*, dated 5 September 1762, the author urges the quick conclusion of a peace, observing that in Germany "we have, notwithstanding our repeated victories, a wolf by the ears" (p. 2). The proverb was picked up by controversialists in debating what to do with the French in Germany.

4. "one of the papers of the Briton": In *Briton*, no. 7, Smollett had discussed the legality of entering into treaties repugnant to a nation's interests. The *Monitor* had responded immediately in no. 365 (17 July 1762), not discussing the legal principle but asserting that the alliance with Prussia was beneficial and served the interests of Britain. This remained one of the major points of debate between ministerial and antiministerial forces, as can be seen in the present elaboration. *North Briton*, no. 14 (4 September 1762), had quoted from the *Briton*'s earlier argument and attacked it as "beyond Machiavelian politics."

5. "*non compos mentis*": A standard Latin legal phrase to describe one not in his right mind.

6. "the manœuvre of his P——n Majesty": Frederick invaded Saxony in August 1756, quickly secured his conquest, and added the Saxons to his own armies. The dep-

redations of the Prussians in Saxony during the next few years became notorious.

7. "the convention of Closter-Severn": In September 1757 the duke of Cumberland, finding himself in a difficult military situation in his defense of Hanover, signed the convention of Klosterseven, which would have greatly narrowed the English field of operations and left the Prussians much more exposed to French power. Frederick wrote a letter of expostulation to George II suggesting that Great Britain appeared to be weakly withdrawing from a conflict it had encouraged Prussia to begin. Soon thereafter George II angrily repudiated the convention and recalled his son from his command.

8. "The number of people in Great Britain and Ireland": See *Briton*, no. 17, n. 8.

9. "Martinique, Guadaloupe, Senegal, and Goree": These were all French possessions that had been captured by the British during the course of the war. The two West Indies islands, Martinique and Guadeloupe, had been captured in 1762 and 1759, respectively; see *Briton*, no. 4, n. 8, and no. 5, n. 10. Part of Senegal, on the west coast of Africa, and the island of Goree, off the coast of Senegal, had been captured in 1758.

10. "swords into plough-shares and pruning-hooks": The phrase echoes Isaiah 2:4.

No. 19. Saturday, 2 October 1762

1. "that he is a Stuart": *North Briton*, no. 16 (18 September 1762), was the latest issue of that paper to reiterate the attack on Bute as a Scot and a Stuart: "We have suffered enough from the whole race of [Stuarts]: but I find we are for ever at least to be reminded of them. I have heard of a vain inscription at the family-seat of *Mount-Stuart, Not they from kings, but kings from them.* . . . I will affirm, because the English history proves it, that it had been happier for this country, if every *Male Stuart had been strangled in the birth*." Mount Stuart was on the island of Bute.

2. "giving his eldest daughter in marriage to a Scotchman": Henry VII gave his eldest daughter Margaret to James IV of Scotland in 1499 to help promote amity between the two nations.

3. "the Egyptian custom . . . judgment": Before the discovery of the Rosetta stone in 1799 and the deciphering of Egyptian hieroglyphics that it made possible, little was known about the details of ancient Egyptian religious beliefs. Smollett would have shared with his contemporaries the notion that the Egyptians believed the souls of the dead had to pass a place of judgment before entering their immortal state.

4. "*manes*": L. The ghost or shade of a dead person.

5. "Sommers, Godolphin, Cowper": The treaty of union between England and Scotland was negotiated in 1706. Sir John Somers (1651–1716), a former lord chancellor, was one of the chief spokesmen for the union in the House of Lords. Sidney Godolphin, first earl of Godolphin (1645–1712), was lord treasurer from 1702 to

1710; a former Stuart loyalist who carried on a friendly correspondence with the deposed James II for many years, he fell under the influence of John Churchill, first duke of Marlborough, when their families were united by marriage and became a staunch supporter of Whig efforts to unite the two kingdoms. William Cowper, first Earl Cowper (d. 1723), was lord keeper and lord chancellor from 1705 to 1710 and was one of the commissioners negotiating the union.

6. "wish with Caligula . . . at a single blow": Caligula is reported to have wished that the people of Rome had but one neck; see Suetonius "Caius Caligula" 30.3. The *Spectator* had cited the wish in three different issues: nos. 16 (19 March 1711), 246 (12 December 1711), and 435 (19 July 1712).

7. "the great Duke of Marlborough . . . Scots parliament": The first title of John Churchill, the great English military hero of the War of the Spanish Succession (see *Briton*, no. 10, n. 11), was Baron Churchill of Aymouth in the peerage of Scotland. The title was bestowed in 1682.

8. "John Duke of Argyle, John Earl of Stair": John Campbell, second duke of Argyll (1678–1743), was one of Marlborough's chief commanders during his continental campaigns of 1706–9; later he led the government forces against the Jacobite rebels of 1715. John Dalrymple, second earl of Stair, was an important military figure from the reign of Anne well into that of George II; he was still active as late as the battle of Dettingen in 1743. See *Briton*, no. 4, n. 7.

9. "an action of trover": "An action at law to recover the value of personal property illegally converted by another to his own use" (*OED*).

10. "*Ni fallat fatum*": *Political Controversy* translates the Latin phrase as "Unless fate proves fallacious."

11. "in right of a Stuart": See above, n. 1.

12. "the act of settlement": The parliamentary act of 1701 limiting the succession to the English throne. The act provided that, after William III and the future Queen Anne and their possible descendants (neither had living children at the time), the succession should fall to the Electress Sophia of Hanover and her Protestant descendants. Sophia was named because she was the granddaughter of James I, the first of the Stuart monarchs and the successor to Elizabeth I. George III was the great-great-grandson of Sophia. The act is still the legal basis for the royal succession in Great Britain.

13. "a right by conquest to the crown of England": Gilbert Burnet, in *A Pastoral Letter* (1689), advanced the argument here cited. In January 1693 the House of Commons ordered a pamphlet entitled *King William and Queen Mary Conquerors* burned by the hangman and then pronounced a similar sentence on Bishop Burnet's work for its having first asserted the dangerous idea.

14. "Edward the Fourth . . . his sign": Smollett refers to this story in *Complete History*, 2:378, where he reports that the man was a grocer: "The first act of sovereignty that distinguished the reign of Edward, is said to have been the execution of one Walker, a citizen and grocer, who jocosely said to his neighbours that he would

make his son heir to the crown, meaning the sign of the crown that hung over his
door: this innocent jest was construed into high treason, and the unhappy man
suffered death; though in all probability, his chief crime was his adherence to the
house of Lancaster, which Edward resolved to punish with the utmost rigour."

15. "a poor Prince . . . a goose": Edward, earl of Warwick (1475–99), nephew of
Edward IV and last male in the Yorkist line, was held prisoner in the Tower
of London from 1485 until he was beheaded in 1499 for supposedly conspiring
against the king. Kept in ignorance of the world about him, he has usually been
described in terms similar to the *Briton*'s; *DNB* quotes the unascribed phrase: "he
could not discern a goose from a capon."

16. "the gallant Earl of Surry . . . a day or two longer": Henry Howard, earl of Surrey
(1517–47), the well-known poet, was executed in 1547 on a charge of conspiring
to keep the future Edward VI from the throne. One of the main points in his trial
was that he evidenced his own ambitions by changing his arms and quartering
them with those of Edward the Confessor. His father, Thomas Howard, third
duke of Norfolk, was included in the charge and would have met the same fate
had not Henry VIII died the night before his scheduled execution.

17. "the two only uncles he had": Thomas Seymour, Baron Seymour of Sudeley
(1508?–49), was executed on charges of treason in 1549. His older brother, Edward
Seymour, first earl of Hertford and duke of Somerset (1506?–52), was named pro-
tector of the realm when Edward VI became king in 1547, but he eventually was
defeated in the struggle for power among the king's councillors and was executed
in 1552 on a charge of felony. It does not appear that the youthful king was actively
involved in promoting the trials of his uncles, but he readily acquiesced to their
executions.

18. "lady Jane Grey": Lady Jane Dudley, née Grey (1537–54), was the cousin of
Edward VI. Upon Edward's death in 1553, a group of councillors headed by
Lady Jane's father-in-law publicly proclaimed her queen. But within less than two
weeks, Mary Tudor's claims to the throne were established and Lady Jane's re-
linquished. A few months later she pleaded guilty to charges of treason, and both
she and her husband were beheaded on 12 February 1554.

19. "the Earl of Gowry, the lady Arabella, and the Duke of Monmouth": William
Ruthven, first earl of Gowrie (1541?–84), was beheaded in 1584 on charges of
treason against James VI (before he became James I of England); his son, John
Ruthven, third earl of Gowrie (1577–1600), was killed by James's attendants—
possibly by James himself—in 1600 because of suspected treason. Arabella Stuart
(1575–1615), cousin of James, was mistrusted by him as a potential claimant to the
throne and was imprisoned in the Tower, where she died in 1615. James Scott,
duke of Monmouth (1649–85), Charles II's famous natural son, was beheaded by
his uncle James II in 1685.

20. "an inscription . . . *from us*": See above, n. 1.

21. "*sciatis* . . . 11th Nov. 1400": The words of the charter are translated in *Political
Controversy*: "Know ye that we have granted, and by this our present charter con-

firmed, to John Stuart of Bute, our beloved brother, the office of viscountship of Bute and Arran, dated November 11th 1400."

22. *"pro aris et socis"*: Cicero *De Natura Deorum* 3.40: "On behalf of our altars and hearths." *Political Controversy* translates the phrase as "For our civil and religious liberties."

23. "the battle of Poictiers down to that of Minden": The battle of Poitiers was fought in 1356, during the Hundred Years' War; Edward the Black Prince defeated a French army under King John II. The battle of Minden, during which the French were defeated by an allied army of Germans and British, was fought in August 1759.

24. "The new acquisition of the Havannah": Havana was taken by British forces on 12 August 1762.

No. 20. Saturday, 9 October 1762

1. Motto: Horace *Satires* 2.3.48–51. *Political Controversy* quotes the popular translation of Philip Francis, first published in 1743:

> When in a wood we leave the certain way
> One error fools us, though we various stray
> Some to the left, and some to t'other side.

2. "the treaty of Utrecht": The treaty of 1713 ending the War of the Spanish Succession. As news of preliminary negotiations for the treaty was published, controversy flared between Whigs and Tories over what appeared to be an abandonment of continental allies and over possible consequences of the proposed peace for the future of the British monarchy and nation. The controversy was marked by a spate of printed partisan material, much of it inspired by Jonathan Swift's *Conduct of the Allies* (1711), which propagandized the Tory ministry's proposals for peace terms. As the *Briton* perceives, many of the circumstances and issues of this earlier controversy were similar to those fought over in the struggle to bring about a peace in 1762.

3. "the rival ministers of Queen Anne": Robert Harley, first earl of Oxford (1661–1724), who was head of Queen Anne's Tory ministry from 1710 until shortly before her death in 1714; and Henry St. John, Viscount Bolingbroke (1678–1751), who was secretary of state in the same ministry.

4. "the death of the Emperor Joseph": Joseph I, Holy Roman Emperor, died suddenly of smallpox in April 1711, and was succeeded by his brother Charles VI. See *Briton*, no. 10, nn. 5, 10.

5. "scale now kicked the beam": A proverbial phrase based on the observation that when scale pans are unbalanced, the one with less weight will fly up and hit the beam. In chapter 9 of *Roderick Random*, a landlord observes that if a parson and an exciseman "were weighed together, a straw thrown into either scale would make the ballance kick the beam."

6. "the fires of Smithfield": See *Briton*, no. 10, n. 4.

7. "The individuals concerned . . . abandon their country": In 1715, the Whig-dominated House of Commons resolved to impeach Oxford and Bolingbroke (see above, n. 3), James Butler, duke of Ormonde (1665–1745), and Thomas Wentworth, earl of Strafford (1672–1739), for the parts they had played in effecting the treaty of Utrecht. Bolingbroke and Ormonde, a popular general, fled into exile in France. Oxford was imprisoned in the Tower of London for two years. The charges against Strafford, who had been a plenipotentiary in the peace negotiations, were eventually dropped.

8. "during the ministry of his predecessor": *Monitor*, no. 367 (31 July 1762), had bemoaned the loss of Newfoundland earlier in the year and asserted that under Pitt's administration it had been defended by six or seven ships of war. See *Briton*, no. 12, n. 14.

9. "another paper": *Auditor*, no. 9 (5 August 1762), replied to the *Monitor* by maintaining, "it is false *that six or seven ships were Always stationed there under Mr. Pitt's administration.*"

No. 21. Saturday, 16 October 1762

1. Motto: Horace *Odes* 3.2.21–24. *Political Controversy* quotes the translation of Philip Francis:

> To him, who not deserves to die,
> She shews the paths, which heroes trod,
> Then bids him boldly tempt the sky,
> Spurn off his mortal clay, and rise a God.

2. "The Havanna . . . Great Britain": News reached England on 30 September that Havana had been captured by British forces on 12 August.

3. "devoted": "Consigned to evil or destruction" (*OED*).

4. "empirics": Medical practitioners who lack scientific knowledge; thus, quacks or charlatans (*OED*).

5. "Isthmus of Darien": An area in the eastern part of present-day Panama.

No. 22. Saturday, 23 October 1762

1. Motto: Horace *Satires* 2.3.46–47: "Now learn why all, who have given you the name of madman, are quite as crazy as yourself." The translation in *Political Controversy*, apparently influenced by the quotation from *Macbeth* with which the number begins, reads, "Now swallow that poison which maddens all that use it."

2. "*had eaten . . . prisoner*": *Macbeth* 1.3.84–85: "Or have we eaten on the insane root, / That takes the Reason Prisoner?"

3. "those who have been bit by the tarantula": "An Essay on the Tarantula" appeared in Smollett's *British Magazine* 1 (April 1760): 185–89. The author remarks on the first page: "it was supposed and taken for granted, that the only remedy which could expel this poison [of the tarantula] was dancing and music." The essay makes several further references to this practice.

4. "collate . . . negotiation": *Auditor*, no. 15 (16 September 1762), had provided just the sort of comparison suggested here. See *Briton*, no. 17, n. 2.

5. the French sugar-islands": Presumably Martinique and Guadeloupe. See *Briton*, no. 18, n. 9.

6. "on a former occasion": See the latter part of *Briton*, no. 18.

7. "the capitulation of Closter-Severn": See *Briton*, no. 18, n. 7.

8. "a noble D—ke": The duke of Newcastle.

No. 23. Saturday, 30 October 1762

1. "bully-backs": A bully-back is "a bully who supports another person" (*OED*).

2. "the first of May 1761": This was about the time when representatives of France and England were exchanged to begin discussion of possible terms for peace.

3. "cognoscible": Or *cognizable*, "capable of being, or liable to be, judicially examined or tried" (*OED*).

4. "*swallowing the cow, and choaking on the rump*": A common proverb, usually found in a form such as "to swallow an ox and be choked with the tail."

5. "*what is done, cannot . . . be undone*": *Macbeth* 5.1.68.

6. "*crassa Minerva*": Horace *Satires* 2.2.3: "rough mother-wit."

7. "The earl of Salisbury": Robert Cecil, first earl of Salisbury (1563?–1612), served James I as his chief minister from that monarch's accession in 1603 until the earl's death in 1612.

8. "a formal treaty with Spain": Salisbury negotiated an uneasy peace with Spain in 1604.

9. "the treaty of Munster": A treaty of 1648, concluded at Münster in Westphalia, establishing the Peace of Westphalia. The treaty resolved for a time the series of continental power struggles known as the Thirty Years' War.

10. "squib": "A short composition of a satirical and witty character; a lampoon" (*OED*).

11. "the treaty of 1667": A lengthy commercial treaty between Spain and England was negotiated in Madrid in 1667 by the earl of Sandwich (see below, n. 22). This treaty remained the basis for most commercial relations between the two nations for the next several decades.

12. "Another treaty . . . in 1670": A treaty signed in Madrid in 1670, supplementary to that of 1667 and known in some sources as the Treaty of Madrid, clarified the rights of both Spain and England in the West Indies and confirmed English possession of Jamaica.

13. "*felo de se*": L. Suicide. *OED* quotes Blackstone: one who "deliberately puts an end to his own existence or commits any unlawful malicious act, the consequence of which is his own death."

14. "*the turn of the scale*": To turn the scale is "to cause one scale of a balance to descend: said of an additional weight, usually a slight or just sufficient one" (*OED*).

15. "*Pons asinorum*": The bridge of asses; the fifth proposition of book 1 of Euclid was

humorously so called because of the difficulty dull students had in getting over it. At Winchester School, Peregrine Pickle "had scarce advanced beyond the *Pons Asinorum* when his ardour [for Euclid] abated" (*Peregrine Pickle*, chap. 16).

16. "honest Baucis and his wife": A confusing allusion. In Greek mythology, Baucis was not the husband, but the wife, of Philemon, a peasant of Phrygia. In Ovid's version of their story (*Metamorphoses*, book 8), Baucis and Philemon were rewarded for their hospitality to Jupiter and Mercury by the granting of two wishes: first, that they might be priests of the temple into which their hut had been transformed; and second, that they might remain forever together. Upon their death they were changed into trees, an oak and a linden, which grew from the same trunk and stood before the temple they served.

17. "clubbed": The context suggests the meaning "added"; *OED* gives these definitions for *club* as a verb: "To combine together"; "To combine, or contribute, to a common end."

18. "*get the ladle out again*": Apparently a proverbial or allusive expression, but its source has not been traced. Smollett may here refer to a version of the story of Midas attributed to Plutarch and sometimes confused with the more familiar legend of his wish, later retracted, that everything he touched might be turned into gold. In the alternative story, Midas became lost in a desert while traveling in a distant part of his kingdom of Phrygia. The earth, pitying him, sent forth a spring for him to drink from, but the spring spouted gold instead of water. Midas prayed to Dionysus, asking that the gold might be changed to water; his prayer was answered, and he was able to drink again. See Pierre Grimal, *The Dictionary of Classical Mythology*, trans. A. R. Maxwell-Hyslop (Oxford: Basil Blackwell, 1986), 290.

19. "Northern": Scandinavian.

20. "prescriptive": "Derived from or founded on prescription or lapse of time, as *prescriptive right* or *title*" (*OED*).

21. "the bay of Campeachy": The Gulf of Campeche, the southwestern part of the Gulf of Mexico.

22. "the Earl of Sandwich . . . Lord Sunderland": Edward Montagu, first earl of Sandwich (1625–72), was in 1666 appointed ambassador extraordinary to Madrid, where in the following year he concluded a commercial treaty with Spain. Sir Richard Fanshawe (1608–66) was English ambassador to Spain from 1664 until his recall upon Sandwich's appointment. Sir William Godolphin (1634?–96) assisted Sandwich in the negotiations leading to the commercial treaty of 1667; in 1671 he became ambassador to Spain. Robert Spencer, second earl of Sunderland (1640–1702), served on a brief diplomatic mission to Spain in 1671–72.

23. "a right of indulgence": A right acquired by the delay in enforcing a legal right; indulgence is similar to forbearance, "abstinence from enforcing what is due, *esp.* the payment of a debt" (*OED*).

24. "the celebrated family compact": There were at least three eighteenth-century

treaties between Spain and France known as family compacts because the family of the Bourbons possessed the thrones of both France and Spain. The reference here must be to the compact signed secretly in August 1761, the discovery of which helped cause Pitt to demand a declaration of war against Spain, a demand which in turn resulted in Pitt's departure from office. Pitt probably learned of the family compact through secret correspondence from Hans Stanley, an English envoy in Paris, but the discoverer of it, ironically mentioned in the next sentence of the *Briton*, is probably intended to be recognized as Pitt himself.

No. 24. Saturday, 6 November 1762

1. Motto: Cicero *Pro Rabirio* 5.15: "I have ever shewn the greatest reluctance at, and have always resisted, to the utmost of my influence, understanding eloquence and abilities, the tamely suffering even the smallest act of despotic cruelty" (*Political Controversy*).
2. "the conquest": The Norman Conquest of 1066, when William, duke of Normandy, made good his claim to the English throne by defeating King Harold at the Battle of Hastings and being crowned as William I.
3. "The reign of William the Conqueror . . . from the lawful proprietors": William I (1027?–87) ruled England from 1066 until his death in 1087. Odo (d. 1097), bishop of Bayeux, was named earl of Kent at the time of his half brother William's coronation. William Fitzosbern (d. 1071), a chief supporter of the conqueror, and Odo were appointed viceroys when William returned to Normandy for a few months in 1067. During these months they provoked outbursts of revolt by their severity in securing William's conquered realm. Geoffrey (d. 1093), bishop of Coutances, accompanied William and his fellow-bishop Odo during the Norman invasion of England. For his services, he received numerous estates throughout England.
4. "As for Odo . . . William's death": For an account similar to that given here, see *Complete History*, 1:226, 237. Much of the historical matter of this number of the *Briton* is drawn from the pages of Smollett's *Complete History*; several of the early passages are almost verbatim borrowings.
5. "That prince's son . . . the King's coffers": William Rufus (d. 1100), so called because of his ruddy complexion, was the third son of William I. He reigned as William II from 1079 to 1100. Ralf, or Rannulf, Flambard (d. 1128) early in life gained the favor of William I and quickly became an important figure when William Rufus gained the throne. He was named bishop of Durham in 1099 and was especially notorious for contriving and forcing exactions from the king's subjects.
6. "he raised the proportion of the taxes accordingly": See *Complete History*, 1:245.
7. "Henry I. . . . useless implements": Henry I (1068–1135), the fourth son of William I, quickly seized the English throne upon the death of his brother William Rufus in 1100 and reigned until 1135. Roger of Salisbury (d. 1139), be-

cause of his excellent management of the king's affairs, was consecrated bishop of Salisbury in 1107 and shortly thereafter the king's justiciar (a political and judicial officer who acted as the king's deputy and as regent in the king's absence).

8. "Sarum": Old ecclesiastical name of Salisbury.

9. "the usurper Stephen . . . grief and vexation": See *Complete History*, 1:273, 275, 284.

10. "The usurpation of Stephen . . . William d'Ypres": Stephen (1097?–1154) was the son of William I's daughter Adela. Although he had sworn to support Henry I's daughter Matilda and her son (the future Henry II) as successors to Henry, he successfully claimed the English crown immediately after Henry's death in 1135 and reigned until 1154. On Stephen's becoming king, he surrounded himself with a force of Flemish mercenaries, with William of Ypres (d. 1165) at their head. William quickly became a confidant of the king, helping him to maintain his uncertain throne with a good deal of violence and terror.

11. "massacre all the foreigners in the kingdom": See *Complete History*, 1:281.

12. "Henry II. . . . government and life": Henry II (1133–89) was the grandson of Henry I and the eldest child of Henry's daughter Matilda and Geoffrey Plantagenet; he was thus the first of the Plantagenet monarchs of England. He became king upon Stephen's death in 1154, reigning until 1189, and was noted for setting the administrative affairs of England in much better order than they had previously been.

13. "many excellent laws and regulations": See *Complete History*, 1:378–79. Henry II is one of the few kings from the two or three hundred years after the Norman Conquest of whom Smollett has much good to say in his history.

14. "While Richard . . . the realm": Richard I, Coeur de Lion or Lion-Heart (1157–99), was the son of Henry II. He left for the Third Crusade within a few months of securing his father's crown in 1189 and, while returning, was captured and imprisoned on the Continent; he did not get back to England until 1194, after he was ransomed by the English. He remained at home only a few months and then left for France, where he was killed in 1199. Altogether Richard spent only about six months of his reign on English soil. William of Longchamp (d. 1197) was a Norman who served Richard's interests in France before Henry II's death. Upon Richard's coronation, he was named chancellor of the kingdom and bishop of Ely. His loyal pursuit of what he considered Richard's interests during Richard's absences brought upon him much hatred from the natives of England.

15. "legatine": "Of or pertaining to a legate [i.e., a deputy or emissary]" (*OED*).

16. "his brain was disordered": See *Complete History*, 1:391. From here on, Smollett's historical summary is more sketchy and does not use verbatim passages from *Complete History*.

17. "John . . . fixed principles": John (1167?–1216) was the youngest son of Henry II. He succeeded his brother Richard I as king in 1199 and reigned until 1216. His struggle with the barons of his kingdom brought about his signing of the Magna Carta in 1215.

18. "Henry III. . . . own persons": Henry III (1207–72) was only nine years old when he became king in 1216, after the death of his father John.

19. "Hubert de Burgh . . . his subjects": Hubert de Burgh (d. 1243) became justiciar to John in 1215 and continued in the office under the young Henry III. He was opposed by a coterie known as the Poitevins (natives of Poitou in France), led by Peter de Roches or des Roches (d. 1238). Peter had served both Richard I and John and became bishop of Winchester in 1205. He was appointed guardian of Henry III when Henry became king. In 1232, Peter succeeded in getting Hubert dismissed and had his nephew Peter de Rivaux or Rivaulx (d. 1258?) appointed treasurer. But two years later, public clamor against Peter and the Poitevins resulted in another revolution in the king's councils, leading to their dismissal. In 1236 Henry married Eleanor of Provence (d. 1291). She was escorted to England by her uncle William (d. 1239), bishop elect of Valence, who gained and maintained considerable influence over his nephew-in-law until his death.

20. Edward I. . . . and success": Edward I (1239–1307) succeeded to the throne of England immediately upon the death of his father, Henry III, in 1272. His reign was generally well administered.

21. "but his son . . . the barons": Edward II (1284–1327), who succeeded his father, Edward I, in 1307, has historically been regarded as one of the most unfit of English monarchs. Piers Gaveston (d. 1312), of Gascon origin, was brought into Edward I's household as a young boy and from an early age was an intimate of Edward II. Edward's extreme fondness for him both before and after becoming king gave Gaveston an ambition and insolence that incurred the resentment of most of Edward's other associates. His enemies managed his execution in 1312. Hugh le Despenser (1262–1326) and his son, also Hugh (d. 1326), gained ascendence over Edward soon after Gaveston's death, but their influence helped to precipitate a revolt by Edward's consort, Queen Isabella, and the barons. The Despensers were apprehended and executed as traitors in 1326. At the same time the king himself was deposed by Isabella and her lover, Roger Mortimer, and in the following year the king was murdered, presumably with their connivance.

22. "This was also the fate . . . hatred and vengeance of the people": Edward III (1312–77) was crowned king of England in January 1327, while his deposed father was still in prison. He was fourteen years old at the time. His mother, Isabella (1296–1358), and Roger Mortimer, earl of March (1287–1330), who had become her lover in France while they were planning rebellion against Edward II and the Despensers, were virtual rulers of England for the next few years. However, in 1330, the young king, resentful of Mortimer's power, secretly arranged his arrest. Mortimer was charged with numerous crimes and was shortly thereafter hanged, drawn, and quartered. Alice Pierce, or Perrers (d. 1400), was in the service of Edward's queen, Phillipa, and sometime around 1366 became Edward's mistress. She used her intimacy with the king to accumulate considerable wealth. The king is reported to have bestowed upon her a large collection of jewels, including those

that had belonged to Queen Phillipa before her death in 1368. In the 1370s, a struggle to control Edward's government developed between parties led by two of the king's sons, Edward the Black Prince (1330–76) and John of Gaunt, duke of Lancaster (1340–99). With the support of Alice, John of Gaunt was able to gain and keep control until shortly before his father's death.

23. "All the world . . . his life": Richard II (1367–1400) was a grandson of Edward III and son of Edward the Black Prince. He was ten years old when he came to the throne in 1377. Michael de la Pole, earl of Suffolk (1330?–89), was chancellor of England from 1383 to 1386, when parliamentary opposition forced Richard to dismiss him. Robert de Vere, ninth earl of Oxford and duke of Ireland (1362–92), was a special favorite of Richard, whose generous grants to him created much parliamentary opposition. While Richard was abroad in Ireland in 1399, his exiled cousin and rival, Henry Bolingbroke, duke of Hereford, landed in England, took control of the country, and deposed Richard. Richard died or perhaps was murdered in prison the following year. While in Ireland, Richard had left the affairs of England in the hands of four councillors: William le Scrope, earl of Wiltshire (1351?–99); Sir John Bussy (d. 1399); Sir Thomas (not Henry) Green (d. 1399); and Sir William Bagot (dates unknown). When Hereford arrived in England, he arrested the first three of these men in Bristol and had them summarily executed. Bagot managed to escape arrest but was afterward apprehended and committed to the Tower, where he presumably died some time later.

24. "the fourth and fifth Henrys": Henry IV (1367–1413) reigned from 1399, when he forced the abdication of Richard II, to 1413. He was succeeded by his son Henry V (1387–1422), whose short but celebrated reign ended in 1422.

25. "this weakness . . . Somerset": Henry VI (1421–71) was not quite nine months old when his father, Henry V, died and he became king of England. His father's younger brother, Humphrey, duke of Gloucester (1391–1447), although denied his claim to be the infant king's guardian, was an important power in the king's affairs for at least two decades. Henry Beaufort, bishop of Winchester (d. 1447), an illegitimate son of John of Gaunt and thus Henry VI's great-uncle, was chancellor during the reign of Henry V, an office he retained in the early years of Henry VI's reign. He and Gloucester often contended as rivals in the king's councils. He was made a cardinal in 1426 and remained an important advisor of the king almost until his death. Henry VI married Margaret of Anjou (1430–82) by proxy in 1444. She came to England in 1445, escorted by William de la Pole, fourth earl and first duke of Suffolk (1396–1450), who had negotiated the marriage and who remained her close friend as well as a councillor to the king. Later he was accused of betraying English interests in negotiating the marriage and was murdered by his enemies. Edmund Beaufort, second duke of Somerset (d. 1455), was a military leader and an ally of Suffolk in the king's councils. Antagonism between him and the duke of York, great-grandson of Edward III and claimant to the throne, led in 1455 to a battle in which Somerset was slain. This battle was the beginning of the

War of the Roses. The Lancastrian Henry was deposed by the Yorkists in 1461 and eventually murdered in 1471.

26. "Edward IV. . . . rebellion": Edward IV (1442–83), son of Richard, duke of York, was crowned king by the Yorkists in 1461, after the deposition of Henry VI. Richard Woodville, first Earl Rivers (d. 1469), had been a supporter of Henry VI, but he switched his allegiance to the Yorkists at about the time Edward became king. Rivers's daughter, Elizabeth, was married to Edward in 1464, an event that brought the Woodvilles into prominence in the king's councils.

27. "Every body has heard . . . master's tyranny": Richard III (1452–85), known to history as Crookback because of a slight physical deformity, was the younger brother of Edward IV. He had himself proclaimed king in 1483, a few months after his brother's death and the announcement of a claim that Edward's two young sons were illegitimate. His short reign ended in 1485, when he was slain at the battle of Bosworth Field and the victorious Henry Tudor became Henry VII. Among Richard's closest associates during his reign were Francis, Viscount Lovel (1454–87?); Sir Richard Radcliffe or Ratcliffe (d. 1485), slain with his king at Bosworth Field; and William Catesby (d. 1485), taken prisoner at Bosworth Field and beheaded three days later. The three were immortalized in doggerel verse affixed in public places throughout London by Richard's enemies in 1484: "The rat, the cat, and Lovel our dog / Rule all England under the hog." *Cat* and *rat*, of course, are wordplay on the names Catesby and Ratcliffe.

28. "Nor is any historical fact . . . substance": Henry VII (1457–1509), first of the Tudor monarchs, reigned from 1485 to 1509. Sir Richard Empson (d. 1510) and Edmund Dudley (1462?–1510), both trained in the law, became important as financial councillors to Henry VII. Both were accused of corrupt policies and of working together to extort taxes and fines from the king's subjects. When they lost the protection of Henry VII at his death and Henry VIII came to the throne, widespread charges against them caused the new king to commit both to the Tower, where they were beheaded in 1510.

29. "The pride . . . has expatiated": Henry VIII (1491–1547) succeeded his father, Henry VII, in 1509. Thomas Wolsey (1475?–1530) accumulated vast wealth as a prince of the church and as a diplomat and minister for Henry VIII. He was made both a cardinal and lord chancellor in 1515, giving him almost unprecedented power, both political and ecclesiastical.

30. "The Duke of Somerset . . . popular detestation": Edward VI (1537–53) was only nine years old when he succeeded his father, Henry VIII, in 1547; he died six years later. Edward Seymour, first earl of Hertford and duke of Somerset (1506?–52), uncle of Edward, became lord protector of the child king but was removed from office in 1549 and beheaded in 1552 by his rival, John Dudley, duke of Northumberland (1502?–53). Northumberland was executed in 1553 for his attempts to proclaim his daughter-in-law, Lady Jane Grey, successor to Edward.

31. "The administration of Mary . . . Bonner": Mary I (1516–58), an ardent Roman

Catholic, succeeded her half brother Edward in 1553. Stephen Gardiner (1483?–1555), bishop of Winchester, was made lord high chancellor of the realm by Mary shortly after her accession. Edmund Bonner (1500?–69) was bishop of London. Gardiner and Bonner have historically been linked together as responsible for much of the persecution of Protestants during Mary's reign.

32. "Elizabeth . . . friends of the public": Elizabeth I (1533–1603), who came to the throne in 1558, after the death of her half sister Mary, was generally fortunate in her ministers, most notably William Cecil, Lord Burghley (1520–98), who served her throughout most of her reign.

33. "The administration of James I . . . personal beauty": James I (1566–1625), distant cousin of Elizabeth and first of the Stuart monarchs, became king of England upon the death of Elizabeth in 1603.

34. "In the reign of Charles I. . . . haughty disposition": The reign of Charles I (1600–49) began in 1625 and ended with his beheading by Puritan rebels in 1649. George Villiers, first duke of Buckingham (1592–1628), had been a favorite of Charles's father, James I, and had also so thoroughly ingratiated himself with Charles that, when Charles came to the throne, Buckingham gained virtual control of the English government. His reckless policies created numerous enemies, one of whom assassinated him in 1628. Thomas Wentworth, first earl of Strafford (1593–1641), was a military leader and a minister to Charles. The Long Parliament that led to the civil war forced Charles to assent to Strafford's execution.

35. "After the restoration Clarendon . . . popular execration": Charles II (1630–85), son of Charles I, was in exile in France for eleven years after the execution of his father. The Restoration of 1660 brought him back to England. Edward Hyde, first earl of Clarendon (1609–74), shared Charles's exile with him and was made lord chancellor upon their return. He served as chief minister to Charles until 1667, when personal and political enemies convinced the king to dismiss him. Soon he was impeached in Parliament and fled again to France, where he lived the last years of his life.

36. "It was not without reason . . . his expulsion and ruin": James II (1633–1701), the Roman Catholic brother of Charles II, reigned only from 1685 to 1688, when he was driven from the throne and into exile by the Glorious Revolution. Robert Spencer, second earl of Sunderland (1640–1702), was lord president and secretary of state during James's brief reign. Richard Talbot, earl of Tyrconnel (1630–91), was viceroy in Ireland. George Jeffreys, first Baron Jeffreys of Wem (1648–89), was lord chief justice and was very serviceable to James in conducting trials for high treason.

37. "the liberty of the press": An act passed by Parliament in 1662 (13 & 14 Car. II, cap. 33) decreed that no book could be printed without first receiving a license. The act, intended to control publication of works thought to be seditious, was renewed a number of times but finally was allowed to expire in 1694.

38. "the whole reigns of William and his successor": The Glorious Revolution of

1688 brought William III (1650–1702) and Mary II (1662–94), the Protestant son-in-law and daughter of James II, to the English throne. When William died in 1702, James's younger Protestant daughter, Anne (1665–1714), succeeded to the throne and reigned until 1714.

No. 25. Saturday, 13 November 1762

1. Motto: Cicero *Phillipics* 3.4: "Dear citizen and native of this commonwealth, perfectly regardful of her reputation, and a respectful imitator of his own ancestors" (*Political Controversy*).
2. "*they will blow us up in a trice*": A recent pamphlet entitled *A Letter to the Right Honourable the Lord Mayor, the Worshipful Aldermen*, . . . had attacked the preliminary peace terms that were being published. Dated 6 October 1762 and signed by George Heathcote, the pamphlet warned that some terms quoted "will, like Gunpowder, blow up this Nation in a Trice" (p. 8). Smollett refers to this same pamphlet in the opening paragraph of *Briton*, no. 27.
3. "now stands with his dark lanthorn and match": The image of Guy Fawkes, holding a dark lantern and getting ready to ignite his explosives, had long been used in prints to accuse others of treason. See George, *English Political Caricature*, index under "Fawkes, Guy."
4. "Brief let me be": *Hamlet* 1.5.59.
5. "*myself will mount the rostrum . . . to gain his pardon from the people*": Addison, *Cato* 2.2.36–37.
6. "Lacedemon": Another name for ancient Sparta.
7. "Augusta": London.
8. "pretors": Roman magistrates.
9. "Cripplegate grenadiers": Cripplegate was one of the old gates to the city of London. No record has been found of any regular military group bearing such a name. The satiric context here suggests that it may have been a nonce nickname for municipal watchmen or other minor officers.
10. "*Equites*": L. Horsemen or knights. In early Roman times, the term specified a military distinction; later it specified a social or political upper class.
11. "*Curiones and the Decuriones*": *Decuriones* were Roman local municipal councillors. *Curiones* may be interpreted as priests presiding over a voting assembly, but there may be a bit of wordplay here, suggesting that *curiones* were a distinctive rank of *decuriones*.
12. "the chief magistrate of the metropolis": William Beckford became lord mayor on 9 November 1762. See *Briton*, no. 8, n. 14.
13. "Caboceiro": A caboceer, a native chief of West Africa (*OED*).
14. "the modern Demosthenes": William Pitt, who enjoyed the unflagging support of the wealthy and influential Beckford. *Auditor*, no. 4 (1 July 1762), quotes words Pitt was supposed to have spoken in defense of Beckford on a certain occasion

when Beckford's language had raised laughter in the House: "I am glad I was born in an age that produced such a man, so able a senator, so good an orator, so rich a planter, and so excellent a physician."

15. "to cast the water": "To diagnose disease by the inspection of (urine)" (*OED*).

16. "mayor of the palace": *Major palatii*, a medieval French royal office roughly equivalent to that of prime minister. See below, n. 26.

17. "*tributim . . . centuriatim*": L. Tribe by tribe . . . by companies.

18. "tything": A small rural administrative division, originally one in which the members (apparently ten men or ten families) were bound to support one another.

19. "*magister equitum*": L. Master of the horse or of the knights; sometimes used to identify a dictator's lieutenant.

20. "Colonel Jack": John Wilkes was appointed colonel of the Bucks militia in June 1762.

21. "Lilburn": John Lilburne. See *Briton*, no. 16, n. 20.

22. "The present town-clerk": Unidentified.

23. "the two reverend augurs": Probably Charles Churchill and Robert Lloyd (although Lloyd was not a clergyman). The *Briton* on earlier occasions (see nos. 13, 14, and 15) had coupled the two as Wilkes's lieutenants in the propaganda war against Bute.

24. "*vox et præterea nihil*": L. From a Greek proverb, originally said of the nightingale: "a voice and nothing else." Smollett earlier used the same proverb in chapter 11 of *Roderick Random*.

25. "the Dairo of Japan": A dairi, or dayro, is "a respectful mode of speaking of the mikado or emperor" (*OED*). The term is used satirically throughout *Adventures of an Atom* to refer to George II and George III, kings of England.

26. "*Faineans*": The seventh- and early-eighth-century kings of France have been called *rois fainéants*, "do-nothing kings," because of the dominance of the *major palatii* (mayor of the palace) during their reigns.

27. "the cubay": The term *Cuboy* appears frequently in *Adventures of an Atom* as a satiric designation for a chief minister.

28. "eat, drink, and be merry": Luke 12:19.

29. "*Junius Brutus Cockney*": Junius Brutus was the legendary hero and Roman patriot who drove out the Tarquins and put to death his own traitorous sons.

30. "the preliminaries . . . actually signed": The preliminaries of the peace were signed on 3 November 1762. See *Briton*, no. 28, n. 2.

31. "Mr. H——'s prediction": George Heathcote's warning mentioned in the second paragraph of this number. See above, n. 2.

No. 26. Saturday, 20 November 1762

1. Motto: Translated in *Political Controversy* as "Insolence is the child of prosperity."

2. "the case of one Mr. Fitz-George": *Political Controversy* of 2 August 1762 had re-

printed a letter to the *St. James's Chronicle* in which one Thomas (*i.e.*, Newcastle) laments the passing of the old master of Albion manor (*i.e.*, England), of which he was the steward, and his replacement by "a dirty Scotch boy." Immediately following this reprint is an answer addressed "To the *Editor* of the *Political Controversy*," which continues the fiction of Albion manor, but, being signed by the new steward, John (*i.e.*, Bute), attacks the practices of the old servants and defends the new master. This number of the *Briton*, with its story of the estate of Mr. Fitz-George (*i.e.*, George III), was probably suggested by these allegories.

3. "Will Pitot": William Pitt. Smollett here seems to be punning on one or both of two French words: *piteux*, which means pitiable, woeful, miserable; and *pitaud*, which means peasant.

4. "by publishing a letter": A few days after Pitt's resignation in October 1761 a single sheet had appeared entitled *A Letter from a Right Hon. Person, to —— in the City*. In it Pitt (although there is some question whether he was actually the author) justified his resignation, stating, "I resigned the Seals . . . in order not to remain responsible for Measures, which I was no longer allowed to guide." His opponents quickly picked up the word *guide* to use in taunting him.

5. "Tom Give-place, or Buy-vote": Thomas Pelham-Holles, duke of Newcastle, who was notorious for his "management" of Parliament and parliamentary elections by giving supporters money as well as appointments to office.

6. "The case . . . left his place": In March 1762 Newcastle, then first lord of the treasury, was preparing to ask Parliament for a vote of annual credit of two million pounds for the war, the largest sum ever proposed. Bute and the other ministers considered that one million pounds would be sufficient, a consideration based in part on a proposed reduction or elimination of the annual English subsidy to Prussia, an action that Newcastle could not accept. At the beginning of May, Newcastle presented his case to the king, but the king would not hear of Newcastle's figure. A few days later, Newcastle announced his resignation.

7. "Jack Scot": John Stuart, earl of Bute.

8. "disquisitions upon cockle-shells, plants and flowers": Bute was well known as an amateur botanist.

9. "Jack-a-boot": "A jackboot and a petticoat, the popular emblems of Bute and the princess [George III's mother], were frequently burnt by excited mobs" (*DNB*). The emblem of a jackboot was also used in satiric prints to point at Bute. See, in the present volume, "The Scotch Butt" (p. 399); see also "The Jack-Boot Kick'd Down or English Will Triumphant. A Dream," included (print no. 3965) in the Georgia Edition of Smollett's *Adventures of an Atom*.

10. "Harry Chamberman": William Cavendish, fourth duke of Devonshire (1720–64), resigned (or was dismissed) as lord chamberlain of the household sometime toward the end of October 1762 and soon retired to Chatsworth, his estate. The *Gazetteer* for 1 November 1762 included a note about Devonshire's dining with Newcastle the previous week.

11. "Charley Check": Charles Watson-Wentworth, second marquis of Rockingham (1730–82), who, following Devonshire's lead, resigned as first lord of the bedchamber around the first of November 1762. It is not clear why Smollett calls Rockingham "Check." Possibly the name refers jokingly to his keeping of the checker-roll of personal servants to the king while he was first lord of the bedchamber.

12. "Peter Post-boy": William Ponsonby, second earl of Bessborough (1704–93), who, also following the lead of Devonshire, his brother-in-law, resigned as postmaster general around the first of November.

13. "Patriot": The *Patriot* was an antiministerial paper that survived for only five numbers during the early summer of 1762.

14. "Charles Say": Charles Green Say (d. 1775) was a printer and publisher of the *Gazetteer and London Daily Advertiser*. In its issue for 3 November 1762, after alluding to Devonshire's dismissal, the *Gazetteer* stated that several other persons were soon to be dismissed from the king's service. Perhaps the reference to Say's eldest brother in this sentence is a mistaken reference to his father, Edward Say (d. 1769), also a printer and publisher of the *General Evening Post*. Charles Green Say inherited his father's property, suggesting that he was himself the eldest son. See Robert L. Haig, *The Gazetteer 1735–1797: A Study in the Eighteenth-Century English Newspaper* (Carbondale: Southern Illinois University Press, 1960), 30, 87, 95.

No. 27. Saturday, 27 November 1762

1. Motto: Horace *Satires* 2.6.77–78: "He tells stories like an old woman" (*Political Controversy*).

2. "a pamphlet": The pamphlet was written by George Heathcote. See *Briton*, no. 25, n. 2. Neither Heathcote's pamphlet nor the answer in this number of the *Briton* is very well organized, but they are good examples of the kind of bickering that characterized public discussion of the preliminaries to the Peace of Paris.

3. "examination of African-traders . . . old African company": Smollett refers to deliberations in the year 1748, when the Royal African Company was subjected to parliamentary scrutiny as a result of alleged mismanagement and corruption. Petitions were submitted to the House of Commons on behalf of merchants of London and Liverpool, who requested that the African trade be opened to all who wished to pursue it and that the old joint-stock company be dissolved. A bill was presented in the Commons, where it passed; but it failed in the House of Lords. See *Continuation*, 1:26–29.

4. "Mr. H——": Mr. Heathcote. See above, n. 2.

5. "a *penny saved, is a penny got*": The favorite maxim of Sir Andrew Freeport as reported in *Spectator*, no. 2 (2 March 1711).

6. "Goree": A small island southeast of Cape Verde and off the coast from present-day Dakar in Senegal.

7. "Gum Senega": A variety of gum arabic, a water-soluble gum obtained from

acacia plants and used as a stiffener or filler for fabrics and in the manufacture of adhesives, confections, and pharmaceuticals. Smollett here echoes his earlier reference to this valuable gum in *Briton*, no. 17. He elsewhere frequently emphasizes the economic importance of preserving the Senegal gum trade. See *British Magazine* 1 (April 1760): 179–81; see also *Continuation*, 2:270–78, and *Adventures of an Atom*, 70–71.

8. "CRITO": A friend of Socrates; in Plato's dialogue *Crito*, Crito's proposal that the condemned Socrates escape is rebutted by Socrates himself.

No. 28. Saturday, 4 December 1762

1. Motto: Livy *Ab Urbe Condita* 30.13.17–18: "The rejoicings for victory are now become so common among the Romans, that they are worn out and utterly disregarded; the great extension of whose empire is owing more to their generosity to the vanquished than to the power of their arms" (*Political Controversy*).

2. "preliminary articles of the peace . . . in some of the daily papers": Preliminary articles of peace were signed at Fontainebleau on 3 November 1762, and the papers of London began publishing reports of them a few weeks later. The order in which the terms are here discussed corresponds closely to their order in the published accounts.

3. "New-France . . . insidiously represented": New France was the name for seventeenth- and eighteenth-century French colonial possessions in North America, which were located mainly along the North Atlantic coast and the Saint Lawrence River. Smollett may be responding to the *North Briton*, no. 24 (13 November 1762), which had described French Canada as "a miserable wretched country."

4. "inquiries . . . in the year 1748": Smollett refers to investigations promoted by merchants of London, Great Yarmouth, and Wolverhampton who sought to break the monopoly of the Hudson's Bay Company. Petitions accused the company of failure to pursue the fur trade aggressively and of barbarous treatment of the Indians, with the result that a great share of the trade was controlled by the French. A committee of the Commons considered abolishing the company, but decided that the public treasury could not bear the expense of maintaining the forts and settlements necessary to protect ship traffic. See *Continuation*, 1:31–32.

5. "St. Peter and Miquelon": Saint Pierre and Miquelon are two small islands off the southern coast of Newfoundland. Originally occupied by the French in 1660, they were captured by the British in 1702 but returned to the French in 1763 as the sole remnant of their North American colonies.

6. "Tobago, St. Vincent, and Dominica": Possession of these three islands in the West Indies was confirmed to Great Britain by the Peace of Paris in 1763. Previously they had supposedly been neutral, that is, left in possession of the natives. But France had more or less controlled Saint Vincent and Dominica until the British captured Dominica in 1761 and Saint Vincent in 1762. At various times,

Tobago had been claimed and partly colonized by Spain, France, the Netherlands, and England.

7. "the Spanish plate-fleet": "The fleet which annually brought the produce of the American silver mines to Spain" (*OED*).

8. "CURIO": See *Briton*, no. 11, n. 17.

No. 29. Saturday, 11 December 1762

1. Motto: Horace *Epodes* 16.41–43. *Political Controversy* quotes the translation of Philip Francis:

> For earth-surrounding sea our flight awaits,
> Offering its blissful isles, and happy seats,
> Where annual Ceres crowns th' uncultur'd field,
> And vines unprun'd their blushing clusters yield.

2. "the peace of Aix-la-Chapelle": The treaty signed in 1748, ending the long War of the Austrian Succession (1740–48).

3. "governor of Barbadoes . . . island of importance": Smollett here substantially repeats, though more briefly, the account given in *Continuation* (1:42–44) of British attempts to forestall French settlement of the island of Tobago in the West Indies. According to Smollett the governor of Barbados at the time, one Mr. Greenville, dispatched Captain Tyrrel, a naval commander, to discourage the landing of French troops and settlers. Tyrrel engaged in no hostilities but instead returned, reporting that settlement had already begun. British protests at Versailles led to the evacuation of the island.

4. "the noise . . . it produced": Minorca, in the western Mediterranean, was captured by the French from the British in the summer of 1756, when its Fort Saint Philip surrendered. Public indignation at the loss of Minorca and at the failure of Admiral John Byng's fleet to provide relief to the besieged fort led to the notorious court-martial and execution of Byng in 1757.

5. "an address to the King": This address was presented on 20 August 1756 and subsequently printed in *Gentleman's Magazine* 26 (August 1756): 408. The "&c." in the quotation that follows indicates omission of a few lines from the original.

6. "judge-advocate of the court of admiralty in New-England": The capture of Louisburg by colonial troops in 1745 was conceived and promoted by William Shirley, earlier appointed judge of admiralty but at the time governor of Massachusetts. See *Briton*, no. 12, n. 11.

7. "their address of congratulation to the King": This address was presented to the king on 20 October 1759. The text, of which the second paragraph is here quoted, is found in *Gentleman's Magazine* 29 (October 1759): 495.

8. "General Oglethorpe": James Edward Oglethorpe (1696–1785), founder of Georgia in 1732, led a successful repulse of Spanish forces attempting to invade and gain control of his colony in 1742.

9. "the treaty of 1750 . . . the Assiento contract": In October 1750, Sir Benjamin Keene concluded a commercial treaty with the Spaniards in Madrid that resolved some trade issues left over from the Treaty of Aix-la-Chapelle. The *assiento* (or *asiento*) contract was a treaty between Spain and England signed in 1713 in the wake of the Treaty of Utrecht. It gave England certain trading rights in the Spanish West Indies, most notably a monopoly on the slave trade. The treaty of 1750 rescinded the *assiento* contract on condition of a Spanish payment of one hundred thousand pounds.

10. "The last complaint . . . this condition": The shibboleth of "no search" had long been a battle cry of the English commercial rivals of Spain. English traders in the West Indies were often guilty of smuggling activities, which the Spanish authorities tried to control with a coast guard that maintained the right to board and search any suspected vessel. The exchange in Parliament between Sir John Hynd Cotton (d. 1752) and Henry Pelham over failure to include in the Treaty of Aix-la-Chapelle any provision prohibiting the search of English vessels is reported in *Gentleman's Magazine* 19 (November 1749): 483–84.

11. "Mr. P— justified the treaty": William Pitt defended the commercial treaty of 1750 in a speech delivered in Parliament on 17 January 1751. He admitted that in 1739 he had spoken out for the principle of no search, but he justified his about-face by claiming that he was now more mature and more experienced in matters of foreign policy.

12. "MILO": See *Briton*, no. 5, n. 11.

No. 30. Saturday, 18 December 1762

1. Motto: Virgil *Aeneid* 5.465–67: "Unhappy people! what strange infatuation possesses you? are ye not sensible of the strength of other nations, and the power of opposing gods? yield to reason" (*Political Controversy*).

2. "*Petuita . . . anilitatem generat et inde matronisatio*": Supposedly in Quintilian, but not located; Smollett seems to have erred in his attribution. The remainder of this paragraph may well be an indirect sally against the duke of Newcastle, who was frequently represented as an old woman in political prints of the day.

3. "Mecœnates": Plural form of *Mæcenas*, generic term for a patron. The historical Mæcenas was the patron of Virgil and Horace.

4. "a doctor, who is well known": But not well enough known to be identified.

5. "my publisher, Mr. Coote": John Coote (d. 1808), publisher of the *Briton*, was a bookseller and publisher in Paternoster Row from 1757 to 1774, when it is presumed he went bankrupt. See *Briton*, no. 3, n. 14.

6. "this curiosity before my reader": The ensuing ironic confession of the Magdalen Monitors is an allegory relating both to the *Monitor* and its support of William Pitt and to Pitt's change of position on the question of English support for Hanover and Prussia. *Magdalen* denotes a reformed prostitute, a denotation derived

from the belief that Mary Magdalene of the New Testament was a harlot who became a faithful disciple of Christ.

7. "Will the coachman": Allegorical figure standing for William Pitt.

8. "High-Wycomb": A market town about thirty miles northwest of London on the road to Oxford.

9. "we still ate . . . asparagus": Although this seems to be a proverbial expression, no source or previous use of it has been traced.

10. "Bucephalus": A fiery steed, Alexander the Great's favorite horse.

11. "John": John Stuart, earl of Bute.

12. "Palladium": "Anything on which the safety of a nation, institution, privilege, etc. is believed to depend" (*OED*).

13. "the birth-day . . . Plutus and Lucina": The first son of George III, George, Prince of Wales, was born on 12 August 1762, the same day British forces captured Havana. Plutus personified wealth, and Lucina, childbirth.

14. "our patron . . . Bay of Honduras": Despite George II's personal dislike for him, Pitt was brought into the administration of Henry Pelham as paymaster of the forces in 1746 and proved to be a fairly staunch supporter of the policies of the Pelham brothers over the next decade. For Pitt's defense of the commercial treaty of 1750, which seems to be alluded to here, see *Briton*, no. 29, n. 11.

15. "*guiding*": See *Briton*, no. 26, n. 4.

16. "surprisal of Newfoundland by the French": See *Briton*, no. 12, n. 14, and no. 33, n. 8.

17. "Timariots": Holders of Turkish fiefs obligated to the military service of their overlords (*OED*).

18. "*food* for its *powder*": "Food for powder" is Falstaff's phrase for his recruits in *1 Henry IV* 4.2.65–66.

No. 31. Saturday, 25 December 1762

1. Motto: Virgil *Aeneid* 1.574: " 'Tis equal to me Trojan or Tyrian." This translation is from the reprint of *Briton*, no. 34, in *Political Controversy*, where the motto is repeated.

2. "Hydra faction": The Hydra was a many-headed water serpent of Greek mythology. When one of its heads was cut off, two more were supposed to sprout in its place. Smollett allegorized the mob as the Hydra in *Adventures of an Atom*.

3. "an address from the Cocoa-tree . . . in answer to it": The two pamphlets here referred to, both of which seem to have been widely read, were *A Letter from the Cocoa-Tree to the Country Gentlemen* (London, 1762), warning of a new Whig faction supposed to be forming around Newcastle, Devonshire, and Cumberland; and *An Address to the Cocoa-Tree from a Whig* (London, 1762), defending Whig principles. On the Cocoa-Tree, see *Briton*, no. 15, n. 17.

4. "I shall presume . . . disavowed by you.": *Address*, p. 2.

5. "scepterly": Apparently this word is Smollett's own coinage from *sceptre* (or *scepter*, in an eighteenth-century variant spelling). The ironic suggestion is that the Tories have assumed royal prerogatives.

6. "*Thou can'st not say I did it*": *Macbeth* 3.4.49.

7. "like the lady . . . *there lay* MY *feet*": Obviously a quotation or paraphrase, but the source has not been traced; perhaps from a jest book or (more likely, given the error in number agreement) a grammar book.

8. "Pye-corner": Pye Corner was at the southwest corner of Smithfield in London. One saying about the Great Fire of 1666 was that it started in Pudding Lane and ended at Pye Corner. The "barley-broth woman" seems to be no particular person, but rather a general reference to an ordinary street vendor.

9. "three very great names": Newcastle, Devonshire, and Cumberland.

10. "As to the third name . . . royal n — w": William Augustus, duke of Cumberland (1721–65), uncle to George III. Smollett continued to hold Cumberland in contempt because of his merciless persecution of the Scots during and after the Jacobite Rebellion of 1745–46, persecution memorialized by Smollett in *The Tears of Scotland*. His ironic praise of Cumberland here is echoed in *Humphry Clinker*, where the duke is described as "that illustrious hero, who trod rebellion under his feet, and secured us in possession of every thing we ought to hold dear, as Englishmen and Christians" (Jery Melford to Sir Watkin Phillips, London, June 2, p. 95).

11. "That the King . . . no right to oppose them": *Address*, p. 3.

12. "*sylva rerum*": Cicero *De Oratore* 3.26: "a supply of matter."

13. "the names of High-church, Ormond and Sacheverel": James Butler, second duke of Ormonde (see *Briton*, no. 20, n. 7), and Henry Sacheverell (1674?–1724) were defenders of High Church, Tory principles during the last years of Queen Anne's reign. Although strongly attacked by the Whigs — Ormonde was eventually forced into exile as a Jacobite — they both, Sacheverell particularly, had a large, excitable following among the London populace.

14. "We . . . *generally admitted*": *Address*, p. 3.

15. "Such a minister . . . Charles the Second of England": Adrian VI, born Adrian Dedel (1459–1523), was pope from 1522 to 1523. Before being elected pope, he had been tutor to the young Charles V (1500–58), Holy Roman Emperor and, as Charles I, king of Spain. He further served Charles as diplomat and regent. André-Hercule de Fleury (1653–1743) was appointed tutor to Louis XV (1710–74) when Louis became king of France at the age of five. Fleury's elevation to cardinal in 1726 helped him to gain and maintain full control of France's affairs as the king's chief minister until he died at the age of ninety. Maximilien de Béthune, duc de Sully (1560–1641), helped Henry IV of France (1553–1610) secure and set in order his kingdom after the religious strife that preceded and accompanied Henry's becoming king in 1589. Sully was particularly admired as a financial administrator. On Clarendon and Charles II, see *Briton*, no. 24, n. 35.

16. "a draw-cansir": A ranter; see *Briton*, no. 12, n. 17.

17. "the Gavestons and Spencers": Piers Gaveston and the two Hugh Despensers were intimate advisers of Edward II. See *Briton*, no. 24, n. 21.

18. "We cannot . . . in his famous genealogy": *Address*, p. 4.

19. "the story of Fleance": Many of the Renaissance chroniclers of Scotland had traced the Stuarts back to Banquo through his son Fleance. This supposed genealogy was popularized by Shakespeare in *Macbeth*.

No. 32. Saturday, 1 January 1763

1. Motto: Sallust *The War with Jugurtha* 41.5: "Discord reigns every where, dividing the nation into two opposing parties, and tearing her bowels" (*Political Controversy*).

2. "Ithuriel's spear": Milton, *Paradise Lost* 4.810–19, describes how Satan, squatting like a toad near Eve's ear, is revealed in his own shape at the touch of Ithuriel's spear. Ithuriel was one of the cherubim sent by Gabriel to seek Satan in Paradise.

3. "One superannuated original": Newcastle is the statesman lampooned in this passage.

4. "the famous Conde d'Olivarez": Gaspar de Guzman, count of Olivares (1587–1645), controlled Spanish policy during the first two decades of the reign of Philip IV, who came to the Spanish throne in 1621. But Olivares lost the royal favor in 1643 and spent the last few years of his life in virtual exile.

5. "Mughouse-mob": A mughouse was an alehouse; in the middle decades of the eighteenth century, the term was used to identify particularly any alehouse where groups supporting the Hanoverian succession would gather.

6. "a Westphalian rat": Newcastle had strongly advocated support of the war in Germany. On Westphalia as an important battleground of the war, see *Briton*, no. 4, n. 8.

7. "marrow-bones and cleavers": "Instruments of 'rough music,'" for the vulgar (*OED*).

8. "those who are bit by the Tarantula": See *Briton*, no. 22, n. 3.

9. "when they heard that M——r": The minister referred to is Bute. Debate on the preliminaries of the Peace of Paris opened in both houses of Parliament on 9 December 1762. Bute's speech in the House of Lords was one of his more noteworthy public performances.

10. "the great methodist": The connotations of *methodist* for Smollett are clear from a passage in *Continuation*, 4:121–22: "Weak minds were seduced by the delusions of a superstition stiled Methodism, raised upon the affectation of superior sanctity, and maintained by pretensions to divine illumination. Many thousands in the lower ranks of life were infected with this species of enthusiasm, by the unwearied endeavours of a few obscure preachers."

11. "mounted the rostrum . . . courted popularity": During the afternoon of the first day of parliamentary debate on the preliminaries, Pitt, suffering severely from

gout, appeared before the House of Commons to oppose them. He entered the chamber supported by two friends and, while sitting, spoke for more than two hours on the articles of the peace. Owing to his illness, he rambled and repeated himself; the speech, one of his least effective parliamentary addresses, did nothing to impede approval of the preliminaries. See Basil Williams, *The Life of William Pitt, Earl of Chatham* (London: Longmans, 1913), 2:146–49. If Pitt wore a flannel gown on this occasion, it would have been because of his illness; Smollett here makes the flannel a sign of Pitt's continual efforts to cultivate the support of ordinary people, or the "mob"; *frowzy* means dirty, slatternly, unkempt (*OED*). A "candidate of ancient Rome," aspiring to the senate, would have solicited, not the "mob," but his patrician peers.

12. *"that witnessed huge dismay"*: Milton, *Paradise Lost* 1.57: "That witness'd huge affliction and dismay."

13. "planet-struck": "Stricken by the supposed malign influence of an adverse planet; blasted" (*OED*).

14. "Ringwood": Probably John Wilkes. Ringwood is apparently a traditional name for a foxhound, as in John Woodcock Graves's "John Peel": "Yes, I ken John Peel and Ruby too, / Ranter and Ringwood and Bellman and True" (*The Oxford Book of Light Verse*, ed. W. H. Auden [London: Oxford University Press, 1938], 364).

15. "The shameless scribbler": The author of the *Monitor*.

16. "the village-idiot . . . silent": Although this passage seems to echo a proverb or folk tale, no source has been traced.

17. "The weekly libel": The *North Briton*.

18. "those delicate pictures": See *Briton*, no. 16, n. 16.

19. *"in terrorem"*: L. By way of threat; a legal term.

20. *"forcibly to prescribe . . . are T——n"*: Smollett possibly refers to a statute of 1350–51 (Act 25 Edw. III, Stat. 5, c. 2), which defines treason in much this way. In 1795, after long years of controversy over the appointment of ministers, and in the wake of the French Revolution, the offense of treason was extended to include actual or even contemplated use of force to persuade the king to change his councils.

21. "SCRIBERE EST AGERE": L. To write is to act.

22. "CURIO": See *Briton*, no. 11, n. 17.

No. 33. Saturday, 8 January 1763

1. Motto: "He turns pale with envy, and malice gnaws his entrails" (*Political Controversy*).

2. "the identical words of the North Briton and Monitor": Despite this assertion, the words appear to have been invented for the purpose of expressing sentiments attributed to the two antiministerial sheets.

3. "the North Briton of last Saturday": Actually *North Briton*, no. 30 (25 December 1762); the words in quotation marks a few lines farther on paraphrase the contentions of the *North Briton*.

4. "the years fifteen and forty-five": The Jacobite rebellions occurred in 1715 and 1745.

5. "*vox populi* is *vox Dei*": See *Briton*, no. 16, n. 12.

6. "*à qua parte hunc Proteum capiemus?*": L. By which part shall we seize this Proteus?

7. "*concio populi*": L. A common expression for assembly of the people.

8. "the observation . . . minister's temples": In *Briton*, no. 30. The recovery of New-foundland occurred during September 1762. Alexander, Lord Colville (1710–70), leader of a naval squadron at Halifax, responded at that time to the presence of a French squadron under Commodore (or Chevalier) Charles d'Arsac Ternay that had captured Saint John's, Newfoundland, during the preceding June. The English squadron drove off the French without an engagement.

9. "Lord Colville's letter . . . he had received orders": The account given here seems self-contradictory, as Smollett says first that Colville had received orders to sail for Newfoundland, and then that he had not received them. See *Continuation*, 5:152–54, for a clearer account. In any event Colville did retake Newfoundland; see above, n. 8.

10. "Mr. Elliot . . . squadron he took": In February 1760, acting quickly on informa-tion from the lord lieutenant of Ireland (John Russell, fourth duke of Bedford), a British squadron under the command of John Elliot engaged and defeated a French squadron foraying off the northeast coast of Ireland. The French squadron was commanded by François Thurot, a privateer.

11. "*Guide*": See *Briton*, no. 26, n. 4.

No. 34. Saturday, 15 January 1763

1. Motto: Except for the last word, Smollett here repeats the motto to *Briton*, no. 31.

2. "No fewer than three . . . compliment of hands": The tone of this letter suggests a certain hyperbole in the details the writer cites. The proponents of peace often complained about the increasingly high cost of the war in both money and men, but the figures cited here have not been traced to any particular source.

3. "It would become . . . languishing in captivity": In 1760, despite reports of cruel treatment of British prisoners by their French captors, a successful public sub-scription was launched to raise funds for the relief of French prisoners held by the British. Both Oliver Goldsmith and Samuel Johnson remarked upon this inci-dent. See Goldsmith, *Citizen of the World*, Letter XXIII, in *Collected Works of Oliver Goldsmith*, ed. Arthur Friedman (Oxford: Clarendon Press, 1966), 2:97–101; and Johnson, "Introduction" to Proceedings of the Committee on French Prisoners, in *The Yale Edition of the Works of Samuel Johnson*, vol. 10, *Political Writings*, ed. Donald J. Greene (New Haven: Yale University Press, 1977), 285–89.

4. "this severe weather": According to *Gentleman's Magazine* 33 (January 1763): 42, on 25 December 1762 "a most intense frost set in with a north-easterly wind, which has continued with very little intermission till the end of *January*."

5. "Cosmopolite": Greek for "a citizen of the world."

6. "the public papers": The satiric observations that here follow may have been prompted by a report appearing in the *Gazetteer and London Daily Advertiser* for 22 December 1762: "An officer lately arrived from the Havannah declares, that there are not three hundred men left alive of the regiment of Highlanders, commanded by Lord John Murray, which regiment consisted of two battalions of one thousand men each."

7. "a certain infallible political sage": The *North Briton*, as the ironic voice of John Wilkes, had spoken slightingly of the Scots in its attacks on Bute, especially in its early numbers. Wilkes could very well be the "political sage" here referred to, although the exact phrases of the passage cannot be attributed to him.

8. "*natale solum*": Ovid *Metamorphoses* 7.52, 8.184: "Native land."

9. "the Gazetteer": The *Gazetteer and London Daily Advertiser* for 5 January 1763 had printed the following from the *St. James's Chronicle*: "A Person, whom I take to be a Scotchman, frequents most of the coffee-houses about town, where he purloins the news-papers as fast as they come out, whenever they contain any thing in the least remarkable against a certain great man. In order to do this the more effectually, he is always early in the rooms, where he catches the papers as soon as they come in, and running immediately over the contents, if he finds them fit for his purpose, takes the first opportunity of pocketing them slily, and then walks off."

10. "generation of vipers": Christ's phrase in denunciation of the Pharisees and others, as in Matthew 3:7 and elsewhere in the New Testament.

11. "Who is so deaf . . . sing in the wind": Apparently a proverbial saying, but no source for it has been traced.

12. "naturalizing the Jews": In June 1753 Parliament passed a bill allowing the naturalization of Jews, but public and parliamentary agitation forced its repeal within a year.

13. "the *Anthropophagi that one another do eat*": *Othello* 1.3.143–44: "the Cannibals that each other eat, / The Anthropophagi."

14. "Benjamin Hempley": The name suggests a joke based on Hempley's offer to hang himself with a cord of his own twisting. Hemp was the fiber commonly used in making cords.

No. 35. Saturday, 22 January 1763

1. "the Tale of a Tub": The allusion is to Jonathan Swift, *A Tale of a Tub* 4.

2. "the treaty of Utrecht": See *Briton*, no. 2, n. 11, and no. 20, n. 2.

3. "Billingsgate faculties": Capacities for vituperative language. Billingsgate, the fish-market located near one of the old city gates of London, was known for loud vulgarity; the name was synonymous with verbal abusiveness.

4. "Convention": One of Sir Robert Walpole's most notable achievements in parliamentary management was gaining House of Commons approval of the Con-

vention of the Prado, settling certain disputes between Spain and Great Britain early in 1739. The minority were loud in pointing out how many of the majority had places under the court. In *Complete History*, 4:589–93, Smollett describes the dramatic debate and the "pathetic remonstrance" of Sir William Wyndham, a spokesman for the minority.

5. "a place-act": A parliamentary act restricting officers of the Crown (placemen) from being elected to Parliament. One such act had been passed in 1743 after Walpole was forced out of office.

6. "the majority that was against them . . . the minority against the present minister": According to accounts recorded in *Parliamentary History* 10:1293, the division on 8 March 1739, at the end of a long day and evening of debate on the convention, was 260 for, 232 against. The figure of a majority of only twenty-eight was used by Wyndham in his remonstrance a few days later. The division in the House of Commons on the Preliminaries to the Peace on 9 December 1762 was 319 for, 65 against.

7. "knaves . . . fools": Numerous proverbs and literary passages combine a reference to fools and knaves. Most of them represent some variant or elaboration of the proverb recorded by John Ray in his *Collection of English Proverbs* (1670): "Knaves and fools divide the world."

8. "In a long and fruitless opposition . . . country-party": During the 1730s the opposition to Walpole was largely voiced by the *Craftsman*, a journal directed at first by Bolingbroke, the old Tory minister of Queen Anne, and William Pulteney, leader of a group of opposition Whigs and Jacobites who styled themselves Patriots, or the Country Interest. Although parliamentary opposition forced close divisions on occasion, Walpole managed to stave off any serious opposition to his administration until his ouster in 1742.

9. "they met again": See below, n. 13.

10. "Out-herod Herod": *Hamlet* 3.2.14.

11. "Walpole was an honourable man": An echo of Antony's ironic praise of Brutus, *Julius Caesar* 3.2.82.

12. "the addresser to the Cocoa-tree": See *Briton*, no. 31, n. 3.

13. "to widen the bottom . . . the late minister": In 1744, two years after Walpole's downfall, Henry Pelham and his brother Newcastle succeeded in forming a "Broad Bottom" administration, so called because of Pelham's endeavor to include representatives of several parliamentary cliques. Pitt was brought into this administration in 1746.

14. "*cujus contrarium est verum*": L. The opposite of which is true. Apparently this is a legal phrase for which there is no exact source.

15. "flead": A past participle form of *flay*, still in use in the eighteenth century according to *OED*.

16. "Earl of Oxford": Robert Harley, first earl of Oxford. See *Briton*, no. 20, n. 3.

17. "the act of succession": See *Briton*, no. 19, n. 12.

18. "natural property": Property in land.

19. "much may be said on both sides": *Spectator*, no. 122 (20 July 1711). Smollett's letter writer cites Sir Roger's humorous opinion, given after he is appealed to in a dispute between two companions.

20. "descendants of the Russels . . . the Manners": Members of the Russell family had been earls and dukes of Bedford since the sixteenth century. The Campbells were a powerful Scottish clan whose importance can be traced back at least to the twelfth or thirteenth century. They held numerous titles; John, fourth duke of Argyll, and John, fifth duke of Argyll, were especially important political and military figures in the middle decades of the eighteenth century. The Churchills were a prominent family of Dorset and Devon with a history of distinguished military and state service. John Churchill, the famed victor of Blenheim, was the first of the family to be ennobled as earl of Marlborough in 1689 and duke of Marlborough in 1702. Members of the Spencer family, originally of Warwick, gained prominence as earls of Sunderland. An important alliance between the Churchills and Spencers came about in 1699 when Anne, daughter of John Churchill, married the third earl of Sunderland. The Douglases, like the Campbells, were an important Scottish family whose members included Gavin Douglas (1474?–1522), a distinguished poet and churchman, and James Douglas (1662–1711), second duke of Queensbury, who favored William III and worked for Scottish-English union. The Montagus came into prominence during the time of the early Stuarts and had possessed the earldom of Sandwich since 1660. The Percevals were an Anglo-Irish family distinguished by their possession of the earldom of Egmont. The Percys traced their lineage back to an ancestor ennobled by William the Conqueror and were one of the most powerful families in the north of England, where they had been headed by a long line of dukes and earls of Northumberland. The Manners family had also been important in the north of England since the fourteenth century, with hereditary titles as earls and dukes of Rutland.

21. "Did he ever . . . remained unsatisfied": This series of rhetorical questions in defense of Bute is intended to contrast him with Pitt, the accusations against whom in the *Briton* and elsewhere are well summed up here.

22. "a short story": The anecdote that follows is probably proverbial, but no printed source for it has been discovered.

23. "PHOCION": Athenian general and statesman (402–317 B.C.) who helped accommodate matters between Alexander the Great and the Athenians.

No. 36. Saturday, 29 January 1763

1. Motto: Virgil *Eclogues* 3.93: "A . . . snake lurks in the grass."

2. "A short ADDRESS . . . WHIGS": This *Briton* was probably prompted by *North Briton*, no. 33 (15 January 1762), which considered the "true and original meaning of the word" *Tory*.

3. "the administration about that time": The administration of Sir Robert Walpole, which lasted until February 1742.

4. "A broad-bottomed plan": See *Briton*, no. 35, n. 13.

5. "treasurer . . . secretary of state": Henry Pelham became treasurer and chancellor of the exchequer in 1743 and retained office until his death in 1754. His brother, the duke of Newcastle, was secretary of state (southern department) from 1724 until 1748, when he became secretary of state (northern department), an office he held until 1754.

6. "examine his accounts": In March 1742, little more than a month after Walpole left office, Parliament appointed a secret committee of twenty-one members to inquire into Walpole's administration over the preceding ten years, particularly his handling of secret-service money. But the committee failed to uncover any substantial evidence to support charges of corruption against Walpole (now earl of Orford), and the inquiry was dropped by the end of the year.

7. "a certain nobleman . . . turn him out": In February 1746, during the midst of the Jacobite rebellion, the Pelhams resigned their offices. The inability of Lord Granville (who died 2 January 1763) and Lord Bath to create a working ministry forced the king to recall the Pelhams within two days to form a new administration. The episode helped the Pelhams to consolidate their power at the time. See *Briton*, no. 8, n. 2.

8. "a certain Right Hon. gentleman . . . about that time": In the ministerial shake-up of 1746, Pitt, who had gained George II's enmity by his outspoken opposition to subsidies for Hanover, was made vice-treasurer of Ireland. Shortly afterward he became paymaster general and altered his position on Hanover, a turnabout that his enemies were never to let him forget.

9. "a certain nobleman . . . the last insurrection": Probably the reference is to Simon Fraser, Lord Lovat, a Scots nobleman whose shift to the government side during the 1715 Jacobite uprising was an important factor in the collapse of the rebellion in Scotland. Ever a restless figure, Lovat became one of the early conspirators in laying the groundwork for the rebellion of 1745. He was beheaded for treason in 1747.

10. "You may remember too . . . his own and family's destruction": No written account of this episode has been traced.

11. "handles": Figuratively, a handle may be "a fact or circumstance that may be 'laid hold of' or taken advantage of for some purpose" (*OED*).

12. "a war with Spain": The War of Jenkins' Ear, begun in 1739 and leading into the War of the Austrian Succession. It was so named because England declared war against Spain after one Robert Jenkins testified in the House of Commons about the search of his ship by the Spanish coast guard and the cutting off of his ear by the searchers.

13. "A certain gentleman . . . you had done": On Pitt's turnabout on the issue of no search, see *Briton*, no. 29, n. 11.

14. "*commiscere cœlum & terram*": L. To mix heaven and earth; a common phrase for the attempt to combine things of contrary kinds. See Juvenal *Satires* 2.25.

15. "*nunc inter hos . . . pars omnium virorum*": L. Now of one, now of another; a man of many parts, and a part of many men. The source, if any exists, has not been traced.

No. 37. Saturday, 5 February 1763

1. Motto: Livy *Ab Urbe Condita* 37.50.8: "When liberty is equally diffused, the cause of a Plebeian has the same prospect of success as that of the Noble" (*Political Controversy*).

2. "a late performance": *The Doctrine of Grace*, by William Warburton, bishop of Gloucester. The title page bears the date 1763, but the work seems to have appeared a short time before the new year. Warburton had been made dean of Bristol at the instance of Pitt in 1757 and was elevated to the bishopric of Gloucester in early 1760.

3. "faulchion": Falchion, "a broad sword more or less curved with the edge on the convex side" (*OED*).

4. "Scipio . . . Nevius": In the preliminary advertisement to *The Doctrine of Grace*, Warburton refers to a report that he was writing in defense of Pitt but maintains that Pitt's own words, like those of Scipio Africanus (see *Briton*, no. 16, n. 6), are all that is needed for his vindication. On Nevius, see below, n. 5.

5. "Livy says . . . Nævius": Livy *Ab Urbe Condita* 38.56. Two cousins, each named Quintus Petillius, were tribunes in 187 b.c. Marcus Nævius was a tribune in 184 b.c. Modern critics note that Livy contradicts himself on the time and circumstances of Scipio's impeachment and death.

6. "*Nebulo* and *Nugator*": L. Rascal and swaggerer.

7. "broad-buckler": A buckler is "a small round shield; in England the buckler was usually carried by a handle in the back" (*OED*). *OED* gives no entry or citation for *broad-buckler*.

8. "this venerable P——te": Warburton's writings, most notably *The Divine Legation of Moses* (1738–41), had gained him a reputation as an arrogant and dogmatic controversialist, a reputation ironically pointed up here in the following passage.

9. "By his spirit . . . to impose": Scipio's eloquence helped to rally the Romans after they were defeated by Hannibal at Cann in southeastern Italy in 216 b.c. His army captured the important Carthaginian city of Carthago Nova (New Carthage, today Cartagena) in 209. After conquering Spain, Scipio invaded Africa, where he defeated Hasdrubal, one of several Carthaginian leaders by that name, and Syphax, chief of the Numidians and Hasdrubal's ally and son-in-law, in 203. In 202 Scipio's forces defeated those of Hannibal in the climactic battle of the Second Punic War. Zama is the name traditionally given as the site of Hannibal's defeat. Modern scholars are unsure as to the exact location of Zama, but they are

quite certain that Scipio's defeat of Hannibal did not happen at, although perhaps it happened near, a place of that name.

10. "Tiberius Gracchus": Probably the Roman Tiberius Gracchus (d. 133 B.C.), whose father, also Tiberius Gracchus (d. 154 B.C.), had married Cornelia, daughter to Scipio. The elder Tiberius was a distinguished and admired political leader who held numerous important offices during his lifetime; but his son and namesake, also a political leader, was the more dramatic and controversial public figure. Smollett may have inadvertently conflated the lives of the two men. The younger Tiberius was murdered during electoral riots because, as a popular tribune, he was successfully agitating for reforms in land law; his opponents accused him of seeking tyrannical powers, and the violence against him began a period of political bloodshed in Rome.

11. "his own brother-in-law": Earl Temple; see *Briton*, no. 15, n. 2.

12. "Col. W——kes . . . Ch——ll": On Wilkes and Churchill, see *Briton*, no. 4, n. 18, and no. 25, nn. 20, 23.

13. "Jacob Henriquez to the Duke de Sully": Jacob Henriques was author of several notices and tracts proposing to pay off the national debt by a lottery scheme. The duc de Sully was minister to Henry IV of France; see *Briton*, no. 31, n. 15.

14. "The frame . . . ne'er been born": *1 Henry IV* 3.1.16–19.

15. "Were not the admirals . . . a former M——": Edward Hawke (1705–81), although naval commander of the ill-fated expedition to Rochefort (see below, n. 17), received high praise for containing and defeating a French invasion fleet sailing from Brest in November 1759. Henry Osborne (1698?–1771) was commander in chief in the Mediterranean from May 1757 to July 1758. He succeeded in forcing a French squadron intending to sail from Toulon to North America to retire to Cartagena in Spain, where the British successfully blockaded it and fought off reinforcements. Edward Boscawen (1711–61) commanded the fleet that protected English land forces at the successful siege of Louisburg in 1758. In 1759 he was assigned to the Mediterranean. In August of that year his ships met with a French squadron sailing from Toulon to join the Brest invasion fleet. The British were victorious in the ensuing battle, but five French ships escaped and sought harbor in the neutral waters of Lagos Bay, Portugal, where Boscawen followed and destroyed or captured them. Charles Watson (1714–57) was in 1756 appointed naval commander in chief in the East Indies. There his forces helped to defeat a pirate force at Gheriah in February 1756, and they assisted Sir Robert Clive in taking over the French settlement of Chandernagore in March 1757. Sir George Pocock was second in command to Watson in the East Indies and succeeded him as commander in chief when Watson died in August 1757. He fought several engagements with French ships in Indian waters over the next year and a half, but none was decisive. After returning to England, he was appointed commander of the expedition to Havana, which succeeded in capturing that Spanish stronghold in August 1762.

16. "Was it he . . . are owing?": In December 1758, Pitt assigned James Wolfe (1727–

59), who had previously shown his abilities at the siege of Louisburg, to command the forces attacking Quebec. Wolfe's famous defeat of the French on the plains of Abraham took place on 13 September 1759. Both Wolfe and the French general Montcalm were killed in the battle. Sir William Johnson, or Johnston (1715–74), emigrated to America in 1738. He led provincial forces that defeated the French at Lake George in 1755. In 1759 he was second in command of an expedition against Fort Niagara and concluded the expedition successfully by taking command after its leader, General Prideaux, was killed. Sir Robert Clive (1725–75), commissioned as a lieutenant colonel in the Royal Army, secured the British interest in Bengal by defeating a native army at Plassey on 23 June 1757. Stringer Lawrence (1695–1775) was made civil governor and military commandant of Fort Saint David in India in 1750. He led British forces in a number of engagements with the French until poor health forced his return to England at the end of 1759. Sir Eyre Coote (1726–83), having distinguished himself at the battle of Plassey, was given command of an army in Madras that defeated the French on 22 January 1760 at the battle of Wandiwash, a battle usually considered decisive in assuring British dominance over the French in their struggle for control of India.

17. "the gentleman who declined landing at Fouras": Fouras was the site of a fort near Rochefort, which had been the object of a costly expedition to the coast of France in 1757, shortly after Pitt's assumption of leadership. The expedition had returned to England without carrying through a landing. Although public indignation was strongest against Sir John Mordaunt, commander of the expedition's land forces, public opinion also attacked Admiral Sir Charles Knowles, second in command of the naval forces. In *Critical Review* 5 (May 1758), Smollett severely criticized Knowles's published defense of his actions. The criticism resulted in Smollett's conviction for libel in 1759. See Paul-Gabriel Boucé, "Smollett and the Expedition against Rochefort," *Modern Philology* 65 (1967): 33–38.

18. "a glorious retreat from the bay of St. Cas": See *Briton*, no. 12, n. 7.

No. 38. Saturday, 12 February 1763

1. Motto: Horace *Odes* 4.4.61–62. *Political Controversy* quotes the translation of Philip Francis:

> Not Hydra stronger, when dismember'd, rose
> Against Alcmaena's much-enduring son,
> Grieving to find, from his repeated blows
> The foe redoubled and his toil begun.

2. "Reverend Father": It is difficult to detect in the first few paragraphs of this satirically arcane letter any specific allusions beyond the general one equating the opponents of the ministry with crafty, seditious groups such as the Jesuits.

3. "a Campian, a Parsons, and a Garnet": A trio of English Jesuits active in the Roman Catholic cause during Queen Elizabeth's reign. Edmund Campion (1540–

81), a controversialist and missionary, was convicted of high treason and then martyred for his illegal Jesuit proselytizing and his attacks on Protestantism. Robert Parsons, or Persons (1546–1610), was, with Campion, a Jesuit missionary and an extremely effective writer on behalf of his faith. He owned a printing press and issued from it controversial tracts, including his own and Campion's. When Campion was seized in 1581, Parsons escaped to the Continent, where he set up schools for English Catholics. Henry Garnet, or Garnett (1555–1606), was also a Jesuit missionary; he was wrongfully executed for his supposed part in the Gunpowder Plot of 1605. In *Complete History*, 3:65, Campion and Parsons are said to have been "the first jesuits that ever set foot in England."

4. "13": Charles Churchill.

5. "14": John Wilkes.

6. "*O sancte* 14 . . . *cum sancto* 14": L. "O sacred 14! O would that my spirit (not my body, Lord, but my spirit) O would that my spirit be with sacred 14." Just what is being parodied here is not clear.

7. "L— M—": Lord Mayor William Beckford.

8. "an old pilot": The duke of Newcastle.

9. "a plebeian orator": William Pitt.

10. "a B—": Bishop William Warburton.

11. "flummery": Literally defined, flummery is a kind of food made by coagulation of wheat or oatmeal; but Smollett here uses the term in its figurative sense, meaning nonsense, humbug, empty trifling (*OED*).

12. "cicatrised": To cicatrize is "to heal . . . by inducing a cicatrice or scar; to skin over" (*OED*).

13. "*Guelph* and *Ghibelline*": Rival factions in thirteenth- and fourteenth-century Italy.

14. "*Abraxas* and *Abracadabra*": *Abraxas* is a name for God used by the followers of the second-century Gnostic teacher Basilidés. The name is also rendered *Abrasax*. It has been found carved on amulets, the supposed power of which was derived from the fact that the Greek letters of the word can be made to add up to 365. In *Adventures of an Atom*, Smollett has a passage citing authority for stating that the magic term *Abracadabra* was formed from *Abrasax*; see *Adventures of an Atom*, p. 65 and nn. 717–19.

15. "hesitate dislike": A phrase from Pope's *Epistle to Dr. Arbuthnot*, line 204.

16. "St. Ignatius . . . the blessed Xavier": Saint Ignatius Loyola (1491–1556) founded the Society of Jesus (the Jesuits), of which Saint Francis Xavier (1506–52) was one of the original members. In Protestant countries the Jesuits were commonly suspected of sedition.

17. "the beatified Borgia": Rodrigo Borgia, who, as Pope Alexander VI (1492–1502), had a reputation as one of the most worldly and corrupt of Renaissance popes.

18. "go at large or close-hauled": Sail off the wind or close to the wind.

19. "main-top-bowling": A rope attached to the maintop sail and to the ship's bow to help keep the sail steady.

20. "our Master": The duke of Newcastle.

21. "old bumboat woman . . . Mother Shipton's chickens": A bumboat hauled vege-
tables and other provisions to ships lying in the Thames, a service once provided
by the "dirt" boats, formerly also called bumboats, charged with removing filth
from anchored ships (*OED*); in the 1760s the older application of the word re-
mained familiar, and a "bumboat" man or woman was thus associated with filth
and meniality. On Newcastle as an old woman, see *Briton*, no. 30, n. 2. Mother
Shipton, probably a figure of folklore, was a witch-prophetess who supposedly
lived early in the sixteenth century and made many startling prophecies that were
fulfilled in the succeeding centuries. Her connection with chickens has not been
established, but a common phrase suggested by the *Briton*'s nautical context is
"Mother Carey's chickens," the name given by sailors to the seabirds known as
stormy petrels and, figuratively, to snow. The *Briton*, for reasons not very clear,
may have mixed the two allusions together.

22. "Will Timoneer": Another mask for William Pitt. A timoneer is a "helmsman, or
steersman" (*OED*).

23. "two glasses": One glass was the time required for the sand in a glass to run out,
usually a half hour.

24. "Weser": See *Briton*, no. 2, n. 9.

25. "clapped the helm a lee": Turned the helm (steering apparatus) toward the side of
the ship away from the wind.

26. "the lizard": Peninsula in Cornwall; the southernmost tip of England.

27. "overhaul the logline . . . lead might be hove": The logline is "a line of 100 fath-
oms or more to which the log [for ascertaining the rate of a ship's motion] is
attached" (*OED*). The lead is "a 'bob' or lump of lead suspended by a string to
ascertain the depth of water" (*OED*).

28. "best bower": *Bower* is the name given to "two anchors, the *best-bower*, and *small-
bower*, carried at the bows of a vessel" (*OED*).

29. "a cypher in my own ship": *Auditor*, no. 12 (26 August 1762), in its ironical "Politi-
cal Dictionary for the year 1762," noted under the entry "The King": "It means at
present one who ought to enjoy the painful pre-eminence of being a mere cypher
in this kingdom." The ministerial writers often put this figure into the mouths of
their opponents.

30. "I'll be damn'd . . . take the helm for me": A last echo of Pitt's declaration upon
resigning in October 1761; see *Briton*, no. 8, n. 4.

31. "the Black-joke": A bawdy song, best known as an item carried by a street singer
in the brothel scene (plate 3) of William Hogarth's *The Rake's Progress* (1735). In
chapter 53 of *Roderick Random*, Smollett has one of his characters whistle and hum
the Black Joke. The date of the song is given as 1730(?) in the British Library
Music Catalogue: G.315(99) and G.316.e(99).

32. "Rotherhithe": Dock area on the south bank of the Thames, much associated with
common sailors.

33. "Jack North": The earl of Bute.
34. "the chest at Chatham": The Chatham Chest was a fund administered at Chatham for the relief of disabled seamen. For Pitt's connection with Chatham, see *Briton*, no. 3, n. 17.
35. "Captain Swabber, and Jack i'the bread-room": Charles Churchill and John Wilkes. A swabber is "one who behaves like a sailor of low rank . . . a term of contempt" (*OED*). The bread-room was a room below the lower deck of a ship where the ship's bread was kept. *Bread-room Jack* was sailors' slang for the purser's assistant.
36. "AUGUSTUS ALBION": Albion is one of the ancient names for Britain, usually used poetically; Augustus is the title conferred on Octavius as emperor in 27 B.C. and subsequently borne by his successors.

Appendix: Doubtful Attributions

ODE ADDRESSED TO THE LATE GEN. WOLFE, WRITTEN AFTER THE REDUCTION OF LOUISBOURG

1. Title: The source for the attribution is Buck, *Poet*, 63–68. The poem appeared in the *British Magazine* for February 1760, p. 98. Buck reprints it (pp. 67–68) and assigns it to Smollett largely on grounds of internal evidence, specifically the evidence of the third and fourth lines of the final stanza, which strongly echo the references to Drake and Howard found in the concluding lines of the prologue to *The Reprisal* (see above, p. 176 and nn. 6, 7). General James Wolfe (1727–59) died heroically at the capture of Quebec during the Seven Years' War, but the poem makes no reference to that fact; instead, it treats the siege of Louisbourg in July 1758, when Wolfe led the attack under the command of General Jeffrey Amherst and Admiral Edward Boscawen. On the basis of its specific historical subject matter, Buck gives the date of the poem's composition as 1758.

THE JUNTO

1. Title: The source for the attribution is Buck, *Poet*, 60. The poem appeared in the *British Magazine* for April–May 1760, p. 265. Buck assigns it to Smollett because he finds in it echoes of two recent works, *The Reprisal* (produced in 1757) and *Peregrine Pickle* (second edition, 1758), noting specifically the poem's anapestic meter, which resembles that of "the verses of Mr. Jumble in *Peregrine Pickle* and of a song in *The Reprisal*." Further, Buck argues, the "rhythm, the humorous turn, the bad French rimes," together with "a culinary metaphor paralleled in the Prologue to *The Reprisal*," all suggest Smollett's authorship. The attribution is further confirmed by the poem's precise references to the political and military leaders and the concerns of France, a country whose politics and policies greatly interested

Smollett. It is doubtful whether any such meeting as that parodied in the poem ever took place, but the people mentioned were figures of real importance. Among them are Madame Pompadour, the notoriously influential mistress of Louis XV; Etienne François Choiseul, secretary of state; Etienne de Silhouette, controller general; and duc de Richelieu, marquis de Contades, duc de Broglie, and prince de Soubise, all important military leaders.

MORNING, IN SPRING, A FRAGMENT

1. Title: The source for the attribution is Buck, *Poet*, 60–63. The poem appeared in the *British Magazine* for April–May 1760, p. 265, immediately following "The Junto." Buck suggests (p. 62) that the verses are "a fragment left stranded by one of the many revisions of *The Regicide*," the youthful tragedy which was never produced but which Smollett published in 1749.

A PASTORAL BALLAD

1. Title: The source for the attribution is Buck, *Poet*, 58–60. The poem appeared in the *British Magazine* for October 1760, p. 604. Buck assigns it to Smollett because of its echoes of the "Ode to Blue-Ey'd Ann" (see above, p. 52), published in the April 1760 number of the same magazine, and because of its reference to "Anne" as the object of the poet's love. Smollett was married to Ann (or Anne) Lassells.

ON SIGNIOR TENDUCCI'S SINGING JUBAL'S LYRE. BY A PRISONER IN THE KING'S BENCH

1. Title: The source for the attribution is James G. Basker, *Tobias Smollett: Critic and Journalist* (Newark: University of Delaware Press, 1988), 201. The poem appeared in the *British Magazine* for January 1761, p. 48. Smollett was imprisoned for libel in the King's Bench for some eleven weeks beginning in late November 1760; Knapp, 235–36, suggests that while there he met Tenducci, the famous Italian tenor, who had been in the prison for debt since June 1760. Knapp also assigns the poem to Smollett, but somewhat more doubtfully than Basker. See also Claude E. Jones, "A Smollett Note," *Notes and Queries* 174 (1938): 152. The title of the poem refers to the biblical legend (Genesis 4:21) that Jubal was the inventor of the harp.

KEY TO *THE BRITON*

Smollett, or perhaps his printer, inserted dashes into numerous words in the *Briton*. This practice, called "gutting," was originally used with the printing of names to avoid charges of libel; see Carl R. Kropf, "Libel and Satire in the Eighteenth Century," *Eighteenth Century Studies* 8 (1974): 153–68. In *Continuation*, 5:200, Smollett remarks that the practice was "now laid aside" as no longer necessary, and so his use of it in the *Briton* may simply be intended to satirize the convention. Alternatively, his printer may have automatically gutted certain words spelled out fully in the manuscript.

Many of the gutted words in the *Briton* are easily understood from their contexts, but the following list is provided as a convenient guide to clarify any ambiguities. If a word appears in different instances with either a capital or a lowercase initial letter but has the same meaning in every instance, it is given in this key with the capital letter only. For the purpose of this list, the length of dashes has been normalized. Possessive forms have not been included.

A—n	Alderman
Ad—n	Administration
adm—n	administration
Af—n	African
Antim—l	Antiministerial
B—	Bishop; Bute
B—d	Board
b—dy	bawdy
B—e	Bute
B—n	Britain
B—p	Bishop
b—r	brother
B—sh	British

B—t	Bute (perhaps a pun with *butt*)
B—te	Bute
C—	Churchill
c—b—t	cabinet
C—l	Council
C—l—d—ian	Caledonian
C—ns	Commons
c—rs	councillors
C—s	Commons
c—t	court
Ch—	Church
Ch—ll	Churchill
Cl—em—t	Claremont
d—	duke
D—ke	Duke
d—n	damnation
D—ne	Divine
E—d	England
E—r	Elector
E—te	Electorate
El—r	Elector
El—te	Electorate
F—x	Fox
G—	George; German
G—d	God
G—le	Grenville

G—lle	Grenville
G—n	German
g—nized	germanized
G—t	Government; Great
G—y	Germany
H—	Heathcote
H—n	Hanoverian
H—r	Hanover
H—y	Hungary
K—	King
K—g	King
K—gs	Kings
k—ly	kingly
L—	Lord
L—d	Lord
L—ds	Lords
L—n	London
L—p	Lordship
M—	Mayor; Minister; Monitor
M—h	Monarch
M—l	Ministerial
M—r	Mayor; Minister
M—r—y	Ministry
M—rs	Ministers
M—s	Ministers
M—tre	Mitre

M—y	Ministry; Majesty
N—e	Newcastle
N—le	Newcastle
N—n	Nobleman
n—w	nephew
P—	Pitt; Prussia
P—a	Prussia
P—ce	Prince
P—e	Prince
p—e	prime
P—l—t	Parliament
P—n	Prussian
p—n	pension
P—s	Pelhams
P—ssia	Prussia
P—t	Parliament; Pitt
P—te	Prelate
P—ts	Parliaments
P—tt	Pitt
Pr—ce	Prince
r—d	reverend
r—g	reigning
R—l	Royal
r—t	right
S—h	Scotch (or Scottish)
s—ls	seals

S—n	Sovereign
S—ns	Saxons; Sovereigns
S—sh	Scottish
S—te	Sodomite
S—y	Saxony
s—y	secretary
So—n	Sovereign
St—n	Statesman
T—	Temple
T—le	Temple
T—n	Treason
T—ne	Throne
T—y	Treasury
Th—e	Throne
Th—ne	Throne
U—r	Usurper
W—	Wilkes; William
W—es	Walpoles
W—kes	Wilkes
W—ph—a	Westphalia

TEXTUAL COMMENTARY

EDITORIAL PRINCIPLES

The autograph manuscripts for the poems, plays, and *The Briton* are no longer extant. In fact, no printer's copy for any of Smollett's works has survived. The nature of the manuscripts can only be deduced from letters, never intended for publication, and from an examination of manuscript revisions the author made in a copy of the 1766 first edition of *Travels Through France and Italy* for a new edition that did not appear.[1] The revisions for the *Travels* include additions, translations of passages in foreign languages, and corrections to the printed text. It might be argued that Smollett, by the mid-1760s largely free from his numerous editorial tasks, had new leisure to correct the *Travels*; but an examination of other works he saw through the press shows much the same care, for he left uncorrected only the kinds of errors that none but the most exacting proofreaders might have caught.[2]

The revisions to the *Travels* are written in Smollett's neat hand, which, after more than two centuries, can be read with ease. A compositor, then, would have had no difficulty reading the author's manuscripts, but in the process of setting the type an overlay of normalization occurred. As John Smith notes in *The Printer's Grammar* (1755), "By the Laws of Printing, indeed, a Compositor should abide by his Copy, and not vary from it. . . . But this good law is now looked upon as obsolete, and most Authors expect the Printer to spell, point, and digest their Copy, that it may be intelligible and significant to the Reader; which is what a Compositor and the Corrector jointly have regard to, in Works of their own language." The compositor peruses his copy but, before beginning to compose, "should be informed, either by the Author, or Master, after what manner our work is to be done; whether the old way, with Capitals to Substantives, and Italic to Proper names and Emphatical words," and nothing "in Italic but what is underscored in our Copy." When composing from printed copy and "such Manuscripts as are written fair," we "employ our eyes with the same agility as we do our hands; for we cast our eyes upon every letter we aim at, at the same moment we move our hands to take it up; neither do we lose our time in looking at our Copy for every word we compose; but take as many words into our memory as we can retain."[3]

In the lengthy manuscript additions to Letter 11 of the *Travels*—the English translation of a Latin letter to Antoine Fizes and of the professor's reply in

French — Smollett followed the old practice, though somewhat inconsistently, of capitalizing nouns and some adjectives. Schooled to capitalize substantives, he continued in his habitual way.[4] But he certainly knew that his capitalization and his use of the ampersand for "and" would be brought into conformity with the rest of the book. He seems to have accepted this styling by the printer, or at least acquiesced. In the printed text of the *Travels* he corrected such small matters as a transposed letter, "muscels" (the bivalve mollusc) to "muscles," and a verb tense "affords" to "afford"; at the same time he allowed to stand variant spellings such as "paltry" — "paultry," "ake" — "ach," and so on. Smollett was not consistent in his spelling, although he did have a preferred spelling for some words; but the compositors, by taking as many words into their memories as they could retain, sometimes introduced their preferences. Smollett appears to have been content with the resulting inconsistencies in spelling as long as they were correct, and he did not attempt to restore his capitalization and punctuation.

The works included in this volume were printed in both the old and new ways. Those printed in the new way are likely to have the greatest number of changes, since much of Smollett's original capitalization may have been eliminated. Compositors were paid to be accurate and were highly consistent in capitalizing substantives; Smollett appears not to have been consistent. But even those works printed in the old way must have introduced numerous changes between the manuscripts and the printed books, including normalization of spelling and punctuation.

In the present edition no attempt has been made to achieve a general consistency in spelling, punctuation, or capitalization, because in the absence of the manuscripts one cannot determine whether Smollett or the compositor was responsible for their variations. Hence the spelling, punctuation, and capitalization of the copy-text for each work have been retained except when they are clearly in error, or when they obscure meaning or distract the attention of the reader. Hyphenated words at a line-end have been adjusted according to the usual practice of the copy-text insofar as that practice may be ascertained from other appearances or parallels. Only the following changes have been made silently: all turned letters or wrong fonts have been corrected, the long *s* has been replaced by the modern letter *s*, and "ae" and "oe" have been treated as digraphs. The display capitals in the works have not been exactly reproduced. Quotations have been indicated according to modern practice, and the punctuation in relation to the quotation marks has been normalized. The length of dashes and the space around them have also been normalized according to modern practice.

No attempt has been made to produce a variorum edition. The history of variant readings and editorial emendations of an individual work is recorded only through the first collected edition, *Plays and Poems Written by T. Smollett, M.D. With Memoirs of the Life and Writings of the Author* (1777), printed for T. Evans and R. Baldwin. An extensive search has been made of poetical miscellanies, song books, collections of song sheets, and periodicals in an attempt to locate as many printings as possible of Smollett's poems through 1777.[5]

Particularly important is the discovery, if possible, of all authoritative texts. An "authoritative text" is a particular text the author wrote or approved.[6] In the case of the poems included in Smollett's early novels, *The Adventures of Roderick Random* and *The Adventures of Peregrine Pickle*, for example, it is relatively easy to determine an "authoritative text." Sight collations of the novels clearly indicate that Smollett made extensive revisions for the second, third, and fourth editions of *Roderick Random* and the second edition of *Peregrine Pickle*. Later editions show no authorial intervention, only an accumulation of compositorial errors. For purposes of establishing the text for the poems in the novels, only variants from the authoritative editions have been used, although variants from later editions may be included in the historical collation. In the case of many of the other poems, and particularly *The Tears of Scotland*, it is almost impossible to determine which texts have authority. In the headnote to each work (see below) an attempt has been made to sort out authoritative from non-authoritative versions of the text, but a record of substantive variant readings is given for all versions of the text through 1777.

Bibliographical descriptions for those of Smollett's works not described in other volumes of the Georgia Edition are given following the historical collations, except for the *Briton* discussed below (pages 576–77). No bibliographical description is provided for *The Union*, the poetical miscellany which provides the copy-text for *The Tears of Scotland*, but the copies examined are identified below, in note 19. Other poetical miscellanies, song books, collections of song sheets, and periodicals examined are given in the notes. Place of publication is London unless otherwise stated.

CHOICE OF COPY-TEXTS

The choice of copy-text is discussed in the headnote to each work (see below), but a few general observations should be made. A number of the works included in this volume present no difficulties. Both *The Regicide* and *The Reprisal* were ignored by Smollett after their initial printings, so the first editions, set from the author's holograph manuscripts or from copies made from them, have been chosen as copy-texts. With the exception of two numbers, the *Briton* exists in only one printing. Likewise, the poems in the *British Magazine* survive in one printing. *Ode to Independence* was published posthumously from Smollett's manuscript. Since the manuscript has not survived, the first edition must serve as copy-text.

The traditional view that the first edition should be chosen as copy-text because it is closer to the author's lost manuscript and is more likely to retain its formal features must be reexamined, however, in light of Smollett's involvement with later printings of some of his works. The little surviving evidence, the not very extensive revisions Smollett made in the *Travels*, suggests that many of the formal features in his works probably derive from the compositor. Whether Smollett desired the many compositorial changes in spelling, capitalization, and punctuation, or acquiesced in accepting the changes because they were inevitable, is not known. It is known, however, that the first printings of Smollett's works required few emendations to correct them, indicating that proofs were read carefully by someone. Since the high level of accuracy is consistent, no matter who printed a work, Smollett must have been responsible. When a second or later edition was revised by Smollett, he not only made verbal changes, but corrected errors and adjusted some of the formal features.

The second editions of his two satires, *Advice* and *Reproof*, for example, have lines added, deleted, and revised, and notes deleted and revised, but also small adjustments such as those made in the letters and dashes in the names printed "in clear."[7] Although it is impossible to know whether a given spelling or punctuation mark originated with Smollett or with the compositor, the attention to details in the texts places the presumption in the author's favor. Choosing the first editions of *Advice* and *Reproof* as copy-texts would force the editor to make dozens of emendations to establish a text. If the second editions are chosen, only a few corrections are required.[8]

The text of *The Tears of Scotland* is particularly difficult because no edition can be assumed to have been supervised by Smollett. In fact, it is difficult to know whether all forms of the text have been discovered. The poem was extremely popular and was much copied and, although an extensive search has been made of poetical miscellanies, song books, collections of song sheets, and periodicals, other copies may await a chance discovery. *The Tears of Scotland* and other Smollett poems set to music present additional difficulties not found in more conventionally published poems. Song sheets frequently are not dated, and indeed can be dated only generally as 1750(?) or 1790(?).[9] The texts of the poems often lack punctuation since the music indicates the phrasing. Are small changes in the text an attempt by someone to make the lyrics fit the music, or are they revisions by the author? The edition containing the earliest state of the text may or may not be the first edition and, hence, may or may not have been set from Smollett's holograph manuscript. The source for the latest state of the text remains undiscovered. In this case, it is impossible to choose one edition as copy-text over another simply on the basis of its formal features. The earliest edition to contain Smollett's final revisions, therefore, has been chosen as copy-text.[10]

The choice of copy-text for poems included in the novels, particularly *Roderick Random*, also presents some problems. Although a detailed history of the publication of *Roderick Random* appears in the Georgia Edition and need not be given here, it should be remembered that Smollett revised the novel three times. The revisions in the three editions are extensive, but the poems did not always receive attention. Whether the first or a later edition of an individual poem is chosen for copy-text is determined by whether it is possible to ascertain that Smollett was responsible for any or all changes introduced.

APPARATUS

Throughout the textual lists and tables, the procedure for reference to the present text is as follows: for the poems, reference is to line numbers; for the plays, reference is to act, scene, and line numbers; for the *Briton*, reference is to page and line numbers. A basic note in the list of emendations provides the appropriate reference and the emended reading in the present text. Except for the line alterations described above, every editorial change in the copy-text has been recorded. Following the square bracket is the earliest source of emendation and the history of the copy-text reading up to the point of emendation. The historical collation follows the same form, except that after the square bracket is given the subsequent history of the substantive variants in the texts examined. This historical collation is confined to substantive variants, whether these are emended copy-text readings or rejected unauthoritative readings. Emendations not found in any of the editions are marked "W" and are the responsibility of the present edition, whether they are originated here or with a previous editor. A wavy dash (~) is substituted for a repeated word associated with pointing, and an inferior caret ($_\wedge$) indicates pointing absent in the present text or in one of the editions from which the variant was drawn. The form of the reading both to the right and the left of the bracket conforms to the system of silent alterations, and there is no record of any variations except for the instance being recorded. When the matter in question is pointing, for example, the wavy dash to the right of the bracket signifies only the substantive form of the variant, and any variation in spelling or capitalization has been ignored. Emendations from catchwords are indicated as *cw*. A (*c*) indicates the reading in the corrected state of the form, and (*u*) the uncorrected state. A vertical stroke indicates a line-end. The titles of poetical miscellanies, song books, collections of song sheets, and periodicals are given by short title at the beginning of an entry for an individual work and thereafter abbreviated.

Some emendations and decisions to retain the copy-text reading are discussed in the headnotes to individual pieces, which follow immediately below. All hyphenated compounds or possible compounds appearing at line-ends in the copy-text are recorded in the word-division list. The reader should assume that any word hyphenated at a line-end in the present text, but not appearing in this list, was broken by the modern typesetter.

Headnotes to Individual Works

A NEW SONG
Set by Mr. Oswald, the Words by Mr. Smollet

This poem exists in two versions. It first appeared in a four-stanza version with the title given above in *Universal Harmony or, The Gentleman and Ladie's Social Companion. Consisting of a Great Variety of the Best and Most Favourite English & Scots Songs, Cantatas, &c. &c. With a Curious Design, by Way of Headpiece Expressive of the Sense of Each Particular Song. All Neatly Engraved on Quarto Copper Plates, and Set to Music for the Voice, Violin, Hautboy, German & Common Flute, with a Thorough Base for the Organ, Harpsichord, Spinet, &c. By the Best Masters. The Whole Calculated to Keep People in Good Spirits, Good Health, & Good Humour, to Promote Social Friendship in All Companys and Universal Harmony in Every Neighbourhood*, published by John Newbery in 1745.[11] The identical engraved plate of Smollett's song was reissued in *Universal Harmony* with a 1746 in the imprint. The song, without the music, also appeared in *The Muses Delight. An Accurate Collection of English and Italian Songs, Cantatas and Duetts, Set to Music for the Harpsichord, Violin, German-Flute, &c. With*

Instructions for the Voice, Violin, Harpsichord or Spinnet, German-Flute, Common-Flute, Hautboy, French-Horn, Bassoon and Bass-Violin: Also, a Compleat Musical Dictionary, and Several Hundred English, Irish and Scots Songs, without the Music, published by John Sadler in Liverpool in 1754. The song, "The Words by Mr. Smollet. Set by Mr. Oswald," has punctuation added and what is most likely a compositor's transposition: the third line of the fourth stanza has "Despair had ne'er her soul possess'd" instead of "Despair her soul had neer possess'd." [12]

The lyrics for the first printing of the song in the 1745 *Universal Harmony* must have derived from Smollett's autograph manuscript or a fair copy of it. Unfortunately, Smollett's manuscript of the lyrics has disappeared, making it impossible to recover his spelling and punctuation. When the lyrics were published with the music in *Universal Harmony*, no punctuation was supplied, as the music indicated the phrasing. It is only when the lyrics were published without the music in the 1754 *Muses Delight* that punctuation was added. Although it is not known whether the punctuation in *Muses Delight* derives from Smollett or reflects his original punctuation, it has been adopted here with a few revisions. Some punctuation is necessary if the song lyrics are to be read as a poem, and the punctuation in *Muses Delight* at least has the advantage of being contemporary.

The copy-text for the first version of the song is the 1745 *Universal Harmony*. The punctuation is supplied, with revisions, from the 1754 *Muses Delight*. The song is printed from copies in the British Library. [13]

The song was revised and shortened to three stanzas when it was included in the first edition of *The Adventures of Roderick Random* (2:31), published 21 January 1748, and in subsequent editions. A second edition of the novel was published 7 April 1748, a third edition 19 January 1749–50, and a fourth edition 10 November 1754. By Smollett's death the novel had reached an eighth edition, and a ninth edition appeared in 1774, but no edition after the fourth contains authorial revisions. [14] The shortened version of "A New Song" is printed here, with the title given as it is in *Roderick Random*.

On Celia playing on the harpsichord and singing.

I.

When Sapho struck the quiv'ring wire,
The throbbing breast was all on fire:
And when she rais'd the vocal lay,
The captive soul was charm'd away!

II.

But had the nymph, possess'd with these
Thy softer, chaster pow'r to please;
Thy beauteous air of sprightly youth,
Thy native smiles of artless truth;

III.

The worm of grief, had never prey'd
On the forsaken, love-sick maid:
Nor had she mourn'd an happless flame,
Nor dash'd on rocks her tender frame.

The deletion of a comma after "grief" in the first line of the third stanza is the only change in the first four editions of *Roderick Random*. It is impossible to tell whether Smollett or the compositor was responsible; the change certainly is not necessary. This second version of the poem was reprinted in the 1777 *Plays and Poems* (page 241) with two spelling and two punctuation changes. The copy-text for this version is the 1748 first edition of *Roderick Random*. It is printed from a copy of this edition of the novel in the University of Iowa Libraries.

THE TEARS OF SCOTLAND

Transcript in unidentified hand in National Library of Scotland (MS 295, f. 56).

Transcript in unidentified hand in National Library of Scotland (MS 2910, f. 16v).

Transcript in unidentified hand in Edinburgh University Library (MS La.II.83/3.12).

Transcript in unidentified hand in Bodleian Library, Oxford (MS Montagu d.26 f. 4).

The Tears of Scotland [1746].

The Land of Cakes, Book the First [1746].

The Thrush, A Collection of Six Hundred Twenty Six of the Most Celebrated English and Scotch Songs, 1749.

The Craftsman, June 1750.

The Mitre and Crown (2 [July 1750]: 460–61).

The Union: or, Select Scots and English Poems, "Edinburgh," 1753, 1753; also London 1759, 1766, and Dublin 1761.

The Art of Poetry on a New Plan, 1762.

The Beauties of English Poesy, 1767.

A Collection of the Most Esteemed Pieces of Poetry, 1767.

Modern Poems, Glasgow, 1776.

Plays and Poems, 1777.

When the news reached London that the Duke of Cumberland had defeated the rebel forces at Culloden on 16 April 1746 there was, Smollett's friend and fellow Scotsman Alexander Carlyle observed, "a perfect uproar of Joy." Fearful of the riotous mob, Carlyle made it home under the cover of darkness with the assistance of Smollett. Carlyle concludes his account: "I saw not Smollett again for some time after, when he shew'd [Robert] Smith and me the Manuscript of his Tears of Scotland, which was publishd not long after, and had such a Run of Approbation."[15] Unfortunately, such phrases as "some time after" and "not long after" are of little assistance in establishing the actual publication date of the poem. The anecdotes by John Moore and William Richardson on the composition of the poem give no hint of a date.[16] Smollett, always quick to anger, probably wrote the poem in an attempt to deal with his feelings in the aftermath of what he considered the massacre at Culloden.[17] In any case, the poem appears to have circulated in manuscript among friends, perhaps first in a six-stanza form and then in a seven-stanza form, before seven stanzas were printed in a four-page leaflet without a title page sometime in 1746.[18] Since the poem was published with no indication of author, bookseller, or printer, no advertisement seems to have appeared in the newspapers. Ordinarily it is assumed that the first edition is printed from the author's manuscript, or a fair copy of it, and that the author has been responsible for seeing the work through the press. Smollett's connection with the printing of this leaflet, however, remains a mystery. Although the leaflet represents the earliest version of the text extant, is it in fact the first edition? Did Smollett pay to have it printed himself from manuscript for distribution to friends? Did he make some financial arrangement with a bookseller or trade publisher to sell the leaflet? Was it printed by some well-intentioned friend from an autograph manuscript or from a fair copy made from one? More importantly, did Smollett see the poem through the press and read proof?

What seems to be the next appearance in print and the first musical setting of *The Tears of Scotland* can be traced to Smollett with a bit more certainty. *The Land of Cakes* was announced in the *General Advertiser* for 3 December 1746:

> This Day is published Price 1 s. The Land of Cakes Book the First. Containing Six Songs set to Musick in the true Scots Taste. To which is added, The Tears of Scotland. Printed for R. Williams, and sold by Mr. Oswald in St. Martin's Church-Yard; J. Newbery in St. Paul's Churchyard; and W. Owen, next Door to the Devil-Tavern, Temple-Bar.[19]

The poem, still anonymous, was printed in full, as set to music by James Oswald, for whom Smollett had earlier written lyrics.[20] This is probably the version referred to by Smollett in his letter to Carlyle of ?1747, where he describes the poem as "a Ballad set to Musick under the name of the Tears of Scotland, a Performance very well received at London, as I hope it will be in your Country which gave Rise to it. The truth is I have a paternal Concern."[21] In addition to the usual variation in spelling and punctuation, attributable to a compositor, there are two revisions from the leaflet text: "round her Head" for "o'er her Head" (line 43) and "And Spite of" for "In Spite of" (line 53). This verbal tinkering is of the kind Smollett often makes in his works, and can be seen, for example, in the revisions made to *Advice* and *Reproof* described below.

The poem was next published anonymously in *The Thrush*,[22] a collection of songs without the music, and this version follows the text in *The Land of Cakes*. Apparently the next publication was in one of the numbers of the *Craftsman* for June 1750, but the number containing the poem is no longer extant. The *Mitre and Crown* for July 1750 reprints the poem, and an introductory letter, from the *Craftsman*. The letter, written by a contributor or, perhaps, by the editor, is dated 26 June 1750. By this period the *Craftsman* was published weekly and would have been issued on 16, 23, 30 June, etc. If the date 26 June is a reference to the day of the issue of the *Craftsman*, "26" must be a misprint for "16." But if 26 June is the date of the letter, it may have appeared in the next issue, that for 30 June.[23] In any case, the anonymous correspondent says, "the Poem on *Scotland* is, I am told, written by the Author of a celebrated Work of Humour."[24] The text is that of *The Land of Cakes*, with the usual compositorial variation, but with some important changes: the poem is divided into thirteen four-line stanzas, omitting the last four lines of stanza five, beginning, "Yet when the Rage of Battle ceas'd"; and in the last line of stanza one, "Cruelty" is given as "C——y." The reason for these changes is not clear, but must be attributed to an anonymous editor since subsequent printings retained the seven-stanza form, including the printing in *The Union* (1753) which incorporates Smollett's final revisions.[25]

The four manuscripts of *The Tears of Scotland*, written in unknown hands, derive their texts, with the usual scribal variations, from those found in the leaflet or in *The Land of Cakes*, the first two printings of the poem. The three manuscripts held in Scottish libraries follow the leaflet, and the manuscript in the Bodleian Library has the two readings first introduced in *The Land of Cakes*. Although it is possible that one or the other of the manuscripts may have been copied from an authorial manuscript or from an undiscovered printed text, there is no convincing evidence that this was the case.

Only in 1753 did *The Tears of Scotland* again appear in print. For this printing Smollett made his final revisions. The poem was published anonymously in *The Union*, an anthology edited by Thomas Warton in Oxford with a fictitious imprint: "Edinburgh: Printed for Archibald Monro & David Murray. M.DCC.LIII." As D. Nichol Smith points out, no printer or bookseller is known with either of these names.[26] No advertisement has been discovered in the Edinburgh newspapers. Although the collection was included in the list of new publications in the *Scots Magazine* for May 1753 (17:263), the list was reprinted from the *Gentleman's Magazine* of the same month (23:250). On 3 May 1753 the following announcement appeared in the *Public Advertiser*:

This day is published, Price 2s. sewed, The Union; or Select Scotch and English Poems, by several Hands; more particularly by Dunbar, Lowth, Shipley, Collins, Grey, Mason, Thomas and Joseph Warton, Hammond, Mallet, Lyndesay and Akenside; with some Originals. Edinburgh printed; sold by R. Baldwin, at the Rose in Paternoster Row, London, and by all the Booksellers in North and South Britain.

The volume, however, was not printed for an Edinburgh firm; indeed, it was not printed in Edinburgh at all, but in Oxford by William Jackson.[27] Thomas Park wrote in his copy of *The Union*: "Mr. Mant, in his life of [Thomas] Warton, says that the 'Union' appeared at *Edinburgh* in 1753. I was informed, however, by Dr. [Joseph] Warton, that this first edition was actually printed at *Oxford*, and that he and his brother were principally concerned in conducting the publication."[28] In fact, two "Edinburgh" editions appeared in 1753. The first edition is readily distinguished by having "Centle-|man" on the first page of "CONTENTS," lines five and six from the bottom. The second edition has corrected this error to "Gentle-|man."[29] The third edition, called "THE SECOND EDITION," and the fourth edition, called "THE THIRD EDITION," are "Printed for R. Baldwin," and the announcement in the *Public Advertiser* suggests that Richard Baldwin was the bookseller responsible for the volume from the start.[30] Even the type and mixture of fonts may have been an attempt to make the book appear Scottish in origin. In the preface Thomas Warton claims that "we have had the favour of some original poems, written by a late member of the university of Aberdeen, whose modesty would not permit us to print his name. . . . Nor must we forget to return our public thanks to this gentleman, for the service he has been to us, not only in making this collection more excellent by his own contributions, but in selecting such pieces of others as were suitable to our design." In the contents are listed an "Ode on the approach to Summer, by a Gentleman formerly of the University of Aberdeen," and "A Pastoral in the manner of Spenser, from Theocritus, Idyll 20. By the same." The poems are by Thomas Warton.[31]

There would appear to be, then, no Scottish connection that might explain Smollett's inclusion in the volume. The "Love Elegy" from *The Adventures of Roderick Random* is identified on the contents page and in the text as "By Mr Smallet." Also, the author of *The Tears of Scotland* is not given. Perhaps this suggests that Smollett was not known to either Thomas or his brother, Joseph Warton.[32] But even as late as 1753 Smollett may not have wished his name to be associated with the poem. In the third and fourth editions (called "second" and "third" editions on the title pages) the "Love Elegy" is said to be "By Mr. Smollet," although the authorship of *The Tears of Scotland*—"by Mr. Smollett, 1746"—is only added to the contents page in the fourth edition in 1766. In 1762 *The Art of Poetry on a New Plan* reprinted the poem and said it was "ascribed to Dr. Smollet,"[33] and in 1764 David Erskine Baker, in a biographical notice of Smollett in the *Companion to the Playhouse*, observed: "The Doctor had a very agreeable Vein of Poetry; as appeared by some little occasional Pieces, particularly the Tears of Scotland." These seem to be the earliest identifications in print of Smollett as author of *The Tears of Scotland*.

The text of *The Tears of Scotland* in *The Union* retains the two revisions made in the poem when it was published in *The Land of Cakes*. Eight more revisions are incorporated, as well as close to one hundred changes in spelling, capitalization, and punctuation. Most of the changes are in capitalization because the leaflet was printed in what John Smith, in *The Printer's Grammar*, calls "the old way," with capitals to substantives, and *The Union* was printed according to "the more neat practice," with capitals for emphasis and for proper names. These changes in spelling, capitalization, and punctuation were most likely the work of the compositor. The revisions are the kind of verbal changes Smollett is fond of making in his works, and have been accepted as authorial.

Nothing is known about any relationship between Smollett and Thomas Warton. Nevertheless, Smollett may have furnished the editor with a revised text to include in his collection. It is also possible that Warton took the poem from some undiscovered publication containing Smollett's revised text. Perhaps the revisions in the poem reveal editorial tinkering by Warton, but no such editorial intervention occurs in Smollett's "Love Elegy," which is included in *The Union*, or in the four poems taken from Robert Dodsley's *Museum*.[34] In the absence of evidence to the contrary, it must be concluded that only the author would have been interested in making substantive revisions in the text.

It is the text of *The Tears of Scotland* from *The Union* that has continued to be reprinted. After the two editions with "Edinburgh" imprints of 1753, editions appeared with London imprints in 1759 and 1766 and with a Dublin imprint in 1761. The poem also appeared in the 1762 *The Art of Poetry on a New Plan* printed for John Newbery (2:76–78), in the 1767 *The Beauties of English Poesy* (2:87–89) with an introductory note by Oliver Goldsmith, in the 1767 *A Collection of the Most Esteemed Pieces of Poetry, That Have Appeared for Several Years. With Variety of Originals, By the Late Moses Mendez, Esq; And Other Contributors to Dodsley's Collection. To Which This is Intended as a Supplement* (pages 285–87), in the 1776 *Modern Poems: Selected Chiefly From Miscellanies Published Lately* printed in Glasgow by Andrew Foulis the Younger (pages 15–17),[35] and in the 1777 *Plays and Poems* (pages 237–40). All of these texts follow that in the first edition of *The Union* very closely, with only an occasional change in punctuation or a typographical error.

The copy-text for *The Tears of Scotland* is that of the 1753 first edition of *The Union*. It is printed from a copy in the Cornell University Library. Given the surreptitious nature of the early printing of the poem and the failure to locate the source for Thomas Warton's text in *The Union*, it is difficult to argue that these texts, or any other text, of the poem have Smollett's punctuation, capitalization, and spelling. These formal features of the text were the provenance of the compositor and, with the occasional exception of spelling, it is rarely possible, without the evidence of the author's manuscript, to determine whether the author or the compositor is responsible. Verbal changes are another matter. Compositors, paid according to the amount of type they set, in general were not interested in emendation and improvement. They normally followed their copy with some care since they knew they would be penalized for failing to do so. Hence the normal assumption is that substantive revisions are authorial. Smollett made verbal changes twice, once for *The Land of Cakes* and again for the first edition of *The Union*. Since the text in the first edition of *The Union* incorporates Smollett's final revisions, it has been reproduced exactly except for the correction of one typographical error.[36] Although the punctuation, capitalization, and spelling may or may not have the authority of Smollett's intervention, they have the advantage of consistency. This text also has historical significance since it is the source for later reprintings of the poem.[37]

ADVICE: A SATIRE

Publication of *Advice* was announced in the *General Advertiser* for 4 September 1746.[38] The poem was first issued as "Printed for M. Cooper" and later issued with a variant imprint: "Printed for George Freer." The later "George Freer" issue appears to be a reimpression, with the inner forme of signature B reset.[39] The text of the poem in both issues is identical. Nothing is known about the negotiations for the sale of the satire or the arrangements for its printing. Smollett does appear to have seen the poem through the press and to have read proof with great care, as there are few errors.

The initial sale of *Advice* must have been good. The reimpression suggests that there may have been a demand for the poem, although an accident in the printing house or bindery may have required machining additional sheets. *Advice* was also published with Smollett's second satire, *Reproof*, in March 1748.[40]

For this new edition, Smollett revised both poems and read proofs with great care. Writing to Alexander Carlyle sometime in ? 1747, he sounds pleased with the reception of his satires: "If I had an Opportunity, I would send you . . . Two Satires called Advice and Reproof which made some noise here."[41]

For *Advice and Reproof: Two Satires* there is an entry in 1747 to the account of John Osborn in William Strahan's printing ledgers:

Advice and Reproof. 4 Sheets No. 750 @ 16s   £3–4–0[42]

By this time, however, the market for the satires had been saturated. Lot 1 of the trade sale of John Osborn, 19 November 1751, was the copyright of the two satires—and 566 books. Andrew Millar bought them for £1–5s.[43] Smollett did not give up on the poems and included lines 91–94 of *Advice* in *The Adventures of Roderick Random* (published 21 January 1748), revised to fit the context of the novel (2:164).[44] When preparing the third edition of *Roderick Random* for the press (published 19 January 1749–50), he made three additional small changes. Perhaps he hoped that reprinting a few lines of his first satire in his first novel might give the sale of the poems a boost. If so, the ploy failed; the satires were not reprinted again in their entirety until 1777, in *Plays and Poems* (pages 203–36). In this reprinting the satires contained verbal changes. Was Smollett or an editor responsible for these changes?

Determining whether substantive revisions in "death-bed" and posthumous editions are authorial is often a problem for the textual editor. The texts of Alexander Pope, James Thomson, and Samuel Richardson, for example, contain non-authorial revisions, but unlike the texts of Smollett's works, the source for the revisions is known.[45]

Tobias Smollett died in Italy on 17 September 1771. He left England for the last time in the fall of 1768, reaching Pisa by the end of March 1769. Little is known about Smollett's activities during the last three years of his life. His major literary activity was the completion of *The Expedition of Humphry Clinker*, published 17 June 1771.[46] Before he left England, however, he completed several other works. Writing and editing may have begun on *The Present State of All Nations* as early as 1760, but proposals were not advertised until 14–17 May 1768 in the *London Chronicle*, indicating that the first number would be published 25 June 1768. *Present State* appeared in eight volumes, volumes 1–2 dated 1768 and the remainder 1769.[47] *The History and Adventures of an Atom*, probably completed in the summer 1768, was first advertised in early December 1768 as to be published "in a few days" but was not in fact published until 1 April 1769.[48] Someone in London must have acted as Smollett's agent, seeing these works through the press.

The same agent may have continued his efforts on Smollett's behalf with both the second edition of *Humphry Clinker*, the reprinting of which began in July and ended in August 1771, and the second edition of *The Adventures of Ferdinand Count Fathom*, printed the following November. Both of these editions contain non-authorial substantive revisions.[49]

Editorial intervention continued in *Advice* and *Reproof* when the poems were included in the 1777 *Plays and Poems*. *Plays and Poems* reprints the second-edition text of both poems with modifications. The most obvious change results from the normalization of all the works in the volume so that they look like each other, thus obscuring the original formal features of each text. For this the anonymous editor may or may not have been responsible. Other changes required editorial decisions.

Since the persons Smollett attacked in 1746, 1747, and 1748 were alive, their names were printed "in clear." In the first edition of *Advice*, for example, Smollett had W—rr—n and H—me, but in the second edition he changed them to W——n and H——, making references to these persons even more oblique. This pattern of making some of the names less ostensibly identifiable continues in *Reproof*. But the editor of *Plays and Poems*, taking advantage of the passage of time and Smollett's death, revises in the opposite direction, filling in the missing letters to fully identify the targets of Smollett's satire. This amounts to providing annotations for the poems. Smollett, in fact, had provided some annotations of his own when the poems were first published, omitting only two footnotes in *Reproof* when making revisions for the second edition. The almost three decades which had passed since the poems were first published meant that some of Smollett's historical annotations needed updating, and other references, which Smollett apparently thought clear, seemed to require amplification or annotation.

In the 1748 second edition of *Advice* Smollett supplies an annotation for R——l [Russell], ending with "he was admitted into Bedlam, where he continues still happily bereft of his understanding" (line 187 n.). The editor of *Plays and Poems* revised and completed Russell's history: "where he continued bereft of his understanding, and died in the utmost misery." Smollett's annotation for "Accomplished W——n" calls him "Another son of fortune, who owes his present affluence to the most dubious qualifications" (line 90 n.). The 1777 editor leaves no doubt about these qualifications: "commonly called Brush Warren, from having been a shoe-black; it is said he was kept by both sexes at one time." To Smollett's annotation on Daniel MacKercher (the "melting *Scot*"), in *Reproof*, the 1777 editor adds information about the identity of the "brother in distress" relieved by MacKercher: "Mr. Annesley, who claimed the Anglesea title and estate" (line 122 n.). In another instance the editor adds to Smollett's sarcasm when "griping *J*——*p*—*r* [Jasper]" is further identified as "A man famous for buying poor seamen's tickets" (line 129 n.). The editor has also added three annotations. Of Smollett's "To coy to flatter, and to proud to serve," in *Advice* (line 235), he says, "This, surely, occasioned Churchill's 'Too proud to flatter, too sincere to lye.'" In *Reproof* he identifies "*W*——*ms*—*n*" [Williamson] as "Governor of the Tower" (line 32), and

"The vanquish'd knight" who has "triumph'd in his trial" as "Sir John Cope" (line 34).

No clear external evidence exists for determining the source of corrections or additions in any of Smollett's works. As has been argued elsewhere, there is some slight evidence that Dr. John Armstrong (1709–79) may have served as Smollett's agent for the *Atom*, and for the second editions of *Humphry Clinker* and *Ferdinand Count Fathom*.[50] Whether or not Armstrong was Smollett's agent, this corrector appears to have ceased activity with the publication of the second edition of *Ferdinand Count Fathom* in late 1771. The perfunctory corrections and the high incidence of error clearly indicate that a new corrector worked on the 1774 edition of *The Life and Adventures of Sir Launcelot Greaves*. The motive for producing this "New Edition, Corrected" is not clear, but it seems to have been little more than a marketing strategy. The changes could have been made by the bookseller George Robinson, but more likely by someone he paid to "correct" the work. Other changes could have been made by the unidentified printer.[51] Whoever the person was, he did not read the novel with the same care exercised by the corrector of *Humphry Clinker* and *Ferdinand Count Fathom*.

With the publication of *Advice* and *Reproof* in *Plays and Poems* (1777), a corrector with Smollett's interests at heart again makes an appearance. The corrector, whoever he was, may have been old enough to remember the two verse satires and their targets or may simply have had an antiquarian interest. He knows that "The vanquish'd knight" who "triumph'd in his trial" was Sir John Cope (1707–60), "vanquish'd" at Prestonpans 21 September 1745 and charged with incompetence and cowardice. The corrector was also familiar with Warren, referring to him as "Brush," a detail not supplied by Smollett. He knows the eventual fate of Russell, whose claim to fame, apart from his sexual activities, seems to have been his subscription puppet show burlesquing Italian opera in spring 1745.

Plays and Poems is prefaced by an anonymous "The Life of T. Smollett. M.D." Presumably the revisions in the annotations were made by the same person who wrote the life. Clear but spare, the life lacks the kind of personal details that would provide clues to authorship. The life is based on an earlier "Some Account of the Life and Writings of the late Dr. Smollett" which appeared in the *Westminster Magazine* for May 1775 (3:225–28) and was reprinted in the *Annual Register* for 1775 (18:45–50).[52] The anonymous author of the life in *Plays and Poems* knew little about Smollett's biography and relied heavily on the novels for details. The author does demonstrate an interest in literary history, providing information on the publication of several of Smollett's works and uncovering details of his life from those who knew him. The most striking addition to this life of Smollett is the three letters from Smollett to David Garrick printed for the first time. The source of the letters was Garrick himself, as the editor indicates in a footnote: "A friend of Dr. Smollett's, desirous of evincing that he was capable of retracting his prejudices, and that his gratitude was equally warm with any of his other passions, prevailed on Mr. Garrick to permit the Editor to take copies of the foregoing letters from several others he had written to Mr. Garrick" (page vii).[53] More important, the editor, perhaps with the assistance of the anonymous friend, helped to establish the canon for Smollett's minor poems. The canon has never been questioned, although in 1927 Howard Swazey Buck suggested additions.[54]

The copy-text for *Advice* is the 1748 second edition containing Smollett's final revisions. It is printed from a copy of *Advice and Reproof: Two Satires* in the Houghton Library, Harvard University. The second edition has been chosen as copy-text because Smollett revised the poem and read proof with care. The emendations to the copy-text follow the procedures outlined in "Editorial Principles," except that the tags for Smollett's notes to the poem have been brought into conformity with the text. The letters and length of dashes in the names printed "in clear" in the notes have also been made to conform to those in the text. Although the possibility cannot be entirely discounted that Smollett left in the hands of a friend a revised copy of the 1748 *Advice and Reproof*, containing the substantive revisions found in the 1777 *Plays and Poems*, it seems improbable. Smollett revised many of his works, and the revisions largely consist of small verbal refinements. He is unlikely to have taken the time to update the footnotes and fill in the names without making any verbal changes in the lines. The 1777 revisions are largely additions and are more likely to have been performed by the anonymous editor.

REPROOF: A SATIRE

Publication of *Reproof* was announced in the *General Advertiser* for 14 January 1746–47.[55] Nothing is known about the negotiations for the sale of the satire or the arrangements for its printing. Smollett seems to have read proof with great care, as there are few errors. The poem was carefully revised when it was reprinted with *Advice* in March 1748. *Reproof* was not reprinted until 1777 in *Plays and Poems* (pages 223–36). For details, see the discussion of *Advice*, above.

The copy-text for *Reproof* is the 1748 second edition containing Smollett's final revisions. It is printed from the copy of *Advice and Reproof: Two Satires* in the Houghton Library, Harvard University, from which *Advice* is also printed.

THUS HAVE I SENT THE SIMPLE KING TO HELL

These verses appeared in the first edition of *Roderick Random* (2:30), published 21 January 1748, and in subsequent editions.[56] Only two changes occur in the verses in the first four editions of the novel. A comma is added after "treasons" in the fifth line in the second edition. In the first edition the last line reads "th'immortal," and in the second edition it is changed to read "the immortal." The first edition readings are retained. The changes for the second edition are unnecessary. In fact, the change in the last line spoils the scansion. In all lifetime editions the second line reads "Without *or* coffin," corrected by the textual editor to "Without *a* coffin." Since Smollett did not catch this rather obvious error, it appears that he did not pay the same attention to these verses as he did to the surrounding prose in his three revisions of the novel. This inattention to the verses suggests that the small changes in the fifth and last lines are most likely compositorial. The poem is not included in the 1777 *Plays and Poems*.

The copy-text for the poem is the 1748 first edition of *Roderick Random*. It is printed from a copy of this edition in the University of Iowa Libraries.

THY FATAL SHAFTS UNERRING MOVE

This poem appeared in the 1748 first edition of *Roderick Random* (2:32). Only four changes to the text occur in the first four editions of the novel. The second edition incorrectly changes the words "my vital," in the fourth line of the first stanza, to "thy vital." Smollett, or perhaps an alert compositor, caught the error and corrected it in the third edition. Also in the second edition, a comma is added after "gaze" in line one of stanza two, and "Unheard" is changed to "Unhear'd" in the third line of stanza four. In the fourth edition the "k" is dropped off "magick" in line three of stanza three.

The poem achieved a measure of popularity when it was reprinted in the *Gentleman's Magazine* for July 1755 (25:322–23) as "A Favourite Air, Sung at Vaux-hall, Set by Mr Oswald. The Words by Dr Smolet," with a running head of "A New Song set to Musick." The *Scots Magazine* for September 1755 (17:446) published "A New Song. By Dr Smollet," omitting the music. The *Literary Magazine* for 15 October–15 November 1757 (2:494) published "A Favourite Air Sung at Vauxhall. Set to Music by Mr. Oswald," neglecting to mention Smollett's name.[57] When the poem was printed in Glasgow by Andrew Foulis the Younger in his 1776 *Modern Poems* (page 123), two substantive changes were introduced. In the third line of the first stanza "thy soft" becomes "the soft," and in the second line of the third stanza "murmurs" becomes "numbers." The first change is unnecessary, but the second has its attraction, as it eliminates the repetition of "murmurs," which also appears in the fourth line. There is no reason, however, to think that the emendation originated with Smollett. Perhaps Foulis, the printer of *Modern Poems*, or the anonymous editor, made the changes. The first change might be compositorial, the second is less likely to have been so.[58] All of these reprints have the usual compositorial changes in spelling and punctuation, but none of the changes is significant.[59] For some reason the poem was not included in the 1777 *Plays and Poems*.

The copy-text for the poem is the 1748 first edition of *Roderick Random*. It is printed from a copy of this edition in the University of Iowa Library.

TRAVESTY

These verses appeared in the 1748 first edition of *Roderick Random* (2:188). For the second edition of the novel Smollett corrected the first line from "Would task the moon-ty'd hair" to "Would *you* task the moon-ty'd hair." He also may have added a comma at the end of the third line; a medial "p" is mistakenly dropped out of "poppling." Although the verbal change and the addition of punctuation may be the work of a compositor, these corrections are consistent with Smollett's habit of revision. Later editions of *Roderick Random* follow the second. The verses are not included in the 1777 *Plays and Poems*.

The second edition of *Roderick Random*, which is the first to contain the two corrections, has been chosen as copy-text. The verses are printed from the Tinker library copy of this edition in the Beinecke Library, Yale University.[60]

LOVE ELEGY
In Imitation of Tibullus

This poem appeared in the 1748 first edition of *Roderick Random* (2:271–72). In the second edition there is what is most likely a compositorial change: "th'empurpled" becomes "the empurpled" in the first line of the third stanza. The third and fourth edition texts, however, have substantive revisions by Smollett in the last two lines. The first two editions have "Wilt thou strew flow'rs," which in the third edition becomes "Strow vernal flow'rs." The first three editions read "bid the turf lie light upon my breast," which in the fourth edition becomes "bid the turf lie easy on my breast." The third edition adds a "k" to "music" in the fourth line of stanza three, but the letter is deleted again for the fourth edition. The third edition changes a semicolon to a colon after "repine" in the second line of stanza five, and the fourth edition adds a superfluous comma after "There" in the preceding line.

The text of the third edition of the poem was set to music by John Buswell and published about 1750. The unrevised version of the text was reprinted in the editions of *The Union* (pages 96–97),[61] and in *Modern Poems* (page 122). The 1777 *Plays and Poems* reprints the revised text (pages 242–43). All of these reprints have the usual compositorial changes in spelling and punctuation, but none of the changes is significant.

The copy-text for the poem is the 1748 first edition of *Roderick Random*. Although the fourth edition contains Smollett's final substantive revisions of the poem, the text also has two compositorial errors and a change in punctuation difficult to attribute to the author. The first edition has been chosen as copy-text because it requires only two emendations, whereas the choice of the fourth edition as copy-text would have required three. The poem is printed from a copy of the 1748 first edition of *Roderick Random* in the University of Iowa Libraries.

ADIEU, YE STREAMS THAT SMOOTHLY FLOW

This poem appeared in the 1751 first edition of *The Adventures of Peregrine Pickle* (1:160), published 25 February 1751, and in subsequent editions. A second edition of the novel, with extensive revisions by Smollett, was published 4 March 1758. This was followed by a third edition 5 March 1765, a fourth about 16 September 1769, and a fifth 16 November 1773.[62] None of the later editions of the poem varies from the first. The Georgia Edition of *Peregrine Pickle* contains a complete history of the printing and publication of the novel.

Another version of the poem, entitled "The Adieu. Sung at the Public Gardens," with music by James Oswald, was published in at least three separate printings in the 1750s. Another musical setting, "A New Song Set by Sgr. Philippo Palma," was also published about the same time. Sheet music during the period is rarely dated, and dating is crucial for establishing the text for this poem. The song has four readings not found in the poem as published in the novel (the novel reading is given first): shade] glade (line 4), charms] smiles (line 7), balmy] gentle (line 12), bright] sweet (line 13). One of the Oswald printings also has "the" for "ye" in the first line of stanza one; another has "springs" for "spring" in the third line of the same stanza.[63] Which came first? Since Smollett never revised the poem after it was published in the 1751 first edition of *Peregrine Pickle*, even though he had an opportunity to do so when he revised the novel for the 1758 second edition, he must have been happy with this version of the poem. Neither Oswald nor Palma uses the text as it appears in the novel. This suggests that there was an earlier version of the poem, probably first set to music by Oswald, which Smollett revised for inclusion in *Peregrine Pickle*, just as Oswald had earlier set "A NEW SONG: When Sappho tun'd the raptur'd strain," which Smollett revised to "On Celia playing on the harpsichord and singing" for inclusion in *Roderick Random*. Palma's setting uses the song as it appeared in Oswald's setting. The song with music was also reprinted in the *Universal Magazine* for June 1751 (8:269).[64] It has the four readings usually found in the song, and the reading "the" for "ye" in the first line.[65] The poem is not included in the 1777 *Plays and Poems*.

The copy-text is the 1751 first edition of *Peregrine Pickle*, for which Smollett carefully revised the poem from an earlier version set to music, and for which he proofread the text carefully. The poem is printed from a copy of the first edition of the novel in the University of Iowa Libraries.

COME, LISTEN YE STUDENTS OF EV'RY DEGREE

This poem appeared in the 1751 first edition of *Peregrine Pickle* (1:183–84). When Smollett made revisions for the 1758 second edition of his novel, he revised line three of stanza four from "For, obliged to his own understanding to trust" to "For, when his own genius he ventur'd to trust." In line four of stanza three a semicolon at the end of the line has been changed to an exclamation point. Since Smollett revised the poem and proofread it carefully, this change is probably authorial. No further revisions were made in the poem in later editions; there are only a few compositorial changes. The poem was not included in the 1777 *Plays and Poems*.

The copy-text for the poem is the 1758 second edition of *Peregrine Pickle*. It is printed from a copy of this edition in the University of Iowa Libraries.

BURLESQUE ODE

This poem appeared in the 1751 first edition of *Peregrine Pickle* (4:117–18). When Smollett made revisions for the 1758 second edition of the novel, he omitted it. It was included, however, in the 1777 *Plays and Poems* (pages 248–49).[66]

The copy-text for the poem is the 1751 first edition of *Peregrine Pickle*. It is printed from a copy of this edition in the University of Iowa Libraries.

SONG "While with Fond Rapture"

This poem appeared in the 1751 first edition of *Peregrine Pickle* (4:148). When Smollett made revisions for the 1758 second edition of the novel he left the poem untouched. He did read proofs carefully, as there is no variation between the first and second editions. Beginning with the third edition, compositorial changes begin to appear, but none of the changes is significant. The poem is included in the 1777 *Plays and Poems* (pages 244–45).

The copy-text for the poem is the 1751 first edition of *Peregrine Pickle*. It is printed from a copy of this edition in the University of Iowa Libraries.

A DECLARATION IN LOVE.
ODE TO BLUE-EY'D ANN

This poem appeared in the *British Magazine* for April 1760 (1:213) and was included in the 1777 *Plays and Poems* (pages 257–58).

The copy-text for the poem is the *British Magazine*. It is printed from a copy in the British Library.[67]

ODE TO SLEEP.
INTENDED AS A CHORUS IN A TRAGEDY

This poem appeared in the *British Magazine* for June 1760 (1:379). In the same month the poem also appeared in the *Scots Magazine* (22:315). It was reprinted in both the 1770 and 1775 editions of *A Collection of Poems*, published by George Pearch (4:138–39; 4:127),[68] and in the 1777 *Plays and Poems* (pages 253–54). The 1770 edition of Pearch's *Collection* identifies the poem as "By T—— S——, M.D." All of these reprints have the usual compositorial changes in spelling and punctuation, but none of the changes is significant.

The copy-text for the poem is the *British Magazine*. It is printed from a copy in the British Library.

AN ODE TO MIRTH

This poem appeared in the *British Magazine* for July 1760 (1:494). It was reprinted in both the 1770 and 1775 editions of *A Collection of Poems*, published by George Pearch (4:139–41; 4:128–29), and in the 1777 *Plays and Poems* (pages 250–52). The 1770 edition of Pearch's *Collection* identifies "Ode to Sleep" as "By T—— S——, M.D." and indicates that "Ode to Mirth," which immediately follows, is "By the Same." All of these reprints have the usual compositorial changes in spelling and punctuation, but none of the changes is significant.

The copy-text for the poem is the *British Magazine*. It is printed from a copy in the British Library.

A NEW SONG "To Fix Her"

This poem appeared in the *British Magazine* for August 1760 (1:549). It was reprinted in the 1777 *Plays and Poems* with one change in capitalization (pages 146–47).

The copy-text for the poem is the *British Magazine*. It is printed from a copy in the British Library.

ODE TO LEVEN-WATER

This poem appeared in the 1771 first edition of *Humphry Clinker* (3:42). It was reprinted in the *Town and Country Magazine* for June 1771 (3:327),[69] in the 1776 *Modern Poems* (pages 24–25) published in Glasgow by Andrew Foulis the Younger, and in the 1777 *Plays and Poems* (pages 255–56). The first two editions of *Humphry Clinker* have the incorrect form "oe'r" in line nine, corrected in the reprints to "o'er." The second edition of *Humphry Clinker* introduced "edges" for "hedges" in line twenty, and *Plays and Poems* has this incorrect reading. The reprints also contain a small number of compositorial spelling changes. The Georgia Edition of *Humphry Clinker* contains a complete history of the printing and publication of the novel.[70]

The copy-text for the poem is the 1771 first edition of *Humphry Clinker*. It is printed from a copy of this edition in the University of Iowa Libraries.

ODE TO INDEPENDENCE

The first edition of this poem was published in Glasgow by Robert and Andrew Foulis in 1773.[71] The "Observations" by Professor William Richardson are dated at the end "Glasgow, February 23d, 1773." The earliest announcement of publication seems to be in "A Catalogue of New Books" in the *Scots Magazine* for October 1773, with a note: "A few copies only of this poem were thrown off at Glasgow" (35:542–43). The *London Chronicle* for 27–30 November 1773 reprints in the left-hand column of the front page the first strophe and antistrophe along with the first footnote of the ode.[72] There is no doubt that the ode is by Smollett. In the first edition, on the recto of a leaf between the title page and the text, is the following note: "The Public may depend upon the authenticity of the following ODE. It is printed from the author's manuscript, which was communicated to the editors by a Gentleman with whom Dr. SMOLLETT was much connected." Additional information was supplied later by William Richardson in a note to his own *Poems and Plays*: "*Ode to Independence* was left in his own handwriting, with some other papers, to the late Robert Graham, Esq. of Gartmore, who was one of his trustees, and who gave it to the author of the present publication, under whose inspection the first edition was elegantly printed, by the celebrated Messrs. Foulis, printers to the University of Glasgow." [73]

The poem was reprinted in the *Westminster Magazine* for November 1773 (1:664–65). Then, in December 1773, a London edition appeared, printed for J. Murray and dated 1774.[74] The poem was included in the 1775 edition of *A Collection of Poems* published by George Pearch (4:121–26), in the 1776 *Modern Poems* published by Andrew Foulis the Younger (pages 18–23), and in the 1777 *Plays and Poems* (pages 259–72). In July 1776, it is worth noting, the *Ode to Independence* was reprinted in America in the *Pennsylvania Magazine* (3:325).[75] All of these reprints have the usual compositorial changes in spelling and punctuation, but none is significant.

The copy-text is the 1773 first edition of the ode published in Glasgow, since it was set from Smollett's no longer extant manuscript. After explaining in a note the circumstances surrounding the publication of the ode, William Richardson confesses:

> It is also proper to mention, that in the fifth line of the third antistrophe, the editor took the liberty of substituting one word in the place of another. The line in Smollett's manuscript was,
>
> > Where insolence her wrinkled *snout* uprears.
>
> No doubt the word *snout* presents a more complete image, and conveys, therefore, a more impressive meaning than the word *front*, which was introduced in its place; but it did not seem so suitable to the dignity of lyric poetry, or the peculiar loftiness of The Ode to Independence. If, however, the more distinct imagery, and consequent vigour, obtained by retaining the original expression, are capable of counter-balancing the considerations that urged the editor to its exclusion, it is proper that future editors may have it in their power to restore to the poet what certainly belongs to him.[76]

Smollett's reading has been restored. The ode is printed from a copy in the Humanities Research Center, University of Texas, Austin.

LYRICS FROM *ALCESTE*

In February 1948, Otto Erich Deutsch published what he believed to be most of Smollett's lyrics for George Frederick Handel's *Alceste*. Only after an independent examination of the manuscripts and printed texts of Handel's music is it possible to recognize the full extent of Deutsch's scholarship. His masterly reconstruction of Smollett's contribution to the opera is here reprinted. It must be noted that none of this material is in Smollett's hand and that the true relationship of this text to Smollett's manuscript is unknown. To put this matter another way, Handel may have begun with Smollett's lyrics, but the extent to which he transformed them to fit the music is unknown.[77]

THE REGICIDE

After ten years of wrangling with potential patrons and theatrical managers in an attempt to have *The Regicide: or, James the First, of Scotland. A Tragedy* produced on stage, Smollett chose another means for bringing his play before the public: "despairing of seeing my old Performance represented, I have at last taken the advice of my Friends, and opened a Subscription for publishing it, which in all appearance will answer my warmest Expectation."[78] William Strahan's printing ledgers for February 1748–49 include an entry to the account of John Osborn:

Proposals for the Regicide. No. 2000   £0–15–0[79]

In the *St. James's Evening Post* for 9–11 February 1748–49 appeared the following announcement:

This Day is Publish'd Proposals for Printing by Subscription on a Superfine Royal Paper, for the Benefit of the Author, The Regicide, or James the First of Scotland, a Tragedy. By the Author of Roderick Random. The singular Manner in which this Performance has been excluded from both Theatres (as will appear in the Preface) obliges the Author to publish it in a Way otherwise not agreeable to his Inclination. The Price to Subscribers will be five Shillings. Subscriptions are taken and Receipts signed by the Author, deliver'd by J. Osborn in Paternoster-Row; A. Millar, in the Strand; J. Brackstone, at the Royal Exchange; J. Jolliffe, in St. James's Street; and H. Chapelle, in Grosvenor Street. N.B. Those who are willing to encourage the above Subscription are desired to subscribe as soon as possible, that the Number to be printed may be ascertained.[80]

A preliminary announcement for the subscription edition appeared 1 May 1749 in the *General Advertiser*: "On Thursday the 11th Instant will be published, and ready to be deliver'd to the Subscribers." The sentence beginning "The singular Manner" is repeated, and another appeal is made for subscribers: "Subscriptions are taken in and Receipts signed by the Author, deliver'd by J. Osborn in Pater-noster-Row; and A. Millar in the Strand. Those Persons who have any Receipts not disposed of, are desired to return them before the Day of Publication to the Author, or to John Osborn in Pater-noster-Row."[81]

Publication was announced in the *St. James's Evening Post* for 9–11 May: "The Subscribers Books are ready to be delivered on their sending their Receipts to the above Places," that is, to J. Osborn and A. Millar.[82] But the play was ready as early as 9 May, the date it was entered in the Stationers' Company register and nine copies were deposited:

		May 9th 1749.
Andrew Millar		Then Entred for their Copy
&	The Whole	The Regicide or James the First
John Osborn		of Scotland a Tragedy
		By the Author of Roderick Random VJ
		Reced nine books[83]

Even though Smollett at the end of his preface to the tragedy thanked the public "for the uncommon Encouragement I have received in the Publication of the following Play," indications are that the subscription was not a success. Absent from the subscription issue is a list of subscribers, suggesting that the subscription did not fulfill Smollett's "warmest Expectations" and that the publication of the list might have proved an embarrassment. In any case, the booksellers gave the five-shilling subscription issue about six weeks to make its way before announcing a trade edition. According to the *General Evening Post* it was published 22 June:

This day is published, Price 1s 6d. The Regicide, or James the First of Scotland, a Tragedy. By the Author of Roderick Random. Printed for John Osborn in Pater-Noster-Row and A. Millar in the Strand. Where may be had, the same on Royal Paper; printed by Subscription for the Author. Price 5s. Where also may be had, The Adventures of Roderick Random. The Second Edition, in Two Volumes. Price 6s.[84]

Although William Strahan printed the proposals for *The Regicide*, there is no record in his surviving ledgers of his having printed the play itself. Alan D. McKillop has suggested that Samuel Richardson "may have had a hand in printing" it, but this requires further investigation.[85]

The most obvious difference between the two issues is in the imprints. The imprint for the subscription issue reads: *LONDON:* | Printed by SUB-SCRIPTION, for the BENEFIT | of the AUTHOR. | MDCCXLIX. | (Price Five Shillings.) | The imprint for the trade edition reads: *LONDON:* | Printed for J. OSBORN, in *Pater-noster-Row*, and | A. MILLAR, in the *Strand*. | MD-CCXLIX. | At some point in the printing process, difficulties arose with the inner forme of signature F requiring that the verso of the first leaf (66) be reset, at least in part. When the page was reset one correction was made: "gloom" was capitalized to "Gloom" to bring it into conformity with the remainder of the text, which capitalizes substantives. Five unnecessary changes were also introduced. The readings of the original setting [a] appear on the left and the readings of the reset [b] text on the right:

5.1.29	Fame,	Fame∧
5.1.36	abroad!—	abroad!∧
5.1.40	gloom	Gloom
5.1.41	th'incessant	the incessant
5.1.49	suppliant.—Ah	suppliant!∧ Ah
5.1.53	you, the	you∧ the

The priority of the readings cannot be established by the order of publication of the two issues. The two states of sheet F appear in both the subscription issue and the trade issue, making it clear that both issues were printed near the same time. Although there is a good mix of [a] and [b] states of the text in the subscription issue, for some reason the first state of the text appears in all but a few of the copies of the trade edition. As the sheets were printed, those containing the first state of the text ended up at the bottom of the stack with the revised second state on top. Perhaps the subscription issues were assembled first, using the copies of sheet F last printed. By the time the trade issue came to be assembled, few sheets containing the second state of the text remained.

Nor is it possible to establish the priority of the readings by examining the paper. As advertised, the subscription issue is printed on special paper with a watermark like Heawood 98.[86] The trade issue is printed on a paper with a watermark like Heawood 1802. Both states of the text, however, are printed on both papers. The original setting was almost certainly that on the left, as it follows the style of punctuation and dashes found throughout the play. It seems unlikely that Smollett was concerned with these changes.

A Dublin edition of *The Regicide* was published in 1749. On the whole it is a careful reprint of the first edition with a sprinkling of compositorial changes. The tragedy was next reprinted in the 1777 *Plays and Poems* (pages xxxv–xlvii, 2–122) with the usual compositorial changes in spelling and punctuation; none of the changes is significant.

The copy-text is the 1749 first edition of *The Regicide*. The play is printed from a copy of the trade issue with the original setting of sheet F in the University of Iowa Libraries.

THE REPRISAL

The printing of *The Reprisal: or, The Tars of Old England* was entered in William Strahan's ledger in February 1757:

1757   Mr Baldwin and Self
Febry   Reprisal, 3½ Sheets, No. 1000   £3–13–6[87]

Although Strahan and Richard Baldwin were partners, apparently each owning a half share, the farce appeared with only Baldwin's name in the imprint. It was published 1 February 1757.

> This Day is Publish'd, (Price One Shilling) The Reprisal: Or, The Tars of Old England. A Comedy of Two Acts, as it is performed at the Theatre Royal in Drury-Lane. Printed for R. Baldwin, in Paternoster-Row.[88]

Smollett is mentioned neither in the advertisements nor on the title page of the first edition. In fact, none of the editions through the "Second Edition" of 1776 has Smollett's name on the title page.[89] In the same year the play was reprinted in what may have been an unauthorized edition: "Printed for Paul Vaillant in the Strand."[90] "The Second Edition" was not published until 1776: "Printed for R. Baldwin, No. 47, Pater-noster-Row." Richard Baldwin had died in 1770 and this edition was published by his cousin, Robert Baldwin.[91] Dublin editions were published in 1757 and 1761, and a Belfast edition in 1767.[92] The farce was reprinted in the 1777 *Plays and Poems* (pages 123–201).

Several of the songs in *The Reprisal* achieved some popularity and were published as song sheets: "The Tars of Old England as Sung by Mr Beard in The Reprisal at the Theatre Royal in Drury Lane"; "Let the nymph still avoid, Sung by Miss Macklin in ye Reprisal"; and "From the Man whom

I love, A favourite Song in the Reprisal Sung by Miss Macklin . . . set by Mr. Oswald."[93] "Let the nymph still avoid" was also reprinted with the music in the 15 August–15 September 1757 *Literary Magazine* (2:396). All of these reprints have the usual compositorial changes in spelling and punctuation; none of the changes is significant.

The copy-text is the 1757 first edition of *The Reprisal*. The play is printed from a copy in the Beinecke Library, Yale University.

THE BRITON

The *Briton* first appeared on Saturday, 29 May 1762, and continued each Saturday thereafter until 12 February 1763, thirty-eight numbers in all. Only six sets appear to have survived, none complete. The set in the British Library is the most complete, missing only the twenty-eighth number. Other sets are in the Bodleian Library (numbers 8–38), University of Minnesota Library (numbers 1–8, 10 [last leaf missing], 11–12, 13 [last two leaves missing], 14–26, 29 [last leaf missing]), New York Public Library (numbers 1–7, 8 [last leaf missing], 9–18, 20–24, 26–38), Wisconsin Historical Society (numbers 1–23), Library of Congress (numbers 1–11).

The second and third numbers are in two editions. The first number and the first edition of the second number each have a large ornamental capital beginning the essay. With the first edition of the third number a factotum of Britannia replaced the ornamental capital for the remainder of the numbers, except for the eleventh number. The second edition of the second number was printed sometime after the Britannia factotum came into use. Thus the two editions of the second number can be readily distinguished, the first having a large ornamental capital and the second the Britannia factotum. The two editions differ in three places; the first edition readings are given on the left:

BL, NN	DLC, MNU, WHS
for the purpose	to the purpose
namely$_\wedge$	~,
mouthed	mouth'd

The order of the editions of the third number is more difficult to establish since both have the Britannia factotum. As might be expected, it is impossible to establish the priority of the editions based on correct or incorrect readings in the text.

BL, DLC, NN	MNU, WHS
idem	*eidem*
nasuris$_\wedge$	~.
Accordingly	ACCORDINGLY
Though	THOUGH
foibles—	~,—
until	Until
not to be joked	not be joked

The edition represented by the MNU and WHS copies, however, has a clause, absent in the other edition, after the imprint: "Where may be had the preceding Numbers." This clause began appearing regularly in the fourth number, suggesting that this edition was probably printed at the same time as the fourth number or after.

The second and third numbers are printed from the British Library copy of the first editions, as there is no compelling reason to think that any of the corrections for the second edition were made by Smollett. All of the other numbers are printed from the British Library copy except number twenty-eight which is printed from the copy in the New York Public Library.

The *Briton* was reprinted in part several times. Smollett's own *British Magazine* reprinted numbers 1, 3, 6–8, with numerous deletions to adapt the essays to their new medium.[94] Since the editorial work was probably performed by Smollett, it is recorded in a separate chart, "Revisions and Deletions in *The Briton* for the *The British Magazine*," at the end of the "Historical Collation" for the *Briton* (below, pages 605–7). Corrections by Smollett in these few numbers are incorporated into the text and identified in the textual tables as *BM*. Most of the substantive revisions, however, were made to smooth over the deletions and have not been adopted.

Extracts and summaries from the *Briton* appeared in the *Gentleman's Magazine* and in the *Scots Magazine*.[95] *The Political Controversy, or, Weekly Magazine of Ministerial and Anti-ministerial Essays. Containing the Auditor, Monitor, Briton and North Briton, entire, with select pieces from the newspapers* (London, 1762–63) published numbers 8–38 with English translations of the Latin mottoes. Extracts from some of the numbers appeared in *The True Flower of Brimstone: Extracted from the Briton, North Briton, and Auditor* (London, 1763), and in *A Collection of All the Remarkable and Personal Passages in the Briton, North Briton, and Auditor* (London, 1766).[96] No evidence connects Smollett with any of these publications and their variants have not been recorded.

LIST OF EMENDATIONS

[The following sigla appear in the textual apparatus of the Georgia Edition: 1 (the first edition); 2 (the second edition), etc., and short titles, as described in the headnote to each work; and W (present edition).]

A NEW SONG

1	Sappho]*Muses Delight*		sappho *Universal Harmony*	
1	strain,]*MD*	~ ∧ *UH*		
2	The]*MD*	the *UH*		
2	pain;]*MD*	~ ∧ *UH*		
3	With]*MD*	with *UH*		
3	strung,]*MD*	~ ∧ *UH*		
4	Like]*MD*	like *UH*		
4	thee]*MD*	the *UH*		
4	play'd,]*MD*	~ ∧ *UH*		
4	thee]*MD*	the *UH*		
4	sung,]*MD*	~ ∧ *UH*		
5	Like]*MD*	like *UH*		
5	thee]*MD*	ye *UH*		
5	play'd,]*MD*	~ ∧ *UH*		
5	sung.]*MD*	~ ∧ *UH*		
6	wire,]*MD*	~ ∧ *UH*		
7	fire;]*MD*	~ ∧ *UH*		
8	lay,]*MD*	~ ∧ *UH*		
11	these,]W	~ ∧ *UH*		
12	please,]W	~ ∧ *UH*		
13	youth,]*MD*	~ ∧ *UH*		
16	ne'er]*MD*	neer *UH*		
16	disdain,]*MD*	~ ∧ *UH*		
17	ne'er]*MD*	neer *UH*		
17	vain,]*MD*	~ ∧ *UH*		
18	ne'er]*MD*	neer *UH*		

THE TEARS OF SCOTLAND

18	wide-spreading]*leaflet*	wide spreading *Union 53a,53b*
36	children's]*leaflet*	childrens *Union 53a, 53b*

ADVICE

15 n.	N—c—tle]W	N—wc—tle 1; N—w—tle 2
17 n.	Gr−ft−n,]W	~ ∧ 1−2
29 n.	*Amus'd, perhaps,*]W	~ ∧ ~ ∧ 1−2
29 n.	*bum.*]PP	~, 1−2
30 n.	*drum.*]W	~; 1−2
62 n.	*fate.*]PP	~ ∧ 1−2
88 n.	L—d.]W	L−yd: 1; L—d: 2, *PP*
90	triumphs]1	triumph 2, *PP*
90 n.	W—n.]PP	W−rr−n ∧ 1; W—n ∧ 2
103 n.	*head.*]PP	~, 1−2
109 n.	*murmurs,*]W	~ ∧ 1−2, *PP*
111 n.	*Dullness*]W	*dullness* 1−2, *PP*
187 n.	oratorios]*PP*	oratorio's 1−2
206 n.	*file.*]PP	~: 1−2
243 n.	243]W	247 1; 238 2; 248 *PP*
244 n.	244]W	248 1; 239 2; 249 *PP*

REPROOF

3	Juvenal]1	IBID.
71	wether]W	weather 1−2
110 n.	110] 2	108 1
110 n.	*worth.*]PP	~ ∧ 1−2
126 n.	L−sc—s]W	L−s—s 1−2; Lascelles *PP*
126 n.	V−n—k.]PP	~, 1−2
129 n.	J—p−r.]PP	~ ∧ 1−2
129 n.	*cent*]1	*Cent* 2
139 n.	*belle.*]PP	~ ∧ 1−2
143 n.	*obsequies.*]PP	~ ∧ 1−2
164 n.	*coloured tutor.*]PP *colour'd tutor* ∧ 1−2
170 n.	*croud.*]PP	~; 1−2
174 n.	174]1	172 2

174 n.	*chair.*]PP	~ ∧ 1–2
174 n.	*board.*]PP	~ ∧ 1–2
186 n.	186]PP	185 1; 187 2
186 n.	*praise.*]PP	~ ∧ 1–2
195 n.	B——ks,]PP	~ ∧ 2
195 n.	B——wby]W	B——w——y 1–2; Barrowby *PP*
195 n.	C——tty.]PP	~, 1–2
197	sagely]1	Sagely 2
214	insipid ∧—]PP	~,— 1–2

THUS HAVE I SENT THE SIMPLE KING TO HELL

2	a]W	or 1–9

TRAVESTY

1	you] 2–4	*omit* 1

LOVE ELEGY

23	Strow vernal flow'rs]3	Wilt thou strew flow'rs 1–2
24	easy on]4	light upon 1–3

COME, LISTEN YE STUDENTS OF EV'RY DEGREE

21	when his own genius he ventur'd]2	obliged to his own understanding 1

ODE TO SLEEP

6	away.]*Pearch 1770*	~ ∧ 1

AN ODE TO MIRTH

11	its]W	his 1; the *Plays and Poems*
23	ray,]W	~ ∧ 1
40	passion's]*Pearch 1770*	passions 1

A NEW SONG "To Fix Her"

19   confess,]W   ~ ∧ 1, *Plays and Poems*

ODE TO LEVEN-WATER

9   o'er]*Town and Country Mag.*   oe'r 1–2

ODE TO INDEPENDENCE

16 n.   *blood.]Plays and Poems*   ~ — 1
53 n.   *isles.]*W   ~ — 1
58 n.   Inquisition]*1774*   inquisition 1
60   domain.]*1774*   ~ ∧ 1
62 n.   *rocks.]*W   ~ — 1
65 n.   Arabs,]*1774*   ~ ∧ 1
65 n.   *sands.]*W   ~ — 1
69 n.   *hord.]*W   ~ — 1
76 n.   *Corsica.]*W   ~ — 1
85   snout]MS   front 1

THE REGICIDE

3.1.48   whither]W   whether 1
4.2.14   Pestilence,]W   ~ ∧ 1
4.2.78   Tempest's]W   Tempests 1
5.1.40   Gloom]1(*c*)   gloom 1(*u*)
5.1.51   Defend]W   Defends 1

THE REPRISAL

1.2.25   "my dear]W   ∧my dear 1–2, *V.1757, Plays and Poems*
1.2.38   monocolos]PP   momocolos 1–2, *V.1757*
1.2.40   honey. But]PP   but. honey 1–2; honey; but *V.1757*
1.3.21   succès]W   succés 1–2, PP; succus *V.1757*
1.6.26   nettle: ∧]2   ~:' 1
1.8.41   you're]*V.1757*   your 1–2
2.1.11   derangée]2   derangeé 1
2.2.5   don't]2   do'nt 1

2.2.22	antiquité]2	antiquitè 1, *V.1757*
2.2.42	France]2	Francé 1
2.5.14	ra, ra,]2	~ ∧ ~ 1
2.11.2	precipitées]W	precipiteés 1, *V.1757*; precipités 2, *PP*
2.12.17	howsomever]2	howsoemever 1
2.14.1	yours]W	your's 1–2, *V.1757*, *PP*
2.15.21	nearer]W	near 1–2, *V.1757*, *PP*

THE BRITON

244.10	malevolence]W	malevolencc 1
247.36	the papers]W	papers 1–2
250.9	war ∧]W	~? 1–2
251.34	*nasuris.*]2	~ ∧ 1
254.26	reproach?]W	~. 1–2
255.33	*Surgis*] (*errata*)	*Surges* 1
255.35	*lasso*] (*errata*)	*lusco* 1
259.1	Ticonderoga]W	Ticonderago 1
259.16	Opthalmiater] (*errata*)	Opthalmeater 1
259.27	ale cellars]W	Ale cellars (*errata*); all cellars 1
260.29	Detected] (*errata*)	Deluded 1
261.1	propagate]W	propogate 1
269.15	impediment]*BM*	impdiment 1
269.32	*Pater-noster-Row*]W	*Pater* ∧*noster-Row* 1
273.21	considerable]*BM*	considerale 1
274.34	17]W	18 1
279.15	Ludgate-hill:]W	~; 1
279.15	Cotamus] (*errata*)	Cocamus 1
281.7	bosom]W	Bosom 1
281.22	disrespect]W	disrepect 1
283.29	the national]W	the the national 1
285.39	the world]W	world 1
286.1	mottoes]W	motto's 1
286.35	Bourbon]W	Bourboun 1
287.35	had]W	had had 1
289.20	arduous]W	ardous 1
291.2	dunghill]W	dunghil 1
294.18	gonfalonier]W	gonfal onier 1
298.17	sagacity.]W	~? 1

298.27	enemy's]W	enemies 1
299.32	fisheries]W	fishery's 1
303.1	Shaftesbury]W	Shaftsbury 1
306.20	28]W	29 1
309.19	disposition.]W	~, 1
310.17	equivalent]W	eqivalent 1
312.32	*horret*]W	*horrret* 1
314.36	are]W	are are 1
315.23	retrograde]W	retrogade 1
315.23–24	he to presume to fall off . . . and to enter]W	he presume to fall of . . . and enter 1
316.4	True]W	true 1
317.35	*sacer*] (*errata*)	*sacra* 1
319.32	terms]W	Terms 1
321.20	called]W	called call 1
322.24	lands]W	Lands 1
322.32	physician's]W	physicians 1
333.27	politeness.]W	~? 1
334.31	their criminality]W	theircrimina-|lity 1
343.31	and abuse]1 (*cw*)	and 1 (*text*)
346.29	ex-|pedition]1 (*cw*)	ex-| 1 (*text*)
347.28	23]W	22 1
351.9	indiscretion!"]W	~? ∧ 1
352.30	BRITON.]W	~, 1
356.13	West-Indian ∧]W	~; 1
357.39	men's]W	mens 1
359.16	formed a]W	formeda 1
360.32	and of]W	of 1
362.27	13]W	10 1
370.8	Will]W	will 1
372.37	Mr.]W	~ ∧ 1
376.32	other day]W	otherday 1
376.33–34	declaiming]W	declaming 1
378.27	Tobago,]W	~ ∧ 1
381.19	11]W	10 1
381.35	declaim]W	declame 1
381.37	declaimers]W	declamers 1
382.39	Mayor]W	mayor 1
383.15	elephants-teeth]W	~ ∧~ 1

384.16	faction?]W	~. 1
386.22	servant,]W	~. 1
387.29	secretly]W	secretely 1
387.32	keep]W	keeps 1
388.5	Doctor's ∧]W	~, 1
388.20	Bucephalus]W	bucephalus 1
394.35	minister's ∧ pretension to power,]W	minister's,
	pretensions to power ∧ 1	
404.33	&c.]W	&c. 1
404.36	K——g,]W	~ ∧ 1
404.36	M——ry]W	M——r——y 1
406.13	*agitur.*]W	~ ∧ 1
414.38	flattery?]W	~. 1
415.18	29]W	28 1
422.18	proceed]W	pro-| ced 1
422.34	plebeian]W	plebian 1
423.14	sphere.]W	~? 1
423.17–18	comparison of]W	comparison 1
424.3	Zama]W	Zuma 1
425.2	had been]W	had 1
425.22	Pococke]W	Pocoke 1
431.12	Well]W	Will 1
432.6	he,]W	~ ∧) 1

THE JUNTO

15	willingly]W	wiilingly 1

WORD-DIVISION

I. LINE-END HYPHENATION IN THE GEORGIA EDITION

[The following compounds, hyphenated at a line-end in the Georgia Edition, are hyphenated within the line in the copy-texts.]

THE REPRISAL

2.8.17	head-|land

THE BRITON

257.15, 351.1	fellow-|subjects
260.7	dram-|drinking
279.25	fellow-|counsellors
284.20	thirty-|six
297.3	wrong-|headed
318.2	mob-|reformers
320.5	King's-|tax
324.17	stock-|holders
328.26	with-|draw
343.24	coffee-|house
346.10	south-|side
367.5	good-|natured
367.17	over-|sea
372.39	letter-|writer
383.12	second-|hand
396.31	under-|value
397.36	village-|idiot
409.17	fellow-|protestants
411.38	conscience-|led
412.17	Out-|herod
412.21	Whig-|minister
412.33	fellow-|subject
413.20	paper-|party
417.34	over-|flowed

421.1	short-|sighted
424.25	over-|whelmed
428.6	re-|establishment
432.17	quarter-|masters

2. LINE-END HYPHENATION IN THE COPY-TEXTS

[The following compounds or possible compounds are hyphenated at a line-end in the copy-texts. The form in which each has been given in the Georgia Edition, as listed below, represents the usual practice of the copy-texts insofar as it may be ascertained from other appearances or parallels.]

THE REPRISAL

1.2.85	puppet-shew
1.6.30	*light-headed*
2.5.30	overblown
2.8.13	wind-bound
2.9.15	pleasure-boat
2.9.26	along-side
2.15.60	leeway

THE BRITON

248.4	beef-eater
251.39	watchman
259.14	ever-memorable
259.27	Bear-garden
262.10	overflowing
278.34	all-perfect
279.12, 311.7	understrappers
300.38	triple-headed
301.11	headpiece
301.13	chop-fallen
304.13	greenroom
312.31	aldermen
321.17	noon-day
329.11	withdraw

337.16	family-claim
338.19	holiday-time
348.1	coffee-house
349.36	withhold
356.35	short-sighted
360.23	outlived
365.31	town-clerk
369.11	cockle-shells
369.28	overwrought
387.31	stage-coach
407.8	fellow-subjects
407.34	merchant-ships
416.14	broad-bottom
423.22	commonwealth
431.20	logline
431.32	North-east

3. SPECIAL CASES

[The following compounds, or possible compounds, are hyphenated at a line-end in both the Georgia Edition and in the first edition.]

THE BRITON

243.29	well-	meaning
315.21	sugar-	canes
416.3	broad-	bottomed

HISTORICAL COLLATION

A NEW SONG

1	Sappho]	sappho *Universal Harmony*
1	strain,]	~ ∧ *UH*
2	The]	the *UH*
2	pain;]	~ ∧ *UH*
3	With]	with *UH*
3	strung,]	~ ∧ *UH*
4	Like]	like *UH*
4	thee]	the *UH*
4	play'd,]	~ ∧ *UH*
4	thee]	the *UH*
4	sung,]	~ ∧ *UH*
5	Like]	like *UH*
5	thee]	ye *UH*
5	play'd,]	~ ∧ *UH*
5	sung.]	~ ∧ *UH*
6	wire,]	~ ∧ *UH*
7	fire;]	~ ∧ *UH*
8	lay,]	~ ∧ *UH*
11	these,]	~ ∧ *UH, Muses Delight*
12	softer ∧ . . . pow'r ∧ . . . please,]	~ ∧ . . . ~ ∧ . . . ~ ∧ *UH*; ~, . . . ~, . . . ~; *MD*
13	youth,]	~ ∧ *UH*
16	ne'er]	neer *UH*
16	disdain,]	~ ∧ *UH*
17	ne'er]	neer *UH*
17	vain,]	~ ∧ *UH*
18	her soul had ne'er]	her soul had neer *UH*; had ne'er her soul *MD*

THE TEARS OF SCOTLAND

2	laurels]	Laurel *leaflet, MS 295, MS 2910, MS La.II.83, Mitre*; Lawrel *Land of Cakes, Thrush, Bodleian MS*

14	once] late *leaflet, MS 295, MS 2910, MS La.II.83, Land of Cakes, Thrush, Bodleian MS, Mitre*
16	Thy] Thine *leaflet, MS 295, MS 2910, MS La.II.83, Land of Cakes, Thrush, Bodleian MS, Mitre*
17	it then, in every] it, that, in ev'ry *leaflet, MS 2910*; it, that ∧ in ev'ry *MS La.II.83, Land of Cakes, Thrush, Mitre*; it ∧ that ∧ in evry *MS 295*; it ∧ that ∧ in every *Bodleian MS*
18	wide-spreading] wide spreading *Land of Cakes, MS 295, MS La.II.83, Bodleian MS, Mitre, Union 53a, 53b, 59, 66, Modern Poems, Plays and Poems*
33	Oh baneful cause, oh!] O baleful Cause! O *leaflet, MS 2910, MS La.II.83, Land of Cakes, Thrush, Bodleian MS, Mitre*; O balefull Cause o *MS 295*
36	children's] childrens *MS 295, MS La.II.83, Bodleian MS, Union 53a, 53b*
43	round] o'er *leaflet, MS 295, MS 2910, MS La.II.83*
47	th' inclement] inclement *leaflet, MS 295, MS La.II.83, Land of Cakes, Thrush, Bodleian MS, Mitre*; the inclement *Modern Poems, Plays and Poems*
49	Whilst] While *leaflet, MS 295, MS 2910, MS La.II.83, Land of Cakes, Thrush, Bodleian MS, Mitre, Plays and Poems*
53	And, spite] In Spite *leaflet, MS 295, MS 2910, MS La.II.83*; And ∧ Spite *Land of Cakes, Thrush, Bodleian MS, Mitre*
56	laurels] Laurel *leaflet, MS 295, MS 2910, MS La.II.83, Land of Cakes*; Lawrel *Bodleian MS, Thrush*; Laurel's *Mitre*

ADVICE

5	O! could I once break loose] O teach me to get loose *1*
7	*H*—] H—*me 1*; H—— *Plays and Poems*
8	*C*—*pe*] Cope *PP*
9	meager] meagre *1*
15	*N*—*c*—*tle*] Newcastle *PP*
15 n.	*N*—c—tle] N—wc—tle *1*; N—w—tle *2*; Newcastle *PP*
17	*Gr*—*ft*—*n,*] *Gr*—*ft*—*n* ∧ *1*; Grafton, *PP*

17 n.	Gr−ft−n,] Gr−ft−n ∧ 1−2; Grafton ∧ *PP*
17 n.	conferred the laureat on *C−lly C−bb−r*] Lord Chamberlain, conferred the laureat on Colly Cibber *PP*
19	*Gr−nv——le* and *B−th*] Granville and Bath *PP*
21	*P——t*] Pitt *PP*
21 n.	*Among the*] *Among* 1
22	*Ch——ly . . . Y——nge*] Chomdly . . . Younge *PP*
25	more the Bard shall claim] more's the poet's claim 1
26	Who] That 1
28	rouze] gain 1
29 n.	*Amus'd, perhaps,*] ~ ∧ ~ ∧ 1−2
29 n.	*bum.*] ~, 1−2
29 n.	R−y−l S−ci−ty] r−y−l s−ci−ty 1; Royal Society *PP*
30 n.	*drum.*] ~; 1−2, *PP*
33	and fell] of old 1
34	Nor the gaunt, growling janitor of hell.] By ev'ry charm unmov'd, but that of gold: 1
34	hell.] *Lines 35–36 of first edition omitted*: Thus at hell gates th' affrighted shade must drop / For ev'ry mouth of *Cerberus*, a sop.
40	base] fell 1
42	who] that 1
43	to captivate] that captivates 1
44	Degrade my talents, and debauch my truth;] (Absorpt at once my talents and my truth), 1
51	Who] That 1
57	who] that 1
60	her] its 1
62	*L——km−n*] Lockman *PP*
62 n.	*fate.*] ~ ∧ 1
68	who] that 1
76	(perhaps)] ∧~ ∧ 1
84	warm] boon 1
88	*L——d*] *L——yd* 1
88 n.	L——d.] L−yd: 1; L——d: 2, *PP*
90	*W——n*] *W−rr−n* 1; Warren *PP*
90	triumphs] triumph 2, *PP*
90 n.	W——n.] W−rr−n ∧ 1; W——n ∧ 2; Warren *PP*

90 n.	who]	that 1
90 n.	qualifications.]	qualifications; commonly called Brush Warren, from having been a shoe-black; it is said he was kept by both sexes at the same time. *PP*
91	his name surround]	the wretch confound *RR* 1–9
92	first that]	first, this *RR* 1–3
93	vice ∧]	~! *RR* 1–9
94	stains!]	~. *RR* 1–3
98	dome]	doom *PP*
99	There only may]	Who starts to find 1
103	*Ch—n*]	*Ch—rd—n* 1; Chardin *PP*
103 n.	*Ch—n*]	Ch—rd—n 1; Chardin *PP*
103 n.	*head.*]	~, 1–2
108	Which]	That 1
109 n.	*murmurs,*]	~ ∧ 1–2, *PP*
111 n.	*Dullness*]	*dullness* 1–2, *PP*
112	lurch:]	*Lines 115–16 of first edition omitted*: Such be the fate of *F—nt—n, Sh—lly, C—pe*; / For swinish bliss the filthy jakes to grope;
124	Who]	That 1
127	If nor by Reason aw'd, nor check'd by Fears,]	*omit* 1
128	He counts his glories from the stains he bears;]	*omit* 1
141	who]	that 1
144	Who]	That 1
148	who]	that 1
154	lewd∧ bosom]	lewd-bosom 1
167	Trophies to her, on others' follies raise]	On others' follies, trophies to her raise 1
177 n.	the *Dea, Bona*]	the goddess *Bona* 1
181	Tool]	fool 1
186	And *Punch*, no longer *Frasi*'s rival squeaks]	And rival Punch no more in terror squeaks 1
187	*R—l*]	*R—ss—l* 1; Russel *PP*
187 n.	*R—l*]	R—ss—l 1; Russel *PP*
187 n.	The person here]	A famous mimic and singer. The person here *PP*
187 n.	oratorios]	oratorio's 1–2
187 n.	continues still happily bereft of his understanding.]	continued bereft of his understanding, and died in the utmost misery. *PP*

199	harm]	dun 1
200	My muse with murders shall the town alarm;]	The town with rapes and murders let me stunn: 1
202	G——ie]	G—th—rie 1; Gutherie PP
205 n.	omit]	205. Snarl like G—th—rie, &c.] A political writer noted for gall. 1
206 n.	file.]	~: 1-2
221	standard]	fatal 1
221 n.	omit]	221. Some changeling heiress steal] Why changeling?—because no woman of common sense, can be supposed capable of sacrificing her fortune and reputation to a passion for a common sharper, the true character of all fortune-hunters. 1
224 n.	omit]	224. A mumbling bear with a claw?] Consequently a very inoffensive adversary. 1
228	That entertains the rude, ungrateful guest]	Of him that entertains th' ungrateful guest 1
234	burst]	spent 1
235 n.	omit]	This, surely, occasioned Churchill's "Too proud to flatter, too sincere to lye." PP
243	who]	that 1
243 n.	243]	247 1; 238 2
243 n.	who]	that 1
244	who]	that 1
244 n.	244]	248 1; 239 2
244 n.	who]	that 1
244 n.	day.]	day: the Hanoverian general, in the battle of Dettingen. PP

REPROOF

	JUVENAL]	IBID. 2
26 n.	omit]	26. To a Jew.] Various have been the conjectures concerning the author of ADVICE, who has been represented as a Jew, a Clergyman, a Templar, and independent Elector; nay, some have not scrupled to ascribe the whole performance to the spirit of the late counsellor Morgan. 1
32	W——ms—n]	Williamson PP
32 n.	omit]	Governor of the Tower. PP

33 n.	*omit*]	Sir John Cope.
41	But lest the Truth too naked should appear,]	*omit* 1
42	A robe of fable shall the goddess wear:]	*omit* 1
62	behind]	~: 1; ~; *PP*
63	While ev'ry]	The fleecy 1
64	fall]	fell 1
71	wether]	weather 1–2
82	May . . . for your]	Will . . . to our 1
83	you]	us 1
90	Which]	Who 1
91 n.	*omit*]	91. *The admiring court.*] The reader will discern a great deal more of the hind than of the hero in the harangue, which, however, is very well adapted to the capacity and disposition of the hearers. 1
108	*L—ck—n . . . H—b—y*]	Lockman . . . Hanbury *PP*
108 n.	L–ck—n . . . H—b—y's]	L–ck—n . . . H–n—y's 1; Lockman and Hanbury *PP*
110 n.	110]	108 1
110 n.	*worth.*]	~ ∧ 1–2
122 n.	D—l M—k—]	Daniel Mackercher *PP*
122 n.	distress.]	distress: Mr. Annesley, who claimed the Anglesea title and estate. *PP*
126–27	*G–d—n . . . L–sc—s . . . V–n—k*]	Gideon . . . Lascelles . . . Vaneck *PP*
126 n.	G–d—n, L–sc—s, V–n—k]	G–d—n, L–s—s, V–n—k 1–2; Gideon, Lascelles, Vaneck *PP*
126 n.	V–n—k.]	~, 1–2
129	*J—p—r*]	Jasper *PP*
129 n.	J—p—r]	Jasper *PP*
129 n.	J—p—r.]	~ ∧ 1–2
129 n.	*cent.*]	cent. A man famous for buying poor seamen's tickets. *PP*
129 n.	*cent*]	*Cent* 2; cent *PP*
139 n.	*belle.*]	~ ∧ 1–2
143 n.	*obsequies.*]	~ ∧ 1–2
143 n.	*W–t—rs*]	Waters *PP*
164	coloured]	colour'd 1
164 n.	*coloured tutor.*]	*colour'd tutor* ∧ 1–2

164 n.	the parents]	parents 1
168	*R—ch*]	Rich *PP*
170 n.	*croud.*]	~; 1–2
174 n.	174]	172 1
174 n.	*chair.*]	~ ∧ 1–2
174 n.	*board.*]	~ ∧ 1–2
174 n.	*board*]	hoard *PP*
183	cannot]	will not 1
185	*T—w—y*]	*T–r—w–y* 1; Tyrawly *PP*
186	*H—ly . . . In—d–by*]	*H–w—y . . . In—d–by* 1;
	Hawley . . . Ingoldsby *PP*	
186 n.	186]	185 1; 187 2
186 n.	*H—ly*]	*H–w–ly* 1; Hawley *PP*
186 n.	*praise.*]	~ ∧ 1–2
187	*Th—p—n*]	Thompson *PP*
195	*C—k, B—ks, B—wby* and *C—ty*]	*M—k–n,*
	B—wby and *Ch—y* 1; Clark, Banks, Barrowby, and	
	Chitty *PP*	
195 n.	*C—k, B—ks*]	*M—k—n* 1; Clark, Banks *PP*
195 n.	*B—ks,*]	~ ∧ 2
195 n.	*B—wby*]	*B—w—y* 1–2; Barrowby *PP*
195 n.	*C—tty.*]	~, 1–2
197	sagely]	Sagely 2
214	insipid∧ —]	~, — 1–2

THUS HAVE I SENT THE SIMPLE KING TO HELL

2	a]	or 1–9
5	treasons ∧]	~, 2–9
11	th' immortal]	the immortal 2–9
11	gods]	Gods 8–9

THY FATAL SHAFTS UNERRING MOVE

3	thy soft]	the soft *Mod. Poems*
4	my vital]	thy vital 2
5	gaze ∧]	~, 2–9, *Scots Mag.*, *Mod. Poems*
10	murmurs]	numbers *Mod. Poems*

11	magick]	magic 4–9, *Gent. Mag, Lit. Mag., Scots. Mag., Mod. Poems*
15	Unheard]	Unhear'd 2–4
16	unpitied]	unpity'd 5–9, *Scots Mag., Mod. Poems*

TRAVESTY

1	you]	*omit* 1
3	poppling]	popling 2–9
3	vow,]	~ ∧ 1

LOVE ELEGY

9	th']	the 2–9, *Mod. Poems*
12	music]	musick 3, 6–9
17	There ∧]	~, 4
18	repine;]	~: 3–9, *Plays and Poems*
23	Strow vernal flow'rs]	Wilt thou strew flow'rs 1–2, *Union*; Wilt thou strew flowers, *Mod. Poems*; Strew vernal flow'rs, *Plays and Poems*
24	easy on]	light upon 1–3, *Union, Mod. Poems*

ADIEU, YE STREAMS THAT SMOOTHLY FLOW

1	ye]	the BL H.1994.c
3	spring]	springs BL H.1994.b
4	shade]	glade BL 806.d, BL I.530, BL H.1994.b, BL H.1994.c, *Univ. Mag.*
7	charms]	Smiles BL 806.d, BL I.530, BL H.1994.b, BL H.1994.c, *Univ. Mag.*
12	balmy]	gentle BL 806.d, BL I.530, BL H.1994.b, BL H.1994.c, *Univ. Mag.*
13	bright]	Sweet BL 806.d, BL I.530, BL H.1994.b, BL H1994.c, *Univ. Mag.*

COME, LISTEN YE STUDENTS OF EV'RY DEGREE

12	skill]	skull 5
13	an housewife]	a housewife 5
19	was]	were 3–5

21   when his own genius he ventur'd]   obliged to his own
            understanding 1

BURLESQUE ODE

39   lay]   ray *Plays and Poems*

ODE TO SLEEP

4   rod]   road *Scots Mag.*
6   away.]   ~ ∧ 1
15   Or]   Nor *Plays and Poems*

AN ODE TO MIRTH

11   its]   his 1; the *Plays and Poems*
13   unremitting]   unremitted *Pearch 1775, PP*
23   ray,]   ~ ∧ 1, *Pearch 1770,1775, PP*
40   passion's]   passions 1

A NEW SONG "To Fix Her"

19   confess,]   ~ ∧ 1, *Plays and Poems*

ODE TO LEVEN-WATER

9   o'er]   oe'r 1–2
20   hedges]   edges 2, *Plays and Poems*

ODE TO INDEPENDENCE

8   bleached]   blanched *1774*
16 n.   *blood.*]   ~ − 1, *1774, Mod. Poems, Penn. Mag.*; blood, &c.
            Pearch 1775
53 n.   *isles.*]   ~ —— 1, *1774, Mod. Poems, Penn. Mag., Plays and
            Poems*; isles, &c. *Pearch 1775*
57   Batavian's]   Bardavian's *Pearch 1775*
58 n.   Inquisition]   inquisition 1, *Pearch 1775, Mod. Poems,
            Penn. Mag.*
60   domain.]   ~ ∧ 1, *Mod. Poems*

62 n.	*rocks.*]	~ — 1, *1774, Mod. Poems, Penn. Mag., PP;* *rocks,* &c. *Pearch 1775*
65 n.	*sands.*]	~ — 1, *1774, Mod. Poems, Penn. Mag., PP; sands,* &c. *Pearch 1775*
65 n.	Arabs,]	~ ∧ 1, *Pearch 1775, Mod. Poems*
69 n.	*hord.*]	~ — 1, *1774, Mod. Poems, Penn. Mag., PP; hord,* &c. *Pearch 1775*
69 n.	remoter]	remotest *Pearch 1775*
69 n.	could]	would *Pearch 1775*
76 n.	*Corsica.*]	~ — 1, *1774, Mod. Poems, Penn. Mag., PP; Corsica,* &c. *Pearch 1775*
85	snout]	front 1, *1774, Pearch 1775, Mod. Poems, Penn. Mag., PP*
90	stale]	state *Pearch 1775*
91	bloated]	blasted *Pearch 1775*

THE REGICIDE

2.8.34	happy]	*omit Plays and Poems*
3.1.48	whither]	whether 1
4.2.14	Pestilence,]	~ ∧ 1
4.2.78	Tempest's]	Tempests 1
4.3.15	not th']	not all th' *PP*
4.3.52	the Dust]	dust *PP*
5.1.22	Soul]	fond soul *PP*
5.1.51	Defend]	Defends 1

THE REPRISAL

1.1.17	master]	maister *V.1757*
1.1.42	trust to their]	trust their *V.1757*
1.2.5	for]	far *Plays and Poems*
1.2.9	I'm]	I am 2
1.2.9	saoul]	shoul 2
1.2.10	pleasure]	peasure *PP*
1.2.18	happing]	happin *PP*
1.2.25	"my dear]	∧~ ~ 1–2, *V.1757, PP*
1.2.26	will]	shall *PP*
1.2.30	speechless]	spaichless *V.1757*

1.2.32	St.]	Shaint *PP*
1.2.38	monocolos]	momocolos 1–2, *V.1757*
1.2.40	honey. But]	but. honey 1–2; honey; but *V.1757*
1.2.70	ye]	you *V.1757*
1.2.71	countryman]	countrymen *PP*
1.2.78	St.]	Shaint *PP*
1.2.83	Pritish]	British *PP*
1.2.89	saoul]	shoul 2, *PP*
1.3.3	gloire]	glorie 2, *PP*
1.3.17	renonce]	renounce *V.1757*
1.3.21	succès]	succés 1–2, *PP*; succes *V.1757*
1.4.5	a proper]	proper *PP*
1.5.7	terribly]	terrible *PP*
1.5.25	variance]	a variance *PP*
1.6.16	acquanted]	acquainted 2, *PP*
1.6.26	expact]	expect *PP*
1.6.26	nettle: ∧]	∼:' 1
1.6.40	man]	mon *PP*
1.6.43	edge; to]	edge. To *PP*
1.6.59	our canvas]	our own canvas 2, *PP*
1.7.9	saoul]	shoul *PP*
1.7.19	saoul]	shoul *PP*
1.7.20	tree]	three *PP*
1.7.27	choose]	chuse 2, *PP*
1.7.35	saoul]	shoul *PP*
1.8.12	or his power]	or power 2, *PP*
1.8.15	easy]	aisy *V.1757*
1.8.18	saoul]	shoul *PP*
1.8.27	all past]	past all 2, *PP*
1.8.41	you're]	your 1–2,
1.8.42	saoul]	shoul *PP*
2.1.3	answar]	ansar *V.1757*
2.1.5	meurtre]	meurtrier *PP*
2.1.5	vous]	vouz *V.1757*
2.1.8	man]	mon *PP*
2.1.11	derangée]	derangeé 1
2.1.23	sa]	sae *V.1757*
2.1.44	Si]	Oui *PP*
2.2.5	don't]	do'nt 1

2.2.6	saoul]	shoul *PP*
2.2.11	offisher]	officer *PP*
2.2.13	ave]	have 2
2.2.22	antiquité]	antiquitè 1, *V.1757*
2.2.23	saoul]	shoul *PP*
2.2.29	saoul]	shoul *PP*
2.2.35	St.]	Shaint *PP*
2.2.42	France]	Francé 1, *V.1757*
2.3.3	may]	my 2, *PP*
2.3.8	man]	mon *V.1757*
2.3.11	part]	parts *PP*
2.3.17	tak]	take *V.1757*
2.4.2	your master]	you master *PP*
2.5.3	procure you de]	procure de *PP*
2.5.10	wat]	vat *PP*
2.5.14	ra, ra,]	~ ∧ ~ 1
2.5.15	languisse]	languish *V.1757*
2.5.26	wid]	vid *PP*
2.8.4	'un]	'um *PP*
2.8.12	cutlash]	cutlass *V.1757*
2.9.2	sweat he]	sweat ye *PP*
2.9.4	fechting]	fetching 2
2.9.23	lieutenant]	lieftenant *PP*
2.9.25	demand]	command *PP*
2.9.29	Lioni]	Lionne *V.1757*, *PP*
2.9.30	Goluat]	Golliat *V.1757*
2.9.31	ave]	have *PP*
2.9.32	you]	your *V.1757*
2.9.33	escadre]	scadre *V.1757*
2.9.43	who]	wo *PP*
2.9.50	soupe]	soup *PP*
2.10.1	pas]	par *PP*
2.10.4	vil]	will] *V.1757*
2.10.5	juge]	judge *PP*
2.10.6	wen]	vere *PP*
2.11.2	precipitées]	precipiteés 1, *V.1757*; precipités 2, *PP*
2.11.5	pitie]	pitié 2, *PP*
2.12.8	saoul]	shoul *PP*
2.12.17	howsomever]	howsoemever 1

2.13.4	pigeon—Ah, master]	pigeon—master *PP*
2.14.1	yours]	your's 1–2, *V.1757, PP*
2.14.4	saoul]	shoul *PP*
2.14.8	answar]	answer *PP*
2.14.10	salvation]	shalvation *PP*
2.15.19	pitie]	pity *V.1757*
2.15.21	nearer]	near 1–2, *V.1757, PP*
2.15.22	taught]	tort *PP*
2.15.38	Belokke]	Blokke *V.1757*
2.15.60	that ever reefed]	that reefed *PP*
2.15.71	ordres, wich]	orders, which 2, *PP*

THE BRITON

244.10	malevolence]	malevolencc 1
247.36	the papers]	papers 1–2
248.28	for the purpose]	to the purpose 2
250.9	war ∧]	~? 1–2
251.3	namely ∧]	~, 2
251.25	hard-mouthed]	hard-mouth'd 2
251.33	*idem*]	*eidem* 2
251.34	*nasuris.*]	~ ∧ 1
252.32	*foibles*——]	~,—— 2
253.8	until]	Until 2
254.26	reproach?]	~. 1–2
255.22	not to be joked]	not be joked 2
255.33	*Surgis*]	*Surges* 1
255.35	*lasso*]	*lusco* 1
259.1	Ticonderoga]	Ticonderago 1
259.16	Opthalmiater]	Opthalmeater 1
259.27	ale cellars]	Ale cellars (*errata*); all cellars 1
260.29	Detected]	Deluded 1
261.1	propagate]	propogate 1
269.15	impediment]	impdiment 1
269.32	*Pater-noster-Row*]	*Pater* ∧*noster-Row* 1
273.21	considerable]	considerale 1
274.34	17]	18 1
279.15	Ludgate-hill:]	~; 1
279.15	Cotamus]	Cocamus 1

281.7	bosom]	Bosom 1
281.22	disrespect]	disrepect 1
283.29	the national]	the the national 1
285.39	the world]	world 1
286.1	mottoes]	motto's 1
286.35	Bourbon]	Bourboun 1
287.35	had]	had had 1
289.20	arduous]	ardous 1
291.2	dunghill]	dunghil 1
294.18	gonfalonier]	gonfal onier 1
298.17	sagacity.]	~? 1
298.27	enemy's]	enemies 1
299.32	fisheries]	fishery's 1
303.1	Shaftesbury]	Shaftsbury 1
306.20	28]	29 1
309.19	disposition.]	~, 1
310.17	equivalent]	eqivalent 1
312.32	*horret*]	*horrret* 1
314.36	are]	are are 1
315.23	retrograde]	retrogade 1
315.23–24	he to presume to fall off . . . and to enter]	he presume to fall of . . . and enter 1
316.4	True]	true 1
317.35	*sacer*]	*sacra* 1
319.32	terms]	Terms 1
321.20	called]	called call 1
322.24	lands]	Lands 1
322.32	physician's]	physicians 1
333.27	politeness.]	~? 1
334.31	their criminality]	theircrimina-| lity 1
347.28	23]	22 1
351.9	indiscretion!"]	~? ∧ 1
352.30	BRITON.]	~, 1
356.13	West-Indian ∧]	~; 1
357.39	men's]	mens 1
359.16	formed a]	formeda 1
360.32	and of]	of 1
362.27	13]	10 1
370.8	Will]	will 1

372.37	Mr.]	~ ∧ 1
376.32	other day]	otherday 1
376.33–34	declaiming]	declaming 1
378.27	Tobago,]	~ ∧ 1
381.19	11]	10 1
381.35	declaim]	declam 1
381.37	declaimers]	declamers 1
382.39	Mayor]	mayor 1
383.15	elephants-teeth]	~ ∧~ 1
384.16	faction?]	~. 1
386.22	servant,]	~. 1
387.29	secretly]	secretely 1
387.32	keep]	keeps 1
388.5	Doctor's ∧]	~, 1
388.20	Bucephalus]	bucephalus 1
394.35	minister's ∧ pretension to power,]	minister's,
	pretensions to power ∧ 1	
404.33	&c.]	&c. 1
404.36	K——g,]	~ ∧ 1
404.36	M——ry]	M——r——y 1
406.13	*agitur*.]	~ ∧ 1
414.38	flattery?]	~. 1
415.18	29]	28 1
422.18	proceed]	pro-| ced 1
422.34	plebeian]	plebian 1
423.14	sphere.]	~? 1
423.17–18	comparison of]	comparison 1
424.3	Zama]	Zuma 1
425.2	had been]	had 1
425.22	Pococke]	Pocoke 1
431.12	Well]	Will 1
432.6	he,]	~ ∧) 1

REVISIONS AND DELETIONS IN *THE BRITON* FOR THE
BRITISH MAGAZINE

242.1–	[Heading and first five paragraphs]	296.a.11–19 *omit*;
243.34	*substitute*: This author, after setting forth what he thinks	
	his duty as a writer, and inveighing against the Monitor,	

on the subject of court favourites, says, "I shall take the trouble to examine the particulars of this honest essay, and I doubt not, shall be able to convict the author, not barely of falacy, but of fraud; not of weakness only, but of wickedness also."

244.1	for, every	296.a.30 for every
244.27–245.19	"Without merit . . . infamous untruth.]	296.b.25 *omit*
251.33–253.3	[Heading and first three paragraphs]	298.b.1 *omit*
253.19	hath attended	298.b.30 has attended
254.3	M——l	299.a.20 Ministerial
254.5	although	299.a.24 altho'
254.26–255.28	[Last three paragraphs]	299.b.32 *omit*

264.35– [Heading and first three paragraphs] 368.b.10–19
265.37 *omit; substitute*: This paper is addressed to right hon. earl of B——, wherein the writer, after recounting the wounds he has received by espousing his lordship's cause in the present political fray, says, he flatters himself he has, by refuting the allegations and detecting the malice of his opponents, been in some measure instrumental in rendering their schemes abortive; and then proceeds as follows:

265.38	Your enemies	368.b.20 Your lordship's enemies
266.17–29	By the English people . . . hath imposed.]	368.b.54 *omit*
267.5–31	After mentioning . . . to retain.]	369.a.26 *omit*
268.2–5	The country . . . not know.]	369.a.44 *omit*
268.23–35	It is . . . baffled party.]	369.b.21 *omit*
268.36	those pseudo-patriots	369.b.22 pseudo-patriots
268.36	equivocate;	369.b.23 ~,
269.15	impdiment	369.b.47 impediment
269.27–35	[Last paragraph and closing]	370.a.12 *omit*

270.1–37 [Heading, first two paragraphs, and heading]
372.b.13–16 *omit; substitute*: The chief design of this paper is to refute the principal arguments urged against a speedy conclusion of peace between Great Britain and France.

270.38   objections which the enemies   372.b.17–18 objections,
                 says the *Briton*, which the enemies
271.37–   It would be . . . this digression,]   373.a.31 *omit*
272.20
272.20   To return from this digression, *salus populi*   373.a.31
                 The *salus populi*
273.6–10   Who is . . . jurisdiction.]   373.b.19 *omit*
273.21   considerale   373.b.37 considerable
273.30   through   373.b.54 thro'
274.6–30   The army . . . ATTICUS.]   374.b.26 *omit*
274.33–   [Heading and first three paragraphs]   375.b.17–22 *omit*;
275.36   *substitute*: This author compares the behaviour of a late
                    M — r, with that of the two Brothers, who, he says, threw
                    up their places in disdain, during the last rebellion, in
                    order to distress the hands of government at that critical
                    conjuncture.
276.10   c — rs   375.b.44 C — rs
277.9–38   These circumstances . . . candour.]   376.a.55–58 *omit*;
                    substitute: The *Briton* undertakes to refute an assertion of
                    his antagonist the *North-Briton*, in his paper of July 10, in
                    the following manner:
278.7   minister   376.b.14 Minister
278.13–16   If then . . . subjects.]   376.b.25 *omit*
278.22   house of commons   376.b.35 House of Commons
278.30   house   376.b.50 House
278.34   m — r   376.b.57 M — r
279.3–39   [Last two paragraphs]   377.a.14 *omit*

THE JUNTO

15   willingly]   wiilingly 1

BIBLIOGRAPHICAL DESCRIPTIONS

1. THE TEARS OF SCOTLAND

1a. THE FIRST EDITION
[*Caption title*:] THE | TEARS | OF | *SCOTLAND.*
Collation: 8° (176 × 110 mm.). A^2. Pp. 1–4.

Copies: Textually collated Harvard University, Houghton Library (*EC75.Sm792.746t), Huntington Library (135507), Oxford, Bodleian Library (Don.e.230), Yale University, Beinecke Library (Bz25.22).

2. ADVICE

2a. THE FIRST EDITION, FIRST ISSUE
ADVICE: | A | SATIRE. | *Sed podice levi* | *Ceduntur tumidae medico ridente Mariscae.*— | *O Proceres! censore opus est an haruspice nobis?* | JUVENAL. | [printers' ornament] | *LONDON:* | Printed for M. COOPER, at the *Globe* in *Pater-* | *noster-Row.* MDCCXLVI. | [Price one shilling.]
Collation: 2° (335 × 225 mm.). A^2 B-D^2. Pp. *1* title page, 3–16 text.

Note: Foxon S531. Horizontal chain-lines in A and B.

Copies: Textually collated Pennsylvania State University Library, University of Illinois (Nickell 400), Harry Ransom Humanities Research Center, University of Texas, Austin (Am. Sm79.+746a), Beinecke Library, Yale University (Z78.093s). Additional copies bibliographically collated: British Library (840.m.1 (37), 643.l.25 (26)), Cambridge University Library (Syn.2.74.6), Harvard University, Houghton Library (*fEC75.Sm792.746a), Huntington Library (89240), Oxford, Bodleian Library (Frith C.9 (18)).

2b. FIRST EDITION, SECOND ISSUE
ADVICE: [*as in* a *except:*] *LONDON:*   Printed for GEORGE FREER, at the *Bible* in *Bell-* | *Yard,* near *Temple-Bar.* MCCXVI. | [Price One Shilling.]
Note: Foxon S532. Sheet B reprinted with at least the inner forme reset.

Copies: Textually collated British Library (11630.h.3), Harvard University, Houghton Library (*fEC75.Sm792.746aa).

2c. SECOND EDITION

ADVICE, | AND | REPROOF:| TWO | SATIRES. | First Published in the Year 1746 and 1747. | — *Sed podice levi* | *Caeduntur tumidae medico ridente Mariscae.*— | *O Proceres! censore opus est an haruspice nobis?* | JUVENAL. | — —*nam quis* | *Peccandi finem posuit sibi? quando recepit* | *Ejectum semel attritâ de fronte ruborem ?* | IBID. | [double rule] | *LONDON:* | Printed for W. OWEN, at Homer's Head, near Temple-Bar. | [single rule] | MDCCXLVIII.

Collation: 4° (270 × 200 mm.). *A*¹ B-D⁴ E³. *1* title page, *3*–*18* text of *Advice*, *19*–*32* text of *Reproof*.

Note: Foxon S533. The collation of E is complex and varies among copies examined. William Strahan printed 750 copies for John Osborn.⁹⁷

Copies: Textually collated Harvard University, Houghton Library (*EC75.Sm792.B748a), University of Illinois (x821.Sm7a 1748), Newberry Library (Case Y.195.S702). Additional copies bibliographically examined: British Library (11631.g.31), University of Chicago Library (PR3694.A35 1748), Yale University, Beinecke Library (Im. Sm79.+7466).

3. REPROOF

3a. FIRST EDITION

REPROOF: | A | SATIRE. | THE | SEQUEL to *ADVICE.* | —*nam quis* | *Peccandi finem posuit sibi? quando recepit* | *Ejectum semel attritâ de fronte ruborem?* | JUVENAL. | [printers' ornament] | LONDON: | Printed for W. OWEN, at Homer's Head, near Temple-Bar, Fleetstreet; | M. COOPER, at the Globe in Pater-noster Row. 1747. | [Price One Shilling.]

Collation: 2° (340 × 250 mm.). *A*¹ B-D². Pp. *i* title page, *1*–*12* text.

Press figures: 2–2 7–1 11–1.

Note: Foxon S534.

Copies: Textually collated British Library (840.m.1/38), Harvard University, Houghton Library (*fEC75.Sm792.746aa), Pennsylvania State University Library, Yale University, Beinecke Library (Folio Pamphlets 33).

3b. SECOND EDITION

Published with *Advice*. See 2c.

4. ODE TO INDEPENDENCE

4a. FIRST EDITION

ODE | TO | INDEPENDENCE. | BY THE LATE | T. SMOLLETT, M.D. | WITH | NOTES | AND | OBSERVATIONS. | GLASGOW: | PRINTED BY ROBERT AND ANDREW FOULIS, | M.DCC.LXXIII.

Collation: 4° in 2s (288 × 220 mm.). π² A–C². Pp. *i* title page, *iii* [advertisement to the reader], *1*–8 Ode, *9*–*11* Observations, *12* blank.

Note: Gaskell 561. Issued stabbed in blue-gray wrappers.

Copies: Textually collated British Library (11630.d.18 (9)), Huntington Library (322329), University of Illinois (x821.Sm70), Harry Ransom Humanities Research Center, University of Texas, Austin (Am.Sm79.+7730), Yale University, Beinecke Library (Im.Sm79.+773).

4b. SECOND EDITION

INDEPENDENCE: | AN ODE. | By the Late T. SMOLLET, M.D. | [double rule] | LONDON: | Printed for J. MURRAY, at No. 32, Fleet-Street. | MDCCLXXIV.

Half-title: [row of flowers] | INDEPENDENCE: | AN ODE. | [row of flowers] | [Price Sixpence.]

Collation: 4° in 2s (290 × 200 mm.). A² B–E². Pp. *1* half-title, *2* Entered in the Hall Book of the COMPANY of STATIONERS, *3* title page, *5* ADVERTISEMENT, *6* AN INSCRIPTION *To . . . the late Dr.* TOBIAS SMOLLET, *7*–18 text, *19*–*20* BOOKS printed for J. MURRAY.

Copies: Bibliographically collated British Library (11630.f.59), University of Chicago (PR3694.I4 1774), Houghton Library, Harvard University (*EC75.Sm792.7730b), University of Illinois (Nickell 118), Yale University, Beinecke Library (Im.Sm79.+773b).

5. THE REGICIDE

5a. FIRST EDITION, SUBSCRIPTION ISSUE

THE | REGICIDE: | OR, | *JAMES* the FIRST, | OF | *SCOTLAND.* | A | TRAGEDY. | [single rule] | By the Author of RODERICK RANDOM. | [single rule] | – *Τόν ϑ᾽ ὑμνοποιόν, αὐὴς ἂν τίχτῃ μελῃ,* | *Χαιντα τίχτειν.* – Eurip. IKETIΔ. | *Hunc — | Anxietate carens animus facit, omnis acerbi | Impatiens, cupidus silvarum, apturque bibendis | Fontibus aonidum —* JUVENAL. | [double rule] | *LONDON:* | Printed by SUBSCRIPTION, for the BENEFIT | of the AUTHOR. | MDCCXLIX. | (Price Five Shillings.).

Collation: 8° (250 × 162 mm.). A⁴ B–F⁸. Pp. *i* title page, *iii–vii* PREFACE, *viii* PERSONS of the DRAMA, *1–80* text.

Typography: Catchword 32 Assuasive] Asswasive. No catchwords *vii, viii,* 15, 31, 40, 50, 64.

Note: Leaf Fiv (p. 66): [a]=first state, [b]=second state.⁹⁸

Copies: Textually collated Harry Ransom Humanities Research Center, University of Texas, Austin (Wm.Sm79.749ra [b]), Yale University, Beinecke Library (Plays, 424 [a], Plays, 522 [b], Plays, 810 [a]). Additional copies bibliographically examined: British Library (Ashley 4271 [a], 841.d.36 (3) [a]), Cambridge University Library (S721.d.70.98 [b]), Leeds University, Brotherton Collection [b], Oxford University, Bodleian Library (M.adds.108e.177 [a]), Harvard University, Houghton Library (*EC75.Sm792.749r [a]), Huntington Library (147761 [b]), University of Illinois (822.Sm7r [b]), Rice University, Axson Collection (PR3694.R4.1449a [b]), Williams College, Chapin Library (Engl. Lit. 17; signature F missing).

5b. FIRST EDITION, TRADE ISSUE
[*Same as above except:*] LONDON: | Printed for J. OSBORN, in *Pater-noster-Row*, and | A. MILLAR, in the *Strand*. | MDCCXLIX.
Copies: Textually collated University of Iowa (xPR3694.R4 [a]), Harry Ransom Humanities Research Center, University of Texas, Austin (Wm.Sm79.749r [a], Am.Sm79.749r [a], Am.Sm79.749r, copy 2 [a]), Yale University, Beinecke Library (Plays, 148 [a]). Additional copies bibliographically examined: Leeds University, Brotherton Collection [a], Oxford, Bodleian Library (M.adds. 108e.136 (6) [a], Malone B.34 (11) [a], Malone B.136 (1) [a]), Harvard University, Houghton Library (*EC75.Sm792.749r [a]), Huntington Library ((147761 [b]), University of Illinois (x822.Sm7r 1749 [a]), Newberry Library (Y135.S68 [a]), Rice University, Axson Collection (PR3694.R4 1749 [a]).

6. THE REPRISAL

6a. FIRST EDITION
THE | REPRISAL: | OR, THE | TARS of Old England. | A | COMEDY | Of TWO ACTS, | As it is PERFORMED at the | THEATRE ROYAL | IN | DRURY-LANE. | [printers' ornament] | LONDON: | Printed for R. BALDWIN, in Paternoster-Row. | MDCCLVII. | (Price One Shilling).
Collation: 8° (220 × 138 mm.). A–C⁸ D². Pp. *1* title page, *3–4* PROLOGUE, *4* PERSONS represented, *5–50* text, *51* EPILOGUE, *52* blank.

Press figures: 13–3 15–4 27–8 48–5

Typography: Page 35=53 45=4. Catchwords 24 OCLABBER∧] ~. 32 gers,] ~. No catchword *4*, 50.

Note: William Strahan printed 1,000 copies of the first edition for himself and his partner, Richard Baldwin.[99]

Copies: Textually collated Harry Ransom Humanities Research Center, University of Texas, Austin (Wm.Sm79.757r), Yale University, Beinecke Library (Plays, 112, Plays, 71. Additional copies bibliographically examined: British Library (643.h.3 (10)), Cambridge Univerity Library (S721.d.7056), Oxford, Bodleian Library (Malone B.136, M.adds.108e.98 (11)), Harvard University, Houghton Library (*EC75.Sm792.757r), Huntington Library (152867), University of Illinois (Nickell 257), Rice University, Axson Collection (PR3694.R45 1757), Williams College, Chapin Library (Engl. Lit. 17).

6b. PIRATED (?) EDITION
THE | REPRISAL: | OR, THE | TARS of Old England. | A COMEDY, in two ACTS. | As it is ACTED at the Theatre-Royal in *Drury-Lane.* | *LONDON:* | Printed for Paul Vaillant in the *Strand,* | M.DCC.LVII.

Collation: 12° in 6s (170 × 100 mm.). A–D⁶. Pp. *1* title page, *3–4* PROLOGUE, *4* PERSONS represented, *5–47* text, *48* EPILOGUE.

Typography: Catchword 14 SONG∧] ~. No catchword 47.

Copies: Bibliographically examined Harry Ransom Humanities Research Center, University of Texas, Austin (Ak.F460.737h), University of Toronto (B–10 3682).

6c. SECOND EDITION
THE | REPRISAL: | OR, THE | Tars of Old England. | A | COMEDY | OF | TWO ACTS, | As it is PERFORMED at the | THEATRE ROYAL | IN | *DRURY-LANE.* | [single rule] | THE SECOND EDITION. | [double rule] | LONDON: | Printed for R. Baldwin, No. 47, Pater-noster-Row. | MDCCLXXVI. | [Price ONE SHILLING.]

Collation: 8° in 4s (240 × 150 mm.). A² B–F⁴ G². Pp.*i* title page, *iii–iv* PRO-LOGUE, *iv* PERSONS represented, *1–42* text, *43* EPILOGUE, *44* blank.

Press figures: 2–1 12–2 22–2 28–2 40–2

Typography: Headline 2 Reprisal: 24 Reprisal: 38 Reprisal:. No catchwords *iv*, 42.

Copies: Bibliographically examined Oxford, Bodleian Library (Vet.A5e.2420), Rice University, Axson Collection (PR3694.R45 1776), Yale University, Beinecke Library (Plays, 764).

7. PLAYS AND POEMS

7a. FIRST EDITION

PLAYS AND POEMS | WRITTEN BY | T. SMOLLETT, M.D. | WITH MEMOIRS OF THE | LIFE AND WRITINGS OF THE AUTHOR. | [engraved portrait of Smollett] | LONDON: | PRINTED FOR T. EVANS, IN THE STRAND, | AND | R. BALDWIN, IN PATER-NOSTER ROW. | M DCC LXXVII.

Half-title: PLAYS AND POEMS | WRITTEN BY | T. SMOLLETT. M.D.

Collation: 8° (193 × 123 mm.). π^2 a-c^8 B^8 (-B1) C-S^8. Pp. *1* half-title, *3* title page, *i*–xxix THE LIFE OF T. SMOLLETT, M.D., *xxx* blank, *xxxi* contents, *xxxii* blank, *xxxiii* fly title: THE REGICIDE, *xxxiv* blank, *xxxv*–xlvii PREFACE to The Regicide, *xlviii* PERSONS OF THE DRAMA, *3*–122 THE REGICIDE, *123* fly title: THE REPRISAL, *124* PERSONS represented, *125–126* PROLOGUE, *127*–199 THE REPRISAL, *200*–201 EPILOGUE, *202* blank, *203* fly title: ADVICE AND REPROOF, *204* blank, *205*–220 ADVICE, *221* fly title: REPROOF, *222* blank, *223*–236 REPROOF, *237*–240 THE TEARS OF SCOTLAND, *241*–247 POEMS, *248*–265 ODES, *266*–272 OBSERVATIONS ON DR. SMOLLETT'S ODE TO INDEPENDENCE.

Press-figures: ix–2 xiv–4 xviii–2 xli–2 xlii–4 15–4 16–2 20–1 30–2 47–2 48–1 50–2 68–1 78–2 88–1 95–2 111–4 112–2 118–2 142–1 144–2 146–4 148–2 164–1 171–2 187–1 192–2 194–2 205–1 218–2 224–4 230–2 250–1 268–1.

Typography: Page 17=71. c1, F4 unsigned. Headline 212 ADVICE. 214 ADVICE. 216 ADVICE; 270 OBSERVATIONS$_\wedge$. Catchwords 19 ANGUS.] ~$_\wedge$ 48 SCENE$_\wedge$] ~. 107 ANGUS$_\wedge$] ~. 109 DUNBAR,] ~. 148 BRUSH,] ~. 211 "Sir$_\wedge$] ~, 219 FRIEND,] ~. 232 Pleas'd$_\wedge$] ', 245 SONG.] ~$_\wedge$. No catchword xxix, *xlviii*, 71, *124*.

Note: Fly title for *The Regicide* is in various positions in the copies examined. The proper location is at c1 as it appears in the uncut copy in original boards at the Huntington Library. B1 has been cancelled. Most copies follow this pattern. Evidence from another uncut copy, formerly in the Robert Hoe Library and now in the Chapin Library, Williams College, seems to indicate that the missing leaf B1 may have been a fly title. The University of Iowa copy has the fly title following the title page; i.e., gatherings a and b have been inserted between c1 and c2. In 1784 the sheets were reissued with the title and half title page cancelled and replaced with a new title page: "LONDON: | PRINTED FOR T. EVANS IN THE STRAND, | AND | D. OGILVY, MIDDLE-ROW, HOLBORN. | MDCCLXXXIV."

Copies: Bibliographically examined British Library (11779.ff.26), Cambridge University Library (7720.d.153), Oxford, Bodleian Library (Vet.A5.e.1624, Vet.A5.f.161 [1784]), University of Chicago (PR3690.084 [1784]), Harvard University, Houghton Library (*EC75.Sm792.B777p), University of California, Los Angeles, Clark Library (PR3690 1777), Huntington Library (146593), University of Illinois (x822.Sm7p 1777, Nickell x822.Sm7p 1777), University of Iowa (x828.S666pl), University of Minnesota (Y824Sm7.OPl), Newberry Library (Case 3A 1582, Y 12.S6677), Williams College, Chapin Library (Engl. Lit. 17), Yale University, Beinecke Library (Im.Sm79.C777, 2 copies).[100]

Notes

1. This copy of the *Travels* is in the British Library, shelf mark C.45.d.20, 21. Apart from the manuscript revisions of the *Travels* and a relatively small number of holograph letters, little survives in Smollett's hand: a one-leaf holograph note on the reign of Edward III in the Berg Collection, New York Public Library, and about a dozen signed receipts and documents. See *The Letters of Tobias Smollett*, ed. Lewis M. Knapp (Oxford: Clarendon Press, 1970), xvi–xvii.

2. Smollett was content to make small changes because the *Travels*, written at a relatively slow pace, did not require the extensive stylistic revisions of the earlier works. In the works of his later career, revision seems to have been carried out before publication; by this time he was a more experienced writer. For discussion of the composition of the *Travels*, see the introduction by Frank Felsenstein, ed., *Travels Through France and Italy* (Oxford: Oxford University Press, 1979), xxxv–xli.

3. John Smith, *The Printer's Grammar* (London, 1755), 199, 201–2, 209.

4. Bertrand H. Bronson, *Printing as an Index of Taste in Eighteenth Century England* (New York: New York Public Library, 1958), 17.

5. For a discussion of the 1777 *Plays and Poems*, see pp. 562–64, below.

6. See Peter L. Shillingsburg, *Scholarly Editing in the Computer Age: Theory and Practice* (Athens: University of Georgia Press, 1986), 13.

7. See the discussion below, pp. 560–64.

8. What I call the "traditional view" was formulated by W. W. Greg in "The Rationale of Copy-Text" (*Studies in Bibliography* 3 [1950]: 19–36) and extended in its application by Fredson Bowers and G. Thomas Tanselle. But Greg indicates that there are cases "in which an editor would be justified in taking a revised reprint as his copy-text." One such case would arise as follows: "an author, wishing to make

corrections or alterations in his work, may not merely hand the printer a revised copy of an earlier edition, but himself supervise the printing of the new edition and correct the proofs as the sheets go through the press. In such a case it may be argued that even though the earlier edition, if printed from his own manuscript, will preserve the author's individual peculiarities more faithfully than the revised reprint, he must nevertheless be assumed to have taken responsibility for the latter in respect of accidentals no less than substantive readings, and that it is therefore the revised reprint that should be taken as copy-text" (33–34). For a good summary of various editorial positions, see Shillingsburg, *Scholarly Editing*. In Shillingsburg's terms the texts of *Advice* and *Reproof* have "a strong historical orientation" (p. 20). A strict "historical orientation" would have followed the texts of the second editions exactly, reproducing them as historical documents with no emendation. Although here and elsewhere the editor has produced an eclectic text, emendations have been kept at a minimum in order to respect as much as possible the copy-text as historical document. See Shillingsburg, especially chap. 2.

9. I am extremely grateful to members of the staff of the King's Music Library and the British Library for their assistance in helping me to locate songs and to date them.

10. See the discussion below, pp. 554–60.

11. *Universal Harmony* is no. A598 in S[ydney]. Roscoe, *John Newbery and His Successors, 1740–1814. A Bibliography* (Wormley, Herts.: Five Owls Press, 1973). Roscoe reproduces the title page on p. 382. Page 86 of *Universal Harmony*, containing "A NEW SONG," is reproduced in Lewis M. Knapp, *Tobias Smollett, Doctor of Men and Manners* (Princeton: Princeton University Press, 1949), 195. The song collection was issued serially. See Roy M. Wiles, *Serial Publication in England Before 1750* (Cambridge: The University Press, 1957), 242, 344, 347. See also Otto Erich Deutsch, "Poetry Preserved in Music," *Modern Language Notes* 63 (1948): 74–76. Little is known about the Scottish composer, James Oswald. See the article by David Johnson in *The New Grove History of Music and Musicians*, ed. Stanley Sadie, 20 vols. (London: Macmillan, 1980), 14:15; Lewis M. Knapp, "Smollett's Verses and Their Musical Settings in the Eighteenth Century," *Modern Language Notes* 46 (1931): 225–26; and Deutsch, 76–77.

12. In 1795 the song was published with a new setting by Philip Hayes (1738–97), professor of music at Oxford. There is a copy in the British Library, shelfmark G.366 (10). I have checked this setting and later eighteenth-century settings and reprintings of the song listed by Deutsch (pp. 74–77), but they are of no textual significance.

13. The shelfmark for the 1745 *Universal Harmony* is K.8.k.6, and for the 1754 *Muses Delight* E.872. A 1746 *Universal Harmony* is E.364.

14. O M Brack, Jr. and James B. Davis, "Smollett's Revisions of *Roderick Random*," *Papers of the Bibliographical Society of America* 64 (1970): 295–311; and Albert H. Smith, "The Printing and Publication of Early Editions of the Novels of Tobias

George Smollett, with Descriptive Bibliographies" (Ph.D. diss., University of London, 1975), 1:1–34.

15. Alexander Carlyle, *Anecdotes and Characters of the Times*, ed. James Kinsley (London: Oxford University Press, 1973), 98–99. Kinsley notes that Carlyle "wrote his *Anecdotes and Characters* during the last few years of his life, in part from diaries and journals but mainly out of his remarkable memory" (p. ix). Carlyle died in 1805.

16. See above, the introduction to the poems, p. 6, and Knapp, 58–59.

17. His anger had cooled little when he came to write his account in the *Complete History* more than a decade later. See above, the introduction to the poems, pp. 5–6.

18. An anecdote of William Richardson, received secondhand from Robert Graham and published as late as 1801, and then reported by Robert Anderson in the fourth edition of his *Life of Tobias Smollett, M.D.* (Edinburgh, 1803), suggests that Smollett wrote "the first sketch of his Tears of Scotland, consisting only of six stanzas" at one setting, and then almost immediately "subjoined the concluding stanza" (Knapp, 59). The stories of hasty composition are legion, often fostered by the authors themselves, as in the case of Smollett's story of the speed with which he composed *The Adventures of Roderick Random* (*Letters*, 8). Credulity must occasionally make a stand. A more likely explanation is that the two versions (if there were two) were written over a longer period of time. No copy of a six-stanza version appears extant. See also David F. Foxon, *English Verse, 1701–1750: A Catalogue of Separately Printed Poems with Notes on Contemporary Collected Editions*, 2 vols. (Cambridge: The University Press, 1975), no. S535; 1:739. Foxon says, "The typography appears to be Scottish; it has a good text and may be authorized."

19. *The Land of Cakes* was also advertised in the *Salisbury Journal* for 5 January 1747. For purposes of collation of printed versions of *The Tears of Scotland*, the following have been used: *The Land of Cakes*, National Library of Scotland (Glen Collection 361); *The Thrush*, British Library (11601.a.63); *The Mitre and Crown*, Princeton University Library (1421.646); *The Union, 1753* (1st ed.), Cornell University (Rare PR1171.U58, cop.2), British Library (11631.aa.29, Cup.500.ii.20), Oxford, Bodleian Library (Vet.A5f.2171, 280kj.37), Harvard University, Houghton Library (*EC7.G2523.Z732g v. 19 no. 2, *EC75.Sm792.A753w), Huntington Library (139559), Rice University (WRC PR1171.W3 1753), University of Texas, Austin, Harry Ransom Humanities Research Center (Am.W267.753u), Yale University, Beinecke Library (Ib55.t753); *The Union, 1753* (2d ed.), Cornell University (Rare PR1171.U58 cop.1), British Library (992.g.2 (2)), Oxford, Bodleian Library (HARDING C236 (1)), University of Iowa (xPR1171.W3 1753); *The Union, 1759*, Cornell University (Rare PR1171.U58 1759), British Library (11602.b.42 (1)), Oxford, Bodleian Library (Douce P433 (1), HARDING C237 (1)), Bliss B167 (1)), University of Texas, Austin, Harry Ransom Humanities Research Center (PR1171.W3 1759), Yale University, Beinecke Library (Ib55.t753b); *The Union, 1766*, Cornell University (Rare PR1171.U58 1766), British Library (11602.c.46),

Oxford, Bodleian Library (HARDING C238), University of Iowa (xPR1171.W3 1766), University of Texas, Austin, Harry Ransom Humanities Research Center (PR1171.W3 1766), Yale University, Beinecke Library (Ib55.t753c); *The Union, Dublin 1761*, British Library (1507/1195 (1)); *The Art of Poetry on a New Plan*, British Library (1091.c.26); *The Beauties of English Poesy*, British Library (11609.p.22); *A Collection of the Most Esteemed Pieces of Poetry*, British Library (11601.dd.18); *Modern Poems*, University of Oregon.

20. See the discussion below, pp. 552–54.

21. *Letters*, 5. There are other musical settings of the poem, but these are exceedingly difficult to date. See Knapp, "Musical Settings," 224–32, and Deutsch, "Poetry Preserved in Music," 73–77. In the British Library (I.530 (100)) is a single music sheet, tentatively dated 1750 in the catalogue, which contains the first two stanzas of the poem. The text for these two stanzas follows that in *The Land of Cakes* exactly. Knapp and Deutsch list other musical settings, but they appear to have been printed after 1777. I have examined these settings, but they are of no textual significance.

22. It appears as Song 388.

23. William Scott, "Smollett's *The Tears of Scotland*: A Hitherto Unnoticed Printing and Some Comments on the Text," *Review of English Studies*, n.s., 8 (1957): 38, states that it "is obviously a misprint for June 16."

24. *The Mitre and Crown* 2 (July 1750): 460.

25. The four-line stanzas suggest that the copy-text for *The Mitre and Crown* and, presumably, *The Craftsman* may have been some undiscovered musical setting.

26. D. Nichol Smith, "Thomas Warton's Miscellany: *The Union*," *Review of English Studies* 19 (1943): 263. In a search of ESTC on 12 July 1992, the names in the imprint were not found on any other publication.

27. See D. Nichol Smith, "Three Scottish Ghosts," *Transactions of the Edinburgh Bibliographical Society* 2 (1942–45): 429–32.

28. Smith, "Thomas Warton's Miscellany," 264.

29. See Smith, "Thomas Warton's Miscellany," 274: "There are two states of the original edition. The whole book was reset in the same type, page for page and line for line. The second edition corrects at least twenty misprints."

30. For a discussion of the career of Richard Baldwin (1724–70), see C. Y. Ferdinand, "Richard Baldwin Junior, Bookseller," *Studies in Bibliography* 42 (1989): 254–64. Richard is often confused with his cousin Robert (1737–1810), who took over Richard's business in 1770. Richard Baldwin at the Rose in Paternoster Row was involved in numerous publications by Smollett, including *The Reprisal* (see below), the *Critical Review*, *A Complete History of England*, the *Continuation*, the *Works of Voltaire*, and *Present State of All Nations*.

31. Thomas Warton had carried out a somewhat similar ruse two years earlier when *The English Poems collected from the Oxford and Cambridge Verses on the Death of His Royal Highness Frederick Prince of Wales* was published with a fictitious im-

print: "Edinburgh: Printed for Hamilton Bruce, MDCCLI." See Smith, "Thomas Warton's Miscellany," 264–65.

32. Samuel Johnson was acquainted with the Wartons by 1753, but his "On a Lady's presenting a Sprig of Myrtle to a Gentleman" appeared in all editions of *The Union* as "By Mr. Hammond."

33. The headnote to the poem reads: "We have already observed that any dreadful catastrophe is a proper subject for Elegy; and what can be more so than a civil war, where the fathers and children, the dearest relations and friends, meet each other in arms? We have on this subject a most affecting Elegy, intituled the *Tears of Scotland*, ascribed to Dr. Smollet, and set to music by Mr. Oswald, just after the late rebellion" (1:76). *The Art of Poetry* is no. J16A in Roscoe, *John Newbery and his Successors*.

34. See below, pp. 566–67, and see also Scott, "Smollett's *The Tears of Scotland*," 41. D. Nichol Smith indicates that here and there Warton did Anglicize some of the Scottish poems in the anthology, but these are special cases. He also praises Warton for having chosen the best text for William Collins's "Ode to Evening," noting that in his attempt to identify Warton's sources for the poems he actually compared Warton's version with his source. Other than for the Scottish poems, no mention is made of editorial intervention by Warton. See "Thomas Warton's Miscellany," 269–70.

35. Philip Gaskell, *A Bibliography of the Foulis Press*, 2d ed. (Winchester, Hamps.: St Pauls' Bibliographies, 1986), no. 605.

36. Line four of stanza five has "childrens" for the possessive in *The Union*. The other two possessives in *The Union* version of the poem have an apostrophe before the "s" (lines 38, 51). The compositor's failure to add an apostophe may have been influenced by his having set "fathers" immediately above "childrens" in the preceding line. Although possessives in the eighteenth century appear with or without an apostrophe, in this instance it seems likely to be a typographical error. The earliest text of the poem, that in the leaflet, has "children's," and the copy-text has been emended to restore this reading.

37. See Shillingsburg, *Scholarly Editing*, 23.

38. Publication was announced in the *British Magazine* (1:245), the *Gentleman's Magazine* (16:444), and the *London Magazine* (15:428) for August 1746. The August issues would have been published in early September. It was still being advertised as late as 30 August 1746 in the *London Evening Post*.

39. Foxon, nos. S531, S532, S533; 1:739. No advertisement for the "George Freer" issue has been discovered.

40. Advertised in the *British Magazine* for March 1748 (18:143).

41. *Letters*, 5.

42. The entry was made between August 1747 and January 1748. British Library Add. MS 48800, opening 63.

43. Patricia Hernlund, "Three Bankruptcies in the London Trade, 1746–61: Riving-

ton, Knapton, and Osborn," in *Writers, Books, and Trade: An Eighteenth-Century English Miscellany for William B. Todd*, ed. O M Brack, Jr. (New York: AMS Press, 1993), 77–122.

44. The variants of the *Roderick Random* text are recorded in the Historical Collation.

45. William Warburton's collaboration with Alexander Pope, Lord Lyttelton's revisions of James Thomson's poetry, and the posthumous revised editions of Samuel Richardson's three novels continue to cause difficulties for textual editors. See David F. Foxon, *Pope and the Early Eighteenth-Century Book Trade*, rev. and ed. James McLaverty (Oxford: Clarendon Press, 1991), 144–52, 176–80, 217–19, 227–30; *The Seasons*, ed. James Sambrook (Oxford: Clarendon Press, 1972), lxiv–lxxxiii; *Liberty, The Castle of Indolence and Other Poems*, ed. James Sambrook (Oxford: Clarendon Press, 1986), passim. According to Sambrook, Patrick Murdoch also made revisions in posthumous editions of Thomson's poetry. For a summary account of the problems surrounding Richardson's novels, see O M Brack, Jr., "*Clarissa* Bibliography: Problems and Challenges," *The Clarissa Project* (New York: AMS Press, 1993), 10:44–69.

46. See Knapp, chap. 14, and *The Expedition of Humphry Clinker*, ed. Thomas R. Preston (Athens: University of Georgia Press, 1990), xxi–xxii.

47. Louis L. Martz, *The Later Career of Tobias Smollett* (New Haven: Yale University Press, 1942), 104–8.

48. *The History and Adventures of an Atom*, ed. Robert Adams Day (Athens: University of Georgia Press, 1989), lvii–lxiv, 325–28.

49. *Humphry Clinker*, 447–48; *The Adventures of Ferdinand Count Fathom*, ed. Jerry C. Beasley (Athens: University of Georgia Press, 1988), 444–47.

50. See *Ferdinand Count Fathom*, 445; *Atom*, 327; *Humphry Clinker*, 447. For details on Armstrong, see Lewis M. Knapp, "Dr. John Armstrong, Littérateur, and Associate of Smollett, Thomson, Wilkes and Other Celebrities," *PMLA* 59 (1944): 1019–58.

51. Smith, "Printing and Publication," 2:86; Barbara Laning Fitzpatrick, "The Text of Tobias Smollett's 'Life and Adventures of Sir Launcelot Greaves,' the First Serialized Novel" (Ph.D. diss., Duke University, 1987), 135–37.

52. John Nichols, in his "Biographical Memoir of the Late Isaac Reed, Esq.," states that Reed was "a valuable contributor to the *Westminster Magazine* from 1773–4 to about the year 1780. The biographical articles are from his pen" (*Gentleman's Magazine* 77 [January 1807]: 80). Not all of the biographical articles in the *Westminster Magazine* during these years read as though they came from the same pen. Although other authors may have contributed lives to the magazine, Isaac Reed (1742–1807) must be considered a strong candidate. See *The Early Biographies of Samuel Johnson*, ed. O M Brack, Jr. and Robert E. Kelley (Iowa City: University of Iowa Press, 1974), 295. See also Paul-Gabriel Boucé, "Eighteenth- and Nineteenth-Century Biographies of Smollett," in *Tobias Smollett: Bicentennial*

Essays, ed. G. S. Rousseau and P.-G. Boucé (New York: Oxford University Press, 1971), 204–7.

53. This note would seem to rule out Isaac Reed as the possible author of the life, as Reed knew Garrick and could have obtained the letters himself. In a manuscript note on the flyleaf of Reed's copy of Samuel Johnson's translation of Father Jerome Lobo's *A Voyage to Abyssinia* in the Arizona State University Special Collections, for example, Reed records: "15 Augt. 1776 I dined with Mr. Garrick at Hampton . . . IR." An anonymous reviewer of *Plays and Poems* in the *London Review* observes that "the writer, however, appears to have had chiefly in view, not the character of Doctor Smollett, but that of Mr. Garrick." He suggests further that Garrick wrote the life himself, as "no other writer would be so extremely solicitous to exculpate that comedian from the charge, brought against him by Dr. S. in regard to his managerial shuffling about the author's tragedy, the *Regicide*" (*London Review* 5 [March 1777]: 206).

54. Howard Swazey Buck, *Smollett as Poet* (New Haven: Yale University Press, 1927), 52–68.

55. Publication was also announced in the *British Magazine* (2:47), *Gentleman's Magazine* (17:52), and the *London Magazine* (16:56) for January 1746–47. The January issues would have appeared in early February.

56. See above, p. 553 and n. 14.

57. For purposes of collation the copies of the *Gentleman's Magazine* and *Scots Magazine* in the Arizona State University Library, and the copy of the *Literary Magazine* in the British Library, have been used.

58. In line four of stanza two, *Modern Poems* also has "transport" instead of "transports." The version of the poem with a musical setting by Philip Hayes has the same readings.

59. This song was also set by Philip Hayes and published about 1790. I have checked this setting and later eighteenth-century settings and reprintings of the song listed by Deutsch, "Poetry Preserved in Music," 74, 77, but they are of no textual significance.

60. Robert F. Metzdorf, *The Tinker Library: A Bibliographical Catalogue of the Books and Manuscripts Collected by Chauncey Brewster Tinker* (New Haven: Yale University Press, 1959), no. 1925.

61. See the discussion of *The Union* under "The Tears of Scotland," pp. 557–60, above. For a list of copies examined see n. 19.

62. Smith, "Printing and Publication," 1:146–77.

63. The change of "ye" to "the" is almost certainly an engraver's error. It is found in British Library H.1994.c (56). The change from "spring" to "springs" is found in British Library H.1994.b (1) and is unnecessary. Another Oswald printing is British Library 806.d (16). The Palma setting is British Library I.530 (126). See Knapp, "Smollett's Verses and Their Musical Settings," 231. There are the usual variations in spelling and punctuation, none of which is significant.

64. For purposes of collation the copy of the *Universal Magazine* in the Huntington Library has been used.

65. This version of the song contains the same textual readings as British Library H.1994.c (56).

66. The anonymous editor of *Plays and Poems* added the following footnote to the poem: "Dr. Smollett, imagining himself ill treated by Lord Lyttelton, wrote the above burlesque on that nobleman's monody on the death of his lady."

67. The British Library copy of the *British Magazine* has been sight collated with copies in the Beinecke Library, Yale University, and in the Harry Ransom Humanities Research Center, University of Texas, Austin. No internal variation was discovered in any of the copies.

68. For purposes of collation the following copies have been used: the 1770 edition of *A Collection of Poems*, published by George Pearch, in the Harry Ransom Humanities Research Center, University of Texas, Austin; the 1775 edition in the Huntington Library.

69. For purposes of collation the copy of the *Town and Country Magazine* in the Beinecke Library, Yale University, has been used.

70. *Humphry Clinker*, 441–45; "Ode to Leven-Water" appears on pages 241–42.

71. Gaskell, *A Bibliography of the Foulis Press*, no. 561.

72. Luella Fredericka Norwood, "A Descriptive Bibliography with Notes Bibliographical and Biographical of the Creative Works of Tobias Smollett, M.D., 1746–1771, with the Posthumous Ode to Independence" (Ph.D. diss., Yale University, 1931), 296–300. See also Norwood, "The Authenticity of Smollett's *Ode to Independence*," *Review of English Studies* 17 (1941): 55–64.

73. William Richardson, *Poems and Plays* (Edinburgh, 1805), 1:124. See above, the introduction to the poems, p. 17.

74. Publication was announced in the *Gentleman's Magazine* for December 1773 (43:612) and in the *Monthly Review* for the same month (49:500–502). The December issues would have been published in early January 1774. The verso of the half-title of the 1774 edition published by John Murray reads: "Entered in the Hall Book of the Company of Stationers." A search of the "Entries of Copies at Stationers' Hall" for 1773 and 1774 has failed to discover an entry.

75. The headnote to the ode as it appears in the *Pennsylvania Magazine* reads: "That this Poem has high merit no one will doubt, who has the smallest pretension to taste. It has all the enthusiasm and poetic colouring which suit the ode; and it breathes a spirit of liberty that would not have disgraced a citizen of Sparta, or of Rome." A footnote has also been added: "See his epitaph in the first number of this work:—A very few copies only of this poem have been printed in Britain" (3:325).

76. Richardson, *Poems and Plays*, 1:124.

77. Deutsch, "Poetry Preserved in Music," 80–84. Deutsch, it should be noted, has normalized spelling and punctuation, and smoothed out some of the lines. A few

of Handel's manuscripts are very rough drafts. A recording of *Alceste*, directed by Christopher Hogwood, was released in 1980 by The Academy of Ancient Music, Editions L'Oiseau-Lyre, Decca, DSLO 581. Excellent program notes are supplied in English by Anthony Hicks.

78. Letter to Alexander Carlyle, London, 14 February 1748–49 (*Letters*, 10). The best account of Smollett's experiences with *The Regicide* is still Howard Swazey Buck, *A Study in Smollett Chiefly "Peregrine Pickle"* (New Haven: Yale University Press, 1925), chap. 3. See also Knapp, 49–57, 106–8; and see above, introduction to the plays, pp. 69–73.

79. British Library Add. MS 48800, opening 63. No copy of the proposals is known to be extant.

80. The announcement also appeared in the *General Advertiser* for 11 February. It was repeated in the *St. James's Evening Post* for 11–14 February and in the *General Advertiser* for 13, 14, 15 February and 9, 10, 11 March. This announcement, apart from the technical information supplied by the booksellers, may have been written by Smollett. The second sentence, beginning "The singular Manner," is almost certainly his. Smollett was not above promoting his own work; later, he prepared advertisements to puff his historical writings. See O M Brack, Jr., "Smollett Puffs His Histories," *Writers, Books, and Trade*, pp. 267–88.

81. A similar preliminary announcement appeared in the *St. James's Evening Post* for 29 April–2 May, repeated 2–4 May.

82. The notice also appeared in the *London Evening Post* for 9–11 May. It was repeated in the *St. James's Evening Post* for 11–13 May.

83. *List of copies, 1746 to 1773*, f. 62. The entry is signed by the Clerk, Nathaniel Cole. "VJ" refers to the entry fee of 6d. See Cyprian Blagden, *The Stationers' Company: A History, 1403–1959* (London: George Allen & Unwin, 1960), 42–43.

84. The publication of the trade edition was also announced in the *St. James's Evening Post* for 22–24, 24–27 June, in the *London Evening Post* for 24–27 June, and in the *Gentleman's Magazine* for June 1749 (19:288). When John Osborn went bankrupt, Andrew Millar bought one-half share of *The Regicide* for £0–10–6 at the sale of 19 November 1751. On 12 March 1752, in a catalogue entitled "the entire Stock of Mr. Tho. Woodward, Deceas'd," seven lots appear near the bottom under the heading, "Books and Copies left unsold at Mr. John Osborn's Sale." Lot VII is "The Absent Man, a Comedy, wrote by Mr. T. Smollet, half the Copy-Right, and Profits in the Acting. The Copy is in the Possession of Mr. Smollet, and the Purchaser is to run all Risks of its being ever acted, or printed." It went unsold. See Knapp, 92, and Hernlund, "Three Bankruptcies in the London Trade," p. 107.

85. On 13 April 1749 Margaret Collier wrote to Samuel Richardson: "I return you my thanks for the play you sent me; and by what I have read of it, I think Mr. Garrick is very much obliged to the author for shewing the world how much he was in the right for refusing it" (Anna Laetitia Barbauld, *The Correspondence of Samuel Richardson* [London, 1804], 2:65). Alan D. McKillop states that "the reference

seems to be to Smollett's Preface of grievances." Almost certainly he is correct, and this means that Collier had a copy of the play at least four weeks before it was published on 11 May. Richardson may have had an early copy of the play because it was being printed in his shop. See McKillop, *Samuel Richardson: Printer and Novelist* (Chapel Hill: University of North Carolina Press, 1936), 180. See also T. C. Duncan Eaves and Ben D. Kimpel, *Samuel Richardson: A Biography* (Oxford: Clarendon Press, 1971), 510. Richardson printed for both Andrew Millar and John Osborn. In the University of Illinois Libraries Special Collections is a copy of the trade issue of *The Regicide* untrimmed in the original blue wrappers. On the inside of the wrapper is the top half of the proposal for printing the "Ancient Part" of *Universal History* in twenty volumes octavo, dated "London, May 30. 1746." Both Millar and Osborn owned shares in the *Universal History*; Richardson certainly printed the early volumes, and perhaps the later volumes, of this octavo edition. See William M. Sale, Jr., *Samuel Richardson: Master Printer* (Ithaca: Cornell University Press, 1950), 101–2, 331, 332–34. Sale makes no mention of *The Regicide*, and the printers' ornaments in the play are not to be found among those reproduced by Sale in chap. 9. See also Hernlund, "Three Bankruptcies in the London Trade," pp. 100–108.

86. Edward Heawood, *Watermarks, Mainly of the 17th and 18th Centuries* (Hilversum, Holland: Paper Publications Society, 1950), no. 98.

87. British Library Add. MS 48803A, opening 23.

88. A preliminary announcement appeared in the *London Evening Post* on 29 January with publication announced 1 February. Publication was also announced on 1 February in the *Public Advertiser*, the *General Evening Post*, and the *London Chronicle*. The *General Evening Post* repeated the advertisement in its issues of 1–3, 3–5 February. Publication was also announced in the *Gentleman's Magazine* (27:94) and the *Scots Magazine* (19:112) for February 1747. The February issues would have appeared in early March.

89. Perhaps Smollett was unwilling to put his name on the farce after his earlier failures to bring a dramatic work on stage. Even in his correspondence with David Garrick he does not mention the farce by name. In a letter of 4 February 1757 he thanks Garrick for his support and expresses the hope that his work will be "acted occasionally that it may have some Chance of being saved from Oblivion"; but he defers to Garrick's judgment as to whether it is "convenient to let the Tars go to the bottom." See *Letters*, 53–54, and also 50–53; and see below, n. 92.

90. Paul Vaillant (d. 1 February 1802), bookseller, was admitted a freeman of the Company of Stationers 7 February 1730 and served as Under Warden, Upper Warden, and Master of the Company in 1768, 1769, and 1770. The unwatermarked paper and the half-sheet duodecimo format suggest that this edition was printed as cheaply as possible. No advertisements have been discovered in the newspapers, lending credence to the assumption that the edition is a piracy. It is unlikely that a bookseller of Vaillant's reputation would have been involved in

piracy, and there is no reason to think he would have put his name in the imprint if he was. Vaillant's connection, if any, with the publication of Smollett's *Reprisal* is unknown. The edition is uncommon. ESTC lists copies at the University of Toronto and at Cornell University. There are also copies at Rice University and the University of Texas, Austin.

91. Ferdinand, "Richard Baldwin Junior," 259.

92. ESTC lists one copy of *The Reprisal* at the National Library of Scotland with the imprint: "London, printed in the year, 1774." Both the imprint and the date may be false. The failure to list a bookseller suggests that the 1774 *Reprisal* is a piracy. It may have originated in Scotland. The title page also indicates that the play is "By Dr Smollet." This copy came to my attention too late to allow me an opportunity to examine it.

93. British Library H. 1994 (54), G. 310 (69), G. 316 (112).

94. *British Magazine* 1 (June 1762): 296–97, 298–99; (July 1762): 368–70, 372–74, 375–77.

95. *Gentleman's Magazine* 32 (June 1762): 280 (no. 4), 282 (no. 5); (August 1762): 367 (no. 9), 368 (no. 10), 368 (no. 11); (November 1762): 530 (no. 21), 534 (no. 23), 536 (no. 24); (December 1762): 580 (no. 25), 584 (no. 26), 586 (no. 27). *Scots Magazine* 14 (June 1762): 286 (no. 1), 290 (no. 2); (July 1762): 349 (no. 1, continued), 350 (no. 3), 353 (no. 4).

96. Although the imprint of this 1766 pamphlet reads "LONDON: Printed in the Year M.DCCLXVI," it was actually printed for John Almon. In the Houghton Library, Harvard University (*EC75 Al682.766s), is a copy of the pamphlet, bound with other Almon pamphlets; a collective title page reads: *A Select Collection of the Most Interesting Tracts, Which Appeared During the Years 1763, 1764, and 1765.* London: Printed for J. Almon, opposite Burlington House, Picadilly. MDCCLXVI.

97. See above, pp. 560–61 and n. 42.

98. See above, pp. 572–75.

99. See above, p. 575 and n. 87.

100. The quality of the edition is higher because of the contributions of Leslie A. Chilton to all its phases. I am particularly grateful for her demonstration of the importance of a sense of humor in scholarly editing. Special thanks to Cyrus I. Dillon III for supervising the sight collations of the poems and plays with the able assistance of Valerie Behrendt and Charles Nelson. Thanks are also due to Guido Weigend, Dean of the College of Liberal Arts and Sciences at Arizona State University, who provided funding for the research assistants. Robert J. Barry, Jr., a special friend, and his son, Robert J. Barry III, have patronized my scholarship at Yale University over many years by providing me room and board. Work on the edition could not have been completed without their help. Paul M. Zall, my friend at the Huntington Library, has been of great assistance in completing this work. J. D. Fleeman and John C. Riely have fielded the odd query but, more im-

portant, have given encouragement and support over the years. Without the staff of the University of Iowa Libraries, especially Frank Paluka and the late Frank S. Hanlin, a Smollett edition would not have been possible. Most of the copies of the works used in the edition were purchased for the Iowa library. When editions of the works were not available from rare book dealers, microfilms were secured. I am also grateful to the staffs of the University of Chicago Library, Special Collections; Houghton Library, Harvard University; Newberry Library; Harry Ransom Humanities Research Center, University of Texas, Austin; Chapin Library, Williams College; Beinecke Library, Yale University; British Library; and the Bodleian Library, Oxford. Friendship and encouragement have been generously given by my fellow Smollettians, Jerry C. Beasley and Tom Preston. Eric Collum has been of great help with numerous details during the final stages of work on the texts. Gay Brack read drafts of the commentary, corrected proofs, and listened to Smollett tales with the patience only love can give. I hope that the return is satisfactory.

INDEX